Keeping Karis

KC McGee

Pengate Publishing

Keeping Karis

Pengate Publishing

www.pengatepublishing.org

ISBN 978-0-9998931-2-8

Book Design: Steve Clarke

Cover Design: Jiovonte Marsh and Linda Moua

Printed in the United States of America

Table of Contents

The Beginning

They seemed to have been waiting for me; I rushed to them. I went over to bed A; I rushed over to get him water. His little lips looked chapped, after getting him taken care of I rushed over to the other little guy. I sat the bed up and turned on his TV; he watched me instead." I'm Andy. What's your name?" He asked. "I'm Karis," I told him as I tucked the other little boy in.

"I wonder if you could stay with us for a while and talk?" He asked. "Well I have a little time, what would you like to talk about?" I asked. "I can't believe some of the things I've been hearing," he says while shaking his head. "Really" I respond. "What are the things you hear?" Well for starters I hear there is no heaven, I hear there is no God is that true? Is what they say true?" He says as he points his finger at the kid in the other bed.

"Well, I'm not sure about what they think. What do you think?" I ask. "I don't know what to think; I'm scared because I want to know where I'm going." He said. "My dad is a preacher, and he says if you don't believe you go to Hell, is that true? Is what they say right?" I didn't want to talk too much about it because that was such a touchy subject for me. I began to work faster.

"Well, are you going to answer me, what do you think?" He asked me again. "Well it doesn't matter what I think, I'm not sure about any of it either, and I mean we'd all like to believe that there is a greater place than this. A place we can go and everybody and everything it's beautiful, right? I think if you believe there is a heaven, there will be a heaven waiting for you. You make things what you want them to be just by believing, I think.

"Boy, I was sweating! I don't know what to believe either. I was brought up in a church; I have been trying to figure out things for myself. I rushed out of the room. "Goodbye Andy, I hope I helped you a little, I will see you tomorrow okay." I walked out and just stood outside the door taking a deep breath. As I stood there, I noticed a little boy in overalls standing down the hall staring at me; he waved, signaling me to walk his way. I was just too tired.

What could he want? What could this be and when will this day end? I just stood up and walked his way. I walked towards him, and he walked faster toward the doors ahead. I finally caught up with him, when I did I grabbed his shoulder to turn him around, "Hey you!" I said pulling him around. He smiled, grabbed my arm and pulled me close. He pointed to the surgery room.

I peeked in; a woman was being operated on by doctors, and nurses were all around her. I couldn't see what they were doing, but the little boy pointed at the woman. I moved away from the door; my stomach began to hurt. I began to feel sick all over. I leaned over with my hands on my knees to try to ease some of the pain.

The doctors and nurses came out of the room. I stood there, and the little boy stood beside me as they brought the woman out and rolled her into the elevator. The little boy grabbed me by the arm as he pointed to the woman. "Mom," he said. I was still feeling ill as he pulled me toward the elevator. I could feel pain and sorrow in my heart for him. As we got on the elevator, I felt a little better. We stopped on the 7th floor.

He leads me into a dark room. I stood there and saw a small light shining on the other side of the bed. I began to feel it all over again. I thought I don't want to do this anymore I just want to go home and be normal. I went towards the light as the little boy pulled me. I looked at the woman in the bed. She was pale and very still. It was like she was holding on to something. She was still sleeping. The little boy sat next to her and rubbed her back.

In seconds the pain hit me again in my stomach. I kneeled down toward the floor and just took a deep breath. The little boy looked at me. "She doesn't know I'm waiting." He said rubbing her back. "Please tell her I'm waiting for her." I looked up, and the woman opened her eyes and stared at me. I reached out for her hand feeling sicker than I've ever felt before. She began to weep. I went to her ear, thinking of what little Andy had told me earlier. I don't know her beliefs, so I don't want to pray. I just whispered. "There is an angel here, he says he's waiting." She opened her eyes wide as if she'd seen a ghost. She took a deep breath, and the little boy smiled. He went close to her face and held her hand.

"I'm waiting," he said, and the woman closed her eyes; I touched her hand, and it was so cold. The little boy and the woman were walking away from me towards the door. There was a light around them. She held him close as they walked away. I moved toward the bathroom as the nurse walked in. I went into the bathroom so no one would see me in here. The nurse went over to the woman to check her then ran out of the room. I washed my face and ran out.

I walked quickly towards the elevator. I got in and began to look around. I always get exhausted after every encounter like that. I waited for the elevator to stop it seemed to go forever. When it did stop, there was Dr. Michael smiling and ready to talk. "Hi," he said, smiling and chewing his gum. "I've been looking all over this hospital for you again. "Where do you hide out?" He asked.

"I want to know so we can hide out together. I can tell you're scared; you have that look in your eye, what's wrong? He asked. "Is it too much?" "Am I asking too much of you?" "I bet you have never taken anyone there, have you?" He asked. I kept looking away as if I wasn't interested in his conversation, but he just kept talking. He came close to my face, his breath smelling of mint his teeth so pearly white and straight. I glanced at him from time to time.

"Well, you don't know where I've been," I told him as I began to walk away he put his arm around my back and pulled me close to him.

"Someday Karis, I'm going to make you mine." He said in a whisper. It was warm and soft. I pulled away because I began to get curious. "I want you." He said. I pulled his hand away from my back. "You can't have me like that," I said as I walked away quickly, I was so nervous, and I went to clock-out in a hurry.

Maddy and the other nurses were sitting at the front desk. "Are you going to take me for a ride in your new car?" Maddy asked. "I'm leaving now are you off?" I asked her. "Sure honey," she said. "I'm ready." I grabbed my bag and walked towards the door. Maddy came out behind me, "hey, girl, you're moving so fast! Who are you running from?" She asked. I just looked at her. She got in, and we drove off.

"Hey! I found a couple of places you might be interested in; I circled them in the paper, there is a nice area kind of close to here," she said smiling. "Maddy I don't know if I want to do this job forever, I just don't know," I said. "Well honey you shouldn't want to do the job you're doing forever, you should go back to school and get your degree for nursing or become a doctor or a teacher it suits you better I think, but get the little things out of the way first like finding a place to live." She said smiling. She began touching everything. "This is a very nice car!" she said turning on the radio.

"This is a good investment. That's what you need to be concerning yourself with, investments." She said. "I bet you were planning to rent you an apartment weren't you?" She asked. "Isn't that all I can do?" I asked her. "Well Karis you have money, you can use it to buy something or get some student loans for school, you don't have to pay for that now do you?" I was so baffled by what Michael said I couldn't focus on Maddy's lessons tonight. He said he wants me. What the heck does that mean and why? I wanted to ask her, but what would she think of me? She continued talking, I just drove. We began to head back to the hospital she turned to me and shouted, "Stop! Something is wrong! What is it, Karis? Give it up!" She said.

"Stop the car now!" She yelled. I pulled over. "So, what's the story? Why are you all frowned up, you look confused about something so spill it!" "I don't understand what Dr. Michael wants from me. I kept telling him that I'm not interested in him, but he keeps insisting on being with me, and tonight he told me he wants me." "What!" She said. "He said what? I cannot believe him!" "I'm going to find him and tell him off."

"No please don't do that Maddy, I like Michael I'm just scared to be with him. I don't think I know how to be with a guy." I started to cry. "Maddy, I'm scared because I never had, you know?" "You never had sex before right?" She asked. "Yes, you are right," I said. "You know you don't need to have sex with anyone, you need to get married and be made love to, and your scars Karis, they don't matter when someone loves you. He won't care about any of that stuff; all he will want is you. Your love and affection will be all that matters, and take your time and get to know these guys."

"They might seem ok, but a book cover can be beautiful, you have to read what's inside of it or you will get hurt. So be real careful, and choose wisely. Make sure the cover fit the reading." I was still crying, she came over and hugged me. "You'll be fine, believe me." We got back in the car, and I drove Maddy to her car. "Tomorrow we will go look for those places don't forget."

Maddy is so sweet; sometimes I think she saves me. I have all these things I want to talk about, but I can't. I drove slowly to the house. I'm going to call Michael when I get there and let him talk his sexy talk, I'll let him tease me, and I will tease him back, and when I think I can be with him, I will. I got home and did just that. When I got there, Rose said that James had called me at least ten times. I would call him back, but all he wants to talk about is having babies and what kind of wife he wants. "I want her barefoot and pregnant; I don't care if she never works, I want a lot of children," he says.

I didn't want to hear that tonight. I rushed in, took my bath and called Michael. "Hello, how are you?" I asked him. "I'd be better if you were lying next to me." He said. I could hear him chewing gum." So you like that gum huh?" I asked. "Oh yeah gum is my constant love, double mint gum, I'd like to make you my constant love, I bet you're thinking about how fine I am." "You are very self-centered aren't you?" I asked him.

"Yes, I do love myself to death!" "Don't you love yourself?" He asked. "Sometimes I do, and sometimes I don't." "Why don't you love every inch of yourself? It makes you happier when you can wake up in the morning and look into the mirror and say I'm so beautiful." I laughed. Michael and I talked all night until we fell asleep. I could hear him breathing. It was heavy, but it gave me a certain comfort, I wasn't scared at all that night.

When I woke up the next day, my face was sore from lying with the phone on it all night. Michael must have woken up before me because all I heard was a dial tone. I rushed into the bathroom it was quite cold. I sat down on the toilet and reached out to try and shut the door. As soon as I reached over, something or someone snatched me so fast from the toilet seat and slammed me to the ground so hard. As the door slammed shut, the room got colder. I tried to pull myself up, but I couldn't move.

Something grabbed both my wrists together and pulled me toward the door. I was so scared I began to pray. "Lord, bind this spirit, please, don't let it hurt me, please!" The smell in the room was horrible. It was as if someone or something had died. I was still, and it had my hands so tight that my hands began to go numb. I could feel it's breath it was breathing so hard. I put my head down looking at the floor, and it felt as if it was biting my neck and licking me. I started to scream. I prayed that Rose and Roy were home. "Please, please help me!" I cried out.

Suddenly it dropped me, and I fell to my knees and crawled out to my room. My hands were stiff and cold as if the circulation was cut off. There were red and blue with bruises all around. I crawled away quickly to my room. When I made it to the door, I shut it. I sat up against it so nothing could come through. I just sat there. I felt something dripping from my neck; I touched it and saw that it was blood. I had blood running down my neck; I got up from the floor and went to the mirror on my dresser.

My neck was bleeding, and it looked like something with large teeth bit me. I grabbed a tissue from the box on my dresser and began to wipe the blood off of me. I started changing my clothes as fast as I could and ran to my car. I was going to see my dad. "I have to see my daddy." I thought. I was so scared about what was going to happen to me in that house. When I got into the car, it felt as if someone got in with me. I just drove away, when I got to my daddy's house no one was there. He must be at work. I got back in the car and drove downtown to find daddy.

When I got to his office, he wasn't there, so I just sat down on the couch waiting, he will be here soon. I thought. "Where is that secretary of his?" As I sat there waiting I started to hear noises. I went to the door. Then I heard laughing coming from the closet. "Oh no, daddy's in the closet with the secretary." I knew he had to be here already; he's never late for work. I started for the door, and the secretary pops out. "Hi Karis, umm can I help you in some way?" She asks.

"Oh no, I'm just going to leave my dad a note." I grabbed a piece of paper from her desk and wrote daddy. "Daddy you've been caught again, just when I needed you the most, please don't call me, I'm mad Love, Karis." I put the pen down and walked out. Daddy didn't come out or make a sound. I don't think it mattered to him; I do know he loves me. That note will hurt his feelings. I went to my car and decided that I was going to Daisy's house; she's always cooking and praying. I could see Krystal also. I drove slowly, when I arrived, a lot was going on.

I could see her in the front sweeping. Daisy was very clean she kept everything so neat all the time. As I walked up, she looked at me. "What are you doing here?" She asked. "Oh, I just stopped by to say hi." I was a little nervous because she seemed angry and her eyes said go away. "Is Krystal here?" I asked. "No, she's at the park with some friends." The relationship fighting bug seems to be going around because her boyfriend came outside yelling and calling her names. She ran over to him so fast with the broom and began to hit him with it.

"Ok." I said, "It's not a good time, I will see you later." I said backing away to my car. I waved goodbye and drove to Maddy's house. I sat in her parking lot for hours until I seen her garage open. She didn't come out, but her daughter did. I waved as she drove off. Maddy was at the window watching when she noticed me. She came to the front door. "Hey, come in here girl! What are you doing out here?" "Oh, I'm excited about apartment hunting so I thought I'd pop by," I told her. "Is it okay?" I asked.

"Oh sure come in let's have breakfast." I go to reach for the door, and I looked down at my hands they all bruised, and sore I forgot, I couldn't tell Maddy what happened. What is she going to ask me if she notices it? I had on long sleeves, so I quickly pulled the sleeves over my hands after getting in. "Oh, I'm cold," I said. "Ok I have the heat on, come in honey." She says going into the kitchen. "Maddy, can I use your bathroom please?" I asked.

"Sure honey, you know your way go ahead," she says. I went into the bathroom and looked at my hands and neck. "Ok." I thought. "What could I tell her?" I could tell her that I fell. "No!" I thought. I hope she doesn't notice that I looked bad, I thought. I went into the kitchen, and Maddy was cooking up a delicious breakfast, I was a little hungry. "What

would you like? I have eggs bacon toast and grits. Do you like grits?"
She asked. "Yes, I do," I said.

"Would you like some orange juice, honey? Go ahead and pour
yourself some," she said putting the food on our plates. "I'm glad you
stopped by, I have a new friend!" She said walking towards the window.
"Surprise!" She yelled out, reaching towards the window pulling out a
new cat. "Isn't she beautiful?" She asked. "Yes, she sure is. What kind is
she?" I asked. "Oh she's a Siamese cat, she's exceptional," she handed
her to me. The cat gripped on to me as if it was afraid.

"Her name is Cookie; doesn't she look like cookie dough with those
colors?" She asked. "Oh yeah, she does," I tell her as I put her down on
the floor.   Maddy sat down at the table. "So what happened to your
wrist, it's bruised." "Oh, my wrist?" I asked. "Yeah let me take a look, I
noticed when you reached out for Cookie. So what happened?" She
asked. "Oh I was digging around in some old boxes, and I came across
some old yarn and was winding it around my wrists I didn't know it was
bruising them." "Oh, I see."

Maddy just looked at me. I looked down at my plate feeling bad for
telling that lie. I couldn't tell her what was happening to me because she
would think I was crazy. I ate everything on my plate; I must have been
hungrier than I thought. Maddy drank her coffee walking around; she
didn't eat much she just held that cat and her cup of coffee. "I'm going
to take a shower, make yourself at home, I won't be long," she said
holding her robe and putting her cat down. I walked around the house
just looking at all of her pictures. She loved her cats; she had lots of
pictures of them all over the house.

When she came out, she grabbed her keys. "Let's go hunting girl, off
to a new start!" She said as we walked out. "Do you want to drive or do
you want me to drive?" "Oh, I will it's no problem," we got in the car.
Just then I remembered, "Oh no, she will be to my right, she will see
those bite marks on my neck." I thought to myself. "Oh Maddy I don't

have my driver's license so you could drive us, I know I drove here, but I'm going to get it soon my dad is taking me." "Okay," Maddy said. "Let's take old Betty out then," Betty is what she named her car. Maddy told me she had Betty for years and that she has never let her down, Betty was a station wagon.

Moving Day

We left in Betty. We looked at some reasonably new places. One was a two bedroom, and the other was a one bedroom, both were quite cozy and clean inside. Maddy took me to a real estate office to get a price on the two-bed room. I wanted that one for sure; it was more like a duplex it had a small backyard and a place in the front where you could grow flowers. It had two bathrooms, and in each room, the closets were very spacious. I also loved the kitchen it was clean and comfortable to get around in and the living room was nice and big with a huge window facing the front of the house.

You could see the street, and the houses weren't close. We talked to the realtor and filled out paperwork. I was just following Maddy's lead; she was very sharp, asking all the questions. She looked the realtor in the eye and demanded straight answers. I watched very carefully trying not to miss a beat because Maddy was very serious, it was intense. After talking for hours with the banks, I finally decided on the move in date.

I would pick up the keys on the first of the month and move in; I was so excited that I was finally moving. We went to get coffee and Maddy wanted to take me to my father's house to share with him what was going on. When I saw him last, he was with the secretary in the closet, and I left him that note. I was a little ashamed of him at the time, but Maddy was going there anyway. I wasn't going to tell her what happened that morning; I'd rather keep that to myself. When we arrived at my father's house, he was outside sitting on the porch watering the grass as usual after work. We approached him. "Hello!" Maddy said.

"How are you today Mr. Lawson? She asked. "Oh, I'm feeling great!" He said, "How about yourself?" "Oh, I'm good," she said. "I wanted to come by with Karis, she has a big surprise," she told him. "Is it forgiveness?" He said smiling and putting the hose on the ground. "I hope that's my surprise," he said walking over to hug me. "No," Maddy told him. "She is moving into her own place, and the best part about it is she is going to buy it!" She said with excitement.

"Oh sugar that's great, that's going to be the best thing you have done in your young life." He said. "When does she move in?" He asked. "I can have her brothers help her move if I can keep them out of trouble long enough." He said shaking his head. "Daddy I don't even have anything to move yet, just clothes," I told him. "I'm going to take her to the furniture store this weekend," Maddy said. "You're welcome to join us," she tells daddy. Could it be that Maddy likes daddy? Why was she looking at him like that? No, Maddy isn't interested, I thought.

"Oh yes," daddy said. "You bet I want to come, I need to spend time with my baby girl anyway," he said with a grin, still hugging me. He started to walk over to the back gate, "Hey I have something to show you, come on." We went into the backyard. "Look down there," he said. "There it is, look at the garden." I looked and saw that daddy had been working to keep mommas garden up. There were melons, cucumbers, corn, and tomatoes. "It's nice right?" He asked. I looked at daddy with tears in my eyes, "Thank you." I hugged his neck. "I'm so glad you did this daddy," I told him. "Anything to make my baby happy," he said. "Now get a paper bag over there and take some veggies home, you too Maddy." I kissed daddy's face; I could tell he was so happy with how he smiled.

Maddy took me back to my car. She said she was going to the hospital to see some coworkers, and I should see her when I come to work that evening. I was looking forward to work. I couldn't wait to see Michael after that all night talks we had. I wanted to kiss him, I thought. She dropped me off. "Go home and start packing!" She yelled out of the window waving. "I'll see you later." I got in my car and was dreading to go to Rose's, I hope someone is there, I drove slowly, when I reached

Rose's house; Roy's car was there, but Rose's car wasn't. I sat in the car for a while just looking at the house.

I can't wait to move from here; I have to go in and get my things together. I will just go in and pack everything in my car and just live in my car for a while I thought. I'll just go from place to place or go to Maddy's or try to spend as much time in the hospital as I could. I got out and stood by my car and looked out at the stairs. "Hey!" Roy called out. "Are you coming in or what? I made some tacos do you want some?" I looked up at him. "Sure, why not." I walked in and went to the kitchen. "Where's Rose?" I asked him. "Oh she had an appointment," he said.

"You didn't want to go?" I asked him." Oh, she's fine," he said looking at me handing me a taco. "I'm just not into the baby thing yet," he said. I began to eat my food. Roy walked all around the kitchen. I watched him closely as he put the dishes away and put tacos together for Rose. "Are you going to stay together and get married?" I asked him. "No, I don't think I'm ready for all of that, that's why I don't want kids right now," he told me. "I love your sister, but I'm just not ready to be involved like that."

I ate a bit of my taco and nodded my head to him as if I understood. "I bet you didn't know I was only 25 years old huh?" He asked me smiling. "Oh I don't know, I never thought about your age," I said swallowing my food. I got up from the stool, "thank you for the tacos Roy," I said walking towards my room. "I have to pack now; I'm moving did you know that?" I asked. "Oh yeah, Rose told me you were planning to move out, did you find a place yet?" He asked.

"Yes I did, but it's not going to be ready until the beginning of the month," I told him. I began walking towards the back; Roy was right behind me talking. I turned to look back at him he was talkative today. "So what's your new place like?" He asked. "Oh, it's a great place; it has two bedrooms two bathrooms a nice kitchen and a very nice little yard. I love it." I began packing as he stood in the doorway talking. I pulled everything out of each drawer and began to fold my things. "So did you give your sister any of your money?" He asked me. "Of course I have, why?" I asked him.

"Oh, I just wondered how she was able to pay for some things these days. You know she doesn't make much money on her job," he said. "Well she is making enough for you to live here with her and she pays most of the bills. I tell him in a nice tone. "I'm busy Roy, I need to get this done, and I have to make a call and get ready for work, I bet you have plenty to do right?" I asked looking at him with wonder in my eyes. "Oh yeah I have some things to do," he said backing away from the doorway. "I will talk to you later," I tell him goodbye. As scared as I was of being alone in that room I felt uncomfortable talking to him about things my sister does with her money.

I sat down on the bed after getting all my clothes in order. I lay down, I needed to clear my head, and I took a deep breath. I don't know if I'm able to live alone. I know it is going be a challenge for me, but anything to get me away from whatever has been attacking me in here, I thought, taking another deep breath, I got up to take some things to my car. As I stood there putting my things in the bag there was that smell; it was so foul. I turned my head to see where it was coming from I felt a swift, cold air blowing on my neck.

I closed my eyes and held my bag tight. I felt a hand on my neck and another on my breast. I clutched the bag to my stomach, and I whispered stop, stop, I was feeling so confused, what's happening? It was squeezing harder and harder, my breast started to hurt, and my neck felt as if the grip was tighter as I moved the bag closer to my chest as if I was pushing it toward my breast to move the hands of it away from my breast. As I moved forward the grip on my neck became tighter. "Please stop!" I yelled.

All I could think was stop I don't want you, and it came out. "I don't want you, stop please!" The grip on my neck   became loose, and I felt the hand let go of my neck. I fell to the floor I could still feel the breathing on my back as I fell. I could still smell the foul odor. I just laid there hoping it will leave and I could move. I don't know what would happen to me if I tried to leave before it does so I stayed there clutching my bag to my stomach hoping that Roy would just pop in the doorway and ask me a question. I began to pray closing my eyes shutting them as tight as I could.

No Roy yet, I could still smell it close. I scooted across the floor toward the door I could smell it less and less as I pushed myself closer to the door. I reached for the doorknob while holding my bag with the other hand and I felt it smack my hand a way and hitting me in the face knocking me out. I remember waking up on the floor the next day. I sat up and looked around;

No one came into the room to look for me. The phone didn't ring, and Rose was somewhere in the house. I just sat there in the same clothes I wore yesterday holding my hands to my head, I was shaking, thinking why was that thing touching my breast? If no one ever comes for me what's going to stop it from doing other things to me?

What does it want from me, and how can I escape it? I quickly got my things together moving as quickly as I could. I put everything I owned by the door. I didn't want to leave anything because I will never return after today. I am going to sleep in my car or stay with someone; I can never go back into this house again. I put everything in my car; I got in and looked up at the house. No one or nothing is going to attack me ever again I thought as I drove away. I went to the hospital for my schedule hoping to run into Maddy to at least talk to her. I can't keep hiding these secrets.

Maybe I can tell her without giving her the facts. I will make something up; I will tell her that Rose and Roy want me out. I just need somewhere to stay until I can move into my place. It wouldn't be a complete lie. I walked around the hospital looking around where she usually took time out to talk to her friends. I went to the third floor and looked in almost every room. Some of the nurses said hi as I passed them quickly walking down the halls. They stared at me as if my eyes were telling them something was troubling me; I couldn't find Maddy anywhere. As I walked down the hallway to catch the elevator, I heard footsteps quickly approaching me from behind. I felt a tap on my shoulder. "Hey girl, where have you been?" A deep voice said to me.

I turned to look. It was Michael. "Hi." I said looking up at him. He stood back and looked at me shocked. "What happened? Who did this to you?" He asked me grabbing my face and tilting it back as if he found something terrible on my face. "What do you mean?" I asked him. "What's wrong with my face?" I asked. "What's wrong with your face?" He questioned holding my head back. "There is nothing wrong with your face you have a huge fist print right over your eye by your temple." He said touching my temple where the imprint was.

"Ouch!" I said as he pressed his fingers down to my eye. "Oh, a box fell on top of my head," I told him. "A box with a fist," he said. "No way, it looks awful, someone hit you, you're bruised pretty badly," he said. "Let's go into one of these rooms and take a closer look okay?" He said taking me by the hand.

We went into the room and Michael began to examine the bruise. "What the hell happened to you?" He asked. "I wish I knew," I told him. "I was packing my things and all I remember was waking up on the floor," I told him. "I called you all night," he said. "This must be the reason for you not answering my phone calls. Whoever did this knocked you out cold." He covered the bruises and gave me an ice pack. "Here take this and don't move, did you see anyone?" He asked.

"No I didn't, there was no one else there," I told him. "I don't think so, someone was there, and they hit you," I got down off the examining table and went to the door. "Michael, I don't know what happened to me, I didn't see anyone I just woke up like this." I told him. I didn't even know there were bruises on my face, I came here to find Maddy," I told him. "Thank you so much, Michael, I will see you later. If you see Maddy, please tell her that I will be at my father's house, ok thank you," I walked out into the hall. I kept the ice pack on my head.

My goodness I thought, I never looked in the mirror this morning I just left the house. I should have known something was wrong. My face was a little sore. I was so scared this morning I didn't even think about going to the bathroom. I drove over to daddy's house so quickly I was sure to have violated some laws because of how fast I was driving. When I arrived there Daisy was there and daddy was having a talk with her about her boyfriend. Daddy was very serious. I got out and said hi as I walked past them making my way to the bathroom so that I could take a look at my face before I am questioned by daddy and Daisy.

I walked in and Richard and Randall were sitting on the couch with three women I never seen before. "Hi guys," I say to them in passing. "Hey ears, long time no see," Randall says to me smiling. "Where have you been?" He asked. "I've been around." I replied to him. I rushed away to the bathroom brushing Randall off. I got in, closed the door fast and leaned against it. "Oh my goodness," I said to myself, I went to the mirror with my eyes closed.

"Here goes nothing," I sighed. I opened my eyes it was so bad it actually looked like a fist print on my face. I needed to get somewhere quick so that my brothers and father wouldn't think someone attacked me. I put the bandage Michael covered it with back on and walked out. My brother Richard was standing outside the door. "Are you ok? I have to go bad; he said pushing me out of the way. I went to the front door; I stumbled on the table near the door.

My brother Randall grabbed my shirt, "Hey you need to slow down girl," he said pulling me up. "Oh, I have to get to work." I told him reaching for the door. "I will see you guys later," the girls on the couch waved bye to me. I stepped out the door and daddy was on the porch sitting, watering the grass. I hope that he doesn't notice it; I turned to the side as I walked down the stairs.

"Karis," daddy said, "come sit with me." "Oh daddy I really can't talk right now I have to go," I tell him. "   Karis, where are you going?" Daddy asked. "I have to meet Maddy; I'm staying at her place until mine is ready," I tell him looking down at the grass he was watering. "Why sugar? Why are you staying there until your place is ready? What is going on at Roses house that you can't stay there?" He asked. "Did they put you out?" "No, I just think they need a little space, and I don't mind staying at Maddy's." Daddy handed me the hose. "Here baby," he said while reaching into his pocket.

"I bet you don't have any money do you?" I could tell daddy had been drinking, his eyes were red, and his speech was slurred. "No daddy I'm fine. I don't need any money, I still have enough money left in the bank," I tell him handing him the hose. "Daddy I have to go now," I say walking to my car. "Okay then baby," he said waving his hand to me with a cigarette in it. "I will see you soon, call me when you are ready to go pick out your furniture ok." "Ok, daddy I will." I went back to the hospital to see if I can catch Maddy.

I hope I wouldn't run into Michael again. When I went inside everyone at the front desk was staring at me while a nurse picked up the phone to page Maddy. "Maddy please come to the first floor!" Nurse Cherry walked up to me and grabbed me by the hand. "Honey, are you feeling ok ay?" She asked. "Sure I'm fine." I tell her, "I'm just fine." Maddy comes running towards me. "Are you okay?" She asked. "Sit down, sit down," she says pulling me toward the couch in the waiting room.

"Michael called me after you left," she said. "He said you remember getting hit, but you don't know what hit you?" She began removing the bandage on my head. "Now Karis, you don't have to lie to me," she said with a stern voice. "You know I'm only here to help you so please tell me, who did this to you? She removed the bandage, "Oh god!" She said covering her mouth. "Did one of your sister's boyfriends do this to you?" She asked. I shook my head no. "I don't know what happened to me; I just remember waking up like this with my face hurting a little, but I didn't know it was there," I told her.

"Michael noticed it when I came in looking for you," Maddy shook her head. "Do you have to work today?" She asked. "I can't believe this," Cherry said. "Take Karis off the schedule today and put on for this weekend," she said. "Come on young lady; it's time to talk." Maddy grabbed me by the hand, and we went outside. "You follow me to my house ok ay dear, how's your head? Do you have a headache?" She asked.

"Can you drive?" She looked inside my car. "Karis, what's this? Is it all your things?" Maddy was going in circles with all her questions; she kept asking me was I okay. I wasn't prepared for her to react this way. I watched her as she shook her head with worry, and waited for her to calm down a little. "Yes Maddy these are my clothes, I had to leave because I didn't know what was going on. I was scared I don't want to go back to Roses house," I told her.

"Oh you're not going back there, you can stay at my place until yours is ready," she said. I followed her to her house. I thought, thank you, God, I didn't have to tell her anything, and Michael ran and told her for me. "Thanks, Michael," I said clutching my steering wheel. "Thank you." We arrived at Maddy's, and she made us some tea. "We are going to get your stuff out of the car then you are going to tell me what happened in detail." I thought to myself; she wants a story, what do I do?

We brought my things in after finishing the tea; I sat at the table. Maddy sat down handing me another cup of tea. "So what's the story?"

She asked. "I know you re member what happened." "No, I don't remember Maddy, I was packing my clothes and talking to Roy, and he left, I began to put my things in a bag, and I reached for the door, and something hit me." "Did you see who was there?" She asked. "No, I didn't see anyone, I didn't hear anyone either," I told her.

"Well, I will have to take your word for it I guess," she said shaking her head. She put her cup in the sink and left me at the table. "I will be in the restroom if you need me knock on the door, make yourself at home." I moved the cup away from me. I needed a bath I thought as I put my head down on the table. I must have been exhausted. "Karis! Karis!" I heard someone calling me while shaking my arm.

"Get up dear, go on and take a bath," Maddy told me helping me up by my arm. "Go ahead, I have fixed up the spare room for you, and your bath water is running," she told me handing me a towel. "I'll wait until your done to go to bed, I'll be out here on this couch," I went   into the bathroom and began to take off my clothes. I stared at the bruises in the mirror as I took off my shirt and removed my bra. My right breast had marks and bruises all around the nipple; there were scratches and bruises as if it was pulled and tugged at, I quickly took everything off.

In fear of anything attacking me, I got into the bath water and washed off as quickly as I could still looking all around, I dried off and put on my shirt and pants and went for the door. I bent down to pick up my clothes as I opened the door I thought I heard a knocking noise coming from the shower. I hurried out. Maddy was waiting reading a book, "you know your hair is wet," she told me. "That was a very quick bath, did you get everything," she asked me.

"There are a comb and brush on the dresser in there, she got up and walked toward me. I made sure I covered my chest. I'm glad she followed me to through room. I sat on the bed and brushed my hair out." Maddy, will you please stay in here with me?" I asked her. "Sure I will," she said. She took the hairbrush from my hand and began to brush my hair for me. I sat still as she brushed my hair. I wished I could open up and tell her about these things that I've been going through since the accident.

"So Karis, you never really tell me what's going on with you, how has your body been feeling?" She asked. "Are you feeling any pain or anything?" Oh no, I thought. "Well when the weather changes and it gets cold, I sometimes ache all over, but especially in my arms and legs," I tell her. "I've had these awful headaches too, other than that I'm okay." "Do you ever think about the accident or have any dreams about it?" She asked. "I think about a lot of things, especially when my leg hurts me, I try to wear long pants so that people won't see the way that I walk, and I always feel like people are watching me, so I walk fast."

Maddy began to laugh. "Yes you do walk a little fast, it's almost as if you're skating by," she laughed again. "You do know that you're beautiful. You're a lovely young lady, and if people are watching you, maybe they just want to get to know you better. That's what people do; they stare when they can't find the right words to say." "No, Maddy I'm not beautiful, I've been hiding behind these scars for so long. I pretend to be as normal I can, but I walk; differently, I see people wearing shorts and when it's hot, and I'm envious. I think why this did happen to me, what did I do to deserve this" "Lord, girl."

Maddy grabbed me close to her then she took me by the hand and walked me over to the mirror. "Look at you Karis; you are so beautiful, use what you do have, you are blessed to have what you do have. Some people didn't live through what you did; they didn't get a second chance, so I say stop worrying about what people think. Live for your sister and your niece who didn't get that chance, whatever God brings your way in this life, is all a challenge for you to change and do something better. He saved you for a reason, now I don't know the reason, but I'm sure it's something special that only you can do for him.

So smile for me because you can walk a little funny and show people that you are strong, they may look at you funny, but they don't know why or what happened to you. It's left up to you to tell them." We lay down on the bed, and Maddy called the in cats. "Moving day will be here soon, you make sure you call the utility company tomorrow dear," she said falling off to sleep holding cookie close to her chest. I moved close to her. Maybe Maddy's right I have to just take it all in, maybe there is a reason why these things are happening to me.

I closed my eyes and fell to sleep. I was so comfortable, I felt safe maybe this thing would leave me alone soon. I woke up the next morning feeling so good. I could smell breakfast cooking, and   Maddy was moving all around in the kitchen. "Honey, wash and come eat, I sat the paper out for you please read it, oh and the numbers for you to call for utilities is right on the table," she was yelling out to me as if she was in a hurry. I could see her moving around really fast in the hallway.

She was already dressed up holding her coffee cup. I went into the bathroom and washed my face. I looked in the mirror the bruises looked a little lighter today. I put my clothes on and joined Maddy in the kitchen; she was so busy. "I have to go honey, but you stay here, call those numbers, the address to your place is right over there, make yourself comfortable, and I will be home a little after five o clock this evening." She said hurrying out of the door. I was scared to be alone, but I have to make these calls today.

I turned the TV on and made sure the cats stayed near. I began to call everyone I needed to call because I was afraid, I didn't want to be here alone. I'm going to find daddy, I will follow him all day. I thought. After making all the calls I went into the bathroom to brush my hair. The cats followed. Maddy had face makeup on the counter. I took a little and rubbed it on the bruises on my face. I took a look at the other bruises on my breast they were the same. I was still sore to the touch. I began to wonder what would happen next as I looked over my body.

The cats followed me all over as I dressed to go meet daddy. He would be so surprised to see me. I don't care who he's with today. Daddy will have to put them on the back burner for me. I rushed out. I drove to daddy's house, there was no cars parked in front so I went to the door. I knocked and Randall answered. "Hey Karis, what's up" He asked me with the door cracked. "Oh where's daddy," I asked him. "I think he went with Richard to sign up for the army," he said smiling. "Okay do you know where the place is?" I asked.

"It's on the corner downtown, near the mall," he says shutting the door on me. "Bye," I walked back to my car. I drove downtown to find daddy. I did find him. Richard was taking a test while daddy waited for him in the lobby. I parked and went in. I could see daddy in the window having a pleasant conversation with the lady sitting at the front desk. When he saw me walking toward him his eyes opened wide, "Hi sweetie," he said with excitement in his voice. "What brings you down here?" "You, daddy," I tell him.

"I came to spend time with you, maybe we can do a little shopping as you promised, I'm ready when you are," He said grabbing my hand pulling me toward his cheek. He kissed me and pulled me down into the seat next to him. "Hello young lady, are you interested in joining the military today?" The women at the desk asked. "Oh no," daddy said. "You can't have this one, this is my baby," he said smiling. I smiled at the women; she was in a uniform. "Are you in the military?" I asked. "Yes I am, I love it," she said smiling and walking over to me.

"So what are your plans?" "I'm going to be a nurse," I told her. "She needs to be a teacher really," daddy quickly told her. "She's teaching material," he said. Daddy always wanted one of us to become a teacher because all of his sisters were teachers, but I know that I just don't have the patience for it. I think that being a nurse is for me. "Daddy, can we leave Richard here?" I asked. "I have work this evening, I don't have a lot of time," I told him. "If you guys have to go, we can give him a ride home," the woman told us.

"Oh no honey, we will wait for him," daddy told her. Richard came out an hour later; I read magazines to past the time away while daddy talked with the woman, only to speak to me every so often. I was so glad when he came out; I was tired of waiting for him. When Richard came out, he looked anxious. "I passed dad," he said. "Hey Karis, what are you doing here?" He asked me. "I'm joining the army," he tells me. "I heard; why are you joining?" I asked him as we walked out of the door to the car. "It's Vira, she's having a baby, and I need to do something to take care of them, I needed a career. I can go to school and get paid for doing a job in the army too; I will be able to support my family," he said.

"Oh I see, wow Vira's pregnant huh, it looks like there's going to be a lot of babies born to the Lawson family this year," I said. I must have spoken too soon because daddy looked at me very strange. "What do you mean Karis; the only kid coming into the Lawson family is this kid of Richards, right?" Daddy asked looking very confused. Oops, I guess they don't know about Daisy and Rose being pregnant. Daddy continued looking at me with concern on his face. "Now Karis, what are you saying?" he asked me again. "Oh daddy let's just go and get my furniture," I said pulling him by the arm.

We went to the furniture store right downtown that daddy recommended. There was all kind of furniture to choose from. They had everything I needed in a set. I picked the living room set. It was a brown leather couch, a loveseat, and three tables to go with them. Daddy picked my kitchen table; it had four chairs and a nice cherry wood table with glass in the middle. It was very nice and Richard helped me with the bedroom furniture. He picked a really nice set. It was a cherry wood frame and bedpost with a chest to match, and a white lace valance to cover the top of the bed at night it came with two night stands too.

I bought a mattress and two lamps and a couple of pictures. I had so much fun with daddy and Richard. I paid for it, and the sales guy asked me for my address for delivery. He told me that it would be delivered between 3 to 7 next week; I was so excited I've got my furniture, I'm moving out on my own. When we finished, I asked daddy and Richard to go out to Pofolks with me to eat. I wanted to thank them for coming with me today by buying them lunch.

They were glad I did because we had not eaten anything all day. When we arrived at Pofolks, it was very crowded. The line was out past the door. Richard looked at me and daddy standing in the line. "Hold on you guys," he said walking away. "Excuse me," he said pushing his way through the crowd. He made it inside, we didn't see him for a while, but when he came back, he was with a waitress and the manager. "Hello sir," she said to daddy.

"Follow me," she said walking us through the crowd. "I'm so sorry you had to wait out here," she said, we followed her inside she sat us on the top floor in a balcony seat overlooking the restaurant. I tugged at Richard's shirt. "Um Richard isn't this wrong, those people have been waiting for hours," I said to him. "No Karis, this isn't wrong at all, those people need to get better connected." He said smiling at me and taking the menu from the waitress looking down at her bottom. "It's always good to know the owner's daughter," he said rubbing her backside.

Daddy smiled at him, "yes, you have to keep your connections," he looked down at his menu. We ordered our food and ate, talking and laughing about the crowded restaurant. I was a little worried watching daddy and Richard; I thought who is going to keep an eye on daddy when Richard goes away. Daddy always has Richard around and I know he trust him. Who's going to care for daddy when he drinks now, when we were done I paid the check, and daddy kissed me on the cheek, and they both thanked me. I took off to work right after. Daddy and Richard would get a ride to their car from the owner's daughter.

I made to work a little early so I sat in the lobby outside. I watched the people come in and out looking for family and asking for help. I saw Maddy coming up the hallway looking very angry. She was walking so fast that she walked right past me. I dared to call out to her. She was really angry. I sat back in the seat to watch what was going on. Maddy and another nurse were caught up in a very intense conversation. I could see how mad they were just looking at their faces. The room began to fill with other staff. Soon, there seem to be a big meeting with the administrator. It was intense.

I couldn't stay; it was time for me to go to work. I went past everyone toward the elevator. As I stood there waiting it was freezing. I felt a hand grab my wrist it squeezed it tight. Then I felt someone touch my lower back. I felt nothing but cold air all around me. As the door opened for to the elevator I could feel it still holding my wrist and pushing my back following me into the elevator. It was like I was pushed in, as a couple of nurses walked out. Oh no not again I thought, not here please I said as the doors to the elevator closed.

There was a foul smell in the elevator it was stronger than ever. I began to scream this time, but no one could hear me. I could feel the breathing on my neck. It was heavy. "Stop it I said, stop it, get away from me!" It grabbed me by the waist and pushed me up against the elevator walls. I pushed back from the wall and tried going toward the buttons to open the doors, but it kept me to the wall. Please God let someone come to the door, I thought. Please let the doors open again. I moved my body back and forth so it wouldn't pin me to the wall.

I began to feel it tighten its grip on my waist and wrist. It became tighter and tighter it was rubbing me, I felt it all over my breast and in between my legs. Whatever it is, it is very strong. As I fought it, it began to throw me all around the elevator; I was even thrown up. I began to get very tired. I just prayed, god help me please. The bell to the elevator went off and the doors began to open. I was tossed to the ground. When I woke up I was in a hospital bed. I screamed. "Help Me, God!!"

I sat up, and Michael was standing over me, Maddy was standing with him. Maddy called out to the hallway. "She's awake, get the doctor in here now" I looked around. My whole body was sore again I laid back into the pillow. "Oh no, It's happened again," I thought as looked up. "Hi," Michael said. "Are you okay?" He asked I turned my head. I didn't want him to see me this way,   Maddy came over to me. "What's wrong honey, you can't talk or something?" She asked holding my hand. "No, I'm okay Maddy," I tell her.

"What happened, who was in the elevator with you?" She asked   in a panic. "I was alone, I think," I tell her. "No honey, you weren't alone, someone was with you, you are bruised up badly, we found you on the floor, the police are coming to take your statement, you tell them who was there and what happened." She put covers over my waist, and another doctor walked in. "Hi, I'm Dr. Shain," he walked toward me. "I just need to check your wounds; I hear you were attacked, is that right?" He asked as he checked my vitals. He pulled the cover away from my body and began to look over my body. "So this happened in the elevator, huh?" I leaned back on the pillow and closed my eyes so tight.

I just want them all to go away leave me alone, I don't know who it was nor where it came from, I just want it to stop I thought as they all talked around me. I could hear the police come in. Oh God no, I don't want to lie about the attack. I was tapped on the shoulder. "Young lady, can you look at me for a second," after Dr. Shain was done touching me he walked away. I was sore all over again. I almost cried out stop. "After your talk with the police I need to come in and check if you have any tear s or abrasions on your vagina," he said. The police officer held his note pad. "My name is Officer Benson; can you tell me what your attacker looked like?" He asked. I shook my head no.

"I'm going to need you to tell me everything you saw," he said, and after I had nothing much to give him; he walked away with his notepad in his hand. I looked over at Maddy. The doctor came back into the room. "Okay, Karis I need to do a kit on you, have you ever had a pelvic exam before?" He asked me. I looked over at Maddy. "No, I haven't," I tell him. "I will just be shining a light down there, and there will be some touching, don't be afraid I'll make it quick, I promise." He said helping me to spread my legs open. "If there were any trauma down there I would document it for evidence," I touched my right knee.

"This knee can't go any further," I tell him. I could feel him began to touch me down there with his gloves. He was explaining all that he was doing to me as he went along, Maddy stayed close and Michael left the room. When he was done he said thank you for being so cooperative. Just when I thought it was all over the policeman walked back in with a camera in his hand. "Ms. Karis, I need to get some pictures of your bruises, if that's okay," he said coming up to me. "Okay," I said sitting up on the bed. "I need you to stand for me if you can," he asked politely. He took pictures of my breast my neck my back and wrist even my waist had bruises all around it. I was ashamed and embarrassed.

I covered myself as they all left the room. I began to get dressed. I just want to get out of here; I thought as I dressed up. Maddy came back into the room with me; "going somewhere?" She asked me. "I want to go home," I tell her. "I would like you to go home to, but I think its best if you hang around here, and I'll take you home later, you had a tough day." She sat down on the bed. "I don't think you should be left alone dear,"

"Oh Maddy I'm fine, I just need to get out of here," I tell her while I put on my shoes. "Is there something going on with you that you want to share with me?" She asked. She came over to me and hugged me. "You know there is nothing that you can't share with me; I'm here for you." I knew that Maddy was there for me, but this thing is bizarre and scary I don't think she would handle me fighting something I can't see very well.

So I'd keep this to myself for a while." Maddy I don't know what happened I said standing to my feet, and I think your right I will wait for you, I don't need to be alone" I tell her. It made her happy she walked me out into the hallway, "Go ahead Maddy finish your shift, I won't leave without you." I sat down in the lobby waiting for Maddy; I sat there thinking about it the whole time.

This thing can attack me anywhere, where would I ever be safe, I thought as I watched people come in and out. I continued to tell these lies and keep this a secret, what if I'm hurt one day. I don't know what to do about this, I needed help, but who do I tell without being called crazy? I have suffered enough I thought. The next day I stayed close to Maddy, everywhere she went I was right behind her.

When moving day came Richard and daddy came over to my to see my place, I tried to make them stay all night. I talked about everything I could while they helped me put things away, and when the furniture truck came, I asked them to help me put everything in place just to keep them longer. Maddy stayed and helped hang pictures with me. She bought me dishes and silverware. I was so happy that they were there. I had no fear when they were around.

The minute they walked out one by one I began to get more and more afraid. Where would it attack me next, and will I be saved this time, and is it going to stop, what does it want from me? Maddy was the last to leave. I closed the door and sat on the couch; I turned on the TV, will it ever be peaceful here in my home? I questioned. Will I ever enjoy being alone here?

Settling In

I watched TV and ate a bag of chips. I have my purple phone on the table next to the couch. I haven't given my phone number to anyone yet. I wished that before the night was over, I would get some visitors, and they'd want to stay the night. I picked up my phone and began to call around to all my siblings looking for Krystal. Maybe she'd want to stay the night with me, and I called Martha also. As always she wasn't home, I gave everyone I called my new number.

"Please have Krystal call me as soon as she gets home," I told them. I called daddy too; he was so busy with his women friends. "I just wanted to see how you were doing daddy," I tell him. "I will call you later," I hung up. I just sat back on the couch after no luck with the calls I fell off to sleep fast. I was startled by the loud ringing of the phone. I kept my eyes closed as I reached for the phone. "Hello," I said. "Hello, Michael?" I asked "Yes, He answers back to me "How are you, baby?" He says in his sexy voice, "I missed you today." "I'm better." I tell him. "So I hear that you've moved into your place," "Yes" I answer. "So when will I be invited to come by to see?" He asked.

"I don't know if that's a good idea," I tell him "Oh yeah, why can't I come by and take a peek?" I thought it would be a bad idea because I like Michael and I'm so curious about some of the things he talks about, like making love. "Michael you can't come over because I just don't know you that well yet," I tell him. I think we should talk over the phone for a while, can we do that?" I asked him. He was silent for a second; then I heard him clear his throat. "Okay baby, that's cool." and he began to talk. He made me laugh all night.

Michael was so charming, the things we talked about, things he would say to me would be so interesting, things I never heard before, and he liked to talk a lot about how he would make love to me. I loved to hear about it. He asked me had I ever made love before. He claimed to be the best at it. I told him, "No I haven't." "Really, well promise me you'll let me be the first one to touch your precious body," he said chewing his gum. I didn't say a word. I couldn't do that because I don't know what to expect when it comes to making love.

"I'm not an expert," I tell him. "Then I will be your teacher; you want to be the best, you have to learn from the best," he tells me. "I assure you I will make you the best lover ever known," he says. "Okay, I'm going back to sleep now," I tell him laughing. "Oh, you can't handle it," he says laughing. "Okay then, sweet dreams baby," he says hanging up. I want to kiss Michael so badly after talking to him over the phone.

I do want to learn from him. I wished I could be comfortable enough to show off my body I thought as I got up and went to the bathroom in my room. I took off all my clothes and stood in front of the mirror, looking myself over. Huh, I have a wonderful set of breast I thought, and my stomach is flat, and aside from all the scarring my legs are okay, really pale, but okay, my backside was a little flat, but it matches everything.

What I liked most about me was my breast, my small waist, and stomach they seemed almost perfect for someone as thin as me. Leaving the mirror, I went into my bedroom I still had all my clothes in bags and boxes. I went through them to find me something to wear to bed. Then I will start putting them away. My bed had no sheets. I had one blanket that daddy had brought over; I would use it tonight, I needed so many things for the house; I had no toiletries or food in the house.

Once I put my things away I would write in my journal and make a list of all the things I need to buy tomorrow. Maybe Michael would like to come with me to buy something. I thought. I'm not going to invite Michael over, maybe in a couple of months. Lord, I thank you for watching over me through the day thank you for blessing me with this wonderful place. Lord, I know that these things that are happening to me are to learn by, but I'm afraid, and I know I shouldn't fear anything but you, but this thing attacks me, touching me and bruising my body.

I fight Lord, but I don't understand it, I can't see who I'm fighting, I can feel it. It's powerful lord; please keep me safe from harm. Lord, I'm learning to comfort myself, Lord, please help me to protect myself from the spirit that attacks me. Fight it when I can't, Lord thank you for your many blessings amen. I put my book down and grabbed the blanket. I went back into the living room where I would sleep with the TV on; I made my list and laid on the couch wrapping myself really tight in the blanket.

I have been so tired. I can't wait until tomorrow I thought as I fell off to sleep. It was so hard for me to sleep because I was so scared of being attacked. I tossed and turned all night thinking about the next the next attack all the time. When I woke up the next morning I stretched and went into the bathroom to wash my face and brush my teeth grabbed my clothes quickly dressed and left the house. I went to Maddy's house. She was still cooking breakfast when I showed up. Thank god I thought as I rang the doorbell.

"Come in," Maddy said. "Good morning honey," Maddy says handing me a plate of food the second I stepped into the kitchen. "Maddy I need to buy sheets, pillows, soap, and tissue, do you know where I should go and get those things?" I asked her. "Oh yes, honey we can get these things at K-mart, or Wards." "Okay Maddy, that's where I'll go," I said. "Are you working today, honey?" She asked me. "Yes I have to go in at three today, I'm working on the second floor, I've never worked the second floor before," I tell her. "I don't know what to expect."

"Oh honey, you can handle working anywhere, I've seen you, you are pretty good at adapting to new surroundings well, you will do good anywhere we put you, are you afraid because of what happened?" "I can't be afraid, Maddy, I have to be strong and push through this." I tell her thinking to myself I'm not afraid of it I just never know when it will attack ,the fear is just not knowing if I'm going to make it out of it when it's finished with me I thought.

I have to live my life. I went to work that day with a clear mind trying not to think of that day inside the elevator but that night on the phone with Michael laughing and talking about lovemaking and how he could teach me to be a great lover. I smiled as I walked toward the front entrance of the hospital. The hall to the emergency room was full. You could see the people standing outside talking and waiting. There was an ambulance pulling up into the entrance and standing next it was a short woman, she was standing with her arms folded.

She was standing as if she had been waiting. When I reached the door she came and grabbed my hand. She led me toward the ambulance. I stood back as they took a young girl out rolling her into the hospital. I walked alongside them with the old woman's hand in mine. She pointed at the young girl and the minute I got close to her I began to feel sorrow and pain. The girl needed to Passover. Sometimes I wondered what keeps them.

What makes them lay sick when it's time to pass it seems they can't as if they are waiting in fear of what they might find on the other side. I think perhaps, they do wait for someone familiar to help them journey across to the heavens. I wished I knew why I was chosen to bring them close into the light. As soon as they put the women into the room, I waited as everyone went into the hallway to discuss with the family members what was going on. I went to the young girl, I held her hand. The old short woman touched my face, and I felt warm all over.

The young girl looked up at me and with tears in her eyes, she whispered to me, "Thank you," I walked out fast. I didn't want anyone to see me near her. I was not assigned to that floor. I went into the bathroom to wash my face. I had to take a breather. My body felt weak after that. I don't know what happened to the young girl but I was so weak.

I stayed in the bathroom until my shift started. When I walked out there was Michael in his white coat. "Hey beautiful," he said walking toward me. "I have been searching this place all day for that smile, what time are you off?" He asked. "I would like to take you on a date," he looked me in my face as if he knew I would say no. "Please say yes, I am starving for your company, in person, not on the phone," he said holding both my hands.

"So what's the word, are you my date or not?" He asked chewing his gum and staring into my eyes. I can't say no. I look at him, and he makes me laugh, I like it. I put my guard down. "I will go out with you," I told him. He smiled and jumped up really high. "I've got a date with an angel," he yelled out. "Shh!" I said, "stop it, we're in the hospital remember? I grabbed his coat. "I will pick you up at eight."

"We can leave from here," I tell him, hoping he'd agree. I didn't want him to know where I lived yet. "You don't want to go home and change?" He asked. "I do, I will go home change and come back, and we can leave from here." "Okay whatever you want," he said. "I am good with anything you want to do. I worked my shift smiling thinking about what our date would be like. I rushed to my house took a shower. I wore a nice dress not too long, but fitting and black, I wore boots with it, and I let my hair down.

I put some perfume on, a little bit of eye makeup and lip gloss. I was ready to meet with Michael. I was so excited. When I got back to the hospital, Michael was waiting in his car all dressed up in black slacks and a nice red shirt it was unbuttoned in the front where you could see his bare chest just a little. I could smell his cologne from the window. He got out and walked over to my car. He opened my door and took me by the hand.

"Hello lady" He said pulling me toward his car. He had a very beautiful red sports car. He opened the door for me I got in and he ran over to the other side and got in. "Fasten your seatbelt lady, I'm taking you on a long overdue adventure," he said as we drove off. We drove onto the highway. "I have a huge surprise for you Karis," he said looking at me and chewing his gum. We went up a long hill; it was so dark the moon was full and bright.

"Michael I'm afraid of heights," I told him. "Oh baby, I'm not taking you to high, just high enough for you to feel free to hold on to me," he said. I looked over at him. I was nervous. Michael pulled over alongside a restaurant. He came over to my door and opened it taking me by the hand. "You think we are going there?" He asked me. "Aren't we?" I asked. "No baby, I said I have a surprise for you, not something you're probably used to, right?" He said, "No I'm not, I don't date much," I tell him.

"Oh I see," he says putting his arm around my waist. I don't like to walk when someone is holding me by the waist because I walk with a little limp and I get really nervous. So I kindly took his hand away from my waist and held his hand in mine as we walked. We walked and walked; I had to ask, "Michael, so is this surprise of yours a very long walk?" "I want you to see something; this walk is almost over, I promise. Okay here we are, close your eyes," he said.

"Okay," I covered my eyes. We went walking a little further Michael lead the way. "Open up," he said. When I opened my eyes I was standing in front of a table with candles and wine glasses. There was food on the table and flowers with many colors. "Surprise," he yelled. "I hope you like steak and potatoes," he said pulling my chair out for me. "It was all I could afford," he laughed and sat down. "I do," I tell him looking all around.

It was beautiful out there on the beach. We ate and laughed and talked. Michael had these perfect teeth they made for a great warm smile they looked as if they were made for his face. After we ate we went for a long walk on the beach. I took my boots off and walked barefoot I was comfortable. Michael held my hand as we walked. "I know your old fashion Karis, but when do you think you'll be ready to make love?" He asked me. "I don't know, I don't think I'm going to wait until I'm married, but I would like to wait until I'm in love," I tell him.

"So when do you know you're in love?" He asked me. "I don't know," we sat down on the sand and talked more. Michael reached out for my boots. "These boots are so nice," he said zipping them up and down while I held them in my lap. "Can I?" He asked with his hand on my feet. "I would like to rub them," "I guess it won't hurt," I tell him smiling. "Go ahead," he pulled me close to him and took my right foot.

"They're beautiful," he said caressing my feet. He stopped and took his shoes off. "Isn't this nice baby?" He asked me, "It is nice," I tell him looking down at his feet, wow he even has nice feet. I thought. I looked over at him and smiled. He was staring up at the moon. "How would you know it's nice when you're not even looking up at the moon?" "Oh, I hardly ever look up," I tell him. "Oh yeah, why is that?" Michael asked. "I don't know. I mean I look up sometimes, but I had an experience that scared me some time ago."

"Hmm what kind of experience that might have been, to make you hardly look up at the moon?" He asked. I got up from the sand and began walking. Michael got up and walked behind me grabbing me by the shirt. He was so funny. "Young lady, I want to kiss your lips," he said pulling me back as if we were in an old movie. I closed my eyes. It felt as if he was going to drop me. He quickly pulled me up and held my cheeks tight. He kissed me on the lips and then stared at me. "Did that hurt?" He asked.

"Because I'm going to do it again," this time he grabbed my waist and pulled me so close. He began to kiss me again this time so passionately that my knees were weak. We kissed for a long time. Michael moaned and rubbed my neck at the same time. He sucked on my bottom lip than pulled back. He looked into my eyes. "I'm going to make you fall in love with me," he said begging to kiss me again. We kissed for a long time. I could feel Michaels tongue in my mouth when he took it out he kissed all over my neck again and again.

Michael tasted of double mint gum. As we kissed he held me tight I could feel his penis harden as he caressed my back. I pulled away from him and ran back to the table. He ran behind me. When we made it to the table I sat down. "What's wrong?" He asked sitting down next to me. "Oh, I think you needed to cool down," I told him laughing and pointing at his pants. He took his wine glass from the table. "Are you going to drink with me?" "Oh no, I don't drink." "You don't, wow you're going to make this hard aren't you?" He said.

"If you don't drink, how am I ever going to get you drunk enough to get you in bed with me" He said laughing "Have you ever tried drinking?" He asked. "I never have and never will, "I feel that if I were to drink I turn into someone, I never knew before and acted out badly, I will never try it "I will never act like my father and brothers, I saw it before, and it's not pretty," I tell him shaking my head. "I can't believe that you don't drink, you don't have to get drunk it's just a little wine, It won't hurt, a matter of fact doctors recommend it," he smiled and raised his eyebrows.

"To be honest, I thought I would have had a chance at it if you were a little tipsy," he said laughing. Michael was very honest. He didn't hold anything back. We spent the rest of the night laughing and talking walking on the beach. When he brought me back to my car we kissed and kissed, Michael, made me feel so good when he kissed me, I could feel it all over my body I was warm all over. I can't even imagine what it would be like making love to him he was so gentle never missing a spot on me that made my body reacts to his passion. I drove home thinking about all the things we could do together.

Michael was definitely a ladies man. He'd probably leave me and go over to some other women's house and make love to her. I thought. I drove up to my house. I forgotten to leave the porch light on but there was a car in my driveway. It was daddy's car. I pulled up close to it and there was daddy, drunk and playing his music as loud as he could. Some oldies, "Hi daddy" I said "Are you okay, what are you doing here?" I asked him.

"Oh baby I just wanted to come by and check on you" He said holding his cigarette out of the window. He was shaking his head to the music as I got out of the car. Daddy was so drunk I could smell the alcohol as I approached him. I put my purse around my arm and I helped him to the front door with his arm around my neck. "Daddy you have to put that cigarette out," I tell him as I open the door. "Okay baby," he said taking one last puff from it. He threw it into the dirt near the porch. We went in. I put daddy on the couch. "Daddy I didn't get around to buying more blankets or anything today, but I do have the blanket you gave me," I told him.

"Oh baby daddy will just sit here in the cold, I'm warm anyway," he said slurring his words. He was shaking his head and singing one of the temptations old songs. "I know you wanna leave me, but I refuse to let you go, if I had to beg and pled for your sympathy, I don't mind cause you mean that much to me ain't too proud to beg, oh please don't leave me, honey." Daddy sang the same verse over and over again.

I went into the kitchen and got him a glass of water. "Daddy, will you stay here while I take a shower okay," I tell him. "Don't move please," "okay baby," he says. I hope daddy won't light up another cigarette while I'm in the shower. I thought. I went into my room and began to undress and the phone rings; I wrap myself in my robe and go to the phone. "Hello," I say. "Hello beautiful, you made it home safe huh?" Michael says. "Yes I did, thank you for checking on me," I tell him. Daddy was still singing.

"So I hear you've replaced me already huh," Michael says. "Oh no, that's my dad, he's been drinking, I found him in my driveway waiting when I got here." "Oh yes, he sounds full," he said laughing. "Michael I'm sorry, but I was going to get into the shower just now, can I call you back, when I get out?" I asked. "Sure, I think I'm going to take a shower myself, just to cool down from our date," he said. "I'll take a cold one," I hung up.

I went into the living room to check on daddy one last time he wasn't singing anymore; I wanted to make sure he wasn't trying to leave. I walked in he was falling off to sleep in and out. I reached into his pocket and took his cigarettes and put them in my room. I went into the bathroom took my showered quickly, and got out and wrapped up in my robe. It was so cold in there. I still have yet to learn this house of mine. I went into my bedroom and put on a t-shirt and some shorts. I felt cold.

I took the blanket from the bed and started walking out to the living room where daddy was and something snatched the blanket from my hands and pushed me over onto the floor. The door closed and the room went black. I could smell it. It was back. I covered my eyes this time; it turned me over and laid on top of me. I didn't move. I felt it touching my breast and holding my legs open touching in between my legs. I was as stiff as a board. I could feel it breathing on my neck. The smell was so foul and so rank that I wanted to vomit.

I could feel it squeezing my breast harder. It didn't touch my private area. It rubbed my thighs; I laid still thinking how much longer and what was, is it going to do? When will it go away, I screamed for daddy, I began to wiggle my body unable to keep still and refusing to allow this to happen to me. I moved myself over with all I had in me. I tried to get away from it and grab onto it. It grabbed me harder when I moved; it moved with me. I turned over on my stomach, and it was on my back. It was so heavy it just laid on my back breathing and smelling. It had my shoulders pent down, so I could barely move.

"Don't hit me, don't hit me!" I shouted out over and over again. I held my head to the floor. I waited and waited as my arms began to go numb and cold, my gown was pulled up over my shoulders, I felt as if I was choking. I heard daddy get up. "Karis! Karis! Where's the bathroom baby?" He said. I felt the heaviness lift off me and the smell faded away I got up and ran close to the door. I cracked open the door so daddy couldn't see the panic in my eyes.

"Daddy, go left okay, the bathroom is right over there." I sat down on the floor and struggled to pull myself back up to the bed. I sat down on the bed and put my head in my hands as I leaned over. I could still smell its stench lingering in the room. I could still feel it around me. I looked up at the dresser where I, felt it was, the lamp was thrown to the floor with a crash as if something was angry. I stood up and ran to the door I opened it quickly pulling my gown down. "Daddy, where are you?" I yelled out. "I'm in here!" Daddy yelled back.

"What's going on?" He asked me. I went to the bathroom door and stood there. "Nothing's wrong daddy; I'm just waiting for you to come out, do you want some coffee?" I asked. "Are you feeling better?" I asked him, daddy would sober up quick after a cup of coffee, but it wouldn't stop him from being so sick that he couldn't function all day. He would usually have to lay down after a night of being drunk like this, at least for the whole day.

I would watch him throwing up. He was always really sick the next day and mama would be the one catering to him until he was better. He would do as he always did and praised her and leave her all day again to handle everything while he would work and drink more. Mama would be overwhelmed with all the responsibilities alone. Daddy would be so drunk when he showed up that he never noticed her pain. He didn't want to see it I thought. I stood there thinking of all the things daddy use to do. He never changed not even after mama died.

I wondered if he ever thought about the mistakes he made. I could hear him talking to himself coming out of the bathroom. This meant that he was still a little drunk. "I shouldn't have done it," he said to himself over and over again. "I was so wrong." "Daddy, are you okay?" I asked him. "Yeah baby, daddy's okay," "here daddy, I got you some coffee, just the way you like it, black," I went back into the kitchen and shut the coffee machine off.

Maddy had bought all of the appliances for me; I had never used a coffee maker before. I watched as daddy took a sip of the coffee. He looked over at me. "Baby," he said standing to his feet with the coffee cup in his hand, "daddy can't drink this stuff." He came into the kitchen and stood beside the counter. "Here you go baby, I don't need any coffee," he said scratching his head. It must have been really bad. I thought. "You can just give me some bread and a slice of cheese," he said smiling at me.

"I know you can't make a coffee baby, but you tried," he said taking the bread from the table. I looked all around the refrigerator I had no cheese. "Daddy I'm sorry, I have no cheese," I told him. "Okay baby" He said going toward the couch. "I'll just lay here on the couch. He laid on the couch and turned the TV on the news; he began to fall off to sleep again. I went and sat next to him and watched as he fell off to sleep again. My goodness daddy is never going to change. I thought as I watched him sleeping. I fell off to sleep next to him on the couch. I woke up with my head on daddy's shoulder. He was just staring at me.

"Hey, good morning baby, how did you sleep?" Daddy asked. "Oh daddy, I'm sorry I fell asleep on you huh?" "I was just watching TV, you didn't have to stay here all morning, daddy you could have left, it would have been okay." "No baby, you were so comfortable, I couldn't move away." "Daddy I don't have any breakfast food to make for you," I said getting up going to the kitchen. "I know baby, why don't we do a little shopping today, I will go with you and show you what to buy for the house, just let me go home and clean up and call my secretary to let her know what I'm doing, and we can go.

"Do you mind if I showed you how to shop for groceries?" He asked me smiling at me. "I'd like that daddy," "Okay baby, then it's settled, I will be back soon." He said standing up to go to the door. I walked him out he kissed my cheek and got into his car. "Daddy, come back real soon please," I said looking back at the door. I watched and waved as he drove off. I turned to the door to go back in. I turned off the TV and went into my room to get dressed I looked around the room, there was no smell, I went to pick up the lamp from the floor.

I put the broken pieces into the trash; when I went toward the closet, I began to smell it. It was back. I stood with my back toward the closet door looking all around for signs that it was coming closer to me. I turned my head to the left and I could smell it so strong. Okay, what should I do I thought. I moved slowly out toward the bed, I slowly sat down on the bed. I could smell it. "What do you want from me?" I asked I held the bedpost of the bed so tight thinking I should get out of the house right away. I started to get up. In that instant, I was shoved back down onto the bed, and the smell was gone. My gown went up and I pulled it back down. This time I will fight this thing with all that I have.

"No, I said. No! I won't let you touch me," It felt as if it was on top of me I could feel it's breathing directly in my face, it stopped as if it was out of breath, I felt it move away quickly. I was bleeding I felt my menstrual cycle starting right then. It moved away. This time it snatched mama's picture off the dresser sending it crashing to the floor breaking the frame into pieces. I sat up on the bed. I better get some help I thought.

This can't continue to happen to me. I rushed around the room to get dressed I would wait for daddy outside. He came twenty minutes later I sat on the porch holding the hose to water the grass. He honked the horn as he pulled up to the driveway. I put the hose down and grabbed my keys and purse, and rushed to his car. I got in. "Hi daddy, thanks for coming back," I tell him. "Oh baby, you knew I would, I have to help my baby," he said. I was so happy he came back.

Daddy drove slowly to the grocery store humming the temptations all the way there while smoking a cigarette. He had the windows rolled down because I hated the smoke. It really bothered me. When we pulled up to the store there was fruit in front of the stores entrance and daddy began to look it over. "Get a basket Karis," he said. "Don't get a small one," I pulled the basket alongside daddy the whole time. We got fruit and veggies mostly.

Daddy was big on eating healthy. He picked out steaks and a couple of pork chops. He explained to me how to cook them as we walked around the store. He made me get seasonings too, salt, pepper, onion salt, garlic salt, sugar, and flour. I was so tired when we finished, but daddy insisted we get sheets, blankets, and toiletries. Daddy didn't buy anything cheap nor did he bargain shopped at all. He'd say, "Karis, always get the best, It may cost you a little more, but it will eat better," he said with a smile.

When we were all done daddy stayed at my house and helped put it all away. I was so relaxed. "Daddy, do you have to go to work this afternoon?" I asked him. "Yes, I have court at two, baby; do you want to come with me?" He asked. Oh my god, do I thought. I better go with daddy and then from there go to work myself. As long as I am safe, I took my work clothes and lunch. I grabbed a banana to eat while I watched daddy. I wondered sometimes had he been drinking while he wore that robe.

We were in court until five that day. I went straight from there to work. His secretary seemed eager for me to leave. She kept looking at daddy as if she wanted to eat his clothes off his body. She was undressing him with her eyes over and over again. I rushed away quickly after court feeling like I was pushed out of the door. I could hear them tussling with each other as I walked away from his office door. I laughed at it now.

Daddy was such a ladies man. He played them all. He had women everywhere. He didn't seem to want to be attached to anyone though just have companionship in the bed, I guessed. His emotions seemed to be kept to himself. I think daddy is still missing mama though it seemed he'd moved on. I thought as I drove to work. When I showed up, there was Maddy at the front desk. She was working on the schedule board looking and writing at the same time. "Hello everyone," I said as I approached the desk.

"Hey Karis I would like to talk to you before you go on duty," Maddy said looking at me down from her glasses. "Okay I will wait here then," I said walking over to sit in the chair behind the desk. I was early anyway. I wondered what she wanted to talk about. I twirled around in the chair moving from side to side nervously. She came over to me and tapped my shoulder. "Let's go into the back room," she said. I followed her back. "I want you to get this position coming up, have you started your classes yet?" She asked.

"No, classes start next month," I tell her. "Okay you need that certification so that you can further your career, I'm counting on you," she said. "I'm going to give my recommendation for promotion. You should get the job because you've been here awhile now, and you know the job, and you're going to school to get certified, but let me warn you,

you probably won't see a pay increase until you get those certs," she said opening the door.

"Good luck young lady, now get to work," I had the sixth floor tonight. It was easy all the kids loved me on that floor. I went through each room quickly a couple of bed baths and feedings. I took my break on the patio where I ran into Michael and a nurse laughing and talking at the tables in back. I tried to get as close as I could to hear what he was saying to her. He was so close to her face close enough to kiss her. He was whispering in her ear she smiled and looked my way.

I bet he's saying the same things to her that he said to me I thought as I watched him getting intimate with her. Right after our date, I was a little angry. I picked up my bagged lunch and began to walk back into the cafeteria. When Michael noticed me he got up fast and began walking behind me. I walked as fast as I could. I looked back at him than turned my head quickly looking forward. "Hello sweetie," he said catching up to me putting his hand on my back. I looked back at him and turned my head forward.

"Michael, I don't want to talk to you," I told him as I walked toward the elevators in the hall. "I was just going to tell you, that she's just an old friend that's all," he said. I got into the elevator and push the button to close the doors not even acknowledging what he had just explained to me. He looked at me chewing that damn gum and I waved goodbye to him as the doors closed in his face. I went back to work.

The nerve of him I thought. Michael the lady's man I guess he's not at all who I thought he was, I finished my shift and went home, all I wanted to do was take a hot bath. I wondered if that would even be possible. I drove home fast only to find that I'd left almost every light on in my house. It was so lit up inside. When I opened the door I began turning them off one by one. I started taking off my clothes when I heard the doorbell ringing. I quickly grabbed my robe and went to the door. It was still ringing. "I'm coming!" I shouted, "I will be right there!" I said as I approached the door.

I peeked into the little peephole in the door, "who is it?" I couldn't see anything. "I can't see you," I called out. "Who is it?" I asked again. I looked out again the person moved back with flowers covering their face. The hand looked very familiar holding the flowers. It's James; I know his ring. He wore a nice golden band around his finger with a Virgo birthstone in the middle of it. "James, is that you" I yelled out. "Open up and see," he said taking the flowers from his face smiling.

I opened the door just enough to grab the flowers from his hands. I closed it fast. "Thanks for the flowers," I said laughing. "Hey open up, it's me, James," he said. I opened up the door. "I can't believe your back!" I said as James picked up hugging me. "I missed you, baby," he said. "Aww look at you," he said squeezing my cheeks tightly. "I couldn't wait to see you, I know I should have called, but I just couldn't wait any longer, I was outside of your job almost all day," he said taking me by the hand. I held onto my robe.

"James, what a nice surprise," I told him. "What a nice surprise." "So have you thought about marriage at all while I've been away," he said right away. I stood back from him. "Um James, I was about to take a bath and change, do you mind waiting for me," I asked him. "No I don't mind at all, as a matter of fact, I'll stand at the door and talk to you the whole time, is that okay?" He asked smiling. It was great seeing him; I thought as I went in to the bathroom to run my water.

I was very close to James; he looked so different I thought, he'd grown up a lot, he looked more mature and fit as if he worked out a lot. As I ran the water James began to talk to me. "So are you okay here all by yourself?" He asked me. "I believe I am," I yelled out over the water. "I don't know any of my neighbors yet, but I'm looking forward to meeting them, I hear a dog barking across the fence all the time I tell him. It's not very loud, so it must be a small dog." "Do you get many visitors?" He asked me.

"Only daddy and   Maddy came over so far," I tell him as I turn the water off. "I can hear you better now, so you don't have to yell okay." "Karis, it is so nice to see you," he says. "I have missed you so much baby girl, I have so much I would like to share with you," James always seemed so sensitive at times. "So are we getting married soon, have you thought about my question, while I was gone?"

Oh no I thought, he's going to bring up the married question. I really have thought about it. I don't know a thing about being anyone's wife. I thought washing myself off. I sat there soaking for a while I didn't want to face James. He awaited my answer in silence. "I'll be out soon!" I yelled as I reached for my towel. "Did you hear me, Karis?" He said. "I heard you, James, we'll talk about it when I get out," I tell him. I wrapped up in the towel and got out. I lotion my body quickly and threw on a T shirt and sweats.

I opened up the door and James was sitting down on the floor next to the door. He stood up and grabbed me by the waist pulling me toward him. "Say you're going to marry me baby girl, I need you to tell me that you want to spend your life with me, I want to make beautiful babies and share a home with you, and you'll never have to work or lift a finger again." He said staring into my eyes. I stood back away from him and grabbed his hand pulling him into the living room.

"Come on James, are you serious?" I asked sitting down next to him on the couch. "What do you think Karis, I just don't go around giving out rings and asking people to marry me," he said frowning up at me. "What you and I have is so special, right?" He asked me rubbing my hand. "Oh my goodness, James, I don't know, I am just getting to know myself, I don't know if I'm ready for any of that." "Is there someone else?" He asked me. Oh no I thought, should I tell him about Michael. Well, he will back off if I do tell him.

"I have been on a date with someone," I tell him. "Really" James says, "Do you love him?" "I don't think so, but I do know that I liked him a lot." "Oh you liked him, so it's over?" He questioned. "I don't know James," I say with frustration in my voice. "Can we just talk about you and your journey in the navy?" I asked him. I got up and went into the kitchen. "I have some tea, would you like some?" I asked. I pulled out the tea kettle and began putting water into it. James sat there quiet for a second than he walked over to me.

"You want to hear about my journey, I did nothing in the navy, but took orders and worked hard and dreamed of this very day. Although, it's not at all turning out the way I dreamt it. I just hoped all the time that I would come home and see you and we would start our lives together," he said looking at me. His eyes were so sadden. Oh god, what do I do now? I thought. I put the tea kettle on the stove and walked over to James. "James this doesn't mean that I won't ever marry you, I just think we should take our time and not rush into it," I tell him holding his hands.

"Okay, James I care for you so much," I said hugging him tightly. "I love you, you have always been such a good friend to me," I sat close to him on the couch. "I will always have a special place in my heart for you; can we please just take it slow for a while please?" I hold on to James until I hear the tea kettle whistling. I went over and made our tea as he sat back on the couch with his head back on the couch looking up at the ceiling with so much disappointment and sadness in his eyes. I go over and hand him a cup, "here you go, James."

We sat together and talked. James wasn't happy, but he talked anyway. Telling me funny stories about his time on the navy ship, time flew by soon it was ten o clock, the doorbell rang. I got up. "Were you expecting company?" James asked. "No," I tell him walking over to the window to peek out. It was Martha and Krystal; I opened the door. "Hey girl!" They shout, pushing their way into the house. "Hey James," they both say to him. They both began looking all around the house. "Come on in guys make yourselves comfortable" I say to them sarcastically.

"Do you guys want some tea?" "No, but we'll take some wine if you have any," Krystal says. "Wine, since when did you guys start drinking wine?" I asked them. They made themselves comfortable right away. I sat back down to talk to James a little more about his time on the ship. Krystal grabbed the phone and went into my bedroom, and Martha followed her and laid on the bed watching TV. James didn't seem uncomfortable with them around and I finally have some good company over.

Learning To Love

I managed to keep Martha and Krystal with me all night. I wanted them to come over every night if they could. James went home a little disappointed but somewhat satisfied. I was as honest as I could be with him. I began seeing more and more of him. He came over almost every night. Teaching me his cooking recipes and sharing with me his opinion on everything especially relationships. We would eat and hang out until midnight usually watching TV and laughing.

Krystal and Martha would come and go as they please. I'd given them both a key to my place. I would see Michael around a lot at work, but I was hardly interested in what he wanted to teach me about lovemaking anymore. Although he reminded me of what I was missing every time, he'd catch my eye. I watched him as he spread himself around the hospital with a different nurse almost every day I saw him on the patio whispering in someone's ear. I was not interested in his love lessons anymore. I thought to watch him from afar.

I was assigned to work with him on the sixth floor now. I got the promotion; the job was a bit more challenging for me I had to keep up with all the doctors on the floor. Michael would be a distraction if I had any interest in him. I thought while we waited for the elevator. We rotated to different floors every month. Michael would see me leaving sometimes and shake his head at me. "I bet you miss me," he'd say, from time to time. I'd just ignore him as if I didn't hear him say a word, but Michael couldn't take no for an answer.

He'd follow me around after our shift. He'd tell me all about his great lovemaking skills and warn me that if I didn't together soon and forgave him that I would miss out on him. I'd walk away from him laughing most of the time. But I did wonder about him; he was quite the catch. Should I be mad at him for seeing someone else I thought? I don't know I wasn't making love to him. Maybe that's why he's spreading himself around from women to women; maybe he's just that way a ladies man like daddy.

Maybe he can't help himself. I wondered every day while working near him. I began to understand this relationship stuff more and more. It's just like Maddy says, "have fun, don't get tied up with one guy and you don't have to sleep with them to get their full attention. Just be who you are, make sure they know and respect what you want and have fun." I took her advice although I have only seen Maddy with one man so far and it was a strange encounter.

They seemed so afraid that I knew about the relationship as if it may have been a well-kept secret that they weren't ready to share at the time. I caught them kissing near the front entrance of the hospital one day while coming to work. I asked Maddy about it that day at lunch. "Maddy, was he the love of your life?" She answered back. "No, he's someone else's love, but I do love him," she said sadly. I didn't ask any more questions about it after that day. I was surprised that day by a big bouquet of flowers sent to me by James.

They read. "Hello my beautiful princess, I couldn't help myself, if I can't see you every day I'll have to remind you that you're always on my mind, enjoy your day. Love, James." "Wow," I thought. James is charming. The nurses at the front desk were all smiling at me and saying things all day like "Someone must have gotten a good treat last night to deserve this kind of treatment. Flowers are only given for one of two reasons, they say. Either someone died, or someone got laid."

I was so mad about their comments all day. I worked faster to get my job done. It wasn't until I ran into Michael that I felt better about the flowers. "I see I'm not the only one working hard to get you to love them," he said walking over to me after checking on his patient. "The flowers are nice, but I have something better," he said standing behind me. "Shh!" I said. "Michael I've had enough," I said in a whisper not trying to wake the patient. "What, I can't be the competition?" He asked.

"I don't mind a challenge," he says to me licking his lips. "No," I tell him. "I've been catching heat about those flowers all day," I tell him. "I don't think I can take any more at all" "Oh that, you should be laughing at them," He said chewing his gum. "You know why they're all upset at you, don't you," he asked me smiling. "No, I don't." "Well, baby they're all jealous because they've been sleeping around with men forever and had yet to receive flowers."

He laughed, "baby, you are a special woman they can't understand why you're taking our attention from them." "Michael, now I know you don't expect me to believe that, do you?" I tell him looking into his eyes. "I've seen you giving someone else the same attention that you gave me. I watched you charm her and make her laugh while you whispered in her ear, remember, or doesn't that count?" I asked. He looked at me. "I told you, she was just an old friend." "Yes, I remember, that you enjoyed sleeping with occasionally, right?" I asked.

"Yes, occasionally, she is no one special," he said touching my chin. "Like you," he took my hand and kissed it. "You're going to miss out if I'm involved," he said walking away smiling. Hum, I thought. I don't think I will. I finished up in the room and went down to the front desk to retrieve my flowers. Maddy was sitting down doing paperwork. She looked up at me as I grabbed my flowers from the table. "Karis would you like company tonight?" she asked.

"Really Maddy?" I said happily. "I would love your company tonight or any night." Maddy hasn't been over since the night she helped me put the pictures up. I was honored she would come back. "Should I wait for you?" "Oh no, I won't finish here for a while," she said. "I'll come over when I finish." I rushed home to clean before Maddy comes. I want to make her feel comfortable. When I made it home James was sitting on my porch waiting for me.

"I see you got the flowers," he said as I got out of the car. "Oh yes, thank you so much, James," I tell him kissing his cheek. "I thought you would like them," he followed me into the house. "Now everyone at work thinks I'm sleeping with you" I tell him as we went inside. "Hey your sister and cousin just left, they asked if I wanted to wait inside, but I declined, I knew you wouldn't like that, right," He said looking at me with wonder on his face.

"I wouldn't have mind; I trust you, James," I tell him placing the flowers on the table in front of the couch. "Have a seat I just have to put my bag away," I went into my bedroom through the bag on the floor and came out to begin to clean. "I'm expecting company a little later," I tell him. "Company," he asked. "Is it someone special?" "Oh she's special," I tell him laughing at the thought of him thinking I was having another man over. "It's Maddy, do you remember Maddy?" I asked him. "The nurse right?"

"Yes, the nurse, she's like a mom to me, she wants to come visit, so I would like to make her comfortable." "You always make me comfortable," he said. "I won't say long than; I know you want to spend time with her." "Yes, I would like to," I tell him. She's always been here for me; I want to be here for her no matter what." I can't take my eyes off James as we talk. His eyes are so beautiful and dark his lashes look as if they're made for women's eyes, but they fit his face so long and dark. I wondered if he knew how handsome he was.

James left and I changed into something warm and sat down on the couch waiting for Maddy. I turned on the television to see what was on today. There was another talk show on. The man who was the host was very confrontational. He was having a discussion with his audience about animal cruelty. Whether or not, people who abuse their pets should have the opportunity to get them back. The people on the show were all yelling and screaming.

"No this is abuse, it's not right," it was an ugly scene. I turned the TV off and went over to the window. Maddy was taking a long time. I was growing impatient. I went to the kitchen if there was any left over's from what James and I had cooked days before. I found a couple of things. Beef steak and rice and veggies. I better warm them in the oven. I ate while I waited for Maddy. I am so afraid of being alone. I've done a good job surrounding myself with people so that I won't be attacked.

I went back over to the window when I was done to see if Maddy was coming up the driveway. I opened the front door to allow the cold air to come in while I waited. Soon Maddy was coming up the driveway, Maddy got out of her car waving. "I'm sorry honey, I had some last minute things to do," she said walking up the pathway. "I bet you didn't expect me to show up did you?" "Oh, I knew you would show, I just needed some fresh air." "Well, you looked as if you were scared or something; clutching that doorknob like that."

"Maddy, I'm just waiting for you, that's all," I said opening the screen all the way up for her. Maddy was still in her nursing uniform. She carried her bag with her change of clothes. "Can I change honey?" She asked. "Sure Maddy, go ahead, I will be right here when you come done." I went into the kitchen to turn the tea kettle on for tea. By the time Maddy came out of the bathroom the tea kettle would be whistling.

I put our cups on the coffee table and began to pour the hot water into the cups. Maddy came out. "I have been waiting for this all day, honey," she says as she sat down on the couch. I pulled the foot rest close so that she could rest her feet. "Are you comfortable?" I asked her. "I sure am." she said leaning back on the couch. "Thank you, Karis," Maddy said. I could tell she was so tired. She took a deep breath. I sipped my tea waiting for Maddy to tell me what she needed to talk to me about. I was sure it was about her relationship.

I had the house very quiet for her to rest. After a while she lifted her head. "Karis, why is it so quiet in here?" She asked. "I just thought that you'd like to have a little peace when you came in," I tell her. "Oh, I see," she said. "I wanted to talk to you about what I told you the other day, I told you that the man I was kissing was someone else's love, I want you to know that I do love him, but I can't, and I will never have him." "Why?" I asked her.

"Well I fell in love with him, I didn't know that he was in love with someone else, deeply in love with someone else." "But I don't understand," I tell her. "You were kissing him, and he kissed back, you guys seemed to be in love with one another, that hug said it all." "Oh don't get me wrong, we do love one another," she said. "But he belongs to someone else his heart is there with her." Maddy said sadly, "Is he married?" I asked her. She shakes her head yes. "Oh, I see," I put my hand on hers. "Maddy it's not your fault, you can't control what you feel inside," I tell her.

"He says that he's going to leave her, he's been telling me that for years now. He will never leave her, he won't, he doesn't love me enough," she says crying. I went over to the counter and got her the tissue box for her face. "Maddy you are the sweetest person I know, I can see that you love and care for him, but he's married, you should let him go on with his life. If he leaves his wife than it would be better for you, I think he should decide where his heart lives." I tell her.

I sat back down with her. "Maddy if you love him, let him go, you deserve so much more than that," I tell her. She looked up at me. "Okay Karis, I understand" She said wiping her eyes. "I will consider doing that," she smiled at me. I handed her the tea cup. "I'm glad you came over," I tell her. I turned the TV on. "Oh, this looks good," I say to her. I looked over at her. "Maddy are you okay?" "Yes, I'm fine, thank you, hey I hear you and Michael are going out now," she says smiling at me.

"Is that what you hear, we went out on one date, no Maddy we aren't going out," I tell her. "I have just spent a lot of time with James." "Oh, James huh," Maddy says. "I can see that James love you." "Yes, but James is sensitive, I don't like that at all, I like that he cares a lot about me, but I don't like that he wants so much from me, he wants me to be a mom and a wife all at once. I don't want too many children, and I want to work for a living, you know give back to other people help and all that." I tell her.

"What James wants is some kind of machine" "Yes a baby making machine" Maddy says. We both laughed. "I can see that he's a good man though" She said sipping on her tea. Maddy and I watched TV and talked until she fell asleep. I covered her with a blanket and laid across the couch beside her. I turned the TV off and I immediately began to smell it. It was standing over me. I closed my eyes and began to pray. I could soon feel its breath on my face. Lord please protect me from this thing, Lord please keep me safe from harm. I fell asleep really scared.

I dreamed of a restless spirit I was approached in my dream by a man. His eyes red and his face pale. He pushed and pulled at me. I was running away from him in the dream I woke up just as the man grabbed at my neck. I was out of breath I jumped up from my sleep. I looked around the room for Maddy. She was gone. She left a note by my head. "Karis, thank you for your hospitality, I needed a friend, I will see you at work, Love Maddy."

I got up and went into my bedroom. I took my clothes out for work. I went into the bathroom to run water. I took my clothes off and wrapped up in a towel. As I walked from the bathroom the doorbell rang. "Hold on; I'm coming!" I said walking toward the front window. I peek out to see who it was. It was James. What is he doing here? I thought to myself as I crack the door open. "How can I help you, sir?" I asked. "Hello Karis, what are you up to?" He asked standing with his hands in his pocket.

"I'm getting ready for work, I have to talk to you later," I tell him. "You should call me before coming by, James, I will talk to you later," I said closing the door. I went back into the bathroom and began to get into the tub. As I took off my towel I could smell it near it felt as if it was touching my shoulder. I bent down took the towel from the floor and wrapped up and ran out into the living room. I opened the door and yelled out for James. I could see him pulling out his windows were down, but the music was playing loudly.

"James! James!" I yelled waving my hand for him to come back. He began pulling back into the driveway. Thank god I thought I waved my hand at him to come inside. He got out of the car. "What's up, did you forget to slap me or something?" He said laughing walking up to me. "No, I just wondered if you'd like to stay a while before I head to work, I can cook us something to eat," "Sure, I would love that, what's in the kitchen to eat, baby?" He asked. "Oh, I don't know," I shut the door behind him.

"Make yourself comfortable James, surprise me okay," I walked back into the bathroom to finish my bath. "James, I will leave the door cracked open, talk to me okay," I yelled out to him as I got into the tub. "So, what brought you back over today?" I yelled out to him. "I just missed your face, I had to come over to see you," he yelled back to me. I washed up as quickly as I could. I threw on my clothes and opened the door. James was standing in the hallway, he grabbed me by the hips and kissed my lips.

"I missed you, baby, when will you be mine?" "I don't know." I said pulling his hands away from my waist. "James, I just want to think about it with no pressure," I said. I grabbed his hands and walked with him to the kitchen where he was preparing to make chilly. I watched James as he made the chilly and talked to me about how when we get married I would have to do all the cooking but I would never wash a dish he says. He made it sound so easy and good. I just smiled. "James, these are things that I would want to do if I was married, wash dishes and clean and cook? I want to work too."

We went back and forth while he prepared the chilly. When he was done we put the chilly in a crock pot to slow cook. I needed to get to work so I grabbed my things and we walked out together. James grabbed my hand as we walked out to our cars. "Karis, when are you going to be with me? I am on shore duty now, but I won't be here long, I will be going back to sea soon, tell me something soon please." I got into my car and waved goodbye. I can't keep going through this. I thought as I drove off.

What does he want me to do? I wondered give up all my dreams for his; it's too much pressure. I drove to work slowly. I stopped at the stop light ahead near the hospital. I noticed a senior man standing there staring at me with a senior woman. I drove further up the street and they were there again. When I made it to the hospital, I parked and went walking toward the hospital entrance. I looked up at the second story windows and there they were staring down at me from the window. I went inside quickly.

Michael was standing at the front desk leaning over talking with the desk clerk. Her name was Angie. I smiled at them and walked over to the scheduling table. I looked it over. I had the second floor tonight but only for two hours than it was back up to the sixth floor with Michael I took my charts and headed to the elevator. I hear footsteps behind me. I turn the corner and they became louder. I dared to look back I stopped and stood with my back turned to the wall. I feel hands on my back.

"Hello," I hear a voice say. I turned around "Hello," I say back. "I'm Ben," he says. "Hi Ben, how are you?" I asked. "I'm Karis." "Oh yes, I know, I heard they'd be sending you up to help us today. Are you ready to get some babies born today?" He asked me. "Oh, I love babies." I tell him. "Good because I have eight deliveries today, you can get the moms ready, you have room 716 through 719 you should get started right away, follow me," he said.

I followed him down the hallway where there was at least a dozen nurses and doctors standing around talking. "Okay everyone, listen up, this is Karis, she will be helping us for a little while tonight. So far we have eight deliveries as of now, and we should be expecting more. Mrs. Stanford is here with her sixth birth; she should go fast and easy, Karis you can take her. Then we have Mrs. Taylor," I took notes while Ben spoke. After he was done giving orders I went quickly to the Mrs. Stanford's room.

As soon as I walked into her room I felt ill, I felt really sick to my stomach. Oh no I thought. As I went closer to her my stomach turned over. "Hello" she said Panting and breathing heavy. "Please, I'm in a lot of pain honey, can you please get me something for the pain, please?" She asked. I went closer to her to do her vitals and I began to feel more ill. "I will go and get the doctor for you," I tell her. I started to go and she reached her hand out for me.

She squeezed so tight my hand turned red. She panted breathing heavier. I reached over her with my other hand to push the button for the nurse. "Hello, hello," I yelled out. "Please come in here! We need a doctor in here!" I yelled out. Mrs. Sanford had a grip on my hand, but I had to pull away I was beginning to feel ill as if I was going to vomit. I pulled away and went to the sink to get a cold towel to wipe the sweat from her head. She was dripping wet with sweat.

I wet my face, than took the towel for her head over. "Hello!" a voice yelled out on the intercom. "What's the problem?" "Well, Mrs. Sanford is in a lot of pain, she says she needs something for it, can you please send a doctor in to check her?" I yelled out. "Okay someone will be right in." They yelled back. "Mrs. Sanford, someone will be right in, did you hear that?" I asked her. She shook her head yes. She was panting and crying. I went back over to the sink to wet the towel again. When I came back over to her she was no longer panting, her head was leaned to the side. I immediately felt dizzy I began to get weak. I rushed into the bathroom, I put my head over the toilet and began to vomit, and my stomach was tied in knots.

While I leaned into the toilet bowel I felt a tap on my shoulder. I looked up and there was the old man and the old women. I looked at them. "What are you doing here?" I asked them. "Come," they said. They grabbed me by the hand and helped me up. We walked into the room together. The room was filled with doctors and nurses. They had Mrs. Sanford surrounded "Push! they yelled out to her "Push! they held her legs and hands up as they sat her up to push. She turned completely pale. She looked over at me, and the old man and woman went to the foot of her bed.

I stood next to her hand. They were behind the doctor. I wiped her head with the towel. She was still pushing when the doctor traded places with the nurse to check on Mrs. Sanford breathing. He pushed me out of the way quickly. "Mrs. Sanford! Mrs. Sanford! Hold on please!" He yelled out to her as he checked her. As the nurse began to pull the baby out I watched as Mrs. Sanford passed away.

The room was calm; I felt warm all around me as if I were wrapped in a warm blanket I looked around, and the old man and women were standing with Mrs. Sanford. She was holding her baby and smiling down at me. They all walked away. The doctor was still giving her CPR hoping she'd come back. I stood back and watch the nurses try to revive the baby. It was a very sad moment. I ran out of the room. I went to find Maddy.

I just wanted to go home after that. I had to take a walk or something I thought. I can't take to much more of this. I walked right passed Maddy. She grabbed my arm. "Hey, what's wrong?" She asked. I walked with her holding on to me toward the door. "I'll be okay Maddy." I sat down on the front steps near the entrance door. The air was cold I put my head between my legs. Maddy rubbed my back.

"Karis, this is a hospital, these things happen every day," she said. "I know that you think that there is something you can do, but sweetie there's nothing you can do, you just have to take the bitter with the sweet," she says patting my back more. "Okay Maddy I will get it together," I tell her lifting my head up. I need to let someone know what I'm going through; I thought to myself as I wiped my eyes. It was too much to bear alone. There has to be someone I can truly trust with a secret, the old fashion cross your heart, hopes to die stuff. I thought as I got up to walk back into the hospital.

As I worked I thought about who I could tell. Who would keep a secret without calling me crazy? It couldn't be someone who would come back and throw it in my face later. I thought

Krystal or Martha I ran into Michael again. He watched me from a far chewing gum and smiling. I waved at him and he reached up with his hand as if he was picking up the phone. He said in silence with his lips call me and winked his eye. I smiled and said with my lips I will.

My shift ended a little late this evening. I made it out around midnight. I drove home fast. When I arrived home Krystal and her friends were there. They were on the porch playing music loudly. I pushed through them saying hi to everyone. I wanted to get to my room to write in my journal. I had the worst day all I could think of was Mrs.

Sanford and her baby. I was so upset today. Why would god take the baby to? I thought as I pulled my clothes off in a hurry to write in my journal.

I am sure I can't keep this up I went into the bathroom to get into the shower. I jumped in and out quickly washing with the soap and just spraying it off quickly. I put my clothes on and sat on the bed with my journal after writing I would call Michael. I was really eager to hear what he had to say these days. I had been spending all my time with James. I really hadn't talked to him in a while. I especially hadn't talked to him because of his lover boy attitude. I just couldn't wait. I lay across the bed and began to write.

Lord, today I experienced a terrible tragedy I watched as Mrs. Sanford and her baby were called home. I was hurt, I know that they are in a better place but lord what does it all mean, she had other children, who will care for them Lord, why her? Why her baby? I hurt for them her husband to. Lord, I know that we all have our day to go home to you I know that by your hand we could all be swept away with no warning.

Lord can you please give me an understanding of it all, understanding about what I'm feeling and why they all need me to help them. Lord, I thank you for your many blessings, for waking me in the morning and forgiving me for all my sins. In Jesus name I pray. I closed my journal and went to the side of the bed to look out of the window. As I leaned into the window I began to smell it. I opened the window and called out for Krystal.

"Krystal! Krystal!" I yelled as loud as I could for her. I began to feel it touching my breast it squeezed my nipples. I began to yell out louder. "Krystal, come inside please!" I stayed in the window with my back turned to the door. "Why are you screaming, I'm right here," Krystal said standing at the foot of the bed. I felt it move away fast. Krystal began asking question right away. "Why do you look so scared, what's wrong?" "I was calling you for a while; I needed you to help me with something," I tell her.

"I was in the kitchen eating all of the leftovers that you and James made; that was some great chilly" she said holding a spoon to her mouth. "I have company in there, what is it that you needed help with?" She asked. I could still smell it near. I walked toward Krystal. She stepped back. "What's wrong with you, Karis?" She asked. "I just want to be close to my sister," I explained hugging her neck she pushed me away. "Come on Karis, I have company," she said walking away from me sucking on her spoon. I walked behind her in fear of being alone in the room. As I walked out I could hear things falling down on the floor from the dresser. Krystal looked back. "What was that?" She asked.

"I don't know," I said moving her out into the hallway quickly and shutting the door. We went into the kitchen. Krystal was holding my hand, "I'm so glad you asked me to come back over, I feel so good hanging around here with you." She said going over to the crock pot spooning out more chilly. "So, you do know I own bowels, right?" I tell her reaching for a bowel in the cabinet. "I didn't know where to find them," she said laughing "And besides it taste better right out of the pot," she said spooning more chilly.

I watched as Krystal and her friends ate the chilly and talked. When they were done she walked them outside. I was hoping she didn't stay out there long. I stood at the door staring at them as they all laughed and joked by their cars in the driveway. I could smell its strong scent behind me. I cracked the door opened so that Krystal could see I was waiting for her to go in. She looked back at me from time to time as if she knew I wanted her in.

"All right guys, I'll see you guys in a few," she said waving them away. She came in and sat down at the couch I sat down close to her on the couch and took her by the hand. I felt a whiff of air on my arm. Krystal looked at me and rolled her eyes up as if she was suspicious of

what was going on with me. "So what's going on with you?" Krystal
asked. "What do you mean?" I say to her. "You're acting strange," she
said as the doorbell rang. She took my hand from her hand and went to
the door in a rush as if she was waiting for the doorbell to ring.

I jumped up with her. "Who is it?" I asked. "Oh, it's my friend." She
said going out and closing the door behind her as if she wanted to keep
him a secret. I went over to the kitchen table and grabbed my glass of
water. I went over to the window and stood watching Krystal talking to
this man she called her friend. He was handsome and tall. She was
laughing at whatever it was he was saying to her. As I tipped my glass to
my mouth to sip the water I saw the man fall over clutching his shirt. I
put my glass down and cracked the door open to get a closer look at the
man. I opened the door just wide enough for my head to stick out.

I looked to see if the vision would come back to me. I looked at him
from head to toe. He wore jeans and a T-shirt. I turned my head and
shut the door. I saw it again. This time he was surrounded by people,
other men they had pipes and bats. I called for Krystal to come in
immediately. "Krystal, come in here please," I say from the window. I
wasn't sure why or how but I was sure that the man wasn't going to live.
I didn't want Krystal to be in any harm. He must have been a close
friend because she gave him a very long hug before he left.

Krystal came in soon after that and we sat down on the couch.
"How do you know that guy?" I asked. "I know him from school," she
said grabbing the bag of chips from the coffee table. "Is he in some
trouble?" I asked. "No, he's not in any trouble that I know of, he's a
pretty decent guy, as far as I know, not everyone hangs out with doctors
and sailors Karis," she said sarcastically. "Some people just like ordinary
people; you know the kind that has regular jobs." "Okay, I get it," I tell
her.

"You know I'm not asking because I think he's a bad guy, I just
think he needs to be careful, I had a terrible feeling about him," I tell

her. She sat back onto the couch and snacked on the chips looking at me strangely. "He's fine," she said reaching for the remote. She turned the television on. "Is Martha coming back over tonight?" She asked turning the channels as fast as she could. "I don't know, I think she has a date tonight," I tell her.

"I bet he's hot," Krystal says smiling. Martha always dated the hottest guys but they were always a little on the chunky side, I thought it was a little strange because she was a little tiny thin fare skinned little lady with hair down her back. We would always be surprised at the guys she dated. "I personally thought that it was wise to date what she liked whether or not he was on the chunky side was not relevant as long he was a good guy.

I would think that any guy that I dated would have to love my personality first because I don't have a lot to offer in the looks department," I tell Krystal. "Why do you think that there is something wrong with the way you look, Karis? Some girls would die for your figure," she said staring at me as if I was crazy. "I mean yes, you have some bumps and bruises here and there, but who doesn't, no one's perfect, Karis." She said while she flipped through the channels. "Krystal I know that I just feel that to really love someone you have to get to know them inside and out, don't you think?" I asked.

"Do you think that someone would love the outside of me first?" I asked her. "Yes they would, they'd take one look at your goodies up top and love every bit of you," she said laughing. The phone rang as I began to laugh along with her. Krystal grabbed it before I could. "Hello," she said. I could tell it was for me. "Are you calling to get to know her or do you like the way she looks on the outside?" She asked laughing. I grabbed the phone. "Krystal, don't, that's not funny." I grabbed the phone from her ear and covered it quickly.

"Stop it!" I said putting the phone to my ear. "Hi baby," It was Michael. "Are you feeling better? I heard what happened." "Oh, I'm okay now," I tell him. "Wow, was that your little sister?" Yes, how did you know?" I asked him. "Well she sounded just like you, she sure has the giggles tonight huh, I was just about to tell her that I think you're beautiful on the outside as well as the inside," he said chewing his gum loudly. "And I'd like to get to know you a lot better in every way, especially inside," he began to laugh.

"You're so nasty Michael," I tell him. "I am, I know, I would like to be so nasty with you Karis. I want to say your name while I touch all over your breast," he says. I cringe at the thought of that thinking of what I go through when I'm touched by that spirit. I was afraid that it would never allow me to be comfortable with someone else touching me, I feared that it would never leave me alone no matter where I was. Michael talked more and more about making love to me as the hours went by. I began to think about what it would really be like to make love. I would like to try it someday.

Michael always made me wonder. His sexy voice sometimes made me curl up in my bed and think about making love to him. I fell asleep talking to Michael. When I woke up Krystal was in the bed beside me. She had her back toward me and I could hear her crying. I turned her around I thought that she was dreaming. "Krystal, Krystal! What's wrong?" I ask shaking her as if she was asleep. "Why are you crying?" "My friend, my friend," she said rubbing her eyes. "I was watching the news last night, and they said they found him outside of a club beaten, someone shot him six times," she said crying.

"Are you sure it was him?" I asked. She shook her head yes. "I am so sorry, Krystal," I said hugging her tight. "They did find the guys who did it, but they have them on videotape," she said. "I'm so mad that I didn't believe you when you told me you had a bad feeling about him, maybe I could have warned him," she turned to me and hugged me tighter. I held on to her as she cried herself back to sleep. I couldn't believe that what I seen was real again. I'm learning to believe what I feel and see more and more.

I just needed to learn to except it. I thought. Maybe it's really something special that was given to me I have to learn to live with it I can't turn it off or run from it anymore. I just needed it to share with someone I trusted someone close to me that I could talk about it so that I wouldn't get so upset when things get out of my control. Krystal was too scary, she looked at me funny when I'm afraid and need her close. So I don't think it should be her.

I fell asleep again with her in my arms. I couldn't move at all. I laid the phone down beside the bed. I would see Michael in the morning. Krystal woke me early "I have to go to see my friends family," she tells me wrapping her sweater around her neck. "Do you want to come with me?" She asked me. "I can't Krystal; I have a morning shift with Michael? She asked me smiling. "I'm not even going to answer that question," I tell her. 'Karis, I hope for your sake you give him a little taste of what's on the inside soon because if you wait, he might start chasing someone else's insides," she said laughing.

She threw my shirt at my face. I walked with her to the living room. She took a shower while I straighten up. The whole time I cleaned I could smell it near me it was so foul. I went all around the house picking up and cleaning, it seem to be following my pushing things off the tables and mocking what I was cleaning. I went to the bathroom door near Krystal to try and get it to leave me alone but it stood near me I could smell it close. I couldn't wait for Krystal to come out, I began to talk to her through the door.

When I heard the water stop running I was glad. It seemed as if her shower was never ending. "Hey Krystal, open up!" I yelled at the door. "Why, are you curious about my goodies too?" She said laughing. "No I just want to talk to you," I tell her. "Just open up" I said twisting the door knob. "Okay, okay," she said opening up the door. "What's wrong with you really? Something is wrong with you, I can feel it," she said looking at me.

"What's wrong Karis, you seem afraid of something, tell me," she said drying herself off. "Do I need to tell daddy, is there someone after you or something?" "No Krystal, I just want us to become closer, that's all, is that too hard to believe?" I tell her. "I guess not," she says putting her shirt over her head. "So you'll stay while I get dressed?" I asked her. When I asked her I could smell it closer to me. I could feel its breath on my neck. It was breathing very heavy. I moved closer to Krystal and it moved with me. It was angry and I was afraid.

"Krystal I'm going to be very fast, I'm just going to grab my clothes and get dressed at the hospital," I said in a panic. "Why would you do that? You have plenty of time; I can wait." She said standing back watching me pack my things. We walked out into the living room I held my bag in one hand and with the other I took Krystal by the hand. "Okay let's get out of here," I said to her rushing for the door. Krystal looked at me with her eyebrows lifted.

"Is there a reason why we're holding hands like we're five?" She asked. Just than I could feel it grab my wrist. I walked faster toward the door. "We can pretend we're five again right?" I began to skip as we opened the door. I was too afraid to look back as I closed the door I thought. It didn't get me this time, but when it does, it will probably really hurt me because it was angry. I could feel that it was furious at me. I went to my car. I kissed and hugged Krystal. "Come back tonight," I tell her.

"No, I'm taking a break from you," she says "Why Krystal? Please just come back tonight okay," I begged her. She looked at me and poked her tongue out. "Okay, but I don't like you following me around its creepy," she said driving away. "I won't follow you anymore; I promise," I tell her blowing her a kiss. I drive to work still absolutely in fear of what could happened to me today. I just have to be on my toes I thought don't let it catch me off guard, stay sharp. I was in training to do an IV drip today I had no time to worry about this thing harming me. I just needed to know how I could keep it away for good. It didn't like when other people were around me. It stays away, but I couldn't continue holding people hostage in my home to make me feel safe. What do I do? I thought. I walked into the hospital. Be calm Karis; focus on your job today. I smiled when I walked up to the nurses' station. "Hello everyone," I was going to make it through the day, I thought as I looked over the schedule board.

Let It Out

I started my day working with Michael. Every room he walked into whenever he'd catch my eye he'd wink and stick his tong out at me. I would just smile and turned my head. I at lunch on the patio, Michael joined me from afar. He was having lunch with the other doctors while they talked about surgeries and new medications; Michael made contact eye contact with me, winking and licking his lips. He even hugged himself as if he was holding me. I laughed at him as I finished my lunch. Soon the other doctors would turn and look at me smiling.

When everyone left the table he came over to me. "What are you having?" He said grabbing at the sack paper bag on the table. "I have my lunch," I say taking the bag and holding it close to me. "What are you doing out here don't you need to go back to work now?" I asked him. "I'm trying to keep you focused on all this love you're missing out on," he said winking. He stood up in front of me and began to dance sexy. I turned my head and laughed. "You're too much," I said standing to go put the sack in the trash. I walked away from him.

"See you later," I say waving my hand up at him. He is so funny. I thought as I went inside the hospital. He caught up to me quickly grabbing at my shirt from behind. "Would you like to see a movie or something?" He asked. "I'd like to cook you dinner," he opened the door for us to enter the nurse's station. "That sounds really nice Michael; sure I would like that very much," I said looking up at him. "Great baby, I will pick you up than, right, let's say around seven" He said. "No, Michael, can just go change and we meet back here, is that okay?" I asked him.

"Sure baby that would be fine," he says. "Seven is okay Michael," I said turning to walk away from him. I walked quickly back to the sixth floor. When I turned back to look where he was he was standing in the hall watching me walk away; I waved again trying to move from his sight so that he wouldn't notice my limp as I walked, I could see him began to talk to another doctor. Michael loves his job and it seemed to love him back they were always asking him questions and he was always helpful.

I finished up quickly with no scary encounters. I wondered where I should go to clean up for our date. I was afraid to go home so I set out to find Martha. She would be the one I could tell her about what was happening to me. I knew that she wouldn't tell another soul. She was always very good at keeping secrets. I went to my grandmother's house than to my aunts. Martha was nowhere to be found. I told everyone to have her call me at home is she should show up. I decided to head home maybe she'd show up there.

So I drove the long way home. I parked in the driveway there was no other cars parked in front of my house, I just sat in the car waiting for someone to show, After waiting a while in the car I went ahead and went for the door as I walked toward the door I heard someone yelling for me from across the street. "Hey, Karis, can we come in!" They yelled. I turned to see who it was. Oh my goodness it was Michael. Had he followed me home I thought.

What is he doing here? I ran across the street before he could cross. "Michael, what are you doing here?" I asked. "Did you follow me?" "Yes I did baby, I had to see you." "Why is there something wrong?" I asked. "Yes, you left without me," he said with a sad face. "Can I come inside?" He asked. "You might as well Michael, you're here now," I tell him begging to walk back across the street. We get to the door. "Come in, have a seat," I tell him throwing my bag on the floor.

"I'm just going to change, and we can go," I say walking toward my room. I stopped because something was different. Michael was looking around at everything. "Nice place," He said. "Who decorated?" "Well, Maddy mostly," I tell him. "Maddy, from the hospital?" He asked. "Yes, she's a close friend you know," "Well it's nice." I was yelling from the back room as he talked about my pictures on the wall. There was a certain calmness in the house, no smell following me, no cold, just calm; I never felt this before.

Was it Michael I thought, does it fear Michael. I came out of the room dressed to go. I wore a jumpsuit it was a red halter top that tied around the neck leaving my back out and my breast looking perfect. I spun around for Michael once with my black jacket in my hand. "Oh wee," Michael said standing while grabbing me to pick me up off my feet and spin me around more. "You look gorgeous, baby, you're so sexy." He said putting me down and kissing my face.

"Baby, do we have to go out?" He asked. "Yes Michael we have to go," I said pushing and pulling him toward the door. We drove off in Michael's car with the top off. Michael sang loudly as he drove. We ended up at the beach, "Michael, I thought we were going to the movies?" "Yes baby we are, I just wanted to take some time out to talk to you about something." He said pulling over into the sand near the parking lot. "I feel as if I belong to you," he says to me looking into my eyes. "I know that you're young, I just want you to know that I do care for you," he says kissing my lips.

"I'm not that young Michael," I say to him. "You're a lot younger than I am. I don't want you to be afraid of me; I will never hurt you." He says pulling me closer to him hugging me. "I have to tell you something important; I may be leaving soon. I have finished my residency here, and before I met you, I signed up to do a tour around the world helping people who need medical attention but don't have the money for it. I will be with other doctors from my team." he tells me.

"I'm scheduled to leave in ten days; I wanted to know if you'd like to be with me when I come back? I will call you from wherever I am. However I can, I promise, it will be a whole year that I'll be gone, can you handle that?" He asked. I held his hand tight. "Michael, you have to leave in ten days?" This news so saddened me. Who was going to make me laugh and smile now? He hugged me, "I hope you can forgive me and be here when I come back.

I don't want to go now that I've met you, but I can't back out," He says turning the key to the car. "Do you still feel like seeing that movie?" He asked. I shook my head no and leaned into my seat. "Baby, don't get sad, I will be back, and we will have each other forever, I promise, now let's go see that movie. It would do us some good to laugh," Michael took off into the dark streets for the theater. We sat through the movie holding hands.

I could hardly focus on the movie nor eat the popcorn. All I thought about was Michael leaving me for a year. Who would cheer me up and make me feel good every day? I thought. When the movie was over he drove me home, we glanced back and forth at one another the whole way home. When he pulled up in the driveway he got out and came over to my door and opened it for me. He was so sweet and honest. He took my hand and helped me out. I looked up at him and he moved in close to my face and kissed me with his soft lips.

"Goodnight baby," he said softly in my ear while hugging me. "I will see you tomorrow right?" He asked. "Umm Michael, would you like to come in and have a cup of tea with me?" I asked him. "Come in, sure, a cup of tea, no thank you," he took my hand quickly. We walked into the house, and I put my keys on the table. "Can I use your restroom?" He asked me. "Sure Michael, its right down that hallway and turn right at the end." I went into the kitchen and put on the tea kettle. I stood there and started to look around the house; it was so calm. I couldn't understand it. Was it gone? I didn't smell it at all, I didn't feel it.

I wondered what was going on. Michael came out bathroom and into the kitchen. He grabbed me from behind he began rocking with me in a slow-motion type way while kissing my neck. "Do you have any music around here?" He asked. "Yes I do," Michael held onto me as I walked toward the radio. He took me by the hand before I could reach to turn it on. He turned around. "No baby, we can make our own music, just me and you" He moved me around the floor dancing slowly rubbing against me kissing my neck. Oh gosh did he smell good.

"Michael," I said whispering up to him. "I don't want to go there, I can't make love to you," Michael stopped dancing and looked up at me. "Baby I don't want that, I just want to hold you, if you want me to stop I will," he tells me. I sat down on the couch and he sat beside me. "Baby, calm down, we don't have to do anything that will make you uncomfortable." I kissed Michael on the lips. "Thank you," he kisses me back.

We looked at one another and began to kiss passionately. He held my neck and face so gently, but tight, and kissed me all over. I felt tingling everywhere in my body. He took my hand and brought it down to his lap, he moved my hand up and down his penis it was very hard and very big. I pulled my hand back, "baby I want you so bad." He whispered, "I want you," I stopped kissing and moved over to the other side of the couch. Michael looked at me and leaned his head back up against the couch.

"Baby, you're killing me, would you like me to leave?" He asked. "No," I said quickly. "Please don't leave." I was sure I didn't want him to leave me. I think he's the reason for the calm in my house. I moved back over to him and began to kiss him again. He pulled away from me this time. "Baby I want you to bad, I think I should go." "No, Michael, don't go now, please just stay here with me, I want you to, I'm just scared," I tell him.

He stood up in front of me than sat back down. "I don't know what I'm going to do with you," he grabbed me by the waist, and hugged me and brought me to his chest I rubbed his chest as he held onto me tight. We began to kiss again. Michael kissed my neck and my chest moving closer to my breast. He placed my hand on his shoulders. "Baby, just let me show you something okay, I won't hurt you, I promise."

He kissed me while rubbing on my neck; then he pulled strings tied to my jumpsuit exposing my breast and began to touch them looking them over, I put my head back on the couch. I felt a little ashamed; he lifted my head with his hand on my neck. "You're so beautiful, and they're so beautiful." He said rubbing his hand on my nipples; soon he was licking them. I laid back I didn't stop him; he pulled my jumpsuit down to my thighs.

I grabbed the sides of it. "No, please don't pull it off," I said. He didn't; he started to kiss my stomach, then he looked up at me. "I won't baby I promise," Michael began to kiss me all the way down to my vagina. I laid there as he licked all over it I was so stunned but aroused at the same time. It made me so nervous. "Stop shaking," he said lifting his head up from time to time.

I covered my eyes as Michael kissed his way up from my vagina to my lips. "See, I told you I wouldn't hurt you," he said. "I just wanted a taste." He took my chin and put his forehead to mine, and we rubbed noses. He got up from his knees and helped me with my jumpsuit. I looked down at his pants there was still a big bulge and it was wet near the center of his zipper area. He looked down. "See what you did to me baby, I want you so badly, but I'll accept what just happened as an invitation for next year, that was a great preview." He said smiling,

"I'm going to go to the restroom baby; I need to run some cold water over this head of mine." I tied my jumpsuit back around my neck and ran to the tea kettle it had been whistling for some time. We didn't even hear it. I was sure there was no water left in it by now. I can't believe that just happened. I thought as I could see it all over again Michaels head in between my legs. I shook my head and smiled, Michael just gave me my first sexual experience.

I turned the tea kettle off with the biggest smile on my face. I waited for Michael to come out of the bathroom. "Well baby, I need to go home and change," he said standing in front of the door smiling. "Come over here and give me a kiss baby," he said with his arms stretched towards me. I walked over to him, "Do you have to go Michael?" I asked him. He looked at me and then looked down. "Baby, do you want me to stay like this?" "Yes, I want you to stay with me," I said hugging him by the waist.

"If you'd like, you can come to my place, and I can change, and I'll bring you back later, you've never seen my place before. It would be nice for you to ride with me, I'd like that," he said taking me by the hand. I grabbed my jacket and went for the door. We got into his car and drove. Michael lived so far we went onto the highway and across the biggest bridge I'd ever been on. I was afraid going over the bridge because I'm afraid of heights. Michael knew that, he held my hand as we went over.

I was eager to see how he lived. We made it over the bridge. Michaels place was two blocks down from the bridge exit right near the water. He had underground parking. It was a beautiful place he lived in a condo. His neighbors were standing outside looking at some flowers in the front yard. It was a very small area where the flowers grew. "Hello," Michael said as we walked by grabbing my hand and pulling me behind him toward the door.

The man stared at us and moved his head down as if to say hello back. Michael opened the door, and I could smell his cologne all over the house. "Come on in," he said to me I stood at the door looking around, "Make yourself comfortable" Michael's place was spotless, it looked as if he was never home. He had a couch and a table and exercise equipment all over the living room area. It was quiet, he had very nice art, lots of pictures of angels and clouds and beaches. I didn't walk around too much; I didn't want to seem nosy.

There were mirrors everywhere, but I was expecting that, Michael loved himself so much. "Hey you!" He yelled out. "Come back here." I followed his voice to the back room. He was laying across his bed watching TV. His TV was mounted onto the wall above the dresser. "Come join me, baby," reaching his hand out for me to help me onto the bed. I took my shoes off and joined him. He hugged me close. "Let's just rest awhile," I laid my head on his chest, soon I fell off to sleep on Michael's arm.

I woke up to Michael kissing my forehead. "Hey, baby I got called into the hospital. You can stay here and rest if you like." "No Michael I better go home and change," "Okay well we have to hurry, I can't be late," he says putting on his shoes. We arrived at my house quick he drove very fast. I kissed him goodbye and went for my door. On my porch was a basket with Cookie, Maddy's cat in it, and there was a note. "It's time for her to come home, please take care of her." I picked cookie up from the basket. "Hello Cookie, welcome home," I said opening the door carrying her in with the basket.

I put the basket on the coffee table. I carried Cookie on my side. "This is it; this is your new home." I walked her into the kitchen. "I bet you'd like a bowl of milk wouldn't you?" I felt so good; I must have needed that sleep I thought as I poured Cookies milk. I put Cookie down and went into my room to look in the mirror; I looked very well rested. I walked over to the dresser to get my bed clothes out. The feeling was back.

I could feel it near me. I began to panic; I grabbed my clothes and went to the bathroom. As I crossed the hallway Cookie was standing looking up as if she was stuck, her eyes were focused, and she was hissing. I picked her up and began to walk toward the bathroom, "what's wrong?" I said rubbing her back. As I began to look her in the eye, I was struck suddenly in the face so hard that I fell to the floor. I couldn't see nor smell it, but I could feel it close to me, so I began to crawl.

It was hitting me; it felt as if I was being attacked by more than one. I tried moving faster toward the bedroom door, but it seems to have a hold on my hair. It pulled me to the couch; it felt as if it was pulling my legs apart as Michael did, I couldn't move my feet or my legs. It was if it had me tied down in every way, I screamed, my hands were being held tight above my head. When I moved, and it became even tighter, I cried out. "PLEASE LET ME GO!

My clothes were pulled down as I was choked, I could smell it, I could feel it all over me it was breathing heavily. "God, please help," it pulled my hair harder. I rolled over with all my might; I began to move my bottom and shoulders trying to wiggle my way to the table. It grabbed my neck; my feet were being held down. I kicked and began to crawl toward the bathroom, it felt as if it was hanging onto me, I felt I was pulling something heavy, I made it to the tub and held onto it. It was a struggle.

It began to pull my legs, trying to turn them over. I felt it grabbing my neck and squeezing it. I would not allow it this time; I shook my head all around making it hard for it to grab my neck. I could feel it try to turn my body over, but I twisted and turned so that it wouldn't succeed. I won't let it have me I thought as I fought it. I won't let you have me I screamed out. I held onto the tub screaming, soon the light went off. I screamed louder.

I grabbed onto the shower curtain, and for a second I thought it was over, the room was dark and quiet. I felt it let go of me, but I continued to hang onto the shower curtain. Soon It felt as if something was ripping me apart I felt the scratching of long nails, something was pulling my legs apart it held onto my hands so tight they began to go numb. I started to scream out louder when it grabbed my neck and squeezed until I couldn't scream out at all. It shook me violently, squeezing tighter and tighter.

I couldn't scream or move anymore, the darkness became pitch black as I began to fade away not able to breathe or see anything, but darkness. I started to see spots of light. There was one then two then three, they were moving all around in front of my face faster and faster soon there were at least eight of them. It let go of me, and for the first time, I heard it sigh out loud as it let me go. I felt it move away from me, but still, I laid there, the lights were still around, and the air filled with the smell of flowers.

The light became brighter and brighter. I felt as if I was surrounded by flowers in the garden. I closed my eyes. I didn't want to move; I couldn't. I just laid there as if I was hopeless thinking of the smell of the flowers. Soon I hear my name being called. "Karis, Karis, what the hell happened to you?" It was Martha. She was standing over me I covered my face and peeked out at her "Karis, what happened?" She asked grabbing me by my shoulder to pull me up.

Martha was very short. She was too small to pull me up. I was taller than her. I struggled to get up. She put my arm around her neck. "What the hell happened in here?" She asked me. "Wait I'm going to get you some water," she said. "Should I call uncle Earl?" She asked scurrying around the room in a panic. She was shaking her head and talking to herself. "I don't know what happened, but you are all messed up."

She came back into the room with a glass of water for me. She held it to my face as I took a couple of sips. My head hurt, my body ached I felt as if I was empty inside. I lay on the bed beginning to cry. I took Martha by the hand. "Martha, you can't tell anyone this because they will think I'm crazy okay, promise me you'll never tell anyone," she shakes her head yes at me. "I promise," she says. "Something keeps attacking me, I don't know what it is or what it wants, but it keeps attacking me, and it's getting stronger and stronger."

Martha look baffled at what I was telling her. "What, what are you talking about   Karis?" She said reaching for the phone. "I think I should call uncle Earl; you need the police here." She touched my head. "Did you get smacked on the head with something? You're talking crazy," she said. "No, really Martha something is attacking me, it won't leave me alone, it's some spirit, I don't know what to do, I can't keep going through this." "Karis, okay, don't worry then, we will find a way to get some help," Martha grabbed me and held me for a while.

She waited then went to the bathroom to get a warm towel. She wiped my head with the towel. "Martha, I'm only safe when people are around, I can't be alone, I think it will kill me," I tell her. "It beats me and touches me; it's strong, I can't stop it." "It touches you?" She asked. "Yes, it touches my breast, and tonight it tried to touch me in between my legs." "Okay I will do some research on this, I heard about this before," she said rubbing her head.

"Martha please don't tell anyone," I begged her. Martha assured me she wouldn't tell. Martha laid in bed next to me. She was my big cousin, I trusted her I thought as I fell off to sleep, I had to tell someone. "Karis, Karis," I hear. "Wake up, we have to get those bruises checked out," she said. "We won't tell what happened, but we have to get them checked out, we'll just say you were attacked somewhere out in town," she says lifting her eyebrows.

"No, Martha I used that line before, if I go back to the hospital they will start to think that I'm hurting myself, Michael won't believe it, and Maddy will be upset." "We can go to a different hospital, where no one will know you, we will just tell them you were mugged at the mall okay." She began to fall off to sleep. We were woken up again by the doorbell ringing. Martha jumped up to her feet and looked down the hall.

"I'll get it," she said going to the door. I didn't want anyone to see me. I laid in bed thinking about how good it felt to get that off my chest. I got up to go to the bathroom. I felt as if my body had been hit by a heavy truck. I limped a little worse today because I'm sore all over. I just want to take a hot bath and soak. I could hear Martha talking at the door to someone. "Hey next time, just call," she said shutting the door. "Karis, where are you?"

"I'm in here," I was sitting on the toilet. "Martha, I don't feel so good," I said as I got up to turn around and vomit. "We have to get you to the hospital Karis, you need to be checked out, you have marks and scratches all over," she said pulling my hair from my face. "I want you to get washed up, I'm going to get you something to wear, and we are going to the hospital." It was horrible trying to get my clothes on.

I hurt everywhere, lifting my arms up, moving around and my head was pounding as if someone hit me in the head with a bat almost like a beating drum inside my head. I took Martha's hand as we walked to the car. We went to a hospital way across town. It was very busy in the emergency room. I sat down while Martha went to talk to the nurse. When she came back out with a nurse, a doctor and two police officers followed "Hello Karis, how are you feeling?" They asked. "I hear you were attacked tonight, did you see who did it?" I shook my head no.

"Okay can you tell me what happened, did they take anything, like your purse or your car?" While the police questioned me the nurse inspected my body in the emergency room, people were watching me, listening and whispering. I pulled Martha close to me. I whispered to her. "Martha can they take me in back, I don't want to talk about this out here." "Could we go in the back somewhere, to a room or something? She's a little embarrassed talking about this out here."

"I'm sorry, are you able to walk to the back?" The doctor asked. "Yes, I am," I tell her getting up from the chair. We followed them to the back. "We need a rape kit and the camera," the police officer yelled out down the hall. I pulled Martha down to my ear. "A rape kit, Martha?" I thought oh my goodness, I'm doomed; I gave them blood, the policeman took his pictures than for the worse part, the checking of my vagina.

I felt embarrassed; I had bruises and scratches all over me. Some of them looked like small handprints, and some were big hand prints. It was very bad this time. My neck was blue and black as if there had been a rope there for hanging. They even took an x-ray of my body to check for broken bones. We waited for the doctor to come back into the room. "Martha, are you afraid?" I asked her. "We told a lot of lies," she said shaking her head. "I'm so sorry you had to lie." I told her as the doctor walked in.

"Hello, I'm Dr. Thatcher, nice to meet the both of you," he said smiling taking a seat on the stool in front of me. "I want to explain to you what we found, is that okay?" He said as he flipped through the pages of the chart he was holding. "It looks like more than one person was attacking you, its confirmed that the handprints on your arms and ankles don't match, even the handprints between your thighs don't match. They tell me that you didn't see anyone, is that true?" He asked.

I believe that because you have a mild concussion from the blow to your head, do you recall being hit over the head at all?" He asked checking my eyes. "You also have a cracked rib; we will be wrapping you up, you should probably take some time off from work, maybe three weeks." He says pushing down on my stomach, "I suggest you rest for a while so that you can heal." I looked over at Martha, how on earth am I going to explain this to anyone without having to tell this same story, I thought, this is what I didn't want to happen.

"You, young lady, you were fortunate and I'm glad that you are strong, what do you weigh?" He asked. "I weigh 120 pounds I believe." "Yes that's probably about right you're so lucky to have made it through that." "Yes she is fortunate," Martha said. I was sent home that night with pain medication, my waist was wrapped in white like cast material. I was still sore. When we arrived at my house James was sitting on the porch waiting for me. We pulled up, I looked at Martha. She immediately pulled back out. "Scoot down, scoot down!"

She drove off quick. I don't think James seen us drive up or out. We went around the block and up the street. "What the hell is he doing there?" Martha asked. "Damn! He can't just pop up at your house like that all the time, does he call you at all?" She asked. "No, I'm going back," Martha pulled over. She moved my seat way back. So that he can't see me. She took a cover from her back seat and covered me from head to toe.

"Hey Martha, this blanket stinks," I tell her. "I'm going to have to hold my breath the whole time," we pulled back onto the road, Martha drove quickly toward the house James was still there sitting in his car now listening to the radio. Martha got out. "Hey James," she said. "Oh hey Martha, how are you, I'm just waiting for   Karis, have you seen her?" He asked. "Oh yes, she told me she'd be working late tonight, have you been to the hospital to check for her?" Martha asked him.

"Oh no I haven't I just came here straight from work, I figured she'd be home by now," he said backing up toward his car. Martha went to the front door. "I will tell her you stopped by," she tells him. "Sure, please do, I appreciate it, maybe I'll call her tonight," he said. "That sounds great," Martha says waving him off as she pretends to go into the house. He was still in the driveway when Martha went in and shut the door. I sat still.

I heard him drive off, but I didn't move until I could no longer hear the car. I was so glad I pulled the cover off me and got up. Martha ran down the stairs to the car and opened the door for me. "Come on before he decides to come back, hurry," she said. "I bet that little moment was like an hour for you huh Karis?" She said laughing. She laughed as I walked slowly inside. The house was so cold. I went to my bedroom and lay across the bed.

"I'm going to call your job first and tell them that you went out of town, a family emergency and that you will be back in a week." "No, just talk to Maddy," I tell her. "Just tell her I'm sick, tell her that I'll be at daddy's and she won't come looking for me," I covered myself with a blanket. "Martha you can watch what you want, I need to sleep," I tell her closing my eyes. "Please don't leave okay," Martha took the remote and the phone and began making calls and flipping through the channels. I make sure I can hear her voice.

I lay so close to her I am almost laying on her chest. "Hey, tomorrow we will hit the library," Martha says rubbing my back. When I woke up I could hear Martha in the kitchen. Lionel Richie on the radio and she was talking to someone. I could smell the food cooking. I wondered who she had over. I got up and poked my head out into the living room. I see her standing over the stove she sees me and waves. I still can't see who's there with her. I go back into the bedroom. She follows me with a plate in her hand.

"Hey you, eat up we have lots of work to do today," she says putting the plate down beside me," I can't shower Martha, I have this wrap remember," I tell her. "Oh yes, damn it, well wash up then. Take you a good old fashion whore bath." She danced around the bed than out to the kitchen laughing. "Martha!" I yelled out to her. "Come back here," she came back in. "What is it?" "Who do you have out there?" I asked her. "Oh that's Chad, remember Chad Randall from school?" She says smiling and dancing, "I'm dating him now."

"You are?" I asked in disbelief. "Does he still have that terrible haircut," I asked. "Or has he stepped out of the eighties?" I asked her laughing "Shish, he'll hear you," Martha said smiling as though she wanted to laugh with me. "I'll stay close to the door while you wash up okay?" She was still dancing and prancing around. I'm so glad she's here I thought to myself as I scarfed down my food. When I was done I went to the bathroom I stood in the mirror at the sink.

I closed my eyes at first before really looking at myself. When I opened them I just cried. My neck and face were swollen, I was hurting, what did I do to deserve this Lord, I asked looking up. I washed up quickly so that Martha could get back to her company. I put my clothes on in the room and sat on the bed waiting for Martha to finish her breakfast with Chad. The phone rang. I picked it up. "Hello?" I say. "Hello baby, I hear you're sick, you don't sound sick." "Hello, Michael? I'm just a little under the weather, that's all," I tell him.

"I haven't heard from you since the other night, I hope I didn't scare you," he says chewing gum. "No I'm not afraid, I just have a little cold that's all." "Aww, do you want the doctor to come by and check you out, baby? I'm certified you know; I can give you a diagnosis and a prescription." "I'll be fine Michael, please don't worry, you don't have to come by, I don't want you to catch what I have," I tell him. "We can just talk on the phone tonight," I tell him. "Sure baby I could listen to your sweet voice all night if I could, I can't believe that you became sick that fast, you were fine the other day, maybe it was that ocean breeze that night?" He said.

"It was chilly out there, and you were sexy in your red baby, you are so sexy to me." Michael said. "I can't wait to get into you; I enjoyed myself that night." "You did?" I asked him. "Yes baby, it was fantastic." "You know Michael, I felt guilty, because you did all that for me and I didn't do anything for you, except kissing, how did I make you feel good?" I asked him. "Baby there are so many things that we are going to together, I felt good just thinking about that," he tells me.

"When you marry me I will show you how we can please one another, guilt-free." My heart just dropped, "Michael, you want to marry me?" I asked him. "I didn't know you liked me that much; I thought I was just a fling or something." "Oh baby, when I come back from my trip I want you, I want you to carry my children, when you're ready, I want you to be my one and only," he says to me. "Michael I would love that." I was so stunned at Michael's pouring of affection for me.

All I could do was say, "Michael I like you so much, I hope that you want this" "I never tell the lies baby, I want you all right, you just wait and see" Michael began to talk to me about his plans to have his very own practice. He plans to have free health care at his practice on special days to help the poor. He said he'd make me his right hand. I believed he was sincere. I fell asleep listening to him talk. I woke up to Martha tapping me on the cheeks.

"Wake up girl, we need to go to the library before it closes" She took my plate to the kitchen. I wiped my face with the towel next to the bed "I'm sorry Martha" I said sitting straight up. "Don't be, just hurry" She said. I got up and we went to the library. Martha what am I going to do if I can't get rid of it" I asked her. "We will get rid of it one way or another." At the library, we went into the section where they had science fiction, and paranormal activities were listed, then in the section were ghost and spirits.

We took all the books we could carry and checked them out and went back to the house, there was a book about spells and demonic spirits and what they meant, we made tea and sat down at the table, Martha had a book about evil spirits and how sometimes they can invade your soul and haunt you. Where they come from and how to get rid of them, there was so many ways to get rid of them.

We read that we could perform an exorcism and try to allow the spirit to go away on its own or we could seek a spiritual guidance counselor to get a better understanding of why it was haunting me. We could find them most likely on an Indian reservation. "Indians," Martha said. "Does uncle earl still hang out with Mr. Red?" She asked me. "Mr. Red? I don't know of any Mr. Red," I tell her. "Yes, you do, he used to come over to all the family holiday parties."

"The Indian man, remember, his skin was red, he had red hair too." "I'm going to call uncle Earl and ask him if Mr. Red is still around, maybe he could help us find someone to help you," She said grabbing the phone. "Martha, how are you going to explain to daddy what we want from him" I asked. "We can't just ask these questions, daddy will become suspicious, don't you think?" "No, I will deal with uncle Earl," she called over to the house.

"Hello may I speak top uncle Earl," she asked it's Martha." "Okay hold on," "hi uncle Earl, How are you, have you seen, my mom?" She asked. "I know she was with you and Mr. Red the last time I saw you guys, Is Mr. Red still living on the reservation?" She asked him. "Okay let me write it down," she took a pen off the table and began to write whatever daddy was telling her. "Thank you uncle," she hung up the phone.

"I got it," she said waving the paper around in the air. "Okay let's call Mr. Reds house, I'm going to pretend I'm looking for my mom," she said about to call Mr. Reds house. She was about to pick the phone up when it rang. "Hey Martha, it's your uncle Earl, now I don't want you going over to that reservation looking for your mom alone, you hear me." "Mr. Red is always drunk and those Indians over there are all nuts, if you need to go over there looking for your mother I have to go along with you, you hear me," he said in a stern voice.

"Yes uncle Earl, I hear you," she says hanging up the phone. She looked at me. "Hey, we might have to include uncle Earl in our plans because he says we can't go alone." "Well, will it be so bad, they'll probably start drinking, and we can go searching around the reservation for a spiritual doctor.

There has to be someone over there who knows how to find one." "Yes that will be the plan, we go to uncle Earl's tomorrow," she closed the book and came over to me. "I love you.

Karis, we will find a way to get rid of this thing, I promise you." I must have looked scared to her because I could only remember Martha being this close to me when we were younger. She was always around when I needed a friend. So tomorrows the day, we turned the TV on waiting for the next day; we didn't talk about it for the rest of the night.

Smoking Spirits

The next day would come quicker than we anticipated. At 3 am that morning, we were awakened by the doorbell ringing over and over again. I pushed at Martha. "Martha gets up someone's ringing the doorbell," we both got up from the bed quickly to get the door. I walked behind Martha. She peeped from the peephole in the door. "It's uncle Earl," she said pulling the door opened. He walked in covered with dirt from head to toe.

"Daddy where have you been? I asked him. He was mumbling, "I went to get her Karis, I want her back." "Who daddy, who do you want back? I asked him "I need her Karis, I need her," he said crying. "Uncle Earl, what's wrong, where were you tonight?" Martha asked "I went over to her," he said. "Daddy are you telling us that you were at the graveyard, digging?" we both said at the same time.

We looked at one another and shook our heads. I went to get daddy a glass of water. "Daddy you can't do that, I know you miss mama, we all do daddy, but you can't go try and dig her up, she's not even there daddy, but she's with us in spirit all the time." I tell him. "I know baby, I just miss my wife," he said holding his hands together. "Daddy, drink some water," I said holding his glass to his lips. Daddy had been drinking we could smell the alcohol on his breath. "I'm going to stay on the reservation for a while," he told us.

"Red and I are just going to stay over there, he lost his wife to some years back, and they have some spiritual classes over there that we can go to, to help us through this, because baby, I don't think I can continue on this way." "Okay daddy," I said holding his hand. Martha stood beside me looking down at daddy. I went to get him a blanket and pillow for the couch. I gave daddy a white T-shirt and some old sweats and took his clothes to the bathroom to soak them. I made him lay across the couch.

Martha and I went back into the bedroom. She got on the phone again, and I began writing in my notebook. Lord thank you for bringing daddy to my house, he could have gone anywhere lord and gotten into trouble,   but you brought him here to me, thank you Lord for getting him here safely, I hope that he does get the help he needs on the reservation tomorrow. In Jesus name, I pray Amen. I fell asleep listening to Martha giggling on the phone. When we woke up daddy was in the kitchen cooking breakfast.

"Good morning young ladies, I have breakfast all ready for you two, have a seat," he said. "Karis baby, you had these green tomatoes in the fridge, and I see you didn't know what to do with them, so I fried them up." I grabbed a slice of toast from the plate on the counter. I took a butter knife from the drawer and Martha and I sat at the table. "Daddy, how did you cook them?" I asked him spreading apricot jam over my toast, Martha stood near him watching him cook. "I want these recipes," "I do to daddy, I need to learn to cook for myself," I tell him eating toast and a couple of slices of bacon. Daddy put the green tomatoes on a plate in front of us.

Then he joined us at the table for breakfast, "Good eats, you two," he said as he sipped his cup of coffee and read the paper. We dared to talk about last night. If daddy was really going to stay at the reservation he probably would have already gone to get Mr. Red. When we were done Martha and I went to get dressed. "Daddy I'm turning the television on for you." I tell him as I go back into the room daddy shook his head as if to say yes.

"Karis, I'm going home soon, will you girls call me if you still plan to go over to the reservation with Red and me?" He said flipping his paper over. "Oh yeah daddy, we're going with you, we'll be over as soon as we get dressed." The phone rang, Martha answered. "Karis it's for you, its

Michael," she said yelling out. "Hello," I said putting the receiver to my ear. "Hi baby, how are you feeling today, sweetheart?" He asked.

"I'm feeling a little better," I tell him. "I miss you, baby, when can I come see you?" He asked. "Well I'm headed out to the Indian reservation with my daddy today, I don't want you around me until I know that what I have is gone for sure," I told him. "Baby I'm a doctor, I'm around sick people all day, you know that, are you sure you just don't want to see me because of the other night?"

"No Michael, I'm sick, and I don't want you to get sick because of me. The other night was so great, and I know we didn't talk after you dropped me off, but I'm okay Michael I promise, I'm curious about my next encounter with you," I said laughing. "I was a little scared too." "Okay baby I get you," Michael said laughing. "I will call you later baby" "Okay Michael, I will miss you until then." "Yes baby, I will miss you too," he said hanging up. I put my clothes on in the room while Martha put her lipstick in the dresser mirror.

"So, are you and Michael a couple?" She asked. "You guys seem close, have you had sex with him yet?" "Oh my goodness Martha, no we haven't," I told her. "Well what was all that, the other night stuff about, what did you guys do the other night?" She asked looking at me smiling. "My God, Martha, were you listening in on the phone?" I asked her. She smiled "Were you?" I asked her again.

"Yes I was, girl and it sounds like you guys are in love," she said. "I'm going to get you back," I said throwing a pillow at her head. "You're in love," she said. "Let's get out of here before uncle Earl leave without us." We drove over to daddy's house. It was short drive; Martha always drove her car as if she was flying an airplane we made it there in seconds. Daddy was in the room lying across the bed. "Daddy, we're here, are we still on for today?" I asked standing by the door. "Baby let me rest a while, I'll be out, I'm still a little tired," he said with his head on the pillow.

"You and Martha go check on the ducks for me, or water the garden," he said muffled. My brother Lee was home. He had girls all over the living room. They all seemed at home as if they lived there. Martha knew some of them from school. We quickly went out back to check on the ducks in the pond. Martha grabbed some bread from the cabinet in the kitchen and we sat on the porch feeding the ducks until daddy got up. I didn't go over to the garden, but I could see that daddy had been watering it.

"So Karis, don't you get bored just working and hanging out with the same guys all the time?" She asked me. "No, I kind of like having the same guys around all the time, I don't know Martha I'm just a little scared of any affection from a man," I tell her. "They are all so hard to trust, don't you feel that way sometimes?" "Well little cousin, I will never give anyone the chance to get close enough to me to worry about it," she said.

"Are you afraid because of what happened to you?" "No, Martha, well yes, I'm a little worried that I may not be able to give them what they want or need." "What do you mean?" "I

can't give them children." "Do you think that will matter to them?" She asked. "I don't know if it will matter or not, all I know is that I will never allow anyone to get that close, I will probably never marry," I tell her throwing my last crumb to the ducks. I got up and walked up to the top of the stairs and sat on the rail.

"You know what, who says that children will make a man happy anyway Karis?" Martha asked still throwing breadcrumbs at the ducks. "You never know Karis, a man just might just want you for you, just plain old you," she said getting up. "Let's go get uncle Earl, I'm burning up out here in this sun," she said. "We need to get out of here before it gets too late." We walked back into the house to get daddy. Martha's right we better go. Getting to the reservation was like driving down a terrifying obstacle course, and it is very dark over there at night.

One way up and one way down, daddy came into the living room with his bag on his shoulder. "Let's go, girls," he said. "Lee you guys keep up the house, I'll be back in a couple of days." "Can I have some money dad?" Lee asked. "Here you go," daddy said reaching down into his wallet handing Lee money. "Get a job and you won't have to ask me for any money," he raised his eyebrows at Lee, and we walked to the car. Martha parked her car on the street.

"I hope you girls don't think that you're staying because you're not," daddy tells us as we get into the car. He drives off onto the road. "I want you guys to drive my car back home." We were on the highway then soon off into the hills to the reservation. Daddy played the radio the whole time, mostly news. Martha and I talked and laughed the whole drive up. 'So Martha, who do you think you'll marry?" I asked her.

"I don't know, but he will have to have a lot of money." "He does, why?" I asked her. "Because I don't ever want to worry about my bills being paid." Martha seemed always to have things together; I never hear her complain about money or a job, she was always shopping. She loved to buy clothes, both her and my aunt dressed like movie stars on TV all the time. I really liked their style. We must have been in the car a little over an hour.

When we went high up on the hills Martha would tease me. "Look! Look!" She said. I would put my hands over my eyes. "I don't want to look, Martha, cut it out, you know I'm afraid of heights." We finally made it to the reservation. The houses around us looked normal. I thought I would see teepees and feathers and bear skinned blankets all over, moccasins and lots of babies being carried around by their mothers in a pouch around their waist.

I was taken by surprise at what I seen. Normal houses, close together, but big, no fires were burning outside with rocks around it an there, and there was no circle of Indians singing by fire either. Martha began to laugh at me. "You look shocked, what were you expecting?"

She said pointing and laughing at me. "You girls follow me," daddy said. "Red should be somewhere around here." We followed him through an open side area where it was dark and quiet; daddy led us to the very back of all the houses.

Mr. Red lived in the back wooded area. Daddy knocked on his door softly, then he yelled out, "Red, you in there!" He knocked harder. Suddenly the door cracked open. We all leaned back to look and see who it was. We didn't see anyone at all, then a little boy with bushy red hair appeared. "Hello," he said standing looking at us with his tiny little clothes on. He looked really dirty and unkempt, even his hair looked dirty. He was wearing an orange shirt and a pair of jeans that were   too short for him. "Hello little man," daddy said.

"Where is your pop?" Daddy asked him. The little boy kept his eyes on us as he pointed daddy in the direction of his dad. "You girls come in." Daddy said pushing the door open, "go sit down, and I will see if Joann's back here," he told us looking at Martha. We walked in. The floors were wooden and it looked as if they'd never been cleaned and the couches looked to dirty and old to sit on, by now Martha and I were holding each other by the arm as we walked closer toward the kitchen.

We could smell a foul scent as soon as we got closer, there was trash everywhere. I could never see why Aunt Joann would want to be with Mr. Red. We stood up until daddy came back into the room. The little boy stood there with us staring. He didn't say a word. When daddy walked in, he had a woman with him. "Hey girls, Joann's not here, but Red said she was here yesterday, she was supposed to come back and take little man shopping, but she never did."

Martha looked at daddy and shook her head. "Okay uncle Earl, we're going to go then."

We held each other by the arm as we walked toward the door. "Where are you guys going from here?" He asked us. "We're just going home daddy," I tell him. I looked at Martha and she looked at me.

"Well, why don't you guys take the little man here with you?" He said grinning with his hand on the little boy's shoulders. "What, uncle Earl, I don't think I can do that," Martha told him. "Yes, I think you guys will be okay, just take him, get him some clothes and a bath and keep him until you guys come back to get me," daddy said frowning at us.

"Uncle Earl, I know what you mean, but I am swamped during the day," Martha told him. "And daddy, you know that I work, I can't be responsible for a child daddy" I tell him. "He's a good boy, please," daddy said pushing the little boy toward me. "Karis," daddy said looking at him. "Just take the boy and clean him up for me" I reached out my hand for the little boy. Martha was so angry. She shook her head at daddy as we walked out.

"You girls be careful going out of here it's dangerous, if you don't take your time" We rushed out of the front door. It was darker out. We took off down the side pathway than we stopped. "Now Karis, how are we going to get you some help if we have him with us" She asked pointing at the little boy. I shrugged my shoulders. "Martha I don't know it's kind of scary out here anyway, don't you think, maybe we should do this when we bring him back?" I suggested.

"No," Martha retorted. "We have to get this done, I can't keep staying with you, I have school, I have a life," she said walking faster out near the front walkway. "Do you hear that?" I asked, "What?" "Shh shh! Listen," Martha looked up, "I hear it." We could hear drums beating and singing. We walked closer to the sound of the drums. It was begging to get very dark by now and the sound was coming from in the woods. "Wait" I said grabbing Martha's shirt.

"What?" She said. "Let's go!" The little boy clutched my hand tight. I looked down at him. He looked so frighten. "Hey, are you okay" I asked him. The little boy looked at me and took his hand to one side of his neck to the other and pointed into the direction we were walking in. He then shook his head no. "Can you talk?" I asked him. He shook his head yes. "Well, talk then," Martha said walking ahead of us. "In the woods, there is a headhunter, if we bother him, he will cut our heads off," he said with his eyes opened wide.

"Sure he will," said Martha. "No, he will, he's a witch doctor, and daddy said I must stay away from the woods," the little boy told us. "He doesn't like people," we walked on into the woods. "Martha, are you sure about this?" I asked her. "I mean this kid lives out here, I think we should believe him," I told her. "He probably has never been outside, just look at the fear in his eyes, how would he know what's in these woods?"

Martha said as she walked through the trees and branches crunching under her feet. There were so many leaves and trees we could heat them more and more as we made it deeper into the woods rustling and crunching under our feet with every step we took the drums became louder. "Martha we need to think this over." "Wait, shh," she said holding her finger to her lips. "I don't hear anything anymore," we strolled toward the trees in the wide brush ahead. Soon we couldn't see what was ahead nor hear the drums anymore. Just the rustling of the brush under our feet, I could feel a presence near us.

I looked around into the darkness holding onto the little boys hand, I seen nothing, I held the back of Martha's shirt and clutched the boys hand tighter. Martha didn't say a word. The little boy pulled down on my hand. "Stop it," I said whispering to him. He pulled again this time he twisted my wrist. I turned and grabbed him by his shoulder. He looked up at me with his eyes wide and quickly pointed up. I turned and looked over my shoulder, and all I saw were two eyes looking back at me in the darkness, two eyes and a white painted face just staring back at me. I pulled Martha's shirt hard enough to pull her to the ground. "What's wrong with you?" She yelled rusting through the brush trying to get up. When she looked up I pointed my finger for her to look behind me.

She quickly got up and grabbed my other hand and we ran as fast as we could with the little boy. I was pulling him so hard and moving so fast that his feet were barely touching the ground. We stopped to take a breath. "What the hell was that?" Martha asked trying to catch her breath. "I don't know," I say looking around us. "He was just standing there"

We were both breathing heavy. The little boy stood in front of us. He pointed up. We both looked up and there stood a man in a skirt with a white painted face. He held his arms folded to his chest, he was barefooted. I stood there speechless. Martha grabbed my hand. "Don't run," she said. "He's probably the one we need to talk to," Martha stood up. "Hi sir, we are here because we need," the man quickly put his hand over Martha's mouth and grabbed her wrist.

He pulled her forward, suddenly there were two more big men standing before us with white painted faces. One of them grabbed me. We were speechless. The other one picked up the little boy. He began to cry. They walked us into the darkness of the woods. "Wait a minute!" Martha yelled trying to wiggle her way from the man's tight grip. Every time she began to talk the man would cover her mouth with his big hand. Martha was held tight with her mouth covered the whole time.

The little boy stopped crying and was very quiet, and so was I. We stopped in a very dark area lite only by the moon, the stars shined down on the water. We could only hear the sounds of the woods, the man stood back and folded his arms, and the other men stood with him. Their faces were serious. They seemed very upset that we were there. They sat down on the dirt. "Sit," the man said in a stern voice. "You are here to learn about the spirits within you," he said pointing his finger at me. I didn't say a word I started looking at Martha. She's always got all the answers.

He picked some dirt from the ground in front of him and held it in his hand. He held his hand over his mouth and began to blow the dirt as it fell from his hand. He blew the dirt went upward toward the sky; it went up in a swirl as if the wind was blowing it. Martha grabbed me by the hand. "You come to learn about the spirit?" The man asked again. This time I shook my head yes. The men stood up, grabbed each other by the hand and began to dance around us in a circle.

They all had heavy voices singing and dancing. The men stopped dancing and reached out their hands to me. I stood up and walked over to the circle grabbing the man by the hand, he pulled me into the middle of the circle and we all sat down with our back turned toward the little boy and Martha. They scooted close to me, they all reached their hands to the sky and over and over again they began to chant something in the native tong that I didn't understand.

As they shook their hands and heads up to the sky, I watched, intensely afraid of what would come next, the man sat in front of me and took me by the hands. "You have a haunting spirit, taunting you, it is around you all the time, it can't rest. It's violent, and it will hurt you until it gets what it wants." I squeezed his hand as if I understood and knew it was going to continue haunting me, what I didn't know was how to get rid of it. I thought as he chanted more.

"Where did it come from, and why me" I asked him. "He wants you, he came from out there in the universe, his soul never laid to rest, someone close to you knows why" he got up and went over to a tree. He came back with a bowel, it was smoking. He stood over me and began to move the bowel around my head in a circle chanting while the other men danced around me. He sat back down and opened my hand he placed what looked like a fig from a tree inside of my hand and chanted as he squeezed my hand tight.

"I can't make it go away; I can give you protection from it, this spirit is violent because it died violently, only you can make it go away. You have the strength of the true spirit inside you; you have to learn to use it, my child, my protection is nothing compared to what you have. This spirit that haunts you knows you, it wants to be free of you, but it doesn't know how. You have the power within you. The power to free it, you have to learn to look into the lights, only they will tell you the stories of the spirits that come to haunt you.

The light saved you; it has given you all the answers to save them all, soon you will be haunted by them all." He said looking up, "you have a connection to a higher source of light if you learn to follow what you feel when these things are happening to you. You will soon learn how to reach the souls of the spirits around you. They will only harm you when you can't reach them, the spirit of the light will teach you all things, just follow the light."

The man took the bowel and stood in front of me, he blew the smoke directly into my face, but instead of it hitting my face it flew upward into the sky. "Look up," he said. "See what I see." When I looked up quickly and in through the dirt was a light shining into my eyes. "There," he said pointing up, they watch you," he said looking serious. "They protect you," I watched as the smoke began to swirl and twist into a bigger cloud with light shining through it.

I felt like I was dreaming this the whole time. We could hear whispers in the smoke. I put my head down in fear of what would happen next. The man took my chin and held my head up. "You have to look up don't fear the light," he said. "Go where it takes you," I closed my eyes. I began to feel afraid, where would the light take me, I thought I'm afraid of what's up there; I'd rather fear the unknown than face the truth.

He squeezed my face harder, "open up," he said. "Look into the light and free your spirit," He blew smoke into my eyes and everything went black. All I could see was light it was quiet and all around me was light, there were lots of people in the light. I couldn't move or think I just stared into the light. The people were people I knew, people I've met before. I felt as if I was in a different world, I felt so much joy, I felt so happy, I could do nothing, but smile at the things I saw there.

Suddenly the darkness came when the man took his hand from my face. I grabbed his shoulders and began to cry because I felt sadness. "No, no," the man said. "Sufio wants you to remember that feeling that the light gave you, that light will always guide you there, remember when that spirit comes to haunt you look into that light and they will come to guide you through." He pulled me up. "I will be a guide in the light for you look for all the good," he said wiping my face with ash from the bowel.

Martha took the little boy by the hand and began walking ahead of me like usual. I walked as fast as I could to keep up with her as the sun began to come up, we didn't have such a hard time walking through the trees and brush. Martha knew exactly where to go. I was somewhat confused. "Martha do you know where the car is" "Yes, we came through here from the west, so we need to exit south, that's where the car is," she said pointing south.

"We've been here all night, I don't know what they said to you, but I hope it helped, did it?" She asked. "Yes Martha, I have a better understanding of things," I tell her. "I have to learn how to use my instincts better; I have to look beyond my fears." "What was with all the smoke and the whispering?" She asked. "What exactly did they do to you?" "Martha, you wanted me to come here, now you want me to explain to you what happened to me. I thought you were watching; I can't explain it, all I know is that this thing is connected to me somehow, it's lost, and I have to help it back somehow." I tell her.

On the way home we barely talked. The little boy was very quiet to. He smelled so bad. We kept the windows down the whole way to daddy's house. "So, he's going with you, right?" Martha said looking at me out of the corners of her eyes. "I guess so, he's probably no problem, he doesn't seem to talk much," I tell her. We pulled up to daddy's,

Martha went to the door to give Lee daddy's keys. We got into her car, and she drove me to my house quickly as if she was in a hurry. We were so tired.

"I'm only staying tonight because I can't drive any further, I am beat." Martha said taking her keys from the ignition of the car. I opened the door to the house and cookie came running out to greet us, I went to the kitchen to get her a bowel of milk. "You can have a seat on those chairs over there," I tell the little boy pointing at the chairs to the kitchen table. "I'm going to run you a bath, and get you something to wear until we can get you some new clothes," Martha sat down on the couch.

"I'm going to watch Oprah today because she knows it all," she said flipping through the channels. "Oh, you watch Oprah too, huh?" I said smiling. "Who's on there today?" I asked her. She found the show quickly. "It's about people living in fear of their spouses," There are a lot of people in the audience, "mama would watch Oprah every day," I told her. "Mama said she was the most confident women she'd ever seen."

"But she doesn't enjoy being overweight," Martha said. "How do you know?" I asked her sitting on the edge of the couch watching. "She seems comfortable to me," "no, she's not, look at the way she holds the microphone, how she's taking cover with her movement, her arms closed tight. Almost like she's squeezing her body so that it would look a bit smaller, she's trying to hide herself." "No, Martha, that's just the way she stands," I tell her going to the bathroom to check on the little boy's bath water.

I took him by the hand. "Come on, young man, it's time for your bath," I grabbed a T-shirt and a pair of sweats. "Here you go, you take your time and soap up, the towels are over there when you finish, okay." I could hear the applause everywhere in the house I went back into the living room with Martha while the little boy took his bath. "Oh, I forgot to tell him to wash his hair," I ran back into the hallway and knocked on the bathroom door.

"Hey, can I get your name?" I cracked the door. "My name is Paul, but everyone calls me Scooter!" He said yelling. "Okay Scooter, can you please wash your hair?" I yelled back to him. "There's some shampoo on the counter, don't hurt yourself getting out," I tell him. "I need help, can you help me please?" I walked in and went to the bathtub. "Here you go," I said putting shampoo into his hand I even put a little on top of his head. "There, wow you look cleaner already," I tell him walking out of the bathroom.

"Take your time, okay Scooter," I went back in to check on him after Oprah went off. He was sitting in the tub just soaking. "Are you done?" I asked him. He shrugged his shoulders. I walked in he was cover in soap, his hair was still full of shampoo, the water was dirty I reached in the tub and pulled the plug to let the water out.

I ran the water while the water drained. "I need you to lean under the faucet while I wash this soap out of your hair," I tell him. I took a clean towel off the counter and washed the soap off his little body. He was so pale underneath all that dirt. He was so cute. "Scooter, my you're such a handsome little boy," I said helping him out and drying him off. "You look good, and you smell great." I told him handing him the clothes I had for him.

"After you get those on coming in the kitchen to get something to eat okay, do you like mac n cheese?" I asked him. He shook his head yes, "good that's what I'll make for you," I tell him walking out. He came out and Martha had to look at him twice. She pointed at him and smiled. "You look brand new," she said smiling. He ate his mac n cheese quickly. I made him a bed on the couch with plenty of blankets and pillows so that he'd be comfortable.

I brushed his hair before I put made him go to sleep. He was so happy. I knew he would sleep well. He was so clean I rubbed his small back and left him to join Martha in my room she was in bed talking on the phone as usual. I could tell she was ready to be at her own house in her own bed. I laid down in bed with my clothes on from the day before I fell off to sleep quickly listening to her talk about what flavor ice cream she wanted to have with her boyfriend on their next date.

The next morning we all started getting dressed early. We ate breakfast quickly and headed out to take Scooter shopping. "Let's just take him to Wards," Martha said turning the key. "We'll buy his clothes and shoes there, and we won't have to worry   too much about crowds or lines, kill two birds with one stone," she said driving off quickly into the street. We made it to Wards soon after.

"You can buy all the pants, I'll get the shirts and shoes," Martha said. She threw things into the basket as we walked talking about what we would put on him to wear that day. We paid for it and took it all into the bathroom with Scooter. We bought him socks and underwear too. Martha would ask him from time to time if he liked some of the shirts putting them up to his chest. We bought more than what we came to buy.

He smiled as we dressed him looking in the mirror at himself. On the drive back to the reservation to pick up daddy, I looked back at him from time to time. He was checking out his clothes and shoes. "Thank you guys so much," Scooter said looking out of the window as we drove. "   Aww sweetie, you are so welcome, maybe soon you can come back and hang out with us again," Martha said to him. It was taking a while to get to the reservation today because of the weekday traffic.

I thought about how at home I didn't feel it presence around nor did I smell it. Maybe what the Indian men did to me really worked and just maybe I'll have some peace. I thought. But what did it all mean for me to go deeper and let it happen. I did just stop fighting and allow it to do what it wanted; I have to figure out a way to fight it so that it will leave me alone for good.

I'm guessing that he means to allow myself to open up and go where the spirit has been or where it comes from. When we made it to the reservation daddy and Mr. Red were waiting outside. Mr. Red was waiting. Mr. Red was working on some old car and daddy was assisting him. "Hey girls," daddy said. "Hey daddy," "hey uncle Earl, Mr. Red," Martha said. We put Scooter behind us covering him so that they couldn't see him. "Guess what's behind us?" we both said. "Little Scooter," daddy said.

"Yes, maybe," we said pushing Scooter out in front of us. "Hey, it's me, dad, Scooter!" He said jumping up and down in front of his dad. Mr. Red grabbed Scooter by the shoulders. "You look, wonderful son," he said hugging him tightly. "Thank you, so much, girls; I appreciate this, what do I owe you guys?" He asked. "Owe us, what do you mean?" I asked. "What do I owe for the clothes?" He asked reaching into his pocket.

Martha took the other bag from the car and handed it to him. I didn't say anything. "I don't know what you owe her, but you owe me about 45 bucks," she said with her hand out. I slapped her hand away. "No, Mr. Red you don't owe us anything, we were happy to do it," I told him looking at Martha out of the corner of my eyes. "No girls I have to give you something for taking such good care of my boy," he said reaching back into his pocket.

He pulled out two hundred dollars and handed us both one hundred each. "Now, you girls go and have some fun, buy you something nice for yourself," he told us putting his wallet back into his pants. Mr. Red was so dirty. It was like he just woke up that way. It didn't seem to bother him at all. His hair was very wild and he had a beard that looked as if he cut it every now and then but unevenly. "Daddy, are you ready?" I asked. "Yes," daddy grabbed his bag and shook hands with Red, and we walked to the car.

"Thank you, girls" Mr. Red yelled out to us. "Thank you for the money Mr. Red!" I yelled back. "Goodbye!" Scooter yelled waving at Martha and me. "Goodbye Scooter, be good okay." When we got into the car Scooter ran over to us. He grabbed me by the wrist. "Thank you, Karis," he said. Then he did the same thing to Martha, we both kissed his little cheeks and told him anytime. Daddy was the driver now and Martha sat in front. I wanted to sleep on the way home but daddy talked all the way there.

"So what did you girls do last night?" He asked us. "We just watched a little TV and took care of the kid." Martha told him. "He was perfect, no bother at all," "yes," Daddy said. "You know Red takes good care of that boy, you know his mother died during childbirth, so Reds been raising him all alone," he told us again. "Yeah daddy, but he needs to keep him cleaned up, don't you think," I said.

"Well baby, sometimes us men only do what we can, Red cooks for the boy and makes sure he goes to school, and he puts him to bed at night, that he may be capable of doing   . You know as a man there are just some things we can't do, that little boy is just lucky his dad is there, it broke him to see his wife die like that, I had to hall my ass up here almost every day to see about him.

He wanted to die with her and believe it or not that man was once one of the most powerful lawyers out here. He defended most all of the Indians on the reservation; he was the reason they have what they have over there, all their money and land he helped them get it all. Then the tragedy with his wife, that just about killed him." Daddy shook his head and lit a cigarette. He placed it in his mouth and took a big puff. "What about other family members, don't they want to help him?" I asked.

"Baby, sometimes people just don't come through the way you would like them to. That little boy has one auntie on his mother's side, and she wanted him to move to Arizona to live with her. Now you can't split the boy from his dad; he already lost one parent." Taking another puff from his cigarette, "Red's all that boy has," he shook his head again and continued smoking. It was quiet. I fell off to sleep.

I dreamt of a woman I have never seen before; she was smiling at me standing with my mother. "There she is," my mother said to her. "Say hi and thank you," she said. They were standing in a very warm light, I could feel the warmth from it as they walked up close to me. My mother took me by the hand. She kissed both my hands and they were pulled back into the light. When I woke up we were in daddy driveway. "Get up, Karis," Martha said tugging at my shoulder. "We're here, I'm going in to use the bathroom," she said handing me the keys to her car. "Okay   Karis," daddy said. "I will see you guess later," he said.

"What are you doing for the rest of the day daddy?" I asked him. "I think I'll just have me a drink and work out in the garden," he tells me lighting up another cigarette. "What are you doing baby, you should be going to work soon, right?" He says looking down at his watch. "Okay, I'm about ready," Martha said running down the porch stairs. She got into the car and we took off into the street. We arrived at my house quickly after. Martha left the engine running.

"Well, I guess I'll see you later," she said. I opened my door. "So you're not coming in?" I asked her hesitant to get out of the car." Karis, I need to get home to take care of some things, I've been here with you for a while, you should be fine with what we did, right? If you want me to, I will come by tonight and check on you okay." I looked at her with sadness in my eyes. " I promise you I will Karis" She put her hand on my back and pushed at me to get out of the car.

I stood outside the car waving bye to her. Cookie was waiting for me in the window I turned around and went into the house. I picked her up at the door and rubbed her back. I went to the couch and sat down. It was very cold in the house. I went into the hallway and turned on the heat. I placed Cookie on the floor. She followed me all around the house. I began to pick things up here and there straightening out the house. It seemed as if I had been gone from the house for a long time everything was so unorganized almost everything was out of place.

After straightening up I started my dinner. I took out veggies and turkey legs. I would eat lite tonight. I wanted to change and get comfortable but I was so afraid to. I don't know if it would happen to me again. I'm afraid to find out. I just decided to stay in the front room where the television was. I put the tea kettle on for tea and sat down on the couch and watched TV.

Today Oprah's show was about people who have claimed to have seen things like ghost or spirits. There was a man on who took a picture of the sky on the plane and the picture captured Jesus in the sky. I watched it intensely thinking, okay I'm not the only one then, and there are more people out there like me. I thought as the tea kettle went off. I was still watching the man shared the picture it was similar to what I saw I was amazed.

I ran over to the tea kettle and turned it off and ran back I didn't want to miss what was next, maybe someone will say that they experienced more. I wondered why no one thought that he was crazy, was it because he had proof. I thought watching. I wondered if God had left him something like a gift. I only wished I could tell my story without people thinking that something was wrong with me. I turned off the TV and went to get my tea ready. Standing in the kitchen I felt a presence next to me. I couldn't smell anything though.

I could just feel it close to me, I stood back from the stove just so I would be safe if it attacked me. As I moved toward the with my tea cup in my hand, it seemed to be in my face, I felt air blowing in my face as I walked over to sit down. I moved over to the far end of the couch clutching my tea cup. My hand began to shake as I took a sip of the tea it was very hot. The steam hit my lips and nose as I turned the cup up. I began to place the tea cup down on the table as I placed it down it was being pulled from my hand.

I let go of it and it was placed on the table. I watched as it went back in forth in front of me from one side of the table to the other than it was like something picked it up and threw it to the wall. I quickly got up and went for the phone. I will call daddy and tell him to come over for dinner I thought. When I went for the phone I could feel it breathing on my neck. I reached to get the receiver I moved slowly closing my eyes as I feel it about to happen to me again. I would be attacked I know it. So instead of me being afraid I turned to it.

I closed my eyes and I let it breath into my face. It was breathing so hard that it blew my hair back from my face. I dared to open my eyes. I thought about what the Indian man said to me. Open, let it show me what I need to see; allow it to free itself through me with no fear. I reached out to it, my hands were shaking, I was so afraid. I began to smell its presence. I think Cookie could feel it or see it. She began to hiss. I couldn't see her; I kept my eyes closed reaching out to it as it continued to blow air in my face in anger.

It began to get heavier and heavier than I felt it. It took my hand and it felt as if I was being lifted from my feet. I began to feel light all over, my hands and feet were tingling and shaking. I just kept thinking. Tell me what you want, tell me what you want, take me to where you need to be, show me the truth and maybe we can set your spirit free. I don't know where that came from, but I kept repeating it over and over again in my head.

When I opened my eyes I was in another place. It was cold and dark. I could only see a few things. I could hear whispering and the sound of digging. I was being pulled forward it guided me toward tress it was a forest or park it was so dark, there were two men one was digging and the other was beating on the ground. "Die," he said. "Die." I pulled back; I don't want to see any more. I closed my eyes trying and tried pulling away from it but it clutched on to me tighter pulling me forward.

When we went up closer it grabbed the back of my neck and directed my head down. I opened my eyes. When I did I was shocked it was Frank. My eyes opened wider. He was all bloody. The two men were beating him and kicking him. He was gasping for air. I began to fill as if I couldn't catch my breath I was gasping for air also and my body began to feel pain as if I was being beat. I was hurting all over. I couldn't scream or yell out I just felt pain. Franks pain. I tried to cough but it felt as if I was suffocating. It freed my hands. It felt as if I fell to the ground. I was coughing so hard my throat was dry and hurting as if it was filled with dirt.

I held my hands to my throat. When I opened my eyes Cookie was staring into them. I was breathing heavily as I pulled myself up from the floor. I sat on the couch to catch my breath I needed a drink of water but I couldn't move I had to catch my breath. After a while I got up and went to the kitchen sink I slashed cold water on my face and drank the water from the faucet. I drank it until my throat began to feel a little better.

I grabbed a cup from the cabinet to catch the water in. I stood there allowing the cup to fill up over and over again after each drink. When I sat down at the table Cookie sat in my lap I put the cup down and the phone rang loudly. I jumped in fear. Cookie jumped down off my lap. I went to get the phone "Hello," I said clearing my throat. "Hello love, it's me, Michael, how's everything going?" I sighed. "Michael, can you come over?" I asked him. My eyes filled with tears.

Fly With Me To Heaven

Returning to work wouldn't be so bad. I would be working with Michael today; I thought as I began to get myself ready for work. I can't wait to see him. He always had a way of making me feel good about all of it. Everything could be going wrong in my life, but when I was around Michael, it seemed it went away. I thought thinking about how he came to me that night and held on to me while I cried.

He didn't ask me why I was crying and he didn't pressure me to be with him he just held on to me and comforted me. I rushed out to my car and drove to work playing my favorite songs in the tape player. Holland Oats, I could never get enough of them. God, I love them I thought as I moved my head to the rhythm of the music. When I pulled up to the garage area of the hospital, there was Michael parking his car too. He waved to me smiling. I waved back.

As I slowed my car to park, I noticed that he wasn't alone. He had a passenger with him. She cut her eyes at me as I approached Michael getting out of his car. "Hello, you," he said grabbing me by the waist side. "You're back huh, you look fabulous," he said twirling me around by my arm. "It's good to see you too," I said kissing him on the cheek. I looked over his shoulder as he hugged me tightly. His passenger pierced her eyes at me as I held onto Michael, he smelled so good.

I stepped back and looked at him and then her. "Oh, oh," Michael said nervously. "This is Shelia, I gave her a ride this morning, her car is in the shop," he said staring me in the eyes. "Nice meet you, Shelia," I said reaching out to shake her hand. She grabbed her things from Michael's car looked at my hand and walked away quickly rolling her eyes. Michael smiled at me and took my hand. "So you're back huh?" He asked.

"Yes I'm back, are you going to tell me what was going on the other night?" "Michael, I don't want to talk about it at all," I say to him walking toward the hospital. "Thank you for coming to rescue me last night, I didn't want you over sooner because I didn't want you to get sick" I smiled at him. "You know what I think," He said. "I think you had a visitor and you just wanted me to keep away."

"No, Michael, I promise I didn't have any visitor," I tell him as I walked into the hospital together. "So old James didn't stay with you huh?" Michael asked. "Michael I was sick," I say pulling my hand away walking over to the nurse's station. "I will see you later," he said smiling pulling at my shirt. He pulled me toward his face as if he wanted to kiss my lips. I stood back. "Oh now you want to be shy," He said beginning to walk away.

I wasn't shy I was scared all eyes were on us. I was too nervous to kiss him in front of everyone, so I walked away. "I will see you soon," I said blowing a kiss at him. When I went over to the nurse's station, Maddy and all the nurses except for Shelia were singing. "Michael and Karis sitting in a tree K.I.S.S.I.N.G." I smiled at them, Maddy came over to me and hugged me.

"Hey girl it's good to see you, we missed you around here," Neil the male nurse said patting me on my back. I looked on the board my name was plastered up in bold letters with a smiley face beside it. Just like I thought I was working with Michael all day today. I grabbed my list of rooms and walked out onto the floor with Maddy by my side. "Do you feel any better?" She asked. "Oh yeah, I'm okay now," I tell her. "You look well rested too," she said rubbing my back. We went to the elevator.

"You know James came up here a few times looking for you, are you hiding from him?" She questioned. "He was very concerned; I felt kind of bad for him, I saw his grandmother yesterday, she been admitted with a broken hip, did you know about that , he must have expected you to be here while she was cared for," she tells me smacking her lips. "I will give him a call later," I tell her. "His grandmother means the world to him; she raised him." "Well, his mother called the nurses station and told us that she was coming up to visit her."

"I don't know anything about his mother except for that she wasn't welcome to come over to the grandmother's house before," I tell her. "But Maddy how can that be, it's her daughter, maybe James just told me things to get me to feel bad for him. "Karis sometimes people don't ever recover from the hurt of a loved one, you can forgive them but never forget enough to move forward with them, they can only love them from afar," she says cleaning her hands at the sink.

I went on to my assigned rooms following Michael and all the interns. They were all talking about Michael's big trip to Africa. How great it was going to be helping all those people over there and how he had to be careful in some parts of Africa because they had tribal wars and some Africans didn't want them to be in the country. I looked at Michael's face as they told him all these stories. He didn't look afraid at all.

He was totally up for the challenge I felt so bad listening because I will miss Michael like crazy. He is so sweet to me. I will miss everything about him, his smile his walk and especially his soft touch. I was just daydreaming about that night on the couch when I was shoved in the back by a nurse walking by; it was the nurse from Michael's car that morning. She stared and smiled I went over to Michael and stood close to him staring back at her.

She turned her head quickly. I knew that would hurt her feelings I grabbed on to his coat and gave him a very sexy wink. He winked back and smiled telling me he wanted me with his eyes. I went on listening to the interns telling Michael all the stories they'd heard about Africa. I really don't want him to go there but I know I can't stop him. I thought listening as I turned down a few beds and checked a few patients.

I know there's a chance he won't come back. He could get sick or fall in love with someone else. I thought as I watched him from a distance. I would be lost without him here. What if he marries someone else, without that walk on the beach or that calmness that I felt when he came by I don't know. I looked down it was like I was having some sort of panic attack thinking about Michael leaving me. I began to sweat and pant as if I couldn't catch my breath I was breathing faster and faster.

Oh no I thought, I'm in love with Michael. I have never felt this way about anyone ever. I put my clipboard down and my head in my lap. I sat down in a chair and stayed behind in the patient room, it was dark and quiet. I just sat there trying to catch my breath hoping that they wouldn't miss me and began to look for me. When I pulled myself together I went over to the sink and wet my face with cold water.

"Pull it together Karis," I said to myself looking in the mirror, you have plenty to do yourself, you can't marry Michael anyway. He wants more, like someone he can make love to and have children with I told myself. He could never be in love with you. I dried my face and went to the door. I stepped out into the hallway. I saw two women; one very fair skinned the other a very pale women walking toward the elevator.

As I walked passed them the really pale skinned women gave me a very funny look and with her eyebrows raised she shook her head at me as if she knew about something I did. I tried walking by them quickly but we all stopped at the elevator together. "Hello," I said to both of them. "Hello," the pale-skinned women replied. "Do you happen to know where we can find the cafeteria?" She asked.

The doors began to slide open. "Oh sure, if you just take this elevator down to the second floor go right then a quick left, it will be on your right-hand side. You'll start to smell the food as soon as you turn the corner from the elevator," I tell her smiling. When the doors opened they got off. "Thank you, Karis," the pale-skinned woman said to me as the doors began to close the pale-skinned woman stared at me walk away slowly.

How did she know my name? I wondered I reached for the buttons to stop the doors from closing. I wanted to get a closer look at them. Did I know them from somewhere I thought as I watched them walking away from the door, holding the door open with my foot I stepped back in and leaned against the railing of the walls. The woman did look familiar; the other woman was wearing a hat looking down a lot, so I didn't get a good look at her, but they knew me. The elevator stopped on the fourth floor. I got off and began to walk toward the front desk.

It was so quiet on this floor I walked quickly to the front desk when I made it passed the room doors almost into the hall I was snatched by the arm into a room at the edge of the hallway. I was startled and shocked, "shh , don't say a word," it was Michael. He put his hands over my mouth and pulled me close to him and removed his hand. "I have been looking all over this hospital for you baby, where have you been?" He asked.

"Shh," he said kissing my neck. "I want you so bad Karis, I want to taste you," he said as he pulled my pants down. I just looked up into the darkness of the room as he went down on his knees. I could feel his hands moving all over my bottom, he pulled my bottom to his mouth, my body began to tingle all over. I didn't say a word until I felt his tong on my vagina. "Michael, stop please," I whispered holding his head in my hands to push him away. "Oh, my goodness, Michael stop," I say to him as he pulls me closer to his mouth not letting my bottom go.

He squeezed my bottom tight as he licked. When he came up from his knees he was sweating, he began to kiss me all over my neck again he held onto me really tight I could feel his penis pressing against my vagina. He reached down and unzipped his pants. I shook my head no. "Michael, I'm not ready," I tell him. "I know, I know baby," He says in a whisper kissing my neck and lips softly. "Trust me," he took my hand and placed it on his penis.

"I just want you to feel me," he says. "See how much we need you, baby," he says moving my hand slowly up and down his penis. I didn't look at it I just allowed him to guide my hand to do what made him feel good. It was exciting. Michael's penis felt smooth it was pulsating as my hand moved up and down it. Michael breathed heavily with his head smashed into my chest, soon my hand and stomach felt wet all over.

Michael stopped moving and grabbed my hand. He began kissing me holding on to my hand. "Karis, I love you so much," he tells me begging to pull up his pants and fixing his shirt. "I'm going to miss you so much," I stood up straight. "Don't move baby, don't move, I'm going to get you something to wipe off with." I stood still with my hands covering my vagina; the room was so dark I wanted to see what my hand looked like, what the wet stuff looked like; I put my hand close to my face to see if it would appear when Michael appeared with a warm wet cloth.

I stared at him as he took the cloth and began to wipe me off down there; he then turned the cloth over and wiped my hands. "You can wash off in the sink if you like, I don't know if I got it all," he said staring up at me. I will miss him so much I thought as he finished wiping me. He laid his head on my chest. "I'm going to miss you so much baby, I love you," he kissed me on the lips, " Karis when I come back, we have to get married okay, will you marry me when I come back?" He asked looking into my eyes. I just looked up at him and shook my head yes.

When I began to speak out, he covered my mouth. "Please baby, don't say a word, I know what you're thinking, I know that it will be too much to ask, for you to marry a guy like me. I just want you to know that there is no one else for me, you are it, all I want, just say that when I return you'll be my wife, you'll be mine Karis, just say it please." "Yes Michael, when you return I will be your wife," I tell him.

Michael smiled so wide I thought his cheeks would burst. He grabbed me and held me close. "I love you, baby, don't change, please don't change," he said squeezing me tight. I pulled my pants up and we held hands and kissed walking away from the room. When we stepped out into the light of the hallway Michael fixed my hair and I straightened his shirt. He looked around than kissed my forehead. "Goodbye baby, I'm off now, can I come by later?" He asked. "Okay," I said walking away. I was so happy.

Oh, my goodness, I never said I love you back to him, what must he be thinking. I wondered as I walked to the rooms down the hall, how could I have been so silly, how do you forget to say you love someone back? I went into the bathroom to look over myself and freshen up a bit, I walked in, and there was the woman with the hat and the other woman washing their hands, "Hello," I said to them. "Hello," the younger women replied. The women with the hat just stared back at me with a frown on her face. "Hey," she says with a quick wave of one hand.

She puts her head down. I went into the stall to use the restroom. When I came out the younger women was still there standing by the sink. "Hi, I'm Teresa, James little sister, it's very nice to meet you finally," she said with her arms crossed. How ironic I thought. "Oh yes, nice to meet you   too finally," I never knew the James had a little sister. I thought to myself as I washed my hands. After drying them I reached out to shake her hand. "I was wondering how you knew my name," I tell her smiling.

"Yes, James has told us so much about you, I'd know you anywhere, your all he talks about these days   , I guess that's why my mother feels the way she does about you." "Oh I'm sorry I had no idea that he talked about me to her, I can't imagine what he says," I tell her. "I've known James for a very long time; he's very nice." "Yes he's lived with my grandmother since he was small, it's a bit hard on my mother, she never really had time for us; we just made contact with her this year after James joined the Navy."

"Oh, I didn't know that," I told her going for the door. "It was a pleasure meeting you Teresa," I said. "I'd like to keep in contact with you if you don't mind," she said reaching into her purse for a pen and paper. "That would be nice," I tell her standing at the door. "You know we all plan to move back to North Carolina when James gets out of the Navy, it's just better for all of us, and you know James loves the country, did you know that?" She asked me. "No I didn't, but you learn something new every day, I guess," she handed me the paper with her number on it.

"I will call you sometimes okay" I tell her pushing the door open. "Can I have yours?" She asked following out behind me. I looked at her. "Mine?" "Yes your phone number, you do have a phone right?" She said waiting for my answer. "Yes I do," "Okay well, here, write it on this," she said handing me a piece of paper with the pen rolled in it. I wrote it down quickly trying to seem in a rush. She took it and looked at it, squinting her eyes. "Is this 2633873?"

"Yes I'm usually home by 10 pm, okay, but you can call me anytime you like," I tell her. I walked away quickly so that she couldn't catch up to me I walked faster through the halls. Wow that was pretty interesting, her wanting my phone number, and all that information she gave me about James, I wondered what else he hadn't been telling me, wow and a little sister, she seemed really bright too. As I walked closer to the front desk I began to see people running everywhere. I ran toward everyone to see what was going on.

I looked over at the desk and there was a nurse on the floor shaking in convulsions. There were doctors all around and Maddy was on the floor beside her. I looked around to see if I saw anything, there was no light nor warmth anywhere around. I got down on the floor with Maddy. "What happened is there something I can do?" I asked her. "She was walking past, and she just fell and began to convulse." They said, "she was coming out of one of the rooms, and the door swung back and hit her in the head very hard, she was fine until she fell.

That's all we have," she said looking down at her. We held onto her to keep her from hurting herself. She had seizure after seizure Michael came running with a gurney and a team of other doctors. They all circled around her picking her up and lifting her onto the gurney. Maddy and I stood back watching. It was very intense. Everyone was very afraid for her. I knew she would be fine. I walked away from the area just to take a deep breath. There was so much excitement when this happened I didn't even notice James standing at the front desk with his mother, but they noticed me. He began to walk toward me with her.

I stood leaning against the wall holding my clip board. I looked down at the clip board as they approached me. I hope he doesn't come over to me, Just keep walking I thought. Just keep walking. I was hoping he'd keep walking and pass me but he didn't. "Hello Karis, how are you?" He asked me leaning in to hug me, kissing me on the cheek. "I'm good" I tell him holding the clipboard to my chest. "How have you been, long time no see," I say clutching the clipboard even tighter. "Well you've been off work, I hear."

"Yes, I was sick." "Oh too bad, I came to your house, but Martha always had some reason you couldn't come to the door, you didn't call me." I shrugged my shoulders. "Well, my dad took good care of me," I said smiling. I put the clipboard down on the desk and began to walk away. "It was nice seeing you," I told him. "Wait, I want you to meet someone," he pulled his mom forward. "Mom this is Karis." She looked at me very crossed frowning and trying to give a smile at the same time. "Yes son, we met before," she said. "

Really?" James asked. "Yes, I met her with your little sister in the restroom earlier, it was a pleasant encounter," I told him smiling. "Well, I have to get going, it was very nice seeing you again ma'am ," I tell his mom. "Honey, don't ever call me ma'am again, I'm no old lady, just call me Mrs. Harrison," she said with a frown. "Oh, I'm sorry Mrs. Harrison, I won't forget next time," I said walking away from them. She made me feel very uncomfortable. I walked as fast as I could to go see Maddy.

I wanted to hear what she thought of my encounter with James and his family. I hoped that by meeting his mom he wouldn't think that I change my mind about being with him, like a girlfriend or anything. I went up to the seventh floor where Maddy was working tonight. Ma Maddy and all the other nurses were getting ready for shift change. I was very eager to share this with her so I stood there waiting for her to finish. I went over to her chair and picked up her bag and began to fill it with her things from the desk.

"What's going on Karis?" She asked. She noticed me moving very fast. "I'm just helping you get your things ready for when it's time to leave." "I still have quite a while before I can leave Karis, what's wrong?" She asked me. "Oh, well, I can wait for you, it's no problem." "You know what? Karis, you can meet me at my house in an hour, bring Cookie okay, I have a dinner date, you can talk to me while I get dressed, maybe give me a few pointers. How does that sound?" She said moving all around the desk with papers in her hand.

"That sounds good, in an hour then," I said walking away from the desk. I went to my station to get my bag as I bent over to pick it up Michael came up behind me and grabbed me by the waist side. "Hey sexy," he whispered in my ear. "I love you," he said kissing my neck. "What did you say?" I asked him smiling as I put my bag over my shoulder. "I won't repeat it, I know you heard me the first time," I laughed. "I love you too Michael," I said just moving my lips.   "What was that" He said. I whispered it into his ear. "I love you, Michael," I told him softly.

I took a deep breath waiting for his reaction. I stood back and stared at him. He took my hands and squeezed them tight. His hands where so big compared to mine. Compared to me he was like a giant. I loved the feel of them on my hands though I squeezed back onto his fingers. He hugged me as tight as he could without breaking me. With my head buried into his chest muscles, I could hardly breathe. "I will still see you later, right?" He asked me. "I'm going to   Maddy's for an hour after work, but I'll be home right after okay," I tell him walking away from him.

"Hey, do you mind coming over to my place?" He asked. "I'd like to cook for you, one last time," he said smiling. "Okay, that sounds great, I'll be there right after Maddy's," I tell him smiling. Good I don't have to be home alone. He winked at me; I could feel him watching me as I walked away. I walked fast to my car. People were crowding the emergency room already it was only 6 pm. As I reached the stairway I began to feel someone walking with me. I turned to look on each side of me. There was no one there. I made it to my car and got in quickly.

I saw a very dark shadow standing near the window. I put the keys into the ignition starting the car as quickly as I could before I drove off I closed my eyes and opened them quickly hoping it wasn't there anymore. I drove off looking from the rearview mirror to see where it may have went, I looked over at the passenger seat and all the other windows checking for any signs of it in or around the car. When I pulled into my driveway I turned the car off and reached for my bag I seen it again it was a dark shadow of a person standing near my door.

I was afraid to get out and go in but I told Maddy I would bring Cookie over for a visit and I wanted to change into something more comfortable, get out of my scrubs. I sat in the car looking at it. I wondered what it wants. I turn the engine back on. The figure of the shadow stood under the light and tilted its head back and forth at me. Suddenly there was a knock on my driver side window; I jumped so high in fear, he startled me by knocking. I turned to the window, "Hello," an old man said to me waving his hand at me.

I didn't roll down the window. He began to move his hand up and down as if to tell me to open the window. I shook my head no. He smiled. Who might he be I wondered. I cracked it just a little because he didn't move. I wanted only to hear what he wanted. "Sir, how can I help you?" I asked him. "Young lady, are you okay?" He asked. "I'm fine sir, this is my house," I told him pointing to my house. "Well if it is you might want to go inside, it's getting late out," he said zipping his jacket. He wore a member's only jacket and a small little hat that fit his head perfectly, I smiled at him, "I will be fine sir, thank you again," I said.

"I guess I'll be going on my way," he said walking away. I turned back to look at my door and the shadow was no longer there. I looked down the street for the old man to my surprise he wasn't there he was gone I looked all around for him. I man was too old to move that quickly, there is no way I thought looking at my house. The curtains were moving all around. I put the car in reverse; I decided to just drive over to Maddy's house I couldn't bear the thought of another attack. On the drive over to Maddy's I thought about what a crazy night this was turning out to be.

I began to get chills just thinking of the shadow standing by my door. I had never seen him before around the neighborhood. He had a very nice face and his smile was nice it was like he was shining. When I made it to Maddy's I sat in the car. I looked at my watch it was only 6:58 pm it would be a while before Maddy would be home. I turned the engine off and stared at Maddy's door. I could see all her beautiful cats sitting in the window; they were waiting for her to. I was so tired.

I kept nodding off to sleep then looking at my watch to see what time it was. Time sure goes by slowly when you're eager to see someone

I thought as I sat there falling asleep. I was awaken by a hard knock on the window. "Girl, what are you doing in there?" Maddy said screaming through the window. "Get your butt inside," I opened the door and walked out following her up to the house. "You know you could have just come over and got the spare key, see I keep one right here," she said reaching down into a flower pot full of dirt. She blew on it.

"Here you keep this one for yourself okay, when you want to come over just use that," my head was hurting now. I followed Maddy through the door. "Wow, were you tired?" She said. Putting her bag on the floor and reaching for one of the cats in the window. "I would have gotten here earlier, but you know that hospital, all work no play for us," she said. "Look at my babies, they are always waiting for me," she was kissing the tops of the cat's heads, one by one she kissed them."

Karis you can put your bag on the floor over there" She said pointing into the hallway. She began getting milk bowels for each cat. "So Karis, what's the big urgency, what is it that you wanted to talk to me about?" She put the tea kettle on for tea. I walked over to the kitchen table and sat down and with my hands on my head." Maddy do you have anything for a headache?" I asked her. "Sure I do, hold on a sec." She went over to the cabinet and got out two teacups and sat them on the counter, then over to the bathroom to get me two aspirin.

"Here you go honey," she handed me the pills and went over to the sink and gave me a cup of water. I took the tablets and laid my head down onto the table. She came over to the table and sat with me sitting the tea cups down on the table. "So, what's the story?" She asked sipping her tea. "I think I'm in love with Michael," I tell her lifting my head and sipping the tea. "Really, how do you know you love him?" She asked me.

"I feel good around him, he makes me laugh and smile, I can't stop thinking of him when we're apart, and when I think of him leaving, I feel sick all over." I tell her. "I almost did it; you know made love." "Did it huh," she says with excitement in her voice. "Yes, we have been intimate" "Well, tell me what happened?" She sipped her tea blinking her eyes at me. "Well, come on, I don't have a lot of time sweetie, I have my dinner date remember?"

"We were at my house, we began kissing, and we ended up on the couch, I didn't pull my pants down or anything, but he did pull the top of my jumpsuit down and kissed all over my breast, he touched me a lot. Oh, and he licked me down there," I said pointing down at my vagina. "It felt nice." "So, what else did you do anything else?" "I don't know if I should say, it's a little nasty," I say smiling. "Well, we had another moment in one of the rooms at the hospital, this time I felt him down there with my hand," I tell her.

"But we didn't do it at all yet; we want to wait until he comes back, we plan to get married. I think that we enjoy each other more and more every time and Maddy I want more of him, is that bad?" "That last time when he licked me down there I was shaking all over Maddy," she laughed. "Follow me while I get dressed," she said leaving the table walking to the bedroom. "Well now, my dear you're growing up, you have experienced a real good orgasm." She went to her closet taking off her scrubs and wrapping up in her robe.

She reached in and pulled out two outfits for her dinner date. "You like?" She asked, showing them to me on the hanger. "I like the black dress; it's sexy," I said pointing behind her into the closet. "Maddy, what is an orgasm?" I asked her. "Oh honey, don't get scared, that's something most women die to get during intercourse, but can't, they're kind of hard to come by," she said laughing. "It seemed easy for you, it's a feeling that comes over you when you're making love, and it's so great that your muscle down there has like a happy spasm, and you can feel it all throughout your body, it sounds intense." She said going into the shower.

"Honey, talk to me louder, I'll be out in a second, I haven't had one of those in a long time," she yelled from the shower. "So you guys didn't go all the way huh, he didn't put his penis inside you yet?" She yelled out. "No Maddy, I'm afraid, wouldn't that hurt me?" I asked her yelling out to her. The water stopped and she came out of the shower. I sat on her bed and she came out wrapped in robe again. She went over to her vanity and sat down. She began to lotion her body and spray on perfume.

"I'm also afraid to be naked in front of him; I have all these scars what if it's a turn off for him when I undress?" I ask her. "Oh my goodness, listen, Karis if Michael doesn't want you because of the scars on your body, that would just mean that he was very shallow and you don't need anyone in your life. I don't see that in him at all, but maybe you see something I don't. He seems to like you.

I hear him telling those nurses and even some doctors that he's in love with someone and can't date anyone else and believe me, he is a nice looking man, and women are all over them all the time." She said putting her pantyhose on. "I bet he doesn't care about any of that." "I'm still afraid to undress in front of him." "Well, I think you should talk to him about it before you judge him so quickly," she says putting her dress over her head. "Oh wow, Maddy, you look so nice," I tell her. "You're right; I will talk to him."

"That's not the reason you came over here though is it," she asked me while she sat at the vanity doing her makeup. "No, it's James, I met his mother and his little sister today, his mother gives me these looks as if she doesn't like me." "Well, I'm sure she would, leaving her son all those years only to come back and find him in love with someone like you. Someone who could love him back unconditionally and never leave him under any circumstances, she's jealous.

That situation is just too complicated; I don't like it, I would be afraid for you to get involved with him, he's had to live with the constant rejection of his mother all these years. There's no telling what's going on in that mind of his, probably good to just be friends with him, that's all." She says grabbing a scarf from the closet and wrapping it around her neck. "You look wonderful Maddy," I tell her. She came over to me and hugged me. "I love you, honey, you be real careful with him and his family," she tells me again.

"Something about him always gave me a bad feeling." As we were still talking, there was a knock on the door. I stayed sitting while Maddy went to the door. "Maddy, I'm going to the restroom, okay!" I yelled out to her. I was sitting on the toilet when I heard a familiar voice. I got up and went to wash my hands. I came out of the bathroom and went into the kitchen to find   Maddy. Oh my goodness, it was the man from earlier. I thought as I walked past him slowly over to the couch, staring at him all the way over.

"Hi," he said smiling at me. I stood up looking at him. "Hello," I said with my eyes wide. I sat back down on the couch. I almost stumbled over the table when he approached me to shake my hand. "Are you okay?" Maddy asked me, you look scared" "Oh it's nothing," I tell her still staring there was the dark shadow standing next to the man. I couldn't take my eyes off him. "Karis, Karis," Maddy called out. "This is my father; you can call him Mr. Simms, he's my favorite person in the world." She said going over to him with a cup in her hand.

"Father, it's so good to see you." I just couldn't take my eyes off the dark shadow beside him. "Um Maddy, I have to go, I'm going to meet with Michael," I kissed Maddy on the cheek. "Thank you for everything Maddy, and sir it was nice meeting you." I say to the old man, when my eyes meet his I immediately hear a whisper, "he will die soon," it said to me. "Oh you too, you too," he said shaking my hand and smiling. Maddy walked me to the door. "He can barely see you, Karis," she says to me in a whisper.

"Oh, I see," I tell her going to my car. "Drive safely, Karis," she waved goodbye to me. I made it to Michaels soon after. I parked right outside his door. I knocked on the door. "Come on in," he yelled out to me. I opened the door and went inside. Michael had the house lit up with candles everywhere. The dinner table was all made up with plates and candles and a bouquet of flowers. Although I didn't drink Michael had two Champaign glasses filled with apple juice. I took a seat on the couch. His place smelled of flowers and burning candles.

"Make yourself comfortable!" Michael yelled out from the shower. "I will thank you!" I yelled back to him. I was really curious about Michaels body, I had a sudden urge to go take a peek at him in the shower, He's probably all wet and soapy, I thought as I waited. I was day dreaming about his body, it must look so nice wet, his perfect skin, and I had to take a look. I walked over to the bathroom door, it was opened so I stood on the side and peeked through the crack of the door through the glass shower doors, and there was a lot of steam.

His body was covered with soap. I waited patiently for him to wash it all off. When he began to wash it off he turned his back to me, he turned back around quickly. "Hey, what are you doing out there?" He yelled. "I can hear you near!" He yelled out. I ran back into the living room and sat on the couch. Michael came right out behind me with his robe on. "Did you like what you saw?" He asked me laughing. "I didn't get to see anything," I tell him.

"Would you like to take a look now?" He says. I shook my head no. "Well, your loss," he walked back into his room and came back out quickly with a pair of pants and a T-shirt on he pulled the drawstring tight to his waist and leaned over to kiss me. "Let's eat sweetheart." He escorted me over to the table, he pulled my chair out for me, and we sat and talked and laughed and ate. "So sweetheart, how about we go on a last minute trip before I leave, have you ever been to the mountains? I have a cabin up at Big Bear; it's wonderful, I think you would just love it."

"But, I thought you wanted to take a break here before you leave," I remind him. "No, I'd rather spend my last night there in the cabin holding you all weekend," I began to blush. He put his hand to my face. "I want you so badly," he said kissing my lips. I looked into his eyes. Michael was so handsome. I wondered what it would be like to really go all the way with him, but I was so scared to take my pants all the way down. I knew it could never happen. I tried changing the subject. "So in Africa, where would you live?"

Michael began to kiss me all over. "Would your place have a phone?" I asked him. "Are you going to be too busy to call me?" Michael shook his head to everything, kissing me was more important. "I am never too busy to call you," he said kissing further down my neck. "I want you so bad." He took a deep breath and brought his head up from my chest. He stopped kissing me and looked at me in my eyes. "What's wrong?" He asked.

"I'm just worried that I will never see you again after you leave." "Of course you'll see me again," he said holding my face in his hand. He took a bite of his steak. "I know you just want to eat, here would you like a piece of steak?" He said taking a piece of steak from the plate and putting it on my plate. "I know you're worried Karis, but you don't have to be. I'm coming back to marry you, Karis. I won't make love to you until you're ready, are you ready for me?" He asked chewing on his steak and looking at me. I shrugged my shoulders.

"You really want to know about my trip huh?" "Yes Michael I do, I mean you're going away for a whole year, what if fall in love with someone over there or what if you get sick? What am I going to do? I love you, Michael." I tell him "Oh baby, I love you too," he said dropping his fork and coming over to hug me. "I'm going to be in Africa for a year; thinking about how much I want to be with you.

I'm not going to be thinking of any other place, but where you are. I have committed myself to this project, and I have to follow through, I wished that I had fallen for you sooner, you know what, it will give us time to get to know one another. We will write to one another, and I'll call whenever I can, do you promise to write me?" "I will write you, Michael, I promise." I said kissing his lips. "Hey, and don't you send me any one-liners either, I know you like to write, I've seen you carrying around that notebook," he winked at me. Michael and I sat up all night talking and laughing. He talked about his trip and I talked about how while he's gone I'll go back to school and get my registered nursing license.

"I like caring for people," I tell him. We kissed and held on to each other all night. When it got darker out we sat on a blanket on the floor. He put out two fluffy pillows for us to lay on. "Karis, tell me what it's like, tell me why you keep hiding behind those clothes. I've never seen you wearing a short shirt or any shorts, what do your legs look like under there, I know there skinny, right?" I looked over at him.

"Yes they are skinny, I just never wear them, I have a lot of scars on my legs and thighs, I was in a terrible accident, and I almost lost the right leg." "Yea, I noticed you have a little switch in your walk; I can tell it's a slight limp." "Yes, my right leg is a little shorter than my left one." "You cover it well; it just looks as if you're switching a little, can I see them?" He asked me. I began to stand up. "Michael I'm not ready, please don't make me do this now, I'm not ready for you to judge me," I tell him.

"Who's going to judge Karis, I just want to see them really," he said pulling me close to him. He kept his hand on my waist the whole time. I just looked up. I wanted to run out of there in fear of what he might think. In that very moment, I was ashamed, embarrassed, and mad. I didn't want to show him my legs, I didn't want to feel bad about me right then. I was ashamed of myself and what he might think I was mad and embarrassed at the fact that I even had to go through that being ashamed. I was mad God why me I thought.

I pushed Michael away from me. "Michael, no, I can't, I'm just not ready to share that part of me yet, I think I'm just going to go now."

"No, stay with me baby, I understand, you don't ever have to do anything you don't want to, baby I promise you will never have to be ashamed about anything with me, I love every part of you, I will never hurt you. I promise," he said. We laid back down on the floor and he covered me with the blanket, I laid on Michael's chest while he held onto me tight. I fell off to sleep praying.

Thank you god, because I know my life spared for a reason, I should never doubt and ask why, forgive me lord and please keep me safe. I began to dream I was being attacked by something dark and everywhere I ran there was light I was fighting when I reached out the darkness pulled me back into the fight. I screamed and cried out but no help came to me. The closer I came to the light the heavier and harder the hits became.

I couldn't breathe and suddenly I was falling everything went black, but as I fell there was light around me that I could see in the corner of my eyes but it was as if I was flying and I couldn't control it. Michael was shaking me. "Karis, Karis, wake up baby, you're having a nightmare." I opened my eyes. "Are you okay; it must have been a bad one huh?" I shook my head yes. Michael turned his back to me and I held onto him from behind. "Every time you have a nightmare hang onto me, and it will go away quickly," he said.

Michael fell off to sleep quickly but I couldn't sleep. I wondered what was happening, I'm seeing shadows and more things are happening than before. I thought laying there holding on to Michael. And what about seeing Mr. Simms, what was he doing at my house, I'm starting to think that trip to the reservation may have been a bad idea. The candles were still flickering in the room. I just held onto Michael I scooted closer to look closely at Michaels back, he had a patch of hair on each side of his back right on his shoulder blades straight white hair with a little bit of black in it.

Underneath, there was nothing, it was smooth all except for those two spots, no hair anywhere else, just those two patches. I began to really look at it. I touched it, it felt different a little course. Michael turned and looked at me. "What on earth are you up to?" "I'm just admiring the patches of hair on your back," I tell him smiling. "Do you know that you have two very straight haired patches on your back, and they're both white, just a tiny bit of black hair in it, did you know that you have hair nowhere else, it's funny?"

"Yes, I'm aware, they're my luck and my strength," He tells me turning to me wrapping me up in his arms. I looked up at him. "What makes them your strength?" "I don't know I just feel that they are." "What makes them your luck?" "I'm sure they're my luck, shh," he said. "Just believe me okay,"   he kissed me. "Let's try and get some rest baby; I'm tired." I stared at him as he fell off to sleep. Michael slept so peacefully, soon I was asleep with him.

I was at ease laying there next to him. I held onto him really tight so that I wouldn't have any more nightmares after a while I felt no fear just comfort. When we woke up the next morning Michael kissed me. "Good morning baby," he said. "Good morning Michael," he admired my lips pinching them with two of his fingers. "So, do we have breakfast or just coffee?" He asked me getting up from our small pallet on the floor. "I will just have coffee thank you." "That's what I thought you'd say, are you cold?" He asked

"No I'm okay," I took the covers and wrapped them around my body and stood up. "Michael, is it okay if I use your restroom?" I asked. "Sure you know where right?" I walked toward him; I kissed him on his cheek, "I won't be too long." I went in used the bathroom and rinsed my mouth and took a look at myself in the mirror and smiled." Karis!" Michael yelled out to me. "I'm going to make us some eggs, just in case you need something to get you through the day, do you like them scrambled?" I came out of the bathroom.

I folded the blanket and laid it on the couch. I stretched out my arms and went into the kitchen to see what Michael was doing. He was standing in his pajamas cooking eggs. "So, how did you like it?" He asked. "Like what?" "Spending the night here with me, how was it?" he sat a cup of coffee down in front of me. It was scorching; I blew on it, blowing the steam up into the air. I looked at Michael and smiled.

"I really enjoyed it, especially the part when I got to hang onto you all night, I was able to sleep without worry" I said. "What do you worry about?" "Oh nothing," I said changing the subject   quickly. "I think I'm going to take this coffee to go, Michael," I said walking over to him kissing his cheek. "I have to be at the hospital early today." Michael grabbed me by the waist and kissed me holding onto me tight. "So no eggs huh?" I shook my head no looking down at the eggs.

"But thank you, I think I'll just take this coffee and have a muffin from home," I tell him. "Will I see you before you leave?" I asked him opening the door. Michael blew me a kiss. "Yes, I will see you before I leave, I promise." I went out to my car Michael was standing in the doorway waving as I drove off. When I got to the stop light up the street from his house there was Mr. Simms again waving and smiling at me. I waved back and drove home. I needed to change my clothes and to check on Cookie.

I couldn't keep leaving her home alone like this. I thought as I pulled up to my house. I could see Cookie in the window just sitting and waiting for me. I walked up to the door. I put my key into the door and before I turned it, it just opened. I went inside and Cookie ran up to me. The house was freezing. I walked over to the heater to turn it on. I was frightened because I knew I locked the door before I left, I held onto to Cookie tight as I walked through the house checking to see if anything was missing or anyone was there.

I opened each door and walked through. My bathroom door was locked. I twisted the door knob. "Who's out there?" Someone yelled out.

"It's me," I was afraid, but I knew that voice. It was Krystal. "Hey, what are you doing here?" I yelled out to her. "I just needed to come over here for a while," she yelled back. "You have a bad habit Krystal; you should never do that." As I walked into my room, I was still yelling out at her. "You left the front door unlocked; you know you shouldn't do that, right?" I yell at her as she steps out of the bathroom. I began to rumble around in my drawer looking for under wear and some clean scrubs.

I hadn't done any laundry. Krystal was wearing my T-shirt and a pair of my old tight gym pants. She looked as if she'd been resting all day. "Hey Karis, where were you all this time, I was expecting you last night, you had a hot date or something?" She asked me laughing. "I know James is back in town." "I wasn't with James, I was with Michael all night, I'm just going to change, I have to be at work early today," I tell her going to the bathroom.

"Are you going to stay here today?" I asked her washing my face. "I will be home at about seven or eight tonight," I tell her turning on the shower. "I don't know; I have a hot date tonight." She said picking at my clothes on the counter I shook my head at her and got into the shower. "Krystal, don't you ever get tired, please Krystal if you leave to come back tonight, I would love to sleep in my bed tonight." I tell her opening the shower curtain to see her face.

"What, you can't stay here alone, why don't you have one of your boyfriends come over and protect you from whatever is keeping you from sleeping in your bed at night?" She said. "Krystal, don't be like that," I said getting out drying off. She was lying on the bed. "Like what, you're asking me do I ever get tired, when you're always running, you're never home, do you ever get tired?" "Yes I do, Krystal I'm always tired, I want to be home, if you don't want to stay I understand," I tell her putting my clothes.

"I'm going to come back, boo who," she said throwing a pillow at my back. "Go to work, I'll come back as soon as my dates over" She said laughing at me. She walked me to the front door. I grabbed her close to me and hugged her. "I love you little sis" I tell her hugging her tight and kissed her cheek. "Yuck" She said wiping her face. "I love you Karis" I left the house just in time to meet James in the driveway. "I can't talk now James, I'm going to be late," I yelled out to him getting into my car.

"I need to talk to you soon okay Karis, tonight," he yelled out. I waved at him. He was tapping his watch looking into my window. I started my car and pulled out of the driveway. I shook my head yes. "I'll see you after work, but only for a little while okay," I said pulling off into the street. I made it to work just in time to catch Michael staring his rounds with all the new doctors who would be taking over when his team leaves. I started working immediately.

I had   to meet the doctor who would take over for Michael because I would be working with him a lot. He was tall and slim and much older than Michael, a bit intimidating to. I thought. I watched him he was anal and tough, he wanted details, absolutely no half stepping with him, "I like this that way and don't do that this way." He was all over us today everyone on the team followed behind him watching him intensely waiting for what he would do or say next.

The day was long. I didn't see Maddy all day today. I guess she stayed out of his way. I began asking around on each floor. I went up to the sixth floor and asked one of her good friends had they seen her today. I went up to her. "Hi, have you seen Maddy today?" She looked up at me from her clipboard. "She won't be in for a while," she tells me. "Her father's ill," she turned her back to the board on the wall. "Mr. Simms, he's ill," I looked on the board.

His room number was there. I just seen him this morning, I thought as I walked away from the women. I finished up with the new doctor and headed straight up to Mr. Simms room. I began to get ill the moment I stepped out of the elevator. I managed to make it to the door without vomiting. I stood there for a while before knocking on the door. There was a sign taped on the door that read family only. So I thought I better knock. "Come in," a woman voice yelled softly out to me. I opened the door and went inside.

The closer I went toward Mr. Simms It felt as if my stomach was being punched it felt like fire was burning inside me. Maddy was sitting in a chair rocking; her head was down into her chest. I went over to Mr. Simms and held his hand. He looked up at me and smiled. He pulled me close to his mouth. He whispered into my ear. "I've been waiting for you" I stood back from him. He squeezed my hand. Maddy looked up at me. I sat down next to him I felt so sick inside. "Karis, how did you find me," she asked me her eyes filled with tears.

"I talked to your friend downstairs, she told me you were to find you, well she told me Mr. Simms was sick, and I just came up on my own, is it okay , I can leave if it's making you uncomfortable," I tell her. "No, he likes you," she said wiping her eyes. "I won't stay long, Mr. Simms needs his rest," I whispered to her. Mr. Simms winked his eye at me, I was feeling so bad inside, I went back over to him and held his hand. "Mr. Simms, I will be back tomorrow okay," I tell him. I walked over to Maddy and gave her a big hug.

"Everything will be okay Maddy, I love you," I tell her leaving the room. I couldn't wait to get out of that door. I went into the hallway and clutched my stomach it was burning so badly. I was bent over holding onto my stomach. I stood there bent over for a while as soon as I got up I went to my car immediately. I stood by the door of my car vomiting. I fell to my knees. I got up and went to put my key into the door of the car and Mr. Simms was standing there.

"Here let me help you," he said taking my keys from me. "No, Mr. Simms, what are you doing out here" He smiled at me. He was so bright eyed. Like he was glowing. "You have to go back to your room I said walking him back. I was still clutching my stomach. When I made it back to his room, it was if I was walking alone Mr. Simms was no longer walking beside me he was gone. I turned away from the door questioning myself, what was going on? Why was seeing Mr. Simms?

I went back to my car. I got in and looked up at the hospital Mr. Simms was staring down at me from the window. He waved his hand gesturing me to come back up. I started my car and began to leave. I made it home and found Cookie outside the door waiting for me. Krystal must have let her out. I picked up Cookie and brought her inside. She was hissing the moment we stepped into the door. I sat her down on the couch. She stood up with her back curled staring into the hallway with her eyes pierced on to the walls I felt a chill all over me.

I began to walk toward the light switch. I feel hands on my back. I turn to run for the front door it felt as if someone snatched me back and threw me to the wall. Oh no, I thought. It's back. I'm in trouble. I closed my eyes tight. I balled my hands into my fist. I just clutched them. I was being tossed back and forth from the door to the wall as if it could only toss me around. I could smell it foul, vulgar, every bone in my body ached at every hit. I could feel the blood flowing from my head to my face.

The room started to spin and everything went black. When it stopped I was laying on the floor. I felt like I was being lifted. I could feel a hand on my back and face. I dared to open my eyes, but I did because I felt a warm feeling all around me. It felt as if someone covered me with a warm blanket as if the sun was shining down directly on me. I opened my eyes as I was lifted off of the ground. I couldn't see a face, but arms were lifting me in a ray of light. Soon there was a face, a beautiful face, wings, and a man smiled at me. "Don't worry I'll always be here."

Fear Within Me

I was being slapped in the face over and over again. I turned my head trying to ignore it until I heard Krystal calling out to me. "Karis, what happened? Wake up! Wake up; I'm scared, Karis!" She yelled out; tears were streaming from her face, she put her face to mine cheek to cheek I could feel her. "Please, please wake up Karis!" She screamed. I sat up and looked around. "Krystal, what's wrong with you?" I asked.

"Why are you crying?" She looked at me. "You were laying here; I couldn't wake you up, what happened to you?" She asked again. "I don't remember," I started to get up from the floor. "I called the police, they should be here soon," Krystal said as she helped me to the couch. "Krystal I'm okay, I just fell, there was no one here, I promise," I tell her. How would I explain all of this to the police, I thought there is absolutely no way to explain this incident.

Krystal handed me a bag of ice for my head. "There is no way that you just fell, Karis, something happened here, something happened to you, would you stop lying and just tell me!" She screamed at me. "Maybe you don't remember what or who did this, but someone did this to you, I mean they must have stricken you that you blacked out," she was frantic. "Krystal, did they take anything from the house?" I asked her looking around. "I don't know; I didn't check anything, I've been trying to wake you all this time."

"Krystal, please don't panic, I'm okay I promise," I said holding my hand to my head. I laid back on the couch; my head was pounding, it was like someone was jumping around kicking in my head. I closed my eyes the room began to spin around as I listen to Krystal rant from one person to the next about how I'd been attacked and we were waiting for the police. I felt nauseous I began to get up slowly, I needed to look at myself in the mirror, my face was burning, and my body ached.

I needed to be close to the toilet in case I did vomit, I strolled to the bathroom with Krystal's help. She turned on the light and helped me sit on the toilet. "You're covered in blood," Krystal said getting a washcloth to help wipe my face, I had a gash on my forehead and cuts on my shoulders that looked like scratches and both my arms hand big hand prints on them they both came in from the front to the back of each arm. I reached over Krystal's arm and grabbed another towel to wash off with; I got up from the toilet and turned around to vomit.

Krystal rubbed my back as I vomited in the sink. I was thinking how I would create a story for the police; my story would be, I came in, it was dark I tripped over the cat and fell and hit my head on the table, and blacked out. I'd rather tell this story than have the police and everybody else in town looking for someone they'll never find. I thought as I leaned over the toilet. Krystal was wiping my forehead and rubbing my back. I went over to the sink to look in the mirror. I had dried blood on the side of my face; I washed my face with cold water and brushed my hair back.

I could feel the swelling in my head as I brushed. When I finished in the bathroom, I went into my room quickly to put on a long sleeve turtleneck and some long pants. I will only show the police the gash on my head, "That's where I fell," I tell them, that's why I blacked out, I will tell them. I began to cry. I shook my head. No crying Karis be brave, I tell myself. I couldn't stop crying I sat on the bed and put my hands in my head and just cried. I didn't expect it this time and it was more intense, I was afraid, this is the time that I needed my mother, I thought as I cried.

Tears streamed from my face I sat up and took a deep breath. I took the towel and wiped my face. I'm going to be all right. I said to myself. The gash on my head was turning into a very big lump. "Are you coming out?" Krystal yelled. "Yes, I will be right out," I took one last look at myself in the mirror, I was sore all over. I opened the door and walked into the living room I sat down on the couch. "I called daddy," Krystal said.

"Krystal, you didn't have to do that," I tell her. I put the bag of ice back on my head. There was a knock at the door. Krystal nearly tripped over the coffee table to get to the door. "Hi, come in please," she said pulling the door open to let them in. It was two policemen, "Hello," One of the officers said, "I'm Officer Dan, how are you?" He asked reaching to shake my hand; I lifted the ice bag from my head and looked up. "I could be better."

"This is Officer Steve," he said pointing at his partner who was walking around the house inspecting everything. "Hello," I said to him. "Can you tell us what happened tonight?" "Sure sir, my sister believes I was assaulted, but officer I assure you, I wasn't, I have been working long hours, I came home and tripped over my cat, Cookie over there," I said pointing to Cookie. "I must have hit my head on the coffee table because when I woke up Krystal, my sister was slapping me in the face crying.

I know it must have scared her, but I'm fine, just a little tired." I tell him putting the ice bag back on my head. He came in close to my face. "Yeah, it looks like you got a good one there," he said pointing to the lump on the side on my face. "What made you think she'd been attacked?" He asked turning to Krystal. "I found her lying on the floor unconscious," she said almost yelling at the policeman, I stood up. "Look, I'm sorry that you guys have wasted your time coming out here, I'm fine now I just need to get a little rest, that's all." I tell them walking over to the door; I reached over to shake Officer Dan's hand he pointed up at my head.

"You have blood on your face" He took the towel from my hand and wiped my face. "You may want to have someone look at that." "Well, if you say that there was no attack then we'll be on our way, please call us if something does happen, and you need police assistance." The other officer said standing by the door. "We're going to be on our way," they said. I walked toward the door. "Thank you guys again, it was all a misunderstanding," I tell them holding the door open for them. "She was just scared, it won't happen again, I'll go get my rest," I said smiling.

I closed the door behind them and sat down on the couch. I took a deep breath and put the ice pack back on my head and leaned back. Krystal was standing over me right in my face. "   Karis, why did you lie? I know your lying; you were attacked, what's wrong? Did they threaten you, did they say they'd come back and kill you or something, what's wrong with you?" She yelled. "Oh, I can't wait for daddy to get here." She sat down on the couch beside me staring at the front door. Daddy came running, pushing his way through the door.

"What the hell is going on here?" He asked yelling. I wished they'd stop yelling my head was pounding. I put my hand up as if to answer daddy before Krystal did. "Nothing daddy, there isn't anything going on, I fell and hit my head that's all, Krystal found me on the floor, she panicked that's all." Krystal looked at me and rolled her eyes. Daddy grabbed my face moving it from side to side. He stared into my eyes. "Are you okay Karis, is that what really happened?" He asked me. "Daddy I'm sure that's what happened, if I were attacked, I would tell you, daddy, you know I would." I tell him looking him in the eye.

I had to look at daddy because if I didn't he'd know I was lying. He always says. "If someone can't look you in the eye, more than likely their lying to you" I assured him that I was okay and got him out of the house quickly. "I'm leaving with him," Krystal said going to the back room to grab her things." Okay Krystal, I understand, I will see you soon." "No you won't I'm never coming back here," she said with tears in her eyes.

"Someone attacked you and you, don't want to tell on them, I know it." She said slamming the door on her way out. That slam was so hard I had to cover my head with the pillow my head pounded even more with every sound. I laid down on the couch my head throbbed so bad I knew wouldn't be able to sleep, I just laid there with my hair covered. I felt Cookie jump on the couch. I took the pillow off and picked her up. "Hey Cookie, let's go to the bathroom and take another look." I walked over to the bathroom I wanted to wet the towel and rewash my face.

I was so mad at this, I was mad that I couldn't stop it and mad that I didn't want to live with it anymore. I stood in the mirror. I placed Cookie on the counter and took off the turtleneck and my pants. I looked my face over and my body, I put my head down and picked it back up. I just screamed out "S.T.O.P.!" I held onto the sink and screamed louder and louder until I couldn't anymore I became dizzy after a while of screaming. I stumbled into my room and laid on the bed clutching the covers; I put my face into the pill ow breathing heavily, I'm done, I thought I am just done, this is never-ending.

I was all screamed out. When I heard a knock at the door, I lifted my head from the pillow. Who could that be, I wondered, oh go away I thought lying back down on the pillow but they continued knocking on the door. I hoped it wasn't Krystal or daddy coming back. I sat up at the edge of the bed the doorbell was still ringing. They wouldn't go away. "Karis, Karis." It was Michael yelling and ringing the bell.

"Karis, open the door," he said. I got up quickly put the turtleneck and the sweats on and started walking as fast as I could to the door. I opened the door Michael came in and hugged me as soon as I opened the door. "Are you okay baby, what's going on?" I laid my head on his shoulder; tears streamed down my face onto his shirt. "Baby, everything's going to be alright, just tell me what happened."

I stood back and stared into Michaels' eyes, I wanted so desperately to tell him everything, but I just couldn't I stood there telling it all to him in my head. I couldn't bring my lips to tell him. I shook my head, "Okay, okay," Michael said rubbing my back, don't worry I understand." He said holding my chin in his hand. "Listen, baby, I'm leaving tonight, I promise you when I come back I will make everything alright, I promise."

"You have to leave tonight?" For a moment I had forgotten that he had prior engagements. He took me by the hand and walked me over to the couch. "I'm scared Michael," I said holding his hand. "What if you don't come back to me, what if you fall in love with someone else?" I looked up at him. Michael reached into his pocket. "I will come back, and I won't fall in love with anyone else, I promise, I love you. I promise I will always love only you no matter what happens I will be back here, you will be the only love I'll be thinking of while I'm gone." Michael held a black box in front of my face he opened it.

"This is a promise ring; it means that all the promises I made will be kept." The ring was so beautiful. "I love you, and I promise I will come back, and we will be Dr. and Mrs. Michael Bernard Phillips. I will love you forever I promise." He said taking the ring from the box placing it on my finger. "Will you wait for me and marry me when I get back?" He asked looking me in the eyes. I dared to say yes. I thought as I looked back at him, but my heart wouldn't allow me not to.

"Yes, Michael I promise I will wait for you and marry you when you come back," I tell him. He kissed my hand and hugged me then he picked me up from the couch and shook me around. "I knew that you loved me," he said laughing. "I knew you did." He carried me back into my room." I love you so much baby," he sat me down on the bed and sat beside me looking at me smiling, he leaned over to me and began to kiss me softly. "I love you so much." I loved his soft lips. He was wearing chaps stick today the bubble gum flavor.

He kissed me again and again. He didn't even question the lump on my head or the gash on my neck. I put my head down embarrassed at what he might be thinking of the lumps and gashes. He kisses me with so much passion pulling my lips into his with every kiss. I want him to touch me so badly too. "I'm so happy baby, I love you so much, I'm going to miss you, baby." We kissed as the night fell; Michael looked down at his watch after a couple of hours of us holding on to one another.

"Baby, I have to go, everyone's meeting at the airport." "You have to go now?" "Yes, you have to go too so that you can bring my car back to my house," he handed me a pair of keys. "This one is for the house, this one is for the car," he explained, "Please take care of these things for me." He handed me a list of things to do for him while he was gone. "Okay, I will Michael," I said shaking my head yes. He kissed me again on the lips. "Come on baby, we have to get going if I want to make my flight," he grabbed my hand and pulled me from the bed.

We went to Michael's car it was packed with at least five bags. "You packed a lot of your things. Can I fit in there?" I asked him. "Well, I tied them down pretty good, there should be enough room for you in here somewhere," he said pushing the bags over toward the window. "Your skinny bones can fit, I'm sure," he said laughing and pushing me into the car holding my bottom in his hand. "Ha ha," I said getting into the car, "hilarious, Michael."

"Yes, bones, hop in." I was taking my time trying to situate myself into the seat when Michael picked me up and sat me in the seat with a kiss on the cheek he shut the door and ran to the other side. "I love you he said. We drove off to the airport. When we arrived at the airport everyone was standing out waiting for Michael. We took his things out of the car. Michael held onto my waist as he checked in. He kissed me over and over again, my eyes began to fill with tears, I didn't want Michael to leave me, and I felt so safe when he was around.

After he checked his bags we went back over to the front entrance where the rest of his medical team where. "Look at me, I love you, sweetie, don't cry, I will be back before you know it," he said kissing my cheek. "There is nothing in the world that I love more than you," he said. "Really, not even rocky road ice cream?" I said smiling. "Not even rocky road ice cream," he kissed me again "I love you, Michael," I said hugging him tightly.

There was an older couple standing behind us. The woman looked at us smiling. "You make such a beautiful couple," I looked up at Michael. "Thank you," Michael said to her pulling me closer to him, he played with the ring on my finger. It was a beautiful diamond ring. He kissed my hand again. "I love it Michael, thank you again." "You don't have to thank me, just remember our promise," he said winking his eyes. His friends began to flag him to go. "I love you, Karis; I will write you every day and call every chance I get okay, I love you sweetheart."

He hugged me tight one last time and walked away to board the plane. He blew me a kiss from the line. I waited until I seen the plane go up into the sky, and then I headed to the parking lot, as I walked closer to Michaels car I could see that someone was sitting in the passenger seat I stopped and stared straight at them, who was it, what were they doing in his car? I stared into the window. The person was wearing a hat. I looked around. Was that Michaels car or did I mistake his car for someone else's car. I thought as I went up closer to it.

Oh no it was Mr. Simms. I walked quickly to the car. I got into the driver's seat. "Mr. Simms, what are you doing here?" I asked him. "What's going on, how did you get here?" I put my hands on the stirring wheel, and Mr. Simms touched my hand, he looked me in the eye. "Come see me, come tonight, I have something to show you." I began to tell him that I couldn't I wanted to go home. When I turned to look at him he was gone. "No way, no," I said out loud as if I was talking to someone in the car. I am going home to rest; if I should get attacked again I will just get attacked I will not fear this anymore.

I was caught off guard the last time, but not again. I thought as I turned the key to the ignition. Why am I not home? I need to be in my space, what am I running from, Krystal is right I need to stop running if this thing can get me anywhere then I might as well learn how to deal with it. I drove home thinking about being brave. I thought about Mr. Simms, should I go there, I wondered, but I'm so tired I need to rest first. I just can't now I thought pulling into my driveway. I took a deep breath and put my head on the stirring wheel.

I'm going in Lord, I will not leave until I'm ready, I took another deep breath and got out of the car I went toward the front door. I could hear Cookie at the door she wanted out. I put the key in and walked inside. "Hello Cookie, hello," I say to her leaning over to pick her up. She licked my hand and I rubbed her back. I turned the lights on; I cringed as I walked through the house. This is my house I will not be afraid to stay in it, Lord please help me to not fear what I can't change, I am here I will not leave. I began to say this all around the house in every room I went into.

I walked down the hallway saying it loudly. I put Cookie down and went back into my room to change my clothes I brushed my hair and went into the bathroom to brush my teeth. After I was done I picked Cookie back up and went to my bedroom, I lay across the bed and covered up with Cookie in my arms. I held Cookie close to me as I fell off to sleep, I prayed more and more. I was awakened by whispers all around me. "That's her, that's her," they whispered I opened my eyes, lights were circling around me eight of them circled the bed.

I couldn't make out all of what they were saying the whispers became faded or like mumbled and some sounded as if they were under water. I just laid there looking at them. I closed my eyes and began to pray. Lord please protect me from harm, blanket me from harm, Lord please keep me safe, I closed my eyes tight and reached over for Cookie. She was sitting above my head, I reached over and rubbed her head as I fell back to sleep I prayed more.

"I am here; this is my house, I will not fear anything or anyone but God, I will stay until I am ready to leave." After a while I was at peace the lights were still there, but I was at peace I didn't fear anything I let go of all fear as I fell off to sleep. When I woke up the next morning my house smelled of flowers all over. It smelled as if I had a rose garden growing all over my house. I went into the kitchen and put the tea kettle on and gave Cookie a bowel of milk.

I took her litter box outside to empty it I went into the bathroom and turned on the shower. I got right in with my tooth brush in my hand. I brushed my teeth then washed all over and got out quickly. I wrapped my body up in a towel. I put lotion and oil all over my body. I cover the bruises with an ointment that I picked up a while back it smelled like aspirin. I began to brush my hair and the tea kettle began to whistle.

I put the brush down and went into the kitchen. "Hello Cookie, you're a beautiful kitty," I said to her while making tea. It felt as if I slept for the first time in a very long time. I want this all the time I thought to myself. "Cookie, I love you kitty, I do," I began singing to her. I took my tea and went into my room to get dressed for work. The phone rang as soon as I walked in. I jumped to get it hoping it was Michael. "Hello," I said. "Hello, how are you?" It was James.

"Are you working today?" He asked. "Yes I am, I'm getting ready right now," I tell him. This was a perfect opportunity for me to let him know I was in love with Michael and that we would be getting married as soon as he gets back. I really don't know how he would react, but he needs to hear it from me not anyone else. I thought as I listened to him explain his day to me. "Do you want to have lunch?" I asked him. "Sure, where do you want to meet?"

"We can meet at the Italian restaurant at 12:30, is that good?" "Sure," James said. "I'd love that." "I'm going to go now I have to get ready for work," I tell him. "I really can't wait to see you, Karis," he says as we say goodbye. I think this is the start of a very good day. I thought as I got dressed for work. I looked in the mirror as I put my shirt over my head I could see what looked like two big red hand prints on my shoulders it looked as if someone was holding on to my shoulders holding me back. I smiled.

I won't allow this to ruin what I was feeling today. I put the shirt on, I rubbed Cookie on the head and locked the house up. I took off to work. When I arrived at work the parking lot was full as it was every shift change. People going and coming, I went to the front desk to check to see what floor I would be working on today. "Hello everyone," I said. Maddy was still not working. Whenever she's off it seemed as if the staff was a little down. I guess having to take orders from someone other than Maddy was a little hard for some of the nurses.

Maddy had a way with people. Today I would start on the fourth floor and work my way back down to the first floor. "Hmm, not so bad," I said writing down all the room numbers on a piece of paper and sticking it into my pocket. "Well, I will see everyone later," I started to the elevator. I was going to see Mr. Simms today to ask him what he meant in the car last night, why did he need me to come see him and I can't forget I have that lunch date with James today.

I thought about these things as I began to work in the first room I was assigned to on the fourth floor. There were three beds in this room, and the adults were here for some orthopedic surgeries. I had to check them using a lot of caution they were all so fragile. They all told me they had been waiting for me to get them things like water, straws, a new set of sheets, extra blankets or something, I work three rooms on each floor today. While I worked I thought about how James was going to take what I had to tell him.

I needed to tell him that there was no chance for us. I was nervous about how he was going to take it. I'm hoping it goes over well and we can still remain friends. I finished up two floors and began going down they were fast and easy. Before I went to the second floor, I went up to check on Maddy, and Mr. Simms People were standing all around his room door talking. They must be family members, I thought. Closest to the door was a tall dark shadow. As I went closer I began to feel sick. I went to the door. "Excuse me," I said trying to push my way closer to the door. "Excuse me," I went into the room.

"Hello Maddy," I said rubbing her shoulders. "I just wanted to stop by and check on two of my favorite people," I said kissing   Maddy's cheek. I went over to Mr. Simms and took his hand. "Hello young lady, I need to tell you something, sit close," Mr. Simms whispered. Maddy walked out of the room. "I knew you would come," he pulled me up close to his face. "I want you to know; you have help, we are all around you all the time," he whispered.

"Don't fear, you have to let us in, you have to open your heart and feel when we're around. I know you're afraid, but that's what they want, they want you to be too afraid to notice us. We're here when you need us, don't lose faith in what you are, holding on to your faith and make it work for you. You will have many, many storms come your way, heavy storms, be aware of them, call out for us when you need us, and we'll come." He looked over at the window and back over at me.

"Maddy's afraid to let me go; you have to be there for her, I need to go now, please young lady, get me home, I'm ready to go, you get yourself ready for the storms. Lots of changes are coming your way dear, be ready for them, don't fear them." He clutched my hands; his hands began to feel cold as if they were frozen. They were skinny, I held his hands tight and began to pray, I watched in pain as Mr. Simms let go, his breathing slowed. He was no longer clutching my hand, I looked up, and he was standing next to me watching and smiling, his hands laid by his side.

He put his hand on my shoulder; he had light all around him. I sat down in the chair beside the bed I felt dizzy for a minute. Mr. Simms stood in the light. "Young lady, come with me," he said reaching his hand out to me. "I want to show you some things, come don't be scared." I stood up, and we walked into the hall. The shadow was no longer there, but everyone else was still there. He shook hands with all of the people; they must have been old friends who were waiting for him to cross over they smiled at me.

"See, these are things you need to know; sometimes we are just waiting around for you to help us, only the lost ones will come to hurt you. The lonely ones will try to destroy you because you're not supposed to be here on this earth at this time; you keep your faith and don't fear them." He said walking away with his friends smiling at me. I watched as they walked away laughing and talking to each other. I went on the second floor to finish up for lunch. I went back down to the front desk and there was James waiting for me.

"Hello," he said standing with his hands in his pockets. "I see you forgot about our lunch date, huh?" "Oh no, I just went up to see Mr. Simms, Maddy's dad, you know he's been ill," I told him. "Is he okay?" He asked. "No, he passed away," I tell him while I fill out my time card. I went to put it back on the desk, and Maddy tapped my shoulder. Oh no, I thought, it's Maddy.

"What did you say about my dad?" She asked me. I looked up at her. I couldn't say a word. I grabbed her and hugged her. "Maddy, I'm so sorry, I'm sorry," I told her, and I looked over at James. She was holding me so tight. "Maddy, let's go up and see him okay," we walked back up to Mr. Simms room. "Hello, Maddy, we were just about to call down for you, he passed on honey, I'm so sorry," the doctor said to her. She went over and sat by his bed rubbing his hand. "Karis, when did he go?" She asked. "When did he leave?"

"Maddy I don't think he wanted you to see him go, that's why he waited for you to leave the room," I tell her hugging her. I walked over to the door. I needed to tell James that maybe he could meet me at my house to talk; I wanted to stay with Maddy. I walked out of the room to give her some time alone with Mr. Simms. James was waiting. "So are we going?" He asked. "James, I'm so sorry, would you like to meet me later?" I asked. "Sure," he said walking away with his head down.

"I hope you understand, I have to be here for Maddy, I'll see you later," I yelled out to him, I stood in the hallway thinking about what Mr. Simms told me. "They're around me all the time," he said. I needed to do what he says and not fear them. I peeked in at Maddy just to see what she was doing. She was lying on Mr. Simms chest crying, I closed the door and went to stand by the window. Boy oh boy, I thought I had the best rest last night. I wondered what to think of all the things Mr. Simms said to me.

He was very serious about me never losing my faith; I do have faith, I just get afraid at times. I feel like I need more than that, these things are attacking me. I feel like I have no control, I pray, I've been to the reservation for spiritual guidance I don't know what else to do. I thought I would have a new begging after the Indians helped me on the reservation, but Mr. Simms says there's more to come. Maddy came walking out of the room with tissue in her hand still crying, I hugged her tight. "Maddy, everything will be okay," I tell her.

"Thank you, Karis; I'm going home now." She tells me, we walked together down to the elevator. It was pretty quiet all the way down; we walked to the parking lot, Maddy was sniffling out loud holding her tissue to her nose and eyes. "Maddy, would you like me to drive you home?" I asked her. "You really shouldn't be driving now; we can come back and pick up your car tomorrow or whenever you feel better. I can take you were ever you need to go." I opened the car door for her.

She didn't say a word. I went over to the driver side and got in, Maddy was sobbing so loudly. I leaned over and rubbed her back. "Maddy it will be okay." "I want him to be okay; I want him to be here with me!" She yelled. "He is here Maddy; he will never leave you." "I can't believe it; I'm going to have to make arrangements for my father to be buried." She sobbed even louder. "Would you like me to help you with that Maddy? I will come pick you up, and we can go make all the arrangements," I tell her.

"I need to go to his house early in the morning and get his insurance policy; I need to call the mortuary to pick him up from the hospital." "Maddy, don't worry I'll be here for you, don't worry," I tell her holding her hand. I drove away from the hospital slowly; I understood what she's feeling, I remembered back when mama died. I felt so lost and confused, the word died or dead, my heart would drop when I heard them. I wished her back so many times; I prayed all the time, I just wanted an understanding of it all, she's gone, she's never coming back.

I wanted to cry just thinking of that time in my life, but I couldn't I had to be strong for Maddy. It was like my heart was ripped away from my chest. Poor Maddy, I thought as I drove her home. I'm going to stay with her until I know she's okay, I will help her make phone calls. We arrived at her house, we went inside, Maddy sat down on the couch and picked up two of her cats, she placed them on her lap. There were cats in the window, and coming out of the room. It looked as if Maddy hadn't cleaned in a while.

"Maddy, do you mind if I picked up a bit for you?" I asked her. She put her head down on the arm of the couch. She didn't answer me. I began to pick up anyway. "Maddy would you like a cup of coffee, I don't know how to make it, but I'll try," I tell her cleaning the living room. I went over to the sink to wash the dishes. "You just turn it on, I'll do the rest Karis, thank you." She said lifting her head off the couch. The cats circled around me as I was cleaning, they must have been hungry I thought. I poured milk in there bowels, I took the kittens and put them in the little kitty bed that Maddy had for them in her room.

Maddy was still sitting on the couch; she stared at the door as if she was in a daze. "Maddy, how do we know when it's done?" I ask her standing by the coffee pot. "Oh, I'll get that Karis don't worry," she said coming into the kitchen. "I remember when my father would come by here just to check on me, he was all I had, my only parent." She explained with tears in her eyes.

"You know my mom ran off when I was just a young girl, I never knew her, it was one of my father's friends that she ran off with, she'd pop in from time to time to tell us she loved us, take daddy's money and run off again. My father never got over that, she was a selfish whore, and I won't call her to tell her about my father, I won't." She said shaking her head. I just listened while I cleaned, I didn't say a word. "Do you know he worked two jobs to put us through school? My brothers and I were fortunate to have him; he always taught us what not to do, I will always love him for that." She said starting to cry again.

I went over to her and hugged her. I guess I'm staying the night with Maddy I thought. I stood by her hugging her tight. "Maddy would you like a hot bath?" I asked her. "Please, I would like that, thank you, Karis, thank you," she said. I went into the bathroom and cleaned the tub, I ran the water hot and added a small amount of the bubble bath she had sitting near the counter. While the water ran I went to her room to get her bed clothes ready. "Maddy your bath is ready," I called out to her when I went into the bathroom. She came into the bathroom with her coffee cup in her hand. "Maddy, is there anything else you need?" I asked her.

Maddy shook her head no, I was afraid for her to shut the door. She began undressing. "Karis, you can wait in the room for me," she tells me closing the door." Maddy, you can leave the door cracked a little, and if you should need me, I'll be out here," I tell her. "No, I'm okay, I just need to bathe," she said waving her hand to me. I waited at the door she sobbed loudly. After I felt she was okay I went into the living room and began to vacuum after vacuuming I mopped the kitchen floor, after I finished cleaning I sat down by the bathroom door and waited for Maddy to come out the cats sat with me waiting.

After an hour of waiting she finally came out. She went into her bedroom, she put on lotion and her bed clothes and came out to the living room with a book and pens and paper. She sat down on the couch next to me. "Karis these are all of my father's friends and family, we should begin to call everyone." "Maddy, its late maybe we should take a break tonight, you need your sleep, I will sleep out here, and we can start calling everyone tomorrow." I told her putting the book down on the table. I went into the hall closet and got out a blanket and pillow. I lay down on the sofa. Maddy got up and went to her room.

"You're right Karis, I do need to rest," she said walking away. I curled myself up into to the couch wrapped up tight in the blanket. I stuffed my face into the pillow and began to pray as I did the night before. I just want to go to sleep. I thought after praying. The cats sat on top of the sofa, I closed my eyes tight with my face in the pillow. I couldn't sleep, I turned and looked up at the cats staring down at me, and I prayed some more. Lord, wrap me up in your warm light, please free me from harm.

I found myself falling off to sleep and feeling very comfortable. I continued praying until I couldn't anymore, I drifted off to sleep, I began to see James face, he was holding on to me, and I was pushing him away from me screaming, stop James, it's not yours. I screamed. Please stop I screamed. I was screaming and yelling at him to stop. He turned me around and pulled my pants down. I jumped up from my sleep and shook my head. James.

I thought, no, I don't think it could have been, what kind of dream was that, what is going on? I lay back down and tried to fall off to sleep; I began to pray again, Lord, please keep me from any harm, I was awakened the next morning by Maddy's son Scott. "Karis, Karis," he said whispering close to my ear. "Get up sleepy head," he handed me a cup of tea. "Thank you for staying with mom, thank you so much, Karis," he said. I sat up and took the cup of tea. I sipped on it.

"She was sad, I just thought I better stay with her, she needed help calling friends and family, I was going to do that, but since you're here," I said smiling at him sipping the tea. "Oh sure I'm going to do all that, but you can still stay over and help," he tells me. "You've done enough; I know you have other things to do, don't worry about it, go on home and get yourself together," he said. "I will keep you updated on everything, my sisters are on their way down here, and they will call you if they need anything." I began to fold the blankets and put them away when Maddy walked in.

"Good morning, Maddy," I said. "How are you feeling this morning?" "I feel okay Karis," she said as she was coming toward me when Scott went behind her and put his hands over her eyes. "Guess who?" He said kissing her cheek. "Scott!" She screamed out. She turned around and put her arms around him, she put her hands on his face. "How? She asked. "How did you know about your grandpa, who called you?" She said looking at me. "Oh Karis, thank you so much, I needed my son here with me."

"Oh no, Maddy, I wish I could take the credit for it, but it wasn't me." She hugged Scott so tight. "Mom, I was called last night by one of the nurses, she called the Red Cross, and they fly me in this morning," he said smiling. "I'm glad they did son," Maddy said holding on to him. "I'm happy to be home mom; I'm going to miss grandpa, was he very ill?" He asked. "No," Maddy said shaking her head. "He was at his best for a while, you know he was always battling arthritis," she said sitting down on the couch. "It's so good to have you home, son."

"Maddy, I'm going to take off," I tell her hugging her. "You're in good hands now," I reached out to shake Scott's hand, and he pulled me in to hug me. "Thank you again, young lady," he said with a smile. I walked to the door "No problem, anything for Maddy." I went to my car, I needed to go home and wash and get ready for work again, I thought as I drove home. I listened to jazz on the radio all the way home; it made me want to sleep more.

I thought about what I would find when I got there, I didn't see James last night, but maybe it was good I didn't. I should probably tell him about Michael and me over the phone, after that vision I had of him, it may be too dangerous to have him over. I thought as I pulled into the driveway. I will call him. Michael, I miss him already I thought, I needed to tell Maddy about the promise ring, but not now. I went inside, and Cookie was waiting in the kitchen next to her bowel. I went to get her milk but when I poured it she ran for the front door.

When I stood up to see why she ran I saw a dark shadow standing next to her in the door way. I went over to her as if I didn't see it; I wasn't going to be afraid. I picked her up from the floor and carried her to the bathroom with me to start my shower. When I turned to go to my room there was the shadow again. I closed my eyes and prayed as I walked toward the room, I prayed out loud. "Lord, walk with me carry me, keep me from harm in my home." I opened my eyes as I turned to my closet to get my clothes as I opened the closet door, there it was, the sweet smell of flowers all over the room. It was beautiful.

I took my clothes out and sat down on the bed with cookie. I decided I would call James before getting into the shower. "Hello," I said when he picked up the phone. "I'm at home now, I'm sorry about last night, I have work today, but you're welcome to come over when I get off, or we can talk on the phone." I tell him hoping he'd settle for talking on the phone. "No, Karis, what I have to tell you is not a phone conversation, I have to see you," he said. "Okay," I said not sounding too sure about him coming over. "Okay, well tonight then, after work," I tell him hanging up the phone.

I took my clothes off and got into the shower. It felt so good to wash away today's troubles. I got out and put my favorite blue scrubs on. I went into the kitchen to make tea. I sat down on the couch with

Cookie; I turned the television on, I flipped through all the channels only to stop where I always did. The Oprah Winfrey Show. today's discussion, women too afraid to leave their relationships, I shook my head at some of them, thinking that will never be me.

Some of the stories were really interesting to hear. I gazed at the television it was always my favorite time when she would go to the audience to see what they thought. After listening to them ask the guest questions I turned the television off and put Cookie in the back room. It was about time for me to leave for work. I took a sip of my tea before putting the cup in the sink, the smell of flowers was everywhere. I took a big whiff of it and went to the front door. I drove to work quickly and made it there on time, I was only working a four hour shift today.

I started on the fifth floor and worked my way back down. It was very quiet there. No Maddy, or no Michael smiling at me and making me laugh. Those four hours seemed like forever to me. I washed a few faces and gave a coupled of sponge baths and joked around with some of the patients about their time in the hospital. They loved the staff, but hated the food; my last patient needed help to eat. He was a senior man in his eighties; his son was there watching me, I fed him slowly.

He asked me was I planning to do this job forever. I answered no. "You're very good with the older people," he said smiling at me. "You can feed me any day." I finished with him and called Maddy to check on her before signing my time card. The nursing station was really quiet. "Hello Maddy, how are you?" I asked her. "I'm good me, and Scott just made it back to the house from the mortuary, we took care of everything. How about you dear, how are you today?" She asked me. "I'm good I'm leaving work soon going home."

"Well, you can come to the house anytime you like, I'll be here, or at my father's collecting his things okay." "Okay Maddy, you call me if you should need me for anything okay, I'm here," I tell her hanging up the phone. I drove home listing to Jazz again. I couldn't get any other radio stations on my radio for some reason that was the only station that came in clear.

When I pulled up into my driveway Cookie was sitting in the window. I got out and went for the door, I opened it and went in. "Hello Cookie," I said pulling the curtain back from the window. She jumped into my arms from the window seal. I took her to the bathroom with me to wash up. I took off my scrubs and put them in the hamper, my bruises were clearing up just a little and what was once a huge lump shrank down to just a gash in my head. I went into my bedroom to change and get ready for James to come over, as I turned to go into the room the phone rang, I ran to get it.

"Hello," I said. "Hello, are you there?" It was James. "Yes, hello, I'm here, what's wrong?" I asked. "I'm on the way to your house." "Okay just give me forty-five minutes okay." I tell him. "Okay, I'll see you in forty-five," he said hanging up the phone. I went to the closet and got out my favorite blue sweater and my white pants, I wore a pair of blue flats. The house still smelled of flowers, it felt so peaceful all around. After getting dressed I brushed my hair and took Cookie into the kitchen to make me something to eat before James showed up. I made sure to wear Michaels ring.

I looked down at it and smiled. I missed him so much, more and more every day. After eating I sat on the couch and waited for James, I played with Cookie twirling a string around in her face, she loved it, running so fast the she would almost fall onto the floor trying to grab it, the doorbell rang, I went to the window to make sure it was James. I looked out, he was standing away from the door staring at his car waiting for me to come to the door, I opened the door, "Hello, James come in," I tell him holding Cookie in my arms.

"Would you like something to drink?" I asked him. "No thanks," he said. "Have a seat," I tell him going over to the couch sitting with Cookie on my lap. "What are you up to?" He asked me. "Oh, not too much, I'm sorry about yesterday, I had to stay with Maddy," I tell him. "Oh, I understand, you're so sweet for doing that, she needed you." I noticed James seemed a little nervous; I was starting to feel uncomfortable so I went ahead and asked him.

"So what was so important that you had to come all the way here to see me and tell me?" I asked. He scooted over close to me and smiled. "You first, you said you had something to tell me too." "Well, James, I know that you are thinking about leaving the area, and I'm going to miss you so much, you've been a great friend to me all these years. I'm so grateful for all that you've ever done for me," I said to him. James put his head on my shoulder and closed his eyes with his face in my neck. I moved over.

"James, I need you to listen to me," I tell him looking him in the eyes. "James I'm going to marry Michael when he comes back from Africa." James jumped from his seat and looked at me. "Are you Karis, you don't love him, you love me," he said. I leaned back on the couch shocked at his reaction. "No, James I love Michael, and we're planning to get married when he comes back," I tell him again. I grabbed Cookie and held her close to my chest.

"James, I don't mean to hurt you, but I'm not in love with you, we've always been friends. I'm so sorry, I wished I did feel the same as you, but I don't I've always loved you as a friend." I tell him getting up from the couch. "So, when you took my ring you didn't love me?" He asked. "James, I took it so that you wouldn't feel bad, I wanted to make you happy. I didn't want to lose our friendship, so I did what I thought was best, I don't want to hurt you." I tell him again rubbing Cookies back. "I hope me marrying Michael won't be the end of our relationship," he looked outraged.

"I hoped you'd understand," I told him. He sat back down on the couch putting his hands on his head, blowing air from his jaws and sighing. I stood up holding Cookie watching him. "I can't believe you,

Karis, I mean, what does Michael have that I don't?" He asked me, "I love you more than anything in this world, does he love you like that? Who loves you more than me? I love you so much Karis," He said with tears streaming from his face. Oh no, I thought lord help me, James was becoming unglued.

"James," I said sitting next to him, "I don't want to hurt you, I just want us to stay friends, I can't give you what you want. You want lots of children and to live in the country, I can't give you that, you deserve someone better than me, someone, who can give you the things you want," I tell him. "When I get older I'll have all kinds of physical problems; I won't be what you want, do you want to have to take care of me because I won't be able to care for myself.

Look, James I don't know if I will marry Michael, I may not be what he wants, I just hope he doesn't change his mind, and I do know that I love him he's all I think about." I told him. He raised his eyebrows at me and I grabbed his hands. "Karis, no one loves you more than me, I don't care about any of those things you said, I don't care if you can't have children, we'll buy them if we have to," he said. "I know that we are good for one another." I reached over and hugged him tight then I stood up.

"James I love you, but I'm not in love with you, I hope we can still be friends, I'm sorry." I walked into the kitchen to get a drink of water. I got two glasses one for him and one for me. I took him a glass, and I went back over and began to clean the countertops with the dish towel. I was nervous, but I had to tell him the truth, I was tired of feeling pressured every time I saw him. I will give him time to collect himself then I'll ask him to leave I thought as I cleaned the kitchen. James kept saying to himself, "okay okay, he leaned his head back on the couch shaking it over and over.

Oh God, I hoped he would leave soon, please let him pull it together and go. I thought as I watched him from the kitchen. I went back into the living room. "Uh James, are you okay?" I asked him. He just stared up at the ceiling. "I need to get some sleep, I have work in the morning," I tell him. "Okay Karis, just let me sit here a minute I need to think," he said. "Okay a minute, I'm going to my room, you can let yourself out when you're ready, alright?" I ask him.

"Yes Karis, I can let myself out," he says looking at me smiling. "Good night," he said. "Good night James," I said walking to my room with Cookie. We went in the room and sat on the bed. I waited to hear the door shut. I needed to use the bathroom, but I wanted James to leave first. I hoped he could forgive me and we could still be friends. After a while I heard the door shut. I took a deep breath and went to the bathroom. Thank God he was gone I thought, I had to use it so bad I almost peed my pants. I ran in and shut the door leaving it cracked for Cookie.

I relieved myself and wiped and got up to flush the toilet. Suddenly I'm grabbed by my waist, my pants were halfway up, I stumbled as I tried not to fall over the toilet seat. "You love me; I know you do." It was James; he didn't leave. I caught my balance and tried to reach to pull up my pants as my bottom was exposed. "James, get out of here!" I screamed at him. "Let go of me please James, let go!" I yelled. He had my waist so tight I couldn't move. "James, please don't, please let go," I said trying to pull his hands away from my waist. I pulled away he squeezed tighter.

"You love me, Karis, I know you do," he said in my ear. I could feel him pulling his pants down. "No James, you don't want to do this, don't please!" I yelled out. I screamed over and over. "No James, no please don't." I started moving all around trying to get away from him, but James had one arm holding me by the waist and the other trying to pull my pants down. I struggled with him, I stopped trying to pull my pants up and I went crazy swinging my arms around and kicking my feet. "James no, please, no!" I yelled.

He took his hand and held my head down with my back bent all the way over. He held my neck down, and with his arm around my waist I could feel him trying to force his penis into me, I screamed and tried to get out of his strong grip he forced it inside me as I yelled and screamed no. "I hate you James! I hate you; it's not yours!" I tell him. "It's not yours to take, James I hate you!" I yelled out as he kept forcing himself in and out of me, I could feel my body rejecting him it hurt so bad.

"James, I hate you I do, I hate you! I yelled out I scratched his arm, anything I could pull on and scratch or hit I did. "You love me," he kept saying. I screamed historically, I squeezed my legs together, I felt as if I was ripping apart, I was burning and ripping. "I hate you James, please stop don't do this to me, Oh god please make him stop!" I yelled. I heard a popping sound and I felt his fluids releasing into my body. I screamed as loud as I could as he let go of my waist. I turned around to him quickly and began to hit him and scream out.

"I hate you! I hate you! why did you do this to me? Get out of here James, get out!" I slapped his face and hit him I was so exhausted I still hit him and yelled and screamed. "You knew I was saving myself for Michael!" I yelled, "I hate you!" I was so hurt. "James, I never want to see your face again! Get out of my house now!" I yelled with tears streaming from my face I looked him straight in the eye. "Did you hear me, get out of my house, I never want to see your dirty face again! Ever! I said pointing to the door.

"I will never love you! I took a towel down from the counter and wiped between my legs just laid there on the bathroom floor clutching the towel, it felt as if I was on fire between my legs, I was bleeding, I moved over to the bath tub and ran warm water over the towel and put it back between my legs, the blood was coming down faster it seemed. I held the towel down there, I sat on the floor holding the towel and looking up at the ceiling. Oh, my God, James hurt me, God he hurt me I cried out, I loved him, and I was so hurt and disgusted with him. I cried holding the towel between my legs with my head in my lap.

Why James! I was sore, but I didn't hear the door shut I had to go and lock the door. I struggled to get up pulling myself up from the toilet seat I held the towel between my legs as I walked I took my pants completely off. I walked into the living room and James was on his knees on the floor crying." Karis," he said reaching his hands out to me. "I'm so sorry, please, Karis forgive me, I'm so sorry." he said crying.

"I didn't mean to hurt you, I love you so much," he said. "Please forgive me." "James if you don't leave my house right now I'm going to call the police," I tell him pointing at my door holding the towel. "Please leave my house, please!" I screamed at him to go. He jumped up from the floor and ran to the door. "I love you," he said shutting the door. I went to my room to call Martha, as soon as I reached for the phone it rang. I had to pull myself together before I picked it up, it maybe daddy or Krystal. I wasn't going to answer, but it rang and rang.

I didn't want to have to explain this to anyone until I could understand it myself. I picked it up "Hello," I said. "Hello," It was Michael "Hi baby, how are you?" He asked. I put the phone to my chest and held my head back to catch my breath, with tears streaming from my face. I cleared my throat. "I'm good Michael; I miss you." I tell him trying to sound normal I was crying inside trying to hold back the tears. "I miss you so much baby, I can't wait to hold you in my arms again," he says. I held the phone to my chest again crying. "I know I can't wait to see your face Michael," Michael went on telling me about Africa.

"The people are sick over here baby, there was a great need for us here, I'm learning a lot and working a lot, but I'm missing you like crazy," he said. "There's a growing virus over here, it's out of control, and the people don't have a lot of resources, it's so sad to watch every day," he tells me. I listen quietly trying not the cry out to him that I need him now. "So baby how have you been, have you started school yet?"

He asked me. "When I come back I expect you to have your degree in nursing, I'm going to start that private practice," he tells me.

"Yes I know, I go back in the fall," I tell him. "Baby I can't talk very long, I love you and miss you very much, you take care of yourself, baby." "I love you, Michael, write me okay," I tell him as we both hang up the phone. I held the phone close to my chest. Michael will not want to marry me after he finds out James did to me. Who will believe that he just took it from me, I thought I've known James for so long we have been close for all these years.

I have to call Martha. I put the phone to my ear and dialed her number. "Martha, please come over," I tell her as soon as she picks up, she stumbled over her words "What's wrong Karis?" She asked, "Martha, I can't tell you over the phone can you please come over here now, are you busy, please say no, come over please?" I begged her. She didn't have time to answer any of my questions as I started with a new one after every breath I took. "Hello," she said. "Calm down; I can't hear what you're trying to say, I have company, Karis."

"Martha I need you. I need you to come over here." "Does it have to do with something attacking you?" She asked me. "No, Martha it's personal, James was here and, I stopped myself, "can you please just come over here please Martha," I said crying "I need you" I said hanging up the phone crying thinking of what James did to me. I went back into the bathroom and turned on the shower. I was sore all over; I sat down on the toilet seat, it was hard to do I was so sore down there, the blood covered my thighs, it was sticky.

I had bruises in between my thighs leading up to my vagina. I was having a hard time coping with what James did, after all these years, he does this to me, and I can't ever trust him again. I'm afraid of him; it was the most disrespectful disgraceful thing he'd ever done, I didn't know how to understand it. How dare he, how dare he I thought crying thinking about it, who does he think he is? Did he think that it would be okay, I hate him I thought as I got into the shower. I washed my body until I couldn't anymore.

I was angry and hurt after washing in the shower I ran the bath water and sat in the tub. I was sore down there I ran the water so hot the it steamed the mirrors, the water was so hot I felt like me skin was burning off. I was red all over. I rubbed the soap all over me. I lay back in the tub to just soak in the scolding water. I put the wash cloth over my face and Cookie came in and stared at me. When she walked in it startled me. "Hello, Cookie," I said to her. She sat next to the tub looking at the toilet.

I soaked until my hands and feet were wrinkled. When I got out I sat on the edge of the tub staring at the toilet seat thinking of what he did to me. Flashes of the moment it happened began to flood my mind. I can't believe it I thought shaking my head crying. James hurt me, he was my closet friend, why would he do that to me if he loved me he would have never hurt me, I could see nothing but that moment, until I heard a knock at the door. I rushed up from the edge of the tub and grabbed a towel from the cabinet and wrapped myself up in it tight.

I took a small one and put it between my legs. I knew it would be Martha, she never let me down, I thought as I went to the door. I peeked through the peep hole in the door, it wasn't Martha, I couldn't make this persons face out. "Who is it?" I yelled out. "Uh, we're just in the neighborhood, we'd like to offer you a new cable service if you have the time I can come in and explain to you what we have?" The man said. He held his clip board to the peep hole. "It's free for a month if you order today," he said.

"No thank you!" I yell through the door. I turn away taking a deep breath, while walking back to my room to get dressed. I can't stop thinking about what James did to me, the moments continued to go through my mind. How could he I thought pulling my clothes from the drawer. I took one last look in the mirror before laying down, my neck was red also as if someone tied a rope around it and pulled it and pulled it, maybe I should just get a rope, why are all these bad things happening to me, I don't know if I should stay here on this earth, I thought. I lay on my bed with Cookie.

I woke up the next day even more sore, I got up and put on a turtle neck and my scrubs over it, I took Cookie to the kitchen for milk and tuna, I ate a piece of toast, I had a glass of water and grabbed an apple from the refrigerator, I left to my car soon after, I guessed Martha was tired of me, she never came over to see about me. I drove to work thinking about what James did. I don't want to ever see his face again. I thought as I pulled up to work. The day went by quickly, I finished up everything and went back home. I didn't call Maddy today and I didn't really speak to anyone. I finished my job and left.

When I arrived at home Martha's car was in the driveway. I pulled up beside her. She was looking out of the window. I walked up to the door and she opened it quickly. "Where you been old time friend?" She said laughing. "I had to work Martha, why didn't you come over last night?" I asked her picking up Cookie. I went over to the kitchen to make tea. Martha followed me in there. "So what was so urgent?" She asked standing in front of the sink. She began to tell me why she didn't make it over but I couldn't listen to her my thoughts were blurred with that day playing over and over in my head like a movie.

"Hello, Karis, do you hear the tea kettle whistling?" She shouted. "Oh," I grabbed it without a hand mitten. It was so hot I burned my hand I quickly put it down and went to the sink to run cold water over my hand, she grabbed a dish towel and wrapped my hand with it, "What the hell is wrong with you, is it still happening?" She asked. "Come sit down and talk to me, what's wrong?" She asked. "What happened, tell me fast because I have to go back to work, be careful though, I'm working with a cancer patient today and I don't know how much more sadness I can take." She said rolling her eyes over.

Martha's a registered nurse already and she's very good at it. She must have been working hard this week because she wasn't as fashionable as usual. "Tell me, hurry," she said. "James came over yesterday after work and I told him about Michael and me," I told her. "Well, what, he was hurt right?" She asked. "Yes he was, then he went mad," "What do you mean, he went mad?" "Well he came into the bathroom when I was using it, and he grabbed me by the back and forced himself on me."

"What! Are you sure Karis! Are you sure?" She asked me again. "Yes! Martha, I'm sure, he put his thing inside me," I told her. I am bleeding and bruised I showed her the bruise between my thighs. "I tried to get away from him but I couldn't, he held me down over the toilet by my neck" I showed her the back of my neck. "Are you sure it was him and not the spirits?" She asked me worried. "Martha it was him, he stayed after I asked him to let his self out; he kept saying he loved me."

"He told me he was sorry when he finished. I was fighting him, but he wouldn't stop." "I'm going to kill him," she said throwing her teacup across the room. "No Martha don't do that, I just wanted you to know what happened to me, I needed to tell someone, I can't tell Krystal or daddy, I know that daddy will kill him. He betrayed his trust. I wanted to know what I should do; I don't know what to do Martha. I don't want him to go to jail, we've known each other for so long, he's not that crazy, I thought maybe it was all my fault maybe I shouldn't have told him about Michael and me and I invited him here." I tell her.

Martha came over to me and grabbed me by the shoulders. She shook me. "Are you out of your mind Karis! He raped you! You were raped last night!" She yelled at me. "No matter what he thought or felt in that moment, he was wrong!" She yelled at me staring at me in my eyes. "He was wrong to touch you anywhere when you didn't want him to" She took her keys from the coffee table and snatched me by the arm.

"We are going to the police station to file a report." Martha said almost throwing me into the passenger seat of the car.

She sped out of the driveway as quickly as she could. My head was spinning. "You can't believe that he didn't know better Karis, he knew better. He just thinks he's going to get away with it because you've known him for so long." She drove faster through the streets catching every light I held onto the door handle. "I'm sure you don't want him to get away with this, right Karis, because if he gets away with it this time, he'll do it again to someone else or maybe even you again, if he gets the chance."

"I can't believe this happened to you, all this time you've spent with him. He should be ashamed of himself, but he probably isn't, I'm going to tell uncle Earl, and he will be sorry he ever met you soon." She said speeding up into the police station parking lot. "Martha I don't want to get him in trouble, I don't want to destroy him, and I know what he did was wrong, but must I destroy him? Isn't there something else that could be done maybe I can make him go to some counseling?" I tell her as she reaches to open my door.

"I wished that I could go back to that night, I would have made him leave before going to the bathroom." I told her as I seen flashes of that night. "Martha, he just went mad, he couldn't take what I said," I tell her. "It's not your fault Karis and really if he went mad because he couldn't take a little rejection, then that's even worse, Karis get out of the car, you can't allow him to get away with this," She pushed my door open and walked over to my side of the car and pulled me out. "I don't care if he went mad, now we're madder," she said pulling me up to the entrance of the police station. "I had to go in and tell them what he did there was no getting around it we were there "Martha, are you sure about this?" She grabbed me by the arm, and we walked into the station.

Mini Miracles

There was a line to the counter. I was unsure of this, I just stood behind Martha, I wanted to run out of there, but I knew that she would run after me. I looked over her shoulders at the people ahead of us. "This is going to take a while," the man in the back of us said. "If you're here to file a complaint it could take all night," he said pointing over to the wall where the clock was. "I've been here since 6:30 am; it's just one line after another." "Well thank god we're not here for that," Martha said rolling her eyes at the man.

"Martha, don't be rude," I told her pulling on her shirt. "It will take time, and after it's filed they do nothing," the man went on talking he turned away from us. We made it to the middle of the line. "Martha, I want to go, I will do this later," I tell her. "No, now," she said. "If we don't do it now we will risk the chance of ever having something done about it!" "I'm just not sure Martha, I'm scared for James; he could go to jail. He could lose all he ever worked for, and I don't want to be responsible for that," I tell her.

"I just think he needs help; something went wrong in his mind." "Yes something did go wrong, and today he'll regret ever letting it get to that point," Martha said. "They will be all the help he needs." She said as we moved closer to the front desk. We talked until we reached the counter, when we made it the policeman stared across the counter at us. "Hello, how can I help you two?" He asked us. Martha came right out and said it. "I would like to report a rape," The policeman stood back.

"Hold on a minute I'll be right back." He said rushing over to the room to speak with another officer. He came back quickly with a female officer. She leaned over the counter and whispered. "Which one of you was raped?" She asked pointing her pen at the both of us, Martha pointed at me, "Come with me," she said guiding me to go around to the back counter. She led me to a very cold small room. "Hi, I'm officer Gracy Bennett," she reached out to shake my hand. "I'm going to be asking you a series of questions, I, need you to tell me in detail what happened when and who did this?" She said in a stern voice.

"After these questions, we will do a physical test to check your body, have you ever heard of a rape kit before?" She asked. I shook my head yes. "Well then, let's get started, do you know the person who assaulted you?" I shook my head yes, where did it happen?" "At my house," I tell her. She went on asking question after question. After she was done another officer came in with a nurse. "We need you to take off everything you have on so that we can get some pictures," one of them said. I took off my clothes and stood by the table.

"Can you show us where the bruises are?" They asked. I turned around and held my hair up so that they could see the mark on the back of my neck, as I stood there showing them all the marks and bruises that night kept flashing through my head. "Here you go," The nurse handed me a blanket. "Wrap up in this and lay back on the table please, this is the hard part." She said looking at the other officers. I lay back on the table and she began to examine me. I was so sore.

"I know honey; it will be over soon," she said. It felt as if she was poking me with something in my vagina. When she was done they helped me sit up. "You can get dressed now," Officer Bennett told me. I was crying. "Honey, it will   be fine we will find this guy and bring him in, and don't worry, everything you told us remains confidential, we don't share this information with anyone until we go to court." She tells me flapping her notepad over. She pulled the curtain around me and walked out.

The other officer came back "Hi, I'm Officer Sharp, I noticed you only gave us his first name, do you know his last name?" She asked. "And do you happen to know where he lives, or any of his relatives?"

She asked me I would tell them about his grandmother, but she just had surgery Mrs. Cotton would be devastated if they went to her home to get James. I shook my head no. "I'm sorry, I don't know where he lives, I know that he's in the navy," I tell her.

"Well, if you should see Mr. James before we do, please call us, don't tell him about this report, just pick up the phone and call us please," she said handing me a business card. I took it and put the blanket I was wrapped up in, that I threw into the hamper on the side of the bed. "Are you ready?" Officer Bennett said. "I'll be escorting you back into the front," I can't believe what I just did. I thought as I walked alongside Officer Bennett. Martha was waiting firmly, clinching her purse tightly as if it was going to be stolen at the police station.

"Hurry up girl," she said to me. I walked toward her quickly. "I have been out here too long, the people coming in here are so scary," she said as Officer Bennett let me out from behind the front counter. "You bet they are," Officer Bennett said to Martha smiling. "I deal with these types every day, but this is nothing, you should see when we do a sweep" "A sweep, that sounds scary," Martha said. "Thank you officer Bennett," I said waving goodbye. "You remember what I told you, if you should see him before we do, please give us a call." "I will," I said walking toward the door. We walked to the parking lot.

"Was it bad?" Martha asked. "No, it was okay." I said getting into the car. "What did they do to you back there, I know they didn't just sit and talk, right?" She said starting the car. "No, they took pictures, and they did a rape kit, they asked me a lot of questions about James, like where he lived and what happened." "Did you tell them?" She asked looking over at me. "I did, I told them everything" I told her putting her mind at ease.

"Good, that bastard needs to get his butt kicked for doing what he's done, of all the rotten things to do," she said shaking her head. She went on about him all the way to the house. When we pulled up Cookie was sitting in the window ceil waiting for me as always. "Are you coming in?" I asked her. "No, I have to get to work, hey Karis can I tell you something?" She asked, "I know I shouldn't ask, but were you a virgin?" She asked holding on to my arm. "Yes, I was," I tell her. "Did he use a condom?" "I don't know Martha; all I know is that it hurt so bad."

"Oh no Karis, Oh my god, you might get pregnant!" She yelled with her hand over her mouth. "No, calm down Martha, that's never going to happen, I can't have children remember. I can't; the doctor told mama and daddy that I will never be able to have them, because of my pelvis. I will never be able to carry them, so don't worry okay," I said holding her hand. "And they tested me for all of the diseases, they'll call me if they find anything, so please don't worry okay." I told her hugging her.

I got out and went into the house. I waved goodbye as I opened the door. I went into the bathroom for another shower, as always Cookie followed me everywhere, I picked her up along the way just to feel her fur, it gave me some comfort knowing she was there with me. I went to the kitchen to give her more milk and tuna. I stood and watched her drink and eat as that night flashed in my mind over and over. I cringed at the thought of ever seeing James again. As I began to walk back into the bathroom to get in the shower the doorbell rang.

I went to the door and looked through the peephole. Oh no, it was James. I turned my back to the door in a panic, what does he want? I will not open this door for him, "Karis, I know you're in there!" He yelled. I didn't say a word, I will give five seconds to leave and then I would call the police. I thought I turned back around to look out of the peep hole; he was standing there at the door ringing the bell over and over again. "Karis please! Please! Talk to me; I just want to talk to you; I was wrong!" He yelled out.

"I know that you're in there!" I stared through the peephole as he explained why he was there. "Don't shut me out   Karis, please don't, I didn't mean to hurt you, please let me explain!" He yelled and yelled and rang the bell over and over. "Please tell me you're listening. After a while he went over to the window trying to look in. I moved over to the wall so that he couldn't see me. "Are you listening to me, Karis? I am so sorry, please say you'll forgive me; I never meant to hurt you."

He went back over to the doorbell and started ringing it again. "Karis please," he said dropping to his knees and crying, "please, forgive me." He cried on the porch with his hands on his head. I watched him and prayed. Lord, please heal James, he has lost his mind lord, please give him understanding, and help him to understand that what he did was wrong. I cannot, and I will not ever forget it, I pray that he gets the help he needs.

I pray Lord have mercy on him, show him the way to your salvation." I put my hand on the door. "James I forgive you, now, please go away." I walked away from the door; I went back into the bathroom and got into the shower. I closed my eyes and let the water run down my face. What a day I thought, Lord, I don't know what to do anymore if it isn't one thing it's another, but I do thank you, Lord, I just don't understand why after all of what I've been through, why more lord. I said to myself washing the soap off.

I got out and dried myself with the towel; I wrapped up in it and walked into my bedroom. I grabbed another towel out off of the bed rail and washed my face off with it, I closed my eyes with it, and when I opened them Mr. Simms was standing in front of me, I jumped startled to see him there. "It's okay sweetheart; it's me, Mr. Simms," he said smiling. I backed up into the dresser. "You're getting it now," he said. I started to talk to him, when I turned around form the drawer he was gone. "Mr. Simms," I said looking all around the room. Mr. Simms.

"What am I getting?" I yelled out. I put on my uniform quickly, and went into the living room brushing my hair, what am I getting I wondered as I looked around for Mr. Simms. I noticed Cookie staring at the bathroom door; I went over to her, hey Cookie, "Mr. Simms where are you?" I said out loud. I put the brush down and left the bathroom. I wore my ponytail tight and up today. I was so exhausted. I took one look at the clock, and it was already getting too late, I ran for the door with my keys, so that I wouldn't be late for work.

I got in my car and drove off when I saw Mr. Simms in my rear view mirror standing in the window waving at me. I waved back I had no time to get the answers to my questions now. Why was he always around? I wondered as I drove as fast as I could to work. He is no relative of mine nor is he a close friend. I didn't know what to think of it. I parked quickly and got out and ran into the hospital. I made it to the front desk to get my assignment, today I worked on the fourth floor and up. No problem I thought, I can handle this today.

There was a posting on the wall with the details of Mr. Simms funeral service, next to it was a family photo all around the photo everyone wrote a pray for them, some wrote more than others. I decided I would write when I finished working today. I didn't want to rush through my prayers. I went to the fourth floor, on the way up I ran into James' sister. "Hello, how are you?" She asked. I looked at her and smiled. "I'm okay," I walked faster to get away from her; I didn't want to talk to her. I went quickly past to catch the elevator. She followed right behind me.

"My grandmother's getting out today," she tells me. "That's great, how is Mrs. Cotton?" I asked her. I felt bad; I hadn't had any time to see her since she's stayed here. "Give her a hug for me please," I tell her pushing the button for the elevator to come down. "Are you going up?" I asked looking at her. She stood there as if she wanted to talk more. "No, I just wanted to say hi," she said walking away. "See you later," she waved.

"Yes, sure, I'll see you later," I said smiling at her while the elevator closed. I would be working with Dr. Green today he was old and liked to do things the old fashion way. There would be no cutting corners today, I was grateful for the experience to work with him, but it would be a long day. I thought as I went to the first room I was assigned to. I met up with him in room 413 he was going on talking to the RN about what medication the patient should have been on and how often he should be checked and cleaned. The patient was very sick, but he wasn't going anywhere for he was a fighter.

"Hello Karis, good to see you are joining us today," Dr. Green said to me. "Hello Dr. Green, how are you today?" I replied back with a smile. "I hear you, and one of my best students will be tying the knot soon," he says smiling looking down at me through his glasses I swallowed hard. "Yes, Dr. Green, how did you know that?" "I keep in contact with all my up and coming students, Michael will be an excellent doctor; I'm hoping he'll stay on board with us." He said moving all around checking the patient.

"If he stays here, he'll become one of the greatest doctors ever lived." He said winking his eye at me smiling. "So young lady you better go back to school so you and young Dr. Michael can make a good living together. For your young children, when you have them of course." He said. I shake my head yes. If only I could give Michael a family. I thought as I listened on to Dr. Green talking to the patient. "Young lady, young lady, are you okay?" He asked. I drifted off into my thoughts.

What if Michael doesn't even want me anymore after he finds out what James did to me? "Oh, Dr. Green I'm okay, I was just thinking about how much I miss him," I told him. "You know   Karis; he's doing something that only a man with a strong heart and soul can do, he truly loves what he does." He tells me. "I know Dr. Green, but can someone tell my selfish heart that, I just want him here with me." I tell him as I take the sheets off of the patient's bed. "I know what you mean; my wife went over there when we first got together.

That year without her here was complete hell for me, You'll find yourself feeling alone and incomplete for a while, but when it all comes back together, it will all be worth the wait believe me." He said winking his eye again. "Yes, I am quite lonely," I said grabbing the water pitcher from the patients eating tray. "But you can go to school while he's gone get your nursing license, and be ready to start your family when he gets back," he tells me. "You could even try getting your doctrine, and come do your residency with me," he said laughing.

"I'd like to see if you're as tough as you pretend to be," he said lifting his eyebrows. "I bet you'd love being under my instruction for a year or two huh?" He laughed again and looked at the nurse standing beside him. She didn't say a word she was focused on the patient. She was taking blood and putting a new IV in his arm. He walked over to the next bed and began checking the patient over. "Sure, Dr. Green I'd love that, but I think I will stick to just being a registered nurse," I tell him following him over to the patient.

After we were done in there we went from room to room. Dr. Green was a stickler for the rules too; we spent most of the day altering things that the team before us changed while he was gone, I try not to make any mistakes with any of his patients. I prayed for lunch to come soon. "Have a nice lunch dear." Dr. Green told the nurse, he tapped on his watched as she stood over the patient trying to straighten out his pillows.

Good, we're finally taking a break, I thought as I washed down the patient's tray table. I put the towel in the sink and headed out to the cafeteria. I would have the special today their serving hamburgers and fries, I grabbed a tray and stood in line when I got the food I held ketchup and mustard packets in my hand and carried my tray to the patio. I just wanted to ta take a nice quick, quiet break; I thought as I walked towards the back door. I went to put my hand on the door to push it opened and someone stepped in front of me.

"I got..." Oh no, it's James' little sister again. "Thank you so much," I tell her walking through the door. I went and sat on the bench near the trees. I began to eat; I tried to eat quickly watching James little sister standing in the cafeteria trying deciding what she was having. Why does she keep trying to talk to me? I wondered I didn't want to talk to her too much. I watched her get her tray she stood looking at the tables inside then she turned back and looked out at the patio. I put my head down as if I didn't see her.

Oh god, don't let her come out here. I thought as I put a fry in my mouth, please, please don't come over here, I think to myself. "Hi again," she said standing in front of me with her tray. "Are you on your break?" She asked. I shook my head yes and smiled. I put another fry in my mouth; Please don't ask me if you can eat with me please don't, I thought to myself. "Hey, if you don't mind, could I eat with you?" I pretended I didn't hear at first then I looked up at her and smiled.

"Sure have a seat, I won't be here long," I say reaching for my plate. "Thank you,   Karis." She sat down at the table and began shaking her bottle of juice. God, I hope she doesn't start talking to me about James. I put mustard on my burger and began eating. She drank her juice slowly watching me to see what I would do next. As soon as she was done sipping she began with the questions. "So how is it working here, do you like the patients?" She went on and on asking questions before I could finish chewing my food to answer there would be another.

I swallowed and looked up at her. "I could never work in a place like this," she explained. "It's not bad," I tell her wiping my mouth with a napkin. "There are so many reasons for loving this job, but if I had to choose one, it would be because I love helping people." I tell her putting all of my trash into my tray. "When I get older, I'm going to be an attorney," she said smiling at me "Really why an attorney?" I asked her.

"I want to defend people who can't defend themselves." "Oh I see, well good luck, it sounds fascinating." "I can't see myself doing anything other than what I'm doing right now," I tell her getting up with my tray in my hands. "I start school in a few weeks I can't wait. I plan to become a registered nurse, but now I have to go back in Teresa, it was very nice seeing you again, have a good day okay and remember to tell Mrs. Cotton I say hello okay." "Karis, I like you, wouldn't it be nice if we became sisters," she said smiling up at me.

"My brother says he's going to marry you soon is that true? You're all he talks about." I looked down; I wasn't going to talk about her brother, that night began to flash through my mind. "I have to go now; I truly enjoyed your company." I told her walking toward the trash can. "I guess, I'll see you later," she said waving. I waved back, oh God I thought, the thought of seeing or talking about James made me feel ill. I wondered if he'd even thought about going to the police station to turn himself in, I went back to work hoping that it would be ending quickly. I was beginning to get tired already.

I went to the sixth floor next; as I approached the doors to room 601, I read the sign on the door. There has been a patient added to this room; please change the bedding before the arrival of the patient, it read. I opened the door and went inside; I have to change the bedding on three beds and check the vitals on each patient. I hoped none of them needed a sponge bath or anything hard tonight; I began to change the sheets on the beds moving as quickly as I could, and I filled all of the water containers, and put juice and crackers on each tray.

While I started to clean each bed, I noticed Mr. Simms sitting in the chair across from the beds. "Hello young lady," he says in a whisper, I ignore him, I know he's not really there. I continue working when I finished, I walked out into the hall, and he followed. "Young lady, what's your hurry?" He called out to me following me down the hall. "I have work to do," I tell him in a whisper. I know he's not really here; people were walking all around the hallway. I didn't want them to assume that I was speaking to myself.

I was trying to be very careful. "Young lady, I don't want anything, I would like to give you something, I've told you what's ahead for you, and would you like to know more?" He asked holding his hand out to me. I shook my head no. He winked his eye at me a turned away. "I'll see you later, young lady," he whispered. I watched as he walked down the hall there was a dark shadow walking beside him. I continued on the sixth floor, two more rooms left after this I'd be done.

I'm heading down to the front desk to write my sympathy note on the wall for Maddy's family. I thought about Mr. Simms; I was certain that whatever had to show me wouldn't help me any more than the Indians did. I made it back up to the sixth floor just in time for shift change, there was doctors and nurses running around everywhere, talking in the halls, updating the other nurses, I stood there watching waiting for Dr. Green to finish up so that he could tell me that we were done for the day, as I was waiting I watched as a dark shadow moves in and out of the crowed making its way towards me.

It doesn't come to close but it stands in front of me, I stand still as the cold air hits my body as if It carried it along with it, I stare at it as if I'm not afraid, it walks past me down the hall toward the other rooms on the floor. "Karis, Karis, are you okay?" Dr. Green asked grabbing my shoulders and turning me around towards him, my head swung around following them, "Hi Dr. Green, yes, I'm okay," I tell him. "You were staring down the hall as if you saw something scary; there's no time for daydreaming on the job," he said placing his pen in his front pocket.

"Good job today young lady, we have one more floor to do and we will all go home," he said with his arm folded. "Get your head together and follow me," he said with his glasses hanging down. I was right; I thought this day would never end. I turned and followed him down the hallway; he talked all the way there. I cannot get a word in, and just when I was going to ask him about the time he began to tell me why he liked me.

"You're good Karis I can see that you love this job as much as I do. You care for the patient's; you're going to make a great nurse." He said looking at the patient's chart. My shift was over; I needed to go home and rest, I thought as he continued talking. "You have a genuine love for this job; you have to love it to do it right?" He says to me tugging at his glasses. "Do you know it's a gift to love people and want to care for them, did you know that it was a gift?"

"Yes, I do love this job Dr. Green, I love everything about it," I tell him following him around the room. Wishing the day would end by now, my feet were hurting from all the standing and walking we did today. "Don't know about being a doctor? Michael works very hard, and he feels troubled when he can't help someone." "Yes well, it's natural for a doctor to have that kind of frustration when they can't cure a patient or get rid of their pain.

It becomes a burden when someone you're trying to treat doesn't get any better. The important thing is always to remember that you did you're best to cure the patient all you could do you try. Michael has to remember that, you keep caring for the patient no matter what the outcome. Maybe, they would be one of his patients." We walked out of the room and down the   hall, Dr. Green walked beside me, he was finally finished with us.

The nurses seemed to be happy; they were walking down the hall as fast as their legs could carry them away from Dr. Green. I was thankful for the lessons but also tired. I finished up and went to the nurse station to sign my time sheet, as I walked toward the front desk I noticed a nurse at the desk talking to a police officer. I walked up closer and grabbed the clipboard from the desk; the policeman had his back turned towards me. I listened in, as he explains to the nurse why he was looking for me. I leaned over the desk and tapped the other nurse on the shoulder.

"Hello Karis, we were just about to page you over the intercom. These nice officers said they need to talk to you," she said with a smile flirting with the male officer. She grabbed me by the hand, "Here she is, Karis, this is Officer Sam and his partner" "Hi, Officer Bennett." I said before the nurse could say anything else. "How are you?" "Hi, Karis can we talk somewhere in private?" Officer Bennett said tapping her pen to her notepad, "Sure, we can go down the hall in the chapel, its quiet there," I tell her walking toward the hallway, we strolled down the hallway.

Their boots stomped loudly over the wooden floors as we walked. We go inside the chapel, I sit in the pew next to the door and they stand over me. "Am I in some trouble?" I asked them. "Did you need something else from me?" "No," Officer Bennett said. "We came to inform you about your case Mr. James Cotton turned himself in," she said smiling. "He confessed to being at your house that night; he tells us that you invited him into the bathroom that night and that you told him that everything was fine between you two.

He explained that you two were making out and you only asked him to stop when he turned you around. He says he did not attack you, is this true, did he attack you?" "Yes, he did!" I yelled out reliving that moment in my head all over again. "He did attack me, I told him to stop, I begged him and pleaded with him to stop. I don't know what he thinks, but he did attack me, it happened, it did, he raped me. I didn't ask for it, we were friends, he betrayed me." "We understand Karis, just calm down and talk to us, how long have you known James?" The other officer asked.

"I've known him for years longer than I can remember, that doesn't make what he did to me okay." "Do you think that this could be all a misunderstanding, maybe you liked him and gave into the friendship, sometimes it happens like that. Do you think that maybe you misunderstood what was going on?" "No sir, there was no misunderstanding," I looked up at him with a frown, "James knew I was a virgin, this was no mistake, I'd never had intercourse before, I was saving myself for marriage, I am engaged to be married, sir." I say to them I began to cry.

Now James was telling lies, I never even knew who he really was I thought as they continued questioning my behavior that night. "So you never consented to have sex with him, is that what you're telling us? You didn't consent to do this at all?" "He has always been my friend, but he just kept pushing for more. That night I told him that I was going to be married soon. I wanted to continue our friendship, but he wanted more.

He was upset and said he would leave, but he didn't. He came into the bathroom after me and forced himself on me," I explained crying. "Okay Karis, okay, don't cry," Officer Bennett said as she handed me some tissue from the table next to the bible. "Karis, we just wanted to make sure your story was the truth. We need to know the truth about that night, we will continue to   investigate, and we will be in contact with you soon, meanwhile stay away from James." Officer Sam says as they walk out of the chapel.

Wow, now he's going to deny what he did, deny that he raped me. I should tell my dad, I thought as I walked out wiping my eyes, but I know what daddy would do to him. Daddy liked to take justice into his own hands at times. I went out to the front desk sauntering, I see coming toward me the dark shadow again. I look straight ahead trying not to acknowledge what I see the hallway grew colder as I walked past it, I could feel its presence closing in on me. I try to focus on what I was going to the front desk to do, which was to finish my time card, I thought.

I was still baffled at what I just heard, all I could do was think about how wrong he was and what went wrong with him. He betrayed me and then lied to the police to save himself; I closed my eyes. He was willing to turn himself in, only to lie I wondered what else he has told them? I dared to tell Martha what he'd done; she would go back down there and make them do something about his lies. I stood close to the wall scratching on a piece of paper.

"What's the matter?" one of the nurses asked me. "Oh, nothing, I'm just thinking, that's all I'll be out of your hair as soon as I finish my time card." I tell her, I finished up the card and placed it in the desk drawer. I said goodbye to everyone and headed down to my car, as I walked toward the door, there standing ahead at the exit was Mr. Simms. He was smiling and waving at me, when I approached him I walk even faster toward the door acting as if I didn't see him. He walked along side me out of the door. "Hello, young lady, how are you doing tonight?" He asked me.

"I'm good Mr. Simms I say walking to my car, "I came back to ask if you noticed yet?" He said smiling at me. "Noticed, noticed what Mr. Simms?" I ask him. "They're always around aren't they?" "I don't know what you're talking about Mr. Simms," I tell him as I got into the car he got in behind me. "Oh, I know you've seen it," he tells me I drove off. "I suppose you mean the dark, cold shadow following me around, right?" I asked him.

"Oh dear," he said laughing "That's not just any old shadow, see that shadow is your eye opener, you watch out for it, study it when it appears, make sure you look around. It's here for you; it won't hurt you at all, I bet you think you're all alone? You're not, young lady; there are many of us out there, you don't know how special you are. It's best you keep praying and do what comes naturally to you, what you feel is what you know."

I looked over to the passenger seat as I pulled into my driveway and he disappeared. I looked over to the front door, and he was standing at the gate waving goodbye to me as he faded away into the darkness. I got out of the car and went inside. I know what I feel most of the time, it still doesn't stop me from being fearful at times, I thought as I go inside and take Cookie from the window seal. The house still filled with the smell of flowers all over. I put Cookie on the floor of the kitchen while I get her cat food and milk ready.

I began to undress removing my shirt and pants to take a shower, as I approach the bathroom; I relive that night all over, closing my eyes as I walk toward the doors to turn on the shower. I cry, James has the nerve to tell them that he was invited in here I thought. I couldn't believe him; I will never speak to him again as long as I live. I showered quickly and went to my bed, I wrote in my journal before covering myself with the covers. Lord, thank you for today, I have never thought that my closet friend could be an enemy, but he is my enemy. Lord, fix him from ever telling a lie again. Lord, he took something precious away from me, he betrayed me, I forgave him, and he betrayed me again.

Lord, please help me to overcome what happened that night, I know I can't change what happened I can't forget it. Lord, give me the strength to overcome it, in Jesus name I pray Amen. I put my pen down, and Cookie jumped on the bed beside me. I fell off to sleep quickly. The next morning Cookie was licking my eyelids. I sat up in bed; I had overslept I jumped from the bed running all over the house trying to do everything all at once. I ran through the house grabbing for my keys and bag. I washed my face and brushed my teeth quickly packing a lunch while walking around the house.

I put more milk into Cookies bowel, and I left for work. When I made it to the hospital, there was a lot of traffic going in the emergency room. So, I took the back entrance instead of walking through the crowd. I came up toward the back approaching the front desk from the back. I saw as I got closer the James and his little sister standing talking to the desk clerk. I had to get to my time sheet. I leaned over the desk for the drawer hoping no one would notice me when the desk clerk turned around. "Hey Karis, we've been expecting you," she said.

I put my finger to my lips to shish her I shook my head, grabbing for my time sheet. I turned my back to look at the door, and they were standing in front of me. "Hi Karis," his little sister said. I looked at James. "Hi Teresa, how are you?" I said signing my time sheet. James was holding a bundle of roses, he reached out to hand them to me, and I grabbed the clipboard from the counter. "Karis, you are working the seventh floor today," the nurse tells me. "Aren't you going to take the flowers?" Teresa said pushing James toward me with them.

"I would, but I can't, I have to start my shift now." I tell her, she was smiling so hard it looked as if her face would crack. "I will see you later Teresa, thanks for coming to see me," I tell her as I walked away. I walked faster towards the elevator. When I made it to the seventh floor there was an old man standing in the hallway with a walker. "Do you need help?" I asked him. He smiled at me. "No young lady, thank you," I started working right away.

I turned down five beds and gave three patients sponge baths. I took my patient's vitals and laughed and talked to them as I worked and cleaned their rooms. The day was going by quickly, I was glad that Dr. Green would be in meetings all day. My day would have become much longer had he'd been there. When I finished the day I went back down the elevator to the front desk to sign my time card, there was James again, this time standing alone. I passed him as if I didn't even see him. I took my time card out and signed it and went for my bag and sweater in the back room. "How dare he?" I said walking towards the door.

"The nerve of him," I said as I passed him. Nurse Cheri was walking alongside me "Is there something wrong Karis, are you okay?" She asked "I'm just a little frustrated that's all," I tell her. "Looks like you should be happy that someone thought of you," she tells me looking at the flowers, "All flowers aren't good flowers," I tell her walking faster towards the door, see you tomorrow, with a wave.

I walked down toward the side door to avoid James and his little sister. When I passed through the side door Teresa was standing at the vending machine buying a snack. "Hi Karis," she said. I walked by quickly. "Hello, again," I tell her hurrying past. She noticed James chasing me and began to yell for me to come back. I got into my car quickly." Karis, Karis," she yelled. I turned my head and turned my radio on really loud as I began to turn the key to the ignition she poked her head into the window.

"Nice car, Karis, when can I go for a ride" She asked smiling, "my brothers looking for you," she said pointing at James coming up behind her. "Maybe one day when I have a day off I'll take you for a ride," I tell Teresa, "but now, I have to go okay." as James walked up to my car I turn the key to my ignition and drive off looking angry at him. Why doesn't he get it? I thought as I drove away from them watching them from my rearview mirror. I don't plan on talking to him ever again.

I will never forget that moment in the bathroom; I feel I might as well had never gone to the police. After what he told them, they would never make him pay for what he did. Now he wants to tell me he's sorry; I don't ever want to see him again I thought as I drove home. I drove faster and faster. I want to hear from Michael; at least I was hoping that he would call me tonight. When I made it home, I pulled up and went inside and picked Cookie up holding her to my chest.

I thought if nothing else Cookie would make me feel better tonight. I walked around the house with Cookie and then back to the couch. I took off my shoes and laid back on the couch, Cookie laid across my stomach purring and rubbing her nose into my shirt. It was freezing cold in the house. I closed my eyes when Cookie stopped rubbing her nose on the shirt I looked up to see why she was staring into the window and there it was again the dark shadow. I sat up and as I breathed in and out I could see my breath in the cold air of the house.

I went over to the window where the dark shadow was, with Cookie in my arms I looked out not fearing what I might see. Cookie looked afraid with her eyes piercing toward the window. I pet her back, comforting her, I would no longer fear it I thought. "Cookie, don't worry," I tell her rubbing her back. I walked toward the kitchen, and I began to smell the foul odor, it was fouler than ever before. It seemed to be fuming through the whole house as I walked through with Cookie. I took her to the bedroom and sat her on the bed; it was getting colder and colder.

I was shivering when I reached the back room I wanted to open the back door to allow in some fresh air. When I reached out to slide it open something grabbed me by the wrist and began to twist it, I twisted my wrist around to grab hold of it. I wouldn't allow it to get the best of me this time. For some reason I felt like fighting back, it pushed me with a strong force. I went flying toward the glass door of the room. I was on the floor, immediately I stood up on my knees and began to pray.

"Lord, protect me today, for this evil spirit has come to play, I will not allow it to stay. I'm closing all doors to hell where he'll go and stay." I don't know where these words came from, but they flowed from my mouth like water streams over the falls. I repeated them over and over again as it shook me with its mighty force. I will fight it this time, trying to pull it in closer to me; I wanted to feel what it was, I wouldn't allow it just to attack and leave I wanted it to face me. I can't see it, but I felt it all around me, it began to shake me I moved my arms around to feel the shape of it.

Soon, I was upside down as if it had me by my legs. Still, I didn't fear it; its force was strong and cold, I closed my eyes and began to grab at whatever I felt. "Take me in!" I screamed. "Take me in; I want to see what you are!" I held on to it, when I opened my eyes there it was not a spirit, but a demon was staring back into my eyes, I looked at its shape. I took my hand and grabbed onto its neck, and with my knees, I kicked into its body sending it to the ground. It roared at me as if to scare me, but I was no longer afraid. I no longer feared it; my knees were planted into its chest.

"You go back to hell!" I screamed "You go back to hell, you go back there! I held onto its throat with my hands, it began to grab at my face as if it was reaching out for my eyes. I went for its eyes, it grabbed onto my hands and placed them on its head, and it was clear, I could see its hell now. Visions of a man violently raping and beating a young man flowed through my mind like a quick picture show; I closed my eyes and began to pray.

"Lord, please lead him back to hell his soul lingers here between worlds bind his spirit lord to bind him back never to return here." I said this prayer out loud. I held onto the spirit and prayed and prayed. "Lord, take him back to hell where he belongs, his path has ended here on this earth now he must go back to hell where he belongs." I prayed and prayed as his grip began to loosen and the odor faded. I felt warmth all around me and then the sweet smell of flowers surrounded me.

Oh Lord, am I free now, did you bind the spirits from me? I prayed for myself, keep me close lord don't let me go. I cried as I laid on the floor praying to God for his mercy. I couldn't move at all. I felt as if my body was tiny. I prayed and prayed until the darkness turned to light; the smell of the flowers filled the air around me. I knew then that I would be alright. Cookie came over to me she lay next to me purring until I moved.

I felt exhausted pulling myself up off the floor was so complicated, but I felt good inside. Once I was up I felt so much joy as if I was a winner of the greatest prize, I smiled and smiled, Glory to god! I shouted "thank you, Lord, thank you," I shouted around the house. "There is nothing like your grace," I walked around my house just thanking God. "I know now, I know." I said aloud; I can face the demon and turn his spirit back, I wasn't afraid anymore I would be ready next time with the Lord by my side.

I went into the bathroom to take my shower. I turned on the water and began to undress I got into the shower and soaped up quickly all over my face and body when the phone rang. I washed the soap off my face and reached for my towel. It may be Michael I thought as I wrap myself up in the towel racing to the phone covered in bubbles. "Hello," I said picking up the receiver, "Hello, how are you?"

It was James; I quickly hang up. I wasn't going to allow him to steal my joy tonight I thought, why was he calling me? I went back to my shower to finish washing, where did he come from I wondered as I washed up, he violated me in the worst way. He hurt me; did he think that I would just get over it? I wondered as I stepped out of the shower, I stood in the mirror looking at my hair and body. Ugh, I was a complete mess; I have to get myself together really.

I thought stretching my eyes and mouth with my hand. I wrapped the towel around my waist and began to brush my hair into a ponytail as I did all the time; it was the easiest hairstyle for me. It had grown so long I'd do anything to keep it from falling into my face, I took the towel off to lotion up, and I noticed two handprints on my chest, I rubbed Vaseline over them and continued to groom myself. I could smell the flowers around the house when I was done. There was a knock at the door as I was walking to my bedroom.

I rushed in to put on some clothes to answer it. "Please hold on; I'm coming," I yelled. I ran to the door and looked into the peephole. "Who is it?" I yelled the peephole was blocked. "I'm not opening my door unless you show your face!" I yelled out. I looked out again, it was James. "Go away!" I yell out to him "Go away, or I will call the police" I screamed. "I will call my dad too; you need to leave me alone, I never want to see you again!" I tell him hitting the door with my fist.

"Go away James, Go away!" I yelled and yelled I walked away from the door I could see the door knob twisting as if he was trying to open it. I walked quickly to my bedroom I went in shutting the door behind me. I could still hear him at the door twisting the knob I cracked the door and looked out. I could see his shadow at the window; I came out of my room to the kitchen to get a knife as I went for the knife in the drawer I could see his shadow moving back and forth toward the window. I went to the door I looked out of the peephole.

"James if your still there, I will not allow you to scare me, I will tell you this, I have the right to defend myself, you are trespassing on my property if you force your way into my home to harm me, I will kill you I have that right!" I yelled out to him. He was holding and twisting the doorknob then suddenly he stopped. "Don't ever come back James or I will do to you what the police should have done!" I screamed. I took Cookie and the knife, and we went back into my room, I lay on my bed taking deep breathes.

"My God, that was so intense," I said to myself breathing heavily. The nerve of this man, I closed my eyes and pictured in my mind, what if what he did to me was done to him? If I could violate him the way he did me, I'd probably be thrown in jail quickly; I thought I curled up with Cookie on the bed I fell off to sleep. As I fell deeper to sleep, I began to dream of two little children a boy and a girl, both beautiful. I was sitting on daddy's front lawn playing with them; they looked happy laughing and playing with me.

I was woken up by the sound of the phone ringing again, I reached over Cookie and picked up the receiver. "Hello," I said still a little sleepy. "Hello baby," Michael said excitedly to hear my voice. "Hi you, how are you?" I asked him "I sweetheart, I miss you so much," he said, and we both began talking to one another at once. "Michael, I have to tell you something," I say to him. "Baby, I can't talk long I just wanted to hear your voice." He says cutting me off.

"We can talk about it when I get back," he said with a sigh, "eight more months, I love you, baby, I will talk to you again real soon, blow me a kiss why don't you," he said. I kissed at the phone loudly for him to hear. He hung up the phone quickly after. I have to tell him what happened to me. I don't know if will still want to marry me after he finds out what James did to me. I'm still sore, and I don't know if I'll ever be able to make love to Michael without visualizing that moment when he attacked me, maybe I should seek therapy at the hospital.

There must be someone there who could help me through this. I thought I couldn't wait to see Michael again; I felt so safe when I was with him, I fell off to sleep. When I woke up the next morning the sun was shined brightly through the windows of the house, the rooms still smelled of flowers, I got up and washed my face and brushed my teeth. Cookie lay at the foot of the bed watching my every move licking her paws. I needed to get to work today a little earlier, the service for Mr. Simms would be held at the church down the street from the hospital.

I got dressed quickly and out milk out for Cookie. I would get to work in time to get all of my assigned rooms done and change into a dress. I would meet Maddy at the church; I wondered would there be a crowd, Mr. Simms was quite old,   I bet he had lots of friends. Rushing out of the door again to the car I had forgotten the black dress that I would wear to the service. I backed up and went back inside to get it. I only had one black dress; I never wore it.

It was long shelves with pockets, it wasn't pretty at all to me, but it was the only one I had. I'd bring a long coat to wear over it; it looked like rain out anyway. I thought as I snatched the dress and coat from my closet and running back out to the front door I had left it open forgetting that I needed to be careful of James. I saw that Cookie had gone out, so I grabbed her milk bowel on the way out and left it on the porch. I drove off to work soon after. Driving to work, I thought more and more about how I'd like to make a difference maybe after I get myself together.

Then I could help other people overcome some of the same things I had to. I'd like to help, this is so hard to deal with, but I won't allow it, or him to break my spirit. I have to live; I thought as I pulled into the parking lot of the hospital. Today will be a good day I thought as I got out of the car, there was a shadow waiting for me at the stairway near the entrance. Don't fear it. I tell myself as I walked up to the entrance. I just watch it, and I did, I watched it's every move. I followed it to the front desk; I checked in.

I went to the back to put my bag in my locker and then back to the front desk to get my schedule. I sat at the front for a while; it stayed close. I must have looked puzzled because the nurses began to stare at me, I wanted to snap out of it, but it wanted to see what it wanted from me. So I followed it with my eyes while trying to direct my attention to the desk and the people around me. Maddy is such a good friend she's always been there for me. I'm hoping that I can do the same for her.

Although her son seems so protective of her, I didn't want to overstep the boundaries. I was just a good friend, not a family member I had to remind myself of that while she's grieving over her loved one. If she needs me I believe she will call me. I thought as I began my shift on the second floor today with Dr. Green. I met up with him inside room 206 I walked into the room I didn't even get close to the patient soon. I began to feel ill; it wasn't good.

As Dr. Green began to talk I noticed the shadow standing near the first bed. I tried to stay focused on what he was saying but my stomach wouldn't allow it. I took the advice he explained about changing the badges on the patients head and rushed over to him. I prayed that he would leave the room soon after he explained because I growing sicker by the second my back began to fold over, I started on the two other patients in the room they just needed water and juice, I was began to get weaker as I approached the patient with the head bandage.

The shadow became clear as I walked up to the old man in the bed. It was a little old women standing there holding her hand out. I went near her and the coldness of her soul gave me a chill throughout my entire body. It was the little old man; he was ready to join her, I grabbed the little old man's hand and hers. I began to pray, "Lord he is ready now, his spirit is rested and waiting. Show him Lord, who is waiting for him on the other side allow him to see Lord, the door of light that's waiting for him."

The old lady looked at me and tears streamed from her eyes she held his hand as the warmth of the light came over him. I walked away; I didn't want to see them walk away this time. I walked over to the door and looked back at them as they walked away hand in hand to the light. I went off to join Dr. Green in the other room. I couldn't help for smiling; my soul felt so much joy it was unreal the way I felt inside. It was like being tickled a little as I walked away. I need that guidance; maybe I won't get ill if I know what to expect already.

Walking down the hallway I thought. I get it now Mr. Simms; I get it thank you, I thought to myself. I caught up with Dr. Green he was explain the patients history to the nurses in the room. "Hello," he said looking at me through his glasses hanging from his nose. "How good of you to join us, hope you enjoyed that short break. I don't suppose you'd like to share with us what you did while you were away, would you?

Whatever it was it must have been terrific you're smile is projecting light all over the room," he said smiling. "I'm sorry Dr. Green I'll get right to work." I tell him taking the sheets from the cabinet to change the beds. "Don't be sorry, you have a beautiful smile," he said turning to the other patient's bed. He was moving a little faster today; I suppose he was going to join us all at Maddy's father's funeral service. We made it to the fourth floor, we were all going into the last room, and Dr. Green stopped us from going in.

"I hope that all of you who know Maddy is going to attend the memorial service for her father if you can. I will be leaving myself to attend here shortly; she needs all the support she can get right now." He said looking over at me. He was a very handsome older man, I know he was married but the way he mentioned Maddy it seemed they had more than a working relationship with her. Maybe he's the mysterious man in her life. I thought as I tucked in the sheet of the last bed before the service.

We all finished and left shortly after. I went straight down to my locker to change into my black dress. I feared getting to the service late so I rushed everything, putting the dress on was easy. I brushed my hair up quickly laying it down it was always frizzy after work. I didn't have a mirror to look at myself so I asked the nurse at the front desk. "How do I look?" I asked quickly spinning around. "You look great Karis, but do you have a pair of shoes to change into?" She asked pointing down at my clogs. "Oh no, I forgot my shoes!" I yelled putting my hands on my head. I knew I wouldn't have time to make it home to get them.

"No worries Karis, what size are you?" She asked going to her locker, "I'm a nine in half" I tell her. She came back out with a pair of black heels. "Here you go   Karis, these should fit you perfectly," she says handing them to me,   "These are my party shoes, try not to scarf them up okay, I'm going to want them back right after okay." "I will bring them back I promise." I tell her taking them and putting them on. I had never really worn high heels before.

They fit loose, but comfortable until I stood up. Oh no I thought to myself this will be difficult because of my right leg is slightly shorter than my left. I am going to have to learn to walk in these quickly without hurting myself or falling. I took off to the parking lot, it was challenging to walk that way my limp was more apparent than ever now, I was ashamed, but I had to make it to Mr. Simms funeral service for Maddy. I walked slowly to my car, when I got inside I took them off, I was afraid to drive with them on.

The service was just about to begin when I arrived. There were people everywhere; I noticed Maddy right away she was with her children and the kind Dr. Green by her side. I walked up close the door where everyone was lining up, I stood on my left leg, but it was becoming uncomfortable for me to stand I was becoming unstable as I stood there in the line waiting to go inside the church. I needed to sit down, so I walked around and everyone toward the church doors and thanked god Scott noticed me in the crowd.

"Hey Karis, come here," he said. I sighed with satisfaction as I walked his way. I almost tripped trying to stay stable in those heels, getting close to them wasn't easy. Dr. Green had Maddy's arm tight, as soon as I reached Scott I grabbed him by the arm. "Thank you so much, Scott," I said "No problem, were you leaving Karis?" He asked me. "No, I wasn't leaving, I was looking for a place to sit down," I told him.

"Sit down, where are going to sit because I'd love a seat, myself," he said smiling "I'm tired of waiting out here, how much longer could this take?" As soon as he began to complain, a man came out and began to escort family into the church. "Could I have all of the family over here?" He yelled out. "Just the immediate family, please," he said again. Scott shook his head. "Uh, sir is it immediate family or all family?" He asked being sarcastic. "Immediate family please," he said looking at him with a glare.

We began to follow his instruction moving slowly into the church, as we walked in I began to get cold. It felt as if a cold wind was hitting my face; I held on to Scott's arm tighter. "Are you cold?" He asked me. "Yes, do you mind this?" I asked as the cold cut through my body like a sword. "I don't," he said with a smile. I was shaking, and my face felt as if it was frozen, then I felt two warm hands touch on my face. My body began to warm up as if the sun had shined in on me with a ray of warm light.

I turned around to look over in the pew, and to my surprise, Mr. Simms was standing beside me. "Did you think I would miss this?" I turned and looked at Scott. We were seated up front with the family; I didn't want to impose, so I slowed down trying to sit in the third row behind them. As I hesitated to continue walking with him he tugged at my arm pulling me to continue walking with him. Mr. Simms was in the casket ahead. "Don't be scared Karis, he's not there nor will he jump out of there to get you," Scott says holding on to my arm tight smiling.

"It will be okay." We sat down with Maddy and the rest of her family. Scott sat right next to her right in front of the casket. "Yes, don't be afraid, young lady this will be short." Mr. Simms says sitting down beside me smiling. "I was a simple little old man." He was looking around smiling at all of the people who came to say their last farewells. His old card buddies were there with their canes and walkers, even the old car salesman who sold him his last vehicle.

He was trying to amuse me by going over to them pretending to shake their hands and high five them. Mr. Simms stood by his casket smiling and making faces. It was so hard to focus on what the preacher was saying while he was standing beside the casket waving and smiling. I kept my composure for the most part until some other friends of his joined him from the back of the podium. They were acting as if they were singing behind the preacher. Mr. Simms came back down and sat next to me.

The service seemed to be going on forever, I was ready to leave but I wasn't looking forward to walking back to my car with these shoes on I thought looking down at my feet. I can't wait to give them back. I looked down at my feet every time they began to stand and pray; I didn't get up from my seat, I would just look down. Mr. Simms put his arm around me and his hand on my knee. "It's okay," I felt ashamed that I couldn't stand and join them in prayer. "Do you think God minds that you can't stand?" Mr. Simms asked me in a whisper as if people could hear him.

"He doesn't mind darling; he's seen your fear, he knows your pain. He's with you always even in your weakest moments, so relax, he knows," he said patting me on the head. Finally, it was all over, the woman on the piano began to play loudly, she sang along to the music. The song was, I'm going up yonder to be with my God, everyone in the church begins to weep and cry. She sang and sang until everyone was out of the church; we all followed the casket out to the cars in front. Mr. Simms stood beside his children especially Maddy; I wondered if she could feel him near her.

The cars were to take the family to the burial grounds. I made the mistake of getting into the car with Scott. I felt so bad, I felt like I was imposing, and I didn't want her daughters to be angry at me. We made it to the burial grounds, and they lowered Mr. Simms in, Maddy threw dirt down over him, we all held hands and prayed. I walked over and gave Maddy a hug when they were done, "I hope I'm not imposing." I whispered into her ear. "I'm so glad you're here Karis," she said to me with a smile.

Everyone began to leave soon after they put the casket down. I watched all around the burial grounds shadows was walking among us; we all walked back to the family car together. The man from the church made an announcement. "We will all be going back to the church   to fellowship with the family and eat." He said escorting us all into the family car. We made it to the church hall, and everyone sat and ate and talked about Mr. Simms. I didn't go up for a plate of food because there was a line. I didn't want to walk over and stand.

Maddy noticed me sitting and looking over. "Scott, go over and get me and Karis a plate and some rolls okay" She winked at me. I whispered thank you to her. He came back over to us with a plate of fruit and food, I ate and looked around the room for Mr. Simms, he was sitting at the table with his only living brother, they looked like twins. He gave me a quick wave, when it was over I said my goodbye and hugged Maddy, and all of her family thanked me for coming.

I took off the shoes as soon as I left the church and I walked to my car bare feet. It wasn't that bad. I thought as I drove home, it was quiet and calm out. I couldn't wait to return those heels I thought as I pulled up into my driveway. There was James again, waiting for me, this time I will walk right by him and called the police when I got inside. I want to forget I ever knew him, I got out of my car carrying the heels in my hand, "James I am calling the police the minute I get inside" I said as I past him "Please Karis can we talk, please" He begged as I walked past into the house.

I went inside and shut the door, I went to the phone and took it to the window while I called the police and looked out at him speaking loud so that he could hear me. "I have an intruder at my house threatening to harm me; please send the police immediately!" I yelled out. He was still standing at the edge of the lawn staring into the window at me. "I screamed into the phone. "Help! Help!" I watched as he walked over to his car and drove off, I was still holding the phone; the operator was still trying to get my attention.

"Hello ma'am, ma'am, what's happening?" She asked. "I'm so sorry, he's gone now," I tell her hanging up. I was able to clean up and go to sleep fine that night. I prayed a lot these days, it seemed to help me get by, when I didn't pray I would have the worst day. As time went on, I saw less and less of James until I didn't see him anymore. I began to go to school, and I worked longer hours, I would go home and go right to sleep.

It had been four months since the incident happened with James, I was getting better at blocking it out. I'd go to work and school and sleep. Maddy came back to work, and things were more settled. I was struggling through school; I was always sick in the morning and fatigued all day. It seemed as if I was dragging myself everywhere I went, the people around me began to take notice, everywhere I went they would make comments." Karis you look pale," or "Karis, you look exhausted."

I don't know why I looked so pale; I thought it might have been because I wasn't getting enough sun. I worked the night shift from eleven to seven in the morning, and I was in the school building all day. I didn't have any time for the sun. I thought, it worked out fine for me I thought because I didn't sleep that much at night anyway, it had its advantages. I would stay in the patient's room and talk to them, and when I was done, I would go to the lounge and do my homework without any distractions.

I would see Maddy from time to time; she was so quiet these days, I never knew what to say to her, she would barely answer questions. She seemed so distant, working with her was different now, I'd see her with Dr. Green more often than ever before. I was working one night, it was late, and my lunch would begin at three am, when it was time to eat I scarf it down quickly as if it was my last supper, but as soon as I got up to put my tray away I felt weak. I felt as if it was all coming back up, I emptied my tray and began walking quickly down the hallway.

I tried not to swallow as I walked, but soon everything just shot out of me like a water fountain of vomit. It wouldn't stop it just kept coming out and coming out until I was on my knees and my stomach was in knots. I thought I couldn't have had that much to eat or drink; soon I was drawing a crowd." Karis, Karis, are you okay honey?" Maddy and Dr. Green were pulling me up from the floor dragging me toward the lounge bathroom. I was so weak; they practically had to drag me down the hallway.

I was still gaging and vomiting a little there was hardly anything coming up by the time we reached the bathroom, they propped me up on a small chair and handed me two napkins. "You guys can go, thank you," I said leaning back in the chair. "Are you sure, you don't look okay," Maddy said. "No, we'll wait here with you," Dr. Green said looking at my eyes. I had to get back to work I thought. What's wrong with me? I laid my head on the back of the chair and closed my eyes; then I sat up. "I have to go to work," I tell them standing to my feet. "No, no, no, young lady you don't look so good," he said as I stood to my feet.

Suddenly the room began to spin around as if I was on a merry go round; I looked around the room trying to focus then everything went black. When I came to, bright lights were shining into my eyes, I couldn't see anything in front of me, but I could hear Dr. Green and Maddy calling out to me. "Karis, Karis!" I hear them say. "Wake up honey," Maddy said. I turned to her. "What's wrong Maddy?" I asked her. I had an IV drip in one arm and a blood pressure cuff on the other arm. There were electrodes all over my chest. "Maddy, what's wrong with me?" I asked her again.

"Honey, you passed out in the lounge, you don't remember?" She asked. "No," I said looking around, my stomach hurt so badly. "We're running some test now," Dr. Green said. I'm going to have the neurologist check you out, is that okay?" He asked. "How long have you been feeling this way?" Maddy asked me. "Maybe a little over a month, I think," I tell her.

"Do you feel weak?" "Yes I do, I have been feeling weak for a few months now." I tell her. She came over to my arm and began to draw my blood into tubes.   Dr. Green came over to me to check me over with another doctor. I was so embarrassed and ashamed. I can't believe this I thought to myself. "Maddy, do you think I'm having problems from the accident?" I asked. "No, I don't, honey, it was so long ago," she says putting labels on the blood tubes. "We'll just do a few more test, and we'll know something, these test should give us some answers," she said walking out of the room.

She popped back in "Hey Karis is there anyone you'd like for us to call for you, maybe your father?" She asked. "Yes, my cousin Martha, please," I tell her. "Okay I'll get her number form your file," She says shutting the door again. She popped back in. "Uh Karis, is there any way that you could be pregnant?" "No, Maddy I can't have children, remember you were there when they told me that it would be impossible" "Okay she said shutting the door again. It took a while for them to come back. I watched Dr. Green in the hallway discussing my prognosis with the neurologist, I could hear him explaining my past history, the head injuries and all of the surgeries I'd had in the past.

I hated thinking back, but it did happen, "Hey girl, what's wrong?" Martha said walking into the door. "Hello Martha," I replied. "It just never ends with you huh?" She said shaking her head. "I don't know what's wrong," I tell her "I just woke up in here this time." I tell her shaking my head. "Well, we have the answers now?" Dr. Green and Maddy came walking into the room talking. "Karis, you're pregnant," he said, Maddy stood by him with this confused look on her face so did Martha. "What do you mean Dr. Green, I can't be pregnant, I can't," I said with tears in my eyes. "I can't be," I sobbed loudly.

"How do you know this?" Martha asked. "The blood test proved that you were indeed pregnant, do you know when your last menstrual period was?" He asked me. "We would like to check inside your uterus to be sure? We could see how far along you are," he said as a man came rolling a big x-ray machine inside the room. "I promise Karis, this won't hurt at all," he said setting up next to the bed. "This is an ultrasound machine we're going to look inside you're uterus with it, it's something like an x-ray machine, but better," he says.

Martha stood beside the bed holding my hand and shaking her head in disbelief. Dr. Green began feeling all over my stomach, "Karis can you pull your shirt up to your chest for me?" He asked. "This is going to feel cold," he said pouring a good like gel all over my stomach "Okay, young lady, let's see what we have going on in here," he said moving the ball like stick around my stomach. "Do you hear that?" He said smiling. "There's a heartbeat." He reached over to turn the machine up louder.

"There it is," he says pointing at the screen, the picture wasn't apparent; there was a little pulsing white circle in there. Then we hear it echoing. "That sounds like two heartbeats," Maddy says. "The baby has two hearts?" I asked. "No, honey, there are two babies." Maddy said pointing out the other heart on the screen. "Two people are living inside you Karis," Martha said.

"Do you want a picture?" Dr. Green said. I was so shocked; I couldn't have thought of anything at that moment everything seemed unreal to me, it was like I was in a nightmare. "I do," Martha said looking at the screen. "So can you remember your last period?" Maddy asked. "No, I can't," I tell her. "Well from the ultrasound reading it looks as if your babies will sometimes come in February may be the twentieth," Dr. Green said whipping the goo from my belly. "We will be able to tell you more in a few months," he said. "But for now, darling, I am prescribing you some vitamins, and I want you to take some time off from work, you will stay here overnight to get more fluids." He said looking at all of us as he walked out of the door.

"Oh my God Karis, you're pregnant." Martha said shaking her head with her hand over her mouth. "This can't be true Martha; I can't be pregnant." "It's a miracle, you are pregnant," Martha said holding her mouth with her hands. "Yes, you've been blessed with a couple of miracles." Maddy said. "This isn't good Martha; it's James, Martha, its James I said sobbing." "What about him?" Maddy asked what's wrong, "He raped me a few months ago," I tell her sobbing. "He did what?" She asked.

"Yes, it's true I took her to the police station, and we reported it, but nothing was done about it," Martha said hugging me. "Have you seen him anywhere?" Maddy asked. "He was coming around harassing me, I told him I never wanted to see him again, and I haven't seen him in a while." "I can't blame you, where was I, Karis?" Maddy asked. "I didn't want to bother you; your father was ill at the time." "Oh, Karis I'm so sorry. I should have been there for you. I should have noticed something was wrong," she said hugging me tightly.

"I will be here for you now honey, whatever you need, I will be here," she said. "Me too," Martha said. "I know it seems like it will be hard, but you can get through this Karis, I'll be here for you." Martha began to cry with me. "It will be alright; women have babies all the time under these circumstances," Maddy said. "Thank you guys, but I can't have these babies, I can't carry them, it isn't right. I was raped. James raped me if I have them he will rape all of my dreams too. I'm in school, and I have a good job and a man, Michael who loves me, I can't risk all that for this evil." I tell them sobbing.

Maddy placed her hand on my stomach. "We'll get through this," Martha kissed my hand. "Karis, there are twins in there, there is two of them," she said smiling. "You're so lucky." I was left alone in the room for the rest of the night, still confused and terrified at the same time. What do I do I thought as I laid there looking around the dim room. I have a home, I'm in school, I have money saved, I could possibly get through this and be okay, but what will my father say, and how Michael would feel.

I knew that this wouldn't go over well, I will never tell James that's for sure, I will never let him know about them ever, and I know that I have options. I prayed, Lord I know that there is some kind of blessing in this, they said that I would never have children and here I am with two of the devils seeds living growing inside me. I pray, Lord that these children will be healthy and bright. I pray Lord that they will understand when they grow up that their father was sick and if took something from me and they came out of it. I prayed all night until I fell off to sleep. I was able to go home the next day.

Maddy and Dr. Green came into the room before I left and reassured me that if I needed anything to just call them and to enjoy this time off. I had a lot to figure out, I drove home that day feeling a little down, I didn't doubt god at all but I was begging to doubt myself, why were all these horrible things happening to me. I thought on the way home. The house was quiet when I got in, Cookies milk bowel was empty, and there was no sign of her anywhere. I took a shower and laid on the bed when the doorbell rang.

"I'm coming," I yelled out going to the door. I looked through the peephole; it was Martha, I opened up and sat down on the couch. "Hello sunshine," she said hugging me. She carried a big bag in with her. "Guess what I have for you," she said holding the bag up. "These will help us both learn about motherhood." She says reaching into the bag; she began pulling book after book out of the bag holding it up and smiling. "This one, the miracle of childbirth, and this one what to expect when expecting"

There were all kinds of books about babies even a baby name book. I looked down and began to sob. She came over to me and placed her hand on my stomach. "Oh Karis, it's going to be okay, we have to prepare ourselves to for these little people to come into this world, come on, we' re going to make this work." We sat down on the couch; Martha put all the books on the table lined up in order. "I will get you some juice; you stay here," she said as she got up from the couch.

She came back quickly with the juice when the phone rang. "I'll get it," she said running to the phone. She came back holding the phone to her chest. "Hey, it's Michael," she said in a whisper. "Tell him I'm sleeping please," I tell her. "I'm so sorry Michael, Karis is sleeping right now. Wake her up? I'll try," she says rolling her eyes. "He wants me to wake you." "Tell him you can't," I tell her. "Um no, Michael it's not working, she's been working long hours lately," Martha says. "Okay, well can you please tell her I called, I miss her, and I will call tomorrow, same time okay," he says "Oh, sure," Martha tells him. "I will." She sat down and began looking through one of the books. How will I ever explain the rape and pregnancy Michael I thought as I looked as I looked at the books on the table, I'm not ready for any of this.

Constant Reminder

Who was I kidding? I knew that the pregnancy was a blessing. I thought as I walked around my house thinking about what I should do about the babies. I stayed home from work for a week after that day, and school was out for summer break. No one came by to see about me, but Martha called me every day to talk about what I should do about the babies. I would tell her I was busy doing something and hang up quickly before she went into detail. I wanted to try and figure it all out on my own. I sat down to dinner late that evening reading what to expect when expecting.

How on earth would I manage to carry these babies while in school? It all seemed so challenging; I thought as I ate my dinner. Maybe I'll find a couple who can't have any children and give them away. I'm sure many couples would want two miracle babies to care for, or maybe I'd find James and give them to him. I never had it in me to use the word hate when I thought of anyone, but James made me feel strongly about changing my ways. Maybe I should be meaner; maybe I shouldn't trust anyone, I thought about being a mean evil deviant person at times. I blamed James for the mess I'm in.

I will have to change every plan I've ever made for my future, even giving up Michael, whom I loved and adored. I will never speak to him again nor will I ever forget, I told myself as I leaned back on the couch. Anxiously I got up to go to the bathroom; I was going more than ever these days. I took my shirt off so that I could get a better look at my stomach when I got up   from the toilet. I stood in the mirror turning from side to side; I was almost nineteen weeks pregnant. I only weighed one hundred and six pounds or less. I looked at my stomach; it poked out a little, would I be able to carry them? How much weight would I gain? I wondered.

I'd probably gain a lot of weight with two babies growing inside me; all the books say that most women gain up to forty pounds or more. Wow, forty pounds so that I could gain up to eighty pounds with two of them inside me. Wow, I thought I could be overweight after they come out. I stood in the mirror looking at myself for a while; I noticed my breast looked bigger, and I was still really pale. I walked away from the mirror shaking my head. I would be going back to work soon. I was glad because I missed work a lot more than I thought I would, I was bored at home, just me, Cookie, Oprah, and food.

I ate a lot all the time mostly healthy stuff though fruit a lot of fruit. I hadn't heard from Michael and daddy hadn't been by to check on me. I was thankful that he hadn't because telling daddy I was pregnant would probably break his heart. Telling him how and who would most likely kill him, I thought, it's probably best to keep it all a secret. I can't imagine daddy's anger. I often wondered if James even thought about what he'd done any more or if he'd move forward in his life leaving it all behind him.

I've been going to the grocery store a lot these days; I ran into Mrs. Cotton a couple of times. She never really talked too much just hi, and bye. I never want to even hear about James, every time I think about him, that day runs through my mind like an awful sick nightmare. I hoped never to see him again. Getting back to work was even more challenging than before I was having a harder time walking from floor to floor. I already looked six months pregnant when I was two months shy of that.

The staff was already taking notice, I didn't want these babies, I didn't plan these babies, and I didn't want to talk about these babies, so when anyone asked I always looked emotionless at them. I tried at times to smile about it, but I just couldn't think of any reason to. I have been violated in the worse way; I was going to court soon. I would have to see James there if he showed; I refused to share anything about this pregnancy with him. I thought as I cleaned up in my last patient's room.

Martha came over every day now trying to cheer me up, it never really worked. She'd come after she'd been hanging out with her girlfriends, she always looked happy and beautiful. At times, I would get so jealous of her, I could scream, she was so lucky; I thought she would never have to have these burdens. I think somehow she knew I felt bad and down, she'd always show up and try and make me happy. One day I came home from work to find my driveway full of cars, my father was there, Randall was there, and as I pulled up,

I noticed Rose and Roy sitting on my porch playing with Cookie. I parked and began to go inside when Martha came running out. "Karis, Karis, please don't be mad at me okay," she said following me to the porch. "Uncle Earl said he hadn't seen you in a while and he was worried, so I had to tell him about the pregnancy," she said walking behind me. "Really Martha, you had to tell him?" "Well, Karis, how long do you think you can keep this a secret, your growing bigger every day," she followed me in. I walked up to Rose and Randall.

"Hi Rose," I said reaching over to hug her and Roy, "Hi Karis, how are you? Long time, no see," they said to me following me into the house. Daddy was sitting on the couch with his hands on his head. As soon as I step in and sat near him he began to scold me. "Karis, how could you?" daddy said holding a bundle of papers up in the air. "How could you let me find out that you were raped? I had to read about it in the court's files," he said sobbing.

He stood up from the couch before I could hug him he walked away from me; I could tell he'd already a few drinks. Then there was Daisy. "You know the court reporter told him, right, what a mess you've made Karis, why didn't you come to us?" She said shaking her head. I walked into the kitchen to sit with daddy; he had already finished cooking for me, he'd made all my favorites. It must have been before he began to drink. I stood in front of him not saying a word; all of my siblings were scolding me.

I didn't say a word, but now daddy knows what James did to me in detail. What would he do to him? I thought, knowing what he did to the last person who tried to attack me. I sat down next to daddy and put my arms around him. "Daddy, I'm okay, I'm okay I promise." Daddy stood in front of me looking down at me; he was so tall, six foot five inches. I looked up at him and began to sob. He sat back down, "don't you worry Karis, I'm going to get that little son of a bitch," he said hugging me.

"I just can't believe you allowed him to do that to you; you should have just gone to the clinic to get rid of it." Daisy said shaking her head eating a tomato. "A baby's going to tie you down; you won't even get to live your life. You'll be stuck caring for it all your life now," she said going back into the living room with Roy and Rose. "Goodness baby sis," Randall says coming toward me to hug me. "Are you okay? I'm so mad that we couldn't have been here for you when it happened," he looked over at daddy.

"It will be okay though, don't you worry." I'd listen to everyone talk about what I did wrong and why I allowed him to do this to me, don't they know that I was raped? "I was raped," I cried on daddy's shoulder for a while before he got up to make a plate for me to eat. "Come sit and eat, baby," he told me helping me from the couch. "I didn't come over here to be angry with you, daddy loves you," he tells me pulling my chair out for me. "You know he left town, right? James left town two months ago, does he even know anything about you being pregnant?" He asked me.

"I went by there to check on Mrs. Cotton one day, and she told me she hadn't seen him in months, and she didn't know where he went" Randall was anxious about me I could tell, he paced the floors of my living room as he talked about where James might be. I didn't want to hear about James, I don't ever want to see him again. I got up from the table to put my plate away, and I noticed that Rose and Roy were standing in the kitchen next to a cake.

"Hey, who's that for?" I asked. "It's all yours Karis; I know how you love carrot cake, so we bought one, surprise!" They said handing me a slice with a fork. "Thank you so much, Rose and Roy," I said taking a piece with the fork to my mouth. "No, one bought me anything when I was pregnant to make me feel good about it, so I figured you didn't need to go through that especially under the circumstances." She looked at Roy as if she was talking about him.

I sat down in the kitchen with Rose and Roy and talked while I ate my cake; Martha came in and took a plate from the dish rack. "Where's my cake?" she said holding her plate up to me. "You can't still be mad at me, I love you, and they needed to know," she said taking the cream from the cake and wiping it on my cheek. We laughed. I ate a little more of daddy's dinner; he made me steak and fried green tomatoes. When I finished, I waited as everyone began to leave, Randall and daddy were the last to leave.

I walked them out and hugged them both. "I will see you soon baby." Daddy said waving his hand at me. I was so tired when everyone left. Cookie had her milk, and I went to the bathroom to shower. I sighed as the water ran over my head; in relief maybe Martha was right. I prayed, Lord I know that I haven't been grateful these days; I have not been able to allow the hurt to go away. I didn't forgive James completely, and until I do Lord I know I will never be happy. I know somewhere in this there is a blessing, please lord allow me to see.

Please help me to overcome this hurt; I cried while the water ran over my body. Lord, help me to forget what I can't, help me forgive. I stood in the shower crying and praying after I washed I got out and laid on the bed wrapped in my towel. There was a knock on the door. "I'm coming!" I yelled out grabbing my robe from the post on the bed. I went out to look into the peephole in the door. It was Martha "Hey, let me in," she yelled out. "Why should I, are you alone?" I yelled out to her through the door.

"You better open up Karis," she said jumping up and down as if she has to go to the bathroom. "Oh, you have to potty?" I said laughing, "Okay, okay, you can come in," I   tell her opening the door. She ran in past me to the bathroom. "I'm staying the night tonight!" She yelled from the bathroom. I went back into my bedroom and put my pajamas on before Martha came out of the bathroom. I was already lying in bed when she came out. "Oh, I almost lost it on the porch," she said straightening out her clothes, she flopped her body down on the bed I was pushed to the side.

"Martha, hey, I'm not in the mood," I tell her. "Oh, don't be a party pooper." She said rolling herself back and forth on the bed; I laughed at her. Martha talked all night; I laughed at the stories she told about dating. I did have something to be grateful for I thought, lying there listening to her. I have a wonderful cousin who loves me enough to come and keep me company when I need someone. Thank you, Lord, I thought as I fell off to sleep, her voice was so soothing. I was in a deep sleep when I heard Cookie purring and hissing loudly in the living room.

I jumped from my sleep and went to the living room to get her; she was on the window sill behind the curtains. I reached in to scoop her out of the window sill, and something grabbed my hand, it was cold, it pulled me into the window through the curtains. I could feel its breath on my face; it seemed as if it was snuffing my neck, I felt something sharp graze across my neck like a knife. Cookie came running out of the curtain as if it had freed her; she jumped at it flying through the air.

I leaned away from the window, I don't know what woke Martha up, but she came into the living room screaming my name. I couldn't hear her, I couldn't move I began to pray. Lord, please don't let this thing hurt my babies, spare them from harm. Lord, please, Lord, help me to bind this spirit. Please Lord, bind it; I could feel the breathing getting heavier as I prayed. I struggled for it to let me go, I prayed and prayed, soon I felt a force of hands on my chest. It pushed me to the floor, the stronghold it had on me was weakened.

I could feel its coldness leave the room; Cookie ran to me and stared at me lying on the floor. Martha came running toward me screaming. "What's wrong, what's happening, why couldn't you hear me?" She said kneeling down to help me up. She helped me to the couch, I was out of breath, but I wasn't afraid. "Martha, can you please get me a glass of water?" I ask her catching my breath. "Stay here, Karis don't move," she said running to the kitchen. I saw the dark shadow still standing near the window.

I stood up and stared at it, I wanted it to know that I wasn't afraid, I sat back down when Martha came in with my glass of water, this thing couldn't scare me anymore, it has no power over me anymore I thought, but why was it here? "I thought that this was all over with, I thought that after we went to the reservation the spirits left," She said frantically. "No Martha it never ended, I mean for a while they did leave me alone, but it came back. It's okay though Martha, I know how to handle them now," I tell her leaning back on the couch.

"They're going to attack you while you're pregnant, that not fair," Martha said. "I will be okay Martha; I found a way to handle it all, I'm learning that if I pray and grab onto it and pray, it will leave." I tell her sniffing the air. "Martha, do you smell that?" I asked her. She sniffed around also. "No, I can't smell anything, remember in the baby book, it says that your senses will become more sensitive." "No Martha, sniff, can you smell it now?" I asked again; the smell became stronger and stronger the air filled with the smell of flowers, Martha had to smell it I thought, "I smell it, where is it coming from?" She asked walking around the room.

"I don't know, it started happening some time ago, they will attack me, and I pray them away, and my house will smell like this afterward." I tell her looking around the room. "Wow, that is the oddest thing," she said looking around. I believe these things are beginning to scare Martha, her eyes were wide open, and she sat on the edge of the couch looking as if she was going to grab her bag and run soon. "Martha, don't worry nothing will harm me anymore, don't you be afraid for me okay." I tell her reaching for her hand.

"I'm okay now, I'm not afraid anymore, someone's looking out for me," I tell her. "Yes, it seems that way, how long does the smell stay around?" She asked "Sometimes days, sometimes just hours," I tell her. "But I feel good when it's around; I feel so much joy, I hope it stays the smell you know." I told her drinking the water. I held Cookie in my arms she was just beginning to calm down, "I know Cookie," I say as I rubbed her back. "Wow, Karis this is crazy, don't you wonder why and where?" She asked me.

"No, I don't, I don't want to be hurt anymore, so I don't wonder about it at all," I tell her still rubbing Cookies back. As I rubbed, I noticed Cookies hair was sticking to my hand. "Martha turn the light on please!" I yelled out, Martha reached over to the light and turned it on. "Oh my goodness," Martha yelled. Cookie's hair was falling off of her body as if someone had ripped it off it was awful. There was blood all over her; it looked as if they tore it like strips at a time.

Martha and I began to cry; we went over to the sink to wash Cookie off. "Oh my God, Martha, how will I explain this to a vet?" I asked sobbing. "Poor Cookie oh you poor baby!" I yelled out while I washed her body in the warm water. Martha went to the bathroom to get a towel to cover her in. I wrapped her up, and we carried her to the room. I just held her in my arms laying on the bed, Martha laid with us. "Karis, you do know what this means right?" She asked, "No, what does it all mean?" I asked sobbing.

"It will attack what you love it can't have you," she said covering her eyes, "Karis I'm staying tonight, but I don't know if I'm coming back," she said holding on to my arm in fear. We finally fell off to sleep we slept close together with Cookie in the middle. Martha woke me early the next day for breakfast. "We'll just have leftovers this morning," she said handing me a plate of daddy's steak and fried green tomatoes. "I hate wasting food," She said sitting down next to me. "Hey, you look like you grew."

I looked down at my shirt; it was tight around my waist. "Yeah, it looks like I may have grown a little." I said eating; soon Cookie came walking from the room slowly. I rushed over to her and picked her up; she looked awful. "Martha we have to take Cookie to the vet," I tell her. "Yes, we do, go get dressed Karis, it looks like still bleeding everywhere," Martha said. I went to the room and changed into my sweats and a baggy sweatshirt. I carried Cookie in an old blanket; she was so quiet. "I'll drive," Martha said as we approached the car.

We drove Cookie to the vet when we went in there were people with pets everywhere. We went to the front desk, and right away Martha began to tell the vet a lie. "Hi, this is our cat Cookie she's about five years old, we had been looking for her for a couple of weeks, she showed up yesterday, and this is what happened to her." She said uncovering Cookie for the lady to see Cookies body. "Oh no," she said, touching Cookie all over with her gloves on. "You don't know what happened. "Do you live near a canyon?" She asked.

We looked at one another and turned back to look at her, "Yes," we both said at the same time. "Yes, we assumed that a car or something had hit her, but she came home this way." Martha tells her again. "Okay, I just need you to fill this form out, and we'll have a good look at her in the back," she said handing us a clipboard. We sat down and worked on the paper work, it took them a long time to come back to tell us what was going on with Cookie. "She looks like something attacked her, she's very weak, we want to keep her hear until she's better," they tell us.

Martha and I sighed with relief; we left the clinic quickly after signing paperwork. "Maybe she'll be better off here Karis because whatever is in that house could kill her," Martha said as we drove off. Cookie stayed at the vet for weeks, and when they called me to come for her, I told them that I could no longer keep her and to find her another family. Martha would come by and drop things off, movies and books and sometimes even food, but she would never stay over.

Daddy came by more often than ever, he would cook for me, and we'd talk about his love life, or the courts and Maddy would come home with me at least twice a week. I think they were all so anxious about having babies around. Unlike me, I hated the idea more than I thought, every time I'd try to be happy about them I would think about how I ended up pregnant in the first place. I just can't get past the hurt of it all, but I do try. I never let the people around me crying or praying. I spent a lot of my time in my room these days.

I was usually doing homework or crying; I write in my journal a lot these days poetry mostly, it always started off nice and then began to get ugly and sad. I'd write things like, "As they grow here close to my heart I think more and more about their troubling start. I think about how he stole my dreams, how he took from me my structured being, I can't go back nor change the past, I carry in me a bundle of hurt, a never-ending feeling of long lost hope. I would write these poems and feel a little better.

I would be able to carry on through the day until someone would approach me, and ask   me if they can rub my belly or questioned me about the father. I'd get a lot of questions at school. "What's the father like?" They'd ask me; I never knew what to tell them, often I was paired up with a partner. I'd always pair up with the same person, she was very nice, a little overweight, fair skinned tall, and she dressed nicely and always smelled good.

She the most beautiful smile I'd ever seen, she lite the classroom up every day with that smile. She would always tell people to leave me alone when they'd ask questions. I guess she could see the sadness and frustration on my face. I would always thank her after class. I wanted to get to know her better, but I was a little afraid to ask her to lunch, I thought maybe she'd get offended. I could tell she was comfortable being overweight. Her name was Tara. Tara and I became closer and closer over time.

I didn't ever get around to ask her out to lunch because she started to bring her lunch to school almost every day. My stomach grew bigger and bigger; I was beginning to feel bad when I walked, it hurt so badly. Tara would bring things she'd made from home, and she'd always ask me to try some. My goodness, she could cook, she made this lovely pasta salad that I craved daily. I would ask her what she needed to make it every day so that I could buy the ingredients for her to make it for me. She'd tell me it was a family secret and she couldn't share it with me. She would laugh and tell me as if she was joking, but I never pushed her to give it up.

Sometimes she wouldn't have her lunch; she said she left home in a hurry and couldn't cook, and those were the days I'd get to take her out to eat. We were working on a project that was due in three days. It was a tough one. It required lots of research; I needed to be at home to do the research. I worked better in the comfort of my own home, so I asked Tara to come by after class one day. "Tara, would you like to come over to my house to work on our project together?" I asked her.

"Sure, where do you live?" She asked me. I wrote the directions to my house down on a piece of paper and gave them to her after class. "Well, if you don't mind, I can ride home with you, I don't have a car, and these directions make for a very long bus ride." She said with a smile. "Sure, I don't mind at all, I can take you home afterward," I tell her. Tara was so funny; she made me smile all the time, as soon as we sat inside of my car she made jokes about it being too tight inside. "I don't know if I will be able to fit in here," she said trying to suck in her stomach.

She took some deep breaths as if she was trying to hold her body in tight. She quizzed inside, it did look very uncomfortable, and so I drove home a little faster so that she could feel better. When we arrived at my house I got out first and ran over to the passenger side and opened her door; she sat there for a minute staring at me from the window. "Karis, come over here and help me get out," she said holding out her hand.

"Help me out of this damn car," she said as I pulled at her trying not to strain and with the help she got out okay. We both laughed as she sprang from the car, she grabbed onto my belly softly. "That didn't hurt you did it?" She asked me. "Oh no, I'm fine," I told her going toward the door. "Hey, so what's that?" She asked pointing at Cookies bowel in front of the door. "Oh, that was my cat's bowel," I tell her. "You have a cat, you know when you have your baby you have to get rid of it?" She tells me walking up the porch stairs.

"Babies, I'm having two of them, and no worries, I already gave her away," I told her. "You never told me that," she said surprisingly. "Oh my goodness you're having twins that is so great aren't you excited?" She asked. I shrugged my shoulders. "Have a seat Tara, would you like some tea?" I asked her putting on the tea kettle. She didn't sit down; she began to wander around the house, she stood in the hall staring at the pictures in the frames on the wall. "So why did you say that I would have had to get rid of my cat when my babies were born?" I asked her.

"Oh, you don't know?" She said looking at me. "They smother babies, they try and get the milk from their mouths," she tells me. I laugh at her. "Tara, you surprise me with the things you say," I tell her sitting at the table. "No, really they don't intend to hurt them, but they do, they lay on top of them and cover their noses and try and take their breath away," she goes on telling me. "Are you for real?" "Yes, this is true, really it is Karis, you should read up on it," she says with her hands behind her head.

"I don't have her anymore, so there's no need for that," I tell her handing her a cup of tea. "So who lives here with you, your husband or your boyfriend?" "No one," I tell her. She was still standing in the hallway staring at the pictures on the wall. "Who are all these people?" She asked. "They're mostly family." She asked question after question that day. We talked all day and when it was time for me to go to work I asked her where she lived. She didn't say a word until I asked her a second time.

"Tara where do you live" She was sitting back on the couch with her head leaned against the pillows rest. "Oh, I'm sorry, I didn't hear you, it's so peaceful here," she said. "I live with my grandmother and sometimes with my mom right now, I'm working on getting my own place, that's why I'm in school." She said with her head back. "Oh, I see, well Tara I have to go to work, I can't be late," I tell her. "Can I give you a ride there?" She took the remote from the table and turned on the TV, ignoring what I said.

"Do you mind if I stick around, what time do you come from work?" She asked me; I went to my room to grab my jacket, I asked God, Lord what do you think? She's so nice, Lord I don't feel like she's going to steal, or do any harm, I feel like she needs me. I went back into the living room. "Okay, Tara, you can stay here until I come home, but don't touch stuff and don't mess up anything okay," I tell her. She smiled so big and leaned back on the couch. "Thank you, Karis; I knew we'd be close."

I went to work, I was a little worried, I barely knew Tara, and she was in my home on my couch. I don't know what I'm thinking sometimes I thought as I worked through my shift. I was on pins and needles the whole time. I went from room to room. I hardly said anything the whole night. I hadn't seen Maddy all night; I knew she was working tonight because her name was on the board at the nurse's station. All night I looked for her in each room that I went into I seen that she'd been in checking the same patients, our paths just didn't cross that night.

After working on the fifth floor I rushed into the bathroom, my bladder was so full it felt as if it would burst it was weaker too. Sometimes I would have to change and wash at work because I wouldn't make it to the restroom in time. I went into the stall closed to the door, when I sat down to urinate I heard a loud knocking noise in the stall next to me. I tried to go fast, but it was a lot, I had waited a while that night before using the restroom. I heard the voice of a man whispering out over and over.

"Oh, Madison oh, Madison." I stood up and tried to look over the stall next to me; there was no one there, I didn't see anything. I stood up and pulled up my pants; I went out to wash my hands. "Oh Madison," he roared it echoed all over the bathroom, and then I hear a woman say, "I love you, Green." Then suddenly it came to me, oh no, I thought, grabbing the paper towel to dry my hands. It's Maddy and Dr. Green; I went walking as fast as I could to the door when the stall door flew opened. It opened by mistake I think, I walked out quickly hoping that they wouldn't see it was me, I clocked out and drove home.

Wow, I thought Maddy and Dr. Green. That's why she never dated anyone else; she loves Dr. Green, he's married though. Oh my, I thought as I made it into my driveway. Tara had all the lights on in the house; I'd almost forgotten she was still there, after seeing Maddy and Dr. Green everything else was forgotten. I couldn't believe those two; I thought, getting out of the car. I went inside, "Hello," I said. "Hello how was your night?" She asked me. "Oh, it went okay." I told her taking my shoes off at the door.

My feet where so tight in my shoes I felt they were being squeezed I had the shoe print on my feet. 'I cooked dinner for us, why don't you shower and I'll warm it up." She said standing at the kitchen counter. "By the time you get out, it will be ready." I went to take a quick shower; I looked at my belly, every night it looked so big, my breast was even bigger. I laughed at myself in the mirror; it looked as if I would tip over if someone should push me hard enough. I checked my weight on the scale; I weighed in now at one hundred and thirty-seven pounds. I put my hands over my mouth.

Oh my goodness, I'm one hundred and thirty seven pounds, I have really put on weight, I thought. I went to eat with Tara, it felt good to have company when I came home I thought as I walked into the kitchen and sat at the table to eat. "So how was work?" She asked me. "It was work, mmm smells good." I tell her lifting the plate to my nose; I began to eat immediately. "Karis, how'd you get this place? It's a lovely place," she says joining me at the table.

"How much is your rent?" She went on asking question after question as we ate dinner. I took a couple of swallows of my juice and a fork full of food again before answering her. "I don't have any rent, and I pay the bank, it's a mortgage, I own my place," I tell her. "Really?" "Yes really, it's all mine, I mean at least it will be mine after thirty years." I laughed and took a fork full of food. "Anyway, I bought it a year ago." "Who helped you buy it?" She asked.

"Well it's a long story," I told her. She looked at me and smiled, Tara looked a mess her hair was all over her head and I knew she wanted a shower. "What time do you need to be getting home?" I asked her She gave me a surprised look; She was beautiful, she just needed to lose a little weight. I thought as I waited for her to answer me. "Oh, I don't have to go home tonight, I know you're tired, you should probably rest and tomorrow after school you can take me home after we work on the project some more," she tells me looking down at her plate.

"Well, what about a shower or clothes?" I asked. "Oh no worries she said reaching over the chair to get her bag, "I have clothes in here." She pulled out a shirt, a pair of pants and some soaps and lotions. I shook my head yes, I was really surprised at her carrying those things in bag. "Do you mind if I take a shower?" She asked putting everything across her arm. "No, I don't mind at all, hey Tara why do you carry clothes in your bag?" I asked. "Do you sleep away from home often?" "It's a long story," she said going over to the cabinet in the hallway.

"Do you keep your towels in here?" She asked. I looked down into Tara's bag; she had all kinds of lotions and perfumes, makeup and all sorts of soaps, I was curious to find out why she carried so much of them around in her bag. "Oh yes, there's face towels and bath towels in there, go ahead get what you need." I tell her still eating, she went into the shower, and while she showered I finished up my dinner and began to clean. When she came out I was sitting in the living room; she was still a little wet, she must have washed her hair, it was wrapped up in the towel.

"Did you enjoy your dinner?" She asked me standing in front of the hallway entrance. "Oh yes, it was delicious, thank you," I tell her, she smelled like perfume, she used a lot I began to sneeze over and over. "Bless you; she said handing me a Kleenex. "What do you call that?" I asked still sneezing. "It was mushroom steak and potatoes, smothered in a raspberry sauce that I made up from some of the ingredients that you have in your cabinets," she told me. "You don't cook much do you?" She asked looking at me.

"No, not really, I don't have a lot of time to do much of that," I say. "I guess you love cooking huh, why don't you go to school to become a chef instead of nursing school?" I asked. "I'd love to do that, but I need to make a lot of money, I don't think I would make a lot of money cooking." She tells me unwrapping her hair "I could still do it on the side sometimes, I like to have fun with food, and you have to be an excellent cook to compete in the chef business." She said turning the TV on; I went into the bathroom to get my brush.

I just had to help her with her hair; it was a mess I thought as I approached her. "Do you mind if I help with your hair?" I asked her taking the brush to her hair. "Hey, what do you think you're doing?" She asked me "I have bad hair, I never know what to do with it," she tells me. "No one has bad hair; you just have to do what you can with it, we can blow dry it out and maybe style it," I tell her. "We will straighten it and style it; it's going to make a world of difference when you style it, you're so pretty Tara." I tell her as I brush through her hair; I was standing over her brushing her hair.

"So, Tara, what's with all of the products in your bag and really why all the clothes, what's your story?" I ask her. I wanted to ask her had she always been overweight, but I didn't want to offend her or hurt her feelings, maybe one day she'll tell me I thought as I began to blow dry her hair. I straightened it and styled it, then took her to the mirror to look. "You look great, don't you think?" I tell her with my hand on her shoulder. She began to cry. "I hate this, I hate it," she cried. "Oh Tara, I'm sorry, you don't like it, but you look so great," I told her holding her hand.

"No, it's not your hair doo" She said. "It's me, look at me, I'm so fat," she tells me crying. "No, Tara, you're still beautiful, you can lose the weight, we can work out together sometime," l tell her. "Have you always been overweight?" I ask "No, and I hate it, I can't get a job, I can't sit in a regular chair, and no one likes me," she says. "What do you mean, I like you, you're a great person so far," I tell her hugging her. "No, Karis, men, I don't have a boyfriend, and they don't even look at me."

She sobbed and sobbed; we walked back over to the couch and sat down. "Do you know that I'm embarrassed to eat in public, I eat in secret most of the time," she tells me. When I was fourteen I ran away from home, I would hang out with my friends all the time, we'd hang out at the beach a lot, one night we met these guys, and we started drinking with them. I went off with one of them, and he told me he needed to get something from his car, some weed." "You mean drugs?" I asked.

"Yes drugs, I went with him to his car and he pushed me in he tore off my clothes, and he raped me," she said sobbing. "I was screaming and screaming, his other friend came to the car, and he raped me too," she was crying historically. "Wait, his friend too?" I asked covering my mouth. "Did you tell anyone?" Who would I tell, I ran away from home, I was disobedient and rebellious, I was stupid. After that I couldn't go back to my moms, so I went to live with my grandparents, my mom had enough," she said sobbing. I got up and handed her some tissues. "Well, at least now I know we have something in common." I told her rubbing her back.

"I was raped too, these babies I'm carrying they belong to a monster, they told me, I would never have children and look at me, the worst thing that could have ever happen to me, happens and Bam! The Lord blesses me with two of them; I didn't know what to do but, here I am," I said sitting back on the couch. "Really, who raped you?" She asked. "A very close friend," I rubbed my stomach, and as I was rubbing I felt some massive kicks, and one roll across my stomach tickled me. I laughed loudly; "what's so funny?" Tara asked.

"They're moving around in here, this is the first time I've ever really felt them moving. Usually, I would ignore them. I would act as if they didn't live in there, I didn't want them there, but they are in there," I leaned back on the couch. "Maybe they want me just to love them anyway," I said rubbing my belly, hoping they'd move again. "Yes, you're too far along now to feel bad about it, they are in there waiting for you just to love them if you don't, who will? It wasn't their fault what happened; you do know that right?" She said coming over to me. "

Can I touch it?" I looked at her and shook my head yes. "Well, I guess that would be one way of looking at it," I told her. She placed her hand on my stomach and waited for their next move. "You have a lot of reasons to be happy Karis, you have your place, you're in school, you have a job, and although it may seem to be a bad blessing, God blessed you with two people to love." She said smiling at me. "You'll be fine, at least you're not fat," she said sadly.

"Tara, you are big, but you're so beautiful inside and out, you should be happy with who you are if not try and change it, you can fix this, it just takes a lot of determination." I tell her, "and have faith in yourself, there are plenty of men who love big women, my uncle has a big woman, she is big and beautiful and proud, I'm sure he wasn't the only man in her life either. I was in an accident that left me with a lot of scarring all over my body, there is absolutely nothing I can do about it, so I live with it," I tell her.

"If there were something I could do about it, I would," I tell her. Tara watched the cooking channel, while I dressed for bed. She enjoyed watching the Chinese chef challenges, they didn't even speak English at all, but that didn't stop her from watching, she watched for hours. After that night our friendship grew, I would watch out for her, and she'd do the same for me, we helped each other through school. I met her family, and she met mine; she loved to go over to daddy's with me to help us in the garden, she even had a love affair going on with my brother Richard.

He loved her company; it was hard to keep her in the garden with us at times, she was so busy going into the house chatting with Richard. Daddy would tell her stories about me when I was younger. He'd tell stories about the veggies he grew; she'd listen attentively, then make fun of him on the way back to my house. She had an amusing sense of humor about everything even her weight, I laughed all the time now; it felt great. I dared to tell her what I saw at times; I couldn't share that with anybody other than myself and Martha.

I couldn't share any of that with her even though she was a terrific friend. She had different beliefs that would overshadow our friendship and maybe even push her away. She didn't believe in spirits, and she hardly talked about God or church, but she calmed to be Catholic, what I heard and felt at night needed to be kept a secret for now I thought. We had one year left until graduation, it was almost time for the semester to end and I was so big now I could barely see my feet.

I couldn't bend over or sit in the front seat of my car, I weighed in at one hundred forty-five pounds, and my doctor says I needed to weigh more. I didn't hear from Michael anymore when he would call I wouldn't talk to him; I think he gave up on me already. I'm in my eighth month, and I'm miserable, Tara would come by every day, sometimes she'd even sleep over. She went to Lamaze class with me, and so did daddy; they thought it was fun, for me it was scary. I could barely walk at times because the babies sat on my pelvic bone where I had surgery, I would be in so much pain.

All I could do at times was pray; daddy began to get scared for me, I was going to the doctors every week because they felt I was high risk. Dr. Green and Maddy were at all of my appointments; everyone was excited that the babies would be coming soon. The hospital staff gave me a big baby shower that everyone attended even my family. Tara cooked all my favorite foods, and daddy bought the babies all the baby equipment they will ever need; a double stroller, two bassinets, and a changing table.

I had so much stuff to take home it took four cars to get it all to my house, most of the staff bought me diapers all sizes, I wouldn't need to buy any for a while. I don't know where I'll put it all. When I arrived at my house, daddy and Tara were both waiting for me at the door. "Cover your eyes," Tara says putting her hand over my eyes, daddy walked me into the house. "I have a huge surprise for you," daddy says guiding me through the house, I stopped, and her hands came off.

"Surprise!" they yelled, "Oh my goodness, oh my goodness," I said looking all around the room, they had transformed the spare room in the hall into the babies room. It was decorated for a boy on one side and a girl on the other. The colors were yellow, orange and blue for the little boy and pink and purple for the girl. I loved it; there were numbers and letters and Disney characters holding balloons. Donald Duck and Minnie Mouse, we stayed in the room while my brother and Dr. Green emptied all of the gifts into the living room.

Tara directed them where to place everything. It was great having her around. I prayed that she would stick around for a while. After Tara helped me put everything away, she left to her grandparent's house. She had been staying there a lot these days because her grandfather had been ill. She would go there every day to help her grandmother with him; he had a terminal illness, Tara would often come over and just cry almost all day. I hadn't gone to visit yet, but I planned to as soon as I get everything set up for the babies. I had a terrible urgency to get it all done, washing their little clothes and putting all their lotions and powder together on the changing table.

I read all the books that this would be the nesting stage in the last trimester; I'd work all day at it sometimes never taking a break. I planned to visit him soon she tells me that he was very ill at times in and out of the hospital. I wanted to give her all the support she needed because she was such an important friend. I don't know what I would have done without her these past months; I would allow her to drive my car back and forth to and from her grandparent's house every day.

She was very grateful; she would come back every night and lay on the couch watching iron chef, I didn't mind at all. I'd watch her sometimes crying from a distance; she was so sad, I didn't think of comforting her, sometimes I would just pray that God will heal her heart. She told me that her grandfather was like a father to her, she never knew her birth father. Her grandfather was the only real male role model she'd ever known. I couldn't dare imagine that a life without my father, it didn't make me feel good to even think of that, I would pray for her and her family all the time.

She became more and more torn as time went on; the meals she cooked became less appetizing. Often, I would eat veggies and fruit so that she didn't cook I'd tell her not to worry I would eat at work or go to daddy's house. One night she was called to go over to her grandparents, they said that the grandfather became incoherent and could speak, for her to come right away because an ambulance was coming to get him. She jumped from her place on the couch quickly and told me to come with her. We went racing over there when we arrived at her grandparent's house her family was all waiting there they were all over the house.

From the front to the back they all looked worried and sad; the grandfather was in the front room closest to the front door. When I walked into the house I immediately I felt sick to my stomach, I asked Tara if I could use the bathroom. I felt as if I would vomit on the floor if I didn't make it there soon. I had to pass the grandfather's room to get to there, her aunt stopped me in the hallway, "Hey, Karis are you okay?" She asked me as I glanced to look at the grandfather lying in the hospital bed they had set up for him.

As soon as I looked at him, I heard a whisper, "He's not going to make it, and he's going today." I looked over my shoulder to see who it was, but there was no one there. I felt even sicker; I went into the bathroom, immediately I began to vomit. The babies moved all around inside me, and my stomach muscles ached in pain from vomiting. I leaned over the sink and washed my face with cold water when I closed my eyes; I could see the grandfather being rolled out of the house by corners.

He was walking alongside them smiling; I had to catch my breath, I sat down on the toilet seat to think before I went back out into the living room with her family. Oh no, Tara will be devastated, I thought. I was so scared to come out of the bathroom, and maybe they would see the worry on my face. Maybe they would know they I knew something more; my expressions sometimes told stories. "Are you okay in there?" A voice yelled in, "Yes, I'm okay," I yell back. "Okay, no babies on the floor of the bathroom?"

It was Tara's aunt Sherry; she was so funny, she would always joke around with me. They all had the same personality always funny and very polite, they were all brilliant. When I came out aunt, Sherry was standing near the door smiling "You didn't drop them off in there did you?" She asked laughing. "No, they're not ready yet," I tell her walking back to find Tara. "They have a few weeks left in here," I rubbed my belly, "And then they'll home free," I tell her. "Where's Tara?" I asked. "She outside sitting with mom," she pointed toward the front screen door. I glanced into the room as I passed by, the grandfather was gone.

"Yea, they took him, to the hospital," Aunt Sherry told me, I walked out the door to the front porch. Tara and her grandmother were sitting on the brick wall; Tara was holding her hand. "Are you two okay?" I asked as I walked up to Tara. "He's not going to make it back here." The grandmother said I shook my head yes unconsciously, as she talked about her husband. Tara didn't say a word, she just looked down at her shoes, shaking her legs was always she'd handle her stress. She was so worried her eyes were red and filled with tears.

"Tara, it's going to be okay," I told her. The babies were kicking all around inside, I rubbed my stomach to try and calm them. "What's going on in there?" Tara said, "I can see them moving all around in there," she said placing her hand on my belly. "Do you mind?" Her grandmother said reaching out to touch my belly. "No, I don't mind at all go ahead," I tell her taking her hand to my belly. "Aw, they're so active, do they always move around like this?" She asked I shook my head no.

"They seem to be moving more often these days," I tell her taking a deep breath. "It feels as if their trying to kick they're way out of there." I tell them. "They're going to be so sweet," Tara said. Her Aunt Sherry came out of the house and sat for a while; we talked until dinner was ready, no one ate much. The grandmother was anxious to get to the hospital to see what was going on with the grandfather. Her children wanted to wait until they got him set up in a room. I ate a little bit of everything; they all could cook, the food was delicious.

The grandmother and two of her aunts left for the hospital they said they'd call us as soon as there was news about his condition. The rest of the family waited anxiously by the phone watching TV and eating; we left after a few hours. I went straight to bed when we made it in; Tara sat up on the couch all night worried about her grandfather. She cried off and on throughout the night I watched her from the doorway, I also watched as the grandfather never left her side when she cried. He sat right next to her on the couch with her; finally early in the morning hours she received a phone call from her grandmother.

They would bury him on a Saturday morning, they were Catholic, the funeral was long and heartfelt, they sang a lot of sad songs and the preacher read a lot of scriptures from the bible. It was a little different from what I was use   d to, they all took turns going up and praying at the alter podium. They went up one by one to say a silent prayer for their loved one, the grandfather laid in the casket next to them. I watched closely as he never left their sides as they prayed he would look into the casket and then smile back at me.

When it was time for Sherry to go up and say her silent prayer, she kneeled down at the podium and began to pray; soon I heard a whisper. "She will be coming with me." I turned around to see where it was coming from this time. Tara's grandfather was sitting next to me   ;

he put his finger to his mouth as to say don't say a word. I put my head down; I wished I'd never heard that, when it was over, I was exhausted. I told Tara that I was going home to lay down for a while, I said my goodbyes to the family with hugs.

When I hugged Aunt Sherry I could see a vision of her lying in bed unconscious flash through my mind; I hugged her tight. I was sure of one thing, I needed to rest, my feet were throbbing from all the standing, and it would be a long drive home from the funeral service. When I arrived at home I was greeted at the door by a bouquet of flowers, I picked them up quickly, I looked around to see if there was anyone around and took them inside I closed the door behind me and locked it. I put the flowers down and began taking off my shoes and clothes; there was a card stuck down in the middle of the flowers.

I prayed they weren't from James; I sat down on the couch, I hoped James would never turn up here again, the card read. "My love, I hoped to have seen nothing but your beautiful face when I came back here, you're all I ever think about, and I'm here, love Michael." "Oh my God! I yelled out, "Michaels here, what am I going to do? He cannot see me like this; he can't." I said I started to get up from the couch; when there was a loud knock on the door. My eyes felt as if they would pop out of my head, oh no, I went over to the door and looked out of the peephole.

It was him, it was Michael. "Love, it's me," he shouted through the door. Oh, my God, I thought as I looked out at him through the peephole, Michael was so gorgeous more handsome than the day he left. His eyes and lips, goodness, I wanted to open the door and hug him so badly. "Open up baby, I see your car, I know you're in there, Lord I have to open up and talk to him, I didn't want him to hear about what happens from anywhere else. I took a deep breath and hesitated for as long as I could, I leaned up against the door with my back turned and counted to five.

I turned and looked out of the peephole to make sure he was still there, and just as I was going to open it, he began to walk down the stairs. The door slowly opened, I peeped my head out, "Hello," I said leaning my head out. Michael ran back up the steps and rushed to the door, he pushed it completely open, and before he could see I was with child he scooped me up in his arms hugging me tightly, I hugged him tight too, trying not to squeeze the babies t too hard, I began to sob loudly. "You're back early," I sobbed. "

Michael, I missed you so much." "I've missed you too." He held me for a long time, "you've gained a little weight," he said as he lowered me to the floor. We both began to hear the sound of water falling on to the floor it sounded as if a cup of water spilled down his pants and mine. "What's this?" He asked backing away from me, I looked down and so did he. "What is it?" He asked again, I put my head down and held my hands between my legs, I was wet, and I felt pressure down there.

"Michael, I have to go now," I told him looking down at my feet they were wet from the water too. "I have to get to the hospital." "What's wrong baby, are you okay?" "I have to explain all of this to you later, right now I have to get to the hospital." I strolled through the water to grab my bag from the room. Michael was still standing in the living room. I was starting to feel as if I had to go have a bowel movement, I rushed to my car leaving the door opened, Michael stood at the door watching me struggle in pain to get to my car, than he came to my side.

"Karis, don't panic, I will drive you okay." He said opening the car door for me helping me in; I started to panic. I was in so much pain; I had sharp pains in my back, I couldn't think straight, all the books that I read were no help at this moment, I would scream out every time. I'd get a heavy pain in my back; it lasted for at least five minutes before another one came. I tried to do Lamaze breathing, but I was so worried and distracted by Michael driving me to the hospital I couldn't. It was such bad timing, Michael drove very fast, I wanted to tell him what happened, but I was in so much pain.

I began to scream all the way there, "Karis, what's wrong baby?" He asked me repeatedly, and I looked at him, he held my hand tightly all the way there. I couldn't talk, I was just trying to breathe, I held my stomach tight, I put my head down as I screamed with every contraction, they began to come faster and faster, It seemed we'd never make it to the hospital. "Karis, are you having a baby?" Michael asked taking his hand off my leg. I shook my head yes as he continued driving; he seemed to be in shock.

"I'm so sorry Michael!" I screamed as we pulled up into the hospital parking lot. "Wait, you're having a baby?" He asked as he turned the car off. "Michael, I'm so sorry." I told him opening the door to get out, I reached over to the back and tried to get my bag out, but I couldn't it was stuck somehow. "Oh forget it," I walked away slowly, stopping a few times to pant and cry with the contractions, by the time I reached the front entrance. I was out of breath again, "I, I, I'm," I said trying to explain to the woman at the desk what was happening to me.

Soon Maddy and Dr. Green were running toward me she had a wheelchair. "Can't you see she's in labor?" She screamed at the front desk clerk. More staff came out, "How far apart are you're contractions sweetheart?" Dr. Green asked me I shook my head. "Maddy please call my dad for me please!" I told her screaming; I screamed all the way down the hallway, we arrived quickly into a big room with bright lights over the bed. They helped me get into the bed, and two nurses helped put my legs into two bars attached to the bed.

"Karis, I'm going to need you to stop screaming, just concentrate on your Lamaze breathing please." She said. "How often are the contractions?" The doctor asked me. "One or two minutes apart they are coming faster and faster," I tell them. I was in so much pain. "Please, can I have something for the pain?" I asked "We are waiting for your doctor to arrive now, she's on her way," Dr. Green tells me. The nurse put an IV drip in my arm. "Dr. Green, I can't wait any longer!" I screamed.

"Please, can I have something for the pain?" I asked. I looked over at Maddy, she was standing talking to Michael he'd finally made his way into the room. "I need some pain medicine." "I know sweetie, but I'm not your doctor, and I'm afraid until she arrives nothing could be done," he tells me "Dr. Green, I know you can give me something, can you stop with the rules already!" I screamed at him, I was burning all over my body, I felt pressure down in my bottom as if I was ripping apart. Finally, my doctor walked in.

"Hello Karis, how are you feeling?" She asked sitting at the foot of my bed. "I'm burning all over," I tell her. The nurse came over to her and helped her put on some gloves. "I'm going to check you out, and then we'll see about the medicine, deal." She said putting the gloves on her hands. "Deal," I told her. The two nurses took my legs from the bars on the bed and held them to my chest. "I can't bend this leg all the way back okay," I tell them. "Okay, Karis we know," the nurse tells me as they pull my legs back.

"Wait there's one coming," I said panting with every breath. She stood back and waited. The nurses held them while she checked me out. "You're feeling a lot of pressure?" I shook my head yes. I could see Maddy still in an intense conversation with Michael, I was embarrassed that he was in the room. She was looking him in the eye. "You are ten centimeters dilated already, Karis," She said shocked. "Now, we know where all the pressures are coming from, we're going to have us a couple of babies soon," she said smiling and ordering the nurses to grab things. They put my legs back up on the bars.

Michael walked over to me and kissed my forehead and took my hand. "I'm sorry baby," he said with tears in his eyes. "I'm so sorry, I'm here for you," Maddy stood on the other side of me "Okay Karis, now here comes the hard part, when you get another contraction you have to push," the doctor tells me. "Wait what about medicine, don't I get pain medicine?" I asked. "I'm so sorry, Karis, but it's too late, you can't have anything, but this is all going fast. Don't think about the pain and let's just get these babies out of here." She said holding the top of my stomach and looking down in between my legs.

"When they come you push hard, push down on your bottom, we will count to ten, and I want you to stop as soon as we say stop okay." I felt one coming I sat up and pushed down, everyone yelled, "Push, push, push!" Then the doctor would count. "One, two, three" She went on to ten, and I stopped. I felt as if I was ripping apart, I pushed so hard I began to cry and scream for mama. I squeezed Michaels hand so hard, I tried to catch my breath every time I would stop, and I looked up and all around the room trying to focus on getting them out.

I saw Mr. Simms and mama standing in the room; they were all waiting for the babies too. I pushed a listened to the doctor's directions. "Okay, Karis the head is there, with this contraction I want you to give me a real big push okay." She said putting her hand down in between my legs. I took a deep breath the contraction came, and I pushed so hard as they held me up I was panting. "Stop! Stop!" She yelled. "Karis I'm going to have to cut you, it's going to sting a little."

Just like that no more talking I felt the scalpel cut me. I screamed. It hurt me so bad but the feeling I felt soon after was of sheer relief. "Okay Karis, she said holding a baby in the air, "Look at her, look what you have," she said holding a baby up in the air. "Oh, she's beautiful." She laid her on my stomach. "Now Karis, we have one more, you just need to give me one more slow push," She said. Michael peeked down there, "there are more babies?" He asked. I shook my head yes.

"Okay push, baby where are you" The doctor said I gave one more push, and I feel her hand down there moving around "Oh, I see," she said. "He was tied up in the cord, and she held up another one "This one's a boy," she said laying him on my belly, the nurse covered the both of them up, and Michael put his hand on their little heads. "Look how beautiful," Maddy said. I put my head back and sighed. I was so exhausted, I didn't want them, but I felt so good about having them I looked down at them and then at Michael.

Lord, give me the strength I thought as I waited for the doctor to stitch me down there. It felt like another baby was coming out. She pushed on my tummy and picked at me, I tried to look down. "Is there something wrong?" I asked. "No honey she said we're just waiting for the placenta to release and then I can get you all stitched up, and you can enjoy those babies." She said, holding on to my leg. The nurses came for the babies; they took them over to a table bright lights were shining on them.

Michael walked over to them, the feeling of them on my belly was so warm. After cleaning them up, they gave Michael the girl and wrapped the boy up and handed him to me. "You look like a pro," the doctor told Michael shaking his hand. "Congratulations you two," she said; all of the nurses came up to us telling us how beautiful they were and how lucky we were. "You have your work cut out for you," Dr. Green said patting Michael on the back, they both were screaming at the same time. Michael took a pacifier from the table next to him and put into the baby's mouth.

Maddy came over and took a picture of us holding the babies, After four hours I was wheeled to another room, the nurses took the babies to the nursery, Michael went with them. The nurses were talking, telling everyone who came to see me how perfect they were. They had perfect noses and straight black hair they even have all ten fingers and ten toes on both their little feet and hands. I would blush at all of the comments they'd have; their little heads were shaped perfectly. I was in the recovery room when daddy came to see me.

"Hey, baby girl," he said kissing my forehead. "My grandbabies are perfect, baby, they look a lot like you did when you were baby," he said smiling. "Thank you, Karis; I'm so proud of you." Daddy put his hands on his hips standing over me smiling. "I am so proud of you," he was holding balloons and teddy bears in his hand. A pink one and a blue one, I began to cry, daddy kissed me again. "Aw, baby, don't cry, it's okay," he tells me. "Daddy, I didn't want them, I didn't, James attacked me, he attacked me, daddy, I don't know what to do with two babies, I don't want them daddy." I tell him still sobbing.

"Aw baby you're just a little scared." I thought about the night James attacked me, I felt worse the moment Michael walked in with them. "I hate him, daddy, I do, how am I going to love them, without thinking of what he did?" I said sobbing. "Hello, Mr. Lawson," Michael said walking over to shake daddy's hand. Daddy got up from the bed and stood next to Michael "Can you take care of my baby, please?" He asked Michael. Michael sat down beside me on the bed and held me.

"Baby, it's going to be okay, I promise you, we'll be fine," he said holding me. "I'm going to take care of you now, I'm back, aren't you happy?" He asked. "I am Michael; I am so thrilled that your back, but I didn't want this, I didn't want any of this, not this way." I tell him crying in his arms. "I know baby, I know, we will work everything out in time, just give yourself some time. I know it's hard, but things will get better," he said. The nurse came in to get me she needed to take me to a private room, as we were rolling down the hallway, there was my mom again.

She waved and smiled as we walked by, she was so bright as if she was standing in the light. I could hear her speaking, but she sounded so far away, as they set me up in the room she stayed close. Michael went down to the nursery to check on the babies again. I was so exhausted I had no interest in seeing them again, the nurse asked me over and over, "Did you want us to bring them up for feeding or should we keep them until you rest a bit?" I didn't answer her I was insulting. "It's not their faults Karis, you need to give them a chance," mama said to me sitting near the bed.

"They will love you, and you can teach them better, no one taught James, no one loved him enough to teach him right from wrong. You have to love them, give those babies a chance, look at them and don't think about the hurt that brought them here. Think about the love that God has for you, the blessings he brought for you, think of his grace, baby." She said putting her hand on my face. "And that Michael, he loves you, he was brought here to love and protect you, trust him." She said walking away as Michael and the nurse walked in with the babies in bassinet together, they had them wrapped up tight in like little rolls.

"I hope you're ready to feed them; they want their mommy." The nurse said, she handed me the boy, and Michael the little girl. "They are the most beautiful babies I've ever seen," she said as I took my baby boy into my arms and looked him over. He is handsome I thought to myself smiling. "Is there anything else you think you need? I'm going on my break soon, but I'll be back just in time for you to change them," she said walking out smiling. Michael waved at her. "Geesh," he said holding the baby up to his face.

"I thought she'd never leave us alone, baby," he kissed her little cheek and rubbed his nose against hers. "I love you, little girl," the babies began to move their little heads around and cry, "I think that means bottle time Michael said taking a bottle from the table trying to feed her. "You feed with those," he said to me pointing to my breast laughing. I untied my gown and tried to get him to eat from me; it hurt so bad he latched on so fast. It felt as if I had a very tight clothespin on my nipple. "That's my boy," Michael said smiling.

"I've decided to name them Kristopher and Kristine, do you like those names baby?" He asked me. "Oh, you've decided, without me?" "Yes, two beautiful names for two beautiful babies." He leaned over and kissed me as he fed the baby. "You look a mess Karis, but I love you anyway." I smiled at him, I knew I must have looked a mess my hair was wet from sweating and pushing, I was exhausted I could barely sit up and feed the baby, but it hurt so bad I couldn't sleep.

"Nothing will ever change the way I feel for you Karis; you do know that right, Karis? Nothing will ever change my feelings for you, I know what happened, I know that he raped you." He said with tears in his eyes, "I wished I could have been here to protect you from him." He leaned over and kissed me again, he held on to Kristine really tight. "I love you too," I told him. We stayed in the hospital for five days the twins were a little early by a few weeks they weighed in at four pounds for the baby boy and four pounds six ounces for the little Kristine.

They were tiny, Michael was there every night and every day to help me. The twins kept us up at night and slept for most of the day, Michael greeted everyone when they came to see us. He made sure I was able to rest. I breastfed them both off and on, it hurt so badly, I was very sore everywhere and ready to go home. People came in all the time to congratulate us and see the twins there was flowers and balloons all over the room, the room was full of gifts and cards. Every time I woke up, there was something new in the room for them.

Martha finally came to visit; she brought everything her little arms could carry from clothes to teddy bears, she was so happy to see them she held on to them for hours switching babies back and forth with Michael. Michael began to take things to the house everyday so that when we left there would be room in the car for the twins. We both had small cars; I didn't know how we'd manage to get them home. The day we were released from the hospital I was surprised when Michael drove up to pick us up in a Volvo; he'd traded his Porsche for a Volvo he pulled up and got out, "Do you love it, baby?" He asked me.

"It has a bigger back seat and lots of trunk space to carry their things around," it was amazing. They wheeled me out to the car. "I do Michael; I love it, thank you so much." I said as the nurses helped me into the car. Michael put them into the car with the help from the nurses, and we drove to my house, Michael had been there off and on I could tell because the babies' things were all over the place. I was still sore; my stomach was still very swollen it was still sticking out from my shirt. I went straight to my room, I took one baby, and Michael took the other, he went into the nursery.

I sat the baby down in the car seat next to the bed and went into the nursery to check on Michael and Kristine. I just peeked in; he was sitting in the rocking chair rocking her. I could tell that daddy had been there, everything was set up nicely; there were two rocking chairs now with footstools. I stood there watching Michael with her, he was singing to her. I guess if he could love them and their not even his, I should try and love them too.

They did come out of me; I thought as I walked back into my room, I will work through all of this with Michael. I picked little Kristopher up from the car seat and went into the nursery to join Michael and Kristine; we rocked them in the chairs all night until they fell off to sleep. Time went by so fast with the twins, they were growing so fast. Every time I turned around they were doing new things. Michael and I worked our schedule out so that he was there when I couldn't be and Tara became a huge help.

She would come over and take over giving us a break, and daddy would come by twice a week and cook for me and Michael he'd hold the twins after he'd cook. He'd talk baby talk to them, and they'd smile at him all the time. Tara and Michael got along fine. The twins were four months old now, and Tara was still complaining about her weight, and I hadn't lost the baby weight yet, so I invited her to workout with me and every night after we'd put the kids down. Daddy would come by to keep an eye on them while we exercised; we walked two miles every night.

Tara was so depressed, she'd cry, and sometimes I couldn't get her to participate at all my weight came off within weeks. I was back down to one hundred and fifteen pounds; I would never tell her that I'd lost the weight because she would have gotten more depressed. She wasn't happy with herself at all because her weight wasn't dropping fast enough and when she wasn't happy she'd eat more. By the end of the summer, she was four hundred ten pounds, Michael and I began to become concerned. Michael even tried working out with her on the weekends too, but she became even more depressed.

One day I came home to find her on the couch she had a bag of fast food and she was crying historically. "What's the matter, Tara?" I asked sitting next to her grabbing the bag. "Are the babies okay?" She pointed at the TV it was Oprah; her show today was featuring her new weight loss. She came out on the stage carrying a wagon filled with fat, she told her audience that this was equivalent to the amount of fat carried in her body, she looked fabulous, and I turned the TV off. I didn't know how to handle this situation at first but I had to try Tara needed me.

"Tara, come on its Oprah, she probably has a great trainer, and you know what else, Oprah has a strong will if it could be done she will do it. You have to want to lose this weight you can't get mad and eat your anger away. You can't eat your pain, you need to change your eating habits now, and we can work out more. It's not going away on its own," I tell her. "Now, get up and go get changed, we will work out until you lose something, it may not be Oprah weight loss, but you know what, it will be something."

"Tara, Oprah did that show so that you can believe that it can happen if she did it you can do it too. I believe that when you're at the correct body weight you are much healthier, I think she believes that too," I tell her. "But, no more Oprah for you, for a while." I tell her smiling, "now whenever you think of that episode think about how good she must feel now, and how good you're going to feel soon," she cried. "And stop crying, nothing will ever change unless you change it, you can't keep having these pity parties."

I was going on and on when Michael walked in, "what's going on, baby?" He asked. "Oh, Tara just had a small meltdown, that's all Michael," I told him. Michael put his things away and went in to check on the babies. "Tara lets go," I tell her "Michael!" I called out "Tara, and I are going for a walk, can you keep an eye on the twins please?" I asked. "Sure, go ahead!" He yelled out. We walked to the park which was about two miles away from the house. "I'm so tired, I don't think I can make it back," Tara said sitting on the curb of the street.

I stood over her looking down at her. "Look at me, look closely," I tell her frowning. "Do you notice something, look close now at my legs, one is much shorter than the other, and I'm still walking Tara. I could be complaining, but I'm not, I can't, I have to move forward and just wal k. You can change, if you just put a little more effort into it, you can change what you look like, please don't complain okay." I told her reaching out for her hand to help her from the curb. "Okay Karis, I get it, I get it, and I can do this."

We walked back to the house almost in silence; Tara was sweating a lot. "I am so thirsty, Karis, you're the best friend anyone could ever ask for, we're like Oprah and Gayle." She said laughing and hugging me as we walked. "Thank you so much; I love you like a sister." "I love you too Tara and you're a godsend, what on earth would I have done without you there to cheer me up?" I tell her taking her hand.

"I love you, thank you." We made it back to the house as we approached I noticed Mr. Simms sitting on the stairs, I looked over at him squinting my eyes. "What are you looking at?" Tara asked me "Nothing," I told her "Goodness, Karis, you're so weird sometimes, it creeps me out," she said with her eyebrows raised at me. We made it into the house just in time Michael had both babies in his arms; they were crying loudly. "I don't know what happened, I was holding Kristopher, and then Kristine woke up and began to cry, I think they're both hungry."

I grabbed Kristine and sat on the couch, I took a napkin and wiped between my breasts, I began to feed her. Tara took Kristopher and fed him with a bottle. "Thank you, Michael," I said. "No problem baby, I'm going to go, I need to grab some things from my house, and I need to shower, I'll see you in a few." He said picking his bag up off the floor and walking toward the door. "We will see you later," Tara called out to him. After kissing me on the cheek he left.

"You're so lucky Karis, Michael is so nice, he helps you with the babies and everything, and he doesn't even complain." She said burping Kristopher. "Have you slept with him yet?" She asked smiling. Wow, I thought, I've been so busy trying to keep everything together, I have the babies and school and work, I haven't even thought about whether or not he'd ever wanted to make love to me. I know it must be a lot for him to overcome; someone else took something so precious from me. Something we both were holding out for, I never even thought about that, but I know he loves me.

I don't doubt whether or not he still wants to spend the rest of his life with me. I thought to myself while burping Kristine. I tried hard not to pay too much attention to Mr. Simms while Tara was around. I didn't want her to get scared of me; I didn't want to take a chance on losing a good friend. I believe that if I shared with her my instincts and visions she'd probably be afraid to talk to me or be near me and I liked having the comfort of her friendship. So I ignored Mr. Simms, but he stayed around following around the house with the babies.

I waited patiently for Tara to start cooking before answering any of her questions she asked about my and Michaels relationship I would watch her off and on while she cooked. She would set everything up around the counters as if she was a top chef; it was hilarious to watch. She was really into it, dashing the salt shaker and all the spices; she'd make faces and talk to the food. I went to the twins room to rock them both in my arms was very difficult, but they loved to be rocked.

They'd go right to sleep afterward; I would take them out to the living room so that we could watch Tara cook I place them both in the bouncy chairs and rock them until they fell off to sleep. "Well, do I have to twist your arm or are you going to give me the scoop on you and Michael?" She said dashing the salt and pepper shaker on the meat. "I don't know Tara, I do love Michael, but I doubt that he could love me now, I had plans to marry him, I have always been afraid to because I didn't think I could have any children for him, but look what happened.

I don't know what he's thinking anymore, he doesn't talk about us getting married as much as he did before and I don't want to bring it up. If he doesn't love me anymore, and just wants to be my friend I'm okay with that." I tell her as I began to cry, "And how can I even think about bringing that up to him, look at these two, they both favor James so much. I'm so hurt that they're not Michael's babies and I think he is too. You know I never expected him to accept them as his children or me as his wife.

I know that's it's all too much to ask of a man, especially after what happened, he says he still loves me no matter what but, I don't know." I told her as she chopped onions and carrots. "So, you think he's just hanging around here?" She asked shrugging her shoulders "I don't know Tara," I said with tears in my eyes. I went over to the counter and grabbed a carrot; I held Kristine close to my chest. "I do love him; I always have, I hate what that monster did to us."

"Karis, I think Michael loves you, I think he's the kind of guy who follows through, whatever he says he's going to do. I think he'll do it, I believe he loves you, and if he said he was going to marry you, I believe he will." She said as she placed the meat in the oven. After she put the food in she took a napkin and wiped her forehead and neck, she was sweating. "I'm done," she said with a smile. "Karis you're so blind, what's keeping you and Michael from going out together, I think is you," she said standing up hanging over the counter.

"I think you're allowing yourself to feel that way because you're still hurting over what James did to you. Let what James did to you go, or you're never going to be able to live your life if you don't. He cannot hurt you anymore Karis, let it go, forgive him, and move on, they're so beautiful, and you and Michael have a good chance. Take it, take this chance, you didn't do anything wrong. Matter of fact, you've done everything right." She said picking Kristopher up from the chair. "So, have you ever made love to him," She asked me again.

"Tara, he barely kisses me anymore, I don't think he's attracted to me anymore at all." "I think that he still loves you, why don't you take him out on a date Karis, ever since he came back you guys have been trapped in the house with the babies. Go out have some fun like you use to do, I am here, and the babies are okay, call him tell him you'll meet him out somewhere. Go to dinner, or walk on the beach." She handed me the phone, "I bet he'd love it, go ahead call him." I took the phone from her hand; I dialed the number, I was terrified, what if Michael isn't interested in me. I thought as I held the phone to my ear.

He has always been upfront about what he felt. "Hello," someone picked up "Hello" a woman was answering Michaels phone, oh my goodness, I was trembling with fear in my voice, who could this be, I thought he's moved on. "May I speak with Michael please?" I said, I felt so embarrassed, I hung up before she could say anything else, I could hear her yelling at him. "Michael, phones for you!" She yelled as I hung up. I walked away not even telling Tara what just happened, I went into my room and sat on the bed.

Mr. Simms was sitting on the other side of the bed; I didn't know what to do next, that wasn't supposed to happen. Michael has another woman at his house; I wondered if he loved her, I wondered if he met someone, my thoughts grew I couldn't think of anything else. I wondered if he was going to ever tell me. I guessed we were over; I was a fool to believe that Michael would ever love me after what happened. I thought as I sobbed I was so hurt; I laid there on the bed sobbing silently. Mr. Simms came over to me, "it's not what you think, be strong, get yourself together troubles coming." He said walking away.

"Karis, Karis!" Tara was calling me. "Yes, I'm coming," I yelled back. "The babies need you, come out here quick, my foods burning, I ran out into the kitchen "What's wrong with my babies?" I said picking up Kristopher. "Mommy's baby is mad," I say to him kissing him and placing his pacifier into his little mouth. I would talk to them the way daddy did, using baby talk, they would always look up at me immediately they would stop crying and pay close attention.

I began to sing twinkle, twinkle little star to them as I rocked them both in the chair. How could even bring myself to worry about Michael, I knew that he wouldn't accept this, he's a doctor, he has a reputation to uphold, and it couldn't include something like this. I needed to focus; if this is all God has for me, I'll take it, I thought there's no way I wanted to mess that life up for him. I rubbed Kristine on the head as I fed her. "Did you get a hold of Michael?" Tara questioned.

"What happened?" "Oh, he wasn't home," I told her "Is he coming over later?" "I don't know, I believe he's busy, maybe too busy," I tell her. "Tara, if he tries to come over from now on please tell him we're not home?" Maybe I needed to separate myself from this attachment, I don't want the babies to be attached to him, I don't want to be in love with someone I can't ever marry, Michaels involved with someone else, I better go ahead and let him go and be happy. I thought looking at my babies. "Tara, I just think he needs his space, I know you're busy with your grandmother, but if you can come by a little more and help me with the twins at night I'd appreciate it, just so Michael doesn't feel obligated to, could you?" I asked her.

"Sure, Karis, no problem, I'll bring my grandma with me, she'd love to hold the babies." She said picking up Kristopher. A week went by, Michael tried calling me every day, but I instructed Tara to tell him that we weren't home and when he'd come by unexpectedly I'd close everything up and act as if we weren't there. I'd take the babies to the back room and wait for him to leave, at work I'd ignore him, I never went to lunch when he did, I stayed far away from him, and everyone began to ask all the time.

"What's going on, why was Michael so sad all the time?" I would always say I didn't know; I have no Idea. I'd tell and walk away. I was hurting too it was so hard to pass him and not say a word, sometimes I would cry in my car before, and after work Maddy approached me one night, "So, you don't love Michael anymore?" She asked me. "Maddy, I don't want to talk about it, Michael and I will always be friends." "I'm disappointed in you Karis," she says to me. "What are you doing, what happened between you two, he loves you, do you know that?" She said staring at me with a frown on her face.

"He's come by my house several times, he tells me you won't talk to him, is this true?" I shook my head yes. "Why Karis, why aren't you talking to him, what happened?" "I don't have much to say, that's all, I'm not angry with him, I just think that he should move on, I can't give him anything, and James spoiled what we once had." I tell her staring down at my clipboard, "he's seeing someone else Maddy, he doesn't love me." I told her sobbing.

"Wait, how do you know that he's seeing someone else, he told you this?" "No, I called his house, and she answered the phone, I made up my mind that night, I can't wonder anymore Maddy. I love him, and we can still be friends, but I don't want the twins to think that we are in love and we'll raise them together. Especially if he's already in a relationship with someone else," I tell her sobbing. "I love him, Maddy, I'm just trying to let go."

"Karis, it's hard to believe that he's seeing someone else, did you even give him a chance to explain himself before you decided to throw it all away? What you two have is so special, try and find out first before you throw it away," she tells me. "Just think about it Karis, I believe he loves you." "Okay, Maddy, I'll think about talking to him," I told her walking into the bathroom to wash my face before going to my last patient's room. Finishing my shift was easy these days, I've learned that less talking and standing around helped, I had done the same job for a while, I couldn't wait to finish school I was to be doing my internship at a mental hospital soon.

I found that interesting, and couldn't wait to do it; I hear the stories about being in the mental ward, it seemed to be challenging. I needed something challenging to keep my mind off of what was happening to me. I filled out my time sheet, Martha met me at the desk, she waited patiently holding a bag in her hand, I hoped there was nothing for the twins in it, she had bought them so much, I was all out of places to put them. I walked over to her after saying goodbye to everyone. "Guess what I have?" She said smiling.

"Oh, please tell me it's nothing for the twins," I said shaking my head. "No crazy, I have movies." She said holding up the bag "Its movie night at your house, and boy do I have the perfect movie for you." Still smiling, "sure, you do Martha, but you know I can't do anything until I get the twins settled, I have to feed them and bathe them and put them to bed first, are you going to wait around for that, it could take hours." I tell her hoping it would discourage her from coming over tonight.

I didn't want any company tonight, I knew that Tara would be leaving the moment I walked in, and I would have some time alone with the babies. Just they and I alone, but it didn't work. Martha followed me home with her movies. When we arrived at the house Tara had made dinner and put the babies down to sleep she was rushing to the door, as I walked in she rushed toward me grabbing my keys from my hand. "I have to get to my grandmother's house to cook for her too." She said with her hand on the doorknob. "I'll be back later, is that okay Karis?" She implored me.

"The house keys are on the key ring if you get back to late just use it and come on in don't wake us," I tell her putting my bag on the floor. She greeted Martha and went out of the door. "Does she always cook for you Karis?" Martha asked. "Yes, she loves cooking, I never ask her, the food has gotten better since her grieving stage passed, her grandpa died a few months ago, you know. Martha, make yourself at home, I'm going to shower before the twins start to get up okay, I will be right out." I grabbed the baby monitor; I took off my clothes, I wrapped up in my robe, I looked in on the twins before getting into the shower, I kissed both of them, they were sleeping so peacefully.

Tara would lay them in bed together all the time both at different ends of the bed. They were both so beautiful; I thought as I headed into the bathroom. I looked into the mirror and stepped on the scale, I was losing more weight, but it didn't look good, I wore a size one, and my face looked too skinny. I think it would benefit me to gain a little weight, but how would I do that while helping Tara with her weight loss? I thought as I stepped into the shower. I washed up quickly and got out, as soon as I stepped out I could hear whispers coming from the babies monitor, what's going on? I thought as I wrap up in my robe; the babies were laughing.

Oh, it's just Martha playing around with them, I thought, putting lotion on quickly. I threw on some sweats and a sweatshirt and walked out of the bathroom; I went into my bedroom. I could hear Martha in the kitchen. But the sounds in the babies' room were still going on; I quickly went into the babies room. It was cold in there; I went over to the window, it was closed, I immediately closed my eyes and began to pray.

Lord, I know that the spirit invading this room is not of you. Lord, protect my babies from harm shield them. Lord, send this spirit back to hell where it belongs, lord cover my babies in the blood, bless them lord spare them from any harm. I prayed and prayed, I stood in their crib as it turned warm and filled with the smell of flowers, I opened my eyes and looked down at the they were up looking at me smiling at me. "Hello, you two," I said. I strapped myself with a baby pouch that I received as a gift; it was like an Indian wrap cloth I could put them in one in the back and one in front.

It was difficult, but it was the only way I could carry them together. I took them into the living room where Martha was sitting on the couch with a bowel of popcorn and lots of candy. "Did you hear them in there, Martha?" I asked her. She shook her head no and continued eating her popcorn. She wiped her hand on her pants and reached out her hand for one of them. I turned around so that she would grab Kristopher from the back. I went into the kitchen to warm a bottle for him. "You can feed him for me right Martha?" I asked her.

I would breast feed Kristine, Kristopher seemed to be eating more these days, he'd get on my breast and when it was time for him to get off he'd latch on tighter trying to stay on my breast all night. I fed them baby food from the jar now; they loved it. Bananas and applesauce they loved it all, I usually gave that to them warmed too. I went over to the couch and sat everything down on the coffee table; I placed Kristine in the baby seat. "Wait, before you get started feeding them, looks in the bag." Martha said smiling; I was feeding Kristopher with a spoon, I reached into the bag, she had brought so many movies, she had a love story, an old classic and a new one called Beloved.

I put the spoon down and looked it over, Oprah played in this one. "This is a good one." Martha said taking it from my hand, "Let's watch this one first, it's about spirits, not the kind of spirits that come after you as they do you," she said. "But I hear it's good." Martha went over to the TV and placed the movie into the VCR. We fed the babies, and I got up and took them to the room to wash them up and put them into their pajamas.

Martha began watching before I was done, "you're going to miss the most important part!" She yelled "I'll just start it over when you come back in okay," she yelled. "Sure, Martha I'll be in there soon," I yell. This movie must be excellent if Martha wants to see it, she's not a movie watcher, I thought as I changed Kristine's diaper. "Girl, hurry up," she yelled out anxiously. "I'm hurrying Martha, remember I have two of them," I tell her.

Just as I walked into the living room with them Tara walked in the door. We all sat together; I held Kristopher and Tara took Kristine as they fell off to sleep we watched the movie intensely. This movie was a little scary, but pretty informative, so it turns out I'm not the only one who believes or have been haunted by spirits. There are people out there who knew about them too; I thought as I watched, It had so many important factors in it. When it was over, I wanted to know what Tara thought, but I didn't want Martha to tell her about my encounters.

Martha was good for spilling the beans and telling people things I didn't want them to know. So I quickly told her to put the other movie in before we got into a discussion about Beloved, as she did Tara talked about how she didn't believe that those kinds of things happen. Martha looked over at me and smiled because she knew better. I wished that Tara was right and that I could believe what she did, those things don't really happen, but I have lived those things already and I knew that those experiences were real.

Martha took Kristopher from Tara and we went into the bedroom to put them down in bed. "So, she doesn't know about your encounters?" She asked in a whisper I shook my head with my finger to my mouth, "shish I don't want her to know. Some people are so afraid of stuff like this Martha, please don't tell her." I said shutting the light off, and I left the small light on near the crib. We went back into the living room, "So, what were you two in there whispering about, how fat I am?" She said holding a hand full of popcorn.

"No," Martha said smiling "Are you okay?" I asked, "We wouldn't do that." I told her cleaning up all the mess. I was so tired by now. "Martha, are you staying the night?" I asked her. "No, I have work in four hours, I'm going home to take a little nap before I go in and I'll call you a little later, okay." She said picking up her bag from the table.

"Do you still want to watch these movies?" She asked "Yes, maybe later I will," I tell her. "Okay, I'll pick them up later." The moment she walked out of the door Tara started with her questions. "Did you guys talk about me in the room?" She asked, "Oh, Tara, I will never do that to you, you're my friend, if I ever have anything to say to you good or bad, I promise, I will come to you and tell you to your face first." I told her she was so conflicted, worrying all the time whether or not someone liked her because of her weight. I often felt bad when other people came around because she would look sad and try and hide out where no one could see her.

I guessed she felt like me at times; I didn't want to look at people in fear of what I might see in them. Or what I might feel would happen to them. I couldn't turn what I had off, and often I'd ignore it, even when I shouldn't. It's hard to turn something off inside you, I thought about how different we were in so many ways, and how alike we were at the same time. Her insecurities were no different than mine; the only difference was that she couldn't hide hers as I could. I thought as I finished cleaning.

I went to bed that night thinking about Mr. Simms, what he said that day about me preparing for something. I had no idea. I try not to get my nerves in a frantic over things I can't change. If I am to be attacked, then I know how to handle it, I won't fear it anymore, he's taught me that much. I prayed to God to bless me and to watch over my babies and me through the night. Tara was getting comfortable on the couch when there was a knock on the door. "Who is it?" She yelled out. "It's me, Michael, and don't tell me that she's not in there because I know she's there" He yelled out.

"I need to talk to her Tara," he said. "They're all sleeping!" Tara yelled out to him. "I don't care, Tara, I need to talk to her now, please let me in," I ran into the living room and signaled Tara with my hands. Don't let him in, I waved to her. "Michael, I'm sorry she's asleep!" Tara yelled through the door. He began to knock louder "Tara I know she doesn't want you to let me in, but I need to talk to her. I have to tell her that I love her, there is no one else for me, we have plans to spend our lives together; why won't she talk to me?"

I turned my back to go back into my bedroom when Tara did it; she opened the door. "Tell her yourself Michael, I can't relay messages all night," she said. "You need to talk to her, there she is," she pointed at me. I went into my bedroom and shut the door; Michael came in right behind me. "Karis, can we talk please?" He asked me kneeling down on the floor in front of me. "What's wrong with you Karis, why are you shutting me out, what did I do to deserve this, please tell me?" He said.

"Michael why are you here, you are under no obligation to stick around here, those babies aren't yours, and I know there's someone else in your life now." I tell him beginning to cry. "You can be with whoever you want; I'm not your girlfriend or your wife, please just go away." "Karis, why are you doing this, you give me a reason a good one and I'll leave," He said standing in front of me. "Michael, I don't want you to have to suffer for what someone else has done, I can't take back what happened, I don't ever want to hurt you."

"I know this seems like a slap in the face, but I have to do this. I know about your girlfriend, she answered the phone when I called you last week." I told him sobbing. "What, what girlfriend?" He asked looking baffled. "I don't have any girlfriend, Karis, what are you talking about, come on Karis what are you talking about, would I do something like that to you, really would I?" He asked. "My mother and my sister are in town they've been here since last month, I was going to bring them over to meet you, but you've been giving me the cold shoulder."

"Is that it Karis, is that why you've been shunning me away?" He asked. "Karis I love you so much baby, I do, there is no one else for me, please don't cut me off." Michael looked me in the eye; I melted, he was so handsome, his lips seemed to be calling me toward them as he talked, he held me close to him. I could feel his muscle protruding from his pants, as he held me closer, he took my head and placed it on his chest? "Do you hear it?" He asked. "Do you hear what my heart is saying, listen close."

His heartbeat was so strong; it pounded louder as he held me, "It's saying, our hearts were brought together for a reason mine beats only for you, and yours beat at the same pace. He held onto me tight with his arms wrapped around my back. "If you let me go Karis our hearts will fail. I love you, Karis, let me back in, allow me to love you and the babies, please let me back into your heart." I looked up at him; he kissed me softly on the lips, I closed my eyes and let him back in, "I love you, Michael, I love you so much."

He kissed me again and held onto me; we made out for a while before we ended up on the bed, my body was warm all over. Michael kissed my neck, and all over my face, he took his shirt off and laid beside me, pulling me close to him. "I love you," he says with every kiss, "I want you." I closed my eyes. Michael caressed my body with his big hands; I tried to keep my mind on him, I couldn't allow James to steal this moment. I began to think about the day James attacked me. I closed my eyes tight and thought Michael is not going to hurt me, I know he won't he loves me. Lord, help me through this, I prayed as he kissed me all over.

He will never hurt me; he loves me, he wants to make love to me, I thought as he began to remove my T-shirt. "Are you okay Karis, is this all right?" He said waiting for me to answer him. "I'm fine," I said shaking my head yes, he took things slow and with every touch he assured me that he loved me, he went to touch my breast. I grabbed his hands and placed them on mine, I shook my head no, "there's milk in them," I whispered smiling at him, "they're sensitive." I tell him lying on the bed removing my underwear; I allowed him to kiss them and touch all over them.

I shook my head yes to it all as he asked me for permission with his eyes; I reached for his face pulling it in closer to mine. I kissed him all over; I was curious about what this would be like, Michael and I had never gone this far. I often wonder about him, and now I will know what it's like to be made love to, I laid there waiting for it to happen. I will not allow James to spoil this moment for me; I will accept what God has given me. A wonderful man who loves me the right way, there was no need for me to be afraid.

I was feeling ashamed of the scars on my body, but I couldn't hide them. Michael was kissing me all over; he didn't seem to mind what he saw. "They just look awful don't they?" I asked him as he rubbed my legs. "No baby, the doctor did a wonderful job, they're not even that visible," he tells me kissing my hand. I followed his lead; I began to kiss all over his body just the same, I loved him back the same way he loved me admiring every inch of his body. I looked into the closet mirror admiring his backside as he lay in between my legs.

He kissed all between my thighs before coming up. "I love you, Karis." He said before he placed it inside me. "Baby, I love you," he said over and over as he made love to me. Michael and I made love passionately all through the night, until the little ones stopped us for their early morning feeding. I started to get up to go to them before I could move he stopped me, "You stay, I haven't seen them in such a long time, I have to go care for them." He tells me putting his pants and shirt on quickly, when he walked out of the room I looked down in between my legs to see if I was bleeding like I did when James attacked me, there was no blood.

It was wet, I was a little sore, but it wasn't so bad. I got up and wrapped myself in my robe; I went in to check on them. Michael was in the chair rocking Kristine, "I thought you missed your boy?" I said standing in the doorway. "Oh, I've missed them both," he said kissing Kristine's little nose. "Baby you're losing too much weight," he said staring at me. "What's going on? You're like skin and bone almost if I hadn't been there to witness the birth of these babies. I wouldn't believe that you'd had any children at all."

"I've been breastfeeding and exercising a lot," I tell him. "I work and go to school too, it's not easy with these two," I tell him taking Kristopher from the crib. I sat down in the other rocker and began to feed him. "You don't like the way I look?" I asked him looking at him feed Kristine. "I love the way you look; I just don't want you to get too small," he said. We stayed in the room feeding the babies until they went to sleep. We laid them in the crib and went back to bed; we made love again until the sun came up.

"Did you have one?" He'd ask me after every time. "Did I have one of what?" I asked him. "An orgasm." "What is that?" I asked him. "Oh you'll know when you get it," he said to me smiling. We held on to one another as we watched the sun come up. "Did you enjoy?" He asked me. I shook my head yes. "I have to be in by five thirty this morning," he tells me getting up from the bed. He put his clothes on. "I'm going to kiss the babies goodbye, and I'll see you a little later baby," he said kissing me softly on the lips.

"Do you mind if I brought my family over to meet you after work today?" He asked. "Remember I get off late tonight," I told him. "Oh yes, then maybe tomorrow huh" He asked. "Yes definitely tomorrow," I tell him. "Baby you know when we get married I don't want you to work anymore." "No, I have to work Michael; I have to take care of my babies." "You don't ever have to worry about them, I will take care of them too, we'll talk about it later baby," he said walking out of the door.

The kids were up I could hear them on the monitor. Tara was playing with them. I went to wash before I went to get them, my shower was quick I thought about my night with Michael the whole time. He touched me everywhere I thought smiling. I want to remember it all, I put my clothes on quickly, I knew Tara had to go to her grandmothers to make her breakfast before coming back here to help care for the babies. Today would be a good day. Michael and I were all right, he does love me I went into the babies' bedroom Tara was rocking in the chair.

"So I guess you and Michael confirmed your love last night huh?" She asked me. "You're happier, and I could hear Michael making love to you last night, these walls are really thin," she laughed. "Karis you're so lucky, someone loves you the way he does." She said holding Kristopher close to her chest patting his little back, "Tara what do you mean, I hear you talking on the phone all the time, and what about Matthew, he's always calling, and I know you've been out with him a few times. You don't think that he has it in him to love you, why won't you date them?"

"Have you seen me, Karis, look at me?" She said I'm too big to fit at the tables in a dine-in restaurant, and when I walk into any place to eat, I'm always stared at, do you even know what that's like?" She asked me. "Yes I do, I know what that feels like, because I' always feel like people are watching me as I walk, because I have a limp, you don't think I can feel them staring at me. Stop complaining Tara please, just go out, try it see what happens," I tell her. "You know it's possible that some people stare because we're beautiful," I tell her smiling.

"Karis, every time I tell you about how I feel you say something about that little leg, you know I never even noticed it until you said something. No one notices you walk funny or with a limp, you look normal in every way. I don't; I can't hide these rolls." She said pinching her side. "You need to stop saying you feel the same way I do. You don't know what it's like to be overweight, you're a stick," she said looking at me. I began to get offended; I'm not going to say another word I thought as I stood over the crib looking down at Kristin.

, "Karis, I hope you're not mad at me." She said grabbing her bag from the floor. "I just think that I'm no comparison to you, you have your place, you have a boyfriend who loves   you, and you're skinny and beautiful." She was upset; she tossed everything into her bag quickly. "Tara, I'm sorry if I made you feel like I was mocking you, I didn't mean to do that, I'm sorry," I told her. Tara laid Kristopher down in the crib, I took Kristine up into my arms.

"I'm sorry Tara, I can't tell you how much it means for you to be here helping me every day, I don't want you to feel bad," I tell her. "Karis I'm going to my grandma's tonight, I'm going to stay there, I think I should stay away for a while, I will help you with the babies, but I won't stay over," she told me. "Can you give me a ride over there?" She asked. "Sure," I said stunned at what was happening, my feelings were hurt, but what could I do, she helped me pack the babies up, and we carried them to the car.

When we began to pack them into the car I thought about how weird this ride would be to the grandmother's house, I stop before opening the doors and handed her the keys. "Just take the car, I have to stay here just in case my father comes by." I tell her. "When Michael comes back I'll come and pick it up." I tell her taking the other car seat from her and walking back toward the house. "Or you can come back, and he can take you home." I opened the door to the house and went inside with the babies, she came up behind me and grabbed Kristopher's car seat and placed it on the couch for me.

I was almost in tears; I felt so bad about having made her feel the way she did. I hugged her, "I'm so sorry Tara, please forgive me, for making you feel that way," I tell her. She shook her head yes with tears flowing from her face she walked out of the door. I sat there thinking about her, God what have I done; I never meant to make her feel that way. I went to the phone to call Michael to tell him what happened but the babies began to cry.

I sat down and cried with them after we cried a while I got up and took them to the nursery one by one I fed them. They fell asleep, and I dimmed the light leaving them for their nap, I walked out into the living room to call Maddy, I was going to call off I didn't want to go into work this evening. I walked toward the phone, and I was shoved in the back with such a force that I fell to the floor and slid on my stomach almost hitting the wall. I struggled to get up as fast as I could; the room was growing darker before my eyes.

I closed my eyes; here it is, I thought Mr. Simms was right, I needed to be ready for it. I closed my eyes and began to pray, and feel around for it; it was so forceful. Every time I'd get up it would push me back down to the floor. I struggled with it; Lord, come quick, I'm in a fight this demon is attacking me with all it's might I need you Lord, please guide me through. I pray you back into the darkness; I could hear my babies crying out for me as I was being flung around the room from one side to the other, I prayed.

Lord help me bind this spirit, send me a sign so that I can feel it, I was flung over near the end of the kitchen table, I just laid still, I didn't try to get up nor do I move, I lay still. I'm going to wait for it; I will hold on to it as soon as I feel it touch me, its heaviness fell upon my back as if it wanted to jump into my body. I quickly turned and grabbed it; it was powerful and big, it felt so cold and smelled foul like they all did, I held onto it as it tugged me toward it, it pushed at me as if it wanted me off.

I prayed, back into the darkness you go, I bind this spirit back to hell down low leave this place you don't belong, I bind your evil it will be no more. While I prayed it flung me all over, I could feel its heavy breath on my face. I closed my eyes and prayed and prayed; I bind this spirit in the name of Jesus Christ. I felt the spirit growing weak; I held onto it as my body hit the wall over and over again, it seemed to grow weaker when I hit the wall. I fell to the floor, I still held onto it was calm, when I felt it was weakening, I began to lift myself from the floor, but it pushed me back to the floor with its strong force.

I began to pray again, go back into the darkness where you belong, I bind you in the name of Jesus Christ, it's evil began to show it's self like a movie as I held onto it; I saw a man prowling the night streets to rape and kill. I see its past as if it was still living in it, its darkness was a horror. I watched as he held a child by his neck and choked him until his little legs stopped dangling in the air his head. I felt as if I was falling into the darkness with him; I was choking and coughing as it grew weak, I prayed in silence, as I felt its force weaken.

Lord, send it back from where it came, close the doors and lock it with chains, I prayed that it never returned. it should go back to hell where it should burn, lead it back in Jesus name. Lord, lead it back into the flames, I was lifted and thrown toward the wall, the force pulled me in as it was leaving, I opened my eyes, and it was as if I was floating in a dark cloud. There was light around me; it was as if I was looking down at the room, I closed my eyes and prayed, Jesus no, it's stealing my body and taking my soul.

I prayed, Lord, lead it back without my soul, the cloud was becoming clear, and I dared to see where I was when the spirit lifted it off me. The room became warm; lights were flying all around me. I could see the spirit leaving it was like a dark cloud dissolving. Lord, thank you, I said still scared to move, I lay still on the floor. Soon there was a figure of a man lifting me up close to its chest with his hand over my face as if it was telling me to rest. I felt good and happy as it held me close, I looked across the room listening for the babies, and they were so quiet.

I began to worry until I saw the room filled with eight lights, they made a circle around the house as if they were shielding us. I laid there catching my breath, the room filled with the smell of flowers again, I watched, and each light faded away. I moved over slowly towards the couch to grab hold of the coffee table so that I could pull myself up on it; my back hurt worse. I sat on the couch with my hands to my head; my neck was also burning, the room grew calm soon I heard a knock at the door. I waited before going to get it; I walked slowly to open it, I looked out it was Michael, he came right in.

"Baby, are you okay, what's wrong?" He asked grabbing me by the arm helping me over to the couch. "I'm okay Michael," I tell him holding my neck. Michael held me in his arms "Baby what happened, you can tell me." "I'm okay. Can you help me to the nursery?" I asked him. I had to see my babies, I hoped they were okay, we walked into the nursery, and they were both standing, holding onto the crib rail looking up in the air. I laid my head on Michael's shoulder watching them from the door; I could see what they did, the lights were above their crib. I prayed silently, Lord, thank you for saving me tonight, and thank you for watching over my babies. Lord, thank you for bringing Michael back into my life. Michael held me, and we watched them smile up at the light.

Shaping Up

Michael never questioned me about that night again, and I never wanted to bring it up. I just went on as if it never happened. I saw more and more of Mr. Simms, but only here and there he didn't say much at all. Working out became a habit for me especially during the night when the babies were sleeping and the house was quiet, and I couldn't wait for Michael to come over through my body craved him all the time now. It was like I needed him to hold me at night to sleep. One morning I awoke, and flowers of all kinds surrounded the house.

Tara had made breakfast, and the children were dressed. I walked into the kitchen, and there everyone was waiting for me to sit and eat. Even daddy, it was a pleasant surprise, Michael was smiling so hard. "Good morning, sweetheart," he said kissing my cheek and pulling my chair out for me. "Good morning everyone," I said. "What's going on? Did I miss something?" I asked. "No." Daddy said smiling; I had to be here.

"It's your day, November first. Today's your big day. I wanted to make sure I was here too." Before my dad could utter another word, Michael stopped him "Uh, Mr. Lawson How's that coffee? He asked. "Yes, daddy told him you think you can pour me a little more? I'd like some of Tara said holding her cup out for Michael to pour her a cup full. She winked at him as he poured her cup full. "So I was thinking Michael said sitting down in the chair next to me.

"You're not working today, and I'm not working today. How about we go downtown and your father marries us?" He opened a beautiful box, and inside it had the biggest diamond ring I have ever seen. I was so surprised. "Really! Michael! Really!" I screamed out, I jumped up hugged daddy and hugged Tara then I ran over to hug the babies. "Oh

God! What am I going to wear?" I said putting my hands on my head running back into the room.

"TARA!" I yelled, "please come help me, I don't know what to wear" Tara came back in the room she stood near the bed then flopped her body down over it as she usually does when she's watching me get ready to leave for work. "Are you happy?" She asked me. "Yes, I believe I am happy Tara, I love Michael." I could hear daddy lecturing Michael all the do's and don'ts of his daughter; I peeked in as I could see Michael sitting shaking his head at daddy intensely to his every word.

"Well, I guess we won't be spending a lot of time together anymore after you guys get married huh? She asked. "Of course we will. What do you mean? You're still my best friend, aren't you?" I asked her; she reached over to me slapped my leg. "Of course I am, Dork, now wear the purple dress. Oprah says nothing speaks greatness like the color purple." "Oh, now you want to listen to Oprah huh?" I said throwing my shirt at her face.

"I love you, Tara," I called Maddy so that she could meet us there and I told her to please bring Dr. Green and a camera. I was so excited that I forgot to call Martha. We were all the way down to the courthouse when she came running in. "Here's your something old," she said pointing down at herself. I'm an old member of the family that was left out, she said with a mad look on her face. Could you believe it, I thought, I'm getting married November today.

Karis and Michael, It was all like a dream as daddy read our vows and we said our vows to one another. Just looking into Michael's eyes, I knew he was a special guy. His smile lit up the room with love and affection for me and mine for him. Michael loved me with unconditionally; I thought. "Look what God brought me, wow. Someone like Michael, when we were finished daddy surprised us with a wedding reception held at his house on the patio. It wasn't anything fabulous, but it was fun. Randall was the DJ, and we all couldn't help, but to laugh at the fact that daddy thought he was a great dancer.

The night ended late I took away almost everyone's keys. There would be no drinking and driving; I told them as I stored them away in a bag for the night. I made sure everyone who had more the one drink had a spot on the floor to sleep with a blanket and pillow. When we left the house was nice and quiet and secure.

Michael and I had yet to discuss where we'd live or where we'd start our lives as a family. He began to talk about it as soon as we started our walk from daddy's house he had one baby in a car seat and I had the other. "I think we should buy a bigger home," he said. "Why?" I questioned. "What's wrong with mine?" "Oh, there's nothing wrong, I just think that it would be better for the children if they lived in a bigger home," he said. "You could rent yours out to Tara."

"What? Michael, no, Tara can't afford to pay for a place by herself right now, and she's helping her grandmother now, remember? "Oh yes I do, I remember you saying that now. Well you know my place is a little bit bigger than yours." Why can't we live there?" He says with no regrets. "No, thank you, Michael; we could all stay at my place until we find another place." I leaned over and kissed his cheek, and that was that.

We pulled up at the house, and there was Cookie at the door purring to get in. "I think we should find cookie a new home," Michael said. "Why, what's wrong with Cookie?" I asked. "You just don't have the time for her. We could find a place where someone can love her you know. Baby, I'm not trying to change things too fast am I?" He asked me laughing as we carried the babies inside. They were so heavy in those chairs. Michael grabbed both chairs at the door so that I could get the key. He loved to joke around.

He started doing curl-ups with babies' seats as if they were weights for weightlifting. I laughed at him, and he kept meowing like a cat. He'd do one and yell out, "meow!" It was funny; the babies laughed at him too. Michael and I took them to them the room to put them down for bed. I breastfed Kristopher, and he bottle fed Kristine we rocked them and talked and laughed. He talked about my dad's dancing skills and how he hoped none of our children inherits any of those skills.

I laughed at him and told him that it would be nice if they inherited his smile; he has a nice smile. We complimented each other until the babies fell off to sleep. Then off to the bedroom to make love all night. Michael undressed me as I undressed him. First I took off his tie and threw it over my shoulders as I stared him in the eyes. He pulled string down from my shoulder and slowly ran his fingers down my chest. Michael kissed me all over my neck; I loved that he took his time to make love to me.

Every inch of my body felt the way he felt about me at that moment. We made love; his passion screamed I love you with every touch. Michael picked me up and carried me over to the bed and laid me down. He kissed me from the bottom to the top. We made love until we were both tired. The next morning I turned over, and both the babies were in bed with me, and there was a note beside the pillow that read. "Karis, I love you, sweetie, I was called into work, get some rest today. See you later."

I looked over, and there was a bundle of lilies. I loved lilies. I got up to get the babies, and the doorbell rang, I wrapped myself in the sheet and went to the window. I took a peep out. It was Tara, I went to the door, "hey you, come on in," I said opening the door. "Hey, married woman, how are we today? She asked. "I thought I'd come over and see how the babies are. Is that okay? Karis." She said looking unsure.

"Of course, if you don't get in here," I said. Snatching her by the arm barely able to grab it my hand couldn't fit around half her arm. She laughed at me." You're so strong, Karis." She walked behind me to the room. I was wrapped up in the sheet; she kept stepping on the sheet as we walked. "Oh, I know what you been doing," she said. "Yes, and I need to shower, could you watch the babies for a couple of minutes, please?"

"Sure," she said "you nasty," she said laughing. She picked up Kristine. "Mommy and daddy are nasty," she whispered to her. "Tara, stop it." I said going to the bathroom. I washed up when I came out Tara was already in the hall bathroom bathing Kristine while Kristopher sat in the chair and watched. I went over to him to pick him up he smiled right away. "Hello baby," I said holding him up in the air. "I love you," I began taking his clothes off, to wash him up alongside Kristine with Tara.

We washed them up and talked about yesterday's wedding ceremony when I turned to grab a towel there stood Mr. Simms. "Hello," he said, I quickly turned to the baby to get him out. "Not now," I blurted out. "Huh," Tara said looking confused. "What are you talking about?" "Oh nothing," I was just thinking out loud I told her. "Oh about how to hold out on; making lovemaking?" She said laughing. "Not now Michael, not now."

"No," I said taking Kristopher to the nursery to put on his clothes. I would put him on a little summer short set outfit today, a one piece with a sailboat on the front of it, with sandals. I applied lotion on him, top to bottom and brushed his hair as he laid on my lap. Mr. Simms sat in the rocker next to me just smiling. "How are you, Karis?" He asked. "I'm fine," I whispered hoping Tara wouldn't walk in to see me talking to someone only I could see.

"That's good Karis, you handled yourself well in with that last encounter, but there's more to come. I want you to know how to handle what's next with ease. The next one that comes will be a big tease." He said getting up from the rocker he reached his hand down to pinch Kristopher's cheek. Kristopher laughed so hard as if Mr. Simms was tickling him. Tara walked in soon after him carrying Kristine in a towel with her little feet dangling out of the bottom. Tara would stay with them today while I worked. She was great; I had to think of something special for her soon, her help was greatly appreciated. I made it to work just in time for shift change.

Dr. Green was yelling at an intern who didn't follow instruction well, I'm guessing. I scrambled to pass them in the hallway to see where I'd be working today. I looked at the scheduling broad, and my name was spelled Mrs. Karis Michael Stevenson, with a smiley face alongside it. I knew right away who wrote it, Maddy. She looked at me and smiled, and everyone said congratulations, and next, a baby huh? "I suppose so," I answered.

I worked through the day wondering when or if I would see my husband all day. I know since he's got back his schedule has been so busy. He's on call, and he's here most of the night I'm fine with it as long as I can see him when I close my eyes at night. I was to be finishing nursing school really soon, to me to be the greatest moment of my life. I don't think that I'd keep the same profession; I'd really like to explore.

I was about done with my shift when I was walking down the hall I felt a cold chill alongside my back. I closed my eyes and turned to look in back of me. It was Mrs. Cotton, "hello," I said walking toward the utility room to get some warm blankets." Hello," she said. "How are you, young lady?" reaching out her hand to me. "I'm fine Mrs. Cotton. Just fine," I told her. "Mrs. Cotton, what are you doing out here?" I asked her, Are you in the hospital? I asked her.

"Yes, I'm here, in the hospital visiting you," she said. She swung my hand back and forth as we walked, "Visiting me?" I questioned. "Really, well what can I help you with?" I asked her.

"You will see later," she said. Swinging my hand way up high and walking away from me she cut her eyes as if she was furious at me. I walked as fast as I could to the patient's rooms to distribute the warm blankets. I went back down to the front desk looking for Michael.

"Maddy, have you seen Michael?" I asked her. "I saw him a little earlier, but he was heading home he said." "Oh, I see." "What's wrong honey?" She asked me. "Have you seen Mrs. Cotton around here at all today?" "Mrs. Cotton?" "Yes, you know you know James' grandmother Mrs. Cotton?" "No I haven't seen her since she was admitted here some time ago. I don't think she's been here in a while. She had a hip replacement right? About a year ago" Maddy asked. "

Yes, I believe so." "You saw her here today? Maddy asked. "Yes, she was here, she said, he had been looking for me." "I didn't see her come through here." Maddy said. "I guess she must have come up through the back I don't know?" Maddy said, erasing the broad for the day. "Well, how are you liking married life so far" She asked. "It's fun, so far so good," I tell her with a smile. "I just think Michael's going to be too busy."

"Yeah that doctor's life is something," she said. "Hey, but the benefits are nice. You can stay home, have babies, and cook and look as sexy as you can for him. He'd love that." "I guess your right; we haven't even had time to sit and talk about anything other than where we're going to live. He wants us to stay at his house, but I like my house." "I think you guys should think about getting a bigger house, don't you? Especially, if you're going to have more babies," she said smiling.

"Maddy, do you think it's possible? I was blessed with the twins, but more? I don't know; I wasn't supposed to have any right?" "Yes, that's right, but I believe that God has a plan for you, and what he says goes. He won't give you any more than you can bear." Maddy said holding my shoulder. "I think that the Lord wants you and Michael to share something special as well." "You're probably right Maddy," I said kissing her cheek. Finally, Michael walked up behind me; he slapped me on the bottom. "Hey, wife, what are you still doing here? You just can't get enough of me huh?" He said while kissing me on the neck.

"No, I can't get enough," I said. I went in the back to get my things ready to head home. Michael followed, "Hey what's for dinner baby? I don't know, Usually Tara has something cooked by the time I get home, It's usually a very good surprise" Yeah Tara can cook, "I feel kind of bad for her though, I want to set her up with someone nice not this guy she keeps talking to on the phone. He's never going come out here to be with her. "I know but she says she loves him Michael there's nothing we can do to change that. It's her choice."

"Your right it is. I kissed Michael on the lips and started to walk away, He pulled me back, "Hey that's not how you kiss your new husband goodbye." He held me close to him and kissed me passionately holding my neck with his soft hands. I felt as if I could just float home. My body started to get warm all over, I pulled away, Michael held my arm tight, "What, ahh, you can't handle it, huh? You gotta run to that cold shower," I smiled at him.

"Yes I can," I said. Shoving him out of my way," I will see you back at home," I said shaking my head and walking away. Goodness, that man is such a kidder, I thought walking away. I walked to my car in the darkness of the hospital halls, It was quiet and cool. I took the stairs to get to the garage. I didn't want to take the elevator tonight; I didn't want to run into anyone. If Mrs. Cotton was in the hospital maybe James was around or his sister Teresa or even worse his mom. So I took the stairs.

No one ever took the stairs; I thought as I began my journey down. I was down three flights when I heard footsteps behind me. I stopped, the footsteps stopped, so I walked down faster, and faster. The footsteps followed me faster and faster. I stopped; something just told me to stop. I kneeled down to pray, "Lord, please, there is a presence near trying to fill my spirit with terrible fear. Stop it, Lord; bind it to go, if it won't make it show." I prayed and prayed; as I prayed the footsteps began to move as if they were dancing in circles around me, faster and faster, I dared to open my eyes.

I prayed over and over as the footsteps began fade into the darkness. I sat on the stairs for a while to collect myself; it felt as if I wasn't sitting alone. I could feel a presence, a good presence all around me. I went on to the garage to my car. When I made it to the house, Tara was waiting sitting outside on the porch with the twins. She had the swing out for them, and she was leaning back rocking herself, she looked sad.

"What's up, Tara? I asked her. "I just feel fat today, I tried working out just ten minutes, and I fell flat on my face out of breath. Can you believe that?" She asked me. "Well, what kind of workout were you doing?" I asked her. "I don't want to talk about it Karis; I really don't. Nothing I do for my weight is working. I tried everything, pills, diets, exercise, starving myself, you name it, I've tried it." She said looking discouraged. "Well Tara, I don't

know, have you ever thought of praying?" I asked her. "Of course I have, you dork I pray every day and night. That doesn't work either. I just think I should give up." "Give up, on life? I think you should rethink what you're saying, Tara? You have a lot to live for, we all love you around here what's going to happen to us? Think about your grandmother what she going to do without you." "I don't care, she doesn't want to help me, I told her that they have this surgery, I can get it done for ten thousand dollars to help me lose weight, but she won't pay for it.

The doctor told me if I lose one hundred and eighty pounds I can get the surgery done. Karis, I can't get a job, people will judge me because I'm fat. When I go to these interviews, they don't look at my resume and my job history or any of that. They mostly look at my appearance. My grandmother says that I don't have a job, so she's not comfortable giving me any money for the surgery. I keep explaining to her I don't have a job because of the weight."

"Tara, I don't know if that's a good excuse either, I mean I know a lot of big people who have good jobs. Maybe it's not that, maybe you're not getting the jobs simply because you aren't really qualified. I will help you, but you have to be willing to lose the weight and pay me back. Just get me the information on it." "Tara began to cry, "Really Karis, Really? You'll help me?" "Yes, Michael and I were just talking about what we could do to help you.

We are both so grateful for you. You help us so much, I mean where we would be; especially me. Where would I be? I wouldn't have been able to finish school or anything without your help." She grabbed me and squeezed me as tight as she could. "Just don't let us down; you have to lose that weight, Tara. I can't tell you how important it's going to be for you to stay with the plan and keep yourself motivated. Don't go to any fast food places, and you have to work out as much as you can every day, or for at least ten minutes at least. Promise me you'll try," I told her. "I will try my hardest to lose it, Karis I promise. I will start tomorrow." She said grabbing her things off of the couch; she was so excited.

          "I have to hurry to grandmas to tell Auntie Sherrie," she whispered her way out of the door as fast as she could. "Oh, you don't have to cook," she said. "I cooked a surprise for you guys." "Uh Tara," I said. "Before you leave can you please help me get the kids inside from the porch?" "Sure, girl," she said in a panic. "I can't believe it," she said as she picked up the Kristine from the swing and brought her inside. I grabbed Kristopher and brought him in we sat them in their little bouncy chairs and buckled them in; they were both smiling and laughing.

"Hello my sweets," I say to them. "I missed you guys today; I missed your sweet little faces all day, my sweethearts." I said as I put them on the floor next to the couch and I locked the door behind Tara. I went to the kitchen to see what she cooked. I warmed the babies' food to feed them before Michael got home. I sat down while the food warmed and played and talked to them. They laughed and so hard. I fed them and got them ready for bed. I laid them in bed and went to my room to get ready for my shower.

I heard footsteps walking down the hall; I left the bathroom quickly to look down the hall. I didn't see anyone; I went to look in the babies' room. There was no one. I walked around the babies room and searched the closet and under the cribs. Where were those footsteps? I went into the living room I looked all around and no one. My water was running for my shower; I went into the bathroom to check my water. I reached my arm in the shower, to turn it off, something grabbed my arm.

The grip was so tight that it stung a little, but I didn't let it frighten me. I pulled the curtains back, and there was Mrs. Cotton with water running all over her night clothes. I snatched my hand back and pulled the curtain back further. "Mrs. Cotton," I said in a frantic, and just as I began to grab her when she opened her mouth wide and yelled. "Liar! They're mine!" She faded away. I held onto the edge of the doorway as the room went colder and darker. I fell to my knees to pray.

"Lord, please spare me from harm tonight. Keep me strong in the light keep me ready and able to fight; I am praying, Lord, to bind the spirit. In your name, Lord, Jesus, I will fight until your blessings come through, I will hold on tight to what I know is true." I rocked back and forth as I kneeled to pray it was like I had a shield around me and there were spirits in it praying with me. It was very warm in there and I could see small lights all around me.

Like bubbles, when I got up from praying, I felt the presence of the Lord, and I could smell the flowers around me again. I got into the shower quickly and washed. I knew that Michael would be calling to tell we he was on his way. I would sit in the nursery and watch the babies and talked to Tara on the phone until he arrived. I was talking to Tara she was ranting about her weight as usual, and I could hear her chewing in my ear at the same time. "Tara? What are you eating?" I asked her. "Oh, Cheetos and dip," she says laughing. Well, I see how serious she's taking this whole lose enough weight for this surgery.

"Tara, are you giving up on our plans?" I asked her. "No, but I can't starve myself until I get to that size," she replied. "Well, how about a few healthy snacks? Like some carrots, celery, salads, peanuts, or water. You know things like that," I tell her. "No, I just can't eat that stuff. It doesn't fill me up at all," she said. "Well, can you try the nutrition bars that we bought the other day with some yogurt and granola? That might satisfy you for a while," I tell her. "No, I'll just stick to what I know;" she said smacking loudly in my ear."

I grew frustrated, as I listened to her chewing away at the chips on the other end. I know tomorrow she's going to call me crying tomorrow about her weight. I hear her talking to her aunty Sherry about a television show that they enjoy watching together. Her aunt began teasing her about her weight and how she needs to get off her fat butt and walk. She began yelling at her aunt to leave the room. "Go on, Aunty Sherry; get out of here," she said.

"Tara, I think you should probably listen to her." I tell her as I hear her aunt struggled to stay and speak with her. She went in and out of the door as we talked. Tara, go ahead and talk to her," I tell her. "She'll be fine," she says. "I have a horrible feeling," I tell her. "Go on; I'm tired anyway I'm going to go ahead and lay down. It looks like Michael is going to have a long night; I'm going to turn in, goodbye." I said hanging up the phone; I held Kristine in my arms rocking her in the chair.

Just thinking about how wonderful she felt in my arms. It was quiet, and Kristopher was sound asleep, and I didn't hear Cookie around the house either. I rocked and prayed, "Lord, thank you for your many blessings; I thank you for what may not seem like much to others, my father, and my mother. Even though she's not here physically, I know that she watches over me. I feel her spiritual light and guidance. Thank you, Lord for blessing me all over, keeping me safe and free from hunger; keeping me from feeling like I can overcome obstacles"

"I know I can because I hold on to you Lord. I prayed and prayed until I fell off to sleep, and when I woke up, I was in bed wrapped in Michael's arms. I turned to look at him, "hello," he said barely opening his eyes, kissing my cheek. "Hello, Michael, I missed you," I tell him. "I bet you did," he said rubbing himself up against me. I could hear the babies waking for their breakfast on the baby monitor.

Tara was usually already in there with them. I waited to hear who was going to start to cry first. They didn't cry; they just played around they are trying to communicate to one another now. So I listened in to hear what they were saying. I heard, "mama, dada," and a lot of spitting noises. It was the cutest thing I ever heard. I kissed Michael and went to their room to get them.

To my surprise, Kristopher had climbed out of his crib onto the floor, and Kristine was standing on her tip toes trying to push herself over the top to get out too. I screamed, "No! Kristine, don't do it, stay in there. Where are you going, baby?" I said picking her up. Kristopher crawled over to me and lifted himself up by pulling on my leg. He waved, "Hello, young man," I say to him. I sat down in the chair as I picked him up. "Hello, little guy. How did you escape from your crib?" I asked him.

"What are you doing out of there?" I asked. He smiled at me. The doorbell rang and rang fast as if someone was in a hurry for me to open the door. I placed Kristopher in my arms and grabbed Kristine and sat her in the chair on the floor. "Hold on I'm coming!" I yelled out. "Who is it?" I asked. I went to the door with my gown on holding Kristopher. They continued to ring the bell. I looked through the peep hole. It's Tara; I opened the door as fast as I could, "What's wrong? Where's your key?" I asked her.

She just stared at me, speechless. "Tara, what's wrong?" I asked again, "what's wrong?" I put Kristopher down in a chair on the floor. I went to the door to see if someone was with her outside, she drove her Aunt Sherrie's car over. Oh no, I thought, it happened, she's gone. Her aunts gone, I shut the door and turned to her. I took a deep breath.

"Tara, Sit down honey, I'll make some tea," I told her walking her over to the couch. "Would you like some tea?" Tears began to stream from her eyes, she didn't say a word. I went into the kitchen and put a pot of water on, and put the babies oatmeal bowls out for their breakfast. I went over to Tara and held her hand. "Everything is going to be okay Tara, I promise. Can I pray for you? Don't cry, Tara, please, let's pray."

She sobbed so hard, "my Aunty Sherrie; where's my Aunty Sherrie?" She sobbed and sobbed; I put her hand on forehead and prayed. "Lord, her heart is heavy, too heavy, Lord, give her the strength to carry this pain. She's struggling to find reason and understanding on why her aunt had to go. Lord, please heal her heavy heat and take away her sadness and pain. In Jesus name, I pray." I held Tara, until the tea kettle whistled; Michael got up from his morning nap and took the babies fed them.

Tara didn't want to go back to her grandma's house she said that it was so much going on and she couldn't look at her little cousin. Her aunt had a child that she left behind. Tara was so torn and hurt after I prayed for her the sobbing was off, and on she was able to tell me how her aunt past over, I took her for a walk down the street. She told me that her little cousin went to wake her mom from her sleep that morning and she wouldn't move when she went in to see why she was stiff as a board.

"She was cold as ice and was not moving or responding to anything," she said as she cried. "Was she on any meds or was she sick?" I asked? "Well, she was taking medications for depression." "Was she depressed?" I asked. "She seemed so happy all the time," I said confused. "Yes, she was very depressed. She hid it very well." Tara said crying more and more; she sat down on the sidewalk, I sat down next to her. "What now?" She said looking up with tears streaming from her eyes.

"I bet even if I get this weight off my body, with the way things are I would still have all kinds of problems. My poor aunt, she was always trying to take care of her daughter, she was overweight, but she worked hard at looking good and staying at a comfortable size. She was able to carry that weight and still have a wonderful job where the people loved and helped her; she had a husband who cared for her. He died in the gulf war. I mean all that hard work she did to get the weight down and you know what killed her?"

"Karis, it was sleep apnea; something she developed during the time she was obese. She could have died many ways before they told her, but no, this is how it happens. I just feel like whatever I do I'm not going to make it, Karis, do you ever feel that way?" She asked me looking at me with wonder in her eyes. "Tara, I don't know why these things happen. I do know that we all live and die, I'm certain that we all serve a purpose and that the Lord loves us all. I don't believe that you leave this earth if it's not your time. I think we all have a special time to be born and a special time to go back."

"We are all spirits in his honor. I feel his presence around me all the time. I can't tell you exactly what's real and what's not, but what I feel spiritually, I believe to be real enough for me." I said. "Karis, I don't know, I've been battling my weight all my life it seems. If God loves us the way you say and we all serve a purpose, what would mine be? Why am I here feeling what I feel? What would I have to give anyone? Besides a bunch of my grief," she said.

"Tara I refuse to tell you again what you have to give back. The Lord has blessed you with lots of gifts to pass on; you have to love those gifts and protect them and learn them. If you don't love yourself how can anyone else love you? Believe it or not, I think when we don't love ourselves the way that God loves us it makes him so angry with us, angry enough to shut us down. You need to catch the spirit of his grace inside of you, know what it feels like, and love it." I reached out my hand to her to help her up.

"Let's go," I looked at Tara, her face was covered with tears her eyes red and filled with more tears. I smiled at her, "Tara you're a beautiful human being," I said slapping her arm. We walked back to the house; I could see Michael outside on the front lawn with the babies. They were playing in the grass while he cleaned the car out. I could see them running back, and fourth round and round laughing and reaching for one another.

As we get closer, I saw Mr. Simms face in the window, standing next to him was Aunt Sherry, waving at me. Her eyes pierced out at me as if they were shinning. I waved my hand at them. "Are you waving at the babies?" Tara asked. "Yes," I said. "They're learning." "Yeah, they're so lucky to have Michael, he's so good to you guys," Tara said. "I know, isn't he the greatest?" I said smiling as we walked up closer to the car; Michael shut the car door and peeked around the car running toward Kristine to grab her before she went for the fence.

"Hey, little one, where are you going" He said, "The grass is this way," she smiled and laughed as he tossed her up into the air, Kristopher hung onto the fence as he danced smiling and laughing. I went to him and picked him up and carried him over to the porch. Michael came right behind me with Kristine, he sat next to me and took him and placed the both of them on his lap and he leaned over and kissed my cheek.

"Hey baby, how was your walk?" He asked. "It was fine," I told him. "How's Tara?" "She seems ok now," I said shaking my head looking over at her. She was standing at the fence just looking out to the street. I looked in the window, and Mr. Simms and Auntie Sherry were still there. "I better go inside and get started on some lunch, Michael, what would you like to eat?" I asked him, holding the door open wide, "I'd like whatever you decide, baby," he said.

"Okay," I went inside to the kitchen, Tara came in behind me. "I can help you make them," she said. "Oh no, Tara, sit down, I'm going to make you the best sandwich you ever had It's going to knock your socks off." I told her. "I have everything I need too." I began taking all that I need out of the refrigerator. I looked over my shoulder, and Aunt Sherry, who loved to cook, was right there to guide me through. I made these sandwiches with all of her love and affection that she carried for Tara.

It had lettuce, tomatoes, onions, a tiny dash of salt and pepper, turkey, salami, Swiss cheese, and one small pickle. I didn't add any mayo, I put just a little on mine and Michaels, and I made a small cucumber salad, just how daddy likes to make. We sat down at the table and ate quietly; Tara played with Kristopher and Kristine. Michael and I winked back and forth at one another as if we were telling stories with our eyes. We hadn't got too much alone time at all this month.

We've been so busy with everything else, and we would be moving to another home soon, something bigger and better for the kids. We were planning to have more children at least two more Michael wants two I only want one more. Time went by soon after laying Tara's aunt Sherrie to rest. She stayed at her grandma's a lot more, she still helped with the twins. Michael and I moved into our new home. We bought a big five bedroom three bath home in a nice kid-friendly neighborhood that my dad loved and approved.

It had a beautiful view, a pool, and an area where could we set up a swing set and sandbox for the kids. It was a beautiful home; daddy came over every weekend to help me set up a spot in the backyard for a garden and in front a rose garden. It was looking pretty good; we'd work on it almost every evening while the twins ran around the yard. Michael would swim with them in the pool. Daddy taught them to swim as soon as we moved in, he spent days after work in the pool with them.

They loved their grandpa; they'd call him papa. I thought it was the cutest thing. Tara was beginning to lose a little weight even eating a little better. When I saw her, I would ask, "how much do you love yourself today Tara?" and she'd smile from ear to ear. I just want everyone around me to be happy, but as I matured, I found out that sometimes impossible to have. People don't want to see you coming if you're too happy because they are so miserable, they'd give you such a hard time when their feeling that way.

Work, which always has been a wonderful place for me, had become a horrible place. Maddy was getting older, and Dr. Green was still married. I don't think he was ever going to leave his wife for her. She grew angry waiting I believe. I could see that she loved him, but I look at her, and I see her many sacrifices. I can see her wasting away her time and energy. It's making her very mean and angry; she's so mad all the time. We wouldn't speak or laugh the way we use too because she's so mad all the time.

Michael and I went out a lot, and we made love all the time. He's working on making another baby, and I'm just making love. I would like to have one, but I say if it's Gods will, it will happen. Fall came, and it was chilly out, I took the day off to go to the doctors with Tara to see if they okay the surgery. It had been a little over two years that we had planned the surgery and it did look as if she lost a little weight. We went to the doctors early after dropping the twins off at the preschool.

They loved preschool so much. We made it to the doctor's office on time, Tara signed in, and we waited in the lobby area for a while. I started noticing that there were people there waiting for hours to be seen. Tara didn't have the best health coverage either she went to a county-funded community clinic in the inner city, or she was anxious about seeing the doctor today. If everything goes well, we will be able to proceed with surgery for weight loss.

After waiting three hours and going to the window several times the nurse came out to get us. "Sorry for the wait, we are swamped today." I looked around and there and looked back at her. "That's probably something you guys should work on, getting more help." I told her as she walked us back into a room for Tara to weigh in. "We're going to need you to remove your shoes," she explained, "and step on the scale." Tara started to remove her shoes and took a deep breath.

"It's okay Tara," I tell her. She got on the scale, and we all looked down. It moved all the way over to the end of the scale, and Tara looked away. "Okay Tara, you can step off now," she's says. "I'm just going to check your blood pressure, take some blood, and we're done. The doctor will want you to wait in that room over there," she said pointing with her pen to a door that looked dirty and old. "Okay," Tara said with sadness in her voice. She brought in a bigger blood pressure cuff for Tara to check her pressure.

"Have you had high blood pressure in the past?" She asked her, "Yes I have." "Okay, its high right now I need to call the doctor in here because it's too high." She checked it over and over again to be sure, and then she got up from her chair and went out of the room.

"Tara, are you okay?" I asked her. "Why is your blood pressure out of control right now? I think you're just nervous, don't worry," I told her.

Just then, the doctor walked in. "She sat down on the stool next to Tara, and said, "Hello Tara, how are you today?" "I guess I'm okay," she replied. She reached her hand out to shake mine. "Hi," I said as she pointed a small light to Tara's eyes. "Are you feeling weak or any dizziness or numbness in your arms or legs?" She asked her, I moved back and began to frown she was very serious. "What's wrong?" I asked. "Her blood pressure is very high right now; we have to find out why."

She pulled up Tara's pants leg and squeezed her; you could see her handprints indented in her skin when she pushed in. "Your bodies retaining water. Have you been feeling dizzy at all? She asked again. "No, I haven't, I've been fine," Tara explained again. She looked at me, "Come with me," the doctor said. We followed her into the room, She turned the light on and told Tara to lay on the table, she checks her all over, then she called the nurse in, she took Tara's clothes and put them in a bag.

"Tara, I'm so sorry honey, but I'm going to have to admit you today," she said. "Why?" Tara asked. "You have fluid on your lungs, and if we don't remove it, you could die. Your heart can't take it, we need to run more test, but I'm quite sure that that's what I'm hearing. I've called an ambulance to transport you over to the county. Would you like for us to call someone, or can your sister do all that for you?" She asked looking at me.

"Sure I can," I said getting the bag with Tara's clothes from the chair. "I don't want to go," Tara said, "I have to take care of my grandma." "You have to tell your mom to go over there Tara. Come on this is very important you have to do what the doctor says." I tell her, "just go to the hospital and at least get your test done if it looks okay then leave if it doesn't, don't leave. I'll call them all for you okay." I tell her, we hear the ambulance coming close. "Tara, don't," I said as she began to cry.

"You're going to be fine, I promise." I took her clothes and walked out. I couldn't watch them take her to the ambulance, so I went to my car before they took her. I made it home as I was leaving the clinic I saw her grandfather and Aunt Sherrie watching me and waving goodbye. A voice said to me, "it won't be long for your friend will be gone." "God, no," I said as I drove off. They kept Tara in the hospital for almost a month before I had the courage to go see her in fear of what I would feel around her.

I had to go see her because the holidays were coming up everyone expected me. I worked the garden with daddy intensely anticipating that moment, daddy knew that something was on my mind because I wouldn't say a word, I would just plant and water and dig the whole time. He would have to tap my shoulder. "Karis," he'd say to get my attention. "Baby what's wrong?" "Oh daddy, I'm fine," I'd say and go on digging and Michael would constantly ask me what was on my mind. I would tell him I was okay too he'd ask about Tara, I'd tell him I spoke to her on the phone.

"Why haven't you been to see her?" He asked. I never reply to him or I just shrug my shoulders as if I don't know why. I get myself ready by praying a lot all day and night. Lord, please give me strength for what I cannot change. Give me peace for when I get mad at what makes me hurt. Lord, please heal my heart don't allow my spirit to break, give me strength, lord, please. In Jesus name, I pray. I go over to Tara's grandma's to meet up with her mother to go with her to the hospital on Christmas Eve.

I have a bunch of gifts for Tara from the children and Michael. I know that he's been up to see her already, but he won't tell me in fear of me being too upset. We get to the county hospital, and it's not what I expected, it's clean, and there are a lot of people walking around. Like it's a normal hospital setting to me. We went up onto the seventh floor it was very clean up there. I took several deep breaths before walking into the room where she was.

   She was lying in bed, the room was huge, there was a nice couch and a big window it was very nice. She had lots of flowers, "Hello," she said when she saw me, "Hello," I said. I went over to her; I didn't feel anything. No stomach ache and no feeling of sorrow anything at all. I didn't even hear anything. I hugged her for a long time, "here," I said handing her the gifts the children made her in preschool, she opened them and cried. "Oh, I miss them so much, I do."

"I know you do," I said, handing her the gift Michael and I got her. It was a picture of the family Me, Him and the children; she was excited about that too. "You guys look beautiful," she said. She began to cough; she coughed so hard, I was so scared I reached over and gave her some water. "Here you go, Tara," I put the straw up to her mouth; she just took a sip of the water and held onto her chest. Tara looked at her mom.

"So what's been going on with you?" I asked. "How'd all the testing go?" "Well, if you had come to visit her you'd know what happened to her." "Yes, I know I'm so sorry Tara, I know I should have been up to see you." "Oh, it's fine Karis, don't you mind my mom, she wouldn't know a thing about taking care of children. She wouldn't know how hard it is or anything. Especially because she never was there for my brothers or me," she said holding my hand. She looked over at her mom.

"Tara that wasn't very nice, now stop," I told her. "Neither was growing up without her there," she said looking at her mom. "Okay, okay, Tara, I just couldn't get away, that's all," I told her. "I understand, but for a whole month, wow right," her mom said walking toward the door. "Some friend you are," she said, walking out angry. "So when is the baby due?" Tara asked looking at my stomach. "What do you mean? There's no baby," I said rubbing my stomach standing up from the chair.

"Yes, there is a baby in there." She said pointing to my belly. I smiled at her, "No, Tara, I have no baby," I looked at her IV. "Are you delirious? Why are you saying all these crazy things? What do they have you on? First your mom now me, I'm not pregnant crazy," I said. "Yes, you are Karis you're very pregnant." "I just want to know what happened to you. What did those test show and why do you all of a sudden think you're a doctor?" I asked.

"I had fluid surrounding my lungs, and they drained off like sixty-five pounds of fluid, and they diagnosed with a chronic heart condition, and I'm going to die soon." She said looking at me smiling, "What are you saying, Tara? What do you mean?" "Yes, this is what they told me, they said that this weight on my body is going to kill me. So, Karis, I don't want to hear it anymore, I don't want to hear how you can help me lose it because you can't. It's over when I get out of here I'm going just to live the best life I can.

I'm going to find some of my old friends and party and run around until I drop." I didn't say a word this time I hugged Tara I pushed her over and laid down beside her. "You know Karis when that fluid was drained out; I felt so light. They came in and weighed me; I did lose weight in here. This food is nasty, and I can't even think straight thinking about whether or not I'm going to heaven or hell. What do you think?" She asked. I can't even tell you what I think right now."

"Yes you can, you don't think I notice, but I do, I see that you feel things. You could probably tell me exactly where I'm going," she said laughing. "No, I really can't," I tell her. "I love you, Tara; I just want you to be healthy. That's all, healthy and happy," I told her, I cried. "Look, don't cry please because we both can't cry at the same time, it's just not a good look and when you cry it's just so damn sad." She said sobbing loudly. She grabbed some tissue from the table next to the bed; we cried and watched television while eating Tara's, Jell-O, it was strawberry flavored.

We each ate with a plastic spoon while watching her favorite show Top Chef. They did not speak English, but the food looked delicious. After it went off, I waited for Tara to fall off to sleep and I slipped away and called Michael to come pick me up. I looked back at her before closing that door; it was not her time, I thought. She would be here for a while longer. Michael picked me up at midnight.

It was Christmas morning. He was wearing a Christmas cap and a white beard. "Ho, ho, ho," he said. When He pulled up, he had a gift for me in the front seat of the car. He opened the door for me quickly trying not to let the cold air hit the children sleeping in the back seat. "Are you hungry baby?" He asked. "No, I had some delicious jello it was strawberry I'm full thank you" "Well, open that up," he says pushing the gift to me next to my thigh near the seat.

"I hope you like it, baby." I unwrapped it quickly it was a small box, I opened it up, and it was dark, but I could feel what it was, It was a gold necklace with two twins and their birthstones in between a heart, I turned on the light to get a better look at it. "It's so beautiful," I told him, "I love it." I reached over and took his hand. "So, did Tara like her gifts?" He asked. "Yes, she did. She enjoyed them very much; the little hands in the clay were her favorites."

"I figured they would be; she loves the children so much." "They love her too," I said. Just thinking about how awful it would be for the kids to have to grow up without her. We all went back up to visit Tara the next day for Christmas. Her family and mine giving more gifts and sharing stories around her hospital bed. She was very happy. We all enjoyed each other as a family should around the holidays. It would be several weeks later when Tara would be released from the hospital.

She would go stay at her moms and then to her grandmother's house. She'd come by from time to time to visit; she soon started to go parting with an old friend that she ran into by chance at the mall. I told her to slow down, sitting on my porch smoking a cigarette, I seen her as I pulled up, I got out of the car. "So, you smoke now?" I asked her. She smiled and threw the cigarette down to the ground and pointed at her friend who was standing by the fence drinking from a silver flask. She walked over to me, "Karis, this is my friend Melissa Brown, and this is Karis, my closest friend."

I reached my hand out to her as she closed the top of the flask and put it into her purse. "Sorry," she said as she shook my hand. "It's so nice to meet you," she said. "I've heard so much about you and your family." "Nice to meet you too," I replied. "Come in you two," she said. "Tara, I haven't seen you in a while," "Yes I know, I've been running around, from club to club," they both began to laugh. "You should come along with us sometimes Karis; we'd have so much fun, have you ever been to a club?" She asked.

"No. I Haven't." "Well, you should come along with us one night, you'd love it, and we'd have so much fun." Tara said. "Tara, you know I won't enjoy that at all." I told her. "I won't be comfortable there." "She might be right," Melissa said. "It is for big girls; she wouldn't fit in there at all. Look at her; she's a little small." She said looking me over, she looked me up and down. "Tara knows that's not my thing. I don't party drink, smoke any of those things," I said. "Well, what do you do for fun then?" Melissa asked. "Oh, I have fun."

"Mostly it involves spending time with my family and friends." "Yes, she's somewhat of a nerd," Tara told her. "So, you must bore your husband," Melissa said, staring at the pictures of Michael and me on the coffee table, "is this him?" She asked. "Yes, it is." I told her. I went into the kitchen to turn the tea kettle on; I was growing angry at this woman that Tara brought to my house. She seemed to be attacking me.

I wanted Tara to take her and get out, so I gave her dirty looks, especially since I knew that Michael would be coming home soon. I went over to the coffee table and took the picture from her hand; she was still admiring Michael's smile, she complimented his teeth and his lips. I looked at Tara again, I was telling her to leave with my eyes, and when that didn't work, I sat down at the kitchen table with my tea and went through my mail. I told Tara that I was tired and I needed to rest before Michael came home with the children. She finally got the hint.

"Well, I guess we'll be going now," she said. "I will see you soon Karis." "Sure you will Tara." I told her. "You need to slow down and take care of yourself okay," I hugged her goodbye. I knew when I closed the door I wouldn't see Tara again until she was well past the weight she was before and miserable crying about making changes. I don't think that the friend she thinks is a good friend has her best interest at heart. Or maybe she doesn't know what I know; I just have to pray for her now more than ever. "Jesus, please cover Tara in your blood, protect her from harm protect her from harming herself in the name of Jesus, I pray Amen.

Setting Up House

I hardly spoke to Tara these days, and as time went on, she grew more distant. No more walks and hardly any visits. I seldom see her or her family. It was as if she didn't care about our friendship anymore either. I spent every moment with Michael and the children. We furnished the house with the beautiful statues we found all over town. We took the children out to the park and the zoo almost every chance we got we went to the zoo, Michael bought us memberships. The children get excited over the same things they saw every time.

They were noticing everything beginning to talk about everything too. Why, was their favorite word to say. By the time Michael and I would get them home at night, they were so tired they'd sleep soundly. I worked at night so that I could stay with them during the day and Michael was at the hospital during all hours. I would usually wake up in the middle of the night and find myself wrapped up in his arms at night as if we'd fallen off to sleep. Daddy would come over on Saturday mornings to help me in the garden usually leaving by the afternoon with bags of tomatoes and carrots.

He loved for Kristopher to follow him around in the garden. He'd question him about all things that he saw including things he'd seen before, just to make sure daddy would answer the same way. "Grandpa, what's that over there?" He'd ask pointing at the tall stems of corn growing up from the ground. "That's corn son," daddy would say. I loved watching them together. I hadn't had too many visits from Mr. Simms, and when I did, it was usually at the hospital. He was walking with someone he knew that had passed on.

He sometimes just came to say hello to me. I hadn't seen Mrs. Cotton and was scared after the incident in the bathroom. I think about it all the time. What could she want from me at work? I feel the spirits around me all the time. I see them and talk to them, I help them cross over, and I feel the closeness of the Lord, and his presence surrounded me more than ever when I'm near certain people.

Some spirits gave me the worst feelings. I would have to run the other way to get away. It   was like they were suffocating me. I felt as if everything turned black around me and I wouldn't see a thing. I couldn't help them, and the force around them was strong enough to knock me off my feet. It smelled awful. I had to pray intensely the moment it began its attack. I am always in fear of it catching me off guard. What would I do?

It was a lot stronger than the spirits that attacked me when I was younger. These spirits could take me into a darkness I didn't know existed. Working longer hours with Maddy now was almost every day, I had stopped working as a nurse and became the hospital's administrator. I was able to be home when I needed to be, and I still was able to have contact with the patients as well as their families. It was a lot of paperwork, but not impossible. I loved the challenges.

The insurance companies were the worse. Michael always came to my office on his break just to say hi. I had an assistant who was very attentive; she saw everything and worked hard at doing her job. Her name was Megan. My dad came by every now and the also just to say hello and take me to lunch daddy was starting to look really thin these days. I wondered why but never asked him. He came by one afternoon and I could tell there was something on his mind. We went to one of his favorite restaurant.

He loved this seafood place on the pier overlooking the ocean. Daddy was a little sad. "What's that matter with you?" I asked him, as he pulled my chair out for me. "Oh baby, I just get a little sad sometimes you know. Your daddy's all alone; I don't have a wife or a steady girlfriend or anything like that baby. And your sisters and brothers still won't let me be with anyone. Every time they see me with someone they get angry and want to fight or curse them. I can't hide all my relationships from them, and I would like for someone to come live with me and take care of me."

"Daddy, I think you gave yourself enough time to grieve and heal. I think that if you find a nice woman who can love you for you and not your money that would be the greatest thing for you. I don't want you to be alone either. I know that you would like to have a companion. It's lonely living in a house not having anyone there to share anything with; I get lonely when Michael's not there with me at night. I know it has to be even lonelier if no one is ever there."

I know that daddy has had his share of the overnight guess, I'm no fool, but by now at his age, he's probably so tired of playing the field it's become more of a hassle than a game for him "So who's this woman that you want to be with daddy, what's her name, where's she from?" I asked. "Hold on Karis; I don't know yet, there are two of them. I don't know which one I want yet." "Wow really daddy, that's very funny, so you're lonely and want to settle down, but you don't even know where to start; daddy that's not a good idea at all."

"I know honey, but they are both so nice." "Well, daddy, only one of them can do. You can't have them both in the house with you right?" Daddy paused and took a sip of his drink. "No, I guess not, I better make my mind up soon huh Karis," he said laughing. "Yes daddy, you should." I took the menu up from the table and began to look it over. "One of them has to have something that you admire more than the other. Right" I said, looking over at daddy.

"I guess you're right, Karis. Let me see, Debbie's funny, and she can cook, and she likes gardening." He said. "What about kids and traveling and work? Daddy does she have a job or career?" I ask. "I guess that's something to think about to sugar," he said smiling. "Now Teri, she's got it all, she's smart and loving, can cook and garden and travel and loves kids." He says looking away at the ocean. "Daddy, I don't like that look you have on your face right now." I told him.

"It's saying something terrible going to happen. What else is going on with you? Why are you so skinny? You look ill daddy." The waiter came over to us as daddy grabbed my hand. I looked at him. "What is it?" I leaned over the table. "I have to have some test done baby. Don't worry okay they're just testing, and nothing's wrong with me." He says shrugging his shoulders. "So if nothing's wrong why would they want to take any test?" I asked.

"Well, baby, I had some bleeding, and they just want to take a closer look at what's going on inside my stomach." He said. "Don't you worry about a thing, order your food" He said waving the waiter to come back to our table, ending the conversation about the test. Well, I can always go through the paperwork. I thought. I will see it before he even takes any test.   But I really can't look over any paperwork without daddy's consent. Our lunch ended quickly. Daddy didn't eat much, and after what he told me, I didn't eat much of what I ordered either especially after hearing of daddy's testing.

I went back to work and finished up a minimal amount of work and went home. Michael and the twins where waiting for me with dinner. "Hello baby, how was work?" He asked me. "It was okay." I tell him throwing my bag down on the chair near the door. I had lunch with daddy today," I tell him. "Yeah, how did that go?" He asked. "It was okay until he started telling me about some test that he has to get; he says he's been bleeding."

"Yeah," Michael says again. He was stuffing his face at the same time. "I don't think it's anything he wanted me to know, but I got it out of him anyway." I said. "Well, maybe it's nothing. Maybe they're just cautious, your dads no young man anymore baby, so every little thing is important now." "Maybe your right Michael," I said. I grabbed a glass of water and sat down at the table with Michael and the children and started to eat with them, mostly off of Michael's plate, he had a mountain of pasta on his plate.

"Hungry weren't you?" I asked him. He shook his head yes. I drank my water and watched Michael eat. The twins sat in their high chairs and enjoyed their pasta also. I looked over at the clock next to the hallway, and there standing next to it was Mr. Simms. He was pointing at it. I looked trying to make out the time he was pointing to as he began to walk away; I got up from the table. "Excuse me, Michael," I said sitting his fork down next to his napkin. I went to the back room to try and catch Mr. Simms, but he was nowhere in sight.

I looked around to see if he could have been anywhere else in the house, but he wasn't. Mr. Simms had vanished; I wondered around the den just checking things out, I stared down at some things on the desk. It looked as if someone had moved pictures all around on the desk the twins pictures where upside down. I turned it back over, and walked towards the door, as I walk out I was shoved to the floor. I turned around quickly to catch myself from being taken into the darkness. When I turned around Mrs. Cotton was standing next to the table, she took the picture and turned it back upside down. I closed my eyes and began to pray.

Lord, bind this spirit, for it comes to harm. It's here to take something that does not belong to them. Please Lord, protect my children and me, guide us from the evil that it's come to do in the name of Jesus I pray. Lord, make it walk away from me never to return, take it back to the darkness and lead it to where it needs to be left to burn. I prayed until I could no longer feel Mrs. Cotton's presence. I got up quickly and went to the dining room with Michael and the twins. Michael was just beginning to get them cleaned up and ready for bed. I took Kristine and went for to the hall bathroom to bathe her.

Michael went into our room with Kristopher and bathed him. We finished and met in their room to put their pajama son and laid them down in bed. They went to sleep soon after. Then Michael began to come on to me. "It's time to get to work on our babies now," he said dancing around me in his underwear. He put on some soft music and began to undress me; we made love until we were both tired. I fell off to sleep in Michael's arms. I was awakened by the cries of Kristopher and Kristine.

I went into their room and looked at the clock in the hallway. It was four am. This was very strange. They usually slept through the night these days. I went into Kristine's room first, she was lying on her back crying, looking straight up at the ceiling. "Oh baby, my baby, what's the matter with my girl?" I say when I picked her up from her bed. She was still crying while I held her carrying her into Kristopher's room. "Hello." I said. "What's the matter with you little man?" I said to Kristopher.

I grabbed two diapers and a couple of wipes and placed them underneath my chin, then grabbed Kristopher and walked them both down the hall to my room. I didn't understand why they were crying, but I knew they needed their diapers changed, and I was worried that they were both afraid of something. They looked as if they had been scared. I took them both and changed their diapers; I laid one on the side of Michael and the other on the side of me. They began to calm when I covered them.

I held Kristopher really close to me and Michael turned toward Kristine and rubbed her back. She began to fall back to sleep. I wasn't sure that Michael was even aware that I'd even gotten out of bed. He never even moved when I got up. By the time Kristopher fell off to sleep I was exhausted. I started dozing off when I smelled a very foul odor coming from the doorway. I quickly sat up and looked at the door a cold breeze followed. I covered Kristopher immediately. I looked to see if it would show itself at all, or a shadow of darkness, or anything.

There was nothing but the odor and the breeze; I sat waiting. After a while, the smell went away, and I leaned back the air was still cold, I relaxed a little. My eyes were wide open in fear,   what was it? I thought. Could this be what Mr. Simms was telling me about the time? Should I be expecting something at a certain time? When I leaned back, I felt someone watching me; it was so dark in the room. The moonlight only lighted it. I looked around the room from the door to the foot of the bed, searching for the presence that I felt.

I couldn't see it at all. I wanted to wake Michael so bad, but what would I tell him? I thought. You married a crazy woman. I can see people who aren't really there and I can help people cross over. Oh sure Karis, tell him your secrets, I thought as I laid my head against the head broad. I looked up; God, help me. Just then in the darkness there she was, Mrs. Cotton. She stood at the foot of the bed. She just stood there looking at me. She wasn't alone this time there were two men in black with her, they had hoods on, and they pointed at me.

Chills went over my whole body. I tried to scream, but nothing came out. I could hear them whispering, "It's her," I couldn't make it all out; I just sang in my head the easiest song that came to mind. Jesus loves the little children all the children of the world. I could not speak, but I sang in my mind. I could see them fade away, but Mrs. Cotton stayed and stared at me. She pointed at the babies. "Mine," she roared as she walked never turning away, looking at me until she faded away. I stayed awake until Michael woke up for work. He got up at exactly five thirty am. He came over to me.

"Hey, baby, what are you doing up?" He asked. "I couldn't sleep." I told him. "The babies woke me up, and I just couldn't get back to sleep." I told him as I watched as he scattered around the room getting things together for work. "I won't be long today, and we have that appointment. Are you excited baby?" He asked. "Yes a little," I told him. "But I'm nerves; I don't think you should get too excited maybe it's a false alarm, I'm only ten days late." "Oh don't you tell me, you don't think you are."

"Baby, I know I can make babies, and that's my baby in there," he said rubbing my stomach." You're carrying my seed now oooh," he said kissing my face and laughing. "I will meet you at the appointment today at three okay," he said walking out of the door. "Okay, I love you, Michael," I tell him. "I love you." He screamed out walking to the car. He was getting into the car when I noticed Mr. Simms standing by the car smiling and waving. What's wrong with Mr. Simms these days?

Why is he not sticking around with me? I thought. I went back into the room to get the children ready for child care. I put on the coffee pot and put the eggs out on the counter so that I could make the children breakfast. Washing them up wasn't easy, I put their clothes on quickly. They ran around a lot now; I had to chase them to put their pants on. When I finally got them dressed, I sat them in their high chairs. I went in the kitchen to start to cook their eggs, to my surprise, the eggs were thrown all over the floor, the coffee pot was turned off, and the coffee cup was broken and thrown into the sink.

I started to clean up the eggs and Mrs. Cotton appeared on the kitchen floor with me. I was on my knees with a towel, as hard as it was already she snatched the towel from my hand and threw it. I got up from the floor ignoring her. I must feed my children I told her. I went back to my refrigerator and reached in for some more eggs. This time she pushed the refrigerator door shut on my hand and I pulled it right back open as if it didn't hurt me. I turned to my children, "mommies going to make you breakfast babies," I assured them. "I have to feed them, and I will not allow you to keep me from doing that. Go back to where you came from," I told her looking her in her eyes.

She stood looking at me. I couldn't show her fear or anything other than my courage and strength. I watched her from the corner of my eyes; I could see that her anger for what she couldn't make me feel was growing. She moved closer to me. I stood back and held the pan close to the fire on the stove. She was old, but she had the strength of five men, and I knew when she wanted to she would use it. I prepared myself. I began to pray.

"Lord, today I want to cook for my children, feed them and get them to child care safe. There is a terrible spirit hanging around here to harm my children and me. Lord, please remove it, and send it back, bind it, Lord, in the name of Jesus. Bind this spirit and send it back to where it could burn. Lord, cover my children with the blood of Jesus." I prayed until Mrs. Cotton back away from me. I was relieved when she turned to walk away; I could see her companions that she brought along with her that night. I immediately made the children breakfast, and I washed for work, then we left the house.

I dropped the children off and went on to work. Michael had a busy day; I hadn't run into him all day. These are the toughest days for me because I sometimes just wanted to see his smile. We met up at three for our doctor's appointment as scheduled; I was nerves. Michael was ready to hear what the doctor was going to tell us. He was sure I was having his baby. For his sake, I hoped he was right. The nurse asked me to take a pregnancy test before we were called back after thirty minutes of waiting.

"Mr. Mrs. Steven son." the nurse said. "Hello, how are you today?" She asked. "Follow me please," we followed her to a small room in the back. She gave me a gown. "When was your last checkup?" she asked. "About two months ago, I had a pap." I told her. "Was it normal?" "Yes, it was, I just had twins a year ago." "Oh, really twins huh." "Yes, they're a handful, but I love them." "Oh I bet you do, I have four children I'm exhausted all the time," she said. "Well, I plan to have as many as I could," Michael said.

"Really, well good luck," she said taking my blood pressure, "The doctor will be in here shortly," she said walking out of the door. Michael sat down on the doctor stool and began spinning around until he was at the foot of the little half bed that I was to sit on. I changed into the gown she gave me. "So, you are going to tease me in here too huh," he said touching all over my breast. "Michael stop," I told him, "someone might come in here." "You know, you're the last one, your appointment was at three, so he's going to take his time to come in here." He said I pushed him away. "Stop it, Michael," the doctor came in smiling.

"Hello Karis, how have you been these days?" He asked. "She's been okay, doc," Michael said shaking his hand. "Now can you give us the news?" Michael asked I was sometimes so embarrassed by Michael's blunt actions. "Michael, just stay calm; he's going to tell us, right?" I asked looking at the doctor. "Yes I am, lay down for me, little lady." I laid flat on my back, and he began to feel around the lower part of my stomach. "You're having a baby," he said, "you're about six weeks along, and you're due around October 26th from the last date of your period. That's the date I got, unless we get some other date with the ultrasound, which won't happen for another five months. I would like for you to start eating a little more. You're a little tiny."

Michael began to jump around behind the doctor turning all around, but not making a sound; he was smiling from ear to ear. "Congratulations sir," the doctor said to Michael. "I'm going to prescribe you some prenatal vitamins, and you are to come back to see me in about a month." The doctor left us in the room. I got down off the table; I didn't know what to feel. I was happy, but also sad. My emotions ran high. I began to take off the gown when Michael grabbed me and picked me up.

"Baby! Baby! Baby!" He said. "Michael! Put me down please I feel like I'm going to be sick you're shaking me all up," I tell him. "Oh baby, I'm sorry. Oh my God, I can't wait to tell everyone!" He said as we left the doctor's office. "Michael, do you think we should do this while I'm still early? I'm only six weeks, let's wait awhile," I said as we approached the car. "Everybody, we're having a baby!" Michael screamed out. "We are! We are having a baby!" I jumped on his back and covered his mouth. "No more Michael, stop it, everyone knows now," I said.

Into The Darkness, Light Shines

I began to show anger toward Michael more and more as time went on. I spent more time away from home, going over to Tara's grandmother's house every day after work with the children and staying until nightfall. I would never eat dinner with them and would spend a lot of my time sitting in a rocker on the front porch, while Tara would water the grass. The children would eat with Tara, but I would just bring snacks in my bag. Michael wouldn't even get angry; he would just say that he missed us and touched my belly. I go right into the bedroom when I get home. "Do you think that this can go on forever?" Tara would ask me.

"I don't know. I think that when Michael decides that he wants to come clean, I'll be ready to stay home, and be a wife to him." I said. "What exactly is he not telling you? Why are you guys angry at each other?" She asked me. I never told Tara about anything that was going on; I would talk about things and leave out details of the story so that she wouldn't catch on to any of the real truth. She'd get frustrated at times and just stop talking and walk away from me.

"Why are you getting so chubby? Your face looks swollen, and your stomach looks pudgy too." She said, looking me over from head to toe. "Wait a minute," she turned to me and shut the water off, "are you pregnant again? Are you?" She asked with excitement in her voice. I got up from the rocker and called out for the children, "Kristopher! Kristine! We need to go now, let's go home, "So you're going to leave without even telling me?" She asked. By now, I was seven months pregnant, and my stomach was sticking way out, but I was so thin you couldn't tell from the loose clothing I wore.

She came up close to me and put her hands on my belly, "Huh!" She sighed, "You are pregnant," she said as the baby moved all around when she touched me. I sat down quickly; the baby kept moving so fast. "Are you okay? How far along are you?" She asked me; I took a deep breathe, "I am seven months," I tell her "Were you ever planning to tell me?" She asked. "Were you going to wait until you were in labor or something?" She asked, helping me to the car with the children. "No, I planned to tell you soon.

Michael and I had planned on telling everyone at a dinner party we were planning. but I'm so mad at him; I haven't planned it all." "Really, a dinner party, was I going to cook at this party? Was I even invited at all?" She asked. Tara was standing in front of me with her hand planted on my belly, I was trying to get into the car, but she blocked my way. "So are you going ever to straighten this out? You have to get over whatever it is that's bothering you. It feels like you don't have much time to ponder on your anger at all."

Tara said. "I'll think about that on the way to the house, I promise," I told her, removing her hand from my stomach. On my way home I did think about it, maybe I should go a little easy on Michael. Maybe he's keeping these things away from me for a reason. I thought. I made it home just in time to catch him; I pulled up into the garage where he met me to help with the kids. We took them inside Michael had dinner ready along with jazz playing on the radio. Tonight I wouldn't go to the room and hide; I would sit and have dinner with my family.

"How was work?" Michael asked me. "Fine," I tell him, "how about you, did you enjoy work today?" I asked him, he looked at me and winked his eye. "Work was work," he says getting up from the table to go grab the tea kettle. "How's Tara doing? He asked me. "She seems to be doing fine, happy as far as I could tell." He sat back down and looked at me and passed me a cup of tea. "Did you tell her about the baby?" He asked. "She figured it out on her own. I didn't have to tell her," I said smiling. "That's good, and now everyone knows huh?"

"I don't think everyone knows," I said shrugging my shoulders. "You didn't want her to know Michael?" I asked taking a sip of tea; I looked at him with suspense in my eyes, the nerve of him, I thought. He doesn't want Tara to know anything, but he's not telling me anything. Oh my goodness, why can't I just let this go? I fed the children the rest of their dinner and took them into the bathroom for a bath. "Michael, are you going to help me tonight?" I asked. "I'm going to need help with them in the tub I can barely bend over," I told Him.

He looked at me while chugging his drink, rinsed his glass and sat it in the sink and followed us into the bathroom. I began undressing the children while Michael ran the bath water. "Don't make it to cold okay. It needs to be a little warmer than usual," I tell him. Michael picks them up and places them in the tub, I sit on the toilet lid, and Michael sits on the edge of the tub. He splashes them with water and washes their hair. I stood over them to lean in and wash their little bodies up. Michael puts his hand on my stomach as I wash them.

He rubs my belly, lays his head on it, and kisses it as if he's comforting the baby. I finished washing them and sat back down on the toilet seat; Michael grabbed my waist and pulled my shirt up to lay his head on my stomach. He was so warm; it felt like a warm blanket, almost as if he had a fever. "Michael," I said lifting his head, "Why are you so warm? Are you sick or something?" He placed his head back down, "No, I'm just enjoying my son. We are communicating; don't you feel him moving around for me in there? He loves me already." He says.

I watched the children play for a while as Michael talked and played with the baby in my belly for about thirty minutes. When the twins were tired Michael took them out and we dried them off and put their pajamas on. They fell right off to sleep with no problem. They loved a bath before bedtime. Michael stood over their beds watching them; he held their hand and prayed with them before leaving their room every night. I stood by the door watching him smiling; I wondered if he'd change when the son of his blood was born?

I don't know what to expect from Michael anymore it's almost as if I'd married a stranger. I thought, as he followed me to our bedroom. I began to get undressed for my bath, Michael began to undress too. He went into the bathroom before I could go in, I sat on the bed with my robe on waiting for him to come out, but he didn't. I could hear water swishing around; I walked in to check on the water, Michael was in the tub soaking with his head back.

"Are you coming in or what? I've been waiting for you to get in here with me," he said, holding his hand out for me. I took my robe off and walked toward Michael; he helped me in, he sat me between his legs so that he could wash my back and holds my belly. "Lean into me baby, all I want to do is protect you and love you until the end of time." He said rubbing my back; he rubbed up and down and all around my neck, it felt so good I lay back on his chest. His body was so warm and cozy that I dozed off a little as Michael washed me and held my stomach.

After a long while, he woke me. "Karis, Karis! We have to get out now baby. The bath is getting cold, and I don't want you to get sick okay." He pushes me up forward, and I held on to the bath railing and pulled myself up, "Thank you, Michael," I said. "That was so good. I haven't felt that good in a while." I tell him wrapping myself in my robe. "You look like you enjoyed it as much as I did baby, and that's what matters the most, is that you enjoyed it too." Michael said, he walked with me to the room, and we lay on the bed, Michael held my stomach and touched my breast too.

I looked away, it had been so long since Michael, and I made love. I'd been holding out because he wouldn't come clean it had been over five months. I couldn't look at him because I wanted him as much as he wanted me if I looked into his eyes I knew I was going to give in to him.

He rubbed all over my breast then licks them, kissing my body all over, and I gave in. He was gentle making love to me until we were both tired. I fell off to sleep in his arms; he held me closer than usual, there was no use in me dwelling on what I couldn't change.

I can't make Michael tell me why he is what he is; I can only hope that he wouldn't leave me or change how he loves us. Tonight, I dreamt of Tara she was in a light and was wearing a flower dress. She was explaining to me how happy she was now. She was thin and was standing in this bright light. She was so happy, I reached out to grab her, but I couldn't get a hold of her, "Tara, let's go home," I say to her. "I am home, Karis; I'm home." She says waving goodbye to me.

I felt like I was falling, so I held my arms because I felt like I was leaving Tara in the light. I screamed her name, "Tara! Tara! Come with me, please!" I say as I fall. "Karis! Karis! Wake up your dreaming." I jumped up and got the phone to call Tara. I dial her grandma's phone number as fast as my fingers could dial, it rang. "Hello," it was Tara. "Hello! Tara, what are you doing today? Could you come over today to be with the kids and me, please?" I asked her; I have to see her I have to know. If I get any ill feelings around her, then I'll know if she's leaving me.

"Um, it's six am Karis, what are you doing up this early?" She asked. I'm just up I tell her, "Can you come or not?" "Um I guess so," she says with suspicion in her voice. "Yeah, I'll come." she said. "Hey what are you doing up?" I asked her. "I'm watching the Top Iron Chef," she said, and you just made me miss the winner." "I'm sorry, they'll show it again tomorrow, I'm sure," I said. I hung up the phone and sat up on the bed, Michael went right back to sleep, he was to be up soon for work, and I sat there.

What was that dream all about, Tara shouldn't be sick she's still overweight I know, but is she ill? She didn't seem to be depressed anymore either at least not as depressed as she usually was, I thought. I stayed awake watching the sun as it grew brighter. Michael dressed for work, the children got up, and I fed them all a healthy breakfast and we waited around for Tara. I cleaned while I waited, she would show after several hours. Lunchtime came soon after, she insisted on making me and the children lunch, she even brought over some of her secret ingredients.

I allowed it only because I was so tired from running around after the children. By now, they were two of the busiest twins I'd ever seen. I sat down on the couch next to Tara's bag and noticed that she was carrying something that looked like a tiny oxygen tank; she still had a pack of cigarettes in her bag right beside it. I didn't say a word; I went to the kitchen and sat at the table to watch what she was cooking. It was always a joy to watch her in the kitchen; she was always so funny; cooking and bouncing around the kitchen as if she's on television.

She was talking to the food as she threw it into the pot, and when she seasoned up the food, she would tell it how it should taste later, and by god, if you were to ever tasted it you would believe that it listen to her because it would make you say wow! The flavors made your mouth sing her praises of joy. Tara certainly could have been a great chef. I wished that she would have stuck with that. She'd marinate her meats with rosemary, sauces, and seasonings unknown.

I'd never ask her because she'd say it was all a secret. I asked her time and time again. When it finished, she'd decorate the plate as if we were eating at a fancy restaurant. She put drinks down and set the table nicely. Who's going to ever be such good of a friend to me as Tara? No one in this world would ever replace her, I thought. Staring at her while she set up the last course of the meal, which was a cheesy bread surprise with a sweet sauce, I was anxious to try that. "Why are you staring at me like that?" Tara asked.

"Oh, I don't know I was just thinking, how lucky I am to have such a good friend. If I haven't told you lately Tara, I love you, and I appreciate you being my friend," I tell her sitting at the table. "Really," she said. She began to cough. She bent over coughing with her apron cover her mouth. "Are you okay Tara?" I asked. She lifted her hand up; I went over to her to pat her on the back. "Do you want water?" She shook her head yes, I went to grab a glass from the cabinet and filled it with water.

"Here you go Tara," I handed her the glass; she stood up and drank the water; slowly. "Tara, are you okay? I saw the oxygen tank; do you need that right now?" I asked. She began to laugh as she shook her head no. I looked at her and asked, "Are you sure?" She shook her head no again. "It's to help me breathe better at night; I've been having trouble breathing at night, so I sleep with it, that's all." She said going over to the kitchen table to sit in a chair. She was breathing really heavy, I handed her the glass of water.

"I'll get the children to the table don't worry," I told her. I finished setting the table and sat the kids down at the table. "When do you go back to the doctors?" I asked as I sat our food out. "I don't; I don't ever want to see another doctor again," she said. "You see all this fat surrounding my stomach? The last time I went, they tried to tell me that it was some kind of tumor." "A tumor, Tara are you sure, I think you need a second opinion." I tell her.

"That's easy for you to say, I don't have the health coverage for a second opinion. So, I'd rather not go and hear any opinion at all; I'd rather die this way." She said with tears streaming down her face. "Tara what about the disability claim that you have going won't they help? I mean they got you the oxygen, right?" I ask. "Yes, but it's not easy to get other things they limit things you should have, and when I say limit, I mean limit. They give you a little here and there, then it all stops, and I have to reapply." She tells me.

"Really why would you have to do that" I asked her. "When I went back to work it screwed up the processing of the disability. They said if I can work I don't need it, and the job I have doesn't have health care benefits. So what could I do Karis? I can't just not work" she says. "But Tara, you can't be unhealthy and work either, can you?" I asked. "I have to live. I have to pay my bills; I have school loans, and now this car note I have to help my grandmother. There is absolutely nothing I can do about it. Nothing! She said wiping her eyes with her shirt as she got up from the table and went over to the couch. I followed her and hugged her.

"Tara, if you tell me what you need help with, I could help you. I have some money saved up, and I can give it to you until you take care of your health problems first then go back to work. How about that? Do you want to do that?" I asked her. "No, I can't take money from you and the babies," she said. "You won't be taking anything I promise. It's a blessing ok, I'm blessing you, and later you can come back and bless me when I need you too. "How about that" I told her I went to the back room to get my purse and grabbed my checkbook.

"Tara, I'm going to give you a blank check, okay, you take it and write up to ten grand, okay. Pay your bills, and take care of your health." I grabbed her hand, "I want to keep my friend," I told her. She got up and went back to the table, leaving the check on the couch beside her bag. "Tara, are you refusing this offer?" I asked her; she shook her head yes. I got up and went back to the table, "I'm not going to beg you to take my money. I'm not; you want to be difficult it will be here for you when you need it. Is it that you don't trust me or something?"

"No of course not, you dork, how can I not trust you? Of all people, I love you, Karis. You're the best friend anyone could ever have." She said. "I know, that's why you better take advantage while you can huh," I tell her, throwing a piece of bread over at her. "Cheer up crybaby, or I'm going to make the kids call you a crybaby instead of Aunty Tara." We laughed and laughed, "the food was delicious, Tara," I told her when I began putting it away.

I sat a plate out for Michael and cleaned the kitchen while Tara took the kids up to read them a story and put them to bed. I was reaching to put the plates away when I turned to the window and saw Mr. Simms. He waved, "hi young lady," he said smiling. I caught a glimpse of him and away he went again. I heard Tara calling out for me, "yes!" I called back; I sat the plates down and went up to check why she was calling for me. "Hey, you needed me?" "No," Tara said, "I didn't call you for anything."

"Are you sure, because I thought I heard you calling out for me a while ago." "No dork, I didn't call you, I'm busy with the children, I don't have time to be calling out for you. Huh, little guy?" She said drying Kristopher off. "Okay, I must have been hearing things then I guess," I said. I went back downstairs to finish up the dishes. I felt a bit of sadness leaving the room coming from Tara. Oh no, this happened to me before, right before Mr. Simms past.

I remember his spirit made a connection with me right before he crossed over. Oh no Lord, please, I stopped in the hall and prayed. "Lord, don't let this be, my best friend has to leave me. I know that this world may not be where she needs to be, but Lord she's all I have, can I keep her here Lord, just for me. I know I sound selfish, and I know I shouldn't be, but Lord, she deserves to live this life out here with me, to laugh, talk, work and live. She hasn't had children Lord or gotten married Lord she wants these things.

Although her will seems to be fading, her heart and soul possibly tore, her spirit broken from what her body won't do for her, but Lord, please change her heart, please Lord give her a new start, help her see that her place is here. Fill her spirit with pleasant thoughts of joy make her want to stay Lord. In Jesus name, I pray." When I opened my eyes Tara was standing in front of me, "Oh, you scared me," she jumped, she had both children in her arms. "I was just taking these little people to their rooms, and I bumped into you. What are you doing standing here?" She asked.

"Oh, I was just thinking about something," I told her. "Just standing in a corner thinking about what? You still have that towel in your hand, so I'm guessing that you're thinking about finishing those dishes," she said laughing as she walked past me. I walked back down to the kitchen, and Michael was pulling up. He took a while to come inside; I went into the garage to see why. He was just sitting in his car listening to jazz. I often wondered about Michael's thoughts, where was his mind sometimes, he had the car running.

That was dangerous I thought. I went to the car window knocked on it, "Michael, do you know how dangerous that is? Please get out of there; you're going to get sick." He turned the car off, "Karis, I know exactly what I'm doing, I wouldn't be in here long enough to get sick or to harm myself enough to die. How was your day?" He says getting out of the car. "It was fine." I tell him. "Tara's here." "Oh good, haven't seen her in a while. What a pleasant surprise," he says putting his bags away.

"What's for dinner?" He asked. "You have a plate in the oven it should still be warm, it's a surprise. Guess who cooked?" I say to him smiling, "wow, sounds interesting." he said as he went to the kitchen to eat. Tara came downstairs too, "Hello Michael, long time huh." He put his plate down, "yes, yes, long time Tara. It's good to see you again really. Where you been hiding yourself these days?" He asked her. "I've just been working and trying to live that's all Michael," she says. "I'm going to make some tea Tara," I told her. "The remote is over there;" I pointed to the coffee table.

Michael went over to her and hugged her, "It is really good to see you," he said, walking back over to his plate. "I'm good," she said smiling at him. "Michael, how's dinner? I asked him. "Mmm, it's so good," he said with his voice muffled. I sat down with Tara at the coffee table waiting to hear the tea kettle whistle. "Looks like you've done some redecorating around here," Tara said looking all around. "New pictures and new frames, I like," she's pointing at the different statues and pictures.

"But I don't see any of me," she said going in her bag, she reached in and pulled out a big picture of me and her sitting on her porch watering the lawn. It was beautiful, "oh my, Tara," I said grabbing it from her hand. "I love it! Is this for me?" I ask. "Yes, I even have a frame," she said pulling out a frame from her purse, It was silver and quoted friendship poetry. It was so nice; I took it and immediately put the picture in the frame. I hugged Tara, "thank you; I love it!"

"Yeah I'm such a good friend, and it's not even your birthday," she said smiling. "And now you'll always have our memories in a frame." We were smiling that day, I couldn't remember what we were talking about, but we were smiling. That is what I know about my friend Tara; she always made me smile. The tea kettle whistled as Michael walked over to take a look at the picture, I sat it on the coffee table and he picked it right up. "Beautiful people," he said smiling, "you guys looked happy that day." "We're always happy," Tara told him.

"I guess you can say that huh?" Michael said putting the frame back on the table. "You guys make one another happy, that's what so great about your friendship." Tara looked sad for a moment, then she got up from the couch, "Karis, I can't stay for tea, so don't bother making any for me okay," she said picking up her purse. "I have somewhere I have to be," "oh really, Tara, I was hoping you'd stick around for a while longer," I say.

"Oh no, I have to pick some things up for my grandma, and I have a couple of other things to do, I'm sorry, but I can't stay," she said rushing toward the front door. I looked at Michael, "Don't worry; she'll return she just needs to take a breather," he tells me. "Have your tea baby; there is nothing more you can do for Tara. She has her mind made up about where she wants to go," he says. I drink my tea alone at the table.

Michael goes into the children's rooms to check on them and to kiss them goodnight. Why would he tell me that she has her mind made up already? I wondered.

He must know how Tara feels too. He gave me a look of assurance; I waited for him to return to the kitchen for me. Michael spent a long time with the children; I finished my tea before he returned, so I went looking for him. "Michael!" I called out, as I walked around the house in the darkness looking for him. I tiptoed into the kid's room to see if he was there, he wasn't. Then to his office, still no Michael, I walked around everywhere in the house. I stood at our bedroom door and went into the bathroom, listening for him. I stood still, and heard Michael whispering; it sounded as if he was far away.

He was in the attic, looked up to see if I could reach the ring to pull the ladder down. I jumped, I wasn't tall enough to reach it, I jumped as high as I could and finally caught a hold of it. I pulled it down and moved back to let the ladder fall to the floor. I could still hear Michael's whispering as I walked up the stairs; I tiptoed up as quietly as I could. I started to feel butterflies in my stomach as I moved in closer to him, I felt like someone was touching my shoulders. The room was lit up by a very bright light, still no Michael.

Now there was another voice following Michaels telling him what he needed to do as he journeyed here in the flesh. I stood close to the end of the door holding my stomach; I began to cramp. It felt like I was pushed back and I couldn't see Michael, but the light was brighter. I walked closer toward it looking for him and calling out to him, but he didn't answer back. "Michael, do you hear me?" I asked. I couldn't see Michael through the bright light, but I can hear him talking. I wanted to go into the light with him, so I began to walk closer to find Michael.

I couldn't think of anything except for losing Michael now. What if he leaves us? What if he does go away? What's going to happen to us and how will I go on without him? I panicked and began to run toward the light, and just as I go to jump into it, the light fades, and Michael appears and grabs me, "Baby! What are you doing up here?" He asks I took a deep breath, "what do you mean Michael, I'm up here looking for you. What are you doing up here? Who were you talking to?" I asked. "Come on baby, it's dangerous up here," he said guiding me down slowly. "Be careful, baby."

"Michael, who were you talking to?" I asked again. "Baby, I was just praying okay. It's nothing to worry about really; everything is going to be okay." He said escorting me to the bedroom. Michael started to kiss me all over, "I miss you, Karis," he says in a whisper. "I want you so bad baby," he says. I put my hand on Michael's chest, "No, Michael, I will not let you have me this way. You have to tell me what's going on; I need to know. I'm afraid you're going to leave us." I said as he lay on the bed and looked up at me with both his hands behind his head.

"Karis, I can't get into this with you right now. You are worried for no reason I will never leave you, I promise I will always be here for you." He said. "Really, Michael, and what does that mean, you will always be here? You'll be here in spirit when you leave, or you'll be here, be here? I need to know Michael, I don't want wake up one day, and you're gone back to the heavens or where ever you've come from, so please tell me, Michael. What's going on?" I ask him.

I lay next Michael and stare at him, he looks me in my eyes, "Karis, please, don't do this now, I can't keep telling you, you don't have to worry, really you don't." He explained I turned my head away from Michael and got up from the bed; I took a pillow and snatched the blanket from the bed. "Okay Michael, I've heard enough, I'm done trying to figure it this out. I won't share this bed or this baby with you until you tell me what's going on Michael." I took my pillow and my blanket and went downstairs. Michael followed me, "Karis, Please!" He yelled out trying to catch up with me as I walked faster and faster to get downstairs, I ignored him all the way down.

"Karis, could you just sleep in the bedroom please, with the baby? I don't want you to be uncomfortable on the couch," he said touching my belly. "It's our precious cargo, Karis, go to the bedroom. I'll take the couch in the den; I won't be able to sleep with you down here baby." He says as takes my pillow and blanket and throws it on the couch, He walks me back up the stairs, "You sleep upstairs if you're mad at me and I'll take the couch baby." He says walking me to the room.

"Michael, can you just explain to me what's really going on and we both sleep in our bed together? This pregnancy is supposed to be a happy time for us, but it's turning out to be the worst. I'm scared and confused; I want to know what's going to happen once I give birth to this baby?" "Nothing's going to happen," Michael says standing at the door facing the stairs. We will have more children, that's all, nothing else would happen, I won't leave. I won't go back anywhere; I'm here until the end of time. I don't understand why you are in a state of panic," he says.

"Michael, I can't believe that you don't understand why I wouldn't be panicking, I am carrying your child Michael, and I have two more in there sleeping. Do you think I should worry later? I don't know Michael; you're making me think I'm crazy for asking these questions." "Well, Karis, I have left before, and I came back. I came back; I have never lied to you or betrayed you in any way. Trust me I can't even think of being anywhere else but here." We fell off to sleep arguing about whether or not Michael would leave me soon.

When I awoke that morning Michael was sitting next to me, "Karis, I love you, I will never leave you, promise. I want you to get some rest today. I called them and told them you wouldn't be in today. Go shopping and buy some pretty things. I love you." He kissed me on the cheek again and handed me his card. "You need to start preparing for the baby," he said, I went shopping that day and bought some things for the baby, but not many things. I just wanted to know what Michael would do next to shut me up so that I wouldn't question him about his life before me. I thought about how I could find out more, where could I get the information I needed to settle my feelings.

As I walk up to the front door of our home, I see Michael through the window playing with the kids. They are running all around him as he's rolling across the floor, just laughing giggling calling out daddy, daddy. "I'm back, guys!" I say as I walk in. "Hello baby," Michael says rolling across the floor over to me. He jumped up and grabs my bags; "you get anything for me?" He asked looking through all of the bags. I laughed.

"Michael, I'm always looking out for you," I said kissing his cheek. "Thank you, baby," Michael said as I walked behind him, we carried the bags upstairs to put the things away. As we walked up I began to feel a cold chill behind me. I turned to look back and standing behind me was an old woman carrying a handbag on her shoulder, she smiled at me as if I knew she would be there when I turned to look back. I walked into the bedroom and placed the bags down alongside Michael; he began taking things out and stuffing them away into the closet.

I started to help him. "Hey, you sit down," Michael tells me, "I will do it, don't you lift a finger," he says. I lay on the bed, the old lady appeared in the chair across from me and stared; I got up to take my shoes off. I stare back at her, wondering where she came from, she's carrying her purse as if she's just come from the mall too. Huh, I bet that's where she came from, I thought as I began to undress for my shower. The twins came in soon after I began undressing, they stopped at the door staring at the chair as if they see what I saw sitting in the chair.

Kristopher even pointed and began to go toward her; I grabbed him catching him by the hand, I don't know what kind of spirit this might be. The woman was very mysterious; she hadn't said a word, she hadn't waved or even batted her eyes at me to give me a clue and her smile wasn't very promising. I wrapped myself up in my robe and took the twins to their room for bed. I read to them; they enjoyed tales of The Three Blind Mice. I read to them as the lady watch me from the doorway, she was wearing a blue flower dress with white spots, and she wore glasses.

Her hair was salt and pepper gray and white; she held onto her purse tight as if she was afraid someone would take it. I looked at her from time to time as did the twins. She was a little heavy build standing in her white shiny shoes. When the kids fell off to sleep, I put my head down to pray before I walked her way I wanted to be sure I was covered by the Lords presence. I began to pray immediately after I closed the book. Lord, in the name of Jesus there is a presence around me be it harmful or be it good I need you to cover me. Blanket me Lord, help me to help this spirit in whatever way is needed. In the name of Jesus, I pray Amen.

I looked up at the woman, and she had tears rolling from her face. I go to walk by her, and she stood still as I walked by, she clutched her purse holding it tight. I went to the room, as I looked back I didn't fear her. I knew that the Lord would protect my babies from her, she was lost. I could feel that her soul was just drifting, I went into the room with Michael, he was looking at some of the things I bought for the new baby. "I like this one." He said holding up some little pink shoes, "but you know they're the wrong color, my baby's a boy."

"No, it's a girl, Michael, just accept it okay," I said going into the bathroom to shower. I took my robe off to get in the shower, and the woman was standing right by the door. I was looking in the mirror, and she was looking with me. I didn't get scared or even move away from the mirror I just kept going on as if I didn't notice her standing there. I let the water run to get warm and waited for those signs that Mr. Simms says I sometimes miss. The water was hot, as she went closer toward the shower the water got colder and colder.

I got in, and it was freezing. I called out to Michael, "Michael, the waters freezing," I washed anyway in the freezing water, not allowing her to know that I was bothered by her presence. I quickly got out after washing the soap off and wrapped up in a bath towel. The woman looked as if she was angry; I walked past her turning the light off behind me. The light came right back on as I closed the bathroom door. I went to the drawer and took a nightgown out and put it on, I spayed on some perfume, and put a little lotion on and lay in bed.

Michael must have gone back downstairs, he was nowhere in sight I hoped for him to be lying in bed, but he wasn't there. When I called out to him was he even there? I thought. The woman was still behind me as I walked around the house looking for Michael; I had no fear of her anymore, as she followed clutching her bag. Soon, I found Michael kneeling in down in the darkness of the attic. I went toward him when I noticed he wasn't alone, standing over him was a large shadow with its hand upon his head. Michaels' head was down with his eyes closed; he didn't even hear me come in, I watched him from the doorway, he was crying out to the Lord deeply praying.

Michael was too focused on his prayers, and the shadow that was standing over him was his angel. I turned away and left him to pray; I have to deal with this on my own for now. I went back to my room with the woman following behind me; I looked in on the children once again before going to my room. I turned to shut their room door, and the glare from the woman glasses shined directly into my eyes making it hard for me to see. I walked down the hall following the glare; I could not fear her spirit.

When I reached my door to turn my doorknob suddenly, she appeared in front my face breathing heavily. "Who are you?" I questioned, she clutched her purse with one hand and swung the other over my head, bringing it down on my head with all of her force. I fell to the ground, and as she appeared bigger in her flowered dress and white church shoes, I sat up quickly scooting myself backward toward an open door to get away from her as she began to stomp toward me clutching her purse. I crawled the rest of the way into the hall closet slamming the door behind me.

Trying to catch my breath I reached for the light, the woman grabbed my wrist and pushed me through the door back out into the hallway, I stayed down this time, "buckle down," I told myself. This is it I have to grab hold of her quickly, she's powerful, and she stood over me. Her glasses were glaring as she clutched her purse, I have to grab that purse, I thought. Lord, guide me through this struggle I prayed, I laid there waiting as she stomped toward me. I closed my eyes; I could feel her spirit getting close. I could smell her evil wanting to do harm to me. I clenched my fist and opened them as she came closer when she began to grab me I reached to snatch that purse.

She stood back quickly, and a roar came from her mouth, I screamed at her. I reached in again still grabbing at her purse, she roared again and began to go further away from me. I stood up as I could see she was in fear of me taking this bag. I went toward her reaching in for her bag every time. "Come on granny!" I called out to her, as she backed away. She began to shake her head no, clutching the bag and holding one hand out toward me, as if she wanted me to stop coming toward her. I then lunged at her, she didn't turn around she clutches her bag when I went close enough, and I grabbed the purse and pulled her into me.

She bumped my stomach, and we fell to the ground together, her glasses fell off, she still held on to the strap of that purse. I took her hand, and she opened her mouth wide and screamed breaking every glass near it seemed. I held her hand and began to see why she came to me; I went with her back to the place where her life was taken. Suddenly we were standing in the path way at the mall, the sun was just setting, and the path was clear. She was walking going to her car when a man approached her from behind grabbing her purse and stabbing her in the back several times.

She wouldn't let go of that purse, and she was fighting him with everything in her, thinking about how she had to get home to her sick husband and her grandchildren. Her drug-addicted daughter left her to care for; she was fighting so hard because she had their rent money in that purse. It was all she had, but there was nothing she could do. This man was an evil spirit on drugs; she could have beaten him until he was black and blue he would have still stabbed her for that purse. It was way too important to him; I held on to her hand and began to pray her spirit up.

"Lord, in her eyes she has no peace; she sees no end to what she couldn't defeat. The devil was on the street the night looking for a weak soul to take; she was in the line of fire and now caught up in a rage. Lord, she can't rest for the trouble in her heart still lye near, she is thinking about the children she left here in this life. Lord, take her in, show her there is light in your warm hands and the troubles pain and struggles she bore here on earth are no longer her game. Take her oh Lord, wash her soul through."

I held this woman's hand, and I closed my eyes I could feel the warmth of the lord come over the both of us. I smelled the flowers all around us, as the woman looked up at me, she took her bag, and I watched as eight small lights began circling us. Soon she became nine, her purse dropped down to my feet, as I sat on the floor in all the glass from the broken windows. I put my head down holding her purse, God, I just don't know, I thought to myself when I lifted my head Michael was standing in front of me with his hand out.

"Come on baby," he pulled me to my feet. When I stood to my feet he immediately picked me up and carried me to our room so that I wouldn't step in the glass, I just rested in his arms. "Baby, don't worry I'm going to call someone to fix the windows early in the morning, you lay down while I try and sweep up all the glass so that you and the kids don't step in any of it tomorrow." He said laying me on the bed; I held the woman's purse close to my stomach. I closed my eyes and thought about how bad that must have been for her, wondering what happened to the family."

"The sick husband and the grandchildren, oh Lord, my heart aches for them, and my soul is tearing apart every time one of these broken spirits come to me. Help me learn to deal with this without too much heartache, Lord I thank you for the guidance." I prayed as I waited for Michael to come back to bed. When Michael returned, he sat at the foot of the bed and rubbed my feet. "Baby you need to know that sometimes these spirits leave more than just purses behind." He stood up and leaned over the bed.

"Baby when our son is born, we have more trouble coming our way," he said going to the bathroom. I sat up, "Michael, what do you mean more trouble? I can't go through any more of this," I tell him. "Baby please, don't worry okay I have it covered." He said coming over to me kissing my for head. "Lay down," he said, I was so tired I just lay on the bed and closed my eyes and fell off to sleep while Michael rubbed my back. That night I dreamt of Tara again this time she was laying in the street gasping for air, I woke up holding my chest.

I turned on the light looked at the time it was three am. I reached over Michael for the phone to call Tara. He pushed my hand back over, "No Karis, she's sleeping," he said. "I have to call her," I tell him reaching over him again. He grabs my hand and sits up with me. "Karis, she's okay I promise you can call her in the morning." He took my hand pulled me close to him, hugging me close. "You need to rest," I rested my head on his shoulder. "How did you know I was calling her?" I asked. "You talk in your sleep more than you know," he said laughing.

"No I do not," I said smiling. "Yes, you do, but it's alright baby I love you know matter what you do," he said. "What was that dream all about?" He asked. I dreamt that Tara fell in the street and no one was there to help her. I'm afraid that she's in trouble or she's not taking care of herself." I tell him. "Baby, its best you just pray about it," Michael said rubbing my back. I waited until he fell off to sleep and I got up to call Tara; I just couldn't go back to sleep after that dream, I had to call her; I had to hear her voice to see if she was okay.

I took the phone and went into the bathroom. I dialed the number silently; it rang, "Tara," I said when someone picked up. "Yes, it's me," she said. "What the hell do you want? It's almost 4 am Karis, I'm sleeping," she sounds angry, "I just wanted to see if you were up that's all, you're usually up watching the iron chef, it's not on this morning?" I asked. "Karis, what's wrong with you?" She asked. "Well, Tara I keep having these dreams about you and there scary. Are you okay Tara?" The phone grew silent for a brief moment. "Hello, Tara, are you there?"

"I am, don't worry Karis I'm still alive, go to sleep please," she said laughing. "Tara this is no laughing matter, I'm serious, have you been to the doctors at all?" "Karis, I'm not going to talk about that right now I'm tired, I want to go back to sleep. Please, can you call me tomorrow?" She was hanging up, and I yelled out, "Tara, can you come over and teach me how to make that dish you made for us with the rosemary sauce please?" I asked her, "Karis, I know what you're doing, it's 445am I can't tomorrow I have to work."

"Don't work tomorrow okay just come over, what are they paying you I'll give you that for the day. You stay with me cook and hang out with the twins. Is it a deal?" I said. "I don't know Karis, will you hang up the phone if I agree to come over tomorrow?" She asked. "I don't know, will you show up" "Oh yeah Karis, I will show up, just go back to sleep," she said. "I'm going to sleep now I just can't take this anymore I'm so tired, okay goodnight," she said hanging up. I put the phone down,

Michael was still sleeping when I returned to bed, and I couldn't sleep thinking about Tara I kept looking at the clock waiting for day light.

Michael had covered all the windows. I must have feel off to sleep, I was awaken by the phone ringing I jumped up and looked at the clock it was 634 am I reached over Michael to grab it. "Hello," I said. "Karis." "Yes," I replied, "this is Karis," I didn't recognize the voice. "Can I help you," I said. "This is Tara's mom, she said sniffling. "Tara died." "What!" I asked, I couldn't breathe, this is some kind of joke, I thought. I couldn't move, "What do you mean? I just talk to Tara," I dropped the phone. Michael got up and took the phone from the floor. He began talking to Tara's mom. I laid in the bed curled in a fetal position.

"Lord, help me!" I screamed out; I cried out to the Lord, I couldn't believe what I just heard Michael came over to me and rubbed my back. "Baby, I know, I know, it's going to be okay I promise," he said pulling me up to hold me. "Baby I know," he said. I cried in his arms for what seemed to be hours. I couldn't move. "She was my soul sister Michael," I told him sobbing. "Who do I talk to now?" "Baby she's your angel now, she will never leave you, never," I sobbed more just thinking about our last conversation. Why would Tara not go to see the doctor?

I just couldn't take it. I got up and got myself dressed and went over to her grandmother's house; I needed to find out how real this was really. It can't be real Lord, tell me I'm still dreaming, I thought on my drive over to her grandmother's house, when I approached the house there were cars everywhere as if there was a party going on. I got out of my car and went to the front door; I was still crying when the grandmother came to the door. "Hello Karis, come in," she said. Everyone was in the back room; when I went to the back room, everyone rushed over to me.

"Oh Karis, how are you?" I shrugged my shoulders at the question this was my closet and only friend, like a sister to me, my stomach was in knots waiting to hear that this was some kind of sick prank that Tara wanted to play on me to get me over here for a baby shower or something. I stood there waiting in odd silence crying; there were boxes of tissues all around. Could this be? I thought to myself. "Why don't you have a seat," her aunt said to me, pointing at the couch. "Sure," I took a seat.

"We were just discussing the funeral arrangements. You were pretty close to her do you happen to know what it was that Tara wanted?" My mind went blank; then I thought about one day a couple of weeks ago when I came to visit Tara, and we argued how she wanted to be buried. She told me that she wanted to be cremated, but I told her I wouldn't do it and I wouldn't tell them. Should I tell them? I thought. "Excuse me, Karis did she share with you what she wanted?" She asked again. "Um, she did. But I don't know if I should say, it's really up to whoever is burying her right?" I said.

"Well no, we need to know what she wanted because it is up to her. "I would like to hear your input, especially because you guys spent so much time together and you knew her best. I know she told you what she wanted right?" I shook my head yes, I got up from my seat, and Tara's grandmother was upset at the thought of her being cremated, but it was Tara's wish. If I didn't tell them I wouldn't be honoring her, so I went over to the grandmother and told her. "I know, I didn't like the idea either, but it was her wishes to be cremated. I'm so sorry, but that's what she told me a few weeks ago right out there in your front yard. I'm so sorry," I said.

I had to leave, I couldn't take it anymore Tara wasn't there anymore, and I felt the emptiness surrounding my heart. The hurt was getting heavier, as I was leaving and Michael showed up. He pulled up when I was walking out to my car. "Baby, I would have driven you over here, you were too upset to drive," he said. "I'm okay, I'm going home now," I told him. Just then Tara's mom came out from the garage. "Karis, would you like to go with us to see her?" She asked me. I looked over at Michael, and he shook his head yes.

"I'll see you later, okay baby." I went in her car; it was me, her mother, and the grandmother. The ride was quiet at first, everyone still in a state of shock; I didn't say a word, not knowing what to expect. "She was going to work, and she passed out on in the parking lot," her mother said. "Was there anyone there?" I asked. "At first no, but someone passing by called for help, and did CPR until the paramedics arrived; they did CPR until they arrived at the hospital.

They said she came back and on arrival, she was in full cardiac arrest, there was nothing they could do, she was gone." She began to sob I reached for her hand and cried with her. When we approached the funeral home, it was hard to get out. I stood by the car for a while; her mother took my hand, "It's going to be okay," she said sobbing, we were both sobbing. I walked with her as we took the stairs to see Tara. Trees were surrounding the place where she was, and she was in a cold room. They had her wrapped up in her favorite blanket it was blue with dolphins all over it.

She looked beautiful, I kissed her cheek and held her hand, and I didn't want to let go. My heart was so heavy with pain, but I felt she was at peace you could see it on her beautiful face. I imagined she looked the same way when the Lord brought her into this life because she had this look of grace on her face just beautiful. We couldn't stay long; her grandmother was so strong, having buried her husband and child just months apart from one another. The lord is so good to her, we went in and planned her funeral service, it was so hard to leave her, and I felt like I left a piece of myself there that day.

I cried all the way home. I tried to stay strong, but my friend was gone and how was I going to go on without my soul sister? I went home that day to prepare myself for whatever was going to happen next. I called daddy, as soon as I got inside. Michael cooked dinner and put the twins to bed, I went into the bathroom and talked to daddy. I cried to him told him all about what happened to Tara and how I felt. He told me to come over to the garden, and we will plant some flowers for Tara out back.

Daddy always made me feel a little better. I went to sleep in Michaels' arms; I didn't talk to him, I just cried all night He didn't complain, he held me and rubbed my back until I fell off to sleep. The memorial service is in three days; I'm going to hate to go to this service to say goodbye to my friend. I woke up the next day, and I could smell breakfast cooking, I rushed up to get my robe. Oh my god, it was I dream I thought, Tara's downstairs.

"Hey, I knew it," I said as I turned the corner going into the kitchen, but to my surprise it was daddy. "Hello baby," he said, coming over to me kissing my forehead and pulling out a chair for me. "I decided to come over here today to cook breakfast for you and hang around here, "You don't need to be driving too much. You're getting too big for that," he said. "I guess it's good, I came over too because Michael had new windows put in all over the house too, so you needed to be here, right?" Daddy said. I shook my head yes, daddy sat a plate of food in front of me.

"Eat all of that you look too thin to even have that baby in there growing. I feel bad for the baby; you're all stomach." I began to cry again, "Oh, Karis please don't cry baby, she's in a better place," he said holding my hand. "You know maybe one day you'll meet again," daddy ate with me. When I was done I went back to my room to lay down; daddy watched the twins until Michael came home from work that night and every day after until that dreadful day finally came when I was to go to the memorial service for Tara.

It was bad enough there was one, but she knew so many people and was loved by so many that they held three memorial services. I could only do one I sat with the family, and it was heart wrenching enough.

There were so many family and friends; I just couldn't believe how many people Tara knew. They all knew who I was and kept calling me her sister, but I hardly knew anyone. The service was very nice, and so was the reception, Michael and I stayed with the twins for as long as we could.

I let Michael take them home while I went with daddy back to the house; he said he had to show me something. I kissed Michael as he got in the car with the twins. I hugged everyone and said my goodbyes to Tara's family; I didn't know how long it would be before I would see them again. Daddy drove me to the house. When we got there he opened the trunk it was full of flowers roses. "There's a rose for every year you spent with Tara in here in every color," he said. "Now grab a couple, and let's get digging."

He kissed my forehead and followed him to the backyard to start our dig. Daddy had a special area already for the flowers to be planted in. "It's beautiful daddy, thank you so much, Tara would have loved this, "I said kneeling down to plant my first batch of roses. I planted the orange colored roses first because she was into nice soft colors. Then I did the red, and onto the white, daddy helped me with them when he saw me struggling to dig.

When I finished, I sat down with daddy and had some fresh lemonade. "Karis, every day is special on this earth, God doesn't make any bad days. If someone tells you they have a bad day they're a liar. If they can breathe the clean air that he provides, then it's a good day. People take everything for granted, look around, baby." He said as I looked down at the ground and all around us it was a peaceful day, and daddy was right we were breathing.

Resting Easy On Sundays

Going over to see daddy was a pleasure for me now. I'd just go to watch the roses grow, while the children played around with daddy. I would prune the roses and cut them down sometimes just to take them home and put them in a vase; it made me feel like I was bringing Tara home with me each time. Little by little, I'd bring her; I was weeks away from having my new baby. More tired every day, I waddled now as my stomach grew to its fullest extent. I'd clean up and down the stairs getting everything ready for the baby, Michael and I painted the babies room. It was a small room close to ours.

The twins would be right across from us now; which was nice I could see them from the chair where I'd sit and read. They played together so well; I wondered how this baby would change the way they played. They were due to start school soon. They hadn't been around too many children; I often wondered if I'd made a mistake not sending them to a preschool for a longer period. Just to see how they'd get along, I was informed that they would be in separate classes, which were fine, but I wanted them to eat lunch together every day.

The principle of the school agreed. "Why not," she said "I'm sure they've eaten together every day since they were born." We laughed about it, and of course, they'd see each other on the playground. I was excited for them. I'd say to them, every day sometimes, "first you learn to tie your shoes, then you're all big, and it's off to school." I'd sing it while I washed them up, I sang the little song everywhere we went around the house. I explained to them about school being the place they would learn, play, and meet friends. They'd ask, "what do we learn mommy?"

"All sorts of things," I tell them. "Mostly reading and math, and they have this great thing called sharing day." Michael bought them lunch pails; he'd bring something home almost every day for them for school. I noticed that he'd sit and talk with them a lot and they'd listen to him so intensely as if he was getting them ready to go off to college. I tried to listen in on the conversation, but when I get close to them, there was a hush that came over them as if they didn't want me to know what Michael was telling them.

Michael would put his finger to his mouth and say, "mommy doesn't need to hear about this, guys. Remember she's very fragile." he'd say to them while rubbing my belly. When I put them to bed sometimes I'd ask them, Kristina would tell me more than her brother would, she was talkative. We'd say our prayers, and I tuck them in, I would sit down on Kristina's bed. "Kristina, how was your talk with your dad? Did he have anything funny to say tonight?" I ask.

She always tells me the same thing, "oh mommy, I forget what daddy said "She would smile kiss my cheek and roll over to her side, I just rubbed her back until I heard the quiet in the room. I went over to Kristopher and kissed him on the cheek and rubbed his back too. "I love both of you," I say as I closed the door, leaving a crack so I could peak in later. When I went to my room it was freezing; I went to check the windows to see where the air was coming from, there were no windows open at all.

I sat on the bed to remove my shoes; as I kicked them off, I felt a colder breeze come over me. I could see my breath as I breathed in and out. I swallowed deep and stood up to get my pajamas out of the drawer. I looked over toward the window, and the frost looked as if it was spelling out words. I turned and walked to the bathroom; the baby would sit so low my bladder that I constantly felt full, at times I thought I would burst. I sat on the toilet; I could still feel my breath, it was still cold. I put my head down and thought to myself.

Lord, I don't have the strength for this at all, I feel so tired, I can't do this now, I can't do this right now. I leaned down to take a breath; there was a cool breeze coming from the doorway. I looked up to see if there was anyone there, and no one so went and sat on the bed. I sat up to lean back onto the headboard, and I felt two hands wrap around my ankles and squeezed them tight. I tried moving my legs, but couldn't get free. I leaned back down and put my hands on my ankles, covering the hands around them.

I was pushed back on the bed with a strong force. I could smell it; I couldn't see over my stomach, I tried lifting myself back up from the bed, but was held down. I could feel it looking at me in my face; I could smell its horrible smell, I wanted to vomit after a while. I began to pray for it to let me go as my legs started to go numb from its grip on my ankles. I put my hands up to feel it; its force pushed them back down toward the bed. I closed my eyes and prayed for it to show its soul. "Open the door for me to feel the spirit near, Lord, please help me send it back. Show me what is holding it back." I reached for it again, I could feel that I had it, I opened my eyes, and to my surprise, it appeared.

My eyes widen with what I saw to be an older male figure staring back at me. I closed my eyes again and prayed. "Lord, please lead his soul to where it belongs; his spirit is worn and ready to rest. Lord, forgive his sins today lead him back to where he will lay." I was still praying when the grip on my ankles tightened, and my wrist was going numb too. I started the Lord's Prayer, I felt like giving into it, I was so tired and started to have cramps in my back, I was in pain.

When it let go, and I grabbed hold of it I went into darkness unknown; I saw this spirits work, he was a doctor before he passed. In this room was another man and a pregnant woman, she was laying on a table screaming for them to help her. The lights from the hospitals ceiling shined on her bed brightly as they stood over her. The doctor sat in front of her on a stool as he was getting ready to deliver her child, but the woman screamed out more and more.

The other person in the room stood by watching, shaking his head in disbelief. "Sir she needs something for the pain," he told the doctor. "No, she's fine this is her fifth child, she can handle this," he uttered back nonchalantly as the woman screamed on. The room was cold and empty, there were no hospital supplies around and no other nurses, the girl looked underage and so did the person with her. The doctor, yelled at her to push, she pushed and pushed as he yelled.

When the baby came out, he cut the cord quickly took the baby over to a small table near the door. He checked it out, and the girl yelled out, "what is it, what is it?" The doctor ignored her. It was a beautiful baby boy; the other person went over to her to calm her down. The doctor came over to him handed him a wad of money. "Thank you," he said. The woman was still lying there bloody, and the afterbirth began to come out soon after the doctor walked away. "What did you do?" The woman asked him.

"What did you do?" The man laid his head on the bed, not saying a word. The doctor walked down a dark hall and met a couple at the end of it, "here he is," he said with excitement in his voice. "Your baby boy is healthy and ready to go home with his new parents." The couple praised the doctor. "Oh my god, thank you," they said the woman quickly grabbed the baby while the man walked off to the side to talk to the doctor. "How much do I owe you doc?" The man said holding his checkbook out with his pen ready to oblige the doctor with whatever he asked.

The doctor looked over at the woman, then down the hall as if he was concerned with the parents of the baby. "I cannot accept anything less than five hundred thousand," he said with a straight face. The man looked over at his wife gazing down at the baby boy and began to write, "no problem doc, none at all." The doctor took the check, shook the man's hand and walked away. "Thank you," he shouted as he went toward an exit leading to the car garage outside. I held onto this spirit as it got colder, the old man's spirit took me in. He drove toward a house on a hill overlooking the ocean.

He went inside straight to the bathroom and cleaned himself up, and back out the door he went. He walked toward his car and stared up at the front window of this home, and into his car. He sat there staring at the check. "I don't know," he said to himself, "I just don't know." He began to drive and ended up at a small gambling shack. Men and women were hanging out everywhere. "Hi baby," a woman dressed in barely anything says to him as he walked by when he turned the corner to go into the dark alleyway where the back door would become his entrance to the hall.

He was approached by two men dressed in leather jackets, "what's up Doc?" They call out to him, they both grabbed him by the arm. "We've been waiting for you far too long." The doctor was pleading with them, "I had to do a job, and I'm here now." He told them, "I have his money right here," he said holding out the check to them. "Doc we don't want your money, the boss wants to see you," the tall one said smiling. "I'll take that," the other man said snatching the check from his hand. "Now, you know that the boss doesn't accept any checks," he said looking at the check laughing.

They took him into a dark room and sat him in a chair. "Oh, I wouldn't want to be you right now," the tall man said. In walked a huge guy surrounded by other men carrying guns, knives, sticks, and bats. "Hello, Doc," the guy in the middle said. "It's time to pay the piper sir, you had too many passes to get me my money," he said smiling. "Boss, this is what he brought you," he said handing the check to the boss. Then, they all took turns beating him one by one; there was blood flying everywhere.

The doctor soon began to lose consciousness breathing less and less. I watched as he drifted into his slow death. The men never stopped beating him, when died they continued to beat him. Soon the boss walked away with the check in his hand laughing and talking to another guy, "Checks, I'm going straight to the bank with this one," he told the other guy. When the men got tired of beating him, they picked him up from the chair and took him outside and threw him into the trunk of a car.

They drove him down a dark road toward a river when the car stopped two of the men got out and took him by the legs and arms and threw him out into the river. "Goodbye, Doc," one man said. "Good luck with the bets you make in hell," the other said laughing. This spirit was destined to roam freely because of this awful death. I held onto him as long as I could, with my back hurting and the pain getting sharper in my belly. I could feel him trying to grab onto my belly, I prayed. Lord take his soul release him right, erase the memories of that awful night give him peace. Lay him to rest; his spirit is weary, lost in distress.

Lord, lay him down where he can be found, where he could be buried in command ground. So he can have peace, and his soul will no longer be beaten. Forgive him, Lord, for he did sin, he's learned a hard lesson, in the end, that evil never wins. In the name of Jesus I pray, I held onto him as I felt him drift further and further away from me with each prayer I prayed. It became easier for me to move, my ankles became free, and I was able to move my legs. The smell of his spirit faded until it was gone. I laid there on the bed with my hands up just as the spirit left me, drained and in pain.

My back hurt me more and more as I tried lifting myself up. I could feel the contractions in my stomach grow stronger. I sat up and held my stomach, oh no, I thought, Michaels in the attic would he even hear me? I got up to go get Michael; I was in so much pain, "Michael!" I yelled out, "Michael!! Help me," I cried out, I was toppled over in the hallway it seemed my contractions were one after the other. Faster and faster they came, Michael didn't hear me calling him. I picked up a vase from the stand in the hallway and smashed it down on the floor, maybe he'd hear that I thought.

I grabbed anything from the table that would make noise. I was feeling so much pressure in my bottom I knew I had to make it to the couch in the den. I walked over bent over, holding my legs open wide as I walked. It felt as if I had to go to the bathroom so bad; the pressure hit me harder as I made it to the couch. I laid on it and put one leg over the top of it; I had on underwear, I struggled to take them off, my body felt hot all over. I wanted to remove all of my clothes, but I had no energy to do it. "Michael!!" I cried out again.

By now tears were streaming from my face, the pain was so bad, I screamed and screamed, at the top of my lungs. "Michael!! Michael!! Help me please!!!" I cried, I began to push, and I put my hand down into there to feel if I had a bowel movement but I wasn't I felt the top of the baby's head instead. "Oh My God Michael" I screamed. Finally he came running down the stairs, "Baby, What's wrong. He asked in a panic. "The baby is coming now." "I'm not going to make it to the hospital," I took his hand and placed it between my legs, so he could feel what I felt, "Oh goodness," he said running over to the phone.

"Did you call anyone baby?" He asked me. "Just you," I told him as I panted, out of breath. I pushed with every pain; it made me feel much better, Michael came over to me with one ear to the phone. He took his hand and felt down there again. "Its head is down; I'm a doctor, I just need an ambulance please!" He told the operator. "Baby stop pushing okay, I have to check you, and you keep breathing," Michael sat down in front of my opened legs and put his hand down there. "Baby, he's almost out with the next contraction just push as hard as you can for me okay." He took my hands placed them with his on my knees.

"Okay," I told him here it comes, I took a deep breath and pushed as hard as I could. Michaels face looked as if he was pushing with me. "Yes baby, yes," he said. He took my hand and put it down there with his, "feel him? Feel our sons head," he said. I smiled, Michael knows that they told us it was a girl, but he insists on believing it's a little boy. I held her little head as Michael reached down and pulled her up and out with both his hands. He grabbed her little neck; that was the best feeling I felt in a long time, it was a relief.

Michael laid the baby on top of me; he covered us up with his shirt. "I have to get some scissors, and I need some hot water," he said running all around the house. Michael came back with the scissors, he turned the baby around to cut the cord, and to my surprise, there it was his little penis, and he started peeing all over Michaels' hands. "See, I told you he was a boy! My boy," he said laughing, I looked down at his little penis, it was definitely a little boy.

Michael cut the cord and tied it with a shoestring, then laid him back across my belly. He was covered in blood; Michael rubbed his back with his shirt. "He's so handsome, just like his daddy," Michael said, "yes, just like his dad," I said. "What should we call him?" I said to Michael, "I like Keagan or Kevin," I told him. He looked at the baby, really good. "Oh, Kegan, I don't know about that one. I like, Jacob or Peter. I don't want him to have a hard time spelling his name." Michael said.

"Michael, I want him to have a K in his name as the other children," I told him. "I will think about it, Keagan, huh," he took him from my stomach and held him up to the light. "Keagan, yes, you do look like a Keagan." He held him close; we could hear the ambulance coming from the back window. Michael went to the door; he didn't open it, he just stood there rocking Keagan in his arms. The children came running downstairs, "mommy, daddy what's wrong?" they said running towards me, they looked over at Michael. "Oh, oh," Kristen said smiling.

"The baby's here! The baby's here!" They both ran over to Michael the ambulance finally showed. The children were all over Michael with the baby in his arm he opened the door for them and pointed to me. They came over to check me out, one of them checked the cord blood and after birth, and the other took my vitals. Michael stood over them with the children each on one side of him and the baby in his arms. "Sir, we will need to check the baby out too," the paramedic told him.

"Okay," Michael said sitting down on the couch with the baby in his arms. "Mrs. everything looks good, you have a little tear down there, but other than that you're fine. Do you want to go to the hospital?" They asked. I looked over at Michael. "No, I think I can handle staying home." I told them. "Well, Mrs. if you start to feel dizzy or sick or if you start to bleed heavy please go straight to the emergency room or call your doctor," he said looking over at Michael. "Oops, your doctors already here," he said smiling at Michael and the baby.

"Sir, everything checks out, she should see her OB-GYN as soon as possible." "Will do," he said to them shaking their hands on the way out the door, "Congratulations," they all said as they left. "Thank you," Michael said. Michael came over to me and kissed my forehead. "I'm taking him upstairs to lay him down I will be back down to get you as soon as I get him into the crib. Come on twins lets go lay him down for a minute. You guys can watch over him while I get mommy." "Yes!" They both yelled out at once, I waited patiently for Michael to return.

The house was quiet, I could hear the birds beginning to chirp the sky began to change as our night turned over into the morning, I reached over the table to grab a note pad, I used the one we used for memos in case someone called and wanted to leave a message. I began to write. Today, this day 23rd of May our baby boy Keagan Oliver was born at exactly one twenty-two this morning, healthy and strong. I wanted to write down the day so that I could put it on his certificate later. Michael returned to get me.

"You all ready?" He asked extending his arms to me. I reached out for him with the note pad still in my hand. He lifted me from the couch; we both looked down as he lifted me to see what a mess I left. "New couch time," Michael said laughing. "No, I think I'll have it cleaned and keep as a reminder for him," he said. "I don't know if that would be a good idea, its blood," I told him. "Yes, maybe you're right, blood is difficult to clean."

We headed upstairs; "baby, do you want to clean yourself up a little? I'll help you," he stood me up in the shower and helped me with my clothes. He ran warm water and took the shower head and a towel and washed me clean. "Today is Sunday, baby. This is the best day of my life," he said washing my body. "Do you even know what you did?" He asked. I shook my head no, "Yes I know baby, God just blessed us so well," he said. He took the shower head and sprayed warm water all over me, especially between my legs; it felt so good because I was so sore down there.

"Thank you, Michael," I tell him as he sprayed the water on me. "No baby, thank you," Michael said. He turned off the water and wrapped me in a towel as he helped me out of the tub. He dried me off and walked me to the bedroom where he already had my night clothes out. "I will be back with the baby," he said. "You need to feed him soon I'm going to wash him up, and then you can feed him. He's starving." He ran out of the room to get the baby. He brought him back in as I lay in bed, I was so tired.

Michael took him into the bathroom to wash him up, Keagan cried the whole time. When he brought him to me, he was trying to eat his hands with his fist balled up. He moved his little head around and around trying to eat those little hands. Michael pulled the strap down from my gown, and put his nose to my nipple, Keagan latched on quickly. "Oh, look at my boy," Michael said. "He's definitely hungry." I rubbed his little head as he sucked on my breast, he was so handsome, I checked him out, his eyes were gray like a cat, and his skin was pale and wrinkly.

I changed sides for him to nurse on both sides; he had very little black straight hair. "Oh my, I bet he's going to look just like Michael when his features come in," I said out loud so that Michael could hear me. "Yes, he is," Michael said rubbing his little head. "I would hate for you to have this straight nose like your mommy's," he said laughing. "I'm going to let you rest with him while I make some phone calls okay baby?" Michael said.

"Sure," I told him, "Go make your calls." "I will bring you up something to drink and maybe a small plate of food okay," he says walking out of the room. "Oh, yes please, hurry with the drink, I need it. Water will be fine," I tell him. "Okay baby I'll be right back up with that," Michael was very eager to call everyone to tell them about his son. I watched the baby eat until his little eyes closed. Michael came back up to the room with my water just as I began to burp him, I laid him on my shoulder and began patting him on the back, his little head constantly moved from side to side as if he wasn't done eating yet.

Michael rubbed his back as I drank some of the water he brought in for me. "Little guy, little guy, you're so handsome," he said, Michael was so proud of him. "I'm so tired Michael," I told him." I need to rest." "Yes I agree, lay him beside you," he said getting a blanket from the drawer to lay on the sheet. "Well, you have all this pink," he said spreading the blanket. "I know I don't know what I'm going to do with it all I thought I was having a girl. I thought I was going to be using all of that stuff," I said.

"Well, I guess we save it for the next one." Michael said. I laid Keagan down on the bed next to me. Michael kissed me on the lips. "I'll be back baby, get some rest," he said closing the door. I have to make the twins lunch I thought as my eyes grew heavy, I have to take them to the park today, it's Sunday. Yawning and looking at the baby, I need to take them to the park I thought deliriously, I turned over onto my stomach; that was something I hadn't been able to do in months. It felt so good as I fell off to sleep when I woke up Michael was in the chair holding the baby with a bottle in his mouth.

"He woke up hungry, I didn't want to wake you," he said feeding and rocking the baby. "Oh," I said sitting up on the bed. "Where are the twins, what time is it?" I asked. "The twins are sleeping, I fed them and gave them their bath already, don't worry I had it covered. They had a wonderful day, baby, you needed that rest. How do you feel now?" He asked. "I feel a lot better; I'm still a little tired though. I need to use the restroom," I tell him getting up to go. I pulled the covers back, and I had bled a little through my gown, but not on the sheets. It was a little embarrassing so I waited for Michael to burp the baby so that his head would be turned.

I got up and held my gown in my hands, just as I went for the drawer Michael looked up. "Baby is there something wrong? Why do you have your gown in your hands?" He asked. "I had a little accident," I tell him as I walked quickly into the bathroom. "You shouldn't be embarrassed, baby," he said, smiling back at me. "A little," I tell him as I closed the bathroom door. "Okay, well, if you're bleeding heavy baby, you need to go to the hospital to be checked okay," he yelled out to me. "Oh, of course, Michael, I know," I said as I washed up after using the bathroom. I started to feel sad while I washed up; I looked in the mirror at myself.

Three kids I thought. Why did I have three kids now? I wiped my face with a towel and stood there looking at myself in the mirror for a while. "Are you okay?" Michael called out. "I'm fine I'll be right out." I tell him. "Okay, I brought the bassinet in for the baby. I'm going to lay him in it and make some more calls, okay baby," he said. "Sure, I will be fine," I said yelling through the closed door. I didn't want to go out where Michael could see me; I knew he would know that I was sad right away.

I missed my friend Tara; I'm not going to be able to share this blessing with her. She won't get to hold this baby nor will she ever be able to care for him like she did the twins, I cried a little more before leaving the bathroom. When I opened the door to my surprise Michael was standing there with his arms out. "Baby, I know what you're thinking, but I'm here, and the twins are here. We have a beautiful baby boy now, believe me, she's around you all the time. I promise you she's around us at all times," he said. I leaned into his chest crying even more. "Baby, we will all be fine."

My emotions were running wild. I missed Tara; I was upset about what happened to me before I gave birth to him. I felt so bad. I sat down on the bed and cried on Michaels' chest, "Oh no." He said. "You have the baby blues, have you ever had these before?" He asked me. I shook my head no. "Well, this is it, but if you feel too sad and hopeless we will have to get you some help," he said wiping my eyes with a soft towel. I lay on the bed and sobbed for a good while, Michael walked around the room holding the baby, and I fell off to sleep again. When I woke up this time, daddy was sitting in the chair holding Keagan.

"Hello, baby," daddy said. "What a smart looking grandson I have, don't you think?" he said holding Keagan up to face me. "Sure daddy, he looks brilliant." I replied. "So, what's the little fellow's name?" Daddy asked. "His name is Keagan Oliver," I tell him. "Wow, what a name your mom has given you. Keagan Oliver huh" He said smiling. "Yes, it just came to me daddy, I wanted him to have a name that could represent his strength."

"Well, he certainly looks strong, baby," daddy said holding him close to his heart. "Little Kegan Oliver, that's most definitely a clever name. I think if I had arrived a little earlier I'd given you the same name," Daddy said. Soon after daddy came, everyone started showing up. First my cousin Martha, I hadn't seen her in a while, she was so happy to see us. Then it was my sister Daisy who had the worst attitude; she seems to only come over because of daddy making her. I barely spoke to her; she didn't bring a gift for him either. It was one person after the other that day; the baby began to get fussy.

I told Michael that we would have to have a get together for everyone to come at once because the baby and I just couldn't handle it. So, he planned it for next weekend before the twins start school. I was so tired I slept more and more. I was up and down all night with the baby now so the mornings came fast and the days where very long with all I had to do. The baby was a good sleeper in the daytime at times; he would sleep for hours while I spent time with the twins. Michael took thirty days off work to help; he held Keagan a lot not wanting his backside to touch the bed or the chair.

"Michael, please, if you continue to do that I won't ever be able to put him down when you go back to work," I tell him. "Oh, he will be fine," he tells me. "Don't you want him to feel comfortable at all times? You have to hold him close to your heart," he says with little Keagan resting on his bare chest. I watched him cuddle him for hours, as the twins sat close to him admiring his little hands and feet. Michael made sure to include them as he held Keagan tight. Keagan eyes rolled up and down as he slept. He would smile and whimper at times while he dreams, but what bothered me most was his constant jumping in his sleep.

I watched him a lot while he slept, Michael would say that the angels were playing ball with him in heaven, we'd laugh about that all the time. As time went on Michael went back to work, and the twins were beginning school, I was left at home with Keagan alone a lot. I was up and down with him. He was a good eater; he'd do thirty minutes on each side every feeding. Daddy would stop by to visit me every other day. He'd bring Kegan all sorts of things, clothes, and toys, I'd tell him to stop, but he never listened to me.

I would take him for walks every day, long walks; he'd fall asleep by the time we'd reach the house. The twins would walk alongside me; they'd sometimes complain that they were tired and wanted to go home. I'd walk them to the park and watch them play until it was almost feeding time for the baby. Keagan would be five months when the twins entered school he was starting to recognize them and Michael more and more; he would reach out for Michael as soon as he would come through the door at night.

The twins would do the same. I would go straight to the bathroom for a shower when Michael got in, sometimes I'd rush to the bath tub just to soak. Michael and the children would come in right behind me sometimes. He would want to know immediately how my day went, "So how was it?" he'd ask, I'd always have the same answer for him. "The day was okay, I'm fine, and still standing." He'd hold little Keagan and stand over the bathtub just watching me. "I would like to wash your back for you, but my hands are full," he'd say bouncing Keagan up and down slowly. "I want you so bad," he says, I grabbed the shower curtain and pulled it back.

"Michael, get out," I tell him laughing. "Baby, when are you going to give it up?" he asked peeking through the shower curtain. "I'm ready when you are," I say back to him smiling. "Oh don't you dare tell me that, I will put Keagan down right now," he says laughing. I washed up and got out fast, I did everything fast these days, cooking and washing. I'd have strange encounters that I would ignore all day. I would go into the kitchen, and cold wind would fly by me or shadows would stand in the bathroom. I would smell the foul odors which always meant that someone was near seeking my attention.

I treated it all as if I didn't feel nor smell; I would pray around the house all day. Michael didn't want me to go back to work, and I agreed, I'd take some time to raise the children, he wanted for me to be there when they come home from school to help them with their homework and talk to them about their day. He didn't want Keagan in childcare at all; he was anxious about him being cared for by strangers. He said that he didn't want him to be picked up by too many people and that their spirit might rub off on Keagan.

Michael was very protective of the children. The twins first day came around fast; they would have the same teacher and be assigned seats across from one another. Michael and I took them to school on the first day. The teacher was a nice lady named Ms. Honey. She wore her hair short, and dressed in a nice flowery dress with a sweater, and wore her glasses on her nose, not looking through them as if they were only for fashion. When we went into the classroom, she greeted us with a smile. "Hello, I'm Ms. Honey, how are you?" She asked.

"This must be the twins I was promised," she went on to say, patting them both on the head. "Would you like to see your seats?" She asked them. The twins both shook their heads yes. "I'm Michael, and this is my wife Karis," Michael said reaching his hand out to shake hers. "Nice to meet you, Michael and Karis" "It's a pleasure to meet you too," Michael said following her around to the twins seats. "Hi, cutie," she said reaching Keagan's cheeks. Keagan smiled and laughed at her; he didn't take his little eyes off her the whole time. It was as if he could see through her.

When Michael finished seating the twins, I handed him Keagan and walked over to them to kiss them goodbye. "Have a nice day you two." I said waving goodbye, following Michael out of the door. "They will be fine," Ms. Honey assured as we walked away. "Well, I guess they'll be fine, right Michael?" I asked. "They'll be here all day now, what if they don't like it?" "Oh baby, you worry too much, they will protect one another, if anything," Michael said. Putting Keagan into the car, I looked back at the classroom window to see if I would be able to see them from the car.

When I looked over there were three kids in the window looking back at me waving; it was the same three I saw at the mall playground weeks before. They looked like adults dressed like children with no faces. I stared at them trying to figure out just what I was looking at. "Hello, Karis, get in the car. Are you coming? What's wrong?" Michael asked me. I was still looking when I got inside the car. I had this sick feeling in my stomach, so I turned around to look back again, and they were gone.

I was ready to go back to get them and take them home. "What's wrong?" Michael asked. "You're so quiet, are you okay? The kids will be just fine, they've been to preschool, so they'll be okay, I promise," Michael said driving toward the house. "Well, here we are," he said. He helped Keagan and me into the house. "I will see you soon baby," he told me grabbing his bag for work. I couldn't get the image of those three faces out of my mind all day. I washed and cleaned and cooked and prayed all day Keagan crawled all over the house while I worked around him. I held him and rocked him to sleep as I watched the clock for school to end.

The phone rang. "Hello," I said quickly. "Hello, how is everything going?" They asked. "It's good, I guess," it was Michael. "I'm going to be running little late so if you can pick up the twins that would be great. "Sure I will," I tell him. When I hung up, I see Keagan standing up in the middle of the floor holding on to something. I ran over to him. "Hey what's going on," I say to him picking him up from the floor. "You can't walk yet," I kissed Keagan's little forehead. "Let's go get your brother and sister," I tell him.

I went to the front door with his bag on one end of my hip and him on the other. I placed Keagan in his car seat and began to drive off when I see the three faces I saw in the classroom window standing behind the car. They were all dressed in dark sweaters and matching pants. They were bald and looked like short old men, but they were the height of five-year-old children. As I drove out, I watched as they waved and moved out of the driveway; I stared at them as I drove off. I was so worried about the children that I drove as fast as I could to the school.

When I reached the school, Ms. Honey was standing with the twins holding their hands side by side they stood with her waiting patiently. I got out of the car and greeted Ms. Honey. "How was their first day?" I asked her. "They both did well today. They're both very bright," she said. "Thank you," I said putting them in the car. She was still talking about the day when I noticed the three-man like children standing across the playground staring over at the children and waving. I looked back at Kristopher he had his little eyes covered at the sight of them, and Kristine watched them with wonder in hers. I said my goodbyes to Ms. Honey and drove off.

"How was your day, guys? Kristopher still had his eyes covered. "Mommy, my day was good, I had hamburgers for lunch, and the teacher let me be the line leader," Kristine told me. I looked in the rearview mirror to see if Kristopher took his hands from his eyes. "Hey you, what's wrong, why do you have your eyes covered?" I asked him. "I don't know," he said removing his hands. "What did you do today? Do you have any homework?" I asked them. They shook their heads no. "I had so much fun, mommy," Kristopher said.

"I have new friends, Nolan and Rodger. They are five like me, mommy, we played on the playground together, and we ate lunch together too, mommy." They both had so much to tell me. They talked all the way to the house. I made them a snack and got them already for Michael to come home for dinner. Michael usually came home the moment I finished dinner and got it to the table these days. He loved being home for dinner and loved hearing the stories the children told while holding and feeding the baby through dinner. It would be the high light of his day it seemed. I wanted to ask the children about those triplets and if they saw them, were they in their classrooms or did they play on the playground with them.

I would bring it up to Michael after we put the children to bed, Keagan was growing so fast. He already knows who we are and follows us around the house with his eyes and reaches out to us as if he wants us to pick him up. Michael was a complete sucker for Keagan. "Hello son," he'd say to him all the time. After getting the children off to bed I was showering when Michael jumped in with me. I felt him washing my back with the warm water.

He pulled me close to him and wrapped me in his arms, e whispered into my ear, "I miss you," I turned around to him and kissed his neck, then his lips, Michael kissed back, " I want you baby" I kissed Michael as I washed his chest. I washed my body quickly, and he washed him, we got out and went to bed barely dry. We fell back onto the sheets and made love. Michael missed me; I could always tell when because he'd hold me closer and kiss me longer. It was like he wanted to get inside me, it was a passionate night.

He held me close all night we didn't talk about the children at all we feel to sleep holding on another. My legs were wrapped around him, and his arms held me tightly, close to his chest. I woke up to his soft kiss early in the morning. He's up by four every morning to go to work. He always kisses me, and I wake up. I'm never able to go back to sleep after that kiss. I spring up and began to start my day. Today I would go to class with the children so that I can watch over them.

I know that they wouldn't want me there, but I had to go in case they need protection. I went to get them dressed for school and fed them breakfast; I told them my plans for today so that they wouldn't be surprised when I hung around the classroom. Kristine was fine with it, but Kristopher was a little annoyed, "mommy, do you have to stay with me?" He asked me. "I'm not going to stay long, I promise," I told him. "Okay mommy, thank you," he said jumping into the car. We headed for school, as I drove we saw those kids again walking and holding hands.

There were four of them all dressed alike; one wore a red jumper with a hood, one had on blue. The other had on yellow, and the last one had green, they stared at us as we proceeded closer to school. They waved at the children, but the twins were too scared to wave back. "Do you guys know them?" I asked. They both shook their heads no. I parked and we went into the school. Ms. Honey was ready to start class, I held Keagan's chair and stood by the door. "Mrs. Karis, will you be joining us today?" Ms. Honey asked me.

"Yes, I would like to stay for just a little while, if that's okay with you?" "Oh sure, it is," Ms. Honey replied pulling a chair out for me. I sat down as I scanned the room looking for the four children we saw walking to the class. They were nowhere to be found. I stood up and told Ms. Honey that I would be leaving soon I couldn't stay too long with Keagan anyway, How would I explain breastfeeding to the class. I began to walk toward the classroom door, and I saw the kids on the playground, playing alone; no teachers and no other children.

I looked back at Ms. Honey, I wanted to ask her about them, but what would she think? I could see that she couldn't see them. My children and I were the only ones who could see them. So I walked out, as I waved bye to my children. As I walked to my car, I stood back and watched them as they played around with each other on the playground. I held Keagan in his chair; it was getting heavier as I stood to watch. I walked to the car worried, why were they there? I felt a horrible sensation come over me, so I put Keagan in the car and strapped him down. I went to get into the car and when I looked up they were in the window of the classroom.

Their faces were distorted, it looked so scary, and I looked at them and got into the car. I don't want to leave the twins here I thought, but what do I do? They have to stay in school. I really can't take them out; I don't want them to miss out on anything. So I drive off, going home worrying about them. I rush home to call Michael to tell him what I seen at the school. When I arrive at the house, daddy was there waiting for me; as I pull into the driveway, he started waving. "Hello darling," daddy says as I get out of the car.

Good, an opportunity for me to go back to the school without Keagan I thought as I greeted daddy with a kiss. "Daddy, what are you doing here?" I asked him. "I just wanted to see my baby," he said taking my hand. "Daddy, do you mind watching Keagan? I have to go back to the school I left something there," I tell him rushing him into the house with Keagan's car seat. "Sure, don't be too long okay darling, I have to be somewhere at around two o'clock," he says going into the kitchen.

"Daddy there's coffee over there and some cheesecake or your favorite strawberry pound cake in the fridge. I promise I will be right back," I said rushing for the door. Keagan reached out to me and began to cry, "Don't cry Keagan granddads here with you." Daddy said consoling Keagan. I shut the door and got in the car. I drove back to the school thinking what I might find there. I pulled up to the school went inside the gate and into the office. "Can I help you?"

The clerk said. "Yes, I would like to visit my children's classroom." I tell her looking around, "Well, whose class are they in?" She asked holding her pen out to me. "They are in Ms. Honey's class they're twins," I said. "Oh, you're the twin's mom? They are so cute; they're always smiling and playing together on the playground. Here's your pass," she says handing me a sticker pass with visitor shining brightly on it. I stuck it to my shirt and proceeded to the classroom. "Um Mrs. hey aren't in class right now they're in the art media room. They have arts and crafts today," she said. "Have a nice day."

"Thank you, you too," I tell her. I began to walk thinking, oh my goodness I forgot to ask her where the art media room was. As I walked, I saw a lot of teachers walking around, so I asked one of them where it was. "Go straight past the cafeteria and down the hall past the restrooms and make a left. You will see a small colorful little building with stairs. Up those stairs is the art media room." "Thank you," I say to them. I finally made it there, when I walked in the kids were all covered with paint and wearing aprons. They had paint everywhere on them except for the paper. "Hello," Ms. Honey said approaching me.

"You decided to come back in huh," she said standing next to me. "Yes, how are the children doing?" I asked her. "Oh, they're doing great, really friendly and very smart. That one especially," she said pointing at Kristine. "She is wise beyond her years." "Yes, I believe so too," I told her scanning the room. "So would you like to stay and help? Today we are painting trees and making forest trees. As you can see the children are really into it," she said smiling looking at them paint each other's clothes and hands. "I can see they do enjoy this, but I can't stay too long."

I left my father with the baby; I just wanted to check on them to see how they were interacting with the other children." I tell her scanning the room in hopes of any glimpse of those kids. "Okay that's fine," she said walking to the front of the class. "Children, children, it's time to get cleaned up and ready for our story. Now everyone put your brushes down, and go over to the sink to wash up, share and help your friends," she said putting music on while they cleaned. "When you're done, take the aprons off hang them up, and come over to the floor as quickly as you can," she said.

"Mrs. Karis came back to hear our story today?" She questioned. "Sure, I would," I tell her. Soon all the children were on the rug. "Boys and girls our story today is about forest trees and why we need them." Ms. Honey began to read the story aloud to the children. I scanned the room as they listened attentively. I gave Ms. Honey a wink I had to get back to the house so that daddy could make his appointment. I stood up and started for the door. I looked out of the window, and there they were playing outside again. I wanted to get a better look at them, but when I walked toward them, they started to run towards the school, I ran after them.

They got on the window railing and stared into the classroom at the children. I was hesitant to get close to them. I could hear them whispering to one another. I tried to make out what they were saying, but I couldn't. I felt a horrible knot I my stomach when I went any closer and I could smell them. It was a rotten smell. I felt sicker by the second so I backed off. I could hear one of them began to growl like a dog would if it was on the attack. So I stood there a minute before turning away from them to head for my car. I looked at them.

The one wearing the yellow jumper was growling, his head was down I stared at him as I walked slowly backward to get away from them. I couldn't see its face yet; I was about to turn away when it looked up at me, "OH!!" I screamed out, his face was all twisted, and his teeth were sharp like a dog's teeth, he growled as I turned and ran to my car as quickly as I could. What are you doing? I thought. "You can't run, you can't run," I told myself getting closer to my car. I looked back at it; I stared into its eyes with no fear in my heart, its head went back down.

Now, what could they want? I wondered. Why are they lurking around the schoolyard? When I got home, daddy was curled up on the couch with Keagan next to him sleeping. I went to the kitchen and began cleaning daddy's mess. There were coffee splatters everywhere; he had cake left on a plate. I heard a noise coming from upstairs; I went to look up there, I could see three shadows moving around like they were running. I ran up the stairs trying not to wake daddy or Keagan. I heard sniffling and followed the sounds up.

I approached the hall and looked both ways for any other shadows. "Hello," I said. It could still hear whispering as I moved closer to the twin's room. I went for the door; I twisted the knob and pushed. They were running out of the window one by one, and the last one had the twins picture in its hand. "Hey!" I yelled out as they jumped out of the window. He dropped the picture on the way out. I looked outside to see where they went. They were running down the street. "Karis!" I hear daddy calling me, so I ran downstairs. "Yes, daddy I'm here I'll be down there in a second," I tell him.

"How was your nap?" I asked him. "It was great. I fed the little fellow, and he knocked out on me. He was exhausted," daddy said smiling. "Apparently you were too daddy," I said handing him his jacket. "Thank you, daddy, the kids were fine," I tell him. "Daddy do you want a washcloth for your face before you leave?" I asked. "I'm just going to go to the bathroom and wash up real fast Thank you, baby," daddy said as he went into the bathroom. I sat down next to Keagan and began rubbing his little back. Daddy left as soon as he came out of the bathroom.

I took Keagan to his room to lay him in his crib for a while he was up from his afternoon nap. I went to the phone to pick it up to call Michael. When I picked it up, there was a voice yelling through the receiver when I put it to my ear. "Hello," I shouted. "Hello, hello, there's been an emergency at the school today, Please come down to pick up your children," the woman said. "What do you mean an emergency? I was just there," I replied.

"Ma'am, I don't have time to explain, there was a teacher attacked and you need to pick up your children." I dropped the phone quickly, and I took Keagan from his crib and walked quickly to the car. I drove as fast as I could to get to the school when I arrived there where parents running everywhere. I grabbed Keagan, and we went to the classroom. When we arrived in the classroom, Ms. Honey was lying on the floor of the classroom covered in blood. I covered my mouth and went looking for my children with Keagan in my arms. I asked the teacher in the classroom next to Ms. Honeys.

"Have you seen my children?" she shook her head with tears streaming from her eyes she pointed me toward the office. I quickly ran toward the office. When I made it there were lots of children lined up in the office waiting for their parents. "Where are my children?" I asked her. She pointed to the office next to the door. "Mrs. Karis," the man at the desk said. "I'm sorry, but they took your children." "What do you mean? Who took my children?" I asked.

"We don't know who they were, no one but the other children seen them come in and they can't explain much. We are waiting for the police now." I sat down in a chair in his office and he closed the door. "I don't understand what you are talking about," I said to him. "My children are missing and you don't know who took them? What do you mean? I asked. "Mrs. Karis, is there someone else we can call?" He asked standing next to me. I was in a state of shock; I leaned over Keagan was crying.

"Lord, where are my children? Lead me to them, Lord," I cried out. I began to pant and pray; I closed my eyes and held Keagan tight. "Lord show me how they came, oh Lord tell where I go to look, lead me to the please Lord, quick. Keep them from any harm; oh Lord, keep them safe until I come." I prayed and prayed until the police came. Daddy came next and then Michael. We were all upset and in shock. Daddy talked to the police; they began asking Michael and I if we had any enemy's. If we owed anyone money, were we in any trouble, Michael grew angry quickly at the questions.

"Look our children are out there. Why aren't you guys looking for them?" The school grew quiet, soon the evening was coming the sun was going down, and my heart grew worried that I may never see them again. I looked out of the office window with daddy; I gave Kegan to Michael and went back to the classroom where I saw Ms. Honey lying in her blood. I watched as the paramedics took her away. As I got closer to her classroom I could feel her spirit near me. I went in and sat down near her blood hoping that Ms. Honey would appear in front of me. I cried out to the Lord. "Help me Lord; help me to find my children."

I heard a noise down the hall, I got up to see what it was and peeked out of the door. It was the custodian's crew. I turned back to go into the room and something grabbed my arm. It was Ms. Honey; I took her hand I wanted to go into that day. "Oh Lord take me in so that I can see where my children could be, I closed my eyes and held on to her arms. Soon I was in the classroom with the children with Ms. Honey. Her back was turned to the chalk board when those children came in with their hoods on in their jumpers.

They were sitting all around the tables with the children when one of them jumped on Ms. Honey's back and began to beat her with a block from the toy chest. She flung it from her shoulders then the others jumped on her with blocks. The children all watched in fear as they beat Ms. Honey until she fell to the floor bleeding. They then took the twins by the arm and walked out of the classroom leaving, Ms. Honey on the floor. She played dead until she felt they had gone, and then she pulled herself up to the table and watched them walk the twins to the playground. Ms. Honey was losing so much blood that she passed out.

I prayed for Ms. Honey to go in peace. "Lord, take her in, she's ready to go. Take her where she can rest her soul. Lord, help her to pass over without any fear let her feel that you are near." I went out near the playground to search for the twins. I ran one way and then the other way. There were trees all around the school. My first look would be to search beyond the trees I went in closer to the brushy areas. It was there that I began to hear my darling Kristina's cry.

"Mommy! Mommy!" I hear. I scream her name; "Kristina! Kristina! I'm here baby; I'm here!" I yelled. "Keep calling out to me baby!" I yelled. Then I hear Kristopher yelling. "Mommy! Mommy! Help me, mommy!!" I ran to their voices as the sun light grew darker. Soon, I could see Kristina in the field ahead. I reached out to her as if she was close, but she wasn't, she was far away from me I looked around for Kristopher as I could still hear his voice yelling at me. "I'm coming babies!" I'm coming I yelled out.

They were both surrounded by the kids with the hoods on they held their hands tightly as I came closer, I could see Kristopher trying to pull away from them. They wouldn't allow him to move away from them. I ran as fast as I could toward Kristina. When I made it close to them, they all started to growl at me as dogs would before attacking. "I am taking my children! I yelled out. They all surrounded me pushing the children behind them. I had no fear of them; they began to growl louder and louder as they drew in closer to me I started to try and get out of the circle formed around me.

One after another they began to come at me closer to my face growling and showing their teeth. I try grabbing them, but they pull back. "Run to the school!" I yell out to the children. "Run together! Keep running until you see your father!" I yell at them. They stand still in fear of them hurting me. "Run babies, please run!" I yell out at them as they growled at me. I'm trying to grab hold of at least one of them. I run toward them jumping toward them trying to grab hold of one; I couldn't they would jump away as fast as I'd jump toward them. I tried to grab one with everything in me, but I failed.

I just wanted out of this circle they surrounded me in. "What do you want from me?" I yelled out. One of them came close to my face and breathed as hard as it could into my eyes, everything went black. I fell to the ground. I could see nothing but could hear them growling around me. I felt the heat of their breath; I could feel them staring at me I couldn't move. Soon they would all try and grab me I felt as if they were dragging me, I lifted up and started grabbing back at them. "Let me go," I screamed.

"Let me go"! I shook my body all around if I could just grab one of them I'd be safe. I moved and moved until we stopped. I could feel them pulling me toward them. I try again to grab one they have sharp nails and wrinkly fingers. I still could only see darkness as I moved around to grab one, just lay here I thought. Get a grip; think about what I want to happen. I want to get my children away from here and safe. I lay there quietly, I could hear them.

Lord, allow me to see them allow me to feel, help me send them back to hell with all my will. I prayed and prayed, I began to have blurred sight. I started to feel them touching me with their sharp nails and growling. I reached out to grab them. I could hear my babies crying out for me, "Mommy! Mommy!" Suddenly I had one of them I held onto him tight. I could feel it scratching me all over I could feel it breathing. The rest of them growled as I struggled to get this one, so my grip grew tighter. I reached out with my other hand and grabbed its hood and pulled it in close to me. Finally I had it.

Lord, help me, help me now, I am in trouble, please don't let me down. Lord, come fast I'm losing ground, what came this time is something wild. Lord, in the name of Jesus, take them back into the darkness send them running, return them to hell. I was tossed all over; my body was like a rag doll. When will this all end, I thought the darkness had come, and I was still in distress praying and fighting. I wanted it to be over soon as the sun turned into a full moon shining brightly over our children and me.

I prayed more; Lord, help me through this as I started to fall off into the darkness along with this being. The children still crying as they watched me, trying to get them out of the circle of darkness; I stopped fighting but held on to it. I allowed it to draw me into the darkness. In an instant, I was in the darkness with them watching as men and women were torching them. They were being yelled at, called freaks and monsters. They were being spit at and kicked. I could feel their pain as if they were torching me. I cried with them; it was a terrible sight.

There were thrown into a room. They were treated like animals; I could see where it all started. They were born in a lab made up of some experimental drugs and cells. I watched as they were brought into this life and suffered until the end. They were thrown into a pit and burned alive. I exhaled as I watched; it was so bad that I cried with them watching them jump to get out of the pit of fire. I watched as the men and women laughed watching them. I could feel there fear and hurt. Suddenly I could open my eyes I could see lights all around me. I looked up and there was Michael with his wings wide open standing over us in the light. I reached for him.

"Michael!" I called out. I could see him moving down closer to me pulling them off one by one into the darkness. I can't say a word I can only reach for Michael. He held me in his arms and covered us with his wings like a shield. They still tried to attack as Michael held us in near him. The light faded and so did they. When it was over, I looked up at Michael; I exhaled loudly and fell off into a deep sleep. When I woke up we were at the police station. There was police all around asking, what happened, and how did we find the children?

Where were they, and that they needed to be checked out, it was loud. I felt like I was hit with a hammer. "Michael, where's Keagan?" I questioned. "Don't worry baby; he's safe." "We'd like to ask you about what happened. Your husband says he found you and the children in the canyon not far from the school. He says that when he came upon you, someone had knocked you over the head and you passed out?" The officer asked. I looked at Michael in a confused way, and he shook his head.

"Um Mrs. we need to know, is this how it happened? Did you get a good look at him? Did he, in fact, have the children when you approached him?" I shake my head yes to it all. We answered the questions as the night goes on the next day which was a Saturday. We go home that afternoon tired and confused; I needed a bath. Michael got the kids off for a bath and a nap, it would be late afternoon. I sat in the tub for an hour before Michael came in. He sat down at the base of the tub and started to wash my back.

"Baby are you okay" He asked kissing my cheek. "I think so," I said putting my head down on my left knee. "Michael, what do we do? We could have lost them forever," I said, crying, "No baby, as long as I am around you will always be safe. You and the children, I promise," he said. "I'm scared," I said sobbing and washed up. "We can't be around all the time to protect them, what would happen if we can't?" I asked. "We will always protect them. These spirits sometimes come to them because they're innocent and harmless and there spirit is pure they have love around them, and you are their protector; you are the way and the light to them."

"I'm sorry, baby, but this light of yours stands out, and you do have a gift to protect them and to cleanse the lost souls that fight to stay here. Just know that the lord is on your side and he sent me to protect you," Michael said. I got out of the tub and went to the bedroom, Michael had my pajamas out on the bed I slipped them on and went into the children's bedroom to kiss the children goodnight. I walked into their room and just held them and kissed them; they were so tired. I laid there beside them until I went to sleep. I woke up to the doorbell. I sprung up and Michael was already at the door. It was daddy with Keagan.

"Good morning pops," Michael said taking Keagan from his arms. "Good Morning, how're my twins?" he asked. "They're fine pops. Go ahead and go upstairs they are up there." Daddy went upstairs, I followed him. "It's early daddy, what are you doing up?" I asked. "Baby, I'm always up early, and that baby doesn't sleep you know, and its Sunday. I want to make us all some breakfast and watch some old westerns "daddy said smiling "The kitchen is all yours daddy; I'm beat." I said falling in the rocker next to the bed. I rocked back and forth while daddy stared at the twins sleeping. "Well, Karis, whatever they saw and felt that day they won't even remember it after today. That's the good thing," daddy said. "I prayed for them to be safe and I believe he heard me," daddy said as he went back downstairs to cook breakfast. I sat in the chair watching the twins.

The Blessing

Daddy was right, Time went on, and the twins didn't remember any of what happened, they went back to school. Ms. Honey recovered, and there was a manhunt for those three juveniles. They had no leads. Michael and I went on after that day as if it never happen. We talked about attending church a lot. Michael said that it would be good for us to go as a family and worship the Lord. "What's our religion?" I'd ask him every morning. "It is what we feel in our spirit," he'd reply. "I've always felt good about having faith in what he is and how it makes me feel. I feel comfort when I pray, and I feel safe when I know his presence is near," I'd tell him.

"How about you, how do you feel about the Lord?" I asked with a smile, knowing that I knew no one is as close to his presence as Michael was. He looked back at me from the table. "Our religion should be spiritual because we can only define what we feel in the presence of the Lord, who is around us all the time," he said. "Hum," I said smiling, "Michael, there are so many churches, of all religions. Do we just walk into any church and become a member? They're going to want us to become a member of the church I use to be in a Baptist church, and I loved every minute of it," I told him.

"Well, why don't we go there?" Michael asked. "Well, the Clemens moved away, and I wouldn't want to go to a different Baptist church. If you don't know the preacher and the family, it's so hard to get in and feel comfortable." "Baby, are you worried about the people in the church or what you feel when you step into the church?" "Both, Michael, I don't want to be judged, and I don't want to get caught up in the church thing. I just want to go there praise the Lord, fellowship and go home," I tell him.

"I understand baby, but it is time for Keagan to get baptized. He's almost a year old; don't you think we need to have him blessed?" Michael asked. "Yes, I think that's a great idea. I will go over and talk to daddy about it later," I say. "He's going to need a nice outfit, all white, okay Karis," Michael said excitedly about the blessing. I knew that daddy would be happy too. After picking the twins up, I would go over to daddy's to tell him the news. I was also egger to see the garden; the roses should be sprouting up right about now I thought.

On the ride over to the school, I would stop at the garden center to pick up some more seed to plant. I always wanted to plant potatoes, just to see how they would grow. I picked the seeds up and headed toward the school. The twins were waiting on the steps with Ms. Honey and the other kids. "How are you Ms. Honey?" I asked. "I'm doing well now," she said. I looked at the gashes on her head still healing and looked away quickly. She was happy to be back at school with the children. "How have the twins been doing in class?" I asked her.

"They have been doing great, they hardly remember any of what happened, and they don't talk about it at all. They've been running around as happy as they always have. They are two of the smartest children I've seen, always smiling," she said smiling down at the twins; I took them by the hand. "Thank you so much Ms. Honey, have a good day," I tell her helping the children into the car. "Mommy, where are we going?" Kristopher asked looking out of the window.

"We are visiting grandpa and the garden," I tell him looking back at them. "Yes! The garden," Kristen shouted. "We need to plant some potatoes today," I tell them driving slowly toward daddy's house. I would meet Michael at the grocery store when we finished. When we arrived at daddy's house there was a lot going on. Daddy was sitting on the porch talking to the neighbors; it seemed there was a burglary across the street at one of the elderly couple's house. They were all standing outside watching the police. I got out of the car leaving the twins and

Keagan inside; I wanted to find out what happened before I brought them out.

"Daddy, what's going on?" I asked him. "Oh baby, there was a robbery over there. They questioned everybody about it, but no one saw anything. I guess they went in through the back," daddy said scratching his head. "Well, there goes the neighborhood," daddy said lighting up a cigarette. He went over to the car to help me with the kids. "Karis, did you come over to tell me about the blessing? I already know, Michael called me earlier, he told me you'd be stopping by here," daddy said. "Oh yeah, daddy, he always beats me to you huh? Well, I came to check in on the garden too daddy, so can you help me with the children?" I asked. "Hello Karis," the neighbors said.

"Look at these beautiful children." They all came over to daddy dotting over the children. I grabbed the seeds from the back seat and followed everyone to the backyard. "Oh Earl, Look at them, you're so lucky," they said to daddy, they were all over him and the children. I walked as quickly as I could, I didn't want to be asked a lot of questions. They would usually ask me about the children, what they like, how they play and do they keep me busier than they should. Oh, and do I dress the twins the same all the time.

The same questions over and over again. I rushed to the back to the garden and kneeled down to plant. Daddy held on to Keagan. The twins began to play with the neighbors. They asked them a lot of questions. "Do you two like school? Who's the oldest? Do you two like the same foods?" I smiled and watched. The roses grew tall; they bloomed out beautifully, it made the garden look even more structured. I put on my gloves and hat and went over the whole garden, the carrots were everywhere, some of them were eaten, and the same with the cucumbers. I could tell that daddy hadn't been watching over the garden at all there were more vegetables on the ground than I could carry.

I out as many as I could into the basket I carried on my arm. I had to throw a lot of them away; they were either rotten or bitten. "Daddy, have you been coming out here checking on the garden?" I asked him. "I think we have a gopher; it has been eating everything. Daddy, there's vegetables everywhere, is there any reason why you haven't been out here daddy? I can tell that you haven't been out here," I tell him. "Oh baby I know, I just haven't had the time," daddy said. "Well, you know honey, your dads been sick lately," Mrs. Kathy said from the porch.

I looked up quickly catching daddy giving her a dirty look and a wink. I got up quickly and walked over to daddy, "What daddy, you've been too sick to tend the garden? Is this true?" I ask. Daddy took one puff of his cigarette and put it out on the cemented steps, he got up with Keagan in his arms and began to walk away from me. "No baby, it's nothing, I was just bleeding a little, that's all. The doctors are going to order some test next week. It's probably nothing," he said. "Daddy, where do you have the bleeding?" I asked.

"It's been my nose lately, nonstop at times," daddy said walking around with Keagan in his arms. I looked at him, I didn't feel his sickness. He's ill, I could tell he'd lost weight, and he looked pale. "Daddy, you have to take care of yourself. No more smoking and drinking," I told him. "Baby, If I give all that up, it won't make a difference. You know, I've known guys who smoked and drank all their lives, the minute they quit they died," he said. "Oh daddy, that will never happen to you," I tell him kissing his cheek, grabbing Keagan from his arms.

"Daddy, you have to stop and get healthy, I want you to stay with me always." I left that evening thinking about how life would be without him. I just couldn't imagine it at all. There was a time when I didn't get along with daddy, but it only made us closer to one another, I looked back at him as I drove away. Daddy has to live I thought. Michael would meet me at the grocery store; when we arrived there, he was standing outside his car looking all around for us. The moment the twins saw him they yelled out.

"Daddy, daddy" He came over to the car and helped me take them out. He brought a shopping cart over, and we put the children in except for Kristopher, he would prefer to walk holding Michael's hand and touching anything and everything he could get his little hands on to throw inside the basket. We shopped for everything that night living with two full baskets and more grocery's than we could carry back to the car. We had to have the grocery store clerk helps us get to the car. I put the children inside while Michael loaded the grocery's into the car with the clerk.

After getting them inside, I thought about how we would get them out when we arrived at the house. Michael grabbed Keagan from my car, and I took the twins inside. When I got inside, I noticed there were footprints all over the house. I took the children upstairs before they noticed. "Come on guys, bath time, then dinner," I tell them. Michael came in right behind me. He noticed right away, "Honey!" He called out, "Come down here a minute please," he yelled from the bottom of the stairs. "I'll be down in a minute Michael; I need to get the children settled in their pajamas," I yell back to him. When I finished washing them up one after the other, I hurried down, leaving them in their rooms to play awhile.

"Do you see what I see?" Michael asked. "Yes, they're all over the house," I said even on the stairs, Michael bent down to the floor sniffing the carpet and wiping the area where the footprints where. They were muddy and still fresh as if the person or persons had just left the house. "All we can do is clean it up," I tell him, while he went around the whole house looking to see where they would have come in from, there were no open windows or broken windows, nor were there any doors tampered. "Should we call the police?" I asked Michael.

"Yes, just to make sure we didn't overlook anything," he said. I went for the phone in the hall, and I noticed that all of the pictures of us in the hall had mud spread across each one, it looked as if someone took their dirty fingers and followed the pictures all the way down the hall, leaving fingerprints all over them. "Michael!" I yelled pointing at the pictures and holding the phone to my ear. "Yes, I see it, baby, call the police now," he said. I called the police.

After all the questioning from the dispatcher, finally, she said they would be on their way. While we waited, Michael and I put all of the groceries away and got dinner started for the children. We ate and fed the children; we tried not to touch too many things around the house. They showed up hours later from the time of the phone call. Michael and I started to get ready for bed when the doorbell rang. Michael ran down to answer. "Baby, it's them," he yelled up to me. I ran down the stairs. "Hello, come on in," Michael said greeting the police.

There were two of them. "What seems to be the problem?" They questioned. "Well, sir if you look around you can see that there are muddy footprints all around the house and handprints on the walls and pictures too," Michael put his hand on his hip watching them look over the footprints and the mud all over the pictures. I stood back and watched from a far; they walked all over the outside and inside and back again. "Sir, it doesn't seem like there was a force of entry, we will dust the prints and see what we come up with, but unless this person or persons had a key, we don't see how they got into the house.

We looked upstairs; everything has been locked up there all day too, right? He asked Michael with his pen and paper in his hand. Michael looked frustrated at him; he was chewing gum and writing everything looking all around the house while the other policeman wandered around the house. "I'm just going to say; we will keep a close eye out in the neighborhood, to see if we had any other break-ins or anything like that. But at this time I'd advise you to make sure you lock up everything when you leave the house and check with any family or friends who may have a key to your place.

Oh, and by the way, this is a beautiful home you got here," the officer said to Michael closing up his notebook and signaling to the other officers to follow him to the door. "Thanks a lot," Michael said walking them to the front door. When he opened the door I looked out and noticed two black shadows shaped like men standing in the doorway. They held their heads down, and when the officers walked out, they looked up, and the officers walked right through them as if they weren't there.

When they looked up their faces were gray, and there were black holes were the eyes nose, and mouth should be. It was something I'd never seen before. I closed my eyes as the officer looked back at me, "Uh sir, is your wife okay?" He asked Michael, Michael quickly walked over to me. "Yes, she's fine," he grabbed me and held me. "Thank you guys for coming out," he said holding on to me tight. I felt as if I was going to fall with my eyes closed. "You guys have a good night," the officer said shutting the door. "We'll be in touch." I sat down on the couch. "Michael, there was something at the door," I said.

"I know baby, don't fear it please," he said walking over to the window looking out. "I know what it is, and by now you should know too," Michael said sitting down beside me. "They know about Keagan," he said. What about Keagan?" I asked. "He special that's all, we need to have him blessed in the church behind the walls of the church in Jesus name." He told me. "We will right?" I asked Michael.

"What do they want?" "They want us, and if they can get to Keagan they will use him to get to you and me," Michael said kissing my forehead. "There are more of them, you need to prepare yourself for prayer," Michael and I went up to bed; I wouldn't rest easy that night. Why wouldn't he tell me this before I called the police? Did he know all along that they were coming to the house? Did he know that this day was coming?

I was up well into the midnight hour just thinking about my faith, I prayed that the lord would watch over us all night and day to. I stared at Michael as he slept, he had a glow that never quit. He slept like he was sleeping eternally; I stared at him until I fell off to sleep. I was awakened by Michaels kiss on my lips. "Baby, I have to go to work, I'll be looking for churches today. You can look too; maybe ask your dad about a good one. It doesn't matter now where we go. It just matters that we get it done," he said grabbing his coat putting it around his arm. He stood over me with his hands in his pockets.

"And Karis, I love you, please keep your faith pure, no doubt. I'll see you a little later, love you," he said as he walked out of the door. I turned over looking out at the moon still lighting the sky. Out of the corners of my eyes, I could see the shadows watching me; they were all in black with their heads held down in each corner of the yard they stood as if they were just standing guard for something. I turned around to face the wall, "Lord, please watch my back as I turn a blind eye to the spirit lying in wait for us. I will not fear it or allow it to intimidate me into losing my faith. Lord, protect my family and me."

I sat up in bed and looked over my shoulder into the backyard, they were still there. I lay back down still tired from not sleeping that night. I looked up and prayed until I fell off to sleep again, waking up to the alarm clock. I got up and went into the bathroom washed my face and brushed my teeth. I could hear the children laughing and playing with one another. "Hey twins," I yelled out. "I hope you washed up already." As soon as I acknowledged that I knew they were up, I could hear them running down the hall toward me. "Good Morning!" I said to them as they ran in and jumped onto the bed. "Good morning mommy!" They said to me.

"We brushed already," Kristopher said jumping on the bed, Kristine started jumping with him, until she glanced out of the window. She took one look out and dashed out of the door. I ran behind her. "Kristine!" I yelled catching up to her and grabbing her arm. "What's the matter, sweetie?" I asked her. She turned to me and then looked towards the window. She pointed out, "they scare me, mommy," she said with tears streaming from her eyes. "Don't worry sweetie; I will never let them get you I promise." I gave her a big hug; "sweetie, do you know how special you are?" She shook her head no.

I picked her up onto my hip, "wow you're getting so heavy sweetheart," she smiled. "Kristine, you are so special, and I don't ever want you to be afraid okay. I know they look scary, but sweetheart they are harmless. Look at them," I told her holding her little face in my hand turning her head toward them. "Sweetheart, don't ever fear them, because we have a special person watching over us, and he will never allow anyone or anything to hurt us. Do you know who it is?" I asked her; she shook her head yes.

"Well, I was hoping that you did, always remember that he has a light all around us protecting us from them. You look at them and just think about that light. Think about how warm it is, how it makes you feel special, and happy all the time, okay sweetie." I kissed her cheeks all over and put her down. "We will be fine," I said as she took one more look out of the glass door and ran to jump on the bed with Kristopher. He was hardly bothered by things. I went into Keagan room to check on him. As soon as I opened the door he was sitting up in his crib smiling. I went over to him.

"Hello son, good morning to you too," I say to him picking him up. He smiles as I carry him down the hall. "Twins come on, let's have breakfast." I yell to them. I could hear them running toward me laughing. "Mommy, I want pancakes and bacon," Kristopher said. "Of course you do big guy," I said sitting the baby down in his highchair. I made them pancakes; they played all around the table making funny faces at Keagan and playing peek-a-boo. The sound of his laugh was so beautiful. It made me smile each time he laughed out loud.

After feeding them I got them dressed and out to the car. I drove the twins to school and Keagan, and I was off to check out some churches in town. I would meet Michael for lunch today. We went to three churches; I just sat outside of them. It wasn't long before I noticed I was being followed everywhere I went. At each church, I stopped in front of they would be standing guard not too close, but close enough to where I could see them standing there. I wanted to go visit Maddy after my adventure with Keagan.

Maddy would be pleasantly surprised. I hadn't seen her in so long; I haven't been to the hospital since having Keagan. I drove up to the hospital thinking; this is where it all started for me. Right here in this hospital, I don't know why or what choose me here, but it did. And now I can't break away from it, I thought, sitting in the car. Keagan was asleep in the back seat as I just sat there for a while thinking back to my experiences there in that hospital. I saw Michael walk by with Dr. Green, as usual, they were discussing a patient they were both smiling and talking.

I waited for them to walk back into the building to get out. I took Keagan inside, from the moment we stepped into the lobby everyone we walked by was staring and walking up to me. "Hi Karis, long time no see," they said. "Is this the baby? No way, he's so big now," they exclaimed. I walked through quickly asking everyone I seen if they knew where I could find Maddy. When I reached the hall I saw her from a far, standing behind the counter writing on the scheduling board. I wanted to surprise her, so I took Keagan behind the counter, and we stood behind her.

I tapped her with Keagan's little hand on the back as I ducked down low, she turned around quickly. "Hello! I'm Keagan," I said in a baby voice. "Oh my goodness, Karis, How are you doing young lady" She asked. She grabbed me by the shoulders squeezing Keagan in between us. "Oh my goodness it's so good to see you, honey, and look at him so big and handsome. You look just like your daddy," she said, pinching his cheeks. "Sit down," she said pulling out a chair from underneath the desk. "Maddy, would you be Keagan's God mom?" I asked her.

"I know that Michael's going to ask Dr. Green to be his God dad. So it would be an honor if you would be his godmother please?" I asked her. She grabbed Keagan and held him tightly in his arms. "Of course, I'd be honored to be his godmother." She squeezed Keagan so tight that he began to pull away from her and reach for me. "I would love to be your God mommy Keagan," she said kissing his cheeks again. I stayed there with Maddy talking about the baby's christening, and she talked about what we would wear and what he'd wear. I had to go before it was too late; I wanted to go by a few more churches before I had to pick the twins up from school. I ran into Michael on my way out of the hospital.

"Hey baby, what are you doing here?" He asked me. "I came to visit Maddy, and to ask her to be Keagan's godmother. Have you asked Dr. Green yet? I know you want to," I said smiling at him. "Yes, I asked him, but there's a problem, you know he's married right?" He asked. "I know, yes, why is it a problem?" I questioned. "Well, his wife is going to wonder why she wasn't asked, and you already asked Maddy," he said. "Do you think she'll be mad at us?" I asked Michael. "Well, I think she'll be a little disappointed. Don't you?" He said. "Maybe," I said walking toward the car.

Michael grabbed Keagan from my arms and carried him for me. "So, I will see you at home then," Michael said hugging me and kissing my lips. "Yes, I'm going to check around for some other churches," I tell him. "Where have you been so far?" He asked me. "Just here and there," I told him taking my seat in the car. "Michael, I have to go if I want to look around anymore, and the twins will be out of school soon." I kissed

Michael once more and drove off. I went towards the downtown area where more people would be, and maybe spirits won't be bold to show. I drove up and down the street to see if anything stuck out.

Finally, at the end of the corner, I noticed a man standing outside of a church door. When I looked around; I saw the church was decorated with lots of beautiful statues. Mary was holding baby Jesus, and children praying; it was just beautiful. It looked like a Catholic Church; the man waved at me and smiled as I slowed down to stop near the front entrance of the church. I came to a stop; I didn't get out of the car I looked at the church watching the man at the door. He started to walk toward the car. He came to the passenger side window and waved his hand. "Hello, I saw that you were cursing the streets, are you lost, honey?" He asked.

I rolled the window down, "what was that?" I asked. "I asked if you were lost. You look a little lost," he said. "No, I have been looking around the area for a good church to get my baby christened. Sir, is this a Catholic church?" I asked him. "No, it's a Lutheran church, similar, would you like to come inside and look around maybe talk about our faith?" He asked. I looked around and then back at Keagan. He was asleep in the back he looked so peaceful. I looked up again at the door of the church, and the shadows were all around just watching. I got nervous.

"Child are you okay?" He asked. I looked at the man at the window. I don't feel good about this do I will just decline for now. I thought. He reached in to touch my shoulder, "Child," he said. I looked at him, and his face changed immediately, he was one of them. I drove off, and he started laughing and pointing at me, as I watched from the rearview mirror. I rushed away from the church driving and watching them all around the church pointing and laughing; soon I could see the preachers white rob turning black. I began to pray as I drove off when I made it to the school the children weren't out yet.

I parked and waited for them. Keagan was up by then so I took him from his chair to feed him. I was still breastfeeding him; I placed a blanket over his head while he ate. I could see them watching me from the playground area. I know there was something for me in that church, I thought as Keagan ate. I'm going to go to the library and search the Lutheran church. I had to tell Michael what happened today. I wondered how he'd feel about it. I watched them watching me as I waited while feeding Keagan. The children came out yelling and playing, and the parking area filled up quickly.

I could see the twins walking hand in hand with Ms. Honey. She always walked them down together. I took Keagan off my breast as soon as I see them walking toward the school doors. Keagan and I got out of the car and began to walk over to the school doors. I approached Ms. Honey. "Hello Ms. Honey, how was your day?" I asked her. "Oh, it was great," she said happily. "The children were great, I did notice, however, that Kristopher was a little quiet today. He didn't want to play outside at all, and wouldn't do any work."

"I asked him if he was feeling okay, he said he felt fine, but I was a little worried about him, he's always the funny, happy, playful one." She said swinging Kristopher by the hand. "So little guy, I hope you feel better tomorrow," she said grabbing his little face. "Thank you so much Ms. Honey; I don't know what I'd do without you. You are such a good teacher." I said. "Come on you two; we have to get home." We walked over towards the car when we approached; I noticed them standing around. Kristopher stood still. "Come on Kristopher," I told him.

"We have nothing to fear." I held Keagan in one arm and took Kristopher by the hand. We walked to the car; they moved backward as we came closer. Kristine wasn't scared at all; she skips most of the way. Her eyes pierced at them with no fear. She skipped and hummed, "yes Jesus loves me." We got inside the car Kristopher gripped my hand so tight that my fingers were red and pulsating. "Kristine, how was your day?" I asked. "I had a good day mommy," she replied.

"Mommy I'm not afraid of them," she said looking through the window as we drove away from the school. She hummed all the way home, I looked back through the rearview window and noticed her holding Kristopher by the hand. They were so cute the way they looked out for one another. I pulled up to the house, I parked in the driveway. The twins got out and ran to the front door while I grabbed Kegan. "Hey wait for me! I called out to them. They held hands all the way to the front door. "Mommy can I have ice cream for a snack" Can I have cookies" They both started at the door with their request for snacks. I turned the key and we went inside.

I noticed on the stairway right away the muddy footprints all the way up. I took the kids into the kitchen, Sat Kegan down in his highchair. I gave the twins the snacks they requested and told them to stay seated at the table and keep an eye on Kegan as I wanted to investigate the footprints. I gave Keagan a baby pretzel to eat, that ought to keep him busy for a while I thought. I went toward the stairway. I leaned over to feel if they were still wet or cold. They were; I could feel the cold coming from the top of the stairs as if there was a cold storm near the top.

I went up the stairs, walking around the footprints. I could see my breath with every step I took. I was expecting the spirits to jump out at me as I approached the top. I could smell them; suddenly I could see on the wall ahead what looked like a big black circle. I went in to look closer; it swirled around fast buzzing like a mad beehive. I turned to run, and two cold hands reached from the darkness of the swarm grabbed me by the arms. I faced it head-on. I began to pray when it formed a circle around me.

I sat down on the floor and covered my head with my legs stretched out straight in front of me. It went around me fast; the buzzing was louder and louder. I closed my eyes as I wanted to feel this spirit, what was it? How can I dispose of it? I prayed to God. "Lord, help me to dispose this spirit back to where it belongs." I wanted to crawl away, I moved in and out, scooting back and forth. Finally, I felt it grab me and pull me in close; I looked straight ahead trying to make out what it could have been, a woman lost or maybe a man. It held me tight, and suddenly I felt cold all over, I began to get chills, biting down on my tongue to stop it from shivering.

I tried turning away from it twisting my body around and around, but it had a strong hold on me. It blew out a loud roar of cold that hit me in the face, freezing my face and pushing me with the hardest force all the way to the back wall. I watched as it swirled around in circles before disappearing into the air leaving a dark black circle on the wall. After I caught my breath, holding onto the wall, I stood up knee after knee. My stomach was turning I felt nauseous, I ran over to the bathroom sink and started to vomit, first water came up then black mucus. I stared down at it holding my stomach as it kept coming up, it wouldn't stop.

The vomiting went on and on until tears streamed from my face and my stomach was in knots. I kneeled down bending over to ease up the pain; I was weak. I held onto the wall as I went closer to the toilet to sit down. "Mommy!" Kristopher called out, "Mommy!" I caught my breath enough to yell back. "Kristopher, I'll be there in a minute sweetie don't worry!" I washed my face with cold water. I could hear Michael come in just as I went down to the down the hall.

I yelled for him. "Michael!" I yelled I could hear him coming up the stairs quickly; his footsteps were heavy as he ran closer to me. I felt weaker as Michael approached me I fell over. I looked up, "Michael when will this end?" I asked him as I fainted. When I woke up, Michael was standing over me wiping my face with a cold cloth, and the kids were all around on the bed with Michael. "Baby, everything is going to be okay," he said holding me close to him until I fell asleep. The next day Michael was downstairs with the children. I could hear them playing around running and laughing.

I can hardly move from the bed when I tried to sit up I still felt weak. I look out of the glass door; the sun is shining brightly through the glass. I try hard to stand up feeling weak and sick to my stomach as I walk over to the door. I just wanted some fresh air to blow into my face. I stood with my face smashed on the side of the glass door to keep myself steady. What happened to me? What was that spirit? I wondered; I stood there trying to figure it out. This was something out of the ordinary for me. I walked back to the bed; I wondered if Michael had to work today I just wanted to lay in bed.

I felt so down; I just want to stay close to the bed. I laid back down on the bed facing the glass door. There wasn't a breeze coming through; I just want some fresh air. I watched as the birds flew around the patio, The hummingbird stayed the longest, it was a peaceful day. I couldn't hear any noises coming from downstairs; the laughter turned into silence, which I found unusual for Michael and the kids. Michael had a voice that carried, deep and stern. I sat up in bed to listen closely for any sounds. I didn't hear a thing, I have to get up from here I thought.

Getting up moving slowly toward the door; I made it to the stairway. "Michael!" I called out; I waited nothing. "Michael!" I yelled again. I walked slowly down the stairs looking at the wall behind me; the black circle was still on the wall. I went down the stairs. When I made it downstairs I could hear them as I approached the front door. Michael had taken them outside in the front to play while he cleaned out the car. I watched them from the window.

I felt so hot all over and still a little weak. I laid my face on the window and watched them play from the window. I could see Keagan sitting in the chair next to the car; he was laughing at the twins they threw the ball back and forth to each other with him in the middle. When one of them missed, it would fall on Keagan's legs or bump his little head. How did he think that was funny? I didn't know, but he loved every minute of it. Michael looked up from the car and smiled and waved at me.

"Come out baby," he said. I shook my head; no Michael walked over to the door and reached in to pull me out. I stood back in hesitation. "Oh Michael, I can't, I am weak. I feel sick all over again with every step I take," I tell him, holding onto his arm. "Baby Just come out here, you can use the fresh air," he said pulling me out of the door to a chair on the porch. "Hi mommy, hi mommy," the children yelled. I couldn't stand for long, so the seat was inviting. It did feel good to be outside. I sat back in the chair; it was a rocker, so I rocked back and forth watching Michael and the children.

I looked up into the clouds as there were very few, Just thinking. There was a time when I wouldn't even look up, I was so frighten by what I saw that I dared to look up. I watched the birds flying by and rocked. I was lost in the feeling quickly, that free feeling I felt when I thought it was over I could look up, and all I would have to have is faith and trust, that the gift I had was going to be easy for me to accept. I was wrong; it's getting so hard to trust and accept what I think is going to happen. There have been surprises around every corner I have had to learn so much more.

I rocked harder and faster, as I thought about the things I've been through these past five years. I look at my children I love them, and I love Michael also. Michael was my strength at all times. I was no longer afraid when he was around, and I could feel his love, and his faith is as trusting and strong as mine. I don't know what to think about what happened to me yesterday, but I do know that it to will pass. "Baby, are you okay?" Michael asked. I shook my head yes. "Can you come with me to a church?" Michael asked. "I went to one yesterday," I tell him.

"It was a Lutheran church, do you know anything about those?" I asked him. "I don't, but we can go find out, what happened when you were there?" He asked. "They surrounded the church, and I was talking to a preacher who wasn't a preacher. He wanted me to go inside with him; I almost took him up on it when I saw the rest of them standing around waiting for us to go inside," I told him. "Did you get out of the car at all?" Michael asked me. Looking troubled by what he was hearing.

"No, Michael I took off, and he was laughing hard, it was the worst laugh that I'd ever heard. I looked back, and he was in black, just like rest of them. But he was taller, and his face was more visible," I tell him. "I will go with you next time, please don't go alone baby, I can't have you getting into any danger," he said. "I was just planning to look at the services they offer and see about the christening," I said. "Baby, don't do it again okay, don't go alone again. I'll make sure I'm off in time to go with you to check them out," he said.

We stayed outside until nightfall, Michael played around the yard with the twins making them laugh until the little tummies were sore. I rocked Keagan in the chair until he fell asleep. It cooled down quickly, Michael suggested we go inside and have dinner. I took Keagan and laid him in the playpen then took the twins to wash their hands. "Baby, what are we having for dinner tonight?" Michael asked while going through the refrigerator. "I would like steak and potatoes with a good salad," I yelled out to him from the bathroom.

"Sounds good baby, I guess I'm cooking it right?" He asked. "No Michael, I'll cook while you get ready for work. You can take some of it with you," I tell him walking over to him in the kitchen. "Thanks, baby," Michael said kissing me on the cheek, the twins watched laughing and making kissing noises. While Michael held me and kissed me more, then slapped me on the butt and walked out of the kitchen. "Mommy, can I please have some juice?" Kristopher asked holding a cup in his hand. "Hey, where did you get that cup from, little guy?" I asked him.

He looked over his shoulder as if someone was behind him. "Did you hear me, Kristopher, Where did you get it from?" I knew that I hadn't given him a cup nor did Michael; Kristopher stood still not answering my question just looking over his shoulder. He had a perplexed look on his face. I went to the refrigerator to get the juice out; when I turned my back I looked at Kristopher from the corner of my eye, he seemed to be communicating with someone. I turned to him quickly. "Kristopher is there someone you want us to meet?" I asked him. "No mommy," "he brought in his friend from outside," Kristine said.

"He, it's a little boy?" I asked them. "No mommy, his name is Shadow and he a cowboy," Kristine said. "So you can see him too?" I asked her pouring them both juice. I went over to the stove to put the potatoes on, they both sat down at the table Kristopher stared up as if he was looking at someone standing in front of him. I didn't feel a thing; I had no clue of the spirit they were talking about. I began cooking and watching them at the same time, I wanted to see if there was really any real interaction with them and this spirit. I cooked and watched when it was time for dinner Michael came downstairs. I set the table, and the children sat together still quiet.

I didn't notice any other reaction except for Kristopher looking as if he was watching someone while he drank his juice, when Michael sat down next to Kristopher. "Hey, buddy, what's going on? What are you looking at over there?" He asked him. Kristopher looked at Michael, "Shadow's gone daddy, and he said he doesn't like you." "Really, why? Why doesn't he like me, Kristopher?" Michael asked. "I don't know daddy; he's gone, he said he has to go home."

We ate and talked, Michael and I didn't pressure Kristopher for answers, but that didn't stop Kristine from giving up all the information she could about their new friend Shadow. "Mommy he's funny, he likes to play ball a lot. He said that he would protect Kristopher from the monsters in his room." "Are there monsters in your room Kristopher?" Michael and I both asked looking surprised that Kristopher never shared that with us. "Is there monsters?" we asked again, he shook his head yes. "Why haven't you told us about them?" Michael asked he shrugged his shoulders.

"Are they hurting you?" He shook his head no. "Have you been praying, as I taught you?" I asked him. "If you pray you don't have to be afraid at all Kristopher." "Mommy, Kristopher said that when he prays they come out more to scare him," Kristine said taking a bite of her steak. "Do you feel like you need Shadow, Kristopher? Does he make you feel safe?" Kristopher shook his head yes. "I'm not afraid when he stays in my room at night daddy. He watches out for them, and they don't come close to my bed either," he said.

Michael and I looked at one another; we didn't ask any more questions. They finished up dinner and headed upstairs for a bath. I started cleaning up while Michael was finished up his dinner. "Keagan will be waking up in a while are you going to be okay with them? Are you still feeling weak?" he asked. "No Michael, I'm okay. Do you think that we should be worried about the twins?" I asked. "No they'll be fine, children see angels all the time, they're open to it they can see what we don't. They will be fine," he said.

"I'm going to put them to bed and then try and wake Keagan and give him dinner and a bath too." I turned to Michael; he was still sitting after eating everything on his plate. "Are you going to be working late tonight? Should I call daddy over tonight to stay with me?" I asked. "Only if you feel you have to," he replied getting up from the table. "I won't be working late tonight, and I won't forget to ask Green to be

Keagan's God dad either." He came over to me and kissed me softly on the lips. "I love you so much Karis; you have to trust that we will be fine, the Lord is always on our side."

"Baby, you have a good night okay, I'll be in a little after one am, promise." He said grabbing his coat and bag. I walked him to the door, as I watched him get into the car I noticed Mr. Simms was back standing in front of the driveway, I waited for Michael to pull off then walked over to him smiling. "Hello Mr. Simms," I say to him. He smiled and grabbed my hand. "Hello young lady, how have you been?" He asked. "Mr. Simms, what are you doing here?" I asked him. We walked together into the house. "I've been watching," he said.

"I don't have long, sweetheart, I've come to warn you." I was afraid then because I've never seen Mr. Simms so serious. He took my other hand. "Don't be afraid, sweetheart. You can't be because everyone is counting on you. You need to get on your knees and restore your faith with all that you have in you; block everything else out," he said. "But Mr. Simms, I have all the faith I can have in me," I tell him looking at him sternly. "You can't have any doubt, every time you have any doubt in him you allow them to gain control. They don't like the power you share with the Lord.

They don't like how you can restore those spirits or what was taken away by their spirits work. You need to be careful, sweetheart, I know that you feel his presence when these things happen, but you're going to need his closeness as well, to hold you. They want you badly, and they won't stop now until they get what they want. They will taunt your family the babies, and whoever gets in the way of what they want, please listen." He said holding my hands with his strong grip. "Mr. Simms I understand, I will be careful, I will make sure that the faith I have will not change. I won't doubt it ever again," I said.

Mr. Simms walked to the door, "Be careful, sweetheart, trust him," he said walking out of the door. I went upstairs to wake Keagan to feed and bathe him for the night. I could see Mr. Simms through the open window leaving the yard. I won't have any fear I thought to myself as I walked up the stairs. I went into Keagan's room and picked him up from his crib. His eyes pierced out at me, smiling and cooing he was ready to eat. We went downstairs to the kitchen, Keagan was happy in his highchair when the doorbell rang.

I placed his finger foods down and went to the door. I looked through the peephole to see who was there. There was no one standing at the door. "Who is it?" I yelled out. I stood there waiting for anyone to say anything, there was still no answer. I turned around to head back into the kitchen with Keagan and standing next to him was daddy, he was holding one of Keagan's treats in his hand giving it to him. "Daddy," I said standing looking at him, Daddy looked pale he also had a glow over him, I began to walk close.

"Daddy, how did you get inside?" I asked. Just as I walked toward daddy and Keagan I began to have a vision of daddy in an ambulance; he was unconscious. His eyes were rolling back into his head; I was in there with him calling out to him, "Daddy! Daddy can you hear me!" I closed my eyes and opened them, and daddy was no longer standing there feeding Keagan. I quickly ran to the phone to call daddy. "Hello daddy," I said. "Hello, Karis how are you?" Daddy asked. I had to catch my breath. I put the phone to my chest before answering. "I'm good daddy, how are you?" I asked.

"Oh, Karis, daddy's not doing so well," he said. "I've been bleeding baby; it won't stop," he said. "Have you been to the doctor yet daddy?" I asked him. "Yes baby they're still running test, I was there all day today," he said. Keagan began to cry; "daddy I'll be over there tomorrow okay." "Oh sure, baby, you can take me to the grocery store. I need to buy a few things for the garden," he said. "Be here at about nine no later, baby because you know I hate to wait around." "Okay daddy, I'll be there." I said hanging up the phone.

I sat down in the chair next to Keagan; he was still crying to get out. I went over to the oven and got his food and began to feed him. He quickly stopped crying. I finished feeding him and took him upstairs for his bath. I bathed Keagan then sat with him on my bed. He was so happy in the sink washing up, he cried when I took him out to clothe him. I leaned back on the bed thinking about daddy. "Oh Lord, I know, I know. I thought to myself, "Daddy's sick. I stayed up reading after Keagan went back to sleep.

I stayed up until Michael came home; it was around 1:30 am when he showed up. I could hear him come in; he was very noisy. He came upstairs after going to the kitchen and getting a drink. I could hear his heavy feet coming up the stairway one by one. "Hello baby, you're up late," he said. "Michael, Daddy's sick," I said hugging Michael. He picked me up by the waist and squeezed me tight, "Aw baby, I know, and I saw him today at the hospital. He's, has some rectal bleeding and nose bleeding as well, Doctor Green checked him in," he told me.

"Well, what are they going to so for him?" I asked Michael. "Right now there's a series of testing he has to do, and afterward we should get a clearer view of what's causing his bleeding. Karis don't worry; your dad will be fine, he's the strongest man I've ever known," Michael said wiping my tears from my face. He held me until I went to sleep, when I woke up Michael was downstairs with having coffee I could smell it brewing from the stairwell. It was 5 am I laid back down but couldn't go back asleep. The phone rang a couple of times before Michael picked it up. "Hello," he shouted, "Yes it is, no she's not," he said, "I will tell her now."

He hung up the phone and came up the stairs; he came up so fast I almost couldn't count the stairs as he walked his footsteps heavily carried the sound of drums beating. "Karis," he said grabbing my arms, "Baby your dads been taken to the hospital, you have to go, are you up?" He asked. "What!" I said leaping up from the bed. I grabbed my sweater and wrapped it around my pajamas and went to the door. "I'll be back, Michael," I said racing to my car. I jumped into the car not knowing where to go or what to do. I stop to think; I'll just go to daddy's house. First, I thought. I drove as fast as I could when I arrived there was the ambulance everyone was outside the neighbors.

Richard and his girlfriend and Rose were there also. I immediately ran up to the ambulance, "Daddy!" I yelled. "Daddy! What's wrong, daddy?" I said to him. I held daddy's hand it was warm, but his eyes were rolling back into his head. "Are you coming?" The paramedic asked me? "I shook my head yes and they closed the doors and we drove off. When we arrived at the hospital daddy was taken into a room immediately. I stood outside waiting for word. What could be wrong with daddy I thought? "Would you like a drink?"

A woman asked me after I sat down. I shook my head no. I didn't feel anything I wasn't sick, and I felt that whatever this may be daddy would make it through this. I waited for them to give me any word, patiently. It was hours before anyone came out to tell me anything, by now all of my siblings where there waiting with me. There wasn't much talk between us; all of us probably had the same thoughts. Thinking of how not too long ago we were awaiting news from the doctors about mama.

I sat there in my sweater and pajamas not afraid. I prayed the whole time to myself, "Lord, please keep daddy in your light, keep him close. Fight for him to be strong and want to continue to carry on in this life. Lord keep him so that I can enjoy him more." I prayed and prayed. Suddenly the doctors came through the sliding doors. They were in surgery scrubs. "Who should I talk to about Mr. Lawson?" He asked. We all stood up quickly, "That would be us," My brother Richard said walking over to hear what he had to say. "Your father had an aneurysm, he bled out on both sides of the brain, left and right, I'm so sorry."

"He came in just in time; we were able to save him from some major damage. We have relieved the pressure and placed on the left side of his brain with a shunt which will release the remaining of the blood flow back into his bodily fluids. He is in a comma; it will be up to him to come out of it. He's heavily sedated and will be for a while," he said standing looking at us. I was floored, I felt like I had been punched in the stomach. I sat down and put my head in my lap, while everyone else asked their questions. I didn't hear anything after him saying he was in a comma. I sat there until Maddy came up to me.

"Karis," she said. "Karis," she reached into my lap and pulled my hands from under my face. "Come with me honey," she said pulling me up from my chair. She walked me down the hall as I began to cry. I wasn't crying because I was going to lose daddy, I was crying because I couldn't stop this from happening. Daddy would be in a lot of pain and I know he has the will to make it through this. I followed Maddy to the chapel. "This is where you want to go, honey," she said going over to light some candles.

"Kneel down honey, start praying." I looked at Maddy. "This is going to be good for you," she said rubbing my arm. "I stayed in here on my knees when my dad was ill," she said. It will make you feel secure in what he can do. I kneeled down and started to pray. I stayed there praying for hours on in until a nurse came in and got me. "Are you Mr. Lawson's daughter?" She questioned. "We have him stable you can go in and see him; all of your other siblings are gone. I was told that you were in here," she said walking quickly ahead of me.

"Your dads a real strong man; he's been responding a little with his hands, you can ask him questions, and he'll squeeze your hand if he understands. I do not doubt that he won't recover," she said showing me into his room. I sat by his bed side. Daddy was so swollen from the surgery he didn't look like himself at all; I took his hand. "I'm here daddy," I tell him moving the chair closer to his bed. "I'm here; you keep fighting, I know you don't want to leave me, daddy," I said in his ear. He squeezed my hand. I stayed there for a while before going back home. When I arrived back at home Michael was waiting up for me.

"Are you okay baby?" He asked. I shook my head no. I sat down next to him on the couch; I was scared. I knew that daddy would make it through, I didn't feel as if he was going home to Jesus, he had some time; it took me all night to fall asleep. I was so worried about how daddy was doing there at the hospital. When I fell asleep I dreamed of how he would come out of it; Daddy was working in the garden playing with the water hose wetting the twins as they ran around him in circles. I awoke the next morning smiling. Michael and I sat out to look for churches today. "Are you okay baby?" Michael asked me peeking out from the shower curtain as I sat down on the toilet.

"I'm okay I dreamed of daddy last night," I said. "It was good huh?" He asked smiling. "Yes, it was I feel better Michael." "Sure you do, are you ready for today? We have some church shopping to do." "I am Michael; I'm ready." I said. "And afterward we can stop in and check on dad. Okay baby, how does that sound?" I nod my head yes, "that sounds great Michael." We got dressed and took the twins to school, Michael took off today which was good I needed him now more than ever, we left the house with no fear. We stopped at two churches in the city first they were right across the street from one another.

We went in, and we didn't feel anything in either one of them. We kept looking, church after church there was no end we had ill feelings about most of them. Until we went way across town, A beautiful white church built like a castle; it was perfect. We sat outside for a while just admiring the structure of the building. "This is beautiful Michael." "Yes baby, but we need to go inside and check it out," he says reaching for the door handle. He got out and grabbed Keagan. I was still sitting in my seat staring at the church.

"Come on Karis," Michael exclaimed, "let's go in," He said wave for me to follow him inside. I got out of the car, and we walked hand and hand toward the church, and we saw them come out as we came closer to the beautiful doors, they became more visible. Michael looked straight ahead as if they weren't there and I followed his lead as we entered the church. We walked in, "My goodness, its beautiful Michael," I said as I looked around. We were greeted by two priests who closed the door behind us.

"Hello son," they said greeting Michael, "Hello daughter, welcome," they said. "Welcome to Gods home of Worship." "Is that the name of this church?" I asked. "Yes daughter, it is, welcome, how can we be of service to you and your family?" "We were looking to have our son baptized," Michael said, "Do you have to become a member of this church first?" Michael went on to say. "Everyone is a member of the lord's heart. Come, son, let's talk," the priest led us to a cold room in the back of the church.

"What's your faith or religion son?" He asked. "My wife is Baptist, and I have no religion I except the Lord as my savior, he is all I am," Michael said. "Son that is what I like to hear. I would like to tell you about us and what we do for the baptism service. We are a Catholic church we will pray for the child and hold him near the blessed waters; then after that, we will pour the holy water over his young head as we pray more." The other priest smiled at Keagan. "He is a beautiful child, he has those eyes," he said.

I looked at Keagan; he did have those funny colored eyes. I thought that they would have changed by now, but they didn't they were still gray and blue like a cats eyes. "Will you have family members to witness the baptism?" The priest went on to ask. "We will have a couple of family members and friends," Michael explained. "But it's not for certain yet." "My dad was going to come, but he became ill," I told them looking around at the many beautiful portraits and sculptures they had all around the church. "We can set a date now if you like," the priest said. "Will we have to pay for this service?" Michael asked.

"Of course not, you can simply bless the church with a donation if you like afterward," the priest told us. "My name is Michael, and this is my wife Karis and our son Keagan. Sir, we'd be honored if you would bless our son this Sunday." "I am Paul, and this is Ken, and we'd love to," he said standing up, He walked over to a table near the podium and grabbed a piece of paper, "Which Sunday looks or feels good for you?" He asked. "This Sunday would be great," I said to him. "This Sunday is open 11 am; does that sound good to you?"

"Yes sir, great just great. Thank You so much," Michael said with excitement in his voice. We took a tour around the church and they explained the holy water and how it's blessed. We were excited and ready. We stopped by the hospital on the way back home. Michael stayed downstairs with the baby. They didn't allow babies in the ICU, Michael was thrilled about the baptism telling all of his co-workers about it and the church, and how beautiful it was, he couldn't be happier. I went upstairs quickly hoping to tell daddy the good news. Praying that his eyes would be open and I could see him smile when I got there.

I walked in and he was still the same as the night before. The nurse was in the room adjusting his medication in his IV. "Hello, how are you? I'm Angie, your dad's nurse today. They told me you'd be here today," she said. "You mean I'm the only one who has come up today?" I asked. "Oh no, Of course not, he had a lot of visitors today, Maddy told me that you would be here. She's a good friend of mine," she exclaimed. "Oh, yea, hello Angie how's my daddy today?" I asked her going close to hold his hand. "He's doing better.

They took him back down this morning to relieve some of the pressure from the blood in his head again. He handled that well," she said with her hand on daddy's leg. "He's a real trooper," she explained. "Nothing's going to stop him from living. I love patients like your dad;

they make my life worth living." I sat down in a chair next to daddy's bed. "Hello daddy, how you doing today" I asked. "We have Keagan's baptism this Sunday, daddy I wish you could be there," I told him. "Do you hear me, daddy?" I asked him; he shook his head. "Did you see that?" I questioned the nurse.

"Yes I did, he knows you're here, and he's responding well to your voice. That's an excellent sign that he'll be getting better soon," she said. "I better go get the doctor," she rushed out of the room. "I love you daddy. Don't leave me please," I told daddy squeezing his hand. Daddy's lips moved as if he wanted to tell me something I moved in closer to see if a whisper or any sound was coming out, there wasn't any. The doctor came in soon after.

I explained what daddy did, and he checked daddy's eyes, shining a light close to his eyeballs. I went to the lobby soon after. When I found Michael, he was standing in the nurse's station holding Keagan and chatting with everyone about how glad he was that Keagan was growing up. "Hey," I said walking up to him. "Hey, how's dad?" He asked. "He's responding to my voice, he shook his head and moved his lips as if he wanted to talk to me. I am so glad he's doing those things. The nurse said it's good," I explained to him.

"Oh yes that's wonderful, baby," he said walking toward the exit to the garage. I followed him talking about daddy. We got into the car and headed toward the school to pick up the twins. We made it to the school just in time the twins were outside waiting with Ms. Honey; I watched as Michael went to get them. She stood there with her hands folded around a book talking to the twins. When Michael approached her she began to tell him how the twins were so excited about the baptism of the baby. "We can't wait either," Michael said walking away from her smiling and waving. Keagan was sound asleep he was so tired from all the excitement at the hospital. "Well, I invited Ms. Honey for tea later," Michael said smiling.

"Tea and cake, would you be all right with that baby?" He said holding my hand in his. "I think she's beautiful," Michael was always making light, of things, knowing how nervous and scared I was just thinking about the baptism. The week was finally over, and Sunday was here, we had everything prepared for this graceful day. We had Keagan in his white suit, and we were all dressed for church in the proper attire, the twins were excited.

On the way to the church the day was calm the sun shined brightly through the car windows as we drove. I was eager to get it over with; we arrived at 1030 am the service for the church was just getting started. The members were walking around greeting one another talking about what the sermon was going to be like today. The congregation was made up of mostly older people at least in there sixty's. They were happy to see us; as soon as we walked in we were greeted with smiles from everyone. We sat in the front pews awaiting the priest to introduce us to the congregation.

The church started at exactly 11 am; the priest began to welcome everyone. "Hello and welcome to this wonderful day. Today is the day that the Lord has made," He said. His sermon lasted at least an hour before he asked us to stand "Can you, please tell us your names?" he said, "Hello everyone, I'm Michael, this is my wife Karis and our children, the twins Kristine and Kristopher and our son Keagan." Just as Michael said Keagan's name we began to see them, they came in there dark robes and fell behind one another walking to the upper area of the church, making a circle around the priest.

Suddenly in the windows above us the sky went black, they never looked up, their dark hoods covered their faces, Michael took my hand, and we walked toward the podium where the priest would bless Keagan. Soon the darkness covers the church it was lit up with candles. The priest came down with his holy water and began to pray. Dr. Green and Maddy came up for the blessing. "Keagan, I bless you in the name of the father and the spirit of the holy ghost," as he began to sprinkle the holy water over Keagan's head.

Michael and I stood still, waiting, soon the priest was no longer standing, his arm went up to sprinkle the water, and he fell back as if someone had pushed him to the ground. A force of wind came soon after, pushing the pews and the congregation out of the church. It was like a horrible storm had arrived. After the pews, the church doors slam with a powerful force that shook us all; the priest laid still, and we stood alone surrounded by them. Michael was being torn away from us by them, and they began to surround Keagan and me, they circled us soon I could smell them and feel their strength.

I held Keagan tight; I placed his head on my shoulders protecting his eyes from seeing them. I turned to look for Michael; he stood in the back of me and what stood in front of him, I thought were two huge angels with their wings spread as big as the room. I screamed, "Michael!" He didn't turn to look at me. They must be here to help I thought. Their wings were black, and they looked at Michael with anger in their eyes, and suddenly I was hit with a great force that took me to the ground. Soon Keagan was no longer in my arms; I tried to get up, "Keagan!" I yelled reaching for him, I was kicked around and pushed and pulled. I lay on the floor of the church, I closed my eyes and thought about God's grace.

"I know that you're here Lord," I said to myself, I opened my eyes, and I looked over to the floor, and Keagan was sitting still. I looked in the middle of the church, and Michael was fighting with all he had in him. The two angels with the black wings took turns trying to defeat him blow after blow; they went back and forth they fought. All I could think about was Keagan, getting to Keagan, I felt them all over me. They held my legs, and my feet pinned down as I swarmed around to get out their grips became tighter. Keagan didn't cry as I prayed. "Lord, I know your here," I prayed and prayed, I closed my eyes I could hear them groaning and roaring the noise of evil. I looked over to see if Keagan was okay again, trying to keep my eyes on Michael and Keagan.

Soon there were seven balls of light circling Keagan; he looked up at them reaching for them and smiling. The room was like a horrible storm, Michael and I were doing all we could to calm it. Keagan was reaching for those lights, and when he touched them one by one, things began to change. He touched one and threw it towards me, and their grip loosened, and they began to walk away. Keagan's eyes shinned, and he threw another towards Michael, and the black winged angels flew away with their heads down.

One by one he changed it all, still smiling, soon everything and everyone was back inside the church. We stood in front of the priest, Michael with Keagan in his arms and me next to him. The priest lifted his arm up once again as Keagan looked up into the light of the sky with his eyes shining, smiling up. The priest was able to bless Keagan. The holy water came down on his little head that day. I looked up to see why Keagan's eyes shined so bright and there in the light of the sky was Keagan's seven lights circling the church. After the blessing, we ate in the church hall. Everyone came up to us and congratulated us on the blessing. I prayed all the way home that evening thanking god for his grace.

The Blessings Rain Down

Things seem to go back to normal after that day, there was a difference in Michael's behavior, he seemed to be on edge about everything. I could tell the fight with the dark angels bothered him, but I didn't ask him. He would come home these days and play with the children, eat dinner and head straight up to the attic, where he prayed. I left him I never went up to see him; I waited patiently, for him to come to bed at night or early morning. He was quiet and seldom, talkative when he lay next to me, he'd just look up staring through the skylight as if he was lost in it.

I'd look at him, and look up too; we fell asleep that way night after night. I wondered about Keagan, he woke up through the night with a loud scream and I'd jumped to go to him. Michael would follow, when we open his door, he'd be standing in his crib with his arms open wide. His eyes would be lit full of color they almost looked like cat eyes, gray with small specks of emerald green in them. Michael grabbed him before I could and sat in the rocking chair with him. I sat next to the chair on the floor. Michael hummed a song, and I would begin to sing along with his humming.

"Yes, Jesus loves me, yes, Jesus loves me, yes Jesus loves me. For the bible tells me so," I stopped when he stopped. He held Keagan close to his chest and rocked and looked up humming for hours until he fell off to sleep again. Night after night Michael and I were awakened by his scream. Sometimes I'd catch Michael praying for Keagan, "Lord in the name of Jesus, watch over our son. Lord, keep him safe from harm, keep him fearless and faithful. Keep my son's heart pure." I would watch him through the crack in the door. He looked so comfortable there with his son.

I wouldn't go in just watching them together put a smile on my face. His love for the kids was so genuine and pure. I started to see changes in Keagan's behavior he was more active than usual, He had a great appetite but loved to eat more fruit than anything. He would stare out a lot, looking down the halls and sometimes through the windows. I'd watch and look out to see if I could see what he saw out there, but there was usually nothing. I'd stand next to him to see if I felt anything like a cold spirit hanging around or would I get a chill.

"Why was Keagan acting so strange?" I questioned Michael who seemed to be in the same mood. "Michael is there something I should know about?" I asked him. "No babe, everything is fine, Keagan is learning things. You saw him that day didn't you?" He said, "We do need to talk. There are some things you should know about Keagan, "He's exceptional. He will be the keeper of our safety, and he'll be more powerful in his light than you, and I could ever be combined. They will always come after him to destroy his light. We need to always be prepared to keep him safe from harm.

If they should ever catch Keagan off guard, they will destroy him. As he grows older, he will become stronger and stronger." Michael walked back and forth pacing the floor explaining to me what was going on with Keagan. "Right now he's studying, he hears and sees things that we cannot see nor hear. His relationship with the lord is far more advanced than ours will ever be. He was born in his light," he exclaimed. "What do you mean Michael, weren't we all born in his light?" I said. "Not like Keagan, he was born of the thickened. His spirit was before he was born out of your womb," he said.

"I don't understand Michael, thickened? What exactly does that mean?" I asked. "It means that in his light he was groomed to be on this earth as an angel, sent to reshape evil here on this earth." He explained. "What do you mean?" I said as I got up from the couch and went over to Keagan; he was sitting on the floor looking out of the window. I put him on my hip and kissed his forehead, "Michael I don't believe you now, all this talk about Keagan having this huge burden on him, he's a little baby."

"He's not even old enough to feed himself yet, I won't hear of him having to deal with such an awful task, Michael, he's a baby." I took Keagan and sat him in his high chair; I went into the kitchen and began to cook. Michael followed me into the kitchen. "Baby, I'm so sorry I want you to be prepared, you asked me what the problem was, and I told you. I'm trying to be truthful, and help you understand what's happening to us. I need you to be strong, baby, that's all," he said, grabbing me from behind and pulling me in close to him.

"I don't want this for our family Michael; I never dreamed that things would be this complicated. I was blessed with children, who knew that everything else would come with it." I said as I prepared dinner with Michael still attached to me holding my hips close to him kissing my neck. I push him away with my hand. "Michael, I don't know, I just don't know if I can go on, "Really, he said, kissing me. I believe that you're strong enough to take this on," I looked at Michael he still had a couple of scratches from the fight on his face. I loved him; this is what I did know.

I couldn't believe that this was our lives, I cooked and thought about my life as it is now and what happened to me in the past. Michael coming into my life was a blessing, the twins the way I love them. I think about how awful James was, and about the night the twins were conceived. There is no use in me crying over any of it anymore, this was it I thought as I made the salad. I went to the refrigerator to get the tomatoes and onion, when I turned to open it there was my mom standing in front of it smiling. I was startled, "Mama," I said, "what are you doing here?" I asked her, she smiled not saying a word at first.

She opened her hand and reached out to me, I took the tomato and onion out and sat them on the counter. She took my hand; her hand was cold and small, smaller than I remembered. She walked me outside to the backyard, and we sat down on the stools on the porch. "Karis, there's going to be some changes in your life soon, some bad ones. I want you to be strong, change is always hard, and this one will be the hardest of them all. Go to your father and help him during this time in his life, he is really going to need your help to crossover.

He's so strong-willed, and he's not going to go without a good fight. It's going to take strength from you to help him be comfortable with living this life," she said as she stood up over me. She took my hand and held it tight, "Karis, I love you, stay strong and go to your daddy, watch him, help him get comfortable." She walked away with her hands closed together smiling. I went back inside to set the table, Michael had already done it. He had the children sitting in their seats and ready for dinner. I served them all and soon it was time for Michael to go to work.

"Baby, I'm going to look in on your dad before I go to work okay, I'll stop there first," he said kissing me on the cheek. He put his plate in the sink and went upstairs to change, I sat there with the children, thinking about going to visit daddy myself. The children finished dinner, I washed them up and put their pajamas on and put them in bed. I said prayers with the twins and rocked with Keagan until he fell off to sleep. While they were all sleeping I took some time out to write in my journal.

I just thanked God for all the blessing that I do have. I prayed about daddy. I was very tired. I went downstairs to watch some television and have a cup of tea. I wanted to take a bath, but I'll wait for Keagan to wake up for his midnight feeding. I watched the late show, it was funny. When I heard Keagan on the baby monitor, I turned off the TV and ran upstairs. I wanted to feed him and go straight into the bathtub. Keagan ate and watched me I dimmed the light in his room so that he wouldn't wake up completely.

He held my hand while I nursed him. One side after the other and when he finished I put him over my shoulder to pat his back and rocked him. He'd usually go right back to sleep afterward. He was so handsome I watched as his little eyes grew heavy. He fell off to sleep quick I laid him on his bed and watched him sleep for a while. He was like an angel sleeping. I went into my room to get myself ready for a bath; I started taking my clothes off as I walked down the hall. I went into the bathroom and turned on the water, I made it as hot as I could.

I poured in some honey and milk bath soap to soothe my body as I laid in there, I went back to my room and got out the bedclothes I would wear tonight. I went back into the bathroom and got in the hot tub, I sighed as my body fell into the water every inch of me was tired. It was so relaxing, "oh thank you God for this bath," I said. I laid my back on the back of the tub and placed a towel over my eyes. The water was steaming hot; I sat in there for an hour. The water was cold when I finally washed up. I got out soon after I washed.

I put on lotion and powder and lay on the bed naked for a while. Oh goodness my body felt good. I must have fallen off to sleep because next thing I knew I felt Michael kissing my thighs. I looked up. "Hello baby," he said kissing my thighs. He was still in his white coat; he kissed all the way up to my lips. When he made to my lips, he held my face in his big soft hands, "hey, I was thinking of you too," he said. "I miss you, baby, I miss you so much. Tell me, can I have you? Can I have your love?" He whispered in my ear. I shook my head yes, Michael took his hand and rubbed in between my legs. "I missed you, baby," I said as I undress him while he kissed me and the lovemaking began.

Michael took me to a different place when we made love, I'd forgotten about all my troubles all my worries were gone away in those moments I was his. While he placed himself inside of me, I was no longer breathing. His passion took me to another world, I felt so happy. Michael made passionate love to me until we were both tired. I fell off to sleep afterwards and Michael went into the shower. When he was done he dried himself off and laid next to me in bed. His body was cold, so he pulled himself close to me and wrapped his arms around me tight, he kissed my neck.

"I love you, Karis," he said to me softly, "I love you too Michael," I told him. I held his hand and fell back off to sleep. It was quiet in the house, we slept well. The next morning I got the children ready for school while Michael made breakfast for us. We fed them, and I took the twins to school. "Michael, I'm going to go see daddy today and then I'm going over to his house to check on the garden okay. Will you and Keagan be okay?" I asked him.

"Sure we will, I'm going to take him for a stroll to the park. Okay, baby, we will see you later," he said kissing my cheek. The twins would giggle when they saw us kissing or doing anything intimate in front of them. It was fun to watch them blush at us, Michael and I would look at each other and then at them after we kissed. "Okay baby, see you later then," I said as I walked out of the door with the twins. We made it to the school soon after, I walked the twins inside the school. Ms. Honey was outside watching the children play; she waved at me from across the playground.

"You two have a good day okay; I'm going to see your grandpa. Is there anything you would like for me to tell him?" I asked them. "Yes mommy, please tell granddaddy that we love him," Kristopher told me in my ear. I kissed him on the hand. "Okay son will do, I most definitely will tell him that," I said to them walking off toward the car. I thought about seeing daddy, what would he look like today? It would break my heart if he were any worse than when I last saw him. I rushed off to the hospital to see him when I made it there I thought I would be the only one there to see daddy, but to my surprise, my brothers were there waiting in the hallway, I always felt uncomfortable around them.

When I saw them, I started to turn back down the hall, but I didn't, I waved hi to them and sat down. I looked at my brother Richard and asked. "What are we all waiting for?" "I just came, and they told me that daddy was taking a test and that they would let us know when he was done, so we've been sitting out here waiting," he said to me. "Oh, I see," I said. I picked up a magazine and sat back onto the chair. "So Karis, how have you been little one?" Richard asked, "I've been fine, how about you?" I asked. "How's my niece and nephews?" He asked me. "They're doing good, how about your children?" I asked him.

"Oh, they're doing good too, I think when daddy gets out of here and gets better we can have a barbecue at the house, and all the kids can be there," he said. "Would you come?" He asked looking at me with a smile. Soon after we finished talking the nurse came out to tell us daddy was done and back in his room. "There might be a surprise for you all when you go in," she said smiling and walking away. I got up and followed Richard to daddy's room. You could hear us trailing one another to the room. We went inside and they had daddy propped up as if he was sitting.

He turned his head when we went all the way in, and waved. I smiled, and it brought tears to my eyes. They had removed most of the tubes from daddy's head, and his eyes were open. His head was still wrapped up and very swollen. He looked up at Richard and smiled. "Hey champ," the doctor said walking in behind us. "I bet you are ready to leave huh?" He picked up daddy's chart and looked it over; he placed it on the bed and walked over to daddy. He flashed a light into his eyes and whistled the whole time.

"Mr. Lawson, can you please tell me your name and what day you think it is?" He asked daddy. He stood over daddy as he shook his head. "Hello, I'm sorry, I'm Dr. Boulder, I have been the neurologist since the surgery your dad had a couple weeks ago," he said shaking our hands. "Your dad has a shunt in the back of his brain; it's draining the fluids down to his rectum. Your dad is able to understand what we are saying to him, but he's unable to speak or eat right now. He has a tube in his stomach and a trach in his throat."

"He can't swallow right now, but we are hoping to see in a few days here is for him to begin to speak little by little. We think with the help of some physical therapy he will improve. We will wait a few weeks to see how well he does off the meds. We will transfer him over to a rehabilitation center, and he will stay there for a few months. We hope he will regain his strength and may be going home from there. He's lost control on his right side, but not complete control. He can move it, it's not stiff, he's so lucky."

"Your father is a true survivor, most people don't survive this. It could have been fatal," he said looking daddy over once more before leaving. "I will keep you guys posted on his progress. Goodbye guys, your dad's doing great." I went over to daddy when he left. "Hi daddy," I said grabbing him by the hand. "How you doing today?" Daddy looked at me with his blue eyes. He shook his head. A tear rolled down the side of daddy's face. I wiped it with my hand. "What's wrong, Daddy?" I asked him.

"Everything is going to be okay I promise, don't be scared. You're only going to be here for a little while longer," I told him holding his hand tight. I sat with daddy while Richard talked to him about work and what he was going to do when daddy gets out. Daddy looked as if he was enjoying the conversation until the nurse walked in. "Hello Mr. Lawson," she said with a smile. "Hello," Richard said to her being flirtatious, "I need to check your vitals today. Also, you have to get a sponge bath later," she said looking back at Richard, she was very attractive.

"My name is nurse Vikki if you guys need anything while you're here visiting, please don't hesitate to call me. I'll do whatever I can to accommodate you," she looked over at Richard and gave him a wink. I looked at daddy as if I didn't see her winking. We stayed in the room with him for a while. I can't wait for him to get better I miss him so much. I thought as I watched as Richard flirt with the nurse outside the room door. I kissed daddy's hand and left the room, I was going to the flower shop before going over to daddy's to check on the garden. I wanted to plant some tulips today. When I made it to the house, everyone was there.

They were cleaning, and the music was playing, and Mary had her friends over. They were hanging out of the door and standing on the porch. I took my tulips and went to the back gate, avoiding Mary and her friends all together. I walked past them waving hi. I made it to the backyard, I could tell that no one had been looking after the garden while daddy was in the hospital. It looked dried out, and a lot of the veggies were nibbled on. I got the water hose to water them as I walked around picking all the dead and bitten veggies. I was working my way toward the tulips soon after. I sat down to take a breather, I looked over at the shed were daddy kept all his tools, I walked over to it, I needed a shovel and a hoe.

When I went toward it, I felt a cold chill come over me, but I didn't stop. I opened the door and walked into the shed, it was dark I tried to turn on the light pulling the string, the clicking noise was loud, but the light didn't come on. I went toward the one window to pull back the curtains, they were dusty, when I pulled them back dust flew everywhere, I held my arm over my eyes. When the dust cleared I looked around the room, there were boxes of mama's old things in there; lamps and a really nice dinner table, it was set up with all the chairs, and it was dust free.

I went over to it, wondering why it was in here and not in the house I wanted to check out the chairs. I pulled one of them out and leaned down to sit when I was pushed so hard to the ground, and the chair was pushed back onto the table. I stood up and grabbed the chair again to pull it from the table. This time it wouldn't budge, I just looked at it, I could feel a spirit around me, it was getting angrier and angrier. I could feel its breath on my neck, I ran my hand across the wood, it was polished and clean, suddenly I felt a slap on my hand. I went toward the door and stood there. I wonder where daddy got that table from, I thought. I went out into the garden and worked on the roses.

I could feel it watching, I looked over to the shed and there it was in the doorway as if it was inviting me to come back. I turned away from it and continued to work on the rose bushes. When I was done I went inside to talk to Richard. "Hey, Richard," I called out walking around the house in search of him. "Hey, Richard, where are you?" I called out. I heard music coming from the den. I followed the loud sound, and I found him in the basement surrounded by three women, smoking a cigarette. "Hey Richard," I said walking up to him. "Where did that table come from?" I asked standing in front of him. The women stared at me smiling. "What table are you talking about?" He asked taking a puff from his cigarette again.

"The one in the shed out back," I said pointing out toward the back. "I don't know what you're talking about," he said grabbing the woman sitting closest to him real tight and kissing her. "Go, baby, make us something to eat," he said to her as he pulled her up by her arm. He slapped her behind and looked at me smiling. "Do you want something to eat Karis?" He asked. "No, Richard, just tell me where that table came from?" I asked him again. He got up and walked toward the basement stairs. "What table are you talking about?" He asked me again. "Oh, forget it, Richard. I mean really, is there something wrong with you?" I questioned.

"I've asked you three times already where it came from, and you keep asking me what table." I walked back upstairs, and he followed me. "Oh the table in the shed," he said as he trailed behind me. "Yes, that table in there, where did it come from?" I asked again. We walked out back together, Richard stood next to me staring at the shed. "Why? Do you want the table or something?" He asked me. "No, I just wondered where it came from, I've never seen it before," I said. "I think daddy may have gotten it from a friend. It's been in there for some time now," he said with his hand on his hip.

"Do you know which friend gave it to him?" I asked. "No, daddy always gets things from people, he'll never use it though, he's comfortable with the things he has," he said. "I'll see you later okay, I have to eat something." "Okay," I said walking out toward the garden. I just wanted to take one last glance at it before I headed home. It was darkness around it, and behind it was a burning fire at last glance, it was showing me what it could do. I wanted to go back to the hospital to see if daddy had made any more progress, but I knew Michael was expecting me back, so I headed home to meet with him.

All the way home I thought about the table in the storage room. Where did it come from and why was it still there? I hope that daddy was a little better I would like to ask him about where it came from. Driving up to the house, Michael was outside with the twins playing around. Keagan was inside the playpen watching them and cooing, the twin ran up to the car as I parked. Michael grabbed their hands and held them close to him.

I looked toward the garage window and there was Mr. Simms again smiling back at me waving. I walked over to Keagan's playpen to pick him up, e was so happy to see me his smile was as big as the sunlight that shined on his face. I raised him up high in the air and brought him down with a kiss. "Mommy's happy to see you too, baby," I said carrying him into the house.

Michael and the twins followed us in. "Do we have anything cooked?" I asked "Oh yea, I made some cucumber salad and sandwiches. Would you like one?" Michael asked me as he went to the refrigerator. "Sure, I would," I said. "I'm going to take Keagan up to get him cleaned. Give me about ten minutes, and it will be ready," I said. Michael winked at me while he stood at the counter fixing my lunch. The twins sat on the floor playing with blocks. As I walked up the stairs, I could feel Mr. Simms presence walking alongside me. I looked over and sure enough he was standing beside me.

I looked at Keagan just to see his reaction the expression on his face would tell me if he can feel him around or not. He was smiling and looking over. Hum, he can see him, I thought. Keagan's smile was so bright, "I love you, son," I told him shaking his little legs as we walked upstairs. We went to the bathroom down the hall and sat Keagan down on the counter near the sink to wash his little face. Mr. Simms stood in the doorway. "Hello, Karis, how have you been?" He asked me. "I'm good," I reply back. "It's about time I checked on you and your son. Have you seen it yet?" He asked. "Yes, I have," I said. "Do you know what it all means yet?" He asked.

"I know that he has a light around him and he is extraordinary," I tell him washing Keagan's hands. "Yes, special indeed, He is as exceptional as they come, he has a unique gift that is more special than any others," he said. "And you must protect him; protect him with everything in you. He's always going to be under attack. Have you seen it yet?" He asks. "Seen what?" I asked. "His brand, he has a brand on him it has been there since birth. They don't have to see it because you can look at him and tell he is one of Gods, but those of the unknown, the ones that come back."

"They will search for that brand on him, be careful of them, search him for it, and protect him with your senses. When you feel something go to him when you see something out of the ordinary go to him, for now, he will need your help. When he turns thirteen, he will have his full strength from above. He will protect you," he explained. "I don't understand Mr. Simms; you say all this and leave me to wonder what's next. Why can't you just tell me what's to come so that I can prepare for it" I asked him.

"I don't know what's to come dear; I'm just giving you the information that was given to me. I wish I could tell you more, but that is all I know," he tells me. Just then Keagan threw his hand up at Mr. Simms as if to shoo him away. "Mr.Simms, where do you belong? Why do you come back to me?" I asked him. He turned and walked away. Keagan looked up at me and smiled. I picked him up and we went back down to eat. "Hey baby, I thought you'd never come back down," Michael said.

"Oh no, I'm hungry," I told him. "Well, sit lady, sit down," Michael said pulling Keagan from my arms. "I want you to enjoy this sandwich, it's the best sandwich you will ever eat, I promise." He said placing the plate in front of me. "Okay we will soon tell," I took a bite out of the sandwich, it was good, but I wanted to play around with Michael. "Ugh! Michael, this is not good," I said. "What did you use? It tastes like vinegar and salt!! Ugh!" I took another bite, then another really fast. Michael laughed.

"See I told you, baby, the best you ever had, right? He asked me. "No, you're the best I ever had" I tell him smiling. I finished my sandwich and Michael fed Keagan his food from the jar, Keagan ate it all, he had an excellent appetite. Michael cleaned his hands and face and took him out of the high chair. I went over to the kitchen to turn on the teapot. "Baby, I thought we should take a long vacation this year." He said. "Really, where would we go?" I asked. "I want to take you and the kids to visit Africa. There is a place over there called Seychelles Africa, it's a beautiful place baby. We will go for two weeks," he said.

"Sure Michael why not" I tell him smiling. "Oh, baby you'll love this place, I'll start planning this week, we will leave next month okay?" Michael was so excited about this trip. He cleaned up all around him and put things away quickly. Then he came over to me and grabbed around my waist, and started to dance with me slowly. "We're going to Africa, where the sun shines all the time even in the moonlight," he sang softly in my ear. "I'm going to make love to you all night to celebrate," he said in a whisper. I laughed at him.

"Anything to get my pants down huh Michael" "Sure baby, anything," he said rubbing mine behind walking away. "I'm going to put the twins to bed, you can put Keagan asleep when you're done," he said running toward the stairway. Michael was so funny to me, one day he's acting strange and the next he's ready for fun and adventure. I really loved the fun and adventurous part of him, but the strange and unknown is taking time to get used to, but when I look at him he lights a fire in me that only he can. I feel closeness to him that I've never ever felt before. There was never a time when Michael made me feel insecure. It was like; he is this soft warm blanket for me.

I finished up the dishes and poured my tea. I turned off the light and went up the stairs to be with Michael, forgetting that Keagan was lying on the couch. He was sleeping so I didn't even think about it. I got halfway up, and something said to me, "Keagan, I stopped in my tracks spilling some of my tea on my foot. Oh, Keagan I forgot about Keagan, I went to the top of the stairs and sat my cup on the table in the hall and went back down for Keagan. When I got to the couch Keagan's eyes were wide open. He looked at me and smiled as if he was waiting for me to come back. I scooped him up and he hugged my neck really tight.

"Handsome, mommy almost forgot about her baby huh, I tell him carrying him up the stairs. I talked to him in baby talk. "Mommy will never forget her baby," I told him. He looked at me all the way up. I took my teacup with me into Keagan's room. I sat down in the rocker and began to rock him to sleep. After singing to him over and over, "Jesus loves the little children," he fell right off to sleep. I laid him down into his crib and sat back down to take a sip of my tea.

I watched him sleeping, Keagan looked as if he was even smiling in his sleep I got up and rubbed his little back while I sipped on my tea. I started walking toward the door when I was startled by Michael standing in the doorway with his robe opened wide, he did a little dance. "We've been waiting for you for a while," I was so stunned, Michael wasn't wearing anything under his robe. Laughing, I stood in front of him. "Michael, you can't do that, I'm afraid Keagan is a bit of a faker, he may not even be sleeping." I told him moving him from the doorway with my body.

"Well, at least he'll know he's blessed if his body is anything like his daddy's," Michael said laughing. I pushed him with my body all the way into the room and onto the bed. I turned on some jazz music because Michael and I can be loud at times and maybe the kids wouldn't hear us over the music I thought. Michael would just think I was romantic, but I was just trying to keep the kids from hearing us. I undressed to the music as Michael lay watching me. He smiled from ear to ear; I could tell he was enjoying me.

He stood up on his knees and started to dance along with me, pulling me closer to him. I could feel him rising as we danced close. Michael kissed me all over until he could no longer keep his composure; he laid me down on the bed and kissed me more. All over my breast and my stomach, we made love to the music, I screamed out his name as his hand caressed my body. Michael held me so tight pulling me into him; his stroke was so gentle but hard and strong. I moaned as he watched my expressions with every stroke. We made love all night. Michael held me tight kissing me over and over when we were done.

"I love you so much Karis," he whispers in my ear as we fall off to sleep together; I spooned in his arms all night. The next day I woke up to Michaels kiss on the cheek. "Good Morning Love," he says holding his bag. "You have to get up, Keagan's up and ready to eat, I'm taking the twins to school before I head to work. What are you doing today?" He asked me. I rolled over and sat up. "I have to take Keagan to the doctors for a checkup, remember? Then I'm going to visit daddy. Hopefully, they'll be some good news about him today," I tell him.

"Okay baby, I'll see you later, you cook tonight," he said laughing and walking down the hall. "Bye, Michael," I said. "Hey, get some information on the Seychelles Islands!!" I yelled out to him. I got out of bed and went into the bathroom to start my shower. I could hear Keagan on the baby monitor Michael left on the dresser. He was up alright playing and laughing to the music Michael left on for him. I rushed to do everything before he became bored with his toys. I got out after only washing once and put on a nice sweater and tights. I went into Keagan's room, he was lying in his crib playing with a small ball throwing it on the pillow and picking it up putting it into his mouth.

I sneak up on him. "Peek-a-Boo!" I say loudly as I pop my head into his little face. He stared at me quickly and laughed. I picked him up and hugged him. "How's mommy's baby this morning?" I asked him. I talked to him the whole while I washed his little face and brushed his two little teeth and we went back into the room for a quick diaper change and change his clothes. "Keagan, we have to go see the doctor today baby," I tell him putting on his socks and shoes. "Do you want breakfast baby?" I asked him looking into his little eyes, he looked at me and shook his head yes.

"Oh my! You're learning," I yelled out. "You're learning baby boy," I hugged him tighter than ever as we walked downstairs to get breakfast. The kitchen was a mess, Michael left everything out cereal and milk and eggs and juice. I put the baby down to clean and make Keagan's breakfast. I put the tea kettle on for my morning tea, as I cleaned and cooked I watched Keagan getting up in down in his playpen. His hand movement would suggest that he was playing with someone. He laughed and grinned as he jumped up and down, sometimes holding on to the railing of the playpen to keep himself from falling over in his laughter.

When I finished cooking, I picked him up and sat him in his high chair. I took my tea over with me to feed him. I sat down and help him eat with the spoon, I fed him oatmeal and chopped bananas he always loved it. He took some in his little hand and tried to give me some. I shook my head, "no thank you, baby, Mommy's full," I tell him scooping more in the spoon and feeding it to him. He put his hand up toward the sky as if he was offering food to someone else.

He looked happy to offer, I turned his little head around. "Keagan, you have to eat okay," I told him as I spooned him some of his food. He ate looking all around sometimes smiling and laughing as I pretended to be an airplane bringing him food into the hanger which would be his little mouth. We finished up and I dressed him. We set off to go to the hospital to visit daddy today. I wanted to tell him about our trip and to ask him about the table in his storage shed in the backyard. Where did it come from? I wondered.

I drove to the hospital slowly with all that I wanted to tell daddy on my mind. I looked into the review window watching Keagan, he looked around scanning out of the window, he looked so happy all the time, I couldn't wait for daddy to see him. When we arrived at the hospital, it was so busy. As we got closer to daddies room, I couldn't help but feel a little scared of what I might find with all the nurses and doctors running around looking in a panic. As I turned the corner to get to daddy's room with Keagan gripped tightly to my hip I looked over at the wall Keagan was smiling and waving hi.

I glanced over, and there was daddy standing holding on to the rail of the wall with the assistant of a nurse on the other side of him holding him steady. I smiled, "oh my goodness daddy, you're up and running today aren't you," I said going toward him. Daddy looked over at me. "Hey Karis, daddy's feeling much better," he said to me. "See baby, I'm walking now." "I see daddy, good job." I cannot describe what I was feeling in that moment, hearing daddy speak and watching him walking, my heart felt heavy with happiness.

My daddy can speak, he's going to be all right, I thought. I hugged daddy, I couldn't even ask the questions or tell him about my trip. I was feeling excited to do whatever it took to get daddy well, and from that day on I was at the hospital every day from 8am until it was time to pick up the twins from school. I'd bring Keagan in his stroller and I'd make daddy walk him around the hospital. I stand behind him as he pushed Keagan around the hospital. He'd get tired at times and we'd stop for a break but most of the time we'd walk right through it.

Every day after the walk he'd meet with the occupational therapist. She made daddy do a lot of speech therapy, it helped a lot he was able to talk a little better every day. Daddy was so strong he never complained and always thanked all who helped him. I tried to be there as much as I could. Michael would come by to check on us every now and then. I would have lunch with daddy. Unable to swallow well, daddy still had a feeding tube in his stomach.

They had a track in his throat for a long time and wanted to make sure he was able to swallow without choking before taking it out. It would frustrate daddy to smell food or watch me eat so I would just skip lunch at times. I'd make daddy feed Keagan which would help him develop strength in his arms again. I would eat when I got home, which was after I picked up the twins from school. Michael would get mad at me at times telling me that I was losing to much weight and it was un healthy to go all day without eating. I didn't go all day without eating but I did eat later in the day.

When I made it home during the day Michael would have a plate of food sitting out waiting for me. I'd sit there and eat while feeding Keagan but at times I didn't feel hungry at all. When Michael wasn't looking I would throw out the food. Michael was so fit his body was so well proportioned with every muscle still intact. He worked out during the day and ran and walked a lot, weight lifting was a must for him. He always talked about staying in shape. I would walk with him, but running was still tough. It felt as if I was straining the calf muscle on my left leg too much.

So I'd always pass when it came to running although I imagined myself running beside him all the time, running fast enough to keep up and feeling the cold air against my face as we ran closer together and laughed about things we saw, I wished so hard sometimes to just be able to do some simple things like squat down bending my knees and running with Michael. The day for daddy to leave the hospital was coming soon. I wanted to take him home with me to take care of him but I heard through Martha that they had gotten together a week ago and discussed where daddy was going.

She said that Rose and Daisy had decided that he would be living with Richard for a while, and Rose would be the one handling all of his affairs. I was never invited to these family meetings. I would always hear what went on through Martha, although I was at daddy's taking care of the garden. Richard never talks to me about family meetings. He'd ask me from time to time had I heard what was going to happen with daddy, and I'd shake my head, no. Not wanting to give up my source, it made me feel like an outsider, but I could deal with it, I guess.

I would still be happy to see daddy come home, and nothing would keep me from going coming to see him at home. I thought as I walked along side Michael. "What are you thinking about, baby?" Michael asked. "Oh nothing, I just wonder sometimes, what's it like not having any family?" I asked him. "I do have a family; I have you and the children. You're my family, and of course, Jesus is my all. If I didn't have anything in this life, I'd have him, his comfort, and his confidence. In him I have it all," Michael said smiling. "Do you believe me?" He asked.

"Oh, yes, I believe you, I think that the lord is the key to me being here, I don't ever think that things are impossible," I tell him. "See sometimes people forget things, they forget the blessings around them." There is a constant blessing in everything, and the lord is there," Michael was so serious. We made it back to the house from the run and I was so tired I almost feel into the door. Michael grabbed me by the waist side and helped me to the floor. We laid down on the floor together, just looking up breathing with our arms spread upward.

"Long walks always did this to me; I was sweaty and felt hot all over. Michael looked over at me smiling. "This is why you have to stay in shape," he said jumping up to his feet standing over me looking down. He scooped me up from the floor with both his arms and carried me upstairs. "You need a hot one," he said walking me up fast. I rested my head on his chest. "I need one too, you know what that means?" He said blinking his eyes in a fast motion. "We getting naked together," he laughed as he placed me on the bathroom counter and ran the water. He helped me undress as I undressed him.

Michael placed me in the shower then got in too. We showered and washed each other and talked about what we were going to cook. I wanted spinach mushrooms with cream cheese and pasta. He wanted steak and potatoes with cauliflower. "We have to toss for it," Michael said. "I'll toss up a box of cereal, and you choose what side you want it to fall on if it falls on that side you win. If it doesn't then, I win and steak it will be." He said while I soaped up his back.

We finished, put our clothes on and headed downstairs after looking in on the kids. I was happy to see that the twins were napping comfortable next to one another and Keagan was standing in his playpen making noises, so I grabbed him and took him with us downstairs. I put Keagan into his high chair and Michael, and I proceeded to the kitchen. Michael grabbed the cereal box and flipped it up and down. "So you ready?" He asked swinging the box back and forth in front of me. "I sure am, let's go," I tell him grabbing at the box.

"I think I should toss it, Michael, you might cheat" "Really, me a cheater? Never," he said tossing the box up in the air. "Here we go!" It flipped up into the air spinning, we watched as it came flying down. We both looked intensely hoping we'd get what we want out of it. When it dropped you could hear the cereal shaking, it was rice crispy cereal. I closed my eyes hoping it would drop on the side I wanted before it dropped Michael yelled. "The front of the box it's mine," I opened my eyes, and sure enough it was the front of the box, Michael wins.

"Ugh, you win I guess we'll have steak and potatoes." I go to the refrigerator and get everything we need to cook. Michael grabbed me by the waist, "Baby, we can have whatever you want really you don't have to eat steak and potatoes if you don't want to I can cook your pasta too," he said holding on to me close. "No, you won fair and square," I tell Michael. He liked his steaks grilled and seasoned well. We went to the patio to grill them it didn't take to long and the patio had beautiful scenery, Michael even put the potatoes on the grill. We sat out there and waited for the steaks to finish.

Michael turned them over and over, the smell was so sweet in the air with the smoke from the grill. I went in with the plate he handed me and put them into a pan on the stove and we cooked them a little more just to make them as tender as we could for the children. When we were done we sat the children down to eat. "Well, we really need to go talk to the travel agent about our trip tomorrow. I'm free after work I can meet you there, its downtown," Michael said eating his steak.

I made a salad on the side I loved tomato and cucumber salad with black pepper. "Yes, after I come from daddy's they're supposed to be taking him home tomorrow. I'd like to be there when he gets home"

I tell him. "Sure, do you know what time they'll be releasing him?" he asked. "You know, I don't, and I should probably call Martha tonight to ask her." I say. "That's a good idea, or I can find out tonight at work." Michael said. "Yes, you can, could you?" I said smiling.

"Hey, I'm going in late, and I'd like to go in calm tonight," he winked his eye at me. "What do you mean? Aren't you calm?" I said with a smile. "Always, but I need you to calm me, all the way down," he said. We talked in code around the children. Michael wanted to make love to me before work. It was becoming a tradition, he said he felt better all day; it gave him something to smile about all night. We put the children to bed late that night because they had taken a long nap during the day. After two stories and running around with Michael in the house they were ready to sleep.

I rocked Keagan to sleep while Michael tucked the twins in and we met in the hallway. "Hello beautiful," Michael said creeping up behind. "I gotcha," he said in a whisper, as he carried me into the room. "I don't have a lot of time baby so forgive me if I go to fast for you." Michael said pulling my clothes off and kissed me all over, he squeezed my thighs as he head fell on my stomach kissing me there felt so good. "I love you," he said. He made love to me quickly, his sweat covered my body as he finished laying his head on my chest and rolling over. "Karis, I love you," he said getting up going to the bathroom.

He washed off dressed up quickly and grabbed his bag. "I will see you later, Karis," he said leaning over and kissed my face all over. "I love you like I love steak," he said. I laughed, "get out of here Michael," I say as he pinched my behind and walked out winking at me. I smiled falling off to sleep only thinking of him. I loved him so much. I thought lying there wrapped in the bed sheet. I dreamed that night of James at my door asking about the twins. Someone had told him that I had the twins and he wanted to see them, he asked was it possible that they were his. I woke up from the dream shutting the door in his face and got up to check on the twins.

That was a nightmare I thought, I never want to see James again. I rubbed Kristopher's back and Kristine's hair. The twins are happy. I didn't want James to know anything. I walked over to the window, it was cracked open just a little so, I closed it and looked out through the curtains. I saw a man standing outside near the parked cars on the sidewalk. It was cold out and a little drizzle. I wiped the window with the edge of the sheet I was wearing trying to look closer. The man was staring up at the window. I closed the curtains. I went downstairs to check all the locks around the house; I went to the back first, then to the front.

I was checking the windows when I heard a knock on the door. The knock was soft at first then really loud. I didn't say a word I walked over to the door and peeked out of the window barely looking out. I didn't see anyone but the knocking was getting louder. I walked back upstairs ignoring the knocking. I called Michael at work. Michael answered the phone immediately. "Baby, what's wrong?" He asked. "There is someone at the door, and I can't see them. But there knocking. I think its James." I said. "James, the twin's father, James" He asked.

"Yes, I think it's him." "Why do you think it's him, baby? Just stay calm baby," Michael said. "Don't go to the door baby, Let them knock. I will see you after work, everything is locked up so you'll be fine I turned the alarm on also so don't worry." He said. "I love you, baby, get some rest I'll see you in the morning." I hung up and lay down on the bed. The knock became soft and it stopped after a while. I fell off to sleep when it stopped.

When I woke the next morning, the twins were in bed with me, and Keagan was lying next to the bed on the floor. I got up quickly and put on a T-shirt and jogging pants. I picked Keagan up from the floor. "Hey you, How'd you get down there, He was still sleeping, laying on my shoulder. I laid him on the bed next to the twins. I laid back on the bed with the children, and we slept a little more until the sun came up. "Mommy, Mommy," Kristopher said tugging on my shirt. "Yes, Kristopher, what's wrong?" I asked. "I'm hungry, mommy," "Okay, okay Kristopher, I'm up," I said climbing over Keagan and Kristine to get out of bed.

I went into the bathroom to use it. I sat on the toilet and Kristopher stood at the door staring at me. "What's wrong?" I asked him yawning. "I'm hungry, I want pancakes for breakfast, mommy," he said. "Okay, after you brush your teeth and wash your face, then we can go make pancakes. I brushed my teeth and washed my face as Kristopher stood next to me brushing his teeth also, we finished and went downstairs. Kristopher turned on the television while I went to make breakfast. I prepared enough for all of them, Keagan was able to have pancakes these days chopped in small pieces, with a little syrup on it, he'd eat it all I'd give him three pieces.

When I was done I went to the front door to check for the paper. I looked out of the window. There was no paper, but a note on the doormat folded just sitting there. I turned the alarm off and opened the door and took up the note. "Hello Karis, I know you don't want to see me, but I have to talk to you, I have to see you. I'm only in town for a while, and we need to talk. I'll be at my grandmother's house cleaning it up, please come over to talk to me. Thank you, James," I crumbled the letter up and threw it back onto the mat.

"Oh, no James is here, my dream was true, he's coming to see the twins. I closed the door and turned on the alarm. I leaned back on the door and envisioned him raping me in that bathroom all over again.

I went into the kitchen and cleaned up. I didn't know whether or not I should even go out today. I was so scared now, Mrs. Cottons house is right next to daddy's and I would see James if I went over there. I needed to tell Michael that he was in town. I went back to the bedroom to change Keagan, he was covered in syrup.

He'd put all in his hair, I walked upstairs slowly looking back at the window through the glass door. There James standing at the end of the doorway looking through the glass. I turned and walked upstairs faster. We made it upstairs and I yelled for the twins to come up after me. "Kristopher! Kristine! Come now!" I yelled in a stern voice. They always came quickly when I used my firm angry voice. I peeked down at them as I heard them trampling up the stairs as fast as their little legs could carry them. "Yes, mommy," they both said with a question in their eyes. "I want you two to help me clean your rooms," I tell them as I place Keagan onto the bed to undress him.

"Okay mommy, no problem, Kristopher says," running down the hall. "Mommy, are you mad?" questioned Kristine. "Oh, mommies not mad, I'm just a little tired Kristine, don't worry" I said, rubbing my hand against her little face I stood there watching them scatter around picking up their toys and quickly putting them away. How beautiful they both were two sweet children, I wondered if he'd left the front porch already, I dared to go and check; I put Keagan in the tub and sat on the edge. He smiled and laughed playing around with his colored ducks. I washed his hair and washed him up after a while I'll remove him from the tub I thought as Kristopher walked into the bathroom.

"Mommy, can I go back downstairs to play?" He asked. I washed Keagan up once more and took him from the tub wrapped in a towel. "Mommy, can I go back downstairs?" He asked again, I walked around him and into the bedroom. I didn't want the twins to go downstairs without me in fear of them looking through the glass door, seeing James. They didn't know him and I never want them to know him. Kristopher followed me around the room as I lotion Keagan and put powder on him before the diaper.

Kristopher stood beside the bed staring at me begging. "Mommy, mommy, please answer me, can I please go downstairs?" "Kristopher, please give me a moment, and we can go together, where's your sister?" I asked him. "She's sitting in the room," he said pointing toward the door. I became suspicious not able to hear Kristine moving around, I yelled out to her, "Kristine! Kristine! Honey, come here," I said. "Yes mommy," she called back my heart skipped a beat just thinking about her not answering. I took Kristopher and Keagan, and we meet her at the doorway.

"Okay kiddos, let's go watch our shows and clean downstairs," I said smiling at them. They followed me downstairs; I carried Keagan on my hip. As we reached the bottom stair the doorbell rang. "I'll get it, mommy," Kristopher yelled out. "No! No! You won't," I said with a firm voice. "You two go in the den and sit." I said pointing toward the den. I watched as they walked to the den, "I'll be with you in a second," I yell out to the door. I quickly walked Keagan into the den to place him in the playpen. I rushed back to the door. I quickly cracked it and peeked out. "Can I help you?" I asked. "Yes, you can, it's me Karis, James," he said.

I act as if I wasn't afraid or wondering why he was there I abruptly blurt out, "it's not a good time James, I will meet you at your grandma's okay." I shut the door and walked into the den. "Hey kiddos, how's the show? They both looked at me and smiled. "It's funny mommy, come watch," Kristopher said. "I'm going to clean up right now and then I'll come over and watch with you guys okay," I tell him picking things up in the kitchen. Michael should be home on time tonight I just going to go meet with him at daddy's house. I will see what he wants I thought as I cleaned. I won't talk too much about anything just listen and pray.

God please don't let him ask about the twins. I don't want to lie to him but I will never allow him to be a part of their lives. I thought watching them as I cleaned. When Michael returned home I quickly took my coat from the chair and walked toward the door as he walked in. "Where are you going?" He asked. "I have to check on daddy," I tell him he comes toward me and kisses me on the lips. "Okay, dinners in the oven and Keagan may need to be changed," I said on my way out of the door.

"Bye mommy," the twins yelled out waving their hands. "I'll be back soon, promise," I said shutting the door. I rushed to my car. "I just want this part of my life over with, I want this door to be closed, God, please help me to close it, please. I thought as I turned the key to start the car. I drove to daddy's as fast as I could. My confidence scared even me; I couldn't wait to finally shut this door on James. Let him know that I am no longer in fear of him and I will never forget what he's done to me nor will I ever trust him again. I arrived to find him standing in front of Mrs. Cotton's house with a bag in his hand.

I paused as I parked in daddy's driveway. My stomach dropped as I thought about what he was going to say. He smiled as I parked the car watching me, waiting for me to get out. He walked up to the car door; I waved my hand to him. I, in no way wanted him to believe that I would fall for his charm without question. I rolled the window down. "Do you mind, I would like to park and run in to say hello to my dad," I tell him rolling the window back up. I get out. "I'll be with you in a second." "Okay I'll be waiting over there okay," he said walking away with his head down as if I hurt his feelings.

I walked over to the house to see if daddy was up I knew he would be. He was sitting in a wheelchair next to the door. "Hi daddy," I said. I hugged him tight. "Hey baby," he said holding my hand, I kissed his cheek. "Daddy, I'm going to be next door talking to James, if I don't return to say goodbye to you, tell Richard to come over and get me, please." I walked out of the screen door slowly; I wasn't looking forward to it anymore. I couldn't feel the confidence anymore; I walked slowly toward Mrs. Cottons house.

I stood at the end of her driveway. I could see James threw the screen door. He stood there for a while staring out. "If you don't come out here, I'm leaving," I yelled out. He came out quickly. "Hi Karis," he said standing in front of me. "I know that I can't get a hug, so I'll get right to it. I just wanted you to know that I know your secret," he said putting his hands behind his back. Oh no, I thought. Here it comes. I started to walk away. "I know that you will never forgive me, would you?" He asked. I shook my head no. I could feel my stomach getting heavier and heavier.

"No, James, I will, I have to, and I'm not going to keep all that inside me. Do you know what you that would have done to me?" I said with my finger pointing to me. I was furious at him and suddenly it came back, Thank you God I thought. I looked James straight into his eyes and with a deep breath I expressed to him what I felt. "James, you have taken something away from the both of us, I trusted you, James, I trusted you cared for me the way I did for you as a good friend, and you snatched it all away in one ugly unforgettable moment. Why, James?" I said looking at him as he held his chin to his neck.

"Karis, I'm so sorry! Please, please forgive me?" He asked. "I can't tell you what I wouldn't give to take it back. Karis, I know you think that I'm some animal, but I'm not, I loved you, I couldn't control myself that night. I don't know what came over me, I wanted you so bad." he explained. "James you could have never loved me hurting me the way you did. I forgive you, I will never forget, I can't ever forget. You believe me when I say, James I'm just going to pray for you and thank you so much for asking me to forgive you, thank you for having the courage to admit that you did something wrong."

"I know that it took a lot to do that. I hugged James as he stood still in front of me with his hands behind his back and tears flowing from his eyes. "I forgave you a long time ago," I whispered into his ears as I hugged him tightly. "Take care of yourself," I say as I walked away from him. I walked over to daddy's with the biggest smile on my face. "Thank you, God," I said. Thank you for the strength. Daddy was right at the screen door in the chair as if he'd been waiting for me. "Hey sweetheart, you okay?" daddy asked. His speech was partially slurred, but I understood him by listening closely. "I'm okay, daddy, I feel good," I said grabbing the back of that chair. I pushed daddy's chair toward the back.

"Do you need anything, daddy?" I asked. "Water Karis, get me a glass of water please," I pushed daddy into the kitchen and got his water. Richard had the kitchen nice and clean as always. "Daddy, have you seen the garden since you been home?" I asked him. He shook his head no. "Oh, good daddy I haven't seen it in a while either, let's go." I felt so good in that moment. I gave James what he wanted I made him feel good about moving on. I made him feel as if I could leave it alone no hard feelings, I let it go. When I walked away, it felt so good, I thought as daddy, and I made it to the garden.

"Well, daddy we haven't been out watering, but look who didn't mind," I said picking up a carrot from the dirt. It was all chewed up with just the stems to prove someone liked it. Daddy smiled. "Oh, Richard can take care of everything else, but he won't water this garden to save his life," daddy said softly. I smiled at daddy and grabbed the hose. I placed it in daddy's hand and while he watered and I would hoe; removing all the weeds and eaten veggies from the dirt. I looked over the roses we planted for Tara they looked dry also so I turned daddy to water them.

I smiled at daddy he was working progress, he was happy I could tell he needed the fresh air. He was so happy just sitting in that chair watering the roses and veggies as I used the hoe to clear the way for new ones to grow. I stayed out with daddy until the sun went down. I took him inside and cleaned him up and helping him go to the toilet and made a liquid drink, while we waited for Richard we watched the news. When Richard showed up daddy was ready to lay down. "Hello Karis, how are you?" He asked me throwing his things to the floor as he walked in.

"Hello Richard," I replied. "How are you?" "I'm good, really good," he said. "Well I'm going to go now," I said standing over daddy's chair. "Richard, I will see you soon," I said blowing him a kiss. I walked out of the door to go to my car. I see James across the street walking out with his bags. I looked over long enough for him to catch me looking. I put my head down as I approached my car door and got in, I start up the car and drove off, taking one more glance at James, I continue on to the house to be with Michael and the kids.

This was a good day I thought, and God does really watch over me. When I arrived at the house, it was dark as I drove up until the security lights came on when I parked. I could see from the bedroom window from the doorway, Michael was still up. The house was quiet I went to the kitchen to grab me a glass of water before heading off to bed. Man, this was a good day. Michael has the kids all sleeping. Wow, I thought it just keeps getting better as I took my glass to my lips I was startled by Michael. I dropped my glass to the ground.

"Hey, why so jumpy" He said turning the light from dim to bright. "Look at the mess you made, good thing the glass fell to the carpet, or it would have awakened the kids," he said bending down to pick up the glass. "So, is there something you'd like to share with me?" Michael asked. "Oh yes, daddy's getting a little better, I took him out to the garden today he's really showing progress, you should visit him soon," I added. As 1 walk away from him making my way upstairs, he steps in front of me.

"Karis, why didn't you tell me about James?" I was stunned, oh no, "what do you mean?" I asked. In shock that he even knew about James visiting. "Yes, I saw James today at daddy's house, he was over his grandmothers, and I'm okay." "Karis, did you see him or did he come by?" He asked as he pulled the note from his robe pocket. "Baby, what's wrong with you? Why are you lying to me? Couldn't you tell me what was going on? What did he want from you? Does he know about the children?" He asked question after question. "Michael, I'm sorry, I didn't want to speak of James in front of the children," I told him.

"I was really shocked that he came by myself." "Did he want the children? Does he want to see them?" he asked. "No, he doesn't know, Michael I will never tell him about the children. I will not ever allow him to know them," I say to him hold his hand and removing the note. "I just had to tie up loose ends I wanted to close that door Michael that's all," I tried to assure Michael as he walked ahead of me towards the stairs. "Karis, I don't want us to have any secrets, and if you should want to tie loose ends with someone, please let me know before you go to do it so that I can at least go with you, especially when it's someone like James." He said sternly.

We went up to bed; I could tell that Michael was furious at me. He didn't come into the bathroom with me, he didn't joke around. He just sat in the bed with his glasses on and his book to his face as if I wasn't there. I washed up and put on my pajamas, I stood in front of the bed to try and get his attention, but he didn't even look up. I went to look in on the kids before I lay down. When I returned Michael was under the covers with his back turned away from me as I walked over to my side of the bed I heard him sigh. I got in bed and turned to him.

"Michael, I love you," I tell him. Please, don't be mad at me," I say holding him from behind. "I love you so much, and I'm sorry if I made you feel bad, please Michael, hold me." He turned to me and kissed my forehead. "Karis, I love you too, just let me in on things, don't shut me out please," he said pulling me close to him. He held on to me for a while before making love to me, I looked up at him, "I love you, Michael, and I won't ever leave you out again." I say to him. We made love until we were both tired.

When we were finished Michael wrapped me up with him in a sheet, falling to sleep came easy that night; we fell off to sleep talking about our trip, we would be leaving in one week. "This would be something great," Michael assured me. "Better than us," he said laughing and squeezing every inch of me tighter. I looked out at the moon shining through the window and fell off to sleep thinking about the blessings God gave me just in that one day. Thank you,

Off To Africa

The day finally arrived; we have been packing all week. Michael put in for his vacation, and we made to the airport on time, thanks to the airport shuttle. I checked everything at the door, passports, and bottles for Keagan, Kristine's favorite dolls, and Kristopher's favorite cars. Packing the children was a lot of work. We made it just in time to the airport the following day. Michael was so excited to be going back to Africa. We checked in quickly and waited for our flight to board in the lobby.

We sat in the area where the kids could play a little and eat our flight boards in an hour. We would have two stops, and it was to be a 24hour flight to Johannesburg South Africa. One stop in New York and another in England, We were to arrive in South Africa and picked up by Michaels co-workers and friends from there to the hotel. I was exhausted already with the children running all around the airport. Michael helped them while we waited. I brought some books in case they wouldn't sleep on the plane.

Keagan looked all over the airport at the people and out of the windows smiling and playing the whole time. It was finally time to board we were able to board first with the children. I took Keagan, and Michael walked Kristopher and Kristine by the hand. They never gave him any trouble at all, he would just look at them, and they would behave. It made me jealous at times because I would have to keep asking them over and over again to do what I wanted. We boarded the plane Michael, and I sat in separate seats, him with the twins and me with Keagan in his car seat. I'm glad he doesn't have to sit in it the whole time.

He was already very fussy. I took out his cup and gave it to him as the plane took off. We were up for a long ride. "Michael, do you think we can switch places at times?" I asked as we settled in the air. "Sure baby, just let me know when." Michael was close to the restroom, and I had to take Keagan in from time to time to change him. There was a woman in the seat next to me. She smiled most pleasantly, but I could tell she wasn't too happy about this long flight sitting next to a small child and a set of twins. I smiled back at her as a peace offering.

"It won't be a problem," she said as she saw that I was worried about making her flight a miserable one. "Your fine ma'am," she was really helpful, she helped me move things around, and she made Keagan laugh throughout the whole flight. After eight long hours of none stop flying, we finally touch down in New York. "Wow," I said as we flew in it was a beautiful sight from where we were. All of the lights and signs shined bright. The kids were so amazed. "Mommy! Daddy!" They yelled out. "Do you see! Do you see!"

They pointed and tripped over Michael trying to look closely as we touched down. The woman sitting next to me began to help me get Keagan altogether. She reached down and picked up all of the toys he dropped during the trip. "Is there anything else I can help you with?" She asked. "By the way, my name is Amy, it was a pleasure riding next to you," she said standing and reaching up to grab her bag from the overhead compartment. "Thank you, Amy, I am Karis, and this is Keagan," we smiled at one another.

"I really appreciated that you were a great help." I followed her as we were escorted by the stewardess to the exits. Michael was ahead of me walking with the twins holding their hands. He walked quickly to the counter while I waited with Keagan in the seating area. I gave him his cup to drink from and a small bag full of cheerio's. He sat quietly and ate them watching his daddy from afar. Michael came walking toward me with the children and two very tall African men. "Karis these men will be helping us with our luggage, they are going to be driving us to our little place.

"Hello," I say to them grabbing Kegan from the chair standing to shake their hands. Michael took the twins by the hand, and the two men took our luggage and escorted us to a small van in front of the airport. They placed our luggage inside the back and helped us into the van; soon we were on our way to our little hut in the country. It was dark, and there were dirt roads even in the darkness I could see the torn and broken down shacks we passed the sky was lit by the moon, I began to worry as we rode alongside the moonlit skies.

I watched Michael smiling as we rode through the country. He held on to the rail on the side door of the van. I began to pray as I could feel the sadness around me. Lord, please watch over my family as we take this journey into unknown territory. Cover us, Lord, with your protection on love and strength. In Jesus name I pray. I looked up into the skies; it was beautiful light thank you, Lord. Michael reached back and grabbed my hand, to reassure me that things would be okay. I looked up again, thank you, Lord I thought to myself. The men took us around every curve there was it seemed, like a very long ride.

When we finally made to our hut all of the children were sleeping the men got out and took them inside; with Michael following them holding Keagan in his arms. I waited inside the van until they came back out. The men grabbed the luggage and carried them inside. I followed them making sure I didn't leave anything behind I carried my purse in my arms and Keagan's bag of goodies. When I got inside there was Michaels friends waiting to welcome us, they had food prepared for us and the hut was beautiful full of colored paintings and wooden statues just like I liked.

I was greeted by everyone in the room with a hug and a kiss on the cheek. A woman was sitting on the sofa next to Keagan, he was sleeping on a blanket that someone had made for him. She quickly stood up and greeted me with a hug, "Hello," she said "My name is Cheron. She was so tall I looked up at her. "Nice to meet you, Cheron" I said hugging her back. "I will be taking care of the children while you're here," she said with a smile. She was very beautiful she smelled of flowers.

Her hair was wrapped in an orange scarf she was wearing a green colored top and a yellow skirt. She took my hand and escorted me around giving me a tour of the house. "Do you like it?" She asked. When she spoke her voice took your breath away she had the loveliest accent I'd ever heard it was an African accent with a hint of French. She spoke softly as if she was trying to whisper. She had the prettiest eyes, and her skin was a honey brown. "I love it Cheron," I told her as we walked back into the front room where everyone was sharing food and talking.

I don't think I'd ever seen Michael this happy ever. I watched him talking to his friends. Telling them about all the things he came there to do. He lit up just talking about it. As the room grew empty, I could hear the sounds of the African night. Michael walked everyone out to their cars, with every goodbye he'd look back at me. I started to put the children to bed one by one. They were so tired they didn't wake up as I laid them in their beds undressing them and covering them. I kissed them goodnight and walked back into the front room to help Michael clean.

He grabbed me by the waist side and began to dance with me swaying my hips with his. With my back turned to him he kissed my neck. "Are you happy baby?" He asked. It struck me just then, I didn't know what to feel about this trip at that moment. I looked up at him, "I am if you are, sweetheart." He grabbed my hands with a spin I was staring him in the eyes. "Baby, I know that this isn't our way of living, but I promise you this is the best trip we will ever take, this is where our joy is, the people here need us, they need our prayers, love, and strength, you watch, you'll thank me later," he said kissing me softly on the lips.

He held on to me swaying my body along with his, we danced and held on to one another closely looking into the African night sky. Michael and I slept underneath the African skies anticipating the next day as if it was Christmas. We were awakened the next day by the sound of the children playing around the hut. Cheron was already inside the kitchen cooking and talking to the children they laughed at her as she sang a silly song to them about monkeys and bananas. They were already comfortable with her. Michael and I both wrapped up in our robes and went to the restroom.

He brushed as I washed my face and began to brush my teeth alongside him. The bathroom was tiny we shared a sink and the shower; we quickly threw on the first pair of clothing we found on the pile of our suitcases and went out to the front room. We greeted Cheron with a hug. "Good Morning," she said "Sit down, sit down, here you go," she said quickly placing two plates in front of us. I looked at Michael and down again at my plate, I am not really big on eating things I hadn't tried before, Michael knows this. It looked like some rice cereal and bananas cooked bananas. I reached for the juice and sipped it.

It seemed to be a mango and orange juice drink it was very good. I watched the children play, they were so happy. "I will unpack you," Cheron explained as she put away the dishes. She cleaned the kitchen and cooked all at the same time. I wondered at that moment, what was I going to do with myself. She's here doing almost everything I'm used to doing on my own at home. I looked at Michael. "Michael, what am I going to be doing while she's doing all of the chores around here?" I asked.

"You won't be here you're going to be coming along with me," he said drinking his juice, getting up from the table. I followed him into the room. "You feel comfortable leaving her with the children right now?" I asked. "I do," he said smiling back at me. "I don't think that would be a good Idea just yet," I tell him. "We just arrived here, and they will be afraid if we just leave them alone with them," I say as my thoughts ran wild. I thought about Mr. Sims, and what he told me about Keagan, I have to watch and protect him.

"You don't have to worry about him here," Michael said getting his bag together. "He'll be fine with Cheron she's very good with children, look out there and watch her for a while. She used to teach at the school in the village until the refuges stormed through killing the people and burning down there homes and schools. Now she just helps at the orphanages in Sudan. She goes all around to different orphanages helping the children. We are very fortunate to have her," he tells me.

I watched her from the bedroom door with Keagan; she was twirling him around singing to him, he laughed and smiled the whole time. I trusted Michael's judgment. However, I wasn't ready to leave them alone with her, I wanted to stay and watch her for a day or two. "Michael, I think I will stay here today, just to make sure that the kids will be okay," I said. Michael looked at me crossed. "Really, Karis, the children will be fine, this mission is ours, and I need you to come with me today and every day. That is the purpose of a housemaid, no worries," he stood in front of me staring me in the face as I stared out into the front room watching Cheron with the children.

"Okay," I said, "I'll go Michael, but don't get upset when all I talk about is the children." He looked at me with a smile and took me by the hand. "I love you, Karis, you, know that I would never put the children in harm's way." He kissed me softly pulling me into the front room. "We are going to be leaving Cheron; the children have everything they need in those bags in there." He pointed towards our room. "I will get everything put away, and the children will be fine," she said in her sweet accent. We were greeted at the door by the same two men who picked us up from the airport. "Hello," they said.

"We come for Dr. Lawson," they said. "Here we are," Michael said. We followed them to the little van outside it was hot I started to regret my choice of clothing. Michael reached into the backseat of the van and grabbed me a big straw hat. "Here baby, you're going to need this, I promise," he said smiling. "Zubeka and Nasdia, I would like to introduce you to my beautiful wife, Karis," he said. "Hello, Mrs. Karis, very nice to meet you," they both said in a solid tone voice. They both have very strong African accents. The roads were really rocky the little van seemed to be shaking and jumping with every turn.

We made it to the village as we pulled into the area I started to get sick, my stomach was in knots. I bent over leaning my head into my lap to catch my breath. Michael grabbed me by the hand. "Baby, are you okay?" He asked me holding my hair back to look at my face. I shook my head yes. "No, you're not Karis, your face is beet red," he said rambling through his bag to get a cold pack for my face. "It will be alright Karis," he took me by the hand and led me into the small village. It was somber, you could hear children crying from afar and singing also.

I looked up at Michael as we were led through the village by Zubeka. He pointed out to us the areas where our help was needed most. Michael held my hand so tight; it was so hot our hands sweated as we walked toward a small shack in the village. A woman came up to us crying holding a small sick child in her arms I couldn't tell whether or not it was a boy or a girl it was covered up to its neck with what looked like an old dirty shirt. The crowd grew larger with crying women and children as we walked closer to the hut people were laying everywhere in the dirt reaching out for help.

I prayed as my pain grew intensely stronger than usual. I let go of Michaels' hand, and we walked side by side together as the people surrounding us seemed to have been waiting for us to help. Michael went in first, and I followed with the two men behind us, they were to interpret the language for us. Michael didn't need any help he seemed to understand them and could speak a little bit of their language as he'd spent several months there before. I watched as he went from patient to patient to help it seemed this was a small place where they would come when ill. I prayed as Michael went from one bed to another.

Some of their spirits just wanted peace from the pain. I held their hands and rubbed their heads as Michael administered shots and touched them where it hurt. A lot of them suffered from constant hunger the babies were tiny; some of them were well over the age of two and looked like tiny infants. I held them and prayed for them. They smiled at me with a look of purity and fear in their eyes. After a while, it hit me seeing these poor children suffering.

I stepped out of the hut to catch my breath. There was a tree in the middle of the village I walked over to it and held on the one branch on it. I fell to my knees in grave pain, I prayed and cried. What I felt there was so intensely strong, and it wouldn't go away. I held my stomach with my head to the ground with tears streaming from my face. I prayed to the Lord reaching out for his guidance. Lord, in the name of Jesus why? I questioned as I was overwhelmed with sadness in my heart for the people in this village. I stayed on my knees for a while praying.

It started to get a little quiet to me; I felt a cool breeze come over me. I sat up straight and looked at the tree and there it was, that feeling of freedom from this fear and pain I carried in my heart. I felt better already asking the Lord to protect me and guide me through this keep me stable on this journey. I stood up and went back into the hut where Michael was. He was still going from bedside to bedside. The people kissed Michaels hand and thanked him. You could feel their spirits lighting up. He sat next to the children on the floor and checked them out explaining as he touched them that they needed medicine for the pain.

He gave them drops, and shots. I held their hands and prayed; I no longer felt pain and was able to smile with them. "Everything will be fine," I said rubbing their hands as Michael worked on them. Soon the women in the hut who were helpers and nurses began to sing the most beautiful song I'd ever heard. It was just beautiful; giving Michael the highest praise of gratefulness they formed a circle around him and danced. It was just beautiful to watch the people looking out at this praise and as ill as they where they tried to clap and whispered the song as they sang to Michael.

When they were done we were escorted to another hut where there was more sick children and women, there was only one hut full of men. It was hidden in the path of the village where the trees were, and you could smell it as you approached the hut. The most horrid smell you could imagine came from that direction. Michael gave me a mask from his bag to cover my nose and mouth the two helpers took one too. We walked up to the hut, and I could hear moaning as if they were in severe pain.

"Karis, these men are very ill and will be dying soon. They all have contracted HIV years, even months ago, and it has been spread throughout the village by them. Their spirits are weak, they don't have much time to live," Michael said walking me in holding my hand tight. "I want you to keep that on your face at all times in here, the air is awful. It's hot, so the germs and bacteria in here are festering and will make you sick just from the smell."

I walked behind him looking around it was dim, and men were lying on small cots, the women around them were either family or the nursemaids who took care of them. They didn't have a lot of supplies to work with so they used whatever they could it seemed. As we approached the first bed in the hut, I started to feel nauseous as we got closer, the man was expiring at that moment his spirit was free of pain. I walked over to him as his eyes rolled back and held his hand. I prayed for his spirit as I felt him around me. I wanted to know what this feeling of relief from constant suffering felt like, so I took it in with my head on his hand I prayed, and the Lord gave me confirmation of the miracle of relief.

The feeling of happiness was all around me, even in my soul I felt so happy that I smiled. It felt like I was being tickled, nothing but happy thoughts. I could see this man as I sat there with my head to his hand smiling and walking down a green path. I looked up knowing his suffering was over. Michael looked over at me and smiled. "That's it, sweetheart, take it in, it's beautiful isn't it?" He asked me as he took the vitals of the man lying on the cot by the door. I shook my head yes. "It's so good Karis, that's the feeling you need to feel, there is nothing much to do here, they are too ill to recover I can only alleviate their pain.

I wish I could do more," Michael said determined to help them all, but he was just one man. We left the village as the night grew closer, the sun started to set as we drove off. Michael put his arm around me as we rode off. "You did good baby, every day you'll get even better I promise," he said putting his head on my shoulder after kissing my cheek. When we made it back to our hut, I went straight to the bathroom to run water for Michael and me to shower. We couldn't touch the children yet until we were cleaned up.

The children were sitting quietly with Cheron, she was reading a story, we could hear them laughing as she read. Without them noticing we were back Michael and I got in the shower together and washed quickly. I wrapped up in my robe and went into the children's room to greet Cheron. "How was your day?" I asked her. "I enjoyed the children, they were so funny," she replied grabbing her scarf from the little chair next to the bed. The two men helpers waited for her in the van. She kissed the twins and hugged Keagan tight.

"Ms. Cheron will miss you until tomorrow," she said to them. I walked her to the door. "Thank you, Mrs. Philips," she added. "Oh no, thank you," I said to her, "you've been great with them, I will see you tomorrow." I shut the door, as I turned Michael was standing in front of me. He pulled me by the middle of my robe and hugged me tightly. "I love you, Karis," he said kissing my neck. "I love you back, Michael," I replied. It felt so different this hug, it felt like Michael was up to something, or he needed to tell me something. "Is there something wrong?" I asked him looking into his eyes. "No, baby everything is fine."

"What, I can't hug you, baby? This is normal for us right?" He asked me walking into the small kitchen. "Let's get something to eat, did you check on the children?" He asked as he walked away. "Yes they're fine," I tell him walking behind him. "Yes, come eat with me." On the table were two plates for us waiting on a heating pan. "She's wonderful isn't she?" Michael asked. "Yes, she seems to be really good with the children." I looked down at the plate, and there was no way I could eat what she made.

I reached over to the bowel on the table to get a piece of fruit. "What, no dinner for you huh" Michael said laughing and taking a bite of whatever it was that she prepared that day. I smiled as he ate it all with a smile on his face with each bite he held his spoon up to my lips. "Yum, this is the best," he said trying to be funny. "You're so picky about your food," he said. "Michael, how long are we planning to stay here?" I asked him. "I don't know baby, there is a need for me here. I feel good when I'm here, I will never get this at home.

There is a great reason why I am able to do this. I am needed here more than anywhere," he said. "I see," I said still wondering how long we were to be here. Our tickets took us through to another month, extending our stay here for at least three months. I wasn't prepared to be here that long, my heart was truly aching for the people, but I needed to get back home to daddy. "Michael, you need to be honest, come clean. What's your plan for us here?" I asked standing over him with my hand on my hip. "Only time will tell," Michael said getting up taking his finished plate over to the sink.

"Only time will tell," he grabbed my hand, and we went in to kiss the children goodnight. I loved to see the looks on their little faces when Michael walked into the room. It was almost as if they hadn't seen him in months, greeting him with big hugs and kisses. It seemed like their little hearts lit up like small Christmas trees when he would enter a room. "Good night little people," I said as we walked back into our room. "I would like to be honest with you Michael, I'm terrified being here. I know that we came here to help, but it seems the help they need is way more than what we can do. It's tough to keep our spirits in good health with so much suffering around us.

Don't you think?" I questioned. Michael looked at me and put his forehead onto mine. "You still can't see it, huh? We are on a mission baby, us together with God," he said looking me in the eyes. He kissed all over my face telling me it would be okay. He held me as I fell off to sleep that night listening to the sounds of the African night. The next day Cheron woke us with a knock on the door. Michael quickly rolled over to cover himself with the blanket from the foot of the bed. "Come in," I yelled out. "Is there something wrong?" I asked. She didn't say a word nor did she enter the room. "Hello," I said again. "Hello, I just wanted to let you know the food is ready, and I fed the children," she said.

"Okay, that's fine, we will be out soon," I yelled out to her. Michael rolled over closer to me putting his head on my shoulder. "Karis, I am exhausted, I guess the jet lag is finally hitting me. I won't be able to function if I don't make love to you right now," he said grabbing me tightly in his arms. He kissed all over my neck, and we made love. Soon after we were up showering, we got dressed and went out to the front room. Cheron had Keagan and the twins all ready for a walk. She had

Keagan with just a T-shirt and a diaper on, and the twins were dressed in short sets that I purchase for them for the trip.

"Cheron, I'd like Keagan to be dressed in a short set also," I went back into the room and went through the luggage to get him an outfit that would cover his little shoulders. She watched as I changed Keagan into the little short set. "I'd like for you to spray this repellant on them before leaving the house okay. It will keep the flies and insect away from their skin," I told her while I sprayed the children down one by one. "You can use some if you like, okay," I tell her putting it into the bag she would be carrying around. Michael came into the room and stood behind me. "Have fun, Cheron," he said kissing the Kristine and patting Kristopher on the head.

"We will, daddy," Kristine told him hugging his neck. "I will be back with them in an hour; will you be here when I return?" Cheron asked. "No, we won't we will be in the village, make sure you feed them lunch." Michael and I stood outside as the driver Zubeka pulled up we both stood in silence thinking about the challenges ahead for us today. "Do you think you'll be okay today baby?" Michael asked me. "I believe that maybe I will," I told him stepping up into the van. "Hello," I said to Zubeka "Hello," he said with his eyes straight ahead.

Michael sat up front with him he placed his bag on the seat beside me. We were off, we planned to visit more of the children and babies today born with HIV and orphaned because of it. There was a woman who cared for a lot of the sick children when they became orphaned, and Michael visited her before giving them free check-ups and shots to keep them healthy. Michael spoke to Zubeka all the way there, he spoke as if he'd been speaking their language all his life. "Karis, there will be a celebration ceremony for us this week in the middle of the village."

"It's to welcome us, it's a celebration of prayers for us baby. It's going to be so wonderful Karis, we will have to dress in the African attire, the kids are also be welcomed," he said. I was worried about this, a real live welcoming celebration I thought. What would that be like? The day was filled with lots of prayers, we entered the small orphanage in the village, and it was somewhat clean. The children were all really tiny some were a little healthier than others, the ones who'd been there for a while looked a little healthier than the new ones coming in.

The woman who ran the orphanage came up to Michael and I and introduced herself. "I am Effie," she said, her hair was wrapped in a red cloth, and she wore a long green dress it streamed down her body until it hit her sandals. She was tall and heavy, her skin was dark and smooth, and she had a smile that would brighten anyone's day. "Hello," I said to her. "I am Karis, nice to meet you, Effie," I told her. She was so happy to see Michael she nearly tripped over Zubeka to hold his hand. She immediately started to greet him with a smile.

"Long time, long time," she said smiling at him. "Doctor, you leave for a long time, I am happy, so happy to see you," she said walking with him hand and hand. Michael was so caught up in her smile that he didn't even notice that I was left standing in a corner surrounded by lots of children. "Effie, you look wonderful, I'm so glad to be back," Michael said. Effie smiled up at him and talked about the children. I sat down next to the doorway the hot air coming in from it. Michael looked over at me and winked. I smile back to assure him that I'm okay. The children came up to me surrounding me touching my hair and clothes. "Hi, little ones," I say to them reaching out for their hands.

They smile back at me so gently. I rub their heads; I reached into my bag to see what I had in there to share with them. I had some candy lemon drops and lots of books. I could read to them while Michael and Ms. Effie were in the back room. I asked the children if they'd like a story, they sat down with me as I read Hansel & Gretel; one of the twins favorite. They seem to be enjoying it especially the lemon drop candy they passed the bag around as I read. I noticed one of the children still sitting on the bed; he didn't come over and engage with the others he just stared at me.

I glanced at him as I read, and the children watched me intensely waiting to hear if Hansel and Gretel would get stuffed into the oven. His eyes pierced out at me, they glared in the light over the bed. Michael and Ms. Effie finally made their way back to the front room I kept reading. Michael sat down beside me putting his arm around me, and Ms. Effie sat in the circle with the children while I finished up the story. "And they lived happily ever after," I said closing the book. Michael looked over at the children and then kissed my cheek. Ms. Effie got up and came over to me, "thank you, dear, that was a wonderful story," she said.

"Yes, it's one of the twin's favorites," I said looking around her to see the little boy sitting on the bed. "You okay dear?" She asked me noticing that I seemed a bit flustered. "Oh, yes, I'm okay," I said looking over her shoulders as she talked to me. I didn't hear a word she said I needed to know whether or not this little boy was really here. I watched him as she looked confused because I didn't answer any of her questions; she walked off walking toward Michael. "Is a school teacher?" She questioned Michael.

"No, Effie, she is a mother, she loves the children," he said smiling at me. I walked toward the little boy, and he got up and walked out of the back door. My instincts were to follow him, but I wasn't sure this was out of my territory. I thought I am not at home in California this is an unknown place. What if I get lost, I stayed there I looked out of the door the little boy stood in the dirt in the doorway and stared at me. "Karis," Michael called out, "come on the vans here," he said with urgency. I walked over to him to say goodbye to Ms. Effie.

"Goodbye young lady," she said kissing my hands. "We will see you again, yes?" She shook her head looking me into my eyes. "Are you okay young lady? You look a little frightened," she said. "Oh, yes Ms. Effie, I am, I will see you soon," I said hugging her and looking over her shoulder to get a last glance at the little boy. I said goodbye to all of the children, they were so happy that we came. Michael and I walked out to get in the van, and there he was, the little boy. He was very small and frail; he had dirt all over him.

I could see his eyes glaring out at me as we drove off. He stood behind and watched us leave. I looked at Michael, he didn't seem to notice him nor did the driver. I looked away and looked back, he was gone. I looked around to see if I could see him walking anywhere, but he was gone just like that. Well that confirms it for me I thought looking up at the sky as it turned to night as we rode along the dirt road. We arrived at the house very tired, Cheron was on the sofa with Keagan in her lap rocking him to sleep.

"Foods on the table," she said putting her finger to her lips, so we don't wake Keagan. "Okay, thank you," Michael said in a whisper. We went to the kitchen and sat down at the table. It looked like we were having some kind of creamy soup. It looked very pasty and bland; we also had a biscuit with a gray spread over it. I was so hungry I took the spoon to my mouth quickly watching Michael's facial expressions; to my surprise it was delicious. Michael and I ate quietly and even had seconds. As I was sitting eating I couldn't help but think about the little boy. He looked so lost. I wanted to find him and help him get to where he needed to be.

"So baby, what did you think about today?" Michael asked me. I looked up from my bowel into his eyes. "Today was just fine, I loved reading to the children they were so happy," I tell him as he put his bowel in the small sink. "Yea, I love the orphanage; it's the one place that's safe and happy." He said as I stood up to put my bowel in the sink behind him. When I walked the room to see Keagan and Cheron, I looked over at the sofa and Cheron had gotten up to take him to bed, I followed quietly behind them. Cheron laid him down so gently and kissed her hand and touched Keagan's little forehead. She turned to come out of the room but was startled by my presence at the door. "Oh, you scared me," she said in a whisper.

"Goodnight, I see you tomorrow," she said very softly. I went in after her, I stared down at Keagan. I wondered if he'd had any experiences while we were gone. I watched him sleeping, he slept so peacefully. I kissed him on the hand and went to the twin's room to give them a kiss goodnight, when I walked in it was dark, but sitting on Kristopher bed was the little boy. He was swinging a stick from side to side; I walked toward him to get a good look at his little face.

It was dark and the twins slept close to one another in one bed leaving the little boy on the bed alone. He watched me with his eyes piercing mine as I kissed the twins one by one. When I was done with the twins I sat down next to the little boy. "Hi," I said as I sat down. He took one look at me and out of his mouth he spewing up a tremendous amount of what looked like flies. I jumped and waved my hands around flagging them away. I tried not to scream and wake the twins. I could feel them all over me. The smell from him was foul I had my eyes closed, Lord, help me I thought to myself.

I opened my eyes thinking of the Lords grace, and the little boy was gone, and so were the flying bugs. I ran over to the bed where the twins were sleeping, and I rubbed their backs. I sat down to catch my breath. I leaned over with my hands on my head. "Lord, I know. I know Lord," I said. When I looked up Michael was standing in the doorway. "So are you coming to bed?" Michael asked. I looked up at him. "What's wrong baby?" He asked. "Oh, nothing," I said getting up following him to our room. "Cheron left us some cake too, baby. I thought we could share some with a glass of red wine."

"Sure, I'd like that," I said. It would help me a lot I thought. "Michael, you know I'm not a drinker. I will be out the minute I take one sip," I told him. "You do know that red wine will not hurt you, it is actually good for you in a lot of ways it has lots of healing power," he said. I walked into the room slowly while Michael made a detour to the kitchen. I sat down on the bed and took my clothes and shoes off I just sat there in my bra and panties it was so hot I walked over to the small window to see if I could catch a small breeze. I put my hands on the window ceil and stood there looking out.

With my back turned toward the bed I could hear Michael's footsteps creeping up closely with the glasses clinging together. "Hello sweetness," he said wrapping his arms around me still holding the glasses. He kissed my back with the wine bottled pushed to my stomach, I cringed. It was so cold. Michael laughed as I scooted to get away from him. "No, no, no," Michael said. "You come here," he grabbed onto my stomach and held the bottle closer still kissing my back and laughing.

I turned around to him and grabbed his neck holding tight for him to carry me to the bed. He sat me down on the bed, and I grabbed the glasses. "Are you okay Karis?" Michael asked. "Of course I am. You're here with me," I tell him kissing his cheek. He poured the wine into the glasses, and we toasted to Africa, "In Africa, baby, I thought I'd never come back here," Michael said. "But after meeting Effie and those kids, I knew they needed me to come back, if not for the children I will always surrender to Gods will, and I do believe that it is his will," Michael said.

We fell asleep that night talking about the children and the celebration that would take place in a few days. I was eager to see what they had planned for Michael. They all seemed very fond of him particularly Ms. Effie. I smiled thinking of her kindness she was a very blessed woman, surrounding herself with all of Gods children. As Michael slept holding me in his arms, I had only one reason to still be up. That little boy, I could still see his eyes dark and cold. I wondered about his story through the night. It could just be that he was lost, I prayed myself to sleep.

"Lord, please guide me to that child allow, me to help him your way. In Jesus name, I pray. I turned my back to Michael and held his hand as I fell off to sleep listening to the African night noises. We awake that morning to a loud knock on the door. "Dr. Michael!" Cheron yelled out, "Please come, we need you!" She said in a frantic. We jumped up and grabbed our robes. Michael opened the door wide. "What is it, what's wrong?" He asked in a stern voice. "They need you in the village, they say to come quick," she said holding Keagan to her chest.

I quickly went to the bathroom and threw on yesterday's clothes while Michael pulled clothes from the bag "Let them know we are on the way," he told Cheron. "Okay sir," she said. We went running out of the door quickly there were five men standing waiting for us. They spoke to Michael immediately telling him that the refugees from another village had come through one of the small villages and started to kill the people. You could hear the fear in their voices. Some of them held on to the side of the truck while the driver went over bumps and rocks in the road shifting the truck up and down. I held on tightly to Michael's shirt and the door handle.

When we made it to the village people were crying, laying on the road bleeding and crying. The driver slowed the truck down as we approached the tiny huts, the men help us out. Michael immediately went over to the people on the ground the men started to pull them into the huts for safety. One after another Michael patched their bleeding wounds and stitched the open cuts. I watched comforting the children, one of the little girls kept pulling my hand to go to the back of the hut, but I couldn't leave the other children. I explained to her.

"Mommy, mommy," she exclaimed. "I know darling," I tell her not really listening attentively as I was so caught up in what was before my eyes, I couldn't pay attention. The little girl stood in front of me tugging my shirt almost pulling it off, she flagged her hand for me to come with her with tears in her eyes. "Okay," I said taking her by the hand. She guided me out of the back door to a field where there were brush, bushes, and tree twigs. I followed her until we reached a dead end there were rocks everywhere big rocks. She led me around the biggest one, and a woman was laying there, she looked like she had been lying there for days.

She was so frail and dirty, her body was nearly bones, she reached out to me trying to speak. I kneeled down to her, taking her hand. The little girl smiled with tears of joy in her eyes, she pointed down at the woman and said "Teacher, teacher." "Go back little one," I tell her waving my hand. "Go back and get the doctor, you understand?" I ask her. She walks away looking behind her. She gave me a look of reassurance. I held the woman by the hand to comfort her. When Michael and the other men arrived two of the men picked her up, she was so frail.

Michael thought if they moved her she would be broken up. Her bones were was so fragile. I followed behind them with the little girl holding her close to me, she cried as we walked. Many people ran up to us as we walked down the road yelling. "Teacher! Teacher!" They cried out loud and some fell to the ground and prayed as we came near the small hut. She must have been a special woman to them, the way they all reacted. Michael started looking her over immediately after they laid her down.

She moaned in pain tears rolls from her face, her body looked like a harden shell when Michael removed her clothes she was what looked like all bones hardly any flesh. I looked away as he checked her out, I took the little girl by the hand and lead her out to the front of the village. The people all stood around, they made a circle and started to chant in a beautiful song prayer, it was by far the most beautiful song I'd ever heard in my life. It sounded beautiful, but they cried as they sang. I put their hands up to the air as if they were reaching high for the Lord to bless them in this time.

I watched and also prayed as I knew he would comfort them. It was all so beautiful, the way they praised Gods name in song and dance. They continued until Michael came out to tell them about teacher. He took the older woman by the hand and put his head to her hand and then to her chest. He then looked her in the eyes and gave her a nod, he backed away, and they sang louder as the woman reassured them the teacher would be okay. Michael grabbed me by the hand and took me over to the hut. "Karis," he said.

He turned to me and put his head to my chest I held him as he cried. "Michael, the lord is with us, don't forget that, please don't forget that." I said as he cried, a light shined on him his wings spread out over us. I stood there looking out to the fields holding him close to my chest as if he was a child. As I held him the little boy appeared again far in the field. This time he waved his stick at me. I tried not to pay him any attention. I closed my eyes and prayed, "Lord, bring him to me," I prayed, "bring him to me and allow me to help him. I won't follow him unless you guide me to." I prayed. Michael picked his head up; "Karis, I love you, baby, and thank you so much for coming on this trip with me," he said.

"I don't know what I would have done without you, the last time I was here, it was so hard for me, thank you, baby." He said kissing my face all over. "Michael," I said blushing, "I love you too." He took my hand, and we walked down the path heading back towards the hut. "I'm going to check on her before leaving," he said. We went to the hut and Michael had an IV set up in her arm, he'd put antibiotics in to help some of her infections go away. The woman was malnourished, so he set another tube up for her to have a food supplement go into her body for nourishment.

She was quiet when we went back in with one of the older members of the village sitting by her side rubbing her back and humming a soft song fanning her body. She seemed a little better; Michael explained to the woman that we'd return in the next day to check one all the people in the village, the men who brought us waited patiently for us to return to the van. When we finally did, they helped us in and thanked Michael for everything. They gave us canteens with water in them to cool us off as we rode through the village.

I prayed the whole time. I was amazed that this was the happening here in Africa. The people were suffering so badly, and their government was doing little to nothing to help. That night I prayed a lot, but I took some time to talk to the twins for I had only been seeing them sleeping since we got here. I ran into the house to wash and change then play with my own children. I wanted to talk to them about how blessed they were to have the things they have, it is truly a blessing. "I want them to come with us to the village next time," I told Michael as we washed up.

"They should see what we see and feel what we feel. They will for sure have a better quality of life that way. They will never take Gods blessings for granted. They will never take life for granted for that matter." I went into the small kitchen and sat down with the twins. "Hello you two," I say to them. "How was your day?" I asked, they both turned to me and spoke at the same time. Kristopher got down from his chair and came over to me hugging me so tightly. "Hi mommy," he says with a wonderful smile.

"Hello again, son." He started explaining that they had a good day, soon I had both the twins on my lap and Keagan in the middle of them in my arms. "Do you have to go mommy?" Kristine asked me. "No, I don't I'll stay around here today, daddy and I have already been to the village." I tell them getting them off my lap one by one taking their hands and leading them to the back of the house. There was a little bench out there it faced the sun directly, but I loved that. They all sat on the bench with me.

Kristine stared out into the field, and Keagan bounced on my lap up and down as if he heard a beat of the music in the air, and Kristopher walked around the bench playing with a little truck that he'd brought from home. Soon Michael joined us we played out there with the children for hours just watching and laughing with them. When it was time for dinner, Cheron came to the door and let us know. "Eat food," she said. We grabbed the children walk into the house. Keagan was mad about going in he kept reaching out toward the field looking at something.

"Keagan, no it's time to eat son," I told him pulling his little arms into his little stomach as he pointed. "You can go back out tomorrow," he yelled even louder as I held him. "What's the matter, big boy?" Michael said to him. He cried even louder, "I take him," Cheron said reaching out her arms to for him. "He just wants more sun," she said taking him from my arms. "I be back sir," she gave Michael a nod and walked back out to the back, I watched as she walked Keagan all the way out into the dirt field she put him down when they approached the fence, and Keagan danced around like he was dancing with someone.

She stood back watching as if this was a normal thing that he was used to doing every day. I watched from the doorway. "Baby, come eat, you need food," Michael said looking at me smiling. I sat down still glancing back at Keagan. "What do you think that's about, Michael?" I asked. "Oh he just likes the outdoors now, he's getting a little older now," he said. "Yes I guess you're right," I said taking my spoon up in my hand. "Mommy, Keagan's really funny, he does all sorts of funny things," Kristopher said chewing his food. "Yes mommy," Kristine said.

"Keagan does, he talks to people we can't see, and he laughs out loud all the time like somebody said something funny," she went on to say, "he really likes trees too," I looked at Michael frowning. "Huh, what do you think that's all about Michael?" I asked. "Oh baby don't start worrying about him he just appreciates his surroundings now that's all," Michael said with a smile. "Maybe you're right." I ate the soup slowly watching him run around in circles with Ms. Cheron. She seemed to be enjoying Keagan; he reached up to the sky as if he was playing with someone. "Would you like more?" Michael asked.

"Oh no, I want to lay down for a while Michael," I tell him, placing my bowel in the sink. "I would love it if the twins come lay down with me, I'd like to read to you guys," I tell them. They immediately went over to the bag I had sitting by the door to get a book out, they both wanted a different story and fought over which story would be better. "I like The Little Red Hen," Kristine screamed put. "No, let's read, The Three Little Pigs," said Kristopher. I watched them for a second to see if they would work it out but to no avail they continued to fight.

"Hey guys, I'll read them both, so let's go kids." We went to the room and the twins laid on the bed with their hands on their chins waiting. I read The Little Pigs first, and Kristine started to cry. "I wanted you to read my book first," she exclaimed. "Kristine, I want to save the best for last, don't you think that that would be a good idea?" I questioned. "If I read yours last you can go to sleep thinking about your book," I tell her. She wiped her eyes, looking up at me. "Okay mommy," she said. "Mommy can you please read mine last then," Kristopher said looking at me with sadness in his eyes. "I want to go to sleep thinking of my story too," he said, sitting up on the bed reaching for the book.

"Okay I see what's happening, I tell you two what; I will tell you guys a real story then. It's a story about a little girl named Kristine and a little boy named Kristopher," I tell them. "Mommy, that's us? We don't have a story," Kristine said. "Oh yes you do," I assure them. "You two have a great story," I tell them. "It's so wonderful to have the connection that you to have. You came into the world together one three minutes faster than the other. I was so excited to see your little faces." "Was daddy there?" Kristopher asked.

"Yes, he was, as a matter of fact, he had just come in from this very place that we're in right now. He was over here working when I was carrying you, and when he came back, you two were born," I tell them. Just then Michael comes in with Keagan. "Hey, little ones what's going on?" He asked flying Keagan onto the bed like an airplane. He sat down and started to tell them more about the day they were born. I watched him take over smiling and laughing with them about how they were little and wiggly. They really enjoyed this story more than I thought they would, before I knew it they were falling off to sleep one by one as Michael rubbed their little backs.

I looked out into the African skies. Thank you Lord for this moment I thought to myself. This is truly a blessing. I thought about the orphans, they may never have this, and it saddens my heart. I felt maybe as Ms. Effie did, she just wants to take and love them all. I could see the small faces, their eyes glossed and yet they still smile, I know the Lord is the reason. We all fell asleep on the bed I held onto the twins and Michael slept with Keagan lying on his chest.

It was comforting to have them in the bed so close to us. I knew Michael needed it. I watched him as he slept, he looked so peaceful. What he must be dreaming, I often thought. I got up to go to the restroom after a while of resting. I went in and shut the door, as I started to pull my underwear down I felt something sharp on my back as if it was tracing the outer part of my spine. I turned to see what it was before I could turn all the way there he was again. The little boy, this time he started swinging the stick across my face hitting me as hard as he could with it.

From my face to my body he kept swinging, I swung my arms and hands following the stick trying to grab it. I knew if I could get my hands on that stick it would tell me his story, and maybe I could help him then I thought. Trying to catch the stick he swung it faster and faster like he knew what I would know had I grabbed it. I fell backward onto the small sink grabbing onto the towel holder to catch myself from falling to the floor. He then swung it harder when I turned around to catch my balance I grabbed the towel; I could hook the stick with it I thought.

I turned around quickly and he was gone. I fell to my knees and prayed. "Lord, whatever this child wants from me, please reveal it. Please, Lord, allow me to help him cross over, he is lost Lord, and I know that you will direct his path. I just need a chance to grab him and help him get back to his path. Lord, I pray that I can help him the way you want me to help him. In Jesus name, I pray." I walked out to the front room and sat down on the couch. I looked out of the window, and there he was standing in the window staring at me, he was as stiff as a board. I wasn't going to go to him I thought, stay here keep praying and he'll come to you.

I got up and went back to the room with Michael and the children. I looked out at him as I shut the bedroom door. I leaned against the door for a while just to see what would happen. After a while, I sat down on the bed. Michael sat up holding Keagan onto his chest. "Karis, are you okay? Have you gotten any sleep at all?" He asked. "Yes, I'm okay Michael," I say taking off my robe and lying next to the twins. "I'm going to get some sleep now, Michael," I tell him looking up at the ceiling. Michael laid Keagan next to the twins and pulled me close to him.

"I love you, Karis," he said kissing my cheek. "I love you too." I said turning to kiss his lips. "You get some sleep we have a long day ahead of us you know. We have to go back to the village and see how everything is going," he said. "Yes I know," I tell him placing my head on his chest, I fell off to sleep soon after. I was so tired that I didn't even feel or hear Michael and the children get up. I woke up to the sound of the winds outside. It was warm but the wind was blowing sand everywhere. I sat up to look out of the window.

My eyes were still slightly closed. I held my head in my hands I had a slight headache. I sat there for a while I didn't hear Michael or the children up front, the door was open I peeked out suddenly I hear them chatting about the food Cheron cooked for them. Michael laughed as they talked to him about bananas. They had these tiny bananas; Keagan ate them fast they were perfect for his little hands and mouth. He'd get really messy stuffing his little mouth so fast. The twins would point and laugh at him. I went to the bathroom to wash my face and brush my teeth to join them before they were done.

My head still was hurting; I stood at the sink for a while with the towel over my head the cold water seemed to help. When I lifted my head up from the sink there was Michael. "Good Morning, baby, I thought you'd sleep the whole day away," he said holding me by the waste looking into the mirror with me. I held my head down, it was pounding by now. He pulled me close with my back to his chest, he kissed my neck. "Are you okay baby?" He asked. "I have a headache," I tell him. "Do you want me to fix it? I have some medicine in my bag."

"No, Michael, I think I should sleep this one off," I said walking away from him toward the bed. I lay on the bed and covered my head with the pillow. "You know the celebrations today?" Michael said in a whisper, "Baby you rest and I will get everything together for us. I'll get the children ready to go," he said. I prayed God please, this headache is the worst, please take it away, and heal me in the name of Jesus. I laid there with a cold rag over my head until I felt a little better.

The pain wasn't completely gone, but I had to make it to the celebration. I wanted to visit the teacher and the children in the village. I sat up. I pulled myself together brushing my hair and getting my clothes, I would wear a long purple dress with red and yellow flowers in small print on it. I put the same color on Kristine she wore a purple dress and

Cheron wrapped her hair in a nice scarf. She looked so beautiful. The boys wore little suits and ties with purple in them. When I was ready, they escorted us to the van waiting outside. We all got in with the help of the driver. We were on our way to celebrate Michael in the village.

We arrived there soon after and were greeted by a circle of children singing and dancing. It sounds so beautiful; all I could think of was how Jesus spirit was in this place; in all this hurt and heartache they still can make time to praise him for his love. Michael and I were escorted to go into the circle of the children; they danced around us and shouted loudly. I was amazed by the voices; it was beyond what I expected. They finished singing, and Ms. Effie came over to us with a bowel, it had some kind of juice in it.

We kneeled down before her, and she came up to us softly pulling Michaels head back, she prayed then poured it into his mouth. Then over to me, she said a prayer in her language and pulled my head back and poured it into my mouth. I almost gagged, it was really bitter. I let it flow down my throat trying not to taste it in my mouth; we lifted our heads forward and were surrounded by the older women in the crowd. They sang and danced around loudly with their hands reaching up to the sky thanking and praising God. I prayed with them, and Michael stayed kneeling with his head up to the sky, tears flowed from his face, he was still there was a bright light around him that was warm like the sun.

These praises went on for a long time. When it was all over I went in to see the teacher. I could see the little girl who first brought me to the teacher standing by the door flagging me her way. I walked slowly over; I could feel my spirit changing as I walked toward the little hut. When I got inside I knew then it was time, the teacher would be leaving the village forever. Ms. Effie came in soon after me, and all that could fit in came in after. The little hut was full, they all watched me go over to her they prayed with tears in their eyes. I took teachers hand, and I prayed out to the Lord, in the name of Jesus, please take her in, her spirit is worn.

Lord, she is tired, Lord. I held her hand; she looked up at me and smiled. She said thank you in a whisper in her language. I kissed her hand and walked out of the hut, giving the children and Ms. Effie, she went to her bedside and kneeled over her throwing both her arms around crying. Ms. Effie's spirit is so full, I thought as I walked away, I went to the field where the celebration took place to catch my breath. I walked in a circle for a while, I looked down the fields of dirt and brush, and I thought about the Lords goodness. I am living proof that he is good. I didn't know any other way to think of it.

As I walked around I heard a loud whistle blowing. I turned to look for it. I noticed it was coming from a hut way down away from the village. It was a small hut it looked abandon, I stared down the dirt road, the whistle began to get louder and louder. I wanted to go down to the hut but I was tired and my head was still hurting. I strolled toward the whistling thinking how I loved the gift that the Lord gave me, but I didn't want to feel the pain that came along with it. How could I feel better about what he gave me? I prayed Lord, please help me that.

As I walked toward the sound of the whistle; it was so loud, and I could see the small boy with the stick. He was peeking around the corner he flagged the stick down at me to come over. I looked at the hut again, and he was gone I could hear still the whistle, but now it was followed by drums. The drums were soft then hard then soft again. As I approached the hut I could see what looked like fire shining through the white curtain covering the opening of the hut. I stood there for a while not wanting to go into the hut. I can't handle to much more today I thought, I stood by the curtain and soon I heard in a whisper my name being called softly.

"Karis, Karis, I turned to see there was no one there and it just felt like wind blowing in my ear. I prayed for the Lord to watch over me,

I have to go in. I went through the curtain to the sound of the drums. It was dark inside, but a man was playing the drums he was painted from head to toe, he stared up and played the drums harder as I approached him. When we were close enough the children were all over me laughing and pulling me toward the floor of the hut. I could feel their hands all over me.

I looked around for something to grab hold of to help me up, but there was nothing they rolled around the floor with me smiling and laughing, suddenly I felt happy, filled with joy I rolled around with them laughing and smiling. When the drums stopped the man came over to me and kneeled down, he reached out for my hands. I took his hands still feeling joy in my soul I smiled as I sat up. "You are blessed; rejoice for you will not feel pain anymore. Your heart will overflow with the feeling of joy and happiness as his blessing guide you to higher ground."

The man touched my stomach and my head. "Grace, feel his grace when he guides you, feel his joy and love for the people, even in these terrible times." When he was done, he looked down at me and smiled. "Go, and be joyful" He helped me from the floor as I walked from the hut I could hear the children laughing I looked back to see them smiling. I would be free of the pain that I felt within me. This will be different for me, I thought as I walked away through the dry, dusty brush of the path.

This will be a real good change for me. When I made it back to the hut, Ms. Effie was preparing for the body of the teacher to be moved to the burial grounds. I watched as the teacher walked alongside them smiling. At that moment I felt so happy inside I felt so happy I too jumped up and down holding my stomach. I felt so much joy. Michael was holding hands with another group of young men; it looks as if he was praying with them. I sat and watch them from the hut. There was a small tree stomp I sat there looking down into the dirt. It was so hot I could feel my face burning from the heat.

I looked out into the path way and saw Cheron coming up with the twins, She carried Keagan on her hip. He was holding her hair and smiling as she sang to them. Her voice echoed throughout the village. She sang beautifully about that accent I thought, but it was way more than that. Her voice was almost like a harp from the heavens clear and sweet. She walked confident and strong when she approached me she handed me Keagan. Her singing went from a song to humming. "Cheron, I love the sound of your voice, it's so beautiful," I tell her.

"Thank you, Mrs. Karis. I'm going to fetch some water for the house, I'll be back to cook dinner for the family," she said walking away. I took Keagan and the twins to meet Michael near the van. As we stood waiting for the van driver I watched as the little girl who first brought me to the teacher stood staring next to the hut. I called out to her to come over to me. "What's your name?" I asked her. "My name is Sasha," she said. "Hello Sasha," I said. "You are Mrs. Karis, I know," she said before I could even tell her who I was.

"You like to read to the children at school," she said. She was so sweet she had sadness in her eyes, but her little heart was already healing from the hurt. I just wanted to take her in and love her. "Do you live around here?" I asked her. "I live over there, Ms. Effie's place," she said smiling. "I use to live with the teacher, till she became ill," she said. "Oh I see. Well, would you like to come along with us for dinner?" I asked her. She shook her head yes, "I should ask Ms. Effie first," she said as she ran toward the pathway looking around. I called her back. "We will get Ms. Effie together," I told her grabbing Keagan by the hand lifting him up to my hip.

Ms. Effie came walking toward us. "Hello, what's going on?" She asked smiling. "We were wondering if we could have Sasha over for dinner, tonight?" I asked her. She looked down at Sasha and held her face in her hands. "Sure you can, Sasha, you go fill your belly." she said laughing. "I will see you soon." We walked back over to the van and

Sasha sat inside with the twins. She was so comfortable there. The men came walking up with Michael. We drove away through the village. Michael held my hand so tight. I looked out into the skies of the evening sunset. Why are so many suffering here, Lord? I thought.

It seemed almost unbearably to take in. but this was places, where the lord is extending his love. I could tell just by the way the people were still able to smile. We made it to the hut. I got the children washed up for dinner, while Sasha sat on the small sofa near the door. "Sasha, would you like to wash up sweetie?" I asked her. "Yes," she said with no hesitation. "Come," I told her to come in here. I gave her a small t-shirt, she was petite. I didn't have much she could wear, but I had a couple of small t-shirts.

"Here you are, sweetie, just wash your hands and face and wear this," I tell her. "You can put your top in the sink, I'll wash it out for you and set it out to dry in the heat, okay," I say to her getting her a towel. "Okay Mrs. Karis," she said. When dinner came around We all sat at the table as Cheron fixed our plates. When we all got our plates we began to hold hands and pray. Michael said grace. "Lord, thank you for all our blessings today and every day." It was fast, we ate, talk and laugh. Cheron took her plate and went toward the patio outside. "No, no," Michael called out to her. "You eat here with us," he grabbed a chair and pulled it out for her, she smiled as she smiled as she took her seat at the table, and said "Thank you, Mr. Michael."

Love Africa

Sasha became a frequent visitor for dinner. We all welcomed her each day as she ran through the small countryside to our hut for dinner. I'd watch her running toward the hut with the sun beaming down on her; she would be smiling the whole way down. When she arrived at the hut door, she'd bend over with her hands to her knees panting for breath. She would take breath after breath before she'd come up. "Hi, Mrs. Karis," she'd say in her small sweet accent, I would hold a glass of water for her every evening while I waited for her to run through the trees.

After we washed and went to the table, she would be the first to say grace clutching her little hands together and saying grace in French, she spoke French fluently. She was a lovely little girl, delightful. As we planned to leave Africa, Michael and I both thought about what would happen to Sasha. Michael said he would talk to Ms. Effie tomorrow about Sasha's placement. I watched her eat, she always waited for Kristine or Kristopher to take a bite, then she would follow their lead. She'd help with Keagan wiping his little mouth, and they would laugh with each other.

She would even teach them new words in French they would teach her words in English. They would wash their hands and head straight for the patio to play. I washed my hands and took a cup of juice to the patio; I loved to watch them play. Sasha loved to teach them a song. Her voice was so beautiful it sounded like a small harp. I am going to hate to leave her behind, I thought as I watched them playing in the field of the patio. It was a hot day, Cheron sat close to me on a stool she hummed and held Keagan in her arms. She reached down pick weeds from the ground under the stool as she rose up I quickly sense that she was ill. I looked at her and turned to look the other way.

Oh God, I thought Cheron is ill. She is ill and its bad, Lord what do I do, I wondered if she even knew how ill she was, I reach over for Keagan. I stood up with him in my hands and straddled him around my hip. "Cheron, can we talk inside," I asked her she looked nervous. "Did I do something wrong?" She asked following me into the front room. "Oh no, I just wanted to ask you something, please sit down, let's talk. Cheron, are you sick?" I ask her. "I am, my husband has infected me with the HIV virus, that's how I met Dr. Michael, I was very ill when he came here before, and he helped to get me better. I will always be grateful to him," she told me.

"I see, are you in pain right now?" I asked her. "Yes, I am I have to go and take my pills, I have to take a lot of drugs to keep me well. I sometimes don't want to get up in the morning, and I don't want to live at times," she said holding her head down. "Oh Cheron, I'm so sorry, is there something I can do for you now?" I asked her. "Mrs. Karis you are doing something. I lost my baby, I get pregnant and over and over, I lose the baby. Being here with the babies, it's good for me. I wanted to die with my babies every time.

I pray, God don't take them and they go anyway. I gave up after my third baby died, the lord is mad at me, I think each time. The doctor tells me there's nothing wrong with me, I should be able to carry babies, but each time I try I fail," she says with tears in her eyes. "Cheron, God loves you, this I know for a fact. He knows your pain and your suffering, it may seem that there was no blessing in it, but believe me Cheron there is a blessing in it all. I want you to know that" I said as I went over to her and held her tight. I began to pray for her.

"Dear God, in the name of Jesus, please bless Cheron with comfort. Bless her to know that, it's not all in vain. Lord, bless her spirit, keep her; Lord, give her peace and strength. Oh God, help her to move past the loss, Lord, give her peace, in Jesus name, I pray." I held onto Cheron as she cried out to the Lord. She cried and cried; I just held her. "Let it go," I told her. "Let him give you the answer, let it go." I got up to get Keagan. He cried, watching Cheron cry made him sad.

"I must go," she said grabbing her bag from the floor. I got up and hugged her. Keagan kissed her on the cheek. "Bye, bye Cheron," I said holding his little hands waving goodbye to her. As I watched her walk off, I felt so much sorrow. I know she won't be well enough to return, although she didn't look like it she was very ill. I watched her walk away off into the sunset clutching her bag, she walked with such confidence. No one would ever know the pain I see in her eyes that day. She kept it in her heart.

I'd never asked her if she had any children before. I felt a little bad not having asked her and her taking care of my children all the time must make her heart even heavier. I took Keagan into the bedroom and changed his diaper. I put his pajamas on and began to get the twins ready for bed also tonight Sasha will sleepover, she was so excited. I gave her some pajamas that I bought at the market for her when I went into the town for the house supplies with Ms. Effie. I planned to take her shopping for more clothing in hopes of Michael getting her paperwork approved for us to take her home with us.

If we couldn't, I wanted to leave her something special like books, pillows, a doll something to remember us by. I washed the twins up and helped Sasha to bed. We read books and said prayers. By the time Michael got in I was in the shower, I could hear him walking all around the room. I bet he was undressing to get into the shower with me. I was facing the water when I felt his hands wrapping around my waist, pulling me close to him and kissing my neck. He just held onto me tight while the water ran over us, he was upset about something I could tell by his eyes.

When he looked up at me, he shut them quickly and laid his head on my shoulder, and held me tighter. After a kiss on the lips I turned around and grabbed his face. "Michael, what's wrong?" I asked him looking into his eyes. "I don't think we will be able to take Sasha with us," he was so sad. "Why not Michael, What did Ms. Effie say to you?" I questioned. "She says that we have to do more paperwork and she's not sure whether or not Sasha was born here, she says that Sasha came to the village with the teacher, and that teacher never said where she came from with Sasha.

She just told them that she was an orphan. "Teacher never told them where she came from, Ms. Effie says she will try and make some contacts tomorrow. Baby, I just don't want you to get your hopes up. I know how bad you want her to go home with us, she is one of many babies, there's a lot of orphans, she is one of many, Karis." Michael seemed as if he'd already given up on the thought of her leaving with us. On that night, before we fell asleep, I took him by the hand, and I prayed with him. He was so hurt at the thought of not being able to take this one child just as much as I was.

We made love that night and fell asleep quickly after. When we woke up that morning I didn't hear the children not even Keagan crying. I got up quickly and wrapped my robe around me and went out into the front room. "Twins!" I yelled out I seen that their bedroom door was open but the children weren't in there I went into the small room where Keagan would be sleeping. I peeked into the room I looked over into the crib and Keagan was not there, frantically I ran into the twin's room. The pushed open the door, and there they all were lying down on a blanket on the floor.

Keagan holding on tight to Kristopher's neck, his little arm was hugging onto his brother. I walked over to them and cover them all with a cool sheet it wasn't warm, but it was a little breeze coming through the window. The sun was coming up soon I looked out into the fields at the trees. I could see Cheron walking up with the sunlight following her. She was wrapped in a yellow and purple shirt, her hair was also wrapped. I watched her walk up, she seemed fine, and I closed the curtains and walked towards the front room, by the time I reached the first room the sun was shining through the front window.

I went to the kitchen to put on a fresh pot of coffee for Michael. I poured me a glass of orange, mango juice and sat at the table. I thought Cheron would be at the door by now, but she still hadn't made it to the door. I could see the sun raising more and more I started to worry, so I went to the front room to greet her at the door. I walked over to the door to open it and peek out when I heard her approach the door. "Good morning, Mrs. Karis, how are you this morning?" She asked.

"I'm fine Cheron, I was hoping to catch you this morning before you became really busy with the children. Come on in here," I said holding the door open for her. We both walked toward the kitchen, she immediately worked around the kitchen, taking things out to cook and I just followed her around helping her with what she needed. "Cheron, I just want you to know that I didn't mean to pry, I just needed to know what was going on because I sensed your illness and I didn't want you to be here working.

You have children that needed you at home; these are things I should have asked you before. I felt so bad that I didn't reach out to you and I am so sorry for that. If there is anything I could ever do for you, please don't hesitate to ask me," I tell her. "I am going to get dressed I'll be back to help with breakfast." I went to the bedroom to get Michael up I laid across his back with my robe open and kissed his neck and cheek. "Michael," I whispered. "You need to get up sweetie." He turned and kissed me back rolling me off his back as he rolled over.

I laid there with my robe open Michael laid on top of me and kissed all over my neck. He made love to me again before we got in the shower again. I rushed back to the kitchen after getting dressed to help Cheron. She was already done the cooking. When I went back into the kitchen, the table was set, and the children were already out in the kitchen eating. "Oh Cheron, I'm sorry I took too long to come out, I'm sorry." She handed Michael his cup of coffee and said her good mornings. "Mr. Michael, I was wondering if I could leave early today. I need to go into the city to see a doctor about my medications," she said with sweat running down her face.

She looked like she was going to fall over, Michael and I both grab one side of her arm, we walked her over to the couch and helped her sit. I fan her with the book from my bag. "Cheron," Michael called out to her, he quickly went to the room and grabbed his bag to check her vitals. I prayed for her, "Michael, what's wrong with her?" I asked him. "She may have been without her meds for a long period of time. It's hard for them to get the drugs they need, and the fall ill," he said. I took her legs and laid them on the couch.

Michael checked her vitals he started an IV line on her carefully. He put two pair of long gloves on and started the line. "Are you going to move her to the room first?" I asked him. "No, Karis she will be fine right here on the couch, this won't take long at all," he said. I rushed over to the kitchen to get a glass of water for Cheron, she hadn't woken up yet, but when she did Michael says she has to take her meds. I sat down with her, I could feel her pain. Michael sat next to her on the floor I sat down beside him and held his hand.

We prayed together, as we were praying, Cheron woke up, she jumped up as if she was startled. She looked around the room. Clutching on to the edge of the couch she seemed lost. I stood up and reached for the glass of water to give to her. She shook her head no she didn't want the water. Then Michael stood up and started checking her eyes and nose. "Cheron, do you know where you are?" He asked her. He asked her over and over again. She just looked up and around as if she was confused. I grabbed her by her shoulders and looked her in her eyes it was if she was looking through me.

"Karis, she's in a state of shock, I believe she may have a high had a high fever the virus may have taken over. I have to get her to a hospital right away if she's going to survive this will be the only chance," Michael said. I went to the door and flagged the driver to the door. "Please hurry," I cried out to him. He came running when he seen the look in my eyes. "Yes," he said in a panic. "It's Cheron, We need to get her to the nearest hospital as soon as possible," I told him.

"Ok, ok," he said nodding his head yes and rushing to Cheron to pick her up from the couch. He scooped her up in his arm as Michael carried the IV tubes alongside him and Cheron. I took Michaels bag from the floor and walked out quickly behind them. The driver placed Cheron into the van and propped her head up on a blanket he had laying on the floor Michael got in beside her holding the IV tube, and I kissed his cheek and kissed Cheron on the head. The driver quickly took off in the van leaving a dust storm of sand blowing in my face.

I wrapped my robe tight around me and went into the hut with the children. "Mommy, what happened to Mrs. Cheron?" Kristopher asked. "She's a little sick son," I tell him taking his hand and walking alongside him into the kitchen. "I want you guys to eat while I get dressed." I made the twins and Sasha sit at the table and placed Keagan into the highchair. I made them eggs and toast. While they ate I went into the bedroom and got dressed, I felt an overwhelming amount of joy come over me like I was being tickled inside I smiled as I wanted to laugh out loud.

It was a very nice feeling I felt so full of joy, I went to the bathroom to wash my face and hands, and as I glanced at the mirror, I saw Cheron smiling back at me waving. I put my head down and prayed. "Lord thank you," I said as I finished up quickly I could hear Keagan getting mad about being in the highchair for so long. When I went back to the kitchen, I could see Keagan reaching out form the chair, the kids were all done with their plates still on the table. They went out back to run around. I went towards Keagan to clean him up and get him out.

He was pretty good at walking around now he could walk without falling down too many times now, he's even trying to run. I would see him, his little legs trying to stay straight. He was every bit of Michael, his smile was so beautiful. I watch him as I cleaned the kitchen, He played around with everything he could find in the kitchen, and he was a busybody. After cleaning the kitchen, I called for the other children to come in to get dressed. They all needed to bathe I took the one by one helped them get clean, I sat them all down we were done and read to them, I knew that soon Michael would be home to confirm to me that Cheron had passed.

I finished reading with the kids and waited for Michael, they played in the front room for an hour before Michael walked in the door, his eyes filled with sadness. I told the kids to go play inside the bedroom while we talked. Michael always loved a cup of tea before bed. I quickly made him a cup of tea while he washed up. He came in and sat down at the table. "I lost her Karis, she's gone," he said. "I know Michael, it's okay." I tell him hugging him at the neck. "It's okay Michael." "We didn't even make it to the hospital, she died in the van."

"I know Michael, but she's fine now, you know that she's in a better place." "I know Karis," he said laying his head on my chest as I stood next to him hugging him. "We have to leave here soon," Michael said with a sigh. "What about Sasha?" I asked him "I don't think we will be able to leave with her. I talked to Ms. Effie, she says that the paperwork can take years, especially since we can't find her parents," he told me. "I see what if she knows where her parents are? Maybe we should ask Sasha where she came from, I can't imagine leaving her here alone Michael.

We have to find a way for her to come with us," I tell him. Michael drank his tea looking out into the back window. "I just hope that we can leave soon, I need to get back to work and you are needed at home also. It's time to move forward. We had been in Africa now for a little over six months there was so much heartache and pain and suffering here," Michael said. I was ready for home also. "Michael, it is about time we go, I know that. However, I feel she needs to be with us when we leave," I said. "If I could, I would take them all, but we don't have enough room for everyone. The others are really comfortable with Ms. Effie, she is what they know.

Sasha doesn't know anyone, nor has she ever been loved outside of what teacher gave her it seems she didn't have anyone. It's going to be tough for her to adjust to our lifestyle. I'm sure, but sooner than later she'll take her place with us," I said to Michael as I washed the dishes. I watched Michael, He got up and went out to the back porch and sat on the chairs, he was torn. I knew his heart didn't want to leave Africa. He felt as if he was losing and he couldn't keep up. I know in his heart he loves the people and can't imagine being anywhere else; there is lots of love here for him.

The people know him they know he's here for them and that he'll do all he can to help them. I finished up the dishes and cooked the kids' dinner. We only had things that Cheron knew how to cook, it was an African cuisine style. I had no recipe book, so I made what was familiar, I thought I was really cooking up something until Michael walked in and came over to my pot. He leaned over from behind me and stuck a spoon into the pot for a taste. He tasted, and with a spoonful in his mouth he ran over to the sink.

"Karis, what was that?" He asked washing his mouth out with a swish of juice. "Baby, no we can't eat any of that. We will take the children out tonight for dinner, I know a great place outside the village gets the kids ready to go, baby," he said walking out of the kitchen area into the bedroom. I stood there, I was in shock He called my food bad, smelled pretty good, I thought. I took the spoon in to taste it myself. I took in a spoonful. Oh no, this is so bad I thought, I gagged, I immediately took the pot out to the trash outside. I dump it; I was looking down into the trash can as it poured in.

I finished tossing it and shut the trash can I looked down at the ground making sure it just went in the trash; I saw a pair of feet standing next to me. I looked up and there was Cheron. She smiled at me, and put her hand onto my shoulder. I felt peace around her as she walked away. When I went inside Michael and the children were all ready to go he even packed Keagan's bag. "Karis lets go," he said as we went to the door. We were escorted to the van with the children and with help from the driver we were off to have dinner. I still had a bad taste in my mouth from the soup or stew.

"You shouldn't be ashamed, baby; you can't cook that kind of food. Stick to what you know," Michael said with a smile, I squeezed his hand and smiled. I looked over at the children, Sasha was so happy with us. I would hate to leave her behind, this would be the perfect opportunity to ask her where she came from I thought as we rode together in the van. We arrived at the restaurant, it seemed two hours later, we were in a small town outside the village it was clean; the people were happy and clean.

The place was filled with richness all around. Why couldn't everyone in Africa live this way I thought as Michael escorted us around. There was a shopping mall right across the road from the restaurant. "Michael," I called out from across the table as soon as we were seated. "Karis, I already know, you're going shopping, no worries," he said with a smile. "I will stay with Keagan and Kristopher while you and the girls take a trip over there, we will wait inside the van, but baby don't take too long okay," he said flagging over a waiter.

"Sir, how can I help you?" The waiter asked looking down at us. "I would like something icy to drink, and please bring the children water," he said. "Sir, is that all?" He asked, passing around menus to the children, "I think that's it for now, we will need a little more time to order." Okay, sir, no problem, I'll be back with your waters and drinks," he said walking away quickly; he had a beautiful accent as well. It reminded me of Cheron. "Michael, why didn't you tell me about Cherons illness?" I asked as we looked over the menu. "I felt you would pick up on it sooner or later. You usually know before me," he said.

"No, she told me you treated her the last time you were in Africa." I said. "Yes I did, she was a patient of mine back then, there was many, but Cheron was really special. She had a heart of gold and a trusting spirit," he said. As I began to ask him why again the waiter came over to us. "Are you ready, Sir?" He asked Michael again. Michael looked up at me; I hadn't even asked him what was good. "What do you recommend?" I asked the waiter. He didn't answer as if he didn't hear me. "The fish here is delicious," Michael said looking at the menu.

"They can't speak to you out here. On this side of town, the men rule, and the women's opinion doesn't really matter," Michael tell me. "We will have the Fish and chips platters with the shrimp on the side. Same for all the children," Michael told him. "Michael, what do you mean they can't take orders from the women? Really," I shouted. "Yes this is where the Somalian border is, the people over here don't really believe in that, the women aren't supposed to make too many decisions over here," Michael said winking his eye.

I laughed at him; he's so funny at times. The children were so fascinated by what they were seeing. The women were wrapped from head to toe in nice colored fancy type dresses with everything was covered in some cases all the way to the nose. I watched Sasha this didn't seem to bother her at all. "Sasha, have you ever been here before?" I asked her, and she shook her head yes. "Do you know where you are?" I asked her. "Yes," she pointed down the road, "there's school," she said. "Oh a school, how far from here?" I asked her. She shook her head yes.

"Did you go to this school?" I asked her. "Yes, I did," she said. "Did you live near here?" She shook her head, yes. "Michael we should look into this, maybe ask around, maybe she has family around here somewhere," I said to him. "I will, I'll start at the hospital down the street," he said. The waiter came back with our food, we ate. Sasha and the twins played around with the shrimp, laughing and joking. "Eat up kids, I want to go across the street before it's too late," I tell them. They began to quiet down and eat. I watched the crowds of people go by, they stared at us eating, some said hello some just smiled.

A woman stood across the street watching us, she never moved. She just leaned against the pole in a sundress watching us eat. She covered her head from the sun with a big paper in her hand. I glanced over at her from time to time just to see if she would move away from the pole. After the waiter came over to pick the plates up, Michael ordered something else to drink. I ordered another salad. The dressing was so delicious, I devoured it. "Come, girls, let's go across the street," I tell them, taking a sip of my drink and grabbing my bag from the chair.

"Michael, give me forty-five minutes, okay," I say him walking away with the girls. We walked across the street in the crowd. Sasha held Kristine by the hand. We walked past the women holding the paper over her head. She gave me the meanest look. I took the girls by the hand watching her closely. She walked across the street as quickly as she could toward Michael and Keagan. I turned the kids around to see exactly where she was going. She kept look looking behind at me. Kristine pulled at my hand. "Stop it!" I yelled down at her.

"Come on mommy," she said. "Hold on Kristine, just hold on," I watched the woman sit across from Michael and Keagan. She immediately started talking to Michael. She stared across at me, I didn't feel anything walking past her. I turned away from them to go back toward the shopping mall. "Alright mommy," Kristine said. "Girls we aren't going to stay inside the store long okay. We'll look around for a bit, get what you guys need and go," I tell them as we step through the entrance of the department store. "Okay mommy," Kristine says. Sasha looked all around as we approached the children department.

"I like these, mommy," Kristine said gliding her hands across the dresses on the mannequin. "Only one, get the color you want and some shorts to wear," I said looking to see what size Sasha might fit. She was very small. I held the dresses and shorts up to her little body in the mirror. She smiled each time. We took the items and went over to the shoe department. Sasha really liked the shoe department her face lit up. She and Kristine went through almost all the shoes on the rack. Sasha loved the colors red and bright yellow. She grabbed all of the shoes and sandals they were red and yellow.

"No, Sasha, please get only two pairs of sandals and one pair of tennis shoes," I tell her. She put them back immediately and grabbed what she wanted. Kristine grabbed the shoes she wanted and we walked over to the cashier's desk to check out. She smiled at the girls, "it's nice to shop huh?" She asked. The girls shook their heads yes. "They love it," I said to her handing her my credit card. I was so eager to get back to Michael and Keagan. I took the bag and walked away with the girls. "Mrs. Karis, you forgot your receipt," she called out.

"You need to sign also," she tells me handing me a pen. I signed the paper, and we went to the front entrance of the department store. As I walked through the doors with the bags in one hand and Kristine holding the other hand, I could see clear across the street, Sasha walked by my side. When we crossed the street, I could see the woman sitting next to Michael looking at Keagan playing with him behind Michael's back. Michael waved as he saw us crossing. I pointed behind him, signaling for him to look behind him at the woman, he looked at him confused.

"Michael," I yelled at as I'd gotten closer to them, "Karis, what is it?" He questioned. As I approached him and Keagan I put the bags on the floor and reached out for Keagan, he held his little arms out and leap into my arms. "What's the matter, Karis?" Michael asked. "Let's go, kids," We grabbed everything and took the kids to the van. The woman stared back at us with a frown; her eyes followed us all the way down to the van. She waved at Keagan; the driver was eating when we made it to the van. "Go ahead finish it up," Michael told him as we strap the children down in the seatbelts.

The van was so old the seatbelts were worn and hard to fasten, sometimes it could take a while before we got it right. The driver hurried up his lunch and hoped inside the van. "Okay we're all ready," he said placing the key into the ignition of the van. As we drove off the woman walked in front of the van making the driver make a sudden hard stop. "Hey watch where you're going," the driver yelled out. The woman stood in front of him for a while before moving out of the way. She stared at Keagan. The driver swerved around her yelling out. "Out of the way Ms." He was so upset.

The woman watched us go down the road. When we made it back to the village the sun was going down. The children fell asleep. Michael and the driver took them out of the car one by one. I stood at the door waiting for him to bring them inside. They laid them in to bed. Michael and I sat at the table with the leftover food from the restaurant. I put on a pot of tea. "Nice day, huh?" Michael said to me. "Especially nice," I replied. He came over to me and kissed my neck. "I love you, Karis, Do you know that?" He asked. "I do, Michael, I love you too," I tell him turning around to look him in the eye.

"Do you know something else?" He asked. I shook my head no. "You're the most beautiful woman I know," I shook my head, no. "Oh yes, you are baby, you're beautiful, I don't think I tell you enough," he said kissing all over my chest. Michael grabbed me by the waist. He held me close to him, and we kissed. I loved kissing Michael, he was so passionate, holding my face close to his and rubbing his nose against mine. I wanted to make love to him with every kiss encounter. He removed my shirt right there in the little kitchen.

I turned around with my back pressed against his chest looking out the window, while he kissed my neck and back I watched the sun going down. When he turned me around, at a glance, I see the woman staring through the window. My eyes stretched, I couldn't believe what I was seeing. I quickly turned to Michael. "Michael, stop." I tell him with my hands to his chest. "Let's go into the bedroom," Michael continued kissing me. "Here, Karis right now," he said in a sweet whisper in my ear. "No," I said turning back around to look out of the window for the woman.

She was gone, but I could still feel her presence around the small kitchen. Michael pulled my shirt down, kissing me all over my chest. "No, Michael, we can go into the bedroom, the kids are all sleeping," I said to him pulling his head up from my breast. I grabbed him by the hand and pulled him away from the kitchen guiding him to the room. When we opened the door to go in there she was on the edge of the bed smiling. I could feel her presence all over she came for something. I stood up as Michael kissed my neck and pushed me into the door.

I stopped him turning to him, "Michael, could we do this some other time?" I asked him. "Karis, please don't do this to me now," he said to me tugging at my shirt. I closed my eyes tight then opened them again to see if the woman would be sitting there. When I opened them she was standing over the bed laughing with her hands covering her mouth. I stared at her letting her know that I didn't fear her at all. Michael kissed all over my neck as I watched her fade away into the dark walls of the bedroom I could still feel her presence around the room as Michael and I made love.

When we finished, I went to the bathroom to wash my face. As I leaned up from the sink, she was standing behind me laughing. I could hear the laughing. Clearly, it was loud and echoed throughout the bathroom. I stood back away from her holding on to the doorknob I looked her straight in her eyes. "What is it?" I say to her. She moved up so close, right in my face and took a deep breath and screamed: "give her back!" Pointing to the door, I stood there in silence. Waiting for her next move when she screamed again I grabbed her by the hand. She pulled away from me taking her other hand and swinging for my face.

I leaned back so that she would miss my face. She violently swung at me with both her hands, I grabbed her by whatever I could she was moving around so fast. She was so angry. She pushed me all over the bathroom up against the door and onto the floor I lost my balance and fell to the floor hard. I could feel her jump onto my back and pull at my neck. I had to get a hold of her somehow I thought. She wiggled out of every grip I could get on her. I tried to get up from the floor, but there was no way to get around her she was powerful.

I laid there as I would do in times the spirit appeared to be too strong for me. I began to pray while she hit at me and screamed. "Lord, please help me now, get this spirit for it is hell bond, I can't seem to tame it to pray it down. Lord come, please help me now." I prayed this prayer over and over again as she grew weak, the hits weren't as heavy as the started out to be. I was able to grab her by the arm. I took her into my arms and hugged her; I could feel her anger and pain. I began to see why she was so angry. I closed my eyes and prayed for her soul.

Tears streamed down my face as I held onto her spirit I could see what she was looking for, she was being held down on a dirt road. There were men all around her, and two of them held her legs open. The others held her by her wrist, she was sexually abused by, man after man, I could see her eyes looking out at something from afar, she cried out to the men to stop, but they kept going one after the other. She laid there looking out after a while at the bush across the dirt road. I held onto her as her spirit became light and weaker.

I had a clear vision of her walking down the dark road she was frightened walking faster and faster this vision followed over and over again as I held her, I held her and prayed. I felt her fear. I prayed for her spirit to go in peace with the Lords guidance as she began to weaken I could no longer see the men. But her walking down the road afraid and then running from the men as her spirit passed over I could see her placing a small child into the bushes, and running across the road so that the men wouldn't hear the child cry out for her.

As I let go of her to say thank you, Jesus, I could see her going over to the bushes and picking the child up smiling, but it wasn't her who picked the child up. It was the teacher when her spirit was free, I realized that she'd come for Sasha. Sasha was her child and she was killed violently being raped by those men. I stayed on the floor of the bathroom thanking God for that blessing. I now know were Sasha came from, I know that teacher must have found her and saved her. She has no family because the teacher might not have known where she came from at all, having found her in a bush like. She just cared for her and loved her not having children of her own.

I stood up after a while of prayer there on the floor. I washed my face and went to get in bed with Michael; I was exhausted after that experience as always. Michael was sleeping when I lay next to him, his body was so cold, and I kissed his back and turned around. I couldn't go to sleep just yet. I wanted to look in on the kids. I went to the kid's room the twins were laying on the bed together, and Sasha was lying on the cot next to the beds swinging with Keagan in her arms. She was looking up at the ceiling swing the cot with her leg hanging out on one side.

She looked up at me when I walked in. "Hey Sasha, how are you feeling?" I asked her, walking over to the cot to pick up Keagan. I reached and took Keagan into my arms. "Did he wake up Sasha?" I asked. "No, he just kept crying in his sleep," she said looking confused. "I just wanted to hold him to make him happy," she said pulling herself up from the cot. "Mrs. Karis, am I going with you to America?" She asked. "Oh Sasha I don't know yet, Dr. Michael is still working on it. He's doing all he can, sweetheart. I know you want to come along with us."

"It's tough because we need to find out where you really came from, I know that you probably don't remember; you were so young. If there is something you remember about where you came from it would be so helpful to us. We would have a better chance of finding the paperwork we need for you to come home with us," I tell her rocking Keagan in the chair beside the bed. She turned to me and cried. "I can't remember where I came from, but I do remember my mother," she said putting her head down.

"My mother was hurt, I watched them hurt her," she said crying. "Oh, Sasha we don't have to talk about it honey really," I tell her. Having seen exactly what her mother suffered through on that dreadful night. I placed Keagan down on the bed beside the twins and went over to Sasha. "Sweetheart, I know that you saw what happened to your mom. My heart aches for you, honey don't you worry now, she's in a better place, and she knows that you are safe with us," I tell her, hugging her tight. "You don't worry, sweetheart, God, is going to work this all out for us."

"I promise he will, and when it's all over you'll be at home with us in America," I tell her, she was so worried about that I felt her sadness every time she thought of us leaving without her. I sat there with Sasha holding her as she cried it out. I took her little cheeks and held her face close to mine. "Little one, I'm going to do all I can to take you home with me," I said to her looking into her sad eyes. "I know you are afraid, I admire your courage, all this time I have never seen you shed a tear, you're so brave, sweetheart," I tell her kissing her forehead.

"You're going to need to stay as brave as you have been in this time, while we get all your paperwork together, you will come home with us. I know you will," I tell her as I walk over to the door. "You get some rest sweetheart, we will go visit Ms. Effie tomorrow," I tell her shutting the door. When I got back to bed Michael was still laying there underneath the sheets I laid beside him and hugged him by his waist. He turned to me and kissed my face all over. "I missed you where were you, Karis?" He asked. "I just look in on the children," I told him.

"Do you think we really have a chance at getting her Michael?" I asked him. "Baby I really don't know, I checked on the status of the paperwork. She was never classified as an orphan; there are no birth records of her parents. I'm hoping that Ms. Effie can come up with something better than I found there," Michael said. I turned to him and kissed his neck. He held me tight. I fell off to sleep soon after we talked about Ms. Effie. My dream that night was of another child, a little boy, he was holding my hand pulling me toward an abandoned building and laughing. I was so happy following him through the school.

He pulled me through a big wooden door where children were sitting in every seat of the classroom, the teacher was standing before them laughing and clapping her hands singing a song. I looked up at the teacher, it was her, and it was Teacher who found Sasha. The little boy tapped my hand and pointed down at Teacher's desk, and there on the desk was a packet of papers with Sasha written in bold black letters on the front. When I went to grab the papers the little boy pulled me back and the classroom was on fire, blazing hot.

He pulled me one way, and I pulled him another way, he screamed out as he let go of my hands and ran from the classroom with everyone running and screaming. I went to grab the papers, and the teacher's desk caught fire; the flames blazed as high as the classroom ceiling. I turned to run and I woke up sweating and clutching my chest. Michael jumped up. "Are you all right?" He asked. "Yes but I think I know where we can find the papers for Sasha," I tell him. "She was going to a school somewhere out near Somalia," I told him clutching his arm.

"How do you know?" He asked. "I dreamt it, wherever it is, there was a fire there and the school maybe burnt down," I told him. I lay back down with Michael. "Just sleep now, baby. I'll go to Ms. Effie in the morning, and we will check into the school. I bet you are right," he said rubbing my back. "Go on, don't worry yourself we will get Sasha home with us," he said. I fell asleep with Michael hands rubbing my back. When I awoke the next morning Keagan was sitting on the bed next to me and Michael was running water to wash him up.

He walked over to Keagan and washed his little face. "Well, hello there sleepy head," he says to me. "You slept in, I have fed the children, and now they're all getting ready to go to Ms. Effie's in the village." He said. "Oh my goodness, is the van here already Michael?" I asked. "Yes they've been out there waiting for a while, but take your time baby," he said kissing my forehead. They've had something to drink and some snacks, I don't think they mind." I sat up in bed with my hand over my head I was a little tired still. Michael took Keagan up from the bed and over to the sink and washed him up.

"It's just going to take me about fifteen minutes, Michael," I said as I went to the bathroom to wash up in the small shower near the sink; I washed up quickly. Michael and Keagan went back into the room, Michael dressed Keagan fast and put his little shoes on his feet and he left the room. I came out and threw on a nice dress brushed my hair up into a ponytail with my bangs hanging over my eyes, I walked over to get my bag of shoes out. "Wear those nice green ones with the straps,"

Michael told me. "They always look so nice on your feet." He winked at me.

I smiled and put on those shoes. I modeled the shoes for Michael with my feet in his face. "I'm going to bite them off," he said grabbing at my ankle. He got up from the bed and took my hand. "I love you, Karis," he said kissing me on the cheek. We walked out of the room and the children were playing on the floor. "Everybody, to the van," Michael yelled out. The kids got up quickly and grabbed their books to read on the trip. I took my bag from the floor and followed Michael out by the hand. Michael talked to the driver the whole way to the village and I sat with the children and read to them.

They wanted the story of The Three Musketeers. It was a long one, but they loved it. We were reading all the way there, and they were eager to hear the rest of the story. We weren't even close to finishing the story when we made it to Ms. Effie's place. When we pulled up, children were playing everywhere. Ms. Effie was in the yard watching them play, she waved at us standing in the van as we approached. The twins yelled out "Ms. Effie, Ms. Effie!" They really loved Ms. Effie. When the van stopped they all jumped out one by one with the help of the driver. They all ran over to Ms. Effie and gave her big hugs.

Ms. Effie smiled and embraced them. She took Keagan from Michael's arms; she hugged him tight and walked away with him toward the front of the house. I followed her with my bag on my shoulder and Michael hugging me by the waist. We went and sat on the porch, Ms. Effie always watch the children while they played outside. She was very protective of all the children in the orphanage. She called them her little angels. We sat down with her there on the porch and watched the children. Michael began the conversation with her about Sasha.

"I wondered if you might have come up with any leads?" He asked. "No," she said shaking her head. "I don't know where to start, I asked around everywhere, no one seems to know anything about the child," she said with a frown. "I can tell you that when the teacher would bring her around, she would tell me that she was her child sent from God," she said pointing up to the sky. "She would say that she saved her life and God wanted her to have this child." Ms. Effie was very clear about the fact that teacher took good care of the child. I listened intensely hoping to get some kind of confirmation of the dream I'd had.

"Well, Ms. Effie do you think that she came from another area?" Michael asked. "I'm sure she did, the teacher taught the children all over the country and was a hard worker she would go all over teaching them." She said waving her hands all around. "You might go to the schools and find what you are looking for, you won't find anything around this school, but in the other countries you might find something," she said rubbing Keagan's head and kissing his little face. "I will look into that," Michael said standing up to grab Keagan from her arms. "No, no," Ms. Effie said.

"I want to play with him, I only have a little time left, I know that you guys are planning to leave me soon," she said holding Keagan up into the air. "Okay Ms. Effie I know what you mean," Michael said walking over to the huts behind us. "I'll go check on the children inside the huts then" He waved bye to Keagan and walked away. I sat there with Ms. Effie watching her play with Keagan. The twins came over and sat on the porch with us, they were tired. Sasha kept playing kickball with the other children. "You guys are tired huh?" Ms. Effie asked. "The twins said yes at the same time.

She smiled at them, "Two peas in a pod huh? You two will always be close, born together in mommy's tummy. I sense you had a tough pregnancy," she said. "Yes," I said shaking my head. I could see Michael going in and out of the huts behind us getting water in a bucket and washing his hands over and over again. I called out to him and waved; he waved back at me and kept filling the bucket with water. Ms.

Effie wondered off into the field with the children. She put Keagan down and let him run around the field with the children.

She chased after him laughing. Michael came over to me soon after he'd finished in the huts. "Is everything okay?" I asked. "Yes, everything is fine; I'm thinking we should take a trip over near the shopping mall where we were, maybe asking the people around there about a school that burned down will help us find something. We have to do something fast we are leaving in a week," he said picking up my bag from the floor. "Ms. Effie, please can I talk to you for a minute over here please," Michael called out to her.

She scooped Keagan up from the field and walked over to us very slowly. "Yes, Doctor, how can I help?" She asked. "I was wondering if you wouldn't mind keeping an eye on the children for a while, we are taking a trip to the town near Somalia to look into the schools for paperwork on Sasha. She told us that she'd been in school over there before; I want to check into it. Could you watch over them, for us, please? He said taking her by the hand and kissing it. She kissed Keagan's cheeks and said, "you go doc, I will watch over the children."

"Thank you so much, Ms. Effie. We will be right back," he said. We walked over to the van and Michael flagged the driver down to come to the van, he was standing talking to another man who seemed to be Ms. Effie's helper. I got into the van and Michael stood there talking to the driver about where we needed to go. He sat down in the front seat with him and we were off. The ride was so long that I was glad I brought along my bag of books. I would go through them to see what books I'd read to the children next.

I would read Oliver Twist, the story of great courage and strength. I looked it over remembering the first time I'd read Oliver Twist. The children are going to really enjoy it. I thought as we rode through the rough roads of the country. By the time we got into town it was a little chilly, Michael and I got out of the van and began to walk up and down the paths of the busy little city. Michael asked people all around him in their language if they knew of any burned down schools around town. No one did.

We walked for what seemed to be miles into the little town. We see children playing people singing and shopping it was a little busy place. I was so tired by the time we reached the end of the business section. There were old abandon buildings, and shacks were people were living in. We saw an old lady sitting down in a chair near an abandoned shack. "Excuse me Ms." Michael said. "I need some help," The woman looked up at him and shook her head and flagged him away. "Ms. I just want to know if you know of any schools around here, schools," he said again.

"Michael, I don't think she understands you at all," I say. "I know she does I seen her talking to someone before we walked over here. She can speak a little English, I'm sure of it," he said putting his hand in his pocket. He pulled out money and waved in front of her face. She reached out to grab it. "Ms. are there any schools around here, schools that have been burned down?" He asked her again. "Yes," she said clearly, "schools down there." She pointed us down a dirt path it looked completely empty no trees no huts no buildings just dirt road. "No, you show me," Michael said to the woman.

"You want money?" He asked waving it in her face again. "I want money," she said. "Well, let's go, you show me, and I'll give you money." The woman got up from the chair. "You follow me," she said. Michael grabbed me by the hand and we followed her through all the brush of the field. We walked for a while down the dirt road. I was exhausted and almost had to stop. I pulled at Michael's hand. "Michael where is it? I am so tired," I tell him. "Baby, just hold on; Ms. are we close at all?" He asked.

We went through a field full of weeds and there in the back of the field stood the frame of an old school. Michael gave the woman the money, and we walked over to the old burnt down school. Michael grabbed my hand as I was eager to go in and look around. "No baby it's dangerous over here, you can't just walk over into the rubble like that the structure of the school is still standing and it could fall at any time," he said creeping around the school. "I want to look around to Michael," I tell him creeping in behind him.

"Okay, but please watch your step, I don't have my medical bag with me," he said. "I will," I said walking over to the front of the classroom. I knew it was the front of the classroom because there was one frame of a chair there and a desk burned to the ground. I walked over to it and leaned down to brush away the black coal like dust to see if by any chance my dream was leading me here to find the papers. I picked up burned book after book, While Michael walked around the rest of the class picking up and turning over the tops of every desk in he could. "Michael, there's nothing," I said. "Let's go."

"No, baby let's look around a little more and then we will leave." I started to get really sleepy just thinking of the walk back to the little town. I stepped out of the school and sat down on a tree stump near the structure while Michael looked around a little more. I could see the sun setting. "Michael you need to hurry the suns going down, and we have a ways to go," I tell him drawing with a stick in the dirt. "Alright!" I heard him yell out. "I found something he shouted running toward me with a bundle of burned papers in his hands. "What is it?" I asked him.

"I don't know yet," he said. He took the papers and spread them out over the dirt. "Michael there all burned up and you can barely see them," I tell him getting up from the tree stump. "I know Karis, but look at what we can see," he said pointing at the top of the page. "Sasha Nuzika, born May 3rd, if we can get them in some light we may be able to read the rest," he said grabbing me by the hand. "Let's get going before it gets too dark." We walked away from the burned school structure for what seemed like hours I was so exhausted and thirsty. "Michael, I don't think I can go on," I tell him stopping to catch my breath.

"Yes you can, look up ahead," he said pointing ahead of us. "There's the van, they came to find us. See you did it, baby," he said. I walked even faster to get to the van; it was like I was running toward the van. "Michael, I need water," I tell him as he hung on tightly to my hand. "It's in the van." When we made it to the van, I grabbed Michael's bag and searched around in it for the water.

It was hard for me to focus on anything other than that water. I was happy Michael found those papers, but I was so thirsty I couldn't think of anything at that moment except for that water. I held it up in the air and drank until it was gone. When I was finished Michael grabbed it. "Hey, none for me huh?" he shook the bottle laughing. "You were thirsty," he reached into his bag and pulled out another bottle. "See I came prepared for this, I knew you would be really thirsty," he said taking the bottle to his mouth.

"Karis lets go," he said after taking one drink. I hopped up into the van, and he came inside behind me. "Alright guys let's get moving," he said waving to the driver and his friend. We drove through the little town really fast. It was hot and humid; I rested my head on Michaels' shoulder all the way to Ms. Effie's. It was a long ride there, but all I could think of was we had the paper that could give us a real chance at having Sasha come home with us.

When we arrived at Ms. Effie's the children were inside, and it was so dark all around the building. Ms. Effie was sitting on the porch with Keagan in her lap rocking him, Keagan was fast asleep. She put her finger to her lips to shush us as we approached her. "He's sleeping," she whispered. Michael waved the papers in her face and smiled. "You found something?" She asked in a whisper. "I did, I will leave it with you, and you can go and find out tomorrow what we can do with it," he said taking Keagan from her arms. "Are the other children sleeping?" I asked her.

"Yes, honey they're inside. They played until they were tired; they sang songs today and eat dinner with the other children." She told us. "Thank you so much, Ms. Effie. You are a saint," I tell her following her inside to get the children. She took me by the wrist and guided me through the room where the children were sleeping. They were all sleeping together. Head to shoulder and it was a picture perfect moment. "Ms. Effie took Kristine and put her over her shoulder to carry her out and I grabbed Sasha and we walked out.

I sent Michael back in to get Kristopher. We all got into the van and the driver drove us back to our hut. It was quiet when we got inside. Michael helped me put the children to bed and then I made him his coffee. I was standing inside the small kitchen when he came over to me and kissed my face. "Thank you, baby, for being so brave," he said. "I don't want any coffee tonight, I just want you, we don't have very long here, let's make the best of tonight. Let's just sit and talk about it all," Michael said. He took me by the hand and we walked out of the kitchen and into the front room.

Michael sat down on the couch and pulled me down with him. I sat on his lap and hugged his neck. "What do you think the weather will be like when we get back home?" I asked him. "Whatever the weather, baby you're always going to be my sunshine," he said kissing my face. "I don't want to talk about the weather Karis; I would really like to talk about you." I smiled at Michael looking into his eyes. "I love you, Michael." We sat there talking into the late night hours until I fell off to sleep. The next day I found myself in bed cuddled up next to Michael it was hot in the room and the sun shined right in my face.

I covered my eyes with the sheet. "Mommy, are you awake?" a little voice said tapping me on my shoulder. I peeked out from the sheet.

"Yes I am, what's wrong?" It was Kristopher, "what's the problem, little guy?" I asked him. "I'm hungry, mommy," he said rubbing his tummy. "I'm sorry Kristopher, I got out of bed immediately and went into the kitchen. I was in a gown, Michael must have dressed me for bed. I must have been so sleepy and tired I don't remember him placing me into bed nor do I remember being dressed for bed. I began to cook Kristopher eggs and sausage right away.

"Sit down sweetie it won't take long, okay." I pulled the chair out for him. "Mommy, can I have toast with my breakfast, please?" He asked. "Of course you can," I told him getting the bread for the toaster. "I hope you're hungry," I said to him I placed a plate in front of him and put his eggs and sausage on the plate. "Thank you, mommy." I went to grab his toast, and I sat down with him at the table. "Kristopher, what do you think of Sasha?" I asked, "She's so fun mommy, I like her a lot, she is my sister?" He said. I rubbed the top of his little head.

"Yes, she is your sister, son. I took some jam from the refrigerator and spread it all over his toast. He was hungry; he ate his breakfast really fast. I waited as he finished up his breakfast, Michael walked into the kitchen. "Good Morning," he said. Kissing my cheek and rubbing Kristopher on the head. "Hello son, how are you this morning?" He asked him going over to the sink to get a cup of coffee. "I'm good, dad," Kristopher said filling his mouth with bread.

"Well, we are leaving soon, are you excited about going home, son?" He asked. "Yes, dad I am. I can't wait to get back to school." Michael looked over at him with a surprised look on his face. "School, son?" He asked. "Yes, dad I can't wait to go back to my school and play with my toys at home," he said turning to me. "Well son, that's great that you're looking forward to going to school," Michael was so shocked by Kristopher's reply. "Why are you surprised?" I asked him.

Michael just shook his head and grab a piece of bread and placed it in the toaster. I went over to the front room to look for the other children, everyone should be up soon. I waited by the bedroom door where Keagan slept for him to wake up. I watched him sleeping in the small bassinet. He was wiggling around so I knew it wouldn't be long before he was up. He was getting so big, his little body was stretched out from the top to the bottom of that bassinet. It wouldn't be long before he was off to school and talking about breakfast too.

When his little eyes opened he looked over at me. "Mommy" He said with excitement in his little voice. He reached out for me and I went to him. "Hello my little sunshine how was your sleep? I bet you saw the angles huh," I say to him carrying him out to the front room to go to the wash sink to wash his little face and brush his little teeth he was ready for breakfast. Soon after, Sasha and Kristine were up and ready too. I waited as Michael went to get dressed and I dressed the children soon after; we left to Ms. Effie's to hear the news about the paperwork that Michael gave her the night before about Sasha.

We packed a snack for the ride this time and we were off. When we made it to Ms. Effie's everyone was outside playing in the field and Ms. Effie was preparing lunch. We were helped from the van with the children. The children went to play in the fields, and we walked into the kitchen with Ms. Effie, "Hello there," Michael said to her kissing her cheek Ms. Effie was in an apron, she was holding kitchen utensils in both her hand. "Hello, Ms. Effie, how are you?" I asked. "I'm doing okay," Ms. Effie says to me stirring the food around in the pot.

"I saw the birth certificate, I know where her father is," she told us. Her father lives in Somalia, and he is worried about the child. He has been in search of her since her, and her mother went missing some time ago. I don't know what he is doing now, but he has been all over looking for her, and you would have to go and see him and ask his permission to leave Africa with her," she said putting the food into a large bowel on the side of the counter. "So we can be sure to find him in Somalia?" Michael asked.

"Yes you need to first go to the police there and tell them who she is, explains how she came to be with you and they will get him." "I'm not sure about this Ms. Effie," Michael said walking over to me looking me into my eyes. He then walked over to the window looking out at the children playing in the field, "Michael, we don't have to worry right?" I asked him. "Yes, Karis, we do have to worry, I think you should get your heart ready to let her go." "Yes, Michael I think your right." I said looking out at the children playing in the fields. Michael took my hand and kissed it.

We left Ms. Effie's that evening a little discouraged. The children said their goodbyes to Ms. Effie and the other children in the village. Michael and I hugged everyone, and he checked on a few patients, and we were off back to the hut where we packed and began to prepare for our trip back to the states. I didn't say a word, and Michael walked back and forth from one room to the other rubbing his head in thought. After I put everything in our bags and sat down on the bed, he came over to me and took my hand.

"Let's go, baby, if we don't do this we will never know, we have to at least give it a try." Michael pulled me up from the bed by my hand, and we went to the front room to get the children. We were heading to the police headquarters in Somalia. Michael was very nervous, and so was I. I was worried about what would happen when we arrived there. Especially the shock it would be on Sasha to find out she had a father who had been looking for her for so long. So I sat next to her and told her about what we were going to police headquarters for.

"Sasha, my dear, I want to share with you the reason for us taking this quick trip back near the school you said you knew. Honey, we found something the other day at the school. It was some paperwork with your full name on it, and it turns out that, your father has been looking for you and he may want you to stay with him. We may not be able to take you with us to America." I tell her. She looked up at me. "Mrs. Karis, I have a father?" She asked me.

"Yes, sweetheart you do, and he's been looking for you all over, he didn't know where you were all this time, and now we are going to find out now if he is still looking for you." She looked at me listening so intensely, her eyes were pierced on mine, and I could tell already she was in a state of shock. "Sasha, are you okay honey?" I asked her shaking her by the hand. She looked down at her lap. "Mrs. Karis I love you," she said. "I don't want to leave you, but I do want to see my father, I want to know him, I want him to tell me about my mother. Do you think he knows about my mother?" She asked with excitement in her eyes.

She was so excited. I hoped now for her sake that she would get to see her father. We arrived to the police headquarters soon after the chat with Sasha. We all went into the station; we sat the children down on the bench in front of the front desk of the clerk. I looked around the office it was very busy, there was a billboard on the wall with missing people and people with wanted signs underneath their pictures. I looked all over it for a picture of Sasha, there wasn't one up.

"These pictures were posted up a month ago," an officer told me standing behind me. "Can I help you with something?" "Yes, my husband and I are looking to find someone who's been looking for a missing little girl. It may have been some time ago," I tell him. "I see, and the person they have been looking for, where are they?" He asked. I pointed to Sasha. She was waiting nervously on the bench. He peeked his head out over the desk at her.

"So where are you from?" He asked. "We are from California," Michael came over to us with papers in his hand. "These are possible links to finding out where her father is," He said sitting down in a chair beside me. The man looked through a book he pulled from the cabinet beside his desk. "I remember this case," he said. "This guy came in over and over again for a long time. He was so frantic, looking for his wife and daughter; he never stopped looking for them.

"Where's the mother?" He asked. "We think she's deceased," Michael told him. "Do you mind if I ask you two some questions?" "Sure you can," we replied to him. "How did you come to having the child?" He asked us holding a pen in his hand. I looked at Michael before answering, "We just came here with my team, I am Dr. Michael Philips, I come here almost every two years or so to help the sick families in the villages." Michael said. "Oh sir, I'm sorry," he said putting his pen down. "I am just trying to find out how you ended up with her," he said looking over at Sasha again.

"She is about how old?" He asked. "I believe she's twelve," I tell him. "Well, I do know where her father is, here's a picture of him right here," he said turning the book to us to see. I looked at the man in the book. Michael looked at me and took my hand. We both knew right off that this was her father; he looked as if she could have been his twin. I looked at it over and over and look back at Sasha. "That's him," he said turning the book to him. He went over to some other officers at the desk and gave them a piece of paper they looked at Sasha and went out of the door.

"Dr. Philips, can you please wait over there, I sent them to get the father, and he doesn't live far from here." "That's it, we don't do anything else?" He asked. "No, because he's been looking for her we don't need anything else." Michael and I went and sat down with the children on the bench. He looked a bit nervous, I was nervous also. We waited there for what seemed like hours. Sasha looked so excited. She didn't say a word she just waited patiently. "Your dad is coming, Sasha," I told her. "Are you scared?" I asked. She shook her head no.

She looked so pretty, she was dressed up in pink and blue she loved those colors her shirt was pink, and her pants were blue. She was ready to see her father I could see it in her eyes. "Don't worry Sasha everything's going to fine," I told her. I took her hand and held it until the doors flew open the police came in with a crowd of people. I could hear crying and yelling a crowd ran toward me and the children on the bench, we all stood up as they approached us. The man was escorted by what I believed to be his whole family.

He stood in front of Sasha as if he knew who she was already. She looked up at him and he smiled down at her, soon after he took her into his arms, he let out a cry of relief. The room was filled with tears of joy. After holding her and looking her over, the man came over to Michael and I and stuck his hand out. "Thank you, thank you, I am forever in your debt. I will never forget your kindness," he said shaking Michaels hand with a tight grip. "You're very welcome, sir I am Dr. Michael Philips, I took care of the teacher she was living with. In the village they found the teacher lying ill in the fields.

Sasha was the one who saved her that day. Unfortunately, she didn't make it through her illness," he told him. "And no one knew where Sasha came from, except for the teacher. We found you through the papers we found at the school right here in Somalia and the reason we were looking for you is because we were looking to take her to America with us. But I see she has love right here in Africa," Michael said hugging Sasha kissing her forehead.

"Come," the man said to us pulling Sasha and me together. "You have to eat with us. You have to come see where she will be living." "I'm sorry, we have a plane to catch tonight, and we have a long drive ahead of us," Michael said looking at his watch. I looked at Michael. "Michael, can we just go by there for a couple hours?" Michael looked at Sasha, and by now she was surrounded by the crowd of people that the man brought in with him. She was all smiles by now.

The children stood by her while the people looked her over and talked to her in their language, the children followed as if they could understand every word. I went over to the children. "Come on children, give Sasha some space," I tell them. "No, Mrs. Karis, can they come with me, only for a little while?" She asked. "Oh, sweetheart, you are going to be fine, we have to go to the airport to check in, I'm sorry, but we really have to say our goodbyes here." I said. "No," Michael said.

"I think we can go over there for a while," he said. "But quickly" We all gathered near the door to get inside the van. Sasha went happily with her father. She was so happy you could see her teeth. She waved at us as he held her close to him all the way to the little car he'd come to the station in. "We will see you soon," I yelled out. "We all caravanned to the home where Sasha call home from now on. When we arrived it was a gated community the houses around it were all very nice I was eager to see what the inside looked like. We all got out and followed Sasha and her father inside.

It was a beautiful place; her father had help in the home to our surprise he was also a doctor and Sasha's mother a teacher. He showed us around the house, he shared pictures of Sasha and her mom he had memoirs everywhere around the house. We ate with them and laughed and hugged Sasha all we could, before leaving their home. When we arrived at the airport, the children were all sleeping. Michael and I got out of the van with the help of the driver; Michael shook his hand and gave him a handful of money.

We walked up to the counter to show our passports and tickets, and it wasn't long before we were off to America. The children slept so well on the plane. When they awoke, it would be breakfast, and then we would be closer to home. "It was great to see that Sasha was happy, wasn't it Karis?" He said looking into my eyes I think he could feel my love for her. I looked at him and smiled. Looking from the window made everything clear.

We never found out why the teacher didn't look to see if Sasha had family there, I felt that maybe in her heart she always knew where the father was. She wasn't that far away from him, teaching at the school, but she chose to keep her and never take her to him even when she became ill. I guess she longed for love also, the love of a missing child. The flight was so quiet I dozed off to sleep. Michael held my hand tight and kissed it every now and then. The children slept on and off also. We were all eager to get back to our home, in America.

Home From Africa

We made it back to America safe, and sound. Michael and I rushed to get the children home from the airport; it had been a very long flight. The shuttle was there waiting for us. They took our bags, and we got in; it was warm and sunny as always in California. The ride home was very long too. When we made it home, I was so excited to see my front door. The kids were also excited. We all rushed to the door. When Michael turned the key and we went in it was like walking into the house for the first time.

Michael dropped the bags on the front porch, and we all walked into the front room the windows were wide open in the back room. Michael went upstairs and all around the house to check everything out. The children and I began to pull the luggage closer toward the stairwell to help Michael pull them up. I went to the kitchen and flipped on the light. Oh, how I missed my kitchen I thought. "Michael!" I yelled. "I'm going to go to the grocery store, we need everything," I told him.

I looked in all the cabinets and the refrigerator, the cupboards were bare. When we got settled and the children were in bed, I left Michael with the children and headed to the grocery store. It was a little chilly out so I grabbed a sweater. I walked out toward the car as I got into the front seat and turned the key I heard a tap on the window. "Hello," the voice at the window shouted. It was Mr. Simms, "hey Mr. Simms," I said rolling down the window. I reached out to shake his hand. "Young lady, welcome home, welcome home," he said with a big smile.

"I'm going to the grocery store Mr. Simms, hop in, take a ride with me," I told him. I hadn't seen Mr. Simms since before we left for Africa; I often wondered why his spirit lingered around. He got inside the car, and we drove to the grocery store. "Mr. Simms you're still around huh,"

I asked him looking over at him. "Yes, I am; where would I be other than here?" He said. "I have to visit Maddy every day, she's not doing well," he said.

"Really, how about we go over and check on her," I said making a detour toward Maddy's house. I hadn't seen Maddy in so long. We pulled up to her house, and it was so dark as if no one was home. "Looks like she's working this evening," I told Mr. Simms. Then he reached over and grabbed my hand. "No, she's in there, can we go knock?" "Sure," I said turning the car off. We got out, and I went to knock on the door. I could see the cats sitting in the window. I knocked hard. "Maddy, are you there?" I called out. "Maddy, please open up," I said.

"You have to open up." I went around to the garage door to see if her car was there I peeked into the garage and her car was there. I went back over to the front door and knocked even harder. "Maddy are you there?" I called out, Mr. Simms leaned on the railing on the porch. He pointed down at the doorknob and moved his hand in a turning motion. I reached down and turned the knob; to my surprise it was unlocked. I walked in, and it was so dark the cats were everywhere. As I walked through the front room, I could hear the cats in every corner.

I walked back into the back room and opened the door I looked for Maddy on the bed, she wasn't there I looked for her in the other rooms of the house. When I turned to go back into the front room Mr. Simms stood in front of me, turn around he pointed back into the bedroom, she's in there. He said. "No, Mr. Simms, I looked in there already." I walked back into the room anyway to check more thoroughly and there she was on the floor in the room sitting staring into the darkness holding one of the carts. I kneeled down to her. "Maddy, are you okay?" I asked her.

She looked at me with tears streaming from her face. I sat down beside her and took the cat from her arms. "Maddy, what's wrong?" "I just keep looking for him," she shouted out. "Where is my father?" She said. "I don't understand why God would take him from me," she said. This was a shock to me because Maddy had taken it so well when she buried her father she cried, and she talked about him. She seemed so well. I took her hand and held it while she cried and screamed out. "Maddy, I know how you feel.

When I lost my mom I was so sad, you need to know that your father loves you, he loves you so much, but it was his time, God called him home. He is safe and free from pain, and he will forever smile down on you and be your angel. You have to allow him to go to his resting place, his soul won't rest as you hold on to him in pain. So please smile and laugh, think of the joy he brought to your life, he needs to know you're okay." I got up and went to the bathroom to grab a box of Kleenex for Maddy to dry her tears.

When I went back into the bedroom Mr. Simms was sitting on the bed looking down at Maddy. He looked over at me and waved his hand he touched the top of her head and she stood up quickly. "Karis, was that you?" She asked in a panic. "No, Maddy I am here," I said to her walking toward her with the Kleenex box. "Here you go," she took a couple of Kleenex and blew her nose. I looked over at Mr. Simms; he was sitting in the light now. It shined so brightly on him. "Goodbye Karis, thank you," he said. I hugged Maddy.

"Thank you so much, Karis, I thought I wouldn't have these moments. I thought I was stronger than this, I guess I was wrong huh?" "Yes, I guess you were wrong, but Maddy everyone has pain, you can turn it off at times, if you try and turn it off it can suddenly consume you," I told her. "Well, I should take it from you huh, I know you know pain." "Yes, Maddy I sure do, So how long have you've been sitting there?" I asked her. "How many of these episodes have you had?" She turned to me.

"Too many since he passed, I was secretly coming home from work and just shutting down, look at my house Karis," she said turning on the lights. "OH No!!" I said as I turned around and around. There were cats and clothes and food and cat pooh. It was a huge mess. "Oh no, Maddy, Oh no," I covered my mouth and looked around the house even more. In every room there was a mess of clothes and trash. I walked into the kitchen. This was so bad. Maddy had been the cleanest woman I'd ever know.

She even slept with towels over her pillows and washed every dish after eating. I was so stunned. I didn't know what to say. I just grabbed Maddy and hugged her again. I just hugged her. What are we going to do, how are we going to clean this up. I thought. "Can you help me?" She asked. "I sure can, but I'm on my way to the grocery store, we just got in two hours ago, and there is nothing there for the children to eat," I told her. "Oh yes, how was your trip?" She asked whipping her nose with the Kleenex. "Oh we can talk about that later," I tell her going toward the door.

"Maddy you come home with me, and tomorrow we will come back and clean the house. I will call a carpet cleaning business to clean the carpets, and we can start from there, okay," I tell her escorting her out to the porch. "Oh Karis I can't impose, you just got back home, I can't do that." "Maddy, you have to come with me. It's unhealthy for you to stay in here, just come tonight, and I'll bring you back tomorrow. We will clean it and get it back for you. I promise you're not imposing," I tell her as we shut the door of her home and walk to the car.

"Okay, okay," she says following me and looking back at her home. "Maddy, I just have to stop at the store, and we will be on our way home." After stopping at the grocery store I drove Maddy to the house. I got the groceries out with Michaels help. Maddy went inside the house and sat in the den. I put everything away. I went upstairs and got Maddy some sweats and a T-shirt, some washcloths, and soap I went into the guest room downstairs to check if everything was as I left it. I didn't usually change the sheets and blankets often because guest was rare for us. I went into the den and got Maddy.

"Here are some clothes to sleep in and there's the restroom, you'll sleep in here." I said pointing to the room. "Thank you, Karis," she said taking the towels and clothes. I went into the front room were Michael was waiting for me. "Is she okay?" He asked me. "Oh yes, she'll be fine," I told him walking back into the kitchen. "I wonder how Sasha is?" I said to him. "She's probably so happy, finding her family and all." "She is happy, I can feel it. I can't wait to get a letter from her; she's starting school soon also."

"That's going to be so great for her if only her mother had been able to escape those men." "I believe her mother still watches over her and keeps her strong," I went back into the room when I heard Maddy come out from the restroom. "Hey, Maddy are you okay?" I ask her. She turned to me, wrapping her robe around her waist. "I am good, I'm so tired," she said yawning. "I know, well, I put some tea on, you go and get comfortable, and I will be in with the tea shortly," I tell her walking back toward the kitchen.

"Thank you for everything Karis, thank you," she said opening the door to the room. I quickly went into the kitchen as the tea kettle whistled. "Hey you," Michael peeked around the counter and kissed my cheek. I made her tea and walked it carefully into her room. I knocked, "Maddy, your tea is ready." "Come in please," she said. I opened the door and went inside the

room. Maddy was sitting on the bed she was still wearing the robe.

"Karis, do you think I should have been over my dad's death?" She asked. "I think you get over things when it's time to get over things. It could take years to get over a death, especially when its someone close to you," I tell her rubbing her back. "You handled your mother's death well, I mean, I can't remember a time when you were ever this sadden by losing her," she said with a frown. "It just feels like in the pit of my stomach there is a hole burning deeper and deeper as the days and weeks roll by.

I miss my dad, more and more as time passes by and as much as I want to let him go, but I feel like if I do I would start to feel empty," she said. "Now, Maddy you are never alone, and you should never feel empty at all, you have to believe that things will get better, with time. You should do something to help you feel better." "I can't feel better Karis, you know what it is, I am in love with Dr. Green, and he's married." "Yes, I know."

"Yes, he is and Karis I feel I can't let him go, I know it's wrong to be with him, he says he's divorcing his wife. I saw the paperwork and all, but where would I fit into his life after the divorce, I'd look to my father to tell me what to do and to comfort me, I feel as if I broke up a happy home." "Well, did you?" I questioned" "No, I didn't, they have been separated for over three years before I started seeing him, and he promised he'd divorce her and he is doing that now." Well, what would be the harm in you being with him after the divorce?" I asked her.

"There would be no harm I guess, he says I'm overreacting, but I feel like I should be because he will be a free man and what if he doesn't want me, the same as he has in the past?" "Maddy, I think you have to let go of all the feelings you have and really open up to God. Ask God to lead your path, ask him to show you what's right and wrong in this situation, you can't keep allowing your emotions to bring you down this way."

"I'm trying not to, Karis, but I am so afraid to let go of the love I feel. My father's love was unconditional, it was something I could always count on, something that didn't confuse me or let me down. It never left me lonely," she said holding her arms together as if she was hugging herself. "I understand you, Maddy, I feel the same way about my daddy.

I suppose you feel no one could ever love you that way, but it can happen, Maddy."

"It can, Dr. Green may just be okay after everything settles and he gets his heart in order, he may just give you the same comfort in love that your father did, but in case he doesn't satisfy that womb you must keep god in your heart for healing and comfort." I tell her holding her hand, "see, we sometimes forget that a heavy heart can kill. The Lord sacrificed his life so that we could be freed from carrying that kind of burden. Like worrying if we're loved enough, we never have to worry about that it should be a constant feeling in our hearts, love.

We should never have to feel like we are abandoned or allow our hearts to get heavy over it. The Lord is there for us in every way," I tell her. "Do you really believe that Karis, do you really believe that you can live this life without your heart getting heavy over something? Without ever feeling pain or sorrow over love?" She asked me. "I do believe that my heart sometimes weakens too, I am not saying that we sometimes won't have to cry or be sad. What I am saying, is that we should feel hurt and sadness and pain, but not forever it shouldn't last a lifetime.

It should only last for a while and after crying or feeling sad is all we can do and nothing changes. We should hold on to what he gave us, and that was his love and his promise that he would never leave us lonely or sad, he will always pull us through." She looked at me and tears streamed from her face. "Karis, if God was or is so wonderful, why am I hurting still? Why won't the pain go away?" She asked me. I took her hands and held them tight. "Maddy the pain won't go away because you allow it to stay there lingering in your heart."

"Let it go, stop thinking about the pain in it, think about the good. Think about the memories of your father and how he made you feel when he was here with us. I know it's all gone the thought of the times to be had, but he's around you still he's watching over you, and I know he wants to see that smile," she smiled at me. "See for each smile you give him, say it, say thank you, Lord. Believe me, he knows your pain and can feel your doubt. Learn how to embrace your past and hold on to what awaits you in the future, there is so much to be happy for," I tell her as I let her hands go.

"You are right Karis, I do need to be fearless and embrace the future and whatever it brings me. Whether it's good or bad huh," she said. "Yes because what can you change about it? how can you fix what happened in the past? You can't, you just have to embrace it, move forward and have peace. Give the Lord praise; he's so happy when we just praise him, by being happy and smiling. Do you think you can pray and just be happy Maddy?" I asked.

She looked at me and smiled, "Karis, I think I will try it for you. I will try letting go of the past and pray more and allowing myself to trust his word." She said giving me a huge hug. I stood up and walked to the door of the room. Maddy took her tea from the table and drank it. "You have a good night Maddy, don't forget to say thank you God before lying down," I tell her before opening the door and going out. When I walked into the front room Michael was sitting on the floor of the den staring at the television.

"Hey, I've been waiting for you to come out of there, I have a surprise for you," he said. "Come," he reached out his hand, and I pulled him from the floor as hard as I could. He laughed, "okay, okay," he said getting up and grabbing me. He covered my eyes with one of his big hands and carried me by the waist upstairs. When we got upstairs and he uncovered my eyes I was standing in front of bathtub. He'd filled it with bubble and it was nice and hot I could see the steam coming up from the tub.

He pulled my shirt over my head and undressed me. I stepped into the tub, and Michael undressed as I sat down in the tub. "Oh, you did this for me, huh," I said smiling at him. "I just wanted to have a moment with you before I have to go to work tomorrow baby," he said sitting behind me. We sat in the bathtub for a while just talking and washing each other. It was great we slept so well that night. I was so happy to be in my bed in my home. I loved Africa, but home sweet home.

We would wake up to the children the next morning laughing and running around the house. Michael came up to me and kissed my face all over. He smelled so good I grabbed him by his tie gently and hugged him tightly. "Michael, have a good day, call me if you'll be late coming home," I say kissing him. "I will, baby," he said. I sat up in the bed it was cool in the house, so I took the sheet and wrapped myself up in it and got up from the bed. I got up and went to the bathroom to wash up before going to feed the children. When I got downstairs I checked in on Maddy before starting breakfast.

The children went into the kitchen and sat down at the table, I placed Keagan in his highchair. He was getting a little too big for it his little legs dangled over the footrest. As I walked over to the room I could hear the children laughing and talking about what they wanted for breakfast that morning. I knocked at the door. "Maddy, are you up? I'm making breakfast." There was no answer. I stood there for a while. I guess she's still sleeping I thought as I walked back to the kitchen. I made the children breakfast.

I made them eggs toast and sausage they all had a small cup of juice. I went out front while they ate to get the paper. When I came back in I thought I'd check in again with Maddy, I knocked harder this time. "Maddy, are you there?" I said loudly. She must have been really tired. I walked away from the door and back into the kitchen and helped Keagan eat his food. The children finished up breakfast. I took them all back upstairs and washed them up and dressed them for the day.

I throw on a pair of sweats and one of Michaels T-shirts, and we went back downstairs. I decided that it was time for me to look in on Maddy because she should have been up by now. I went to the door and knocked again. "Maddy," I called out; still no answer. This time I went inside. I just wanted to peek and make sure she was okay and if she wanted coffee or breakfast. When I opened up, I noticed the windows were open and the bed was still made up. I walked over to the bed and all around the room. On the bed was her robe. She had left a note.

"My sweet Karis, thank you so much for everything, don't worry I took a cab home. I am taking your advice and doing exactly what you said, trusting Gods word. Living and smiling not just for me, but for him too, I am going home to reclaim my life; I love you." She must have slipped out after I left her last night. I walked out of the room and began to clean the kitchen. As soon as I finished, I got the children all together to head to Maddy's to help her clean. I took all my cleaning supplies because it was going to be a tough job.

As we drove over to Maddy's, I thought about her loss and mine. I thought about going to see daddy, I wondered how he was, how he's been since I'd last seen him. I did get a letter from my little sister Krystal telling me he'd moved in with my sister Mary and he was doing okay. I made it to Maddy's. She was sitting on her porch with her cats, there was two vans parked outside her house they were from a cleaning company. She waved at me as I pulled up. I got out, and the twins got out. I picked Keagan up and we walked over to Maddy.

"Hello, Karis," she said. "Hello, so you like sneaking away in the night huh?" I said leaning down to hug her. "Oh no, Karis I was restless, so I decided to just come home and get prepared for today," she said. "I brought my cleaning supplies, I thought you could use my help to clean, but it looks like you have it covered," I said pointing at the trucks. "Oh no Karis, there is absolutely no way we could have tackled that mess," she said smiling. "That was beyond you and I. It needed professional attention," she picked up her cat, and we went walking through the house.

The twins stood at the front door with Keagan. The fumes from the cleaning supplies they used were really strong. "Make sure that the floors are steamed after you clean over them," she told one of the workers. "And I want all of the walls washed down as well." Maddy wanted the house cleaned from top to bottom. It was so good to see her spirit come back to life. She was as demanding and anal as she'd been in the past, as far as cleaning went. "Maddy, are you throwing these things away?" I asked pointing at a bag of things on the floor in the hallway. "Oh no, I'm going to donate them to the Salvation Army," she said.

"Those are my father's old blankets and shirts." As we walked through the house room by room, there was a person in there cleaning and throwing things away. I turned around to go back into the front room to check on the children, I didn't want to leave them at the door alone for too long. When I passed through the hall I looked at the man cleaning the carpet he was sweaty and very focused. "How do you do" He said. I took one look at him and there it was.

I hear a whisper telling me that he was going to die soon. I walked over to the children and take them by the hand. "You guys will have to come in back with me. Now do mommy a favor and cover your noses while we walk through okay." I walk with them and we pass the man, Keagan reaches his hand out to him as if he wants to hold his hand. "No Keagan, he's working little guy," I said pulling him with me. Keagan cried loudly waving his hand at the man. I took them in back with Maddy and sat Keagan down on her bed. "What's wrong buddy?" I asked him, he pointed at the door. "You can't hold the man's hand Keagan, he's working okay.

Maddy, I think I'm going to go, I still haven't gone to see my dad. I need to finish unpacking and clean, but I want to see my dad," I told her, picking up Keagan from the bed. I walked out of the room with the children following behind me. Keagan was getting so heavy I wanted to put him down, but I knew he would go to the man again. I just held on to him and we walked through the hallway. "Goodbye," the man said to us. "Good Bye," I said walking as fast as I could pass him.

I wanted to tell him to go see a doctor, but I always felt strange about doing that. I put the children in the car and Maddy came running out of the house. "Karis, Karis!" she yelled out. "Yes Maddy," I said standing in front of my car door. "I will see you soon right, come have lunch with me, okay, here at around noon tomorrow okay," she said waving at me. "I will Maddy, promise," I said blowing her a kiss. Just then I saw the carpet cleaner walking out of her front door going toward his truck. I wanted to approach him so badly.

What's it going to hurt, if you just give him a warning I thought. I stood at my car watching the man. He probably has a family that needs him I thought. So I walked over to him, he looked startled as I approached his truck. "Sir, I don't know you, and you don't know me but, if you just trust me, I think you should go in to see a doctor," I tell him. "Oh, you heard my cough in there huh?" He asked I looked confused. I hadn't heard the man cough at all, but this would be a perfect way for me to tell him without question I thought.

"Oh yes sir, that cough, you should probably go in to see someone as soon as possible about it, it sounds terrible," I tell him walking back to the car. I look over at him as I am driving off and standing beside him was a woman, she was dressed up like she just came from work. She stood close to him, and she waved to me as I drove off. I felt good that I'd warned him. That was something I'd only done once before and that was with Tara. She was the only person I'd ever warned before, and she didn't listen to me. I drove over to my sister Mary's house to see daddy.

When I get there she was cooking and daddy was getting ready for dinner. He was putting his own clothes on when I entered her house. I hugged her and the children hugged her as well. "How have you been Mary?" I asked. "I've been great, how was your trip?" She asked me making daddy's plate. "It was a great trip," I tell her sitting the children down on the couch. I was anxious to see daddy. When he came out of the room, he walked right past me toward the kitchen. I didn't say a word I wanted to surprise him.

Mary began to say something, but I put my hand to my mouth to shush her. I walked over to daddy he was sitting with his back to the kitchen door. I covered his eyes. "Guess who?" I asked giggling. "Um, it's Krystal," he shouted. "No, guess again," I say still covering his eyes. "It's Rose," he says laughing. "Daddy, guess again," he grabbed me by the nose as he'd done when I was younger. "Aha, it's my Karis," he said bringing me down to his chest hugging me. "Hi, daddy," I said. "Hi baby, how are you? I missed you so much," he said standing from the table.

"Daddy, you have to eat," Mary said. "I know, I know," daddy said to her. "Just let me hug my grandbabies, give me a minute," he said going over to the couch to the children. He grabbed them up one by one and hugged them so tight. "I missed my babies," he said. I was so amazed at his speech. He'd regained everything back dressing himself and talking so well no slurring or breathing funny. He was almost at least eighty percent rehabilitated. I was impressed with Mary she really took good care of daddy. I walked over to her.

"Mary, you have taken such good care of daddy, look at him, he looks so great," I tell her. "He's still going to rehab, but he's much better," she says to me. I watched daddy eat and we talked when he was done. "Where is Michael? He asked me. "He's back at work daddy," I tell him. "Yeah, he's a workhorse that one isn't he?" "Yes he loves being a doctor daddy." "How was Africa?" he asked. I tell him all about it, as Mary cleaned up she asked little too few questions. Mary always seemed to distant herself from me. Even when we were children, I couldn't ever remember her being nice to me or even being a big sister to me.

She was five years older than me. I tried to get her to like me, but she'd always push me away, so I didn't expect her to have a long conversation with me. She cleaned up her kitchen and took a cup of water in her hand and went toward her room. "Daddy, when they leave let me know," she waved to the children and walked away. I continued talking to daddy. We talked for a long while the twins were getting sleepy and hungry and Keagan fell to sleep. Daddy kissed them, he held Keagan for a while before I left.

"When will you come to see me again Karis?" Daddy asked as I went to the door. "Oh, daddy I'll come over every day if you like, maybe we can take a ride to get coffee or something," I tell him opening the front door. I kissed daddy's cheek and went to the car with the children. Daddy watched me from the porch waving and smiling. I couldn't wait to see Michael and tell him about daddy's progress. I was so excited. I rushed the children home to get them settled before Michael came home I wanted to have him to myself to tell him about daddy.

We made it home. I let them run around while I cooked, cleaned, and unpacked. Michael called me to tell me he would be a little late coming home. So I allowed the children to stay up a little longer just to keep me company. They fell asleep one after the other, I put them to bed and took my shower then back downstairs to wait for Michael. I turned the radio on to listen to jazz. I cleaned the kitchen again and the clock dinged at midnight. I sat down on the couch waiting. I was beginning to get sleepy so I went through the house turning off lights and trying to stay busy enough to stay up for Michael.

When I just couldn't anymore, I went upstairs. I looked in on the children one last time and then into my bedroom. When I sat on the bed I heard the door open and shut down the hall, I got up. "Michael," I called out. "Michael is that you?" I yelled out. I walked out into the hallway and I heard the door open and shut again. I walked toward the end of the hallway to check it out. I didn't hear anything else, but I needed to see where this door was opened in the house. I wasn't going to be able to sleep until I knew were the sounds were coming from.

I walked down the stairs and turned on the front room light. I looked around, there was nothing open. I went to the guest room to check if there was an open window that could be causing the door to open and shut. I walked over to the window and pulled the curtains open. As soon as touched the window the door slammed shut. It was so dark I scrambled around the room to find the light, but I couldn't adjust my eyes fast enough. I felt around on the wall for the light switch when I finally reached the switch I smelled something foul in front of me. It breathed heavy, and I could feel its madness surrounding me. I tried to flip the switch on, but I knew what would happen if I did so I stood there. I could feel the spirit standing in front of me waiting and watching me to see what my next move would be. As I began to pray its forceful evil began to push me further to the window, pinning me to it. I prayed harder and harder. I could feel it waiting for me to try and move. I stayed put, and I didn't fear it, I knew the spirit of the Lord was standing right beside me. I had no fear at all.

I just waited; the pressure of its spirit was getting heavier and heavier up against my body. I began to hum a song from church. I was pinned and there was nothing I could do but hum. I knew if I'd moved the spirit would attack. As I hummed the song space loosened more and more. I felt it move away the door opened and the smell left the room. The door closed and I sat on the bed. Thanking God for his favor. I went to the front room after the encounter and waited for Michael, by now it was 2am, and Michael was still not home.

After a while, I just went to bed. I didn't know what the spirit wanted from me I didn't know why it came to me, so I put the children to bed with me. I felt better if I could feel them next to me in bed. They enjoyed waking up in my bed also. I was finally able to sleep by 4am. When I fell off to sleep, I dreamt of an older woman who was looking for her daughter in a small wooded area. Michael appeared in the bed the next morning. He'd placed the children in their rooms and got into bed with his clothes and his white coat still on. I got up and undressed him for bed. He woke up and pulled me toward his chest.

He was half sleep. "Baby, I'm so sorry, it was such a long night," he said holding me in his arms. "Don't worry Michael I understand. I waited up for a while, but I knew you were busy, the first day back and all," I said. He was so tired; I just finished undressing him I threw his clothes on the floor next to the bed leaving him only in his underwear. He grabbed me and rolled me in bed beside him. "Michael, I can't stay in bed with you I have to get up in a few to get the kids breakfast," I tell him kissing his neck.

"I missed you last night," I tell him hugging his waist. "Me too baby, me too," Michael said. With his eyes closed shut. I lay beside him for about an hour before getting up to make the children breakfast. Today I would go have lunch with Maddy I thought. I would have to start preparing the children for school; soon Keagan would be in school also. I would try him out in preschool this year I thought as the twins came into the kitchen. "Did you wash your face and brush your teeth?" I asked them"

"Yes mommy, I did," they both said pulling the chairs out. I made pancakes today and a couple strips of bacon for them. I make smiley faces with the whip cream and butter they loved it. Keagan hadn't gotten up yet. While the twins ate I went up to his room to get him. When I came in he was sitting in his bed looking up at the ceiling. "Hello son," I said to him. "How are you this morning?" I took him out of the crib and took him into the bathroom to wash his face and brush his teeth. He didn't talk much, one or two sentences here and there, but I knew he paid close attention because he would do everything the twins did.

He was sharp when it came to mimicking all that they'd do, good and bad. We went downstairs to eat. Soon after I got them dressed Michael was up in his robe. "Good morning baby," he said to me. "Good morning," I said back kissing his cheek. "Do you want something to eat Michael?" I asked. "No thank you, I'm going to grab a cup of coffee, and I'll get something at the hospital." I walked over to the sink and poured the juice the children didn't drink down the drain. "What are you going to do today?" He asked me.

"I'm going to have lunch with Maddy today, and then check out some preschools for Keagan," I tell him. "Okay baby, if you need me, you know where I am. I will call you again around five," he said heading upstairs with his coffee. Sometimes I'd wish Michael had a different job, one that wouldn't take him away from home for so long during the day and night, but I knew he was doing what he loved and what the Lord sent him here to do. I was beginning to see less of him as we settled in at home. I cleaned up the kitchen and took the children to the childcare center.

I would leave them there to run errands. They provider was happy to see them back there. "I'll only be two hours today," I tell her. "No problem Mrs. Philips," the woman said. I drove off over to Maddy's, I arrived at Maddy at exactly 12pm. She had everything all set up for us to eat on the back patio the house was nice and clean. What I walked all around with her, her spirit was changed she seemed so happy. "Would you like sugar for your tea?" She asked me. "No thank you, Maddy," I tell her sitting in the patio chair, it was a warm day out.

"I made some asparagus and turkey soup. I put some sandwiches on the side for us to share later if you like," she tells me sitting down at the patio table. I was so hot in the sun it was hard to eat the soup I began to sweat. It was very tasty. "So I wanted you to come for lunch because I have something for you," she said reaching into her pocket to get something. She pulled out a gold chain and handed it to me. "Karis, I have to give this to you, no one knew what I was going through, and you came to find me to help me, I just know you're my angel," she said.

"I can't Maddy, I can't take this," I said placing it back in her hand. "There was a time when you came for me and lifted my spirits I can't have you feeling like you owe me something," I said to her. "Karis, I don't feel like that, I just want you to have this necklace it's a symbol of my love for you okay. That's all it is," she got up and went behind me and put the chain around my neck clipping it together. I turned it to look at the symbol it was a gold angel. "Thank you, Maddy," I said to her.

She sat down and we ate our food and talked. She talked about Mr. Green a lot. She was definitely in love with him. It was a great lunch. I drove back to the childcare center to pick up the children. It was a quiet drive. I thought about how nice it was that Maddy gave me that necklace. I looked at it as I pulled up to the childcare center. When I went inside the provider was waiting by the door for me. "Mrs. Philips I wanted to talk to you about Keagan if you don't mind," she said walking toward a small room in the back.

"Oh, I don't mind at all. What is it, how is he, did something happen?" I asked all at once. "Oh no, he's a good little boy. I was just a little concerned about him developmentally," she said. "He's a little behind expressing himself verbally." I knew this was coming I thought to myself. Keagan doesn't talk as much as he should, and he just stares off into to space at times. "Mrs. Philips, I know he will be starting school soon, so I thought this would be a great opportunity to offer you some extra help for him, If you like," she said pulling an information packet from her drawer.

"Thank you so much," I tell her reaching for the packet. "Also you might want to see his doctor for a little help also maybe he might have some learning disabilities that you may not be aware of," she said casually. "Well, I do thank you for your advice, and I value your concerns, but I assure you he doesn't have any learning disabilities, he's just a little nonverbal," I tell her getting up from the seat walking toward the door. "Mrs. Philips, I do want you to know that I am only looking to help your son, I hope I wasn't prying," she said. "Oh no, thank you I appreciate your help, really I do," I said shaking her hand.

I took Keagan and the twins and we got into the car. On the way home I was a little sad.

"Are you okay mommy?" Kristopher asked me. "Oh son, I'm okay," I said rubbing his head. "You know mommy the lady there she kept asking Keagan questions, she was asking him over and over, and Keagan wouldn't talk to her at all, he just kept walking over to Kristine and me and holding on to us, he told me to tell her to leave him alone. Mommy, I was so mad at that lady," Kristopher was so hurt. I was so angry now.

I drove them home quickly hoping that Michael would be there. I took the children inside, got them all together and ready for lunch I was starting to get them ready for dinner when Michael came in, he was so early today. I thought until I heard him going through all of his drawers upstairs he hadn't even come looking for me. "Michael," I yelled out. "Is everything okay?" "Yes, Karis I'm just stopping through, I forgot something I needed today, I will see you soon, I'm coming home early, okay baby."

I heard the door slam shut soon after and he was gone again. The children didn't even see him come in or out. I called them all to the table and we sat down to eat. Tonight I sat with them; I wanted to talk to Keagan. I would make him tell me what he was eating. "Keagan what's for dinner tonight?" I asked him. He looked at me and then his plate. "There are peas and corn and meat," he said pointing down at them with his little fork. "Yes, little man there is," I say to him.

"Why wouldn't you talk to the teacher today Keagan" I asked him. "I didn't want to talk to her, she's mean," he said eating his peas. "She's mean, are you sure?" I asked him. "She's mad at me, I don't want to go back there mommy," he said. "Okay no problem, that can definitely be arranged," I tell him taping his nose with the tip of my fork. "Thank you, mommy," he said eating his food. "See mommy I told you he didn't like her, she was mean," Kristopher said.

We ate and the room was full of smiles I gave them ice cream after dinner. Soon after I got them cleaned up after dinner and I read to them until Michael walked into the room he sat down on the bed and talked to the children before kissing them good night. I went into my bedroom to get ready for bed, Michael came in soon after. He grabbed me from behind and kissed my neck. "I miss you, Karis," he said. "I miss you too, it seems as if we can't see each other enough these days."

"Yes, I know, I am trying to get things together at work, it's hectic there." "I know Michael, I'm not complaining, I just miss you, that's all," I tell him turning to his face and kissing his lips. "Michael, I was approached today by the childcare provider today. She told me that Keagan is not developing as he should because he doesn't talk to any of them or the children in the childcare. I talked to her, but when I got home I talked to Keagan, and he said he just didn't like her, she was mean."

"Baby, Keagan's fine he's just quiet, he likes to keep to himself there's nothing wrong with that at all." "No, but Michael he's so distant at times, it even worries me." "Stop worrying baby he'll be okay I assure you Keagans not disable nor does he have a learning disability" I walked into the bathroom, and he walked behind me. "Are we taking a bath tonight?" He asked me. "No, I'm going to shower and get in bed." "Can I shower with you?" He asked me pulling at my shirt. "Not tonight Michael," I said pulling my shirt back down. I wasn't in the mood for anything except for sleep.

"Are you mad at me?" He asked. I began to take my clothes off and get into the shower. "I'm not mad, Michael, I'm just tired." "I was looking forward to having you for dessert tonight," he said. I shook my head no and began to wash my hair. Michael got into the shower with me anyway. "I just want to help you wash off," he said with his hands in the air. "Don't touch me, Michael," I tell him turning my back to him. "I'll try not to Karis," he said laughing and holding his hands up. "Are you really tired?" He asked washing my back with soap.

"I just want to wash and relax tonight Michael." I got out of the shower and wrapped up in a towel. Michael came out soon after me. "Are you upset with me?" He asked wrapping himself up in a towel also. "No, Michael, I'm not upset I am a little worried that we aren't spending enough time together. I have things I want to share with you," I tell him slipping into my nightgown. "But you're never around for me to tell you." "What is it, Karis, what do you want to tell me?" He asked me.

"I just wanted to tell you that I saw my dad today and he's doing very well over there with Mary. She's doing an excellent job with him, he's able to dress himself; he's talking well and everything." "Yes, I heard about how well he's doing, she has someone bringing him to the hospital once a week for physical therapy. That's so great baby, but don't be mad okay," he said hugging me and kissing my neck. "I'm really trying not to be, I think I've gotten used to you being close to you when we were in Africa. I was always by your side, I feel left out I suppose," I tell him with my head to his chest.

"Listen, Karis, I love you, I am always going to be here for you, and this is what I do for a living. You know that if I could, I'd be here with you all day and night." I was satisfied with knowing that if he had a choice, he'd be there with me all day and night. "I love you too Michael," I tell him kissing his lips. We went to bed holding each other tight. I was awaken by the door opening and closing again downstairs it slammed so hard I jumped from my sleep startled. I shook Michael. "Do you hear that Michael?" I asked. "No I don't hear anything" He said lifting up from the pillow.

I lay down beside him looking out of the door into the hallway. It slammed again. This time he jumped up. "What in the world was that?"

He asked standing up he grabbed a pair of pants from the drawer and went to the hallway. I sat up in bed watching him as he ran to the stairwell he ran so fast I could only see his feet in the air. I could hear him scurrying around down there so I decided to go down there with him to check things out.

"Michael, Michael," I called out. "Yes Karis, I'm in here," he said. I followed the sound of his voice to the guest room. He was sitting on the floor near the bed. "What's wrong?" "I hurt my foot on the edge of the bed," he said holding his foot in his hand. "Oh I'm sorry, can you walk on it?" I asked him. I pulled at his hand to help him up from the floor. "Karis there was nothing opened down here there is no air coming in from the windows or anything. I don't know where that sound came from," he said limping up to the stairwell.

When we put our foot on the first step we heard the door slamming again we both turned in shock looking for where it would be coming from. Suddenly I felt a strong gust of wind, by and then I was pushed down with Michael we both fell to the floor. I could smell this spirits foul odor all around us. Michael took my hand, and we pulled on each other to stand on our feet again. I wrapped my arm around his and we began to walk up the stairs again. This time the spirit snatched Michael up and flung him across the room. He went spinning like a toy doll.

When he hit the wall he dropped down hard. I ran to him but the spirit came to me and just stood in front of me with its force up against my body I couldn't move past it. It was smelly and foul. I stood there; I didn't try and move it out of my way. Michael laid there on the floor waiting for me; he looked up a couple of times to give him the look of comfort. I didn't want him to think I was in any pain or danger, because I knew what this spirit was about to do, it was there to intimidate me. I stood there; I could feel it breathing on my face I covered my nose and mouth to shield from the smell.

I wasn't afraid of this I knew what it was and what it wanted from me, with each breath I stepped back, and toward the stairwell. Michael stood to his feet and came toward me. I stuck my hand out. "Michael, stay where you are, please!" I screamed out, I tried to scream out again, and it was like this spirit grabbed me by the throat, I couldn't speak. I just jester my hands to keep Michael back. I started to choke; it felt like my throat was closing, I reached out into the air as if I was reaching for the spirits throat to grab hold of it.

I know that if I can get a hold of whatever life it has I send it back. I kept reaching and the grip feeling around my neck got tighter and tighter. I kicked at it and hit it with my hands. I see Michael couldn't watch anymore, he bent down to spread out his wings, but just when he was coming up from the floor; it turned to him and held him down on the floor. Michael was pinned with a great force in the middle of his back. I reached out for him more and more as Michael struggled to get up.

Michael pushed himself up and ran toward me again, now I felt like it was squeezing the life from me my whole body felt constricted; like I was being squeezed by a giant snake. I gasped for air and coughed. Suddenly Michael flew in and pulled the spirit over. It was still holding on to me with a great force. I held it as if I was holding a wall back from falling on top of me. I could feel it all over me. When Michael let go he flew up really fast then back down with such force, he grabbed the spirit throwing us all down onto the floor.

I held my arms tightly and embraced the fall so that I didn't hurt too badly. When we hit the floor I laid there, Michael grabbed at the spirit, and they went flying all around the house it was like a terrible wind storm. I couldn't make out what this spirit wanted. When I grabbed on to it nothing came about, I saw nothing, I felt nothing but evil. It didn't seem to be lost or confused about where it was. How could I help it cross over if I don't know why it's here? Michael circled around the house with it and I prayed laying there on the floor confused by its touch.

This was a new thing I would have to overcome. I prayed, "Lord Michaels up there struggling with that spirit. Lord, I know that it isn't of you, send it back down lord to the pits of hell where it belongs. Lord, protect Michael from harm." When I said that, Michael came crashing down to the floor, he was holding on to it. When Michael fell to his back and it was on top. It was revealed; it turned to me and showed its face. It was horrible looking dark eyes and sharp teeth it made no excuses and it had claws it reached up at the ceiling and back down to Michael it had small wings as well.

I turned my head to it. It stuck its tongue out at me, Michael pushed his way up, and they went flying again. I got up this time and hide in the corner to pray on my knees Lord please I prayed. Please remove this spirit send it back to the pit of hell where it belongs Lord in Jesus name help Michael to send it back, All around me I could feel wind and hear Michael fighting. The spirits grunts began to get louder and louder. When I looked up Keagan was at the top of the stairs. He stood there watching.

The room went quiet and I looked over at the spirit and Michael they both turned to Keagan and it began to really struggle to get away from Michael it looked as if it was smiling to see Keagan. I began to run toward Keagan. Going up the stairs as fast as my legs could get me there but it freed itself from Michael and both of them went flying behind me. Michael coming up close behind me and the spirit got ahead of us and pushed both of us back down of the stairs. We both fell to the floor.

Watching as the spirit went for Keagan on the top of the stairs; Keagan smiled at it and reached out his little hands to it. All around Keagan eight small lights began to fly around him. He was smiling and laughing holding on to the railing of the stairs. The lights shined brighter and brighter, and Keagan laughed louder and louder as we watched the spirit being attacked by the eight lights. Keagan kept his small hands out as they went around in a circle around his little body we could hear the spirit sounding further and further away. Michael got up from the floor sitting up watching with pleasure.

I was in such shock. Now I know why Keagan was so special, I thought. When the spirit was completely gone Keagan sat on the top of the stairwell smiling. "Mommy," he said reaching out his arms to me. "Come to bed, I smiled at him and ran up to get him. "Keagan, Thank you, thank you, God," I said holding Keagan up in the air. "Michael, are you coming up?" I asked. It was a bizarre night Michael didn't come up for a while instead he went into the upstairs hideaway room where he often went to pray. I didn't bother him I just held onto Keagan.

When he fell off to sleep I waited for Michael to come to bed. "Michael, when did you get your wings, and why are you here on earth in this life?" "Karis, where's this coming from?" "I just want to know Michael, I've never asked you before; have I? I just think it's time for you to come clean. I would like to know why you have them?" I asked him. "Believe it or not, you have them too, you just haven't gotten them yet. They haven't really come out." "But, how, what do you mean?" I said going over to the mirror to check my back.

I pulled down my shirt. "No, no, I don't have them, Michael, my back is clean." "I was reborn into this world. When I was a young boy my parents took the whole family on a boating trip to Cancun. We sailed every day my father would boast on how good of a sailor I had become. So one day I tried sailing alone before my parents got up for breakfast. I went out to the boating shed to get the boat out so that I could make my father proud of me when he would awake to see me sailing alone.

He'd be so proud I thought so I unwrapped the rope from the wooden post I got into the boat and began to unwind the sail when I did that the wooden sail pole came back and hit me in the head so hard that I fell into the water. It knocked me out, I was trapped under the boat wrapped up in the ropes so when my parents went looking for me, I was nowhere to be found. Until they decided to look for me on the boat when they found me, they did everything they could to revive me, CPR the works.

It wasn't until I was being placed on a gurney going into the ambulance that I came to, but I'd gone there and back. It was a whole other world up there. I was scared at first, but he touched me, he tickled my tummy. It was brightly lit and peaceful, full of smiles there. He told me to always pay attention to what he's doing, always stay on his side he sat me down and showed me what was to come. He handed me a light, and I took it my stomach was filled with laughter for every day after that moment, and I couldn't think of anything but living by what I learned in that time.

Strength in his love and I have never doubted his love nor have I lost my path. I follow him I live through him and him through me I am at his mercy. When I came to that day, it was like I was a brand new kid. I was freed from whatever stronghold that this world would swing in my direction, I was reborn of him I learned about my wings as I got older they didn't come easy. I went through high school than college never knowing that they were there until one summer I decided to go home for a month to visit my parents.

I decided to allow my beard to grow in when it began to grow as it grew in all white like snow I looked as if I was a young cousin of father Christmases." He said laughing, "I would pluck the hairs from my chin while watching television and they would appear to be feathers not hair. After a while, the feathers began to grow on the shoulder blades of my back the same way I would try and shave them, but they would grow back thicker and whiter. I remember hiding the facial hair, shaving it daily and never going swinging that summer in fear of all the questions my family and friends would ask me, they really got a kick out of the white beard before I shaved it."

"I had no idea what to do with the wings, but I can tell you what I didn't do. I didn't question God, I knew that this was all him. It was my destiny, and my mission and I promised I would stay on his path and I have. He called me to you; I was supposed to be at that hospital for you, for us, for those who do believe that beyond this world. There is a place of peace and calm and so much love it will make your stomach hurt with laughter and joy. I won't stop living for him until I make it back to that place," he told me.

Michael was so serious, and the story was so intriguing. I was so tuned into him, his belief was so real, you could see in his eyes that he was reliving all of what he saw in that moment and he really truly was a believer in Gods promise. I was a little taken back by what I heard I just sat up in the bed and thought about how great it must feel to have no doubt. Even I; every now and then doubt what I am doing and why these things happen to me."

"I doubt him sometimes, and that's bad because I know he sent me back for a reason to. I was a little worried now because I could be possibly blocking myself from becoming stronger by doing these things. Michael and I talked more that night about what happened to him. Michael was just so confident that it was a wonderful experience for him and that. The lord held his hand and walked him through things telling him that everything works itself out when you follow the path that he chooses for you.

Sometimes it may seem you step off your pathway, but if you know the Lord and trust him and believe him he will get you back there, all you have to do is ask him to get you there. When Michael was done talking about it we just laid there hugging and I was so happy now because I know now, I know where he came from and why he's the man he is. He never gave me reason to doubt that at all. I would have to learn to be as confident as Michael in his strength there was no fear in Michaels love for God and that's why he could smile and handle the things that come his way everyday with so much grace. I have to learn to be stronger and fearless also never fearing the things I can't change.

We held each other that night, hugging and keeping each other warm. I rubbed Michaels back the hair on his back was just in those two spots and it was so soft and as white as snow. I just ran my hands over it, and then to the middle of his back he turned over after a while and looked me in the eye. "Karis, you can't remember what happened to you in that accident? You don't remember? He asked me. "I remember the accident, I remember seeing the light shining down on me a big bright light I couldn't see through it or around it, but it was there when I came to. I was in the hospital surrounded by people I didn't know.

I didn't have any other encounters with him until long after that. I was outside my house, and I saw him in the sky, I thought I was crazy, I thought that I was dreaming," I told him with excitement in my voice. "I was so afraid after that afraid to look up into the sky." Michael grabbed me and hugged me tightly. "Baby, you're not crazy you were never crazy, it's just so hard for people to accept things like that especially if they didn't witness it themselves.

"Have you ever told anyone about what happened to you?" I asked him. "Yes, I told my mother and my father. I was looked at funny, and my dad told me it was all a dream, but I knew it wasn't at all a dream, I was there with him, and no one could ever tell me anything different because I could feel him I could feel the warmth of his love. I was tickled up there, and I know it was all him all around me. So I never doubted, and when I was told it was a dream, I told my dad that there's no dream like that with that much warmth and joy."

Michael was so happy talking about it. After a while we both fell off to sleep. We were both wrapped up in the covers when woke up that morning. I tried to get up before the children got up, but I didn't hear anyone, and when I moved to roll Michael over he grabbed me. "Aha I caught you, where are you going, baby," he said. "I was going to get the kids breakfast before they get up," I tell him trying to pull the cover from under him. "Oh no," he said grabbing me toward him. He rolled over on top of me and began to kiss me all over.

I was turned on by Michael at times that I would take over and began to make love to him. This was a morning I had to do just that because the kids would be up soon and I know he has to leave for work so I made love to him and I didn't allow him to get me on my back. When I was done I went to the restroom to wash up to greet the children. Michael laid in bed for a while before he got up to get ready for work. I was already done with breakfast by the time he came downstairs. He came over to me and kissed my cheek.

He rubbed the children on their heads and went toward the coffee pot. "Good Morning you," he said to me. He came over to me and whispered into my ear. "You were great this morning; can we do it again before I leave?" He asked. I gave him a smile and he knew I was saying yes with my eyes. I gave the children their breakfast and slipped away upstairs following behind Michael. "What's wrong you didn't get enough?" I asked as he pulled down my pants at the doorway.

"No, I didn't," Michael lifted me up with my back to the wall and made love to me as quickly as possible it was only a matter of time that the children would be upstairs to get dressed. When we were finished, I put my clothes back on and went to the children and Michael got in the shower. The kids were standing by the door when I opened it. "Hello you guys," I yelled out. They were so happy. Kristopher had Keagan by the hand. "Look at his hand's mommy," he said holding his hand s out to me. "He was playing in the syrup mommy, I tried to stop him," Kristine said.

"But he's very fast." "Yes, we have to really keep our eyes on him," I told them going toward the hall bathroom to run some bath water for Keagan. "Mommy it was good," Keagan said licking his fingers. "Son, come here," I said pulling him toward me. I took him by the wrist and took his pajamas off and put him in the warm tub. He began to splash immediately. "Keagan not too much okay, I don't want to have to be cleaning floors all morning," I tell him getting some towels from the cabinets. "Mommy, I'm going to take a shower okay I don't want to take a bath anymore," he tells me taking a towel from the cabinet.

"Oh you're too big for a bath now, huh son," Michael said coming out of the room with his bag in his hand. "Yes dad, I am I don't feel like sitting in the bathtub it seems like the dirt comes right back to me when I do that," he said. Michael squeezed his face and laughed so loud. We looked at each other and laughed. "I love taking a bath," Kristine said. "I love soaking in the bathtub." "Well it's not for everyone," Michael tells her" He leans over and kisses me goodbye.

"Baby, I may not make dinner," he hugged me and whispered; "don't be angry," he winked at me and went toward the stairs. "Bye daddy," Kristine said. "Have a good day, keep everyone well," she said waving him goodbye. "You know that's what daddy does, right mommy?" "Right you are Kristine, daddy's job is so important he's so special." I went over to Keagan to wash him. I finished getting them all dressed, and we went looking at schools for Keagan. I wanted him in a public school, but Michael insisted he goes to a private school.

We went to a private school that was near the hospital, Michael suggested it. We pulled up to the school and immediately we were greeted by a nice very short woman she was to give us a tour of the school today. I had Keagan by the hand and the twins where amazed at the big buildings all around. "Welcome Mrs. Philips," she said. "We've been expecting you and the children, your husband told us he wouldn't be able to make it, but he took a tour a few days ago," she tells me. "Mrs. Philips, please follow me, I want to first take you to the kinder garden classes that are all day, and you can meet the teachers."

"They are all excellent teachers, the children and parents love them." We walked around the school; she showed us the third-grade classrooms also. "Kristopher and Kristine will be attending this school along with Keagan?" She asked. "I haven't decided yet," I tell her. "Oh, I was sure your husband told us that they would attend this year also" "We really haven't discussed what we wanted for the twins yet," I tell her walking around the classroom holding Keagan by the hand. "We do all sorts of things here academically, our scores are very high, and we want every child to get the ultimate educational experience.

When they leave our school for high school, they will be well prepared to tackle any and all this academically," she said handing me three thick packets of paperwork. "Now tuition is a little high. However, there are all sorts of things you can do to lower it, there are volunteer programs that will help bring the cost down, and when you enroll more than one student there is a terrific discount," she said smiling. "It was such a pleasure meeting you, are there any questions I didn't answer for you, Mrs. Philips?" She asked.

"Oh no, you have answered all the questions I had for you except for one," I tell her smiling. "You never told me your name." "Oh I'm so sorry, I am Ms. Barnes, it was a real pleasure meeting you and the children. I hope to see you again real soon." I didn't know that Michael had thought about sending the twins to private school, they seemed to love the school they were already enrolled in, I thought as I began to drive off. "How would you guys like to take a trip to see daddy at work?" I asked them.

"Me, I would love to mommy," Kristine said. "Me too mommy" We drove over to the hospital. When we arrived it was so busy there were cars everywhere, people were running and crying it was a lot for the kids to handle I thought. "Hey you guys, it looks hectic here, maybe we should visit daddy some other time," I told them. Kristopher began to get sad and Kristine started to cry. "Hey, no crying please we can come back when it's not as busy, and daddy can have time to be with us. How about Ice cream" I asked them.

"We can get ice cream from old Misses Sues shop. They were so excited when I said Ice cream the crying stopped immediately. Kristopher smiled and laughed at Kristine we got to the ice cream shop and went in. I took Keagan by the hand and they all choose what they wanted. We sat down and ate the ice cream; their faces were covered with chocolate and strawberry. I cleaned everyone up, and we drove back home, they were so happy. Michael showed up very early which was surprising I was just making dinner when he came in. I heard the children running to him to greet him at the door. "Daddy, daddy" they were laughing and giggling. I watched as they played with Michael at the door. It was so good to finally be settling in at home.

Back To Work

We ate at the dinner table as a family that night Michael and I washed the children up and put them to bed soon after. I wanted to discuss with him the children going back to school and me going back to work. We went to our room I put my bedclothes on, and Michael went to the bathroom to shower. He left the door slightly cracked opened so that we could hear each other talking. "You would like to go back to work huh?" He asked. "Yes Michael I would, I think it will be good for me," I tell him. "I don't want to work in administration. I want to go back on the floor," I tell him.

"Yes, baby I think that would be good for you, having somewhere to go during the day, caring for people, doing what you love talking to people, yes. I think it would be great, baby," he said. Turning on the shower, I laid on the bed and wrote in my journal. I was so happy that we talked about me going back to work, it was time I thought. When he came to bed, he just held on to me. I fell asleep thinking about how great it will be to have work again. I would call Maddy tomorrow and tell her the good news she should be happy also; we could have lunch together every day.

The next morning I awoke late it was about 830am, and the children were all up already in the kitchen. "Mommy, I made you breakfast today," Kristopher said. "Oh, you did huh." I sat down at the table Kristopher brought me a bowl of cereal and a spoon. I smiled. "Thank you, son," I ate; they had Keagan in a chair at the table. He was so happy to be sitting at the table with all of us he was a little too big for the highchair. I ate with the children, and they talked about how late I woke up. "You were so tired, mommy," Kristopher said as he ate his cereal.

When we were all done, we went back upstairs to get they dressed, and I took them to the hospital to talk to Maddy. When we arrived at the hospital, Maddy wasn't there, and the nurse at the front desk said that she hadn't been to work in a couple of days. I walked away very worried. What happened I thought, Maddy was so depressed the last time I saw her. I took the children to her house, and it seemed she was all moved out. I waited in her driveway until someone came to the door.

It was a guy who was packing her things and putting them into a van parked in front when I went to approach him to ask about where he was taking her things Maddy drove up. I was standing on the stairs of the porch she came running up to me smiling. "Karis, hi," she said grabbing my hands. "Maddy; where have you been" I asked her. "You wouldn't believe me if I told you," she said walking back to the car. "Hello kiddos," she said to the children. "Where have you been?" I asked.

"Well sweetheart, if you must know," she said holding out her hand. "You did huh, you and Dr. Green?" "Yes, we are married now, and I'm moving into to a new home, guess where?" She said jumping up and down. "I will be living right around the corner from you!" "Wow, really?" I say to her getting into the car with the children. "Maddy this is so great I was coming to the hospital to tell you that I wanted to come back to work, now that Keagan will be in school."

"That's great, so we will be living around the corner from one another and working together," she said. "Yes, we will." "I am so happy, Karis," she said. "I will call you when I'm getting settled in, it's the big house on the corner of Pickers street. I would love to have you all over for dinner really soon," she said as I drove off. I drove back to the house and let the children play outside while I cleaned the house for dinner. I knew that Michael would not be there until late in the evening. I went upstairs to write for a while.

I thought about the spirit that came to the house and how Keagan handled it. He doesn't talk about it at all, and he's still a baby I thought. I went back downstairs to check on them playing, and to my surprise, Keagan was inside with Kristopher watching cartoons. "Hey boys, where is Kristine?" I asked them. "She's outside mommy," Kristopher answered, she has new friends. "Really" I said going toward the window. I was so excited to see Kristine outside playing she had two new friends they both were so cute, one had ponytails and the other long straight hair with bows tied to the ends she wore lots of bright colors.

I was so happy, I watched her from the window. They played hopscotch with a rock from the yard, it was so cute. I went back into the den to check on Kristopher and Keagan. "When are you two going to play outside with your friends?" I asked. "Mommy, I don't need any friends, Keagan and I can watch TV and play inside where we can be safe," he said looking curiously out of the window. "Who needs friends," Keagan said. When Kristine came inside she went straight to the kitchen for water; "I'm so thirsty mommy," she said taking a cup of water to her mouth.

"You guys need to wash up were going to see your grandfather in a few," I told them. We all washed up and I took them to Mary's to visit daddy. When we arrived at Mary's house it was so quiet. I knocked at the door and she came and peeked out of the window. "What is it, Karis" She asked from the window. "I wanted to see daddy if I could," I tell her. "He's not here today, he's out looking for an apartment," she said. "An apartment" I asked her. "Yes in a like senior living facility, just call later he'll tell you about it," she waved at the children and closed her curtains we could hear her slippers walking away from the door.

"Well, kiddos I guess we came at a bad time," I told them taking Keagan by the hand and walking down the stairs. Just when I'd gotten them all into the car and buckled in my sister Rose pulled up with daddy in the car. "Hey, Karis, where are you going?" She asked. "Oh I was

coming to visit daddy, how are you, daddy?" I said as he opened his
door with a smile on his face. "Hi, baby, what you guys doing over
here?" He said looking and smiling at the children. "Daddy, you looking
for a place to stay now" I asked him.

"Yes baby, it's time for daddy to go," he said rolling his eyes. "Did
you find anything daddy?" I asked him. "Yes I did, I found a nice little
spot not too far from here, and there is a store right next to it. I can
walk down there and buy all my groceries," he said. "Yes, I know how
you like to cook," I added. Daddy got out of Roses car and sat on the
bottom of the stairs. Rose drove off. "Baby, come sit with me," he said.
I left the children strapped in while I sat down next to daddy. "You can't
stay here long baby with the kids in the car like that," he said. "Daddy,
would you like to come over to visit for a while?" I asked him.

"Sure, baby Michael won't mind will he?" He asked. "No daddy he'd
love to see you," I told him going to the driver side of the car. "Let me
let Mary know what's going on, and I'll be right down baby," he tells me.
He came back down quickly after. He had a big bag and a jacket. "I'm
ready, baby," we drove to my house. Daddy talked to the children the
whole way there, he kept them laughing and playing. When we arrived at
the house I was so happy to have daddy over. I called Michael to let him
know.

"Hello, Dr. Phillips, please?" I ask for him. I held on the phone for a
few for them to go get him. I was so happy about it. "Hello Dr. Phillips
speaking," he said. "Hello, Michael, I just wanted to tell you that daddy
was here visiting, I'm hoping that you can come home a little early for
dinner." "Oh baby, I don't know it's busy here, and I have two
scheduled surgeries today. I wish I could promise you, but baby I can't,"
he said in a rush. "I understand Michael; I will see you soon then
Michael." I hung up the phone and told daddy that he may not come
home on time.

"Well, Karis I'll be here in the morning we can all have breakfast together," he said. "I guess your right daddy," I say to him. "You will be here in the morning? I was just hoping that we could all have had dinner together tonight daddy," I said. "I know baby, but I am here so let's just enjoy each other for a while," he said walking into the kitchen looking in the refrigerator, "let's see what you have in here Karis, what can daddy cook for his babies" He said taking out a package of steak and hands full of veggies.

"I know what I would like," he said holding up the steak. "I would like these veggies and all the steak I can eat grilled, you have a grill don't you sweetheart?" He asked. "Yes daddy, I do," I tell him opening up the patio door. Kristopher was so interested in daddy he followed him all over the kitchen and out to the grill. Daddy gave him pans and spoons to carry and help him. I watched as I remembered myself being daddy's little helper at times. I made a salad and Kristine made lemonade; it was a little on the sweet side.

I gave it a little more water and sat it down on the table. I was so happy to have daddy there and so where the children they fought over the seat next to him. It was an amazing night. I cleaned up after dinner and got daddy settled into the guest room. "Daddy I love you so much, thank you for coming over to stay with me," I tell him as we say goodnight. I went back up to get the children ready for bed they were still excited about daddy being there Keagan asked if he could sleep with daddy. "No son, granddaddy needs to get some rest alone tonight, maybe another time sweet pea," I tell him putting him to bed in his room.

"Good night mommy," he said turning over on his side. "Good night my little angel, please don't let the bedbugs bite," I told him leaving a crack in his door for me to hear him through the night. I went inside of Kristine's room she was already half sleeping. "Hello sweetie pie, how do you feel?" I asked her. "I feel really sleepy, I can't wait to see granddaddy in the morning mommy," she said to me. "Oh I know; me either," I tell her. I walked into Kristopher's room. He was sitting up in his bed looking at the walls of the room.

I went to my room to get ready for bed; I sat on my bed and wrote in my journal to tell God all about how thankful I was that he'd brought daddy to the house to stay a   while. I was really tired by that time. I went into the bathroom and ran my bath. I wanted the water hot and steamy. I took off all my clothes, and the door slammed behind me. I looked in the mirror, it must have slammed because of the window in the shower; I was guessing. I got into the bath water and soaked a while.

The water was hot, but it was freezing cold in the room, so I got out and shut the window. When I went back toward the bathtub I could still feel a cold breeze I sat down in the water to warm myself. I laid my head back for a while before washing my body up. I stood up and ran the shower to wash off the soap when I reached in for the shower handle I felt something cold on my hand. It grabbed my wrist tight. I shook my wrist free and got out of the shower grabbing a towel from the wall hanger. I stepped out and wrapped it around me as I went for the door.

The cold hands were on my back again I ignored it. I was barely able to keep my eyes opened I was so tired after a long day with the children and daddy. I went over to the bed and sat down wrapped in the towel I just laid back on the bed. The house was so quiet and I could just stay in this towel I thought until Michael came home. I knew that he would undress me as soon after he'd come to bed. Michael had to make love to me before he went to sleep there was only a few times he'd left me be when he'd come home late and I could count them on my hand. I got up and put my gown on leaving my underwear off for him.

I got in bed and waited for him until I fell off to sleep. I felt Michael all over me his hands went over my back up and down he stroked my back I felt him kiss my back as well when I tried to turn over he pressed down on my back really hard. "Michael, what are you doing?" I asked him. He didn't say a word. "Michael that feels great," I said as I tried once again to turn over onto my back. He pressed down on my back again and I couldn't move.

Suddenly I heard the door creak open, the dim hall light shined through and Michael was standing before me I turned quickly over onto my back and sat up. "Michael I thought that you were already in bed," I tell him with the sheet wrapped around my chest. "No, baby I wasn't I just got in." I looked at the clock it was a quarter past 4am. "Michael, someone was here with me stroking my back and kissing it, I thought it was you, I thought you were here," I tell him looking around the room. "No, baby I just got in, I am exhausted," Michael said. He threw his bag down and his coat over the chair, and he sat down on the bed and took his clothes off, the room began to light up with the morning sun rising.

I laid back down along with Michael, he held on to me so tight, and we fell off to sleep. I got up and went downstairs I could hear daddy playing around with the boys. "Karis, good morning," Daddy said blowing me a kiss as I walked down the stairs. "Good morning, mommy," the children yelled coming up to me hugging my legs and waist. "Good morning kiddos," I tell them. "How's everything this morning daddy?" I asked him. "I was about to make breakfast I have the coffee on Karis, so don't you worry. Did you want me to make something for you and the children?" He asked me.

"No daddy, you let me do that please," I said to him. "I will do all of that daddy, you just have a seat. Would you like me to turn on the news for you?" Daddy loved watching the news in the morning. "Sure baby, I didn't know how to turn that box on, you know I'd rather read the paper myself Karis," Daddy said as I turned on the TV for him. I went into the kitchen to make everyone breakfast. Soon after we all sat down Michael came into the kitchen and sat down for breakfast with us. "What's on the menu pops?" he asked daddy grabbing his hand and shaking it.

"I sure missed you, son," daddy said to him. "I missed you as well sir, there certainly is no place like home," Michael said as he filled his mouth with a piece of toast. "I was hoping to see you today. I know you are a busy man these days," daddy said to Michael. "And you, sir you look great, how do you feel?" He asked daddy. "I feel great," he said smiling at me. "I knew it wouldn't be long before my Karis showed up. I was just asking Mary had they seen or heard from her, no one ever told me a thing," daddy said looking angry.

"I bet you guys been gone a while haven't you?" He said. "Oh yes, sir we've been away for about 8 to 9 months in Africa," Michael told daddy. We all ate and soon after we went our separate ways and began to get ready for the day. Today I would get everything in order for work. The children would be back in school and Michael would take Keagan to meet his teacher. "It's nice having your dad here Karis," Michael said to me; "yes, he's so happy to be here, I don't know if Mary is going to allow him to come back to visit. When I drop him off, I'll ask her."

When we made it to Mary's house, I got out with the twins and we all went to the door to say good bye to daddy. Mary opened the door, she wore her robe around her was a long belt. She quickly took daddy into the house, she waved goodbye to us. I took the twins to the car, and I could see daddy waving from the window I blew him a kiss as he slides the window open. "   Karis, you come back next weekend and pick up your daddy okay," he said waving and smiling. "Sure daddy, I will," I said getting in my car.

I drove the twins to the child care center and dropped them off. I was off to the hospital, where I would be speaking to human resources about the job and hopefully getting started very soon. I made it there just in time to meet up with Maddy and Doctor Green. They waited as I parked my car; Maddy had a smile on her face that could light up the world. I walked up to them and we hugged we all walked in together each of us going separate ways. I was so excited, I had forgotten the feelings I got going to the hospital was no longer there.

I was filled with so much joy smiling all the way I went into the human resource office. I was hired on the spot as a nurse; it was just what I needed. I filled out all of the necessary paperwork and left the office to maybe catch Maddy for lunch. I looked all over the hospital for her she was no were to be found. I decided to find Michael and have lunch with him. I went to the bottom surgery center where I would be sure to find him. After waiting about two hours I gave up. He didn't come out of any of the surgery rooms.

I decided to just go and pick up the children and go home. I could share the news when he came home I thought as I to walk through the parking lot when I was almost at my car I saw Michael, Maddy and Doctor Green walking up to the hospital. Michael walked up to me quickly and grabbed me by the waist. "Hey, pretty lady, where are you going?" I was surprised to see them all walking up together. "I've been looking for all of you, I wanted to have lunch, but you guys were all gone," I told him.

"Oh yeah we just went out to have some Italian for lunch, we didn't think you'd be done in time to come along. Sorry dear, next time," Michael said licking his fingers, "Next time sweetie," I hugged Maddy again. "Did you get everything taken care of?" She asked. "Yes, I start tomorrow," I tell her. "Good it will be so good to have you back," she tells me rubbing my back. Michael kissed my cheek. "Baby, I will see you at home, I love you, sweetie," he said walking away with Dr. Green, he waved at me smiling.

"Well honey, you have that all settled, now what else?" Maddy said. "I don't know Maddy I just wanted to work outside of the home. I think it will do me some good; I've been home with Keagan all this time. It's time I get back to what I know and love, just helping others," I tell her. "Well, I think it's great, it will do you some good. I'll see you tomorrow then," she said walking toward the hospital entrance, I waved goodbye to her as I walked away to my car. This was going to be so great I thought driving to the child care center to pick up the twins and then on to the school where Michael left Keagan.

"This is one of the things that I prayed about. When I picked up the twins they were hungry and ready for lunch as soon as they saw me they ran to me yelling, "mommy, mommy, can we go eat please?" They said together at the same time. "Yes, after we get Keagan I'll take you two out to eat," I tell them. "Buckle up," I tell them as I drove off from the school. I picked Keagan up from the school he was covered in dirt. I looked at him very shocked. "Keagan, what in God's name have you done to your clothes?" I asked him.

"I was playing in the sandbox today mommy, I had so much fun," he said telling us about school, he had details that made me wonder if he had done any school work. It was all about playing in the playground and making new friends. We arrived at the Happy Burger restaurant. I took them inside there were kids and clowns and lots of bright colors covering the walls of the restaurant. I picked a table near the front door and the middle play area where I could watch the children play. I ordered the food, and they ate quickly so they could go to the play area before all of the other children left. I watched them playing and laughing.

It was nearly dark when we left Happy Burger. We arrived at the house a minute before Michael pulled up right beside me. I let the children in the house and waited for Michael at the door. "Michael, you're early, I don't have any dinner for you tonight," I tell him shutting the door after he was inside. "Oh baby, don't worry, I have to go back out to the hospital for surgery in another two hours anyway. I'll just have some coffee and a couple of cookies, how's the evening going?" He asked. "So far, so good, I took the children out to eat, they had a blast at the Happy Burger," I tell him walking behind him into the kitchen.

"Good, are they tired because before I go back, I'd like to make love to my beautiful wife," he said coming up behind me, wrapping his arms around my waist. "I will bathe them and put them down as soon as possible," I said running to the stairs. Michael came up the stairs soon after me and kissed the children goodnight, and we were off to our bedroom where he made love to me, I kissed him and went to the bathroom to run his shower. I got into the shower with him, and he kissed all over me more. Michael had a wonderful appetite for love. We got out together, he put on his clothes, I put on my pajamas and we went downstairs for coffee.

He smiled at me and held me before I walked him to the door. "Goodnight sweetheart," he said as I closed door. I walked back up the stairs and went to check on the children one more time before I would go to sleep. I walked into the twins room first they were sound asleep and Kristopher was in the bed with Kristine they always came together at the end of the night as if they couldn't sleep apart. After checking on them, I went to Keagan's room where he was cuddled up under the covers really tight.

I walked over to him to give him a kiss; he was holding his hands really tight in a fist. I tried to pull his hands apart for him to relax, but his grip was really tight. I took his hand and opened it, inside he held onto a small ring with a red cross on it, he was holding it so tight it was a print inside his hand from his tight grip. I turned on his light to look at it. It was gold around the band, but red in the middle of the cross. I turned the light off and left his room.

I left the door cracked a little so that I could hear him if he was to wake up. When I went to my room, I went to sleep easy. It was so peaceful around the house I could hear a pin drop. It was around four am when I heard a thump in the hall that woke me quickly. I jumped out of bed and ran to the door to see what it was, I didn't see anything. I walked down to the stairwell to see if it came from downstairs. There was nothing down there that I could see. I walked towards the twins door, I cracked open their door and peeked in, they were sound as sleep.

I walked to Keagan's door, and there was the noise again, but louder this time. I opened his door quickly there was a bright light shining over Keagan he was being attacked by

something in his sleep, the noise was him kicking the wall. It was like he was being held down or he was tied to something the bright light around him was circling around him fast, swirling over and over again as Keagan struggled to get out of whatever this thing had him tied up in. In a panic, I went running toward him, only to be pushed down to the floor and held down by my neck.

I prayed "Lord help me, help me lord," I screamed out. I struggled around with it; it was choking me the grip around my neck was so tight that I was coughing and struggling to gasp for air. I could see Keagan getting tired of it he was still fighting and trying to get up. I reached for him as the room grew dim I was going in and out of cautiousness while my baby was left to fight by himself. As I was being choked everything around me started to fade away, I saw the light shining around Keagan. He screamed out and stood up tall on the bed screaming.

"You can't have me! You can't have me!" At that moment eight lights shined around Keagan, he stretched his small arms out and held his head back and a huge light shined through his small body, the eight lights circled around him until the light went away. Keagan sat on the bed, and as I watched in a blur, I could see Keagan take his hand and press it against the back of the spirit holding me by my neck and all the lights around him. The spirit let go of my neck, but I couldn't move at all, I couldn't move or see for a while it was all a blur. Keagan came over to me and kneeled down. "Mommy," he said rubbing my chest.

"Mommy, are you okay?" He asked. "They're all gone mommy," he said looking at me in my face. I started coughing, he grabbed onto my arm. "Keagan," I said holding his little face in my hands, "baby, are you okay?" I asked him. "Mommy I'm fine," he said hugging me by the neck. I got up and went into the bathroom to check my neck. I was bruised all around my neck, it was red and blue. Keagan looked up at me. "Oh no mommy," he said looking down at his small wrist. "Oh no, Keagan," I said taking him by the hand, he was all bruised.

I quickly went to the kitchen to get an ice pack. What will I do now? Keagan can't go to school with these bruises. What will his teacher think is happening to him at home. I thought. I have to start work tomorrow and oh no what will they think if I don't show. I had to call Michael and Maddy right away. I took Keagan to the front room with me and called the hospital to speak to Michael and Maddy. I was so worried, as I dial to call, Michael walks in the door. "What's wrong sweetie?" He asked. I looked up at him and held Keagan's hands out.

"What happened?" "A spirit attacked him in his sleep this morning," I told him. He took one look at my neck and his eyes grew as big as the sun. "Oh no Karis it's happening again." "It is," I told him. "Michael I'm going back to work tomorrow what do we do? I can wear a turtleneck, but Keagan can't wear anything around his wrist. What do we do?" I asked him putting my head in my lap. "Don't worry Karis, I'll stay home during the day tomorrow and keep an eye on Keagan you can go in, everything will be fine baby."

"Oh thank you," I said to Michael getting up to give him a kiss. I was so worried about Keagan with all that was happening to him; I really wanted to keep a close eye out on him. I know that Michael could do it, but he was sometimes only in tune with himself. I went to work the next day on pins and needles all day. I walked around the hospital learning the patients and doing the job not really focusing on what I needed to. I felt badly about having to run through each room.

When I came home that night Michael and the children were all sitting around the table waiting for me, my plate was warm. I wasn't happy at all about my day. I didn't really talk to anyone nor was I able to give my patients the full attention they deserved. I signed a lot of paperwork and sat during lunch most of the time on the phone with Michael. This was beginning to be a real problem. My baby was going to have to deal with these same issues or worse than mine, he'd be attacked to the point where his little body would change.

I looked at the children as they ate, Keagan was especially good always smiling very talkative and genuinely happy all the time. I couldn't see him having these problems throughout his life. It made me sad and angry to think that for the rest of his young life he'd have to be in a constant fight with these sometimes very unkind spirits. I put the children to bed as Michael came up behind me to get himself ready for work. I couldn't think of anything other than what to do about Keagan. I put them to bed and tonight I place them all in one bed together. The twins laid with Keagan in the middle.

I made them hold one another by the hand. I prayed with them, and Michael came in, and we prayed again, I was teaching them the Lord's Prayer. We left the room and Michael took me by the hand. "Karis baby, I don't want you to worry about this too much, after a while he will have no problem handle those things himself," he said. "Michael he's so small, he's five, I don't think I'll ever be at ease about him taking on those things," I say. "Haven't you seen him, he's powerful in his own strength with the Lord, he is of him.

Although it seems hard to believe he's more close to him than we are, children are of an angel, and his light shines so brightly through them. They are in his protection at all times, he never leaves them alone," he says. "I just feel like this is bad for him and for us, will it ever stop?" I asked him looking up into his eyes. "Karis, our resting days are coming, and Keagan knows as well as I do that he's to live a normal life forever in his grace. There isn't any amount of fear in Keagan and baby you need to let your fear go and allow him to use you, let it go. It helps more if you do that."

That night I went to bed thinking about what Michael said to me my fear had always been a problem for me. I was so worried, but about what, I thought. I prayed that night that the Lord give us peace, give us a little break from it all. I especially wanted Keagan to enjoy school; he was so happy about it. I wanted him to be able to go and come home with a normal conversation as he'd done on that first day. I cried out to the Lord tonight. I fell off to sleep that night in my work clothes. When I woke up, Michael was standing over me reaching to take my clothes off. I jumped up, "No, Michael, I can do this," I said grabbing my shirt.

That day things seemed to be so quiet. I watched as Keagan played out in the yard, he was so happy chasing Kristopher around and Kristine playing with her dolls on the stairs of the porch. Time went by so quickly, the Lord did bless us with a few years of freedom there were no spirits. I was back at work and the children at school, this lasted three years. I was so glad we were able to have some really good days and nights. It would always smell of flowers in the house I had never used any air fresheners, but all around the house, the smell of beautiful flowers lingered through the house.

We finally had some peace I thought as time went on. We planned to give a big birthday bash for Keagan, he was soon to turn ten, and the twins were teens now, time flew by. Michael and I didn't see where it went. We talked a lot about the twins getting older and Keagan getting smarter. "Wow, he's turning ten," Michael said as we sat on the back patio set talking until the sun went down. I wrote in my journal still always praising God for his mercy. It wasn't until later that night when I learned that our lives would go back to being what it had always been, soon the house no longer smelled of flowers.

The children were to be leaving school for the summer and Michael and I had plans to send them to camp soon after school let out. We thought it would be a great experience for them; take a break to the campsite to learn about the forest and do some hiking and outdoor sports. The party would take place before they would leave for camp. I was so excited for all three of them. I started to pack their clothes and get their camping gear in order a month before they leave.

On the day before Keagan's birthday party I was to visit Maddy and Doctor Greens house. It was only blocks away, so I decided to walk over. Maddy was to help me with some of the party favors, I'm going to have a   n animal show for him with real live zoo animals. It was the surprise I wanted for him, he loved animals. The arrangements were made easily and the party favors were all I had left to do for this party. I couldn't wait to see the look on Keagan's face when he sees the animals, I thought as I walked over to Maddy's. When I arrived there, she had soft music playing loudly.

"The doors open," she said when she heard me knocking. When I entered the house, I didn't see her anywhere. I walked around calling out to her. "Maddy where are you?" I called out. "I'm here," she shouted. I followed her voice all the way to the back of the house where she was sitting in the tub soaking. "I had to soak these bones," she said smiling. I looked away as I was a little shocked at her in the tub. "Maddy, if you're too busy I can come back another time." "No," she said getting up from the tub.

"I am just soaking for a minute, don't tell me your eyes can't take it," she said laughing and wrapping herself with a towel. "I use to wash your little bones all the time, remember?" She questioned. "Helped you soak them and everything," she said while drying herself. She went to a cabinet and pulled out a pullover sweatshirt and some sweatpants, "Hand it over," she said reaching out for my bag. I sat down on a chair that she had in the hall, it was so beautiful I almost didn't want to sit in it, but she was taking so long to style her hair. It ended up in a ponytail anyway.

I watched her going through the bag and doing her hair at the same time. "Maddy, I'm in no hurry," I tell her. "You're not?" She said. "Not today, the children are old enough to stay in with each other," I tell her. "Look at you all grown up with teenagers and a soon to be ten year old, I am so proud of who you've become," Maddy said. "Follow me, honey." We went to the den area where Maddy's music was playing loudly. She turned it down and we sat and made party bags. She poured us coke, and she had some cinnamon cake that was so good I had piece after piece until she stopped me.

"You are going to gain at least 80 pounds if you continue eating that cake that way," she said smiling. "Oh my Maddy, I'm so sorry, I got carried away. It's so good," I say to her putting my   plate on the table, I was so ashamed. We placed all of the party bags into one big bag, Maddy handed it to me. "Is there anything else you would like us to do for the party?" She asked. "No, this is enough Maddy, thank you so much," I reached over and hugged her tight. I took the bag and went to the door, as I stepped out onto the porch I had a pain so heavy in my stomach it almost knocked me off my feet.

I grabbed onto the railing of the stairs going down to the cemented pathway. I bent over clutching the bag of party favors. Maddy had already gone back into the house. I just stayed bent over to catch my breath and wait for the pain to go away. I knew that this couldn't be what I thought it was, I hadn't felt like this in years. I thought as I stood there bent over clutching the bag. I wanted to scream out to her, but I didn't I knew she would want me to go to the hospital to get checked out. The pain went away after a while and I was able to walk back down the street.

I strolled as I reached the front of the house my head was spinning as if I had been stricken. I sat down on the steps before going into the house when I put my head down on my lap; I had a brief vision of an ambulance. It was pulling up to Mary's house and daddy was in it. I got up quickly and went into the house. "Hello mommy," Kristopher said. "The phone was ringing a lot while you were out mommy," Kristine said. "There's a lot of messages for you mommy." "Why didn't you guys pick up?" I asked them. "Dad told us we aren't to answer the phone unless one of you are home with us."

"Yeah mommy, it's so that strangers won't know we're here alone," Kristopher said laughing and playing a video game. "You think that's funny?" I asked him going over to the counter to check the messages. I placed the bag down Keagan came over and went through it. "Is this all for me mommy?" He asked with excitement in his little eyes. "No, son, it's to give out to all the children at the party," I tell him. "Karis, you need to come to the hospital immediately," I heard a message from Krystal then another from Martha.

"Come to the hospital its uncle Earl," she said in a panic. I was calm because daddy had these episodes all the time now that he was a little older they began to get a harder on him each time. "You guys grab your jackets we have to go to the hospital to check on your grandpa," I tell them. They all put their jackets on while I wrote Michael a note. I was told they took daddy to a different hospital. After getting the children settled into the car I began to drive off from the house when I saw daddy walking up the sidewalk toward the house I was stunned as I watched him walking I almost ran into another car.

The car horn honked loudly at me and the children yelled out for me to pay attention. I knew that it couldn't have been daddy so I proceeded to the hospital where I was greeted by my brother Richard. I hadn't seen him in so long he'd cut his hair really short I almost didn't recognize him. He helped me get the children out of the car and we walked up the hospital steps to the front lobby where I was greeted by more of my family members. Richard sat down with Keagan and began to talk to him. "Do you know who I am?" He asked him. "I'm your uncle Richard, I am your fun uncle," he explained.

"When you want to have fun you call me, I can play baseball and football. Do you play any of those?" He asked him. "No, but I do," Kristopher said. "I bet you do, you look big and strong too, I bet you'd beat me at all the games wouldn't you?" Richard said. "When I get some time I'm going to stop by, and we will play some ball," he said to them throwing soft punches at their little stomachs. I waited patiently by the window to hear the news about daddy. I dared ask any questions about what happened to him. It was a long wait, it seemed to go on forever until the doctor came out, and he was very tall.

"Lawson family," he yelled out. We all stood up. "Yes that's us over here," Richard yelled out. The doctor came walking over he looked a little scared to talk. He cleared his throat, "Mr. Lawson is very ill his cancer has spread all over. I don't know if he's shared this with any of you, but his cancer came back about a year ago, and he needed to do treatment but refused. At this point all we can do is make the patient as comfortable as possible," he said looking all of us in the eye.

"I'd suggest he stay here another two or three days, we'd usually recommend Hospice care for a patient at this stage, but I'm sure you guys would like to take him home." Everyone looked at one another, and Rose and Daisy stood off to the side. "I can't," Daisy said, "I just can't." When Daisy spoke, everyone else looked at one another, and I just smiled. I knew if she couldn't do it then this would be my chance to take daddy in and care for him, I would help him and pray for him until the Lord received him. I stood there for a moment to hear if anyone else would say anything. I walked over to the front desk and waited for the doctor to follow.

"I would like to care for my father," I tell him with a smile. "Your father will be ready after two or three weeks. We want to make sure he's comfortable, so we need your home address to send a hospital bed, and also get a few nurses to come out to manage his care. Do you live close?" He asked. "I do, I would like to have a talk with my husband first," I tell him. I wrote my address down on a paper and gave him my phone number also. "I'll see you soon," I tell him walking away. I took the children back home. When we arrived there Michael was home already he was having dinner waiting for us to arrive.

The children washed up and we sat at the dinner table Kristopher immediately began talking about seeing his uncle Richard. "Dad, he said he'd like to play ball with me soon. Do you think he could come over here and play ball dad?" I couldn't get a word in edgewise, I waited until he was done talking about his day and everything else he could think of telling Michael. When the children were done, they washed up and took Keagan upstairs for a bath. I made coffee for Michael and me, "I have something to tell you, Michael," I tell him getting the coffee cups off the shelf. "Today they told us that my father doesn't have long, the doctor said that he should be in hospice, but I want him with me, Michael. No one can care for him better than me," I tell him.

"Of course baby, your father is more than welcome to come here, but what are you going to do? You just started back at work." "I don't know I didn't think of that, I guess I can explain it to them. I don't know if I'll ever get hired there again, I'm on and off, but it's my dad," I tell him pouring the coffee. "You can take an emergency family leave, talk to Dr. Green tomorrow and tell him he'll understand fully, and if not I'm here you don't have to worry I'll take care of it all baby," he said kissing my forehead. I sat at the table with him and we drank the coffee. I went upstairs soon after he left for work to put the children to bed and get a shower. I thought about where I would put daddy.

I should be close to him I thought there's no room upstairs and the room downstairs is a little small for a hospital bed and all the things daddy would need. I showered for a long while just thinking about where I would place daddy. When I got out Keagan was standing at my door, "Can I come in mommy?" He asked me. "Sure you can," I tell him wrapping up in my towel. I sat on the bed to get dressed. "You can't sleep, son?" I asked as I slipped into my nightgown. He shook his head no. "Come lay with me," I tell him patting the bed. I took a pillow from my side and laid it close to me I hugged him, and he laid his little head on my chest.

"Mommy, sometimes I'm afraid of what I see at night," Keagan tells me. "What do you see at night son?" "I see all kinds of things, but mostly what scares me are the dark faces, sometimes they just stare down at me," he says clutching the pillow. "Do they touch you son?" I asked. "No, they don't, they just stare down at me, I sometimes want them to go away. I'm not afraid all the time, but sometimes I can feel they want to harm me, those are the scariest," he said. "Well, son, you can pray when you see them, you can close your eyes and pray out to the Lord to rebuke that spirit because those are bad spirits," I tell him.

"Hold my hand son," I tell him. "See this is what you do. You hold on to the Lords' hand during those times, and I promise son they will never harm you. Don't be afraid of them, they can never harm you because you are a child of God and he will always protect you." I held his little hand and prayed with him. We fell asleep together and when I woke up all three of the children were in bed with me. I took them downstairs for breakfast. I had a long day ahead of me, talking to Dr. Green would be the main focus.

Hoping that they would understand my position, I needed to care for my father at this time, and no matter what I thought, it's going to be up to them whether or not to allow me a personal family leave. I rushed there that day, and everything went better then I planned. I went home and prepared for daddy to come, I moved things around I felt daddy should be close, so I made room for daddy upstairs in the spare bedroom. I had to prepare the bathroom. The wait for daddy to come seemed like an eternity. He finally came on a Tuesday evening they brought him by ambulance I was so excited to just cater to him in his time of need.

We showed them where to set up the bed and the children and I put all of his things away. I talked to him and sat with him until the night ended. Daddy was very weak at times, but he always had lots to say. This was the start of a great year to come I thought, although the doctor said daddy didn't have a lot of time I say he has one good year left and deep down in my heart I was praying that God would bless me with just that. The days wouldn't be easy watching daddy in so much pain.

It would bring me to tears at times, but I would never cry in front of daddy he was always my hero, and I wanted to be his. I washed his body every day and when it was time to eat I'd feed him if he were too weak to feed himself. I would listen to people, and family members tell me that he was suffering, but he wasn't suffering at all. He was living, and living isn't always a great experience daddy had a deadly disease, and no one but God could cure him of it.

His healing wouldn't come when everyone else saw fit, but when the Lord was ready to receive daddy, he would be healed in his light. There would be absolutely no more pain for him and that same smile that carries daddy through will carry him in. I kept myself thinking this way while I watched daddy at times, just smiling to stay strong for me. It wasn't easy at all, but I

smiled along with him as the days grew longer with him in pain.

Somedays The Sun Shine In

Daddy was comfortable in my home I made sure we went out of the room every day. Sometimes he could walk out on his own and sometimes he had to be carried out in a wheelchair. He was so glad when I would get him up and out. We'd go to the front yard with the children and water the grass, or we'd go for a ride in the car I wouldn't keep him out late he just loves to ride. Day in and out, daddy was smiling and when he couldn't smile he'd pray loudly. Those were the days I knew he was in the most pain.

I'd cater to him even more on those days. Daddy would tell me how brave I was all the time. I would think. You're the brave one daddy. I took him to every appointment, and each time the doctors and nurses would complement me on how great of a job I was doing with daddy at keeping him clean and strong. It took me a while to do all that I needed to do with daddy and the children Michael was a great help. He would make the children dinner and lunch for school the next day and most days when I would nap he would watch the children and daddy outside.

We would have good and bad days, we would pray with daddy all around his bed on the days we knew he was in great pain. Not many visitors came to see daddy, a few of my siblings and more and more I'd see Daisy, although she'd had her issues with daddy in the past, she would show up and make him a couple of his favorite meals. I was grateful for any and all help that came my way. It seemed it wasn't getting any easier, and his mother would call with a request for him to come home to her, but she wasn't well, and daddy was in no way able to fly anywhere. I would kindly tell her that daddy was too ill.

She'd cry every time; I would feel so bad for her. "I won't ever see my baby again," she'd say before I'd hang up. I would let daddy talk to her, and he would smile the whole time talking to her.   He would tell her he missed her. Daddy would hold his hand under his chin and just look out of the window. I often wondered what his heart was feeling. He didn't express all of what he was feeling to me. On some days I'd even ask him, but he'd shake his head and say to me. "Oh Karis, daddy's okay sweetie"

I would say okay, but I could see in his eyes he was wondering about something or someone. He'd usually be very open, but I think when he knew it would hurt me more to hear what was on his mind, he'd just keep it to himself. "Daddy, would you like to watch some television?" I asked him. He loved to watch cowboys and Indians westerns. He was a longtime fan of them so I would put them on for him, especially in the afternoon. Daddy was happy, but being in that much pain, I felt he was sad when he couldn't get up and pull my nose. He'd give me that smile, and I would sit on the edge of that bed next to him.

"Daddy it's okay, you'll be okay I promise," I tell him hugging him by the side. Daddy smiled more and more every day, it was a half-smile just to reassure me that he was okay. Michael would come home and tell us about all the patients he'd have to deal with. Their families and the way they would hug him and tell him what a great surgeon he was. Michael was always a great talker, he'd keep daddy talking most of the time while he checked him over at times. The nurses came in and out of our home while we all tried to keep daddy comfortable.

He would keep us happy telling us that he was in no pain telling us stories of his childhood. It was always a good story, daddy grew up on a farm; he said he had a mule, pigs, and cows. He made the farm life sound spectacular, and I felt like I was there with him when he told the story. This was why daddy loved the garden so much I thought. He would tell me stories of his parents, one Native American one Caucasian, and how they would hide their love in those times because of society. I would listen to his every word, learning the dos and don'ts of life.

It was fascinating to just watch and listen. Daddy was a true storyteller, in detail he told me day by day his life growing up in the country. Time went by slowly, I took care of daddy and Michael took care of me. I would be so exhausted at times. When I needed a break away from home, I would go walking, taking my time in the park. I would sit and watch the children playing, or family's enjoying the day out, people walking their dogs. Sometimes I would feel guilty about coming to the park without my children, but I needed this time for me.

Looking around I'd see how green the grass grew in the park and how some people walk by wonderful trees and never touch them or look at them. Daddy was going to miss all this I thought as I sat on the bench in the park. This would be a every other day event. I'd get the children settled down, give daddy his medication and walk down to the park. Sometimes I would be there so long Michael would come looking for me. Maddy and Dr. Green would join me on their days off, it would be wonderful.

I would have to take in the truth about daddy. On those days when I knew his pain was heavy, I'd be in the park praying Lord have mercy on daddy; please spare him from the pain. Some days I cried all day in the park. On Wednesdays, the pain management specialist was coming to make sure daddy was okay. I watched as she checked and after about an hour daddy asked me to leave the room. "Why?" I asked. "Karis, I just want to talk to her alone," daddy told me shooing me out with his hand. I went out shutting the door behind me.

I stood there in the hallway of the house looking around and waiting for daddy to finish his talk with the pain management specialist. She came out a while after and closed the door. "Karis, I have to talk to you, she said clutching her box in front of her; she carried a red box it was full of needles and drugs for pain. "Have your father shared with you that he's been having a lot of pain urinating?" She asked. "No, he hasn't said a word to me," I explained to her. "I have noticed that his diapers have been a little dry when I change him, he never say's that he's in any pain."

"Karis, I would like to have him go to the hospital to be checked out, he has a full bladder, but he can't relieve himself, it's dangerous for him, we have to relieve him," she said. "Can I use your phone?" She asked. "Yes, but can you tell me why he needs to go to the hospital; can't you do that here?" I asked her. "No sweetie, he needs to be in the hospital, we need to check everything in there, the bladder could be infected, it could possibly be something that we can't do anything about right away until we cure the infection," she said looking at me with sadness in her eyes.

"He will come back home to you sweetie, don't worry." I walked her over to the phone. She called the hospital and told them that I would be bringing daddy soon. I called Martha so that she could tell everyone. When we arrived at the hospital daddy was so pale, he was shaking, and when I touched his forehead, he was burning up with fever. I wheeled him into the admissions office and filled out the paperwork. They told me to wait in the lobby when they wheeled him away.

"Bye daddy," I said to him. I sat in the lobby and prayed for daddy. The doctor came out soon after to tell me that they needed to go into daddy's bladder to cut out the infected areas. I didn't wait around to see daddy, I went in to kiss him before they took him in for surgery. Daddy couldn't urinate without the surgery. I went home to Michael and told him what happened there was so little I could do at this point. Daddy had his trails with his disease, and only God could bless him with the strength to overcome the pain. Michael and I prayed at dinner. It was so quiet at the table; the children missed daddy, and so did I.

We tried talking about school, they hardly responded. Keagan would usually have stories to tell about all his adventures at school, but not this night he was just quiet. "Will granddaddy ever come back home?" Kristopher asked with tears in his eyes. I got up and went over to him I held my son. "Oh son, he will come home he's just having trouble using the bathroom," I tell him as he began to cry. It hurt my heart to watch them worry about daddy. "I am taking you guys out for ice cream," Michael said getting up from the table.

"Really?" Kristopher said looking up at him. "Yes, really, everyone put on your jackets, and we'll head over to the ice cream shop," Michael said getting up from the table. "Michael, I'm going to stay here close to the phone okay," I tell him as I clean up the mess from dinner. No one really ate anything. I stood there looking out into the yard as I did when I washed and cleaned after dinner. I turned away to go and wash the dinner table off and there sitting on the couch was daddy. "Hey daddy, what are you doing here?" I say to him startled.

"I came to see my baby," he said. "No, daddy, you shouldn't be here," I told him I knew if he was here this meant that soon he'd be passing. I went over to him and hugged him tightly, and he smiled down at me. "Karis, I want you to know that you are so wonderful and God will bless you, you took good care of your dad. I know I couldn't have done what you did, changing a grown man's diapers, feeding him, and bathing him. Baby, you really did well, and your blessings are soon to come," daddy said with a smile on his face.

I held onto him until he was gone. I went back over to the sink, I didn't cry, nor was I sad, I was filled with overwhelming joy in my heart for daddy. I was almost finished when the phone rang. I ran to it and picked it up. "Hello," I said. "Hello Mrs. Phillips, I'm nurse Robin the doctor wanted you to know that everything went well and that you can pick your father up tomorrow," she said. "Tomorrow" I asked her. "Yes everything went fine, your fathers comfortable now and he should be ready for you tomorrow afternoon," she said again.

"Okay, I will be there tomorrow to get him." I was stunned at what I heard because I was sure that phone call would be different I thought as I finished up my cleaning. I went upstairs to take a shower. I took off my clothes and stepped into the shower. I washed still baffled by the phone call. I kept hearing sniffling as the water ran as if someone was in the bathroom with me crying. I turned the shower off and listened. It was quiet for a second then more sniffling. I opened the shower door to look around there was no one, I hurried and washed my face and rinsed my hair. I stepped out, and a young boy was sitting on the toilet crying.

I didn't say a word I dried off and wrapped the towel around me. As I walked away from him the crying and sniffling became louder and louder, I sat down on the bed and waited. Was he coming out to tell me or was he just going to linger around me I wondered? I put my pajamas on and waited. Michael and the children showed up soon after, I was still sitting at the foot of the bed when the children came running up the stairs. The crying and sniffling stopped as soon as they stepped into the room. "Hi mommy," Kristopher said.

"Hi Kristopher, how was the ice cream?" I asked him. "I had chocolate, and Keagan h ad orange sherbet, Kristine had strawberry." "Yum sounds so good, what about dad what did he have?" I asked. Michael held up a bag. "I didn't have anything, I saved it for us to share," he said putting the bag on the table. He came over to me and kissed my forehead. "So did you hear from the hospital yet?" He asked. "I did, they said I can pick daddy up tomorrow," I say. "Really, tomorrow?" "Yes, they said tomorrow." Michael took the ice cream from the bag and handed me a spoon.

"Are you ready for him to come home?" He asked. "What do you mean?" I asked looking confused. "I mean are you ready, he may be a little sicker than he was when they took him in Do you need extra help because I can hire someone around the clock to come in if you like," he tells me feeding me a spoonful of chocolate ice cream. I shook my head yes. "I think that will help," I told him. We ate the ice cream and Michael went to the closet to get his clothes out for work. I held the cup of ice cream in my hand and ate while he talked to me from the closet. I was about to take another spoonful when the cup was hit and flipped up into the air.

The young boy stood so close to my face in a flash, he was gone he had tears in his eyes still, but he looked so angry. "What was that?" Michael asked me. "Oh I dropped the cup," I said bending down to pick it up, I looked around for the young man. He was   gone. I stood up holding the cup, and in a flash again the young boy stood close to my face and hit the cup out of my hand again. Then in a flash was gone again. "Michael," I yelled out. I was frustrated I didn't pick the cup up this time I just sat on the bed.

Michael came out of the closet and sat down beside me. "Baby, I know," he said holding me; he held his shirt in his hand. "Everything will be fine I promise," he said holding me and kissing my cheeks. "You will be fine too," he said standing up over me to put on his shirt. "I have to go in a little early tonight, I have two surgeries tomorrow morning, don't expect me home until tomorrow afternoon," he said. I was sitting there thinking about being there alone tonight, Michael waited patiently for me to respond to what he told me.

"Okay Michael, I understand," I told him. He took me by the hand and pulled me up from the bed into him squeezing me tight. "I'll miss you so much baby," he said kissing my chest. "I'll miss you more," I tell him kissing his neck. I closed my eyes as I kissed his neck when I opened them the young man was staring me in my eyes, I closed them tight. Not now I thought to myself, go away. "I love you," Michael said grabbing his bag from the floor. "I love you too Michael," I said walking over to the door to walk him downstairs. "Goodnight kids," Michael yelled out, "I will see you guys tomorrow," he said blowing kisses at Kristine.

"I love you, daddy," Kristine said. Keagan ran over to Michael and hugged his legs, Michael was so tall; Keagan looked up at him. "Daddy stay, stay," he said. Keagan never reacted this way by Michael leaving. "Son, I would stay if I could," Michael told him bending down patting him on the back. "I wish I could stay, not tonight son, I have to go, there are a lot of sick people who need me," he said to Keagan; he grabbed him with his bag still in his other hand.

"I will be back early tomorrow, and we will go to the park, I promise son," he said kissing his forehead and putting him back on the floor. I walked him to the door and waited as he drove away from the driveway waving goodbye. I went around the house turning off the lights and locking all the doors. I went in to put the children in bed. I read them a story until they fell off to sleep then I went to my bed. I was so tired I just covered myself all the way up to my neck and turned down all the lights, I left my door cracked opened and fell off to sleep. I was slept for at least four hours into the night until I heard the crying and sniffling.

I didn't get up nor did I look around the room, I knew it was the young man. I turned over onto my back and looked up. "Lord, please not tonight," I say to myself. I could hear it loudly, I turned over onto my side, and there he was sitting against the bed, on the floor. I dared to touch him, for his burden would be revealed. I turned over onto my other side. Go away I thought to myself I just didn't want to exhaust myself with this spirit daddy was coming home in the morning and whatever strength I had in me I needed to save it for him. "Karis," I heard a whisper.

"Karis," I ignored it until I felt the bed shake. I sat up and looked around and down to see where he was. He was gone. When I didn't see him I laid on my back. I fell off to sleep again watching the clock, by then it was 450 am. I thought I could sleep two more hours and I'd have to get up and prepare everything for daddy to come home. I slept a good hour before I felt little hands hugging my stomach. I opened my eyes and it was Keagan he'd snuck into my bed. I turned over and held him close to me rubbing his hair; I stared outside as the sun came up.

When I couldn't lay there any longer, I placed Keagan on his side got up from the bed. I went in the bathroom to wash. There sitting on the toilet the young boy in a fetal position crying, this time he pointed at me. I washed my face as if he wasn't there. I turned the light out and walked away shutting the door behind me. "Do you think we can have pancakes mommy?" Kristopher says startling me. "Sure, son," I said grabbing my robe from the door. "Mommy I don't want pancakes," Kristine said. "Okay, what do you want then?" I asked her.

"I just want a boiled egg and toast," she said going over to Keagan who was still laid in bed. "Look at Keagan mommy, he's pretending, he's not sleeping mommy, look at his eyes," she said pointing at Keagan's eyes. They were wide open. "Keagan, honey, are you up?" I yelled out to him. "He is, mommy, look at his eyes." Kristine went over to him and began to poke him in the eye. "No, honey, you can't do that," I shouted. I walked over to him and shook him, I'd never noticed that Keagan slept that way, I shook him again.

"Keagan, sweetie, are you awake?" I said pulling him up after a few shakes. "He was limp in my arms, but his body was warm. "Keagan," I said again this time I blew my breath in his face he blinked really hard. "Mommy, what's wrong?" He said dazedly. "You had your eyes wide open, are you okay sweetie?" I asked. "Mommy, I'm really tired, he said pulling away from me to lay his head on the pillow. "Okay son, we'll be downstairs," I rubbed his little back, "I will put your breakfast on the table."

The twins and I walked down the stairs to make breakfast. "Do you think he'll get out of bed soon mommy?" Kristine asked very worriedly. "Oh honey, he's just exhausted, after I make your breakfast I'll go back up and check on him." I made their breakfast fast, I was anxious about

Keagan he'd never done this before. I went back upstairs soon after making breakfast and Keagan was still lying in bed. I went over to him. "Keagan, are you okay son?" I said rubbing his back. I took him into my arms and touched his forehead to see if maybe he could be sick, he wasn't.

I just held onto him, I knew that daddy would have to be picked up real soon. I was so worried about Keagan; I just sat and held him praying. "Daddy appeared on the bed with me he placed his hand over Keagan's head. "He's not ill Karis, pay attention," he said walking away from the room. I looked around the room, and peeking from the bathroom door was the spirit of the young man. He looked at me and began snickering as if it was funny, what was happening to   Keagan? I screamed out to him; "what do you want?" He looked at me and walked away. I laid Keagan down on the bed and walked over to the bathroom, I looked in, and he was gone.

"Mommy," Keagan said. "Yes son, are you okay? I asked him picking him up and placing him on my lap. "I'm tired, mommy, really tired," he said placing his little head on my chest. "Baby, you have to eat something you've been sleeping all day." I took him up from the bed and carried him downstairs to the kitchen. I sat him down on the chair. "Keagan, are you okay?" Kristine asked him going over to his chair. "Would you like some of my egg?" She said putting the egg to his little lips. He turned his head from the egg.

"Mommy, what's wrong with Keagan?" She asked. "He's just a little tired," I told her making him a pancake. I sat down beside him and cut his pancake up into pieces I would have to feed him. This young man's spirit is what's wrong with Keagan I believed. I was determined to make Keagan eat at least a little breakfast before I laid him back down in bed. I was sure that the hospital would call me soon to pick up daddy. As soon as I put Keagan back in bed the phone rang, I didn't answer.

I just waited for it to stop and called Maddy to ask her if she could come over and sit with Keagan for a while. She rushed right over soon after. "Keagan's a little ill," I tell her. "Does he have a fever?" "No, I don't know what he has yet, he's just been lying around in bed, and seemed so weak." I took the new truck that Michael bought and rushed down to the hospital to get daddy, he's really coming home I thought. With all that's happened I never could imagine picking him up. When I made it there, I went to the front entrance it was so cold was in here. "Hi, I'm here to pick up my father, Earl Lawson," I said to the lady at the desk.

"Sign here, I'll go get the doctor for you," she said walking away into the hall. I could hear daddy yelling out "Oh Lord! Oh Lord!" from the room down the hall. I sat the clipboard down and walked toward the rooms in the hall when I approached daddy's room I peeked in at him. He was lying on his side holding the railing of the bed breathing in and out heavily saying, "oh Lord, oh Lord," very loudly. I walked in front of the bed and leaned over. "Daddy," I said looking into his face.

"Are you okay?" he shook his head yes. "Are you sure?" I asked. He looked at me, and right then in his eyes, I knew daddy was gone. I knew that his soul was just lingering in his shell to get him home. I held daddy's hand standing there waiting for the doctor to come in and discharge daddy. When he walked in he gave me this look of worry. "He's ready," he said. He came over to me and grabbed my hand. "Is he able to go home, he seems to be in a lot of pain doctor," I said to him. "Yes, he's going to be in a little pain for a while, your father is in the last stages."

"Oh, I know that doctor," I said stopping him before he could tell me another word about daddy; he knew that I didn't welcome the conversation about daddy's last days. "Doctor, I just want to take him home," I said walking over to daddy's back. "I will get the nurse to bring out a wheelchair for you," he said. "Thank you, doctor," I said as he walked out. He came back quickly with the nurse and the wheelchair. "Mr. Lawson, it was great to see you again sir," he said shaking daddy's hand. "I hope you feel better." He walked out as we put daddy into the wheelchair.

"I hope that you feel better as well," the nurse said to him. We wheeled daddy out to the truck. As soon as we approached the truck I felt joy all over me, and I looked down at daddy in the chair he was pale, and his eyes changed, he just looked as if he was fading away. I held in my cry, I felt the joy, but I wanted to cry. Daddy was leaving me I thought at that moment. I put daddy in the truck and the nurse helped me place the chair into the trunk. I looked back at daddy, he was leaving me. His eyes glossed his skin pale and he didn't say one word all the way home.

"Everything will be fine, daddy, I promise you it will be," I tell him as we pull up to the house. I see Kristopher in the window waiting for us. Maddy ran out to help me get him into the wheelchair, we wheeled him into the house. The chair was so light with him in it, Maddy and I carried him up to his room where I placed him in bed. I first sat daddy up so that I could put him in his bedclothes. As I did, I noticed that he was still breathing heavy, so I reached over him to get him the oxygen mask that hung over the bed. When I tried to place it over his face he grabbed my hand.

"No, Karis, baby thank you so much, thank you," he said breathing heavily. I couldn't cry I wasn't going to allow him to see me hurting I wanted him to know I was brave. I tried to remove his pants. "I can help you, Karis," Maddy said coming over to help me. I took daddy pants down only to find him soiled it looked as if his bowels were running like water. I rushed to the bathroom in the hallway to get a bowl of hot water and towels and soap. Maddy watched me with tears in her eyes.

Oh no I thought I should ask her to leave she just went through this with her father. I went over to her I took daddy's pants all the way down and began to wipe him off. "Maddy, I will be okay, if you like you can go home, I think I can do this alone," I told her. "No honey, I wouldn't dare," she said. "I will stay out with the children, I will take them to their rooms while you get him cleaned up," she said going to the door to close it. Daddy was still smiling as I cleaned him I took a large trash bag and threw his soiled clothes in, he watched my every move.

After I was done cleaning him off, I put a diaper on him his bowels were still running. I put a new pair of pants on him. "I hope it doesn't run through daddy," I said to him. "Daddy, I hope you feel better," I told him. I took him by his legs and lifted them up and laid him straight in the bed. When I did that daddy looked up at me, and his eyes rolled back. "Daddy," I said. "Daddy, are you okay?" He didn't respond. I lifted the bed up to a sitting position with him leaned back a little , and covered him with a light blanket and went out to the hallway.

"Maddy," I yelled out. She came rushing to me. "Yes, honey, are you okay?" She asked. "I need you to please call my family," I went to the children. Kristopher looked so sad I just held onto him waiting for Maddy to come in the room. "I've called the doctor and the family, everyone says that they are on their way," she tells me grabbing onto Kristine. I could feel joy in my belly although my heart was sad. We waited for the family and the doctor to show up. When they did I had a full house. I watched as they went into daddy's room one by one and said there goodbyes. As the sun went down daddy's breathing became more and more, shallow, as if he could hardly breathe.

The doctor kept checking for his heart to stop. Daddy held my hand tight he turned to me and whispered, "I love you, Karis," I couldn't help but tear up. I walked over to the door everyone stood around daddy's bed and watched as he left. I could see his spirit standing next to the bed, he was smiling. His body hardened before them as his soul left the bed. The doctor took one more check of his heart. "He's gone," he said to the nurse. She immediately looked at the clock on the table; it was 7 pm on the dot daddy was gone.

I didn't let the children go into the room; it would have been too much for them to see. It was around 8 pm when Michael came in. He came over to me and hugged me tight. "You'll be fine baby, you'll be fine," he said rocking me close to his chest. It was so upsetting for Krystal, she cried for hours near his bed. I had to go in and take her out before the funeral home would come to get daddy' body. She stood by the door when they came. "I don't want them to take him!" She yelled out. "Daddy, daddy" She yelled. Michael and I held onto her as she cried.

The rest of the family all took comfort with their loved ones as we all watched them take daddy's body out to the van. We would bury daddy on the following Saturday. It couldn't have been a better day. The Friday night before everyone met up at my house to eat and laugh and talk about daddy. They all stayed until at least midnight. I was up cleaning way past than. When I finally made it upstairs I was beat. I took off everything I was wearing by the time I reached the top stair. I went into the bathroom and turned the water on as hot as I could get it. I just wanted to soak. I got into the tub and leaned my head back.

I dimmed the lights in the bathroom and lit four candles. My body was so tired daddy's gone I thought as I laid there in the tub. I put the towel over my head and rested the door was cracked open just enough for me to see into the room. I could hear if Michael moved around a little in the bed. As I drifted off to sleep, I heard the door crack open just a bit, and someone peeked in at me. She was very tall and wore glasses the glare from the glowed as if there was light shining through them.

I sat up quickly; I didn't know what kind of spirit it was. She stared at me her hair was white and she wore a blue dress. I started to get out of the bathtub. When I got up she walked out closing the door behind her. I lay back in the bathtub. I put the towel over my head and soaked a little more. When I got up to wash, she and daddy standing together before me; "I came for him," she said smiling at daddy. She put her hand to the side of his face. "My son," they walked out, and daddy smiled with her by his side.

I was done in the tub by 3 am I got in bed with Michael and held onto him. I had about two hours to sleep before I had to get up and prepare the children for daddy's funeral. Hardly sleeping I was eager to see if daddy would come to me. I just wanted to feel him close to me one last time. It was around 6 am when I woke up. I could hear Michael and the children downstairs already welcoming people into our home. I ran to get my clothes on and rushed downstairs to find the house full again.

We were to all ride in the funeral homes limos together. I would ride with Krystal and Martha and my family. We all got into the limos and rode away to lay daddy to rest. The funeral was filled with many speakers some talked about daddy's kind hearted ways some talked about his work in the community. It was nice to hear the good things daddy did over the years. It was safe to say his life was never lived in vain. The church was packed there were people even standing outside to get there last goodbyes in.

I tried to say hello and thank you to everyone. Especially those who stood outside the church when it was over we all met at the burial grounds. They would put him in with mama. There we all were standing there together again both our parents gone. We needed to stand together this time keeping in touch with one another. This would be it for all of us. Daddy was the only thing holding the family together. It was cool out there at the burial grounds as we all stood around daddy's grave watching as they placed the casket down into the hole.

I watched daddy across the grounds smiling he placed his hands behind his back he waved to me with a wonderful smile on his face and walked away I seen mama waiting for him she was smiling waiting for him to walk her way. I put my head down to watch them throw the dirt into the ground with a shovel. The sun shined down on us so bright that my shoulders were burning from it beaming onto my dress. Everyone came back to our house for lunch there was so much food people were everywhere in the house.

The church family served all of us it was quiet, a little laughter here and there. As the day turned to night the room became more and more empty. Maddy and Dr. Green were the last to leave they helped clean. After a while Michael took the children up for bed and I was left downstairs placing the dishes into the dishwasher. My heart was filled with sadness, but I knew that daddy was home free safe and happy. I just felt so alone no mother or father. I thought about all the time I spent with him and how he could turn my frown upside down.

As he would say this would be a tough experience living without his love. There is no other love like a fathers or mothers love. It is closets to being free from all worries. I put the dishes all away I wiped down the counters after that I went outside to pick up all of the paper plates and napkins that everyone left out. I stood in my garden for a while, I had to cry. I had to express my hurt right than in the garden where daddy and I would often come and work together and talk about the tomatoes and peppers, this was also a place where mama and I spent a lot of time.

It would never be again, us in the garden I thought to myself as I stood there holding the plates in the garden. Soon Michael was standing behind me hugging me tight. "Sometimes, baby its okay, it's hard to accept the fact that you won't see them here," he said. "See, Karis, that's how they receive their wings, they let go and allow God to take them up into eternity where you can only feel joy and happiness. He's going to be so happy, he'll never feel what he felt here, nor will he ever question love or happiness. You have to allow him to go in peace, cry now but celebrate in your heart, you will see him again and their always watching over us."

Michael held me close to him whispering these things in my ear. I cried for a while and we went inside. I went in to check on the children. They were all sleeping, Michael hadn't undressed them or anything they still had their shoes on. I went to them and began taking their clothes and shoes off one by one, I undressed them; it didn't take long. I kissed them all goodnight and went to my bedroom to get undressed. As I walked into the closet, I could hear the crying and sniffling of the young boy again.

I wasn't going to acknowledge him, I was so tired there was no way I could cradle his spirit. I was hoping that it would stop, I took my clothes and laid them on top of the hamper for dry cleaning, and there he was sitting on the floor of the closet crying in the fetal position with his hands to his knees. I looked at him and shook my head no. I walked out of the closet to lay down next to Michael, and put my arms around him. Thinking about all the things to do tomorrow, I would be getting the room that daddy was in cleaned out. Michael says I should wait until I'm ready; to let a few days go by before going in there to clean, but I'm ready I thought.

I need to get everything cleaned out of there. I didn't want the children to have to pass the room and wonder about daddy. I fell off to sleep trying not to think about the young boy lingering around me, I knew his spirit was lost. I had no energy for whatever he needed at this time, but I prayed that God would allow me to rest through this trying time in my life. I knew the young boy just needed my help. I woke up the next day feeling even more drained than the day before.

I could hear the children up with Michael downstairs, I didn't even go to them quickly I laid there in bed with the cover over my face just for a while, I wanted to be still. After about an hour of under the cover silence, I had to get up and stretch. I wrapped myself up in my robe and walked into the room where daddy slept. It was so cold in there. I went over to the window to check if it was opened. It wasn't opened I began to remove everything from the hospital bed; it was to be picked up the moment I finished cleaning today.

I will call them I thought as I was going through his clothing in the closet, I had a box in my closet that I could use to put these clothes in I thought as I walked back out towards my bedroom. I went inside my closet to reach up for the box; it was high on a shelf where I kept my shoe boxes. As I reached up all of the boxes and shoe boxes came tumbling down on my head, and I fell to the floor. The shoes and boxes covered me; I closed my eyes and thought oh my God what did I reach up there for? Lying on the floor covered in boxes and shoes.

I just laid there until Michael came in. When he did I looked up through the boxes and shoes and held my hand up. He laughed so hard at me pulling me up from the floor by the hand. "What happened, Karis?" He said laughing. I couldn't help but laugh too. His smile lit up the room "What were you trying to get from up there?" He asked me. "I was reaching for that big box in the corner," I told him pointing to the box. "It is way back there too," he said reaching up to get it.

I took the box and went to daddy's room Michael followed me. "Baby, you don't have to do this now, you can wait a couple of days sweetie, come on, not now," Michael said pulling at me to leave the room. "No, I need to finish this now," I said placing some of daddy's things in the box. "Okay, I understand," he walked out of the room and left me. I sat down on the bed and packed his pants on the bottom, shirts on top. He had several blankets that he loved to be wrapped up in.

I'll keep only one I thought. I will keep the one blanket that I would spread across his waist at night.

It was a blue blanket it had white stripes going down the middle and horses all around it. Daddy loved horses. I took the blanket and wrapped myself in it. I sniffed it; it smelled of daddy I sat in his chair just holding on to the blanket really tight. I looked out of the window looking into the backyard. How I wished that this had never happened, both my parents died so young, mama in her fifty's and daddy at the ripe old age of seventy three. Would this happen to me I wondered, would I die very young? I laid there quietly thinking about my parents. I was so hurt my heart was so heavy. I knew he was leaving me soon, but it seemed too soon.

I dared to cry when I knew he was free from pain now. I thought as I began to cry. I couldn't help myself, I cried loudly and prayed God, please help me through this time. I don't even know why I couldn't stop crying my heart was just heavy with the thought of never seeing my parents again. I'm here alone without them. My tears fell heavy also. After a while the young boy appeared in front of me, he stood right by the window and he began to cry loudly also. I sat up taller in the chair. He reached out his hand to me.

"Help me," he said crying loudly. I knew if I touched his hand I would be able to see why he was here lingering around in this world. I went over to him, and he grabbed onto my hands as I walked up to him. Immediately I could see him in his bedroom crying. He was hanging onto a picture of another boy in his hand I looked down at the picture. When I looked back up at the young boy there was a rope around his neck. I took the picture and sat down beside him. I held his hand along with the picture and we were soon in a school yard surrounded by other young adults they seemed to be high school kids.

They were taunting him pushing him and spitting at him calling him queer. The young boy was afraid too afraid to yell out for help, he held hands with another young boy who was dressed in girl clothes, and they cried holding hands as the angry young crowd circled them yelling and screaming calling them every bad name you could ever imagine. The boys soon sat down in the circle, the angry group began to kick and hit them leaving them no open space to crawl out.

I could feel their pain both mentally and physically, they felt like they wanted to disappear at that moment. It would be a teacher running over to them that would make the angry mob of young kids run away. The two young men lay helplessly on the ground of the school yard holding one another crying. The teacher helped them both up and escorted them both to the principal office. They were looked over by the nurse, and the counselors came in, both boys crying historically still holding one another.

They separated them and ask their parents to come pick them up. When the parents arrived the young boy who came to me was more frightened about what his father would say about him in the circle being kicked. His father was taken into a room where he and the councilors would talk about the incident. When his father came out, he looked at the young boy with some much anger in his eyes. He snatched him up from his seat and yelled. "Let's go, son!" He pulled the young boy by his shirt. The other young boy watched with fear in his eyes too afraid to even say goodbye to his friend.

They got into his father's pickup truck, and his father took off quickly. He didn't say a word to him at first, but as soon as he was far enough away from the school, he threw a punch at the young boy's face that twisted his neck. When he turned back around he hit him again and again until the young boy screamed out. "Please pa, don't hit me anymore, I'm so sorry!" The father hit him once more. "Do you want everyone to know son, its bad enough that you are swinging your hips around town like a young lady."

"Now you want to have a boyfriend to flaunt around with you. How much, son, how much can I take? Your mom and I can't hold our heads up in church anymore thinking of your dirty sins!" His father hit him again. I was ill with the pain I felt for this young boy, by the time they made it to his house he was bruised and bloody. He rushed inside the house to the bathroom. "What is it? What happened?" The mother asked. The boy sat in the bathroom sobbing for hours. He was so hurt listening to his father explain, how ashamed he was of him.

That it was his fault for being who he was, the reason, he was attacked by the angry mob of young kids. I held onto him. It will be okay I took his hand as he went out of the bathroom and into his room. He took the picture from his drawer and held it to his lips and kissed it. I watched as he went to his closet and took out a rope tied it to the ceiling fan and took it around his neck. I held on to him as we both stood before him watching him take his own life, he cried out loudly.

I held on to him and prayed, "Lord, in the name of Jesus take him into your light. The life he did claim for in this world he became defamed in your words you say to the world judge us not for it is you who will have the last say. Take him into your light Lord for he has no trust. His spirit lingers around waiting for love, let him in and show him, real love. Allow him to be an angel up above, these things which they couldn't understand they couldn't change his heart or the way he felt for another man. Lord, it is not by choice the matters of the heart; allow him to feel it Lord, take his spirit and heal it."

I held onto him, his cry soon turned into laughter as his spirit turned into light. I opened my eyes, I watched as his light became further from the window. I sat down in the chair and thanked God for all that he's done for me. "Thank you Lord for your many blessings," I took the box that I packed with daddy's belongings in them and headed back to my room to put on a pair of pants and a t-shirt. "Mommy, I was looking for you," a little voice said to me. It was Keagan, he seemed all better.

"Oh honey, how are you feeling now?" I asked him leaning over kissing his cheek. "I'm better, mommy," he said holding onto my pants. He did seem fine, I took him by his little hand, and we walked into the hall where the attic was. "Mommy, daddy's up there, he's busy with god" He said smiling. I smiled at him busy with God, son," I said. He shook his little head yes. "Okay, let's go downstairs then, shall we," I said carrying the box in one hand and holding his little hand in the other hand. I was so happy that he felt better. I took him into the kitchen to get a snack.

The twins were sitting out back playing a board game on the patio table. I waved to them as I walked by with Keagan. I placed the box down near the door. I would have to get the rest of daddy's things together after I fed Keagan; he went to play with twins in back. I sat on the sofa and watched them play together until Michael came down. "Karis are you okay?" He asked me walking past me to get to the kitchen. "I'm fine now," I said to him looking at him sadly, I was still hurting, but I didn't want Michael to have that on his mind, I knew he was to return to work soon. He was so worried about me.

"Would you like a cup of coffee?" He said lifting my coffee mug up into the air for me to see. "No thank you, Michael. I'll have some juice instead," I tell him getting up to go in get some juice. "You know I could have gotten that for you," he said. "Are you going to go in today?" I asked. "And leave you?" He questioned. "No, I will be here until you are okay." "Michael, I'm fine really, I just have some cleaning to do, and soon I'll be back at work also, if they'll have me back," I said pouring my juice into my glass.

"No, baby right now you need to rest, we both do, the way we've been working around here keeping your father comfortable he would want us to rest now, don't you think?" He said taking a sip of his coffee. "I suppose so Michael, I really don't know what to do I know that I have you and the children, but I feel so empty there seem to be a hole in my heart where my parents belong," I tell him putting my head to his back. "I'm going to miss him so much," I said. Michael turned to me and grabbed me by the waist.

"You're right, you do have us, and you have the Lord, I know what this feels like, baby. I want to give you some time to heal, so I'll stick around for a few days to watch over you baby," I held on to Michael in the kitchen just thinking about daddy's smile it wouldn't leave my mind I closed my eyes, and there he was smiling again. The memory of him walking over to mama kept flashing in my mind over and over again throughout the day as I cleaned I cried a little here and there.

For days I walked around the house with the blanket after the hospital picked up the bed and I sent his things to the Salvation Army, it felt less and less that he was here. My heart grew heavier and heavier, I just wanted to see them one last time, I felt if I could see them I'd feel better. Michael began to worry about me. Why wouldn't their spirit come to me if I hadn't let them go? Why aren't they coming to me? I thought every day, and I waited and prayed for them to come to me. Soon I was going back to work, the children asked about daddy less and less every day.

I longed to see mama and daddy just for a moment's time. But I worked all day, and when I came home, Michael and I fixed dinner every night together. We put the children down to bed together reading stories until they would fall off to sleep. Michael would ask me if I was okay almost every second of the day when he was home. My spirit was shaken by daddy leaving so soon after I had him here. I felt a part of me thought that I could keep him here by having him in my presence, but God said no. I thought as I would clean up the house at night after Michael left for work and the children were all sleeping.

I would just sit on the sofa downstairs waiting to see if they would come to me. One ni ght I was downstairs sitting on the sofa, Michael had just left for work and soon after I watched him drive off and walked away from the door when there was a knock. I was startled by it and afraid to answer, I peeked through the window to see who it was. I couldn't see, the man's face, he was standing with his back to the door and his hands in his pocket. I yelled out; "who is it?" He turned around. I was stunned it was James, Oh no, I thought. I didn't know what to say, I didn't answer I shut the curtains.

"Hello, Karis, are you there?" He said looking around trying to see through the windows staring at the door. "I know   Karis, you don't want to see me, is that you?" He said with his face to the door. " I just wanted to tell you that I heard about your dad and I just want you to know that I wanted to come see him, but I was afraid. Karis, please talk to me," he said. I cracked opened the door. "What is James?" I asked. "Karis, Mr. Lawson was like a father to me, I know what happened between us was horrible, I know I hurt you, I'm so sorry Karis; I am."

"James, I've already forgiven you for that, there's no need to say that you're sorry every time." James had lost so much weight. "Come on James," I said to him opening up the door a little wider. "Are you sure?" He asked. "Yes, come in," he came in when he stepped in he looked at me and began to sob. "Oh, Karis I can't believe he's gone he was like a father to me," He cried on my shoulder. After he sobbed for a while I offered him some tea or coffee. We sat down in the kitchen I was still a little worried about being alone with James, but I felt at ease.

He talked about daddy, and us growing up, he joked around about him a lot, and I laughed. It was 3 am when I walked him out. I felt so much better sharing those old memories with James, when I closed the door, I watched as he walked down the street to his car. When he drove off, I went up to bed. I fell off to sleep feeling a little better about daddy. He lived a wonderful full life, and God blessed him with the gift of making so many people happy, he was so loved. It was around 5 am when I was woken up by a really bright light shining in at me, it warmed my whole body. When I looked up, there was my mama and daddy smiling at me I reached out to them as they faded away in the light.

Rising Spirits

The next few months after daddy passed seemed lonely. I wondered when I would see James again in spite of what he did to me; he was such a good friend. I asked around about him all the time. No one seemed to have seen him nor heard from him in such a long time they would say, and a good friend of his told me that he lived out of town and had not been here in years. He said he lived near New York and that his sister was the only one who could contact him. It was strange to hear that because he'd come over a few months ago after we buried daddy.

I went on working, soon enough I would call his sister to see how he was. Working at the hospital wasn't as bad as in the past. The spirits would rarely bother me; some would follow me from time to time they would just stare at me and smile. I was comfortable for the first time being me. I've accepted this gift fully, and I wondered when I'd ever been as comfortable as Michael. He was so comfortable with himself always smiling never confused about himself at all. He fully embraced his lifestyle and God truly blesses him.

He has become one of the top neurology surgeons in the world. He was known everywhere they called him from all around for conferences. He had awards all over the house now. We have a special cabinet set up for him in the hallway of our home. He recently has been on the news for saving a child's life. He'd been hit by a bus and suffered brain damage. I watched him from a far sometimes at the hospital walking around with the interns, he was serious as he explained to them the do's and don'ts of medicine.

They would be so into him, especially the young ladies. Michael looked as young as they did, but he was well over thirty. When he would finish, he'd make sure to find me, and we'd have lunch or dinner in his office. He was still a complete bragger, "did you see the young ladies ado ring me?" He'd say to me smiling. "Sure I did, you look so handsome why wouldn't they adore you?" I'd say to him. "You are sexy and smart; they couldn't dare miss a chance at getting you to notice them." He'd always get up from his chair and come over to me and kiss and hug me tight.

"You're the only young lady I ever want," he would hold on to me and feed me bites of his sandwich. We'd eat it together until it was time for me to go back to the floor. I had so many patient's, we were almost always short staffed, especially when Maddy was on vacation. She was getting older and about ready to retire. She was always talking about her and Dr. Green retiring every day just about. She'd show up at work with some pamphlet and vacation brochures, she was ready to travel.

The lady who would be taking over the scheduling was a very tall blonde name Sofia. She seemed very nice at first, but when I would do her shift, the patients would complain about how ruff she was. They would say she was one of the meanest nurses they'd ever encountered. Some of them even wanted to write up complaints, and their families would always come to the front desk to complain about her. Maddy would be so angry at her. Sometimes I'd see Maddy come into work go to her office and immediately call her in.

We'd sometimes all be sitting at the desk listening to her tell Sofia what the patients said about her. She'd come out of the office looking angry complaining to some of the other nurses that it's not her fault, and that the patients we have are spoiled and we cater to them . "Where I come from the patients are here for treatment, and we don't have to talk to them or smile at them. We just go in take care of what they need and move on to another patient," she would say. I wouldn't say a word, but the others would laugh.

"Where could she be from?" They would say in a whisper to one another. It was beginning to be a problem for Maddy with the families complaining, she would take Sofia off the schedule and only allow her to have one or two patients. When she did work; boy, did that cause a problem, day after day would be entertaining for some of the other nurses. They would get a call from Sofia at the nurse's station she would be yelling and screaming at Maddy about the schedule.

I knew sooner than later Maddy would get completely fed up with the encounters and fire Sofia. One afternoon while I was working I saw Sofia sitting out on the patio having her lunch alone. I went out to the patio. At first, I was going to ignore her, but I was worried about her spirit. There had to be a valid reason why she was unable to do this job the way most nurses would, with lots of integrity and pleasure. I walked over to her and sat my tray down on the table. "Is anyone sitting here?" I asked her. She rolled her eyes and turned the other way ignoring what I asked.

"Oh I guess not," I said aloud. I sat down and began to eat, she started to take her tray up and leave. I grabbed onto her tray. "Sofia, can we talk?" I asked her. "No thank you, I don't have anything to talk to you about," she said pulling her tray toward her. "Yes, we have a lot to talk about," I tell her still holding on to her tray. She sat down. "What do you want me to say to you? I don't know you," she said looking angry at me. "I know you don't, shall we get to know one another?" I say to her reaching out to shake her hand.

"My name is Karis," I tell her. She looked at my hand and let go of the tray and shook my hand. "I am Sofia, hi." "Hi Sofia, how are you?" I say to her. "You are friends with the boss, she hates me," she said looking mad. "Yes, I am however I respect her as my boss," I tell her.

"Where are you from?" I asked her. "I am from Russia," she said, she had a solid accent her voice was very raspy. "I come here to work and go to school, to have a better life for my child." "I see," I said to her eating my lunch.

"It must be tough being here in this new country, do you have any other family, I mean other than your child here?" I asked her. "No I don't, my husband brought me over, I don't do what he say he abandon my son and me," she said taking a drink of her canned soda. " Oh, I see," I tell her. "It is sometimes hard dealing with men." "I will find me a new husband," she said in her raspy voice. "I look in the hospital, I marry nice doctor like you," she says smiling. "I know you married to nice looking doctor, I see you go to his office at lunch; how you get him to marry you?" She asked.

"It's a long story, maybe I'll tell you another day" I tell her. "In your country, they don't care for their patients the way we do?" I ask her looking up at her. She was very beautiful and tall. "We care for them we don't pamper them. I don't know what else to do with the patient, just go in give them the medicine and leave, why must I talk to them? Why should I speak with their family?" She said shrugging her shoulders. "I never do that; I leave them in with their family."

"I see, well it won't hurt to smile at them and give them and their families a little conversation," I tell her. "Just let them know you care a little, they like to know that the person caring for their family member cares for them. That's all," I tell her finishing up my sandwich. She took her tray and emptied it. She came back over to the table. "Karis, thank you, I will try to do better," she said reaching out for my tray, "give it to me, I will empty for you," she said taking my tray. "Thank you so much." "Can I say your, my friend?" She asked me.

"Of course you can, if you need help with anything, please don't hesitate to come to me," I tell her getting up from the table. She took my tray and waved goodbye to me. I don't know where they have her working today, but she was happier, I watched her smiling as she walked away. I hope she will do better now I thought as I went to finish my shift. It was late when I finished up as I was walking to the elevator to leave Maddy came to me.

"Karis, I don't know what you said to Sofia, but she's smiled at me and apologized for her behavior. Thank you so much you may have saved her job," she said getting into the elevator with me. "You're off, aren't you?" "Yes I'm done for the day, I'll be back tomorrow," I tell her getting off the elevator at the lobby. I walked toward the front entrance to go to my car. As I was leaving I looked up at the hospital doorway and there standing at the doorway was Tara. I waved at her, and she waved back. I was so stunned to see Tara, I didn't stare at her I continued walking.

I knew if she was watching me that it wouldn't be long before she would appear to me again, I had to rush home to the children. They were home alone for about 3 hours every day until I got home. I would always cook dinner for them the day before in case I didn't make it in time to cook, all they had to do was warm it. Kristine was beginning to love warming the food and acting as if she was the older, of the three. When I would show up she'd be in my apron as if she had just cooked dinner for everyone. I didn't allow them to have friends over after school. That was a problem for Kristopher.

He loved to entertain friends and eat and play video games. "Hi mommy," Keagan said when I walked in the door. "Hello son, how's your day going?" I'd ask him. Keagan would follow me all over the house to tell me about his day. I'd go from the kitchen to the front room to my bathroom to take a shower, and he'd wait at the door to tell me what went on with him that day. I'd always tell him the same thing. "Keagan, maybe you should take some time to think about who your friends really are." His stories would always be about a couple of kids that picked at him at school, but he'd call them his friends.

"I like them, mommy, I can't just stop talking to them," he would say. "Okay son, I understand" He loved everyone; no one was bad in his little eyes. After my shower I'd go down to the kitchen to help Kristine with dinner. "Mommy there's some messages on the table by the phone for you, a woman kept calling you. She says it's important that you call her back," Kristopher said. I went over to the phone to retrieve the messages. There were three messages from James sister.

This was a surprise what could she be calling me about, I thought as I walked back over to the kitchen to help Kristine. She was still placing plates at the table. "Mommy, the lady, was really nice," she said as she helped Keagan over to the table. We waited for Michael to show up for dinner. Kristine was such a young lady now, I watched her do all the things she watched me do for so many years. She took her apron off and laid it across the chair. She sat and reached out her hands to lead us all in a dinner prayer. At the table we talked about school mostly, the children telling us about their favorite teachers and the subjects they disliked most. Michael and I laughed a lot.

"Mommy, did you call her back?" Kristopher asked. "No, sweetie I didn't call her back yet," I tell him. "Who didn't you call back?" Michael asked taking a sip of red wine from his wine glass. "Oh I had several phone calls from James sister. I don't know what she would have wanted from me," I told him giving him a look that I no longer wanted to discuss this. He took another drink from his glass and began to eat his salad. "She seemed like it was very important mommy," Kristopher said eating his food.

"I will call her tomorrow Kristopher, don't worry son," I tell him finishing up my salad. I got up from the table and Kristine followed me. "Mommy I can do this, I will put away all the food and clean the kitchen," she said reaching for my plate. "Oh no Kristine you've done enough, I will clean at least sweetie," I said kissing her cheek. I looked at her little face; she was a teen now looking a lot like James sister. Those big pretty hazel colored eyes, those long eyelashes batting at me with every word she spoke.

I just smiled at her, and thought about what could his sister have wanted and how'd did she get my number? I cleaned the kitchen quietly after the children went upstairs Michael came over to me and kissed my neck. "I know sweetheart, I know what's going on, you don't want to call her back because of the children you think they're after the children, don't you" He asked me. "No, Michael, I really don't know what they want from me, I didn't have a chance to tell you, but James came by here a couple weeks ago to tell me he'd heard about daddy.

It was harmless, he was a great help I was able to talk about daddy and laugh and joke with him. Daddy was like a father to him, and he just wanted me to know that he was praying for us," I told him. "Baby, it's okay that he came by I'm sure he needed to see you also you guys had a long history way before I came along," he said with a smile on his face. "Come here," he said grabbing me. "I miss you, baby," he whispered to me. We kissed when the phone rang again. I pulled away to go and get the phone, he held onto me tighter. "Not now," he said kissing me all over my neck while the phone continued to ring.

"I better get it, Michael," I said pulling away, he held onto my waist as I walked over to the phone. "Hello," I said. "Hello, Karis? Is this Karis Lawson?" A female voice said softly. "Yes, this is Karis, may I ask who's calling" Oh no, it's her, James sister I thought. "Yes this is Karis Lawson Phillips, how can I help you?" I said pretending to act as if I didn't know her voice. "Hi, I am James sister, and I wanted to know if I could come by and talk to you about something important," she said curiously.

"Sure, when would you like to come by?" I asked her. I shook my head at Michael, I didn't really want her to come by, but I knew that it had to be something important. "I'd like to come as soon as possible, I'm going to be leaving town in two days, and I just want to handle this before I leave, how does tomorrow afternoon sound?" She said. Michael shook his head yes listening to her with his ear partially to the phone. "Tomorrow will be fine," I tell her looking Michael in the eye. "Thank you so much, I have your address I hope this is correct," she said as she read my address to me.

"Yes, that's right, then I'll see you tomorrow," I tell her hanging up the phone quickly. "See that wasn't so bad, she probably just wants to talk to you about James, that's all," he said beginning to kiss me all over. He pulled my shirt over my head. "I've missed you, baby," he said undressing himself right there in the den. "Michael, the children," I said in a whisper. "They are sleeping by now, I promise baby they won't hear a thing," he said sliding down my pants, he laid on the carpet and pulled me over him "Oh Karis," he shouted as I began to kiss all over his body.

I missed him as well. We made love until we both were tired. When we were done Michael took the throw from the sofa and wrapped it around his waist. "I have to get ready for work baby," he took my hand and pulled me up from the floor. "You need to get your rest when she comes tomorrow I want to be here," he said kissing my lips softly. "I want you to be here too Michael I'm afraid of what she has to say to me," I tell him pulling my shirt over my head. I grabbed my pants and we headed upstairs to shower. I looked in on the children while Michael went into the shower, I soon joined him.

When we got out Keagan was lying in our bed wrapped up tightly in the blankets. I wouldn't have even noticed he was there except for his little face stuck out of the small hole of the blanket. I went over to him and rubbed his back, I was wrapped in a towel. Michael was in the closet getting dressed. "Baby, have you seen my long sleeve blue shirt?" I took my pajamas from the drawer and walked into the closet with him. "I haven't sweetie, did you go to the cleaners to pick up the dry cleaning?" I asked him as I brushed my hair back, watching him dress.

Michael's body was so beautiful. I stared at his chest as if I hadn't seen it before. "See something you like?" He asked me laughing. "I do," I tell him turning my back to him trying not to blush after saying what I said. He walked over to me and pulled me close to him with my back to his chest he kissed my neck. "Karis, you're the best thing that's ever happened to me." "I know," I said walking away. He kissed my forehead then my lips. "I love you, sweetie, I'll see you soon," he said picking his bag up from the floor. I waved as I walked over to the bed to lay down with Keagan.

I lay beside him and pulled him close to me staring at his little face, I noticed his body was cold, he was covered up in two blankets. "Keagan, sweetie, are you still cold?" I said scooting my body closer to him. He didn't move nor open his eyes. "Keagan," I said shaking his little arms he looked up at me. "Hi mommy," he said in a soft whisper. "Mommy, I don't feel well," he said. I sat up and took him into my arms. "What's wrong sweetheart?" I asked.

"I'm cold, mommy, my tummy hurts really bad," he said, "Do you want another blanket, do you need to go to the bathroom?" I asked him. "No mommy, there's pain all around my tummy," he said pointing to where he felt pain. I got up to go to the hall cabinet to get Keagan another blanket as I was walking back into the room Keagan began to vomit all over the bed and floor nonstop. I ran over to him "Keagan! Sweetie, are you okay?" I asked holding his little belly when sat him up he was still vomiting all over.

"Keagan can you make it to the bathroom" I asked him. He shook his head no. I took him over to the toilet and leaned him over it. "Go ahead sweetie, if you have to, get it all out." He vomited a little more I rubbed his back and reached for a towel to wipe his mouth and hands. I picked him up when he was done and carried him back to the bed. I took the covers and wrapped his little body up tightly. He leaned over and placed his head on my chest. I reached over to call Michael. I was so scared, Keagan wouldn't move around, he was stiff.

I placed him down on the bed as the phone rang to get Michael. "Hi, may I speak with Dr. Phillips?" I asked the woman on the other end of the phone. "Hold on one second please, is this Mrs. Phillips?" She asked. "This is an emergency can you please hurry," I tell her. "Yes can you hold please," she said. I listened to classical music while I waited for Michael to come to the phone. "Hello, baby, what's wrong?" He asked. "It's Keagan Michael he's really sick, I think I'm going to have to bring him in."

Just as I said that, Keagan's body began to shake really hard, his eyes rolled back, and he sat up, and just stared out, as if his eyes were stuck looking at something far away. I waved my hand in his face and yelled his name. I wasn't able to hold the phone for Michael I left it on the floor as I cared for   Keagan. I checked his heart with my ears to his little chest. It was fine, beating strong. I turned him over on his side. No matter what I did for him he wouldn't stop staring out. The twins heard me yelling for him and ran into the room. Kristopher picked up the phone to talk to Michael.

"Dad, I will," he said he hung the phone up and came over to Keagan lying on the floor. Kristine stood by the door looking very scared, she began to cry. I held onto Keagan until I heard the ambulance coming. I put Keagan on his back as I got into something more appropriate for the ambulance attendants to come in. Kristopher let them into the house. They rushed upstairs behind Kristopher they took him from my arms and began to look him over. He was still staring out. I didn't know what to do my baby was just lying there helpless.

"Mrs. how long has he been like this?" The medic asked. "He just started vomiting he was cold all over, there was no fever," I told them standing over him watching them check him over. "Mrs. we are going to take him in, he's not responding he's breathing a little shallow we need to take him in for some testing, would you like to ride along with us? I see that you have other children maybe you'd like to follow us to the hospital," the medic looked a little worried as she went over to Keagan, and began to strap him into the large gurney they brought in to carry him out in.

"I will follow you," I tell him grabbing my shoes from the closet shelf. I took my jacket from the hanger. "Kristopher, Kristine get your jackets and shoes on please, let's go," I tell them rushing behind the gurney and the EMT's "I'll be right behind you," I tell them. Kristine took the keys to the car from the hook on the wall and we were off following the ambulance. Kristine cried the whole way to the hospital. "Kristine it will be okay," I said. "Mommy, what happened to Keagan?" Kristopher asked.

"Kristopher he was fine, I don't know, I think maybe he ate something bad," I really hope that's all it is," I tell him following quickly behind the ambulance. When we arrived at the hospital Michael was waiting for us he quickly went to tend Keagan. He looked very nervous. I parked right behind the ambulance the twins got out. We all followed Michael and the EMT's into the hospital. When we went in Michael told us to wait out in the lobby. Quickly someone came out to talk to us, it was Sofia.

"Hello," she said in her Russian accent. "I want you to fill these out for me while we get your son s   table," I looked up at her. "Karis, it's you," she said as Michael walked into the lobby. "What is it, Michael?" I asked. "I don't know baby they told me I had to wait out here also. I need to be in there with my son," he said angrily. "Dr. Phillips, please don't get upset, I'm sure he's fine with the other doctors," Sofia said. We sat out in the lobby for what seemed to be hours before the doctors came out. "Hi," it was Dr. Tate one of Michaels colleagues.

"Hello," we said to him Michael shook his hand. "Your son in a state shock, we don't know yet what caused it. He's staring out, he's not blinking his breathing and vitals are all fine although at times it becomes shallow, is there a history of Asthma or seizures?" He asked us. "No sir, Keagan has been pretty healthy all his life for the most part just the normal childhood illnesses," I told him. "Can you tell me what happened before you brought him into the hospital?" He asked.

"He was fine, I found him in my bed   sleeping, his little body was cold as ice, so I covered him, he said he was cold I went to get more blankets, and he began to vomit everywhere. I don't know how long he vomited for a while after he was done he laid on my chest and his body went into convulsions. I held him until he stopped, it was like a seizure at first, but he stopped, and his eyes began to stare off as if he was staring at something. I waved my hands in his face for him to respond, but he didn't that when I called my husband," I told him. "I see," he said placing his hand on his glasses.

"We want to keep him here to watch him. We would like to get a scan of the brain sometime tomorrow afternoon, to make sure the brain is functioning well. If you can fill out the necessary paperwork for that, we will call one of you when we're done," he said looking at Michael. "I want to sit in for that," Michael said looking at him in his eye. "Mac, I'd love for you to do that. However, you know it wouldn't be good for you nor our young patient. You know the rules." "But it's my son, Tate," Michael said to him.

"I know, and we all know that it's just not a good idea for you to sit in for that, now, you're welcome to watch from the glass upstairs, it's not a very long procedure," he said. "Michael maybe it best that you don't sit in," I tell him. "Tate, can we go in to see our son now?" Michael asked. "Yes go in, please don't stay too long. We want him to rest I've given him a small sedative to keep him from getting excited," he said. "He seems to be trying to come out of it, his little body is telling us that he's in there fighting trying to come out of it."

Michael shook Dr. Tate's hand, and we took the twins back to see Keagan. I sat by his bed and took his little hand. "I love you, son," I said squeezing his little hand. Kristine and Kristopher immediately went to his side. Kristine was still crying. "Keagan, I love you little brother, please come back to us," she said as she held onto him. Kristopher cried watching him lying there helplessly. Keagan's eyes were still wide open staring off into the room.

We stayed there for longer than we were allowed to soon the nurse came in to check on him. "Hello family," It was Sofia. "I know you want to stay and comfort him, but he really needs his rest, tomorrow is a big day for him," she said to us checking all of the monitors on Keagan's body. "We have to pray for him right now," Michael tells her. "No, I don't think you have time," the nurse said to him. Michael looked at her and stood up. "We will pray for my son before we leave this room if you don't care to listen," Michael pointed to the door.

Sofia immediately walked out giving Michael a really mean stare. We held hands and Michael began to pray for   Keagan. "Lord, in the name of Jesus, please protect my son from harm. Lord we know he is your light, we know that in him lives your spirit and for whatever evil is trying you. Lord, we rebuke that spirit Lord, in the name of Jesus, protect my son. Lord for he is your son, Lord, in Jesus name I pray."

"Amen," we all said at once. We all kissed Keagan on the forehead before walking out. Nurse Sofia was standing at the door when we came out. "Michael looked at her and before she could walk into his room he grabbed her arm. "I don't want you in that room," he said to her. "I will be his nurse tonight Dr. I have been assigned to him," "No, I will not have it," Michael said storming off to look for Maddy. "Michael, what's wrong?" I said following behind him.

"That woman is of evil, and I will not have her spirit around Keagan," he said in a mad whisper. "Michael, she's fine," I said holding his arm. Maddy was sitting at the front desk in the hall. I turned back to look down the hall at Keagans door. I could see a dark shadow lingering near so I ran back to him. When I approached the door the shadow disappeared. I peeked in and looked all around his room. The shadow was gone. I could hear Michael telling Maddy that he didn't want Sofia as his nurse tonight.

"I have to call someone in to replace her than Michael," she tells him. "Do what you have to Maddy, I don't want her near him," he said. We waited an hour for someone else to replace Sofia. Michael drove home with Kristopher and me with Kristine. Kristine was very sad. "Mommy, will he ever come home again? Is he going to be okay?" "I think he will, as soon as they figure out what's going on with him." When we made it home Michael and Kristopher drove up behind us. I went inside and headed upstairs. Michael went to the attic.

The twins stayed in the kitchen. "Mommy, I'm going to make hot chocolate," Kristine yelled up to me. "Do you want some?" "I would like that Kristine thank you," I said as I went into the bathroom and cried out to the Lord. "Lord what now?" I screamed. I stayed in the bathroom crying for a while I didn't know what else to do, Keagan was in the hospital now, and all I could do for him was pray. After a while Kristopher came knocking at the door. "Mommy that woman is on the phone, she wants to know if it's okay for her to come by now," he yelled into the door.

Oh my goodness I almost forgotten that James sister was coming by today. "Ask her to hold on Kristopher, I'll be out in a second," I told him. I went to the mirror to wash my face I didn't want the twins to know I'd been in there crying all this time. I opened the door and went out into the room "Hello, how are you?" I say to her. "I'm good, I was just wondering if now was a good time to come by, I'll be leaving soon, and you're my last stop before I head out," she says. "Um sure, why not," I said still really unsure if I wanted her to come by. "I'll be waiting for you," I tell her hanging the phone up.

I went over to my bed and took the blankets and sheets that Keagan vomited on that night. I washed the floor of and put the bedding into the washing machine. Kristopher stayed close to me, watching and helping with what he could. Kristine was in the kitchen making lunch. "Mommy, should I put on a pot of tea for your visitor?" She asked. "I'm not sure if she'll be up for tea, but warm the kettle just in case," I tell her. I cleaned all around the den and the living room. I figured I'd meet with her in the living room where the kids wouldn't be. It was an hour later when she showed up.

I welcomed her into the house. "Hi," she said giving me a warm hug. "Hello come on in, we'll sit in there, have a seat anywhere get comfortable please," I tell her as I escorted her into the living room. As I began to sit down across from her on the small sofa the twins walked in. "Hello," Kristopher said walking toward her to shake her hand. She was stunned. She did a double look as he came up to her she stood up to shake his hand she stared at him with question in her eyes. I knew she could see that he looked so much like James.

She was still holding his hand as Kristine came walking over to greet her. She nearly came to tears as Kristine favored her mother. She hugged her and sat down. "Karis they're beautiful," she said putting her head down than looking up at me. "Thank you," I tell her offering her tea. "No thank you," she said staring at the twins as they walked away. "Thank you guys," I tell them. "So what is it that's so important that you had to see me?" I asked her choking through my words. She put her hands in her lap and looked at me really crossed.

"I have to tell you that you were the love of my brother's life, there wasn't a day that went by that he didn't talk about how much he loved you." She said beginning to tear up, I went over to her with a Kleenex box. "What is it what's wrong?" I asked her worried. "He's gone, he died in a trucking accident last week," she tells me leaning over crying. I was so stunned. This couldn't be I just talked to James he was just here. "He was in training, and they were going through the mountain when the truck was pushed by the high winds over a cliff.

They were able to pull the truck up, but James fell out of the window down into a mountain creek," she said it was in the newspaper. "I'm so sorry that you had to hear this way," she said wiping her eyes with the Kleenex. I was so baffled by what I was hearing, when James came to me he was fine, he was smiling and he looked as if he was very healthy. I just looked at her with disbelief in my eyes. I couldn't wrap my head around it. "He's dead, is that what you're telling me?"

"Yes, he's gone," she reached into her purse and pulled out an obituary and a small envelope attached to a letter. "He wanted you to have this," she said handing it to me. "How do you know he wanted me to have this?" "You were all he talked about Karis, and in that envelope, it explains why, when I went to clean out his apartment I found that tucked away in his drawer. See, it has your name on the front of the envelope," she said pointing my name out to me. I took the envelope to my chest. "Thank you so much for this, I really appreciate it," I tell her crying.

This was so surprising, I didn't see this coming nor was I warned of his death, I just couldn't believe it, James was gone. Kristine came back into the room holding a glass of water. "Here you go, I thought you might need this," she said as she handed her the glass. She looked up at her. "Thank you, sweetheart, you can call me Ms. Teresa, you are very polite for a young lady your age, and quite beautiful also," she said touching Kristine's hair. "You have such long hair," she took a drink from the glass.

"Thank you," Kristine said walking away. She watched her walk away while she finish ed up her drink. She stood up. "So tell me, Karis, did my brother know about his children?" She asked me. I was caught off guard. I stood up. "What do you mean?" I say to her. "The twins they are a complete replica of my mother and brother," she said handing me the glass and putting her hand on her hip. "Are you going to tell me that they are not his?" She said looking with anger in her eyes.

"I am not, I will tell you that he never knew about them and there's a really good reason why. I will not lie to you, I can't talk to you about it now, maybe some other time when the children aren't around," I tell her beginning to walk back toward the front door. She stood in the living room watching me reach for the door. "Do you want me to leave now?" "Yes, if you want to know what happened I will tell you some other time," I tell her opening my door. The twins both came over to the doorway and stood with me.

"It was really nice meeting you Ms. Teresa," Kristine said to her as she walked toward the door. "It was," Kristopher said shaking her hand. "Thank you so much for this," I tell her holding up the envelope. "Please call me when you have some time, and we can talk," I tell her as she goes out of the door. "Goodbye," she said. I took the envelope up to my bedroom and put it in the drawer. He came to me, he was crossing over, and he came to me. How could I not have known? I thought. I'm going to share the letter with Michael when he comes home I thought closing the drawer.

When I turned around Kristine was standing in the doorway. "Mommy is there something you want to tell me?" She asked with her hands crossed over her little chest. "Kristine, there is something I have to tell you both, but not today sweetie, not now, I promise I'll explain everything later." I told her walking toward her to go downstairs. Oh no she overheard us what will they think of me keeping their real father a secret all these years I thought. I can only hope that they'll forgive me.

I cleaned the house and cooked, thinking about all that was going on. When Michael showed up from work he rushed into the shower and rushed us to the hospital to see Keagan. "I went to check on him today briefly," he told me. "He is so pale   Karis, he doesn't look good and his breathing is shallower than the last time." "What do you think it is?" "They haven't done the testing as of yet, but they will tomorrow. They tell me that his having convulsions over and over again. I don't know what it could be, this is frustrating, I don't know how much I can take watching him like that," he said as he drove faster to get to the hospital.

When we arrived at the hospital everyone was making a fuss over why he was having these attacks. We were greeted by Dr. Tate. "I've been waiting for you, I tried to catch you on your way out, but you got away from me," he said with his hand on Michaels' shoulder. "Your son is   still in the same condition, we did do the testing this morning the brain is functioning well there are no signs of brain damage, and Keagan's not at any risk of anything, at the moment.

We will keep him here to monitor his progress for at least a week," he said. "Then what" Michael asked. "We can't find anything wrong. Keagan's perfectly healthy other than him being in this state of come and or shock. We can't find any other reason to keep him here at the hospital unless of course, you want him to stay here until he decides to come out of it," he says looking at Michael and me with his glasses tilted.

"We can take him home like that?" I said. "Yes in a week if everything stays the same, he will be released to you and your wife. I will come over and check on him at home if you like," he said holding a clipboard in his hand walking toward Keagan's door. We all went inside his room. Dr. Tate checked him over and left us there to talk with Keagan. His eyes were still wide open. I grabbed his little hand and held onto it tight. "Keagan, I love you," I whispered to him. He squeezed my hand. The room was so cold Michael walked around the room looking around at the windows. "It's freezing in here Michael," I said.

"Yes I know," he said. He reached into the cabinet for more blankets. He came over to Keagan and covered him with three more blankets. Michael stood over him and took my hand to pray. "Lord in heaven, please protect our son from all evil, we don't know Lord, what Keagan is feeling. Lord, we ask you at this moment to spare his young soul, spare his young spirit." While we prayed Keagan's hands and feet began to shake as if he was going to say something, although he never blinked or moved his head, his body was trying to tell us something.

Michael continued praying I held his hand in prayer. He squeezed it tight as if he wanted me to help him. I held both his small hands as Michael finished up his prayer. "We have to get him home soon," Michael said with tears flowing from his eyes. "Do you think he'll be better at home Michael?" I asked him looking up at him. "He's just not safe here, while he's here they will come after him," he said leaving the room. I kissed Keagan on the cheek and followed Michael out.

When I opened the door I felt the evil immediately. Michael was standing across the doorway with his hand clutched to the railing on the wall. "What's wrong Michael?" I asked holding his hand on the rail. "Don't you see Karis? It's Keagan who has to want to come out, he's being held under by an evil spirit, if he doesn't pull himself out, or he may never come back to us," he said crying on my shoulder. "What do you mean, Keagan is much stronger than you and I," I said looking him in his eye.

"No Karis, at a certain age he has to control the protection of those eight lights, he has to tune into them whenever he's in trouble. If he doesn't he can be taken in by the darker spirits, they will haunt his soul until they kill him," he said crying, "and there is nothing we can do about it," he continued to talk. "My poor son, what can I do Lord, help him get through this." He was so upset I began to walk him toward the exit when I turned to look back at Keagan's door there were so many dark spirits lingering around the hall.

They just stood around, there were so many I couldn't count. I walked Michael all the way to the car and helped him to get in. I ran back to the hospital entrance door and ran through the hall to get the elevator before it went back up. I got in anxiously waiting to get off. When it stopped, I ran off into the hallway to Keagan's door. As I ran toward his door I could see in front of me nurse, Sofia standing near his door there were other spirits around the door, but hers stood out. I looked her in her eyes, and for the first time, it was clear.

Her eyes were as red as fire and she smiled at me with no fear as if she welcomed my challenge to save my sons soul. I approached the door quickly. "Why are you here?" I asked her. She laughed with her hand to her mouth. "Go away!" I yelled out. She stood in front of me and laughed out loud. "I promise if you hurt my son," I tell her as I reached for the doorknob. She slapped my hand down and from the doorknob. "You think you will grab ahold of me and send me back?" She laughed.

"You will never, I will have him, I will, you call me your friend right?" She said laughing in my face. "Poor Russian girl," she laughed hard, as she laughed the glare from her red eyes became glossier, and it looked as if her nursing uniform became darker and darker. "You will never get him, he is of God, he is strong, and he is covered," I say as she walked away looking back at me laughing as I went inside Keagan's room. When I walked in, dark spirits were flying around Keagan. I ran over to his bed and laid my body across Keagan. I looked up at them and began to pray them away.

"Lord, send them away from my son. Lord, cover him with your blanket of grace, bring him out Lord, and help him become his own strength. Lord, pull him through this." I prayed and prayed until I could see them fly away from his bed. I sat there most of the night after that, trying not to fall asleep. I wondered why this time I didn't get a warning from any of the spirits that have come to warn me in the past. I wondered why this has happened to Keagan. Michael explained it best he could, but I wanted a better understanding. Keagan was always the one to rush in with his light and help us through tough spiritual fights.

Has it weakened him all these years? What would be the cause of his weakness? I thought as I sat in the chair holding his small hand. Keagan was to turn thirteen in two months, would he even be here for his birthday I thought, would he be able to live his young life free of this madness? I started to get mad, it made me want to question all things watching him lye there in that way. "God, help him please," I said out loud as another nurse walked in. "Excuse me, visiting hours are over, we have ask that you leave now," she said walking around me beginning to remove some of his blankets.

I ignored her as I held on to his small hand. I stood up and took the blankets she put to the side and threw them back over him. "His body is too cold, keep these blankets on him please," I say to her kissing Keagan's cheek. "We don't want him getting too hot," she said walking out of the door. I stood up near him and began to talk. "Keagan, son, please fight back, you are strong, use what he gave you son. Fight your way out of there; please, don't allow them to win," I tell him kissing his hand. "I want you to come home and have your party. You're turning thirteen in a couple months," he squeezed my hand.

"Will you fight, son?" I asked him. He squeezed my hand again. "Good, you fight, come out of there show them that you belong to God, tell them that you are his child. They can't have you, son," I tell him as I kiss his forehead. "I'm going now son, remember to tell them who you are. If need be, you show them what you can do son, share with them what God gave you, I love you, son," I said leaving the room. I walked out of his room and standing before me was Sofia. She stood so close I could smell her foul scent of her spirit it was so foul I covered my mouth and nose.

"I will have him," she said to me as I pushed passed her. I walked down the hall watching as she stood up against the hallway wall staring and laughing at me. I stared back at her and with my lips I tell her. "Only God will have the glory," I went to the car Michael was still sitting in there. His head was on the dashboard of the car. "Michael, honey, are you alright?" I asked him getting into the car. "I am now, you think that you can do all things when you walk with him and pray to him, you think that he can change it, I don't know anymore. Karis, what good am I as one of his own when I can't save my sons soul? What good am I?"

"Michael, I know that this is hard, I feel the same way at times, but this is Keagan's fight this it's up to him to come out," I said rubbing the back of Michaels' head. "God is there with him, they can't touch him, Michael, and you must believe that." I looked up and the twins were walking up to the car. "Mommy, were you just going to leave us?" Kristine asked. Oh no I had forgotten about them waiting in the lobby. "I'm so sorry, did you two see me come back into the hospital?" I asked. "No, we didn't see you at all," Kristopher said.

"We wanted to go in to see   Keagan, but no one came out to get us, and when we went into his room the nurse told us   to leave immediately." "I'm sorry guys," I tell them as I began to drive off. When we made it home Michael walked straight up to the bedroom. I went to the kitchen, Kristine followed me, and Kristopher walked into the den to play his video games. I started to cook. I turned on the tea kettle and sat at the table to peel some potatoes. Kristine grabbed a peeler and helped me.

I didn't say a word. I could sense that she had many questions, but knew it wasn't the time to ask. She peeled the potatoes one after another until we had a table full, we both didn't notice that it was too many. When the tea kettle went off, she jumped up and ran over to the cabinet to get two coffee cups. "Mommy do you want sugar?" She asked me. "Sure, not a lot though," I tell her going over to the sink to wash the potatoes and put them in a pot. I put them in a pot, there was so many, I just decided to make a stew.

"Mommy, are you going to need a spoon?" She asked me. "Yes, please," I tell her. "Mommy, I know I can ask at a better time, but it's eating at me." Oh no here it comes I thought as she walked over to the table carefully holding the cups. "I just want to know if that woman was related to me in any way?" She asked. "Yes, she is related to you sweetie," I said rubbing her back. "I wanted to tell you this when you were much older, but I guess now is the best time to tell you," I told her taking the cup to my mouth.

"That woman Teresa was, in fact, your blood aunt. Her brother was a dear friend of mine for many years, he wanted to have a relationship with me, but I didn't want a relationship with him. I often had him over to watch movies and talk, he was a good friend, one evening I had him over, and his urges got the best of him. When he attacked me," she put her cup down. "What do you mean mommy?" She asked. "He attacked me, Kristine, he took my virginity, he raped me," I told her. "Mommy, I'm sorry, why did he do it?" "I first thought it was my fault, Kristine, I did. It was one of the worst things that ever happened to me," I tell her drinking my tea.

"Then I thought he just couldn't control himself. After it happened, it wasn't until much later that I found out I was carrying you and your brother. I didn't want to get rid of you once I had you because I was told that I would never bear children and thank God I didn't, you and your brother are two of the best things that could have ever happened to me," I tell her getting up to take the seasoned meat over to the pot. "Mommy, is he around, do you hate him?" She asked. I knew that was coming, I went back over to her.

"Kristine, I'm afraid not, he was in a terrible accident a couple of weeks ago, that's why she came over." She didn't say a word she got up from the table and came over to me and kissed me on the cheek.

"Thank you, mommy, for being so honest," she said she put her coffee cup into the sink and walked away. I was so worried maybe it was the wrong time for me to tell her I thought as I stirred the meat into the pot. Just then the doorbell rang. I washed my hands and went over to the door I looked out of the window it was Martha, I hadn't seen Martha in so long.

She had gotten married and moved away with her husband she looked absolutely beautiful standing at the door waiting for my response. "Who is it?" I said. She looked up quickly. "Karis, is that you?" She said in a loud screeching voice. "It is," I pulled opened the door and grabbed her in. "Oh thank you, God," I yelled out. "Martha, where have you been, girl," I missed you so much," Martha hugged me so tight. "I missed you more Karis, oh my goodness, you look the same. You look great," she said.

We stood at the door looking one another over for a while before the twins and Michael came down. "Look who showed up here Michael." "I couldn't make uncle Earls funeral I was so upset when I heard, but I had to get down here to you," she said. "Hi, twins," she said going over to them hugging them tightly. "Michael, look at you, you look the same," she said. "Look at this big house Karis, I love it. Where's my Keagan?" She asked looking around the house. "He's in the hospital," Kristine blurted out.

"What, what's wrong with him?" She asked. Michael and I looked at one another before answering. "They don't know right now, he's in a coma state," I tell her. "Come, talk to me," she said grabbing me by the waist side walking me around the house. I felt a little better Martha was always around when I needed someone in the past to talk to. Michael spirit was so shaken, he couldn't help his son it was taken a serious toll on him. I just wanted to crawl in a hole with all that was going on; she came right on time. "How long are you in town for?" I asked her.

"I will be here for about a week, we came to take care of some business," she said.   "Well, I'm just glad you're here," I told her. We stayed up talking all night I needed to vent so bad I told her all about James and his sister. She was so sad to hear about James. "So did he know about the children?" She asked me. "No, I never told him," I tell her going into the kitchen to stir the pot of stew. "He didn't deserve to know Karis," she said. "For what he did, he really didn't deserve them in any way," she said coming into the kitchen.

"No one on this planet would not have supported your decision to keep him away from him" she tells me. "I know, but I had to tell Kristine what happened today, right before you showed up. I had to explain why his sister showed up here and she overheard us talking. Its tough keeping things from them now they're getting to be young adults. They're noticing that they look different." "I'm sure they don't notice those things Karis, Michael has been such a good father to them, and they don't notice anything."

"I know, but I think it's important for them to know where they came from, don't you?" She shook her head no and came over to me and kissed my cheek. "I'm going to go, Karis, I have to get back to the hotel before my honey shows up and I'm gone," she said smiling. "Well, I'd like to meet this great guy," I tell her as she walks to pick up her jacket. Martha was truly fabulous, a great body, she looked like a Hollywood model the way she dressed. Her big sunglasses and her happy attitude, she was always smiling I guess that's why she looked so great.

"Bye everyone, I'll see you soon," she said as she went to the door. "Love the house Karis," she yelled as she shut the door. I took a cucumber from the refrigerator and began to chop it up with onion and sat it on the table. "Hey family, dinners up," I yelled out. Everyone came to the table except for Kristine. "Where's Kristine?" I asked Kristopher. "She was right behind me mommy," he said pointing at the staircase.

"I'll go and get her," Michael said leaving the table. He walked up, Kristopher and I waited patiently at the table for them to return.

When they did Michael looked mad at me. "Can you pass the salad," he asked looking at me. "What is it?" I asked him. "I don't know maybe you can explain to me why my daughter says she wants to know why I never told her," he said. "Michael can I explain later," I asked him. "Mommy, I just wanted to tell him, thank you, for all that he's done for us over the years," Kristine said spooning her soup. "I understand Kristine, Michael, I'm sorry. I really haven't had time to explain to you what happened the other day, you've been so sad about Keagan," I told him.

Just when Kristopher began to speak the phone rang. Michael jumped from the table and walked over to the phone. "Hello," he said in his deep angry voice. He held his napkin in his hand twisting it as he spoke. The conversation must have been intense Michael never seemed that nervous before. He hung up and walked over to me. "Karis, we have to go back to the hospital something's gone wrong with Keagan." He said throwing the napkin on the floor and going for his keys on the hook. "You two stay here," he said to the twins.

"Stay by the phone okay, we'll let you know what's happening." Michael and I went to the front door and stood to wait for Kristopher to lock up. "We'll be back as soon as we can," I yelled out as we walked quickly to the car. We began to drive off, when Michael looked over at me. "Can you tell me how she knows everything?" I'd never seen Michael this upset. "I had to explain to her about Teresa, she came by to tell me about James," I tell him. "What about James, Karis?" He said. "James died in a truck driving accident, and she came to tell me, she saw the twins, and immediately she began to ask about them," I tell him as we pull up to the hospital.

Michael looked over at me. "Karis, never again, don't ever keep this kind of thing from me please," he said staring me into my eyes. "I told her because she overheard us talking, I had to tell her," I told him pulling the door handle. "I understand," he said getting out of the car. We walked into the entrance of the hospital and immediately we were greeted by Dr. Tate. "Hello, Dr. Philips. I need to talk to you alone," he said pulling Michael away from me. They went over to the side and began to talk. I could feel the dark spirits surrounding me.

Never Leave Me Alone

Dr. Tate told Michael that Keagan was moving his hands and feet when he was questioned, he'd respond with hand movement. We spent all night there watching him and asking him questions. "Keagan, do you want us to leave?" Michael asked. Keagan waved his hand out with his palm as if to say no. "Are you in any pain?" Michael asked him. He waved his hand up again as if to say no. I went over to him and sat near his bed. "Keagan, I'm here, I will be here until you want me to leave," I tell him taking him by the hand. "You can't stay here all night," Michael tells me.

"I know, but I can stay until he's ready to let go of my hand," Keagan held onto my hand so tight, my hand was really sweaty. I stayed as long as I could that night when I was ready to leave it was well past the hospitals visiting hours. "Don't worry baby, I'll be here with him all night during my shift, I'll come in and out to check on him, I'll sit with him on my break?" He said walking me to my car. Time went by so fast. Martha visited every day until she had to go. I was finally able to meet her new husband he was tall dark and very handsome. He loved Martha and was a total gentleman.

He would come with her a couple of times just to laugh and talk and hear our stories of the past. When it was time for her to go, I cried. I really needed her   me at this time, but I knew she couldn't stay. "Well, I hate to say goodbye," She said grabbing all of her things off the couch and her camera full of memories. "I'll definitely be back soon, next time I'll stay a little longer," she said. We all kissed and hugged and took more pictures before she headed toward the door. I watched as she and her husband drove off. The twins came over to me and hugged me they knew my heart was saddened by Martha leaving again.

The two weeks went by so quickly it was time to bring Keagan home we all prepared for him to come home. Although he was still not responding with his eyes, we wanted him home. Michael and I had been working so hard to make sure one of us was always there. It had become a struggle to go there every day. When Michael arrived home with Keagan he carried him into the house Keagan was limp in his arms. "Michael is he okay," I asked him at the door. "He's fine baby, he's a little exhausted from the ride," He said. "Did he look around or even blink?" Kristopher asked.

"No, he's the same," Michael responded while carrying Keagan to his room. He laid him on the bed I took his blankets and covered him with them. I put all of his things around him he had a favorite bear that he couldn't ever sleep without. He didn't move around when I sat beside him it was like he knew he was home. He began to move his hands around. "Keagan, do you know where you are?" I asked him he squeezed my hand really tight. "He knows Michael," I said smiling up at him. "We have to make sure we stay with him, I don't want him left alone much," Michael said.

I was thrilled that Keagan was home even though he wasn't very well. Every day we'd switch off; I'd be with him at night, and Michael would sit with him during the day. We both had little time to ourselves. The twins would be so happy to sit and have breakfast and dinner. Both Kristine and Kristopher were a big help, Kristine would sit with Keagan and read to him after school, and Kristopher would tell him all about the new games that came out that month. We all pitched in to help with Keagan.

"Baby, I have to talk to you about something," Michael said walking into the house one night. "I think we should go to my parent's lake house and stay a few weeks out there, just to get away, the kids need it they can boat and hike, and Keagan can get some fresh air," he said picking around in the kitchen. "Baby, it will be great," he said holding a glass of wine in his hand walking toward me. "Are you sure we should take Keagan there, he's still not well, Michael," I tell him kissing his lips softly.

"Um, what was that for?" He asked as he sips his wine. "I just miss your lips," I tell him kissing them again. With all, that's going on Michael, and I hadn't been to intimate we were doing all that we could to bring Keagan back it was very tiring. We both got into bed after a quick shower and going in to check on Keagan. Kristopher slept near him every night in a small bed next to him. He held his hand every night while he slept. I was very impressed by the kids helping with him. I was able to sleep all night.

When I fell off the sleep that night I dreamed that I was fighting in a dark tunnel I was sweating and breathing so hard I couldn't catch my breath. Michael shook me to wake me. I was crying and sweating. "What was that all about?" He asked getting me water from the bathroom. "Are you okay?" He asked coming over to me with the small glass. "I was fighting something, or someone," I told him pulling my hair back from my face. "Was it someone you could see?" He asked.

"No, I couldn't see them I could only feel them all over me tugging at me and pulling at me." I tell him. "I'm here baby, nothing will ever happen to you while I'm here," he said holding me close to his bare chest. I drank the rest of the water and laid down. Michael laid beside me holding, me all night, but it didn't help when I fell back to sleep I heard whispers and voices, "We will have him," they said. "We will keep him," they whispered. I jumped sitting straight up and looking around. Michael turned to me.

"What is it?" He asked. I got out of bed and went to Keagan's room. When I opened the door he was on his side staring out. I walked over to him. "Keagan, sweetie why are you on your side?" I asked him. I began to turn him over when he grabbed on to my gown really tight. "What is it, sweetie?" I asked him; he pulled my gown harder. "Keagan, let me in, tell me?" I asked him. When I placed him on his back he pointed at the window. I went over to the window I opened the curtains and there she was. Sofia she was laughing and pointing at Keagan, I closed the curtains quickly.

"Keagan, don't worry about her, she can't harm you in any way," I tell him. He grabbed onto my gown again and pulled me close to him. "Sweetie, you have to fight to get out of there, you can't let them take you in Keagan. Please fight, show them who you are, please!" I tell him holding on to his hand as he held onto my gown. It wasn't until he fell back onto his pillow that I was able to get free from his grip. I was so afraid to leave him there in bed. I went back over to the window to see if Sofia was still there. She was gone, but spirits were lingering near, I could feel them near.

I didn't go back to bed with Michael. I sat in the chair beside the bed and watched Keagan until he stops moving his hands and feet around it was like he was walking or running around. I rubbed his feet to comfort him from time to time. He would stop, but only for a while before he started again. I was so tired when the sun came up. Michael came into the room. "Baby, you slept here all night?" He asked. I put my hands to my face. "Michael, I barely slept last night," I tell him getting up from the chair.

Every bone in my body ached. I stood up and stretched out my arms. "Michael, I'm going back to bed sweetie, I can't do anything right now I was physically drained." "Baby, the nurse is coming out today, did you forget?" He asked me. "No Michael, I didn't forget I just have to lay down, just for an hour can you give me an hour, please," I asked as I drug my feet to my room. I plopped my body down on the bed. I couldn't do anything I was drained. Michael came over to me and rubbed my back.

"Baby, I know you're tired, but you have to get up, I'll stay and give you an hour, but you have to go in today they don't have anyone to cover you at work remember," he said. "You need to go in because you'll be gone for two weeks remember? You have to tell Maddy," he said. "Maddy will be expecting you." "Michael I know, I know but please let me get an hour," I said getting under the covers. "Okay, okay," he said patting me on the back. I heard him walk away shutting the door behind him. I fell off to sleep. I couldn't have been sleep more than forty five minutes when I was awaken by Kristopher.

"Mom, mom, you're going to be late for work," he said shaking my back. "Okay, son," I said sitting up in bed what time is it," I asked him getting up from the bed wiping my eyes. I walked into the bathroom and washed my face and brushed my teeth Kristopher watched me as I got ready for work helping me to remember all of my things I needed to. "Mom Kristine made coffee for you downstairs," he said walking over to me with my sweater. "Mom, you really need a break," he said kissing my cheek.

"I know son, I really do, you know your fathers taking us to the lake house for a few weeks," I tell him putting on my shoes. "Mom, I will make sure dinners ready when you come home," Kristopher said shutting the door behind me. "See you later, son," I yelled back at him. On the way to work I thought about all the things I wasn't able to escape. I thought about James and that terrible accident. I felt terrible for his family, I should have known that he was gone when he showed up the way he did.

I didn't know what to think of that, but I knew he would show up again someday, but not like that. The twins never will get a chance to meet him even; if I'd wanted to he was gone now. I teared up a little thinking that he never knew his children. When I arrived at work I walked up to the front desk where Maddy was. "Hello, sleepyhead, did you get any rest?" Maddy asked. "You still look a little tired, and honey those bags under those beautiful big eyes don't help," she said coming over to me kissing my face.

"I have to come over there to help with Keagan. I know it's a hard job, how's he doing anyway?" She said handing me a clipboard. "He's doing a little better, he just doesn't want to be left alone in the room," I tell her walking away from the desk. "Why do you think he doesn't want to be left alone?" She asked me. I stood in front of the desk. "Maddy he's probably afraid, I don't know, I just want my son back," I tell her looking her eye to eye. "Michael wants to take us to his family's lake house for two weeks, I don't know if I can unless you have someone to cover me," I say to her looking down.

I didn't want to see her face; I'd just came back from my father being ill. "I will cover you, Karis, I know what you're going through, I was going to be retiring soon. I'll hang on for you honey, don't you worry you just take that time and go on," she tells me rubbing my hand. I went on working that day from room to room I worked, the patients were all very kind, and I felt no sorrow no pain. I was almost done when I went into the room of an old lady they call Ms. Jill.

Ms. Jill was 94 years old, and when I entered her room, she reached her hand out to me smiling. As I walked up to her bed, my stomach hurt from the joy I felt. She spoke in a whisper, "Sweetheart, I've been waiting for you," she said whispering. I leaned over putting my ear to her mouth. "Sweetheart, the day is coming, you have him, and they've come for his young soul. Protect him with the love and joy that you feel inside, don't allow them to get him," she said holding my hand.

"Now send me home," she said smiling. "I know you know how." I stood up I couldn't help for smiling down at her with all the joy I felt; it felt as if someone was tickling me. I held her hands, and she smiled at me as I asked the Lord to take her into his warm light. "Lord, in the name of Jesus, I ask that you spare Ms. Jill. Take her into your warm light at her own will, she is ready Lord. Her soul awaits your loving joy," I held onto Ms. Jill's hands as she began to stare up at the light opening up to her. I watched as the Lord waited for her soul to come through.

I was so filled with joy that I laughed aloud. I felt the tickling inside me guiding her through to her resting place. She let go of my hands and they fell to the side as her spirit began to rise. She stood before me as she began faded deeper into the light smiling and waving me goodbye. I left the room as her heart showed flat line. I walked to through the hallway watching as they ran to Ms. Jill's room. I went to the desk and gave Maddy the clipboard. "I'll see you tomorrow Maddy," I tell her.

"Oh sweetie, I'll allow you the two weeks starting next Friday," she said. "Thank you so much, Maddy," I said walking to get my bag. When I went to the locker I was surprised by nurse Sofia; she was standing there in front of my locker. "We will have him," she said laughing. I ignored her getting my purse and my sweater. "I rebuke you Satan in the name of Jesus," I said staring at her as I walked away. How could I have not known what she was from the very start, I thought as I drove home her beautiful accent and her wonderful smile, I should have known.

I got angry thinking of her betrayal, but why not, it's written that they will be in any form. Demons and evil spirit will rise in every shape and form. I have to remember that I thought as I arrived at the house. I went to the door the twins were waiting for me. "Mommy there's something wrong with Keagan," Kristopher said grabbing my hand and rushing me upstairs. "Why didn't you guys call me?" I yelled out opening his door. "We weren't sure, he's always moving around like this, but this time it's none stop," Kristopher said.

When I opened Keagan's door, it was freezing cold in there like an ice storm had gone through. I went close to Keagan, his little body was warm he wasn't cold at all. I grabbed his hand, "Keagan sweetie, can you hear mommy?" I asked him he squeezed my hand so tight. "Sweetie, that's right, don't you allow them to have you," I said holding both his hands "You fight baby, with all that he gave you, you fight," I tell him. His body was getting warmer and warmer. I was so happy that he was fighting back. I knew he had it in him.

"Mom, what do you want me to do about this room, it's freezing in here," Kristopher said holding his arms together. "Kristopher, let's not do anything sweetie, just pray," I said to him going to the window. "Do you think he'll ever be right again mom?" Kristopher asked me. "He'll be fine," I said looking out of the window to see how many were around him waiting for his young spirit to break. I looked down they were all over, and there were flies all over the outside of the window ceil. I knew as long as they were on the outside, my son was safe from the evil. I walked back over to him and took his hands.

"You're doing it, Keagan, they can't touch you keep fighting baby, the Lord is with you," I tell him squeezing his small hands. He moved all around as if he was running, still not blinking. I had no idea what his little mind was going through, I only prayed that he would be okay and that the Lord would guide him through this. I stayed in his room for a while just watching him and holding his hand. I could tell when they were taunting his spirit, he would act as if he was running and his little hands would sweat, he kept himself warm.

It would be hours later when Michael showed up. "How is he?" He asked coming into the room. "The room was freezing cold Michael, I don't know how much more he'll be able to take," I tell him holding

Keagan's hand. "He has to fight through it Karis, as long as they don't get to close to him he'll be okay. We'll be living for the lake soon, I know up there he'll come back to us." It wasn't easy watching   Keagan suffering, these days I went to sleep praying and woke up praying. I knew only God could carry us through this trying time.

The week went by so quickly, it would be the following weekend when we left for the lake. At work, I would see Maddy the night before we left. I was to give her a key to our house so that she could check on things while we were at the lake house. "Is this goodbye again?" She says as I handed her my keys. "Only for a little while, Maddy," I tell her hugging her around the waist. "Things will be so different here without you." I laughed, Maddy always said that to me whenever I was about to go anywhere. I was going to miss her.

I went home that day and cleaned the house and prepared for the lake house trip. No one had gone up there in a while; I knew we'd have to clean up when we got there, so I packed all of the cleaning supplies up, along with our clothes and toiletries. When Michael came in that night the front room floor was covered with luggage, he tripped over it coming in. I heard him yelling at the door. "Karis!" He screamed out as he fell over all of it coming in. "Yes Michael," I said calling back to him from Keagan's room.

"I wish you had warned me about the luggage, we don't leave for another two days, why is it here?" He asked. "I'm getting everything in order before tomorrow so that I can rest a little before the ride over," I yell down to him. I was busy upstairs putting Keagan's clothes in his suitcase. I was fine until I came across his shoes in the closet. Keagan hadn't worn shoes in so long, I just stared at them when I picked them up and held them. His running shoes, I thought as I held them. Would Keagan ever have the chance to run in them again? I held them close to my chest. I didn't cry.

Poor Keagan, he didn't have to be born into this and who knew that Michael and I would have a child that the Lord wanted to use in this way I thought as I held his shoes. I am taking these shoes,   Keagan will walk again I thought as I walked over to his suitcase to put them in. It was a long night after getting all the luggage prepared Michael, and I were both exhausted, I stayed in the chair with Keagan, the twins came in and asked about dinner. "Please order pizza," Michael tells them handing them money.

"Thank you, dad," Kristopher says walking away closing the door. Michael and I were in Keagan's room all night, him on the small bed, and Michael and I in the chair. We watched him throughout the night. "Good morning," I hear in my ear I jump from my sleep turning my head to the whisper I heard, but there was no one there. I stood up from the chair and went over to Keagan, "Oh Michael!" I screamed out. "Michael, please come here, get up!" I yelled.

"Keagan's eyes are closed," I tell him looking down at Keagan. Michael jumped up and ran toward Keagan's bed. "I need my bag Karis I need to check him out," he said in a panic. He touched Keagan's chest and back. "He seems to be breathing fine, his body is still warm." He pulled Keagan's eyes opened and looked into them. "His eyes look fine, no dilation," he said putting his fingers on Keagan's neck "I'm going to call Dr. Tate," Michael said going downstairs to make his call. He was really in a panic. I watched him come in and out of the room.

He settled down a little when Dr. Tate showed up. He walked into the room. "Hello Karis," he said to me as he passed me going over to Keagan's bed. Keagan was not moving around as he had done since he came home. He hadn't squeezed my hand all day he hadn't moved his feet at all. I was a little worried, but I knew there was something about the calm around him that gave me ease. He was finally fighting them. By being calm I knew that he had to be getting angry. He was calm his eyes were closed they really couldn't touch him now I thought, watching Dr. Tate check him over.

My son would be fine he's finally fighting with what God gave him. After Dr. Tate told Michael that he was fine he just needed to rest. Michael was better; he laid on the small bed beside him and closed his eyes. "Karis, I really can't wait until we go up to the lake house, I'm just tired," he said as he spread his arms up over his head. I stood up to go and kiss his cheek. "Michael, Keagan is fighting now, he's so quiet, he's doesn't seem bothered at all right now, we have to believe that he's a fighter. The Lord can bring him through this; I know that this is hard for you."

"You can't go in and rescue him, Michael he'll do it, he'll come out of this fine. We have to believe it," I tell him walking away from him. I took Keagan by the hand. "Keep fighting baby," I tell him kissing his little hand. I walked out into the hallway to check on the twins, I hadn't really talked to them about James; I hadn't even looked what was in the envelope for me. I had been so busy. When I went down the hall I overheard them talking as I got closer to Kristine's room. "Yes, he was," Kristine shouted to Kristopher. "I want proof, I don't believe you, Kristine," Kristopher tells her throwing pillows at her.

"What are you guys talking about?" I asked stepping into the room. "I was telling Kristopher that we had another dad and how he's dead now. I told him that he attacked you and that you kept us in spite of what happened, isn't this all true mom," she said pointing at Kristopher. I opened the door and called down the hall for Michael to come in. I didn't want to explain this to him without him there again. When he came into the room, he stood at the door still leaving it opened so that he could watch Keagan's door.

"What is it?" Michael asked. "The twins are wondering where they come from," I tell him looking at the twins. "Kristine knows already, but Kristopher doesn't believe her," I told him. Michael sat down beside Kristopher and put his arm around him. "It's true Kristopher, I am not your biological father, I'm sorry it's true. However, I love the both of you as if you are my own," he tells him. "What happened to mom?" Kristopher asked. "Well, I think that what happened between your mom and James was terrible."

"You two are old enough to know that when you're in a relationship whether it's a friendship or you want something more with the person. It is crucial that you respect the other person's feelings no matter how you feel about them. James, your biological father, didn't respect your mother's feelings. He made a mistake and acted on it, it was a terrible mistake that I'm sure he really regretted," Michael said. He hugged Kristopher and stood up beside him. "You guys will be fine," he said walking toward the door. "I love you two brats."

I was really impressed at the way Michael handled that. He didn't say anything terrible about James at all, and they didn't have to feel bad about where they came from. I sighed with relief. "I think you two should one day go and visit your auntie's house in Denver so that you can learn more about where you come from. I think it will be good for you two?" I tell them leaving the room. I was going to go back into Keagan's room to check on Michael and Keagan, but I was so tired.

I walked down the hall to my room as soon as I turned the corner to the door I heard my named being called out loudly. "Kari! Karis!" It was a woman's voice, I turned and looked down the hall it was dark I turn the light on to see if there was someone there. There wasn't anyone there. The voice said my name loudly again. This time it seemed to be coming from my room. I was told long ago never to answer a spirit you can't see. I didn't answer it. I went into my room to get into the shower.

I was in the shower when I began to hear heavy thumping sounds as if someone was walking on the roof of the house. I looked outside of the shower curtain there was no one there. I shook my head. I began to wash my hair. I can't think of anything else Lord, I just need a break Lord, give me a break Lord, I prayed as I washed my hair. "Hello," Michael said stepping into the shower with me; I flinched hearing his voice as he slides open the shower curtains. "Michael

is that you?" I asked running the water over my hair and eyes to wash the soap out. "It better be me," he said rubbing my back.

We showered together for a while, Michael got out before me hurrying to get back to Keagan. I was still washing the soap off my body when I heard my name again. I stepped out onto the rug of the bathroom, and there were the thumping noises again it was even louder now. I wrapped up in my towel and went out into the room. I had my hair wrapped as I walked toward the bed. I was about to sit down when a flash of darkness flew up to me and snatched the towel from my head.

I turned to it trying to follow it as it quickly went for the door with the towel. When the towel dropped it turned to me, it was just darkness. The face moved from side to side as I stared at it. I wanted to run to and grab it, but I knew it wouldn't allow it, so I gave it a taste of its own medicine. I smiled and sat on the bed. I heard my name louder in an echo. I looked behind me, it sound as if it was coming from the outside. When I turned back to the dark shadow, it was gone. I smiled and dried myself off. I put my pajamas on and walked into Keagan's room with Michael the twins were there with him they were all sitting around Keagan.

"We think he's going to get up mom," Kristopher said standing over Keagan. "He sat up in the bed and shook his head," Kristine said excitedly. "Has he opened his eyes at all?" I asked as I went to his bed to hold his hand. "No. he didn't open them at all, but he sat up mom, he sat up and shook his head," Kristine said. We all waited around his bed and talked to him. "Keagan, if you're awake, open your eyes now brother. I'll play ball with you all day outside, any day you like," Kristopher said to him.

"And I'll help you with all of your homework when mom can't," Kristine said. "I'll cook your favorite meal every day," she said. He sat up again. "Yes, Keagan, yes, get up and fight them, you're almost there," I tell him. We all stayed in the room that night until we were all tired. Keagan never opened his eyes nor did he sit up again. Michael and I went to our room, Kristopher slept in the small bed in Keagan's room. When we got into bed, I fell off to sleep quickly. I dreamt I was in a dark tunnel and there was screaming,

I heard hollering, it sounded as if they were saying my name in between the screams. I was sweating it, and I felt like I was falling down into the tunnel deeper and deeper, it felt as if I was being scratched and pulled at the same time. I struggled to wake up from this dream, I tried to yell out to Michael I prayed for the Lord to come. I was on my back, and then on my stomach, as I went deeper down into the tunnel, I saw Keagan being held down there at the bottom of the tunnel.

When I realized that it was Keagan I let myself go I didn't struggle anymore to come up. I tried pushing myself closer to him. I screamed as I went down, and Keagan yelled for me "Mommy! Mommy" His arm reached out for me as I went in deeper. Right, when I was close enough to grab him, I was snatched back. As I was being pulled back up from the tunnel the scratching and hollering began to get louder, there were dark shadows around me I was shoved up really hard on my back as I woke up, it was Michael.

"Baby, are you okay, I've been trying to wake you for at least 15 minutes. I thought I would have to throw water on your face soon," he said sitting in front of me holding my shoulders. "I was there Michael," I said sitting up. "I was where they have Keagan, he's in a very dark place

Michael," I tell him holding him crying. "How are we going to get him back? How will we get him back?" I said. I was sweating and crying so hard I didn't even notice that I was bloody the blood from the scratches was all over the bed and the sheets. Michael turned on the light.

"Oh baby, where were you?" He yelled out, he got up and ran to the bathroom to get the first aid kit. "Oh God," he said running back toward me. I put my arms out, but my whole body burned as if I was scratched all over. Michael help me take off my pajamas I had scratches all over my body. I didn't care about the scratches I couldn't stop thinking of Keagan down in the tunnel. "Michael, how will we ever get him" "I don't know baby, I think that God is giving you a clue how in those dreams. I think he's telling you something baby," he said as he wiped down the scratches with antibiotic soap.

"You're bleeding so bad baby," Michael said. "I don't know when these will stop bleeding, they're so deep almost like they dug their nails into you," Michael said "I'm not going to leave them open, they need to dry out first," he said helping me to lay down on my back. I was still crying when Michael was done with me. He laid down beside me he turned to me. "Baby, I would hold you, but I'm afraid it will hurt you too badly." He covered me with the sheet on the bed leaving me in just my underwear.

"It will be fine, we get him to the lake house, and God will help us bring him back, he will help us, baby." I wanted to fall right back into that dream when I went back to sleep, but I didn't go back into that dream, I was so disappointed when I woke up the next morning. I went into the bathroom to look at the scratches on my body. I wrapped up in the sheet I stood in the mirror holding onto the bloody sheet. I walked back into the room to throw on a shirt and sweats when Kristopher walked in.

"Mom, what happened to you?" He asked. I put my shirt on quickly, then my pants. "Nothing son," I tell him; "did you have breakfast yet?" I asked him as I walked toward the door. "Yes, Kristine made eggs and sausage," I went into Keagan's room to check to see if maybe he opened his eyes yet. When I walked in Kristine was trying to feed him "No, Kristine!" I screamed at her. "He can't, he'll choke." "Mom, he's starving," she said, "No, sweetie, I should have warned you, these tubes hanging over his head." I grabbed the tubes.

"They feed him, he's fine; he's eating. I know he looks so thin lying here, but he is healthy, I promise," I told her going over to him. I just kept thinking of how close I came to get him out. "Is he going to open his eyes soon mom?" Kristine asked. "Yes, he will sweetie soon," I tell her I wanted to wipe Keagan down today give him a sponge bath. "Would you like to help me bathe him?" I ask her going to the hall bathroom to get the washcloth and soap and water in a large bowel. "No, thank you," she said walking out of the room behind me.

"Do you think that you can do me a favor?" I asked as she walked past me. "Sure mom, what is it?" She said. "I need for you to empty the trash in his room?" I asked her. "Okay, I'll get Kristopher for that mom, I can't get my hands dirty like that I'm a lady," she said smiling at me. "Okay, that's fine as long as it gets emptied," I tell her starting Keagan's bath. "I was hoping you were in here," Michael said opening the door.

"I just finished packing some things in the SUV, I just wanted to know if we were stopping to do the shopping or if we were doing it all when we get there so that I can keep some space in the trunk," he said as he leaned over Keagan's bed. "I guess we can stop on the way," I tell him. That's maybe not a good idea I thought we need to get to the lake house as quickly as possible with Keagan. "Michael, I think it will be safer to get there first, and then get the shopping done," I tell him before he walks back out of the door. "I thought that would be better too, baby," Michael said as he walked away.

"See Keagan, moms always thinking of you," I said to him as I bathed him with the soap. I could see his eyes rolling as if he wanted to open them as I talked to him. "I know where you are, sweetie, it's really dark there. I know Keagan, but you have to get out of there you have to fight," I tell him. "You want to come home and be with us, you have to fight. They want you there so that they can keep you from being a part of this life. You were made of him, in his light and they want to take it away sweetie, don't allow them to take it away from you. Be strong Keagan, be as strong as you can be," I tell him.

I finished washing him up and went downstairs to eat breakfast. After I finished breakfast, I helped Michael pack the car. I took some things from the kitchen to make at the lake house. I'll need just cooking utensils and pots and pans. I'd never been to the lake house before I was a little excited to get there and sit on the lake. "One more day," Michael said with a smile "Yes, one more day," Kristopher said as he carried some of his things down from his room. "Remember we're only going to be there for two weeks okay twins," Michael yelled out to them as we both watched them go up and down the stairs.

"They are so excited to be going too," I said to Michael. "They need this as much as we do." The twins don't know anything about why these things happen to us. "I was still hurting from the scratches, and it felt like my clothes were sticking to the scratches and cuts. I tried to be really careful not to run into anything especially doorknobs. It was a long day, we were all tired and needed a break from packing we sat in the den and drank water and talked. Michael kept running up to check on Keagan. It would be nightfall by the time everything was done.

We all went upstairs to bathe and get ready for tomorrows exciting trip to the lake house. "I'm sleeping in with Keagan again mom," Kristopher told me as he went into the room. I was burning; I wanted Michael to cover the scratches right now. I went into the room and took my clothes off. "Michael please come help!" I yelled out

"They're burning Michael, allover," I looked myself over in the mirror I was cover with the cotton from my clothes it stuck to the bloody scratches and cuts. "Uh oh," Michael said.

"You have to get into the shower and wash those off; we can't let them get infected." "Michael that's going to burn more," I tell him looking anxiously at him. "Yes, I know, you'll be fine baby, when you come out I'll cool them off with some ointment cream it will heal it faster," he said. I was afraid to get into the shower. Michael went over to the shower and fixed the water for me. "I'll run it cool for you, you will need to wash gently around them, let the water flow on them so that the cotton will come off of them, okay baby," he said walking me into the shower.

"Do you need me to get in and help you, baby? I will," he said smiling. "Michael you know I can't do it. I can't make love to you right now it will be uncomfortable for me," I tell him. I always knew when he would smile like that what it meant, I went into the shower, I wanted to scream it burned so bad. I did it quickly and got out Michael was sitting on the stool next to the door waiting for me. "You took long enough," he said joking. "Baby that was so quick, are you sure you washed it all off?" he said spinning me around by my arm. "Are you feeling better baby?" He asked while he put the cream on the scratches. "Michael please, be careful, please," I tell him.

"I am, baby, you know I don't want to hurt my baby," he said. "I was thinking, why don't we take the kids up and get them settled in at the lake house and then we find a place to go dancing. We haven't been out dancing in such a long time," I tell him turning to face him so he could apply cream to my stomach. "That sounds great baby," he said kissing my stomach. I wanted to make love to him so badly, but I knew that if I had even touched these scratches, I couldn't take it. "Michael, I want you too, sweetie, I just can't do it right now," I tell him going into the room I looked around inside the drawer to find something that wouldn't stick to me.

I found a nightgown that Michael had bought for me some time ago, it was silk I just slide it over my body and laid down on the bed. Michael came over and laid beside me, I turned over to him. "Michael, I wanted you to tell me that James sister Teresa brought an envelope with something in it from James, I've been waiting for the right time to open it," I tell him getting up to get the envelope. "What do you think it is?" Michael asked. "I don't know I after what happened between us I didn't have much contact with James so I wouldn't know," I tell him holding the envelope in front of him. "Could you open it for me?" I asked.

"Sure, why not?" Michael said taking the envelope from my hand. He opened the envelope slowly. It was a letter and a beautiful ring. "Here you go," he said giving the letter and looking over the ring. "Nice," he says, "looks very expensive and seasoned," he held it up to the light. "Michael, can you read it to me?" I asked him. "Sure, why not?" He took the letter from my hand and opened it. He reached over to his nightstand and grabbed his glasses. Clearing his throat he began to read it.

"My Dearest Karis, I have waited all this time to tell you this because I felt by now you would have forgiven me. It's been so long since I've looked into your beautiful eyes, I know that you have moved on with your life, I just wanted you to know that before I made that terrible mistake and took from you what I should have waited for you to offer me. I don't know what went through my head that day, I just know that I have loved you all my life it seems, I never thought that I'd be living without you."

"This has been the toughest time for me; I felt I was being punished for all the things I'd done to you. I was a sailor in the U.S. Navy, and when I got out, there was nothing for me I went to school to be a policeman and still nothing for me. When I was done and shunned away from any and every job that I applied for, I felt as empty as the day I got out of the navy. I wanted this perfect life with you; I wanted us to have children and live in a big house with both of us happy we could never go wrong."

"I knew that after I did what I did I would never get that chance with you. That's why I moved far away I couldn't ever accept there never being an us, I wanted you to have this ring it's my grandmothers please take it. You never have to wear it, but I wanted you to have it because my grandmother knew how much I loved you and couldn't understand what happened. Karis, thank you so much for never telling her what I did to you. That alone would have killed her."

"I know that I don't stand a chance with you, I know that by now your heart is aching for what you lose. If we never speak again, I want you to know that I love you still Karis, and I will never forget you." "Well, at least we know where his heart was," Michael said as I took the letter from him. "Yes, but it doesn't change what he did to me Michael, it doesn't; I didn't want him to die though." "Oh baby, you know that was an accident, he didn't want to die either, I'm sure." "Yes, Michael I know," I said putting the letter and the ring away. It was a beautiful ring; I looked it over one more time before pushing the drawer closed.

"Michael, I think I'm going to give the ring back to his sister," I tell him getting into bed. "I don't think it's fair to keep it, maybe his sister wants it for herself." "No, I think maybe you should keep it for Kristine keep so that she'll have something that both her father and grandmother cherished. It will probably make her feel a lot better about not knowing him," he tells me about to hug me. "Michael, no," I said closing my eyes tight thinking of the pain that would cause. "Oh "I'm sorry baby," he said laughing.

"I'm so sorry baby really, I won't try it again," he said rolling over on his side. "Goodnight baby." "Goodnight Michael," I said kissing him on the neck. "I love you." "Love you too, baby," We fell asleep quickly after. This time I dreamt I was falling faster into the tunnel, I could hear whispers. "We will have him," they say as I fell through the darkness of the tunnel. I feel them breathing heavy all around me, I can hear crying this time adults weeping and screaming out as I flew down deeper.

I was ready this time when I became close enough I'd grab Keagan I thought as I went down further into the darkness of the tunnel. This time, I was pulled like I was a puppet on a string I couldn't see anything around me, but I could hear. I could hear through all the crying,   Keagan yelling for me to come to him. "I'm coming!" I yelled out to him. "Hang on Keagan! Hang on to the Lords light," I tell him as I was being pulled up. I was being pulled up slowly this time there were no scratching just whispers and darkness. I jumped from my sleep a quickly.

Michael was still sleeping he turned over to me and opened his eyes. "Are you okay baby?" He asked me. "Yes, I just had one of those nightmares again, I think I need to grab hold of something in there maybe I can get to Keagan," I tell him. I get up to get me a glass of water I walk over to the sink in the bathroom. I stood in the bathroom for a while drinking the water. I began to hear the thumping this time it was as loud as thunder. I drop my glass into the sink the crash woke Michael. I looked up at the ceiling. "Karis are you okay!" Michael yelled out.

"Do you hear that Michael?" I asked him still looking up. It was so loud I covered my ears. "No baby, I don't hear anything, please come to bed," He says reaching out to me. "Michael, it sounds like thunder, can't you hear it?" I said to him. "I have to pick this glass from the sink," I said covering my ears again. I walked back over near the sink to get the glass from the sink when I took my hands from my ears, the woman was calling my name out loudly again. The loud thunder sound was gone. I picked the glass out of the sink quickly.

I dropped a piece on the floor I turned on the light all the way up high to see where it was as soon as I flipped the switch a woman was standing in the shower staring at me. I turned the light back off, not tonight I thought to myself as I began to walk out. As soon I stepped out I stepped onto the glass it stung so bad I fell to the floor. "Oh!" I screamed out holding my foot. I was still holding it when I looked up to see if Michael was coming over to me there was the woman in my face it was if she was laying on her back looking me in my face she laughed loudly. I yelled for Michael.

"Michael, come here, wake up please," I yelled out; the woman was laughing so loud I couldn't hear myself yelling for Michael I couldn't tell whether he heard me or not. "Michael!" I yelled out again every time I opened my mouth she opened hers to scream out. "I tried standing, but it was so dark I could see her face I could see around me enough to maneuver myself up from the floor, I could feel the blood gushing from my foot. I was able to hang onto the doorway and pull myself up. When I did, I hopped over to the bed and turned the light on the woman appeared in my face again.

She was still laughing her face wasn't familiar to me at all. I ignored her and began to pull the glass from my foot Michael finally got up and came over to me. The woman went away immediately as he approached me. "Michael, you didn't hear me at all yelling and screaming for you?" I asked him. "No baby, I didn't what's wrong?" He asked. "I broke a glass and cut my foot," I tell him sticking my foot out. "How did you do this baby?" "I heard a loud noise, and I dropped the glass in the sink, I think a piece fell onto the floor, and when I walked back to the bed, I stepped on it," I tell him. He went to get the first aid kit again.

"Baby, you're hurting yourself too much," he said bandaging me up slowly as if he was really sleepy. "I know Michael, I can't help it, I heard a loud noise it sounded as loud as thunder," I tell him, "but it was louder. I had to cover my ears it was so loud," I tell him lying back on the bed. "I want to sleep," Michael said placing the first aid kit down beside the bed. He laid down beside me this time holding my stomach gently. "We need to get some sleep Karis, we have a long drive tomorrow," he said kissing my neck.

"Baby, I'm tired. I'm not at all dismissing your feelings right now," Michael was talking as if I was upset because him being short. I didn't say a word about his behavior. I was just as tired as he was. I wanted to get some sleep as well. I fell off to sleep wanting to dream again just to try and reach out to Keagan, but I knew it was going to be impossible especially because I was too tired to fight. When I woke up the next morning I could hear Michael and the twins shouting back and forth from the window to get everything together.

I got up from the bed and tried to stand up forgetting that my foot had the cut on it. It hurt to stand on it when I walked toward the bathroom to wash up I had to hop there it felt like was splitting open every time I step down on it. I made into the bathroom; I sat on the toilet and looked at the bottom of my foot. It was bleeding through the bandage that Michael put on that night. I took it off and placed my foot into the tub. I ran cold water over it. As I was sitting there the hair on my back stood up as I could feel someone behind me.

"I know you're there," I shouted. I heard them running away from me, it was loud footsteps. I turned around to take my foot from the bathtub and looked underneath the sink for some bigger bandages I would have to wrap it like a homemade cast. I couldn't have it feeling as if it was opening up. I was going to have a lot to do when we get to the lake house I thought as I wrapped the cut up with gauze. "Are you going to be okay?" Michael said smiling down at me. "Where did you come from?" I asked him. "I was up here getting, my shoes," he says coming over to me.

"You know everything is ready to go, baby, we're just waiting for you. As soon as you give us the go ahead I'm going to carry Keagan down the stairs to the car," he said walking over to me watching me wrap the cut. "Perfect baby, it looks good," he walked out of the bathroom. "Remember baby, as soon as you give us the go ahead," he walked out. I got up from the toilet and went over to the sink to wash my face and brush my teeth. I finished up and I limped over to the closet. Oh goodness what shoes would I wear now? I thought as I began to take my clothes off.

I reached up onto the shelf of my closet and grabbed a pair of gym shoes that I wore occasionally when I cleaned. They were always very comfortable. I sat down on the stool in the closet and put them on. It would be about 45 minutes before I was done. I called down to Michael as I closed the room door. "Michael, I'm coming down," I yelled. I walked down the stairs very slow my foot hurt so bad as I was walking down the woman ran past me really fast as if she wanted to push me down. I held on to the railing of the stairs really tight.

"Karis, I think I forgot my jacket, can you please look in the closet to see if it's there?" Michael called down to me. "I will I said going over to the closet door slowly. I grabbed Michael's jacket and the twins too and strolled to the front door. Usually, I'd check to make sure everything in the kitchen was turned off, but I was in so much pain I just took one look around and walked to the car. When I walked, I noticed the woman sitting in the back seat smiling and laughing she was flagging her hand as if she was telling me to hurry.

I walked a little faster when I saw her there Michael and Keagan came right up behind me. Michael placed Keagan, into the car right next to her, he went back inside to get the twins and to lock up the house. When we were all in, he came back out and got in the driver seat. "Are we ready?" He said about to turn the ignition. We began to drive off when we saw Maddy coming up the street. "Hey, hey," she said as she drove up flagging her hand from her car.

"I just wanted to goodbye to you guys before you leave," she said getting out of her car. She walked over to us and kissed everyone on the cheek. "Have a nice trip family," she said as we drove off onto the street. "Well, we're off," Michael said as we went onto the highway. It was quiet at first as we drove along the highway but the twins began to sing and talk about how green it was all around it was really nice driving up there. The lake house was near Colorado it wasn't as far as I thought it would be. It took Michael about 36 hours to get there when we arrived I thought we were in the wrong place.

It was the most beautiful home I'd ever seen. "Michael," I said getting out. "This is so beautiful;" there were trees all around. The air was so clean and fresh the house was beautiful on the outside. It was a huge house just sitting near the lake, with big windows it looked like something out of a fairytale. The twins got out and ran down to the lake. Michael grabbed Kegan out and handed me the keys to the house. "Let's go in," he said we all walked up to the house slowly. As we walked I saw the woman standing by the door waving me inside smiling.

"Are you okay?" Michael asked. "I am, I'm just so happy, this is great Michael it is the best thing we could have done for us now," I said as we approached the door. I put the key in and opened the door. As soon as we all stepped in Michael laid Keagan on the couch, he ran over to the light switch and turned it on. The house was very open; everything was open all the cabinets; the refrigerator was clean inside. The kitchen was so big. I began to walk around the house following Michael.

"Twins come along, I'll show you where you're going to sleep," he said as we followed him from room to room. After he showed us around, he placed Keagan in a room right next to ours. "He'll be safe in here," he said opening the curtains. I covered him with the blankets we brought in from the car. It was getting really cool there. "Michael, can you close the window in here?" I said looking through the window.

"Look at that nice view," Michael said holding out his hand at the window. "It is perfect for him," I said holding Keagan's hand.

"When we get everything inside I'll start us a fire, and we can go to the market down the hill." "That sounds great let's get started," I said following him out of Keagan's room. We worked and worked around the lake house. The twins helped with the sweeping. Michael had to turn the water on from a fuse box outside, and some of the lights didn't work, so he had to turn them on also. I watched him get frustrated over and over again as he tried to figure out what was what. It was growing dark out I had to get to the market before it was closed or we were going to be hungry until the next day. I began to rush Michael.

We went to the market and got everything we needed for the house we bought two baskets full of things candles and extras just in case we forgotten anything. When we came back to the lake house the twins were outside sitting on the stairs in front, I hopped out of the car immediately, I felt something was wrong. "Mom, mom" they ran up to me yelling as I got out. "Keagan, Keagan," they yelled. "What's wrong?" I asked them setting the bag of groceries down running to the room Keagan was in.

I couldn't hear what they were saying I couldn't even see anyone I just wanted to get to him. I could feel the cut on my foot ripping open as I ran toward the door I ran as fast as I could. Michael was right behind me when we opened the door we saw him sitting up, and bed and his eyes were opened he was looking around as if he didn't know where he was. He looked at us as soon as he saw us he blinked and blinked. "Keagan, can you hear me?" I asked him, he blinked his eyes at me. I was so happy. Michael began to look him over and ask him questions about us.

He responded quickly after a while, his voice was like whispers because he hadn't spoken in a while. "I love you Keagan," I said to him hugging him tightly. I noticed his body was cold as ice, Michael listen to his heart with a stethoscope he shook his head. "Karis, step away from him," he said. Michael touched his hand "He's freezing cold, twins go into the front room," He tells them flagging his hands quickly for them to go. "What's wrong Michael?" I asked standing back "This is not Keagan's spirit go and ask the twins if the heard anything before they came in to check on him," he tells me. "Hurry Karis, go ask them!"

Get Him Out

Michael moved so quickly getting me out of the room. "What do you mean, Michael?" I asked as he shoved me out closing the door behind us. "It's not Keagan; he's not in there. Someone has entered into his spirit; we have to pray to get him out." "We pray out here, it wouldn't be safe for us to be near Keagan. The spirits around him are dark, the one inside him is even darker, it is made up of pure evil and Keagan's soul is the perfect resting place for it, if he doesn't fight." Michael grabbed onto my hands, and we stood in the hallway near his door praying.

After a while Michael would go to his knees and put his hands on the door. We heard laughing and crying and sometimes we heard Keagan yelling for help. "What do we do Michael?" I said looking down at him. "We leave him we don't feed it or go near it; we live here and ignore it. Soon it will grow angry and come after us instead of Keagan," he said standing to his feet. "I don't understand Michael, that's our baby; we can't leave him to fight it on his own. We can't right?" I said in a panic.

"Baby trust me, I know what this is, these spirits just want to use Keagan they want his soul and his light and because he's young and kind. They are taunting him, they came for him in his sleep," Michael said. "He didn't have a chance or any control, but he can bring himself out if he fights to come up," "Michael I saw him down there, he is trying, he's trying to get out," I said we heard the woman laughing and crying then Keagan screaming for help. I had to walk away from the door I couldn't take it. Michael wouldn't go in he wanted us to just leave Keagan; I couldn't understand that at all. How would he fight them alone, how would he come out of this alone?

Days went by we didn't go near the room, Michael kept the twins busy every day he took them out to the boat house to show him his father's old boat. He was determined to teach Kristopher to sail and Kristine followed behind them everywhere learning all that Kristopher learned. By the time Michael would bring them in they would both be so tired. They'd eat and wash up and go straight to bed. I cleaned up everywhere trying to keep busy; I wanted to check on Keagan every day Michael said that if we went in, they would have the power over us to keep Keagan under longer.

We stayed away from the room, nurturing him would make them stay there and the spirit growing inside him would stay. But I longed to check on my son every day. I kept busy for the first week. I found the phone plug and was tempted to call Martha a few times just to hear her voice and listen to her stories. She was always so happy never allowing anything to shake her spirit. But I didn't in fear that she would hear what I was going through. I just cleaned. During the weekend it rained and the twins played broad games all day.

I stayed in my room which was so close to Keagan's, I waited for Michael to come to bed and sleep. Tonight I would check on Keagan, I knew that Michael would disapprove. He read until he fell off to sleep. I got up and walked quietly over to the door. I could hear Keagan loudly screaming out for me to come to him. I went to his door. When I opened it the smell was so foul coming out. I went inside and shut the door. "Keagan," I said going over to his bed to hold him.

"Mommy's here son, I'm here," I walked up closer, and when I approached the bed to hold him suddenly, he turned to me his face was distorted, and I couldn't tell whether or not it was Keagan or the woman

I saw in the car. "Get out of here mommy," his voice roared and at the same time her voice screamed out. "I need you, mommy, please stay." In a panic, I stepped back covering my mouth I knew my son was in there. I went close to the door, but before I could get to the doorknob, Keagan sat all the way up in the bed.

"Mommy, look around," he said his voice sounding as if it was under water. I looked around, and dark spirits were running toward me, I tried to get the doorknob, but I couldn't before I knew it they were all over me, I knew I couldn't run, so I took a deep breath and began to yell out for the Lord to help me. "Oh God, in heaven, please come; please help me through this." I knew that I couldn't grab them all, but I could pray.

I could see Keagan on the bed the woman was laughing loudly through him I crawled as they pulled and hit me all over the floor trying to get to the door, I prayed the whole time. "I rebuke your spirit in the name of Jesus," I yelled out. Each time I yelled that they stand back, they would let me go they looked at me with so much evil in their eyes trying to intimidate me to stop praying. I wouldn't I kept rebuking them until I reached that doorknob when I grabbed it one of them was bold enough to hop onto my back and scratched at my neck and eyes.

I yelled out, "I rebuke you in Jesus name, get off me! I rebuke you, you can't have my son, I rebuke you," I said waving my hand in the back of my neck trying to grab onto it. I wanted to grab onto this one because it was bold, it wasn't afraid of the Lord's word at all. When I almost had a good grip on its arm; it pulled away from me and stood back looking at me; staring into my eyes as if it wanted to hurt me. It moved its head from side to side like an animal, I looked into its eyes one more time before opening the door to go out, and I yelled out to it. "I rebuke you in Jesus name, you won't have him!" I said as I went out of the door.

When I stepped into the hallway Michael was waiting in the hall for me I felt my neck burning and the blood flowed down my chest. I looked up at Michael as I began to walk to the bathroom. "I told you to stay out of there Karis," he said checking my neck. "We have to wait for them to come out, and then we can go in and get Keagan," he retorted. "If you try to go in there again they will take him in, and he will never get to come out of there, don't you see this has to be his fight until we can fight with him."

"Michael, when will that happen?" I asked him yelling "When will he come out of there, I feel he needs our help to come out, they're hurting him, Michael, he's suffering in there, I can feel it." Michael started helping me clean the blood off my neck. I couldn't stop crying. I just wanted to save my son. I held on to Michael's shirt and put my head on his chest. I held onto him until we heard the door of Keagan's room shaking it was shaking so hard that the windows started moving, then we heard the sound of thunder and the rain was pouring down Michael looked down at me.

"It's going to happen, the Lord will help us bring him out, and he will have the glory through Keagan." I lifted my head from his chest and looked over at the window I walked out of the bathroom and into the bedroom, the rain and thunder were so loud that the twins came running into our room. "Mom, what's happening, dad what do we do, are we safe here with all this rain?" Kristopher asked. "We will be fine," Michael tell them as they walked towards us in a panic "I have to tell you guys something," Michael said to them.

"There is something that's going to occur here with Keagan that you two may not understand. I want you two to stay in here at all times when it begins and no matter what; don't you dare come out," Michael told them in a stern voice. "But what dad, can we help?" "No, it won't be safe for either of you, just promise that when it begins, you'll stay put in here, no matter what," he said looking at the both of them. Then he looked to me, "Karis, they are going to attack you, they want Keagan."

"They're running out of time to keep him there, and growing angry that they can't keep him down there any longer because he won't stop fighting to come out. We have to pray to help him out, while he's fighting we'll be praying together and they'll come for us and leave him alone. That's when we'll be able to go in and get him, but they won't stop attacking us, and   Karis, I hope you're ready this won't be easy at all. This could mean that if it doesn't get him, it may come after one of us to live."

Michael was very serious he started to walk around the house closing all of the curtains and windows. "I want you two to stay inside no matter what," he tells the twins. Kristopher walked around quickly behind him closing the windows he missed and locking up everything. "Your mom and I will be in the front room when it happens, it will be on the seventh day of the rain and thunder," he said as he went to the drawer in our room, he took out the bible and placed it on top of the drawer.

"I want you to read out loud Genesis chapter 12. "Now the Lord had said to Abram: "Get out of your country from your family and from your father's house. To a land that I will show you I will make a great nation. I will bless you and make your name great and you shall be a blessing. I will bless those who bless you. And I will curse him who curses you. And in you, all the families of the earth shall be blessed." "Twins when the time comes I want you to sit near the window and say the verse over and over until you hear the rain stop," he told them, as he and Kristopher took food and water to the room for the twins just in case it happened right away.

"Michael what on earth do you mean, we can't involve the twins?" I tell him watching him and Kristopher move quickly around the house. "Karis, you have to listen to me and believe me, this has been coming for a long time. We were never to know when it was to come we have to fight for not just Keagan, but for our whole family. We're all at great risk," he said standing near the window. He opened the curtains just enough to see a little through the rain, dark shadows were surrounding the lake house from every end, day and night.

Michael stood and watched, he was not afraid at all, and neither was
I. I knew that whatever happened we'd be able to get Keagan back. We
could hear screaming and crying all through the night and day. Keagan
sometimes screamed through the hollering of the woman for help. Some
nights I couldn't help it I ran to the door with Michael chasing behind
me to stop me from going in. "Just pray," he'd say in his angry voice, he
held my arm so tight it would be bruised. "Karis, you can't go in, you
can't, baby, just pray," he said we stood by the door praying.

When the sixth day of the rain came Michael told the twins to make
sure they remember to do exactly what he told them to. "I don't want
either one of you to get afraid of what you hear, its best you cover your
ears and don't look out of the window no matter what," he tells them
again. We all sat there quietly waiting for Michael's direction, it would be
midnight when he finally settles down. I followed him to the bedroom,
and the twins go into their rooms side by side. The night was dim as we
all tried to sleep. I listen to the rain hit the house from all directions and
over the rain the yelling of the woman trying to grow inside of Keagan's
spirit.

I could tell when she'd get loud that those were the time when
Keagan fought the hardest. I still had the urge to run to him. I cried
instead, holding my mouth with my hand so that Michael couldn't hear
me. I was scratched from my neck to my back and the cut on my foot
was healing just a little. I couldn't sleep thinking about how we would
get Keagan. I only came close to him once; I couldn't imagine what he'd
been going through trying to get out. I had scratches all over me. What
was my son going to look like when he came out?

I just wanted him to come out, and we will celebrate Keagan's
birthday as we promised him before this all happening to him. I laid
there I didn't want to go to sleep at all. I didn't want to think about all
the things we needed to do to get him out. I just wanted to hold my son,
just hug him again and see his wonderful smile I thought as I laid there

listening to the rain. Michael rolled over and hugged me. "Baby, I know it seems like this may never end and we may never get Keagan back, but baby I promise we will." He said holding on to me trying to be gentle because of all the scratches.

I began to pray with him holding me, "Lord, please watch over our family; please cover us in the blood. Lord Jesus, I know that you're here with us; I know that you will come through with us to bring Keagan out. Lord, please bring my baby out okay, I know Lord that he is struggling, he is fighting in your name. Lord, your light shines through him; bring my baby out Lord."

As I prayed the screaming of the woman became louder and louder. I could feel the darkness of the other spirits drawing near me. I was tempted to look up in fear, but I didn't I kept praying as hard as I could. I was praying so hard my fingers gripped Michaels arms so tight he woke up and leaned over to my face. "Baby, are you okay?" He asked me, I didn't open my eyes and he was staring right at them. "Good job Karis you're making them angry that's good, baby," he said.

"Keep it up, pray strong and with conviction at all times, we're going to need it today." I laid there praying for hours, I didn't fear what I couldn't see with my eyes closed I could feel them around more and more of them. I could smell them the smell was becoming so foul I was getting nauseous. I didn't allow that to stop me either, I prayed even harder as the night became day, I prayed more. When I opened my eyes I could see their shadows in the light of the sunset through the break in the clouds. I didn't get frightened, I was ready.

Michael got up and got dressed, he wore a blue shirt and jeans; he put his boots on as if he was going hiking. I got up and went to wash up. I wore a pair of jeans and a red t-shirt, I put the gym shoes on because I didn't know what to expect today. I was ready brushing my hair back in the mirror, I didn't know what to expect today, but I'm following

Michaels lead. He was busy all around the house I watched him stand in front of Keagan's door, he just stood there listening.

I felt he wanted to go in so badly, but he didn't he just stood there watching and listening at the door. After I brushed up my hair, I wanted to talk to Kristopher and Kristine. I needed them to understand that they were safe. I knew that Michael scared them he didn't mean to, but it was scary for them. I'm sure they didn't understand what was happening, but they wanted to help. I went to them, they were both sitting in the front room eating, and I sat down beside them.

"Hello, how are you guys this morning?" I asked them as they ate spoon after spoon of cereal. They shook their heads together as if to say they were okay. "I wanted you two to know that this thing with your dad, I know it seems scary, but he knows what he's doing it is going to be a challenge for the both of us. We have to do it to get Keagan back," I tell them as they continue to eat Kristine took a deep swallow. "Where is Keagan, I hear you and dad saying we have to get him out we have to bring him out, where is he mom? I thought he was just in some kind of coma, I thought maybe he was sick, is he not sick mom?" She said holding her hands up.

"Kristine I'm sorry I know this is hard to understand, he's not sick he's being held in a   very dark place of evil," I tell her watching her reaction. "Mom, what do you mean a dark place, he's in a dark place, I don't understand, and how would you and dad get him out?" She asked me looking confused. "We will get him out Kristen, I can't explain it all right now, but I will soon," I tell her getting up to check where Michael was. Kristopher didn't ask any questions he just continued eating his cereal as I walked away.

I found Michael standing in the rain in back of the house. He was standing there looking out with no umbrella just his hat and Jeans. He was looking out into the rain as if he watching something when I approached him he jumped as if he thought I was someone else or something else. I stood with him looking out into the rain. "Baby," he said pulling me close to him. "This is not going to be easy, I want you to know that I love you very much, I would never abandon you. I'm afraid that you're going to need me and I won't be able to get to you in time."

"Michael, I think I can handle it I'm not going to be afraid, and I won't doubt him. I will do all that I can to get Keagan back with us, I will fight until I can't anymore." "I know baby that's what I'm afraid of," he said holding me close I looked up at him, and we both turned and looked into the rain. This would be the time we needed to reassure one another of our fight. "It should be stopping soon, the rain, and when it does the twins go in the room, and we began to pray," he said kissing me on the nose.

"Baby, I will watch out for you I promise." "And I for you, Michael," I tell him squeezing his hand. We stood out in the rain for a while just holding on to one another. Soon the twins were watching us from the window. I could see the fear in their eyes. They were wondering what was going to happen. I looked up at Michael. "Michael, how will we ever explain all this to them? How will they understand this about us? What we are and how we came to be this way? I really don't know to tell them all of what this is, I barely began to understand it myself, and what on earth will they tell their friends at school about their parents?"

"They tell them what they've always known of us to be, two wonderful loving parents that will protect them with all that we have in us, just as any other normal parents would." I looked up at him, and back at them, it was like they all had the same look on their faces. Michael took me by the hand and we went into the house soaked from the rain. The twins came away from the window. "Mom, are you two okay?" Kristopher asked as he walked toward us.

"We are," I said taking a towel from the cabinet. Michael walked over near me, and I began to dry him off. I wrapped my neck with the towel trying not to rub the towel against my scratches too hard. He dried me. We looked over at the twins and smiled. I think they knew that whatever it was, we would handle it together. "Mom, the rain is slowing down," Kristopher said pointing up to the ceiling; we began to hear less and less of it. Michael went to the window to look out at the rainfall. It was slowing Michael walked away from the window and quickly went to Keagan's door. He stood there listening.

"Michael, what are we listening to?" I asked walking toward him to hear what he was listening for. "Shush," he said standing there listening. He put his hand on the door and his head down, and I held onto his waist as we began to pray Michael prayed heavy, I could feel his back tensing up as he prayed; we stood there a long time just praying. The twins were in the room. We were to pray there at the door until the rain stopped, it went on and on until the clock rang at 12 in the afternoon the rain stopped, and the thunder started.

Michael had both his hands on the door and I had his waist. We were praying and praying until the door blew forward at us and we went flying backward, we fell onto the wooden floor, and we both got up fast. We were forced back down by all the dark spirits leaving Keagan's room. Michael pulled himself up, he was struggling to fight his way through them he didn't fight them back. His goal was to run in and grab Keagan out, I stood up quickly, and while they tried to get Michael, I ran toward Keagan's door.

As I was running, I was being pulled back by the dark spirit I had encountered in the room the day I went in. I was okay I wanted to grab hold of her spirit. I wanted her to go back where she came from. When I felt her grab me I pulled her with me toward his room I knew she would try to hold on to me to keep me from going in, I was running as fast as I could. There were more of them coming toward me, but I was fearless. I fought them all, trying to even grab some of them. I screamed and shouted for the Lord.

It was like I couldn't get around them fast enough I seen Michael struggling with them. The more he fought, the more came at him some were dark some were of pure evil. I had a time trying to catch them, I wanted the woman. I knew she wanted to keep me from Keagan, I was able to grab hold of her, and I just prayed when I did. I prayed loudly, "Lord in the name of Jesus, carry this spirit back to hell where it belongs!" I yelled out as I held it. She was a hard one she looked as if she wanted to spit fire at me. Her eyes filled with redness as I sent her back, she disappeared, and more came one after the other.

They came Michael and I were in a spiritual war, some of them growled at like dogs, and some of them spoke in an unknown language. Some of them would just stare and laugh, but they kept coming it didn't stop. It seemed that the door was so far away. After a while, I laid there and allowed them to attack me while I prayed. I knew I would get a break to run to Keagan. I watched as Michael fought and fought until suddenly he was curled up in a ball on the floor on his knees. I watched as he began to light up, I knew this would be the break I needed to go in and grab Keagan to put him in the room with the twins.

Michael began to light up more and more, his wings came spreading out as they surrounded him. It was if they were afraid to attack him they formed a circle around him leaving me on the floor alone. I watched as they began to take off after him he looked at me and put his head down as if he was telling me to go to the room quickly. I got up from the floor as quickly as possible, the cut on my foot tore open again I could feel it ripping more as I ran as fast as I could to get Keagan. When I made it to his room he was sitting up the woman was inside of Keagan. He yelled out to me as his face kept changing to hers.

"Mommy," I had to grab him even with her in him. I snatched the covers away from his waist and took him from the bed. "Let go of me you bitch!" The woman yelled as I carried Keagan out. She wiggled around in him, and Keagan held onto me his face and body kept changing as I ran faster carrying his body. He would get really light like a feather than very heavy as if I was carrying a dead body. The thunder began to get louder and I could hear Michael fighting them it was like the roof of the lake house was crashing in.

When I made it to the twin's door, I screamed out to them "Genesis Chapter 12 read it now!" I placed Keagan down in front of the door, and I prayed with my hands around him I prayed out loud. "Lord in the name of Jesus, bring him out. Lord oh Lord, I ask you now save his soul, he is made of your light, Lord he is your child. Lord, please pull him close to your light oh Lord. I beg you don't allow them to take him in Lord, he is your light made of you!" I yelled and held Keagan tight in my arms I could feel the spirit of the woman getting heavy, then going away.

I could feel when Keagan was coming out his small hand would hold me tight. I continued to pray. "Oh Lord,   bring him out, allow him to use what you gave him to push himself through. I thank you, Lord, for all your blessings, Lord, bring Keagan back into your light." I rocked as I prayed I prayed and prayed and the thunder was loud and while I was praying the twins recited the verse from Genesis. Soon Keagan began to blink all of a sudden, he let out a very loud holler it was the loudest I ever heard Keagan yell.

"I am his," he said as his body warmed and he pushed me back I tried to hold onto him. The light sat him up, and he yelled over and over again out to the Lord. I looked down the hall, and the woman was standing waiting for me. The woman that I had sent back; she smiled at me and began to run toward me. As she ran I opened the twin's door, and I shoved Keagan in, the twins were still reciting the verse from Genesis over and over they did exactly what Michael asked of them.

I closed the door, and I could hear Keagan crying out to the Lord, still thanking him for his grace. The woman flew into me knocking me off my feet once again. I crawled up and dashed away from the door I yelled back to the twins "Say it louder!" I screamed, soon the door became light, it was bright, and the woman stared down at it and smiled, she knew she couldn't get in. She ran to me along with more of the shadows and out of her came a foul smell.

She came after me flying, I ran to look for Michael the roof of the lake house had a hole in it the size of the moon, it was completely torn off. "Michael!" I yelled out I ran around the front of the lake house all over looking for Michael I didn't see him anywhere. I heard all around me thunder I saw lighting far and near. I ran around and around the lake house looking, soon the rain poured again the clouds formed and the sky became really dark. I looked up, and there I could see the light shining through the clouds as I watched the light I get attacked.

It was like they were carrying me away with the force they had, I wanted so badly to grab them, but they were as fast as the wind. I could see some of them waiting at the window for the twins to stop praying. I knew that when they did they would try and get Keagan again. I fought them one by one and sometimes all of them attacked me at once. I couldn't understand why Michael hadn't come for me my spirit was growing so tired. I needed him with me. It was never ending the woman that I sent back would form more of her. It was if her spirit multiplied, I fought them and prayed.

When I was able to get up I looked around for Michael I was growing worried that maybe he wasn't able to fight them. Maybe they got the best of him, and he was gone. As I fought, I was able to grab two of them at the same time. I took them by the throat and prayed them back to hell. I became stronger as I worried about Michael, I began to grab them one after the other holding them and praying over their spirits.

It seemed I was fighting for hours the thunder stopped, and I heard the crashing of lighting pop as it cracked the earth. Louder and louder it became, I was more powerful as the weather changed I felt as if the

Lord was fighting with me; his strength through me. The evil was heavy it didn't give me time to catch my breath as it attacked I fought them. I took them on two by two now holding onto them and swinging them around by whatever I could hold on to them with.

It would be nightfall when I began to hear the cracking of the lighting and the thunder beat through the sky as if drums were playing. The rain poured over me as I fought them, I stayed in prayer although I worried for Michael. I could see the twins staring out through the window I knew they couldn't see the spirits surrounding them. I could see them growing worried; I wanted to yell out to them to keep praying. I knew Keagan was weak, I could see him staring out at me if he had his strength I knew he'd come to help me. It became dark out; I went on fighting them I ran around the lake house in search of Michael.

They followed, chasing me when I was able to I ran faster to get to the lake house I knew that if I didn't get to Keagan and the twins they'd get them. I ran as fast as I could through the house. When I made to the hallway, I stopped and yelled. "Pray louder please!" I yelled out to the twins I could hear them praying through the door, the door was still lite up. They followed me until I reached it. I was stood in the hallway facing them to see if they would try and come close to it to follow me in.

They stood there growling at me with their eyes filled with redness it was as if their eyeballs were made of pure fire. I didn't fear them, after fighting them I wouldn't fear them, and they knew it. They wanted to get to me, but couldn't as I stood near the door of light. I opened the door and went inside closing the door behind me, watching them every step of the way. When I got inside the twins looked exhausted they dropped the bible down on the bed and hugged one another. I went over to them and hugged them both.

Keagan stood in a corner he looked afraid. I stood up and walked over to him. "Oh, Keagan, son it's you," I said reaching out to him, I missed you," I say to him holding him tight. "Turn on the light

Kristopher please, turn it on." I wanted to see his face, I wanted to see if he was okay. Keagan was so tall I pulled him from the corner. He didn't say a word at first just staring at me. He had scratches all over him I turned him all around to see his body. "Mommy, is it my birthday?" He asked me smiling "Your birthday," I said laughing.

"Oh Lord thank you, Lord," I said holding Keagan in my arms. I stood back from him and looked him over again; he was fine except for the bruising and scratches all over him. The twins came over to him. "Mom is he okay?" Kristopher asked standing in front of him holding his hand. "He is, he's okay Kristopher," I said hugging them all close to me Kristine was crying. "Sweetie, please don't cry," I tell her rubbing her back we were in a circle hugging for a while when I remembered that Michael was still out there somewhere. I knew he didn't want me to go looking for him.

He'd want me to stay here with the children. It was quiet now no screaming or hollering throughout the house it was quiet. The rain stopped the thunder was gone and I was happy that Keagan and the twins were fine. Keagan still had the foul smell of the spirits all over him I had to make him shower soon. I watched out for Michael off and on as I helped Keagan to the bathroom to shower. I was afraid to leave him alone. I watched him shower I removed his feeding tube and helped him into some warm clothes he didn't talk very much while we did this. I began to wonder about what he was thinking. I wanted to be sure he was okay.

"Keagan are you okay?" I asked him as I walked him over to the bed where the twins were. "I am, mommy," he said walking with me holding my hand. He had scratches and cuts everywhere. His face was really bruised; I put cream on him all over. "Mommy where's my dad?" He asked me I covered him with the quilt on the bed and they all laid together there. I went to the window to look out for Michael. Still he was nowhere in sight the sky began to clear I went and sat down on the bed with the children. I started to feel all the pain from the scratches to the cut on my feet.

I pulled my gym shoes off it; the whole shoe was filled with blood as if it had been bleeding for a long time. I pulled the sock off and the cut was wide open. I hopped over to the bathroom and put my foot in the sink near the door. I ran the cool water over it and allowed it to bleed out after a while of that I sat on the toilet grabbed the first aid kit Michael left on the floor. I took the glazes and wrapped my foot over and over with it. When I was done I went back to the bed with the children. I sat down and looked out of the window.

"Lord, please bring Michael back, please bring him home to me," I said aloud "Mom do you want me to go out with you to look for him?" Kristopher asked me. "No sweetie we're safer in here," I said taking his hand. "Mom than you should lay down, you look exhausted," Kristopher said handing me a blanket to cover up in. We all laid in bed together it was so dark around the house. We could hear the wind blowing through the hole in the ceiling up front it blew like a whistle. I wasn't able to fall right off to sleep in fear of what will happen if I did.

I watched as Keagan was able to sleep and the twins held him close to them, they were all older, but it didn't matter they had a closeness that didn't break no matter how old they'd become. After I watched them fall off to sleep I thought about Michael. Where could he be Lord, I thought as I tried to keep myself from falling off to sleep, the window ceil were filled with water. The raindrops still fell from the trees; the sound of the drips hit the floor of the porches wooden frame put me completely to sleep.

I jumped up the next morning at the sound of roaring thunder and lightning the cracking sounded much like the sky was cracked in half. The children jumped up with me. We all looked out to see what was happening in the sky. I stood up. I walked over to the window to see if Michael was there, he wasn't there I stood there staring out I could see far away the lighting sticking behind the trees of the boat house. I wondered if Michael was there. I stared out until Keagan asked me for breakfast.

"Mommy I'm so hungry," It was a true blessing to hear his voice again. "Thank you Lord for bringing my son out I said a loud as I walked over to the small refrigerator that Michael and Kristopher stocked with food before all this happened. Michael must have known that this would happen. But where was he? I wondered. "Where is Michael Lord?" I said as I poured Keagan's milk. I believe that he'll return Lord, but what if he doesn't? He was very worried before he left Lord, as if he knew more, did he know more was coming his way, Lord?

I thought as I went back to the window to watch for him. I stood there with the blanket that Kristopher had given to me last night wrapped around me. I wanted to go out to look for him I stared at the door. The children ate and when they were done they played board games. "Mom, you can't go alone," Kristopher said to me "You can't go out there alone," he said again holding my hand. "I know you want to, but dad told me that when you got in here with us, to not allow you to leave."

"He doesn't want you to go out there alone, I can come with you," he said sitting up taller in the bed. "No, sweetie I think I'll wait one more day, if he doesn't show up today I'll go out tomorrow. I can't take any chances," I told him wiping a tear from my eye with the blanket. What if God wanted Michael back I thought, what if he was done with what the Lord wanted him to do here? "Oh Lord, please bring Michael back to me, please Lord," I said as I stood in the window looking for Michael again through the rain and lighting.

I saw nothing, not a single sign of him or where he may be. The day grew longer and the night came slow as I waited for him by the window. "I think he'll be back soon mom," Kristopher said to me making him a sandwich at the small table near the lamp. "Maybe you're right Kristopher, maybe he will come back soon. I'm just afraid that he may need my help out there somewhere, I don't want him to be alone," I tell him as I walk back over to the window.

"Mom you can't go out there, and you have to eat, do you want a sandwich?" He asked me with one in his hand. "No, thank you, son, I can't eat. I really don't want to sleep; I need to know where your father is. Lord, where is Michael?" I say, throwing the blanket on the floor. "I will stay here tonight again, but I have to go and find him if he doesn't show up today," I said. I picked up the blanket and went to lay across the bed with Kristine and Keagan he didn't sleep as much as he would before I thought.

He would get up and start eating his food right away; he would talk to Kristopher and Kristine about everything he dreamed about while he was asleep. I didn't know whether he remembered seeing me down in the tunnel or not, but I know when he looked at me he smiled as if he knew. It would be three days the rain fell and still no Michael. If he didn't come back soon, I'd have to go and find him. During the day the children would play board games, talk and laugh and play ball hitting the wall with it.

I'd sit and watch looking out of the window, just hoping that Michael would show soon. On the fourth day I watched as the sun came up and the rain cloud spread across the sky. The sun was brighter than usual over the lake. The children were still sleeping when I saw in the lake a flash of light fly up like a leaping shark into the air it was so big and bright I had to shade my eyes with my hand to get a good look. I stood up and went closer, it flew up and spun around in a circle really fast the light became brighter and brighter.

I shaded my eyes and watched as its wings appeared to spread out as big as the sun it went up as high as the sun and came down slowly the bright light began to fade. I took my hand from my eyes watched as it landed to its feet walking on the water toward me the light still shining through it. I became terrified as its head was down and it was larger than life. I couldn't see its face as it became closer to walking on water toward me; it came close when it lifted its head. I yelled out "Michael!"

I dropped my blanket and ran for the door. It was Michael I was so excited to see him I didn't even care about the spirits outside the door. I ran out after him the children jumped up to the sound of my screeching scream for him following me out to the lake to meet him. I jumped up as high as I could. "Michael," I said crying, "I didn't think I'd ever see you again," I hugged him holding his neck so tight. All of the children held onto him also. He carried me inside the children held onto his arms he was fearless even more so than before.

I put my head to his neck crying. "I was so afraid I'd never see you again," I said to him again. Michael put me down when we made it to the porch. His wings were in and the children were all happy. He turned to look at Keagan. "Son," he said grabbing him up off his feet. "I missed you, son." He smiled and spun Keagan around he put him down and tapped the twins on the head kissing and hugging them as we all walked inside. The room was calm the spirits were gone and Michael seemed different.

"Let's get everything together Karis, we must leave soon, we'll stay one more night here." He began to put only our bags in the t ruck leaving everything else to stay at the lake house. He didn't talk about where he'd been for those three days. He was still a little worried about us. He wanted to know our every move around the lake house. The children followed him around most of the night. We didn't talk about what happened the nights before. "I want to leave at the break of dawn," he tells me as he walks toward the front room.

"I want you to be especially careful Karis when we're leaving, they're not going to want you to leave," he said to me while the children were in the back room. I went to him standing in the front room looking up at the hole in the ceiling. "They will try and keep you this time, they will try and destroy you and all that God gave you to use against them they are going to try and take it away. This time they will not stop, and it will be as if the devil himself released the darkness of his soul to defeat you." I stood back and stared into his eyes, I didn't question him at all, his eyes told me what was to come.

"The children need to be prepared to stay safe the twins need to sit Keagan in between them both in the car and lock all window and doors and pray from Genesis once again. That's the only way they'll stay safe," he said looking at them down the hall. The night fell, I wasn't able to sleep at all we all sat up in the front room awaiting dawn the children fell off to sleep Michael began to whisper to me. "I know that you have some fear in you, but don't, call out to him, and he will protect you." As he began to whisper more, the thunder roared.

We heard running in the hall loudly Michael got up from the bed and walked over to the door as if to allow them in. "What are you doing?" I whispered trying not to wake the children. I sat straight up just then I hear my name being called out loudly the voice was as if it was under water. "Karis!" It called out. "Karis!" It said over and over as we heard the running the footsteps were so heavy as if it was carrying thunder under its feet. I looked out into the hall, and a woman was running back and forth calling out to me she was in a white dress I couldn't see her face clearly.

She was barefoot as she ran so fast. I couldn't see what she was running from, but she looked back and ran in fear of something. Michael began to wake the children he carried Keagan out of the door he told them exactly what to do while they walked together. "Karis, you stay here don't move they'll attack us all if you follow us out," he said rushing them out. "Don't look at her, keep your eyes on me," he tells them rushing them to the truck. The clock on the wall reached 5 am, and it rang so loudly that I covered my ears.

I watched Michael through the opened door instructing the children to keep Keagan in the middle and hold on to him tight recite the verse from Genesis that he'd taught them before. He recited it along with them as he walked away from the car. "As loudly as you can children," he said coming back into the lake house. The woman stopped and turned to me; she stood close to the door and waved for me to come out. "Come, Karis!" Michael yelled out to me standing beside her. At first, I couldn't, I stood there, I didn't understand what this was all about. Michael came into the room; he reached out his hand to me to come to him while the woman stood watching, with her eyes piercing out to me. I didn't take his hand at first.

"Karis, they are going to attack you, I know that you can't understand this, trust me you can't fear this," he said walking me to the front room. I wanted to go to the car to get the children home. When I stepped into the front room where the woman was standing I looked up, I heard the thunder loudly it cracked and roared as if it would crack open and suck me in. The woman began to run toward the side of the house, she ran fast looking back and speaking of something I'd never heard. It was like she was afraid.

I watched her run, when I turned to look for Michael; he was no longer standing there. I looked all around the room for him he was gone. "Michael! Michael!" I screamed out loudly all of the windows began to slam the door closed and opened loudly over and over again. He didn't appear I ran to the door, it slammed closed, I ran to the window, it shut loudly. I looked up again, and in a flash, I was being dragged through the front room it began to get darker and darker. I screamed out for Michael again I couldn't turn around the grip on my ankles was so tight I tried holding on to the floor to stop the dragging.

I pulled on anything I could, but I couldn't grip anything I screamed out to the Lord. "Come for me! Help me, Lord!" I said as I was pulled through the dark house. "Lord! I am not without sin come for me!" I said yelling and screaming as I was being drugged through the lake house. I closed my eyes hoping for it to stop somewhere. It held onto me so tight. I could smell its foul scent I knew it was evil. I felt cold wind and I felt dirt and rubbles beneath my skin as my shirt was pulled up from under me my stomach felt scratched from the dirt under me.

When I opened my eyes I was outside on the side of the Lakehouse the wind was cold the trees around were blowing like a heavy storm. The sky was once again filled with darkness. I turned over onto my back and looked around for Michael, I looked up and around. When I looked up again, the trees became calm it was quiet. I sat up to look around me, I could barely see looking out toward the lake suddenly I hear footsteps like thunder walking toward me. I couldn't see anyone, but the footsteps were more than one or two it sounded as if there were more and more and more.

I wanted to stand on my feet I wanted to run, but I didn't I prayed out loud knowing that this was it, they wanted Keagan they couldn't have him, they wanted to stop me and here I was giving them the chance to turn my spirit I laid there thinking. "Lord, come for me; help me through this I can't move without you!" I shouted I could hear them breathing heavy growing I didn't move, and suddenly I was being attacked. I rushed to my feet grabbing onto some of them when I closed my eyes, I could see them. When I opened them they became dark, with them closed I could see them as they were in this world.

I grabbed hold of them, and their spirit told their story. I didn't want to hold on to them to see why they were in the tunnel of darkness. I was being attacked, I had to throw them back quickly, and with the Lord's help, I did just that, some of them spat at me and kicked as I turned them back to the tunnel and some of them beg me for mercy with their eyes. I didn't hold them long at all as they fought me back one after another they attacked me. I opened my eyes, and the darkness became darker all I could see with them open were red eyes.

I tried to keep them close throughout this time, but I couldn't feel them as well as I could with them opened. Soon they began to fade out, and I would get a break of calm, but it didn't last long before I was thrown to the ground with the greatest force. I'd never felt this forceful spirit before. I fell to the ground so hard my body felt as if it bounced, and I lay there looking up at the most evil I'd ever seen it had wings also. Its body smelled as if it was raw sewage something dripped from his mouth and his body as if he was sweating evil.

After it stared into my eyes its mouth opened wide and it reached for my throat. I began to pray as loud as I could with its hand to my throat. "Oh Lord in the name of Jesus, I will fear this evil not, I rebuke you Satan in the name of Jesus Christ, go back to hell where you belong, Lord." It picked me up by my throat and held me to the sky as if I was a doll my legs dangled. I wouldn't give into his evil. "I am of the Lord, I will not turn, you are of evil, and your soul will always burn. The Lord will have no mercy on you" I yelled out all that I could, while held me there.

Each time I yelled out a pray his mouth opened, his head turned, his eyes became redder, and he started out at me squeezing me tighter by the neck. I looked down at his legs each time, his breath was foul and his legs were like the legs of a big bird. I wiggled and wiggled as if I could get away. I couldn't, I just prayed and prayed until my voice wouldn't allow it anymore soon I became faint I began to pass out. He shook me as he held onto my neck. After a while it all went black there was quiet and calm, and I was no longer in his presence.

I felt my soul leaving, my breathing was faint my eyes rolled into the darkness. My body felt as light as a feather as I faded, I couldn't hear anything; I just saw darkness my soul cried out to the lord as it lifted and lifted leaving his hands. I could hear laughter after a while and see the light ahead of me, my stomach filled with joy my heart grew empty of pain. I felt free, and joy covered my spirit, my entire body felt like laughing, as the voices and laughter drew nearer in the light.

I felt as if I was a child again no fear no pain happy and free, when I open my eyes I was sitting in a light and my hands as they were when I was a child. I looked myself over. I was as a child sitting in the light that shined brighter than the sun. Could it be that I was there with my Lord? I wondered as I looked around smiling. It felt as if I was there I looked behind me for the voices I couldn't see   where they were coming from. There was no one, I smiled and when I turned to look in front of me. He appeared sitting in front of me with his hand out, smiling. I was there he came for me I thought as I took his hand, he came for me.

Graceful, I Give In to Him

I sat up taller when his hand touched mine he smiled at me as my hands warmed to his. First, my hands than my body warmed all over. He began to show me things that happened in my life. Like a picture book, one day after the other my life flashed from me fight the spirits from now to then. I was captivated by what I saw; he talked to me through it all. "You are my light; you must never fear things around you that you don't understand. They are not for you to understand, but for your heart to change them in prayer. I brought you here several years ago, I took your spirit in, I gave you something to share with the world. It's not a gift, but the light within you."

"A light that will take you into a spirit to calm it; I gave you a special light, you are so special to everyone in your life, you must never doubt it. Be faithful to it and have peace with it." My head was spinning with all that I saw, I listened to him closely his voice was very clear. "Have faith, and be strong, be true to yourself my dear," he spoke loudly. When I thought it was over I began to see the day I was born, my father looking me over smiling, my mother holding me smiling and the light shining through the window of the hospital room.

I then saw myself as a child running and playing all around with Martha and Krystal I was so happy. He smiled at me as I watched my childhood. The happiness soon faded as I watched the day we went to the fair, that awful 4th of July day. I could see the barbecue, my family, the car ride to drop off Carol. The sitting and waiting at the light, that light shining into my eyes, I watched with him as I flew out from the front windshield of the car. I heard crashing and screaming I saw my sister reaching for Krystal, and soon I was under the car.

I looked up, and there was a warm light just as warm as the one I was with him now. I turned to him and smiled as he began to talk. "You don't remember my child, you remembered all that I gave you but not where it came from. I brought you here many years ago my child, you sat in this very light. I gave you something special," as he talked I seen it all clearly he sent me back here to live in the world with my wings. I didn't have them; I didn't remember being here before. It would have been a lot easier for me to understand if I could have remembered being in his light. He showed me the very day he took me in and explained to me why he brought me back into this word.

"You, my child, you are mine, my light will shine through you forever and your spirit will be filled with riches, and your heart will never weigh heavy. You shall have things in peace," he said smiling at me. He put my hands to his knees and took his hands to his back and pulled from behind him. Two wonderful brightly lit wings, he held them up high above his head and brought them down to me placing them on my back. He leaned his head forward touching my forehead to his he pulled me in close to him. As I began to feel like I was falling the warmth of the Lords spirit, it began to fade.

I was falling, the joy faded, and the laughter in my belly was no longer there. I fell deeper and deeper down into the darkness, I was spinning around and around as the light faded away. I began to feel the evil darkness holding my neck tight. I laughed now, out loud, even with its hands to my throat. I began to take it spinning with me, and soon my wings spread as the darkness became light. I was filled with joy and happiness; the evil freed my neck and fell down. I didn't want to leave the warmth of the light.

I started to wonder if I wanted to stay in this world. I began to fall to the ground I wanted to stay with him, why couldn't I stay I thought. I wanted to go back. I prayed, "Lord, take me back into the warmth of the light. I want to stay with you," I said as I fell to the ground I was sure he'd pull me back into his light. There was still dark spirits all around; I didn't open my eyes to them. I just laid on the ground and allowed them to taunt my spirit so that he pulled me back in.

I became faint after a while not wanting to breathe out not wanting to leave the Lords presence. I knew now why he sent me back, I had my wings now. I don't want them I thought, I'd rather be there with him living in peace; this world has nothing for me. I thought as I laid there refusing to stay in this world. Soon, I could hear Michael screaming my name he yelled loudly. "Karis! Karis, please come back to me," he said kneeling over me. I was slowly going back up into the light where I wanted to be. "Karis, Karis!" He yelled and yelled.

I could see him growing desperate for me to come back; his wings began to spread out bigger and bigger. The light shined through them brighter and brighter as I went up slowly he placed his hand on my chest and began to pray for my soul. He prayed and prayed, his head was down, and his hands covered my chest I was going up, and he was praying me down. He cried over me with his head down, his body lit up as if the Lords light shined through him. I watched him closely, I prayed for the Lord to keep me in his light.

I could feel Michael spirit growing desperate to keep me with him the skies light turned to darkness as he held his hand to my chest. He began to pump my chest and with every pump of my chest we both went up into the light. I was slowly was going back down to Michael, my spirit began to feel his hearts pain; I felt his need for me. He pumped my chest as hard as he could we went up and back down again. Each time we went up the warmth of the Lords light filled us together, we saw each other as children.

I saw him under the boat in the water, and he saw me under the car. We both saw the Lord handing us our wings, the feeling was so real. It was like we were there at the same time with him in his warm light. I watched as Michael stopped, he held me into his chest. He held me so close I could feel his heart beating so hard. He screamed out to the Lord. "Bring her to me, Lord!" I felt his spirit needing me, I saw my children sitting in the car still reciting Genesis chapter 12. The twins holding Keagan close to him.

How could I be so selfish? I thought, how could I leave my family? I know that things haven't always been easy for me, nothing seemed easy for me, but for them. I can be strong enough to stay until the Lord wants me back. Michael was still crying over me with his head into my chest. When I opened my eyes, I placed my hand on his forehead and brought his head up. "Michael, I love you," I tell him lifting his head, he smiled pulling me up from the ground carrying me to the porch. I was bruised and scratched. He held me so tight after placing me on the wooden floor of the porch he began to wipe the dirt from my face with his shirt.

I looked down at my feet the cut burned as if I'd stood on hot coals all day. Michael began to take off my shoes. I wiped his face off with my shirt also, after we tried helping one another Michael carried me over to the car it was time to go home. He placed me down in the passenger seat the children all became really quiet. I held my head back on the headrest, I was exhausted. As he drove off from the lake house, I watched the house and was still able to say, "thank you, Jesus." I was able to look behind me and say thank you Jesus.

We made it home 24 hours later the street was so quiet when we pulled up. We didn't unpack anything out of the car tonight. Michael and I took the children in, and we went to our room leaving them in Keagan's room to get washed up. Michael ran the bath for us. We got in quickly. He sat down; I sat between his legs and leaned on his chest. We lay in the water together silently for a while. Michael went over my back with a sponge, and I rubbed his legs with a towel. "So, how do you feel about them?" He asked me.

"It felt as if my shoulder blades lifted opened when they first came out," I said to him rubbing his legs. "Yes you'll have to get used to that feeling, it will get better, you'll forget that they're even there soon enough," he said. "Do you forget that they're there?" I asked him. "No, I don't I feel better knowing that they are in me." I sat up as he washed my back off. I leaned back onto his chest. "Karis, you're brave." "So are you, Michael," I said taking his hand to mine and kissing it.

We went to bed that night after checking in on the children. I washed Keagan's scratches again putting cream all over him again. We prayed with them and went to bed. We fell off to sleep talking about Keagan's 13th birthday party. It was to be the Saturday coming up. We hadn't been home long enough to really plan a big party and Keagan hadn't been to school in a long while. I know that friends were never a problem for him. I'd planned on inviting a lot of the hospital staff and their children. Michael held me close to him all night.

I dreamt of that talk with the Lord, and how it felt up there near him. It was like no other feeling I'd ever felt. To think my soul could be emptied of all the bad things, no feeling of it. No thoughts of what to do with it. Just pure joy in my soul, I wondered how anyone ever returned from there leaving all that peace behind them. I didn't want to leave it. I wanted to stay, and I almost had the chance. If I'd ever remembered it I would have wanted to go back there sooner. I don't know how I ever forgot that place. I woke from my sleep all through the night.

I'd sit up in bed and look around me I'd get up and walk around the room. It was like I was in a dream. Could this all be just a dream I wondered, it like it was, that would explain all of this I thought. Maybe I didn't make though that accident, maybe Michael didn't make through his either and maybe we are all living in a dream. I thought as I got up from bed and walked all around the house. I walked around looking at the pictures on the wall touching the furniture, after a while, I stood looking out of the front room window. It was a cool night; I walked over to the back patio door and slid it open just to allow the cool air to blow on my face.

I stood leaning on the edge of the doorway I held my robe close to my chest and breathed it all in. I looked down at my foot it was still split open wrapped in a tight bandage that Michael made with gauze. As I was bending forward looking down at the bandage there in the corner of my eye, I saw what looked to be a big white dove. Its wings were covered with an orange tint; it sat on the grass staring at me like it was there for me. I didn't go near it; I just watched it watching me.

I stood there for a long while until Michael came up behind me and kissed my neck. "Hey you, what are you up to down here?" He asked me yawning. "I'm just needed to catch the breeze, the night is cool," I said grabbing his hand. "You couldn't sleep, could you?" He said wrapping his arm around my waist. I shook my head no. "Michael, do you ever feel as if we are still sleeping, maybe we never woke up. Maybe we both never made back from that place, and this place that we call home is all just a trick of our death." I said turning to him still trying to watch the dove.

Michael pinched me on the arm. "See, we are real, baby, this is our home, the children are our lives, and we are among the living," he said kissing me on the lips softly. "Don't be afraid of what the Lord gave you baby," he said holding on to me. "I'm not afraid anymore, Michael, I just wanted to stay there with him. I felt so safe, the feeling that came over me was like no other feeling I have ever encountered, I wanted more," I told him. I turned to look at the dove. "Michael, do you see the bird in the yard?" I asked him.

"I do baby, isn't it lovely, see those are the perks of his love for us," he said kissing my neck. "Just embrace who you are for him, except it in every way, don't speak of leaving too much or too soon. You might miss out on the best part of this life," he said smiling. "What would be the best part of this life Michael?" I asked him smiling back at him. "You don't know baby, the best part is us," he said holding me tight to his chest as I watched the dove spread his wings and fly away. This is the best part. I thought as I watched his wings fly higher and higher into the sky.

I'm not in a dream I'm of him made of in the warmth of his light I thought. I slid the door shut. Michael went over to the refrigerator. He pulled out a bottle of milk and began to drink it. After he drank the whole bottle we headed upstairs to bed. By the time we were asleep it was dawn. When Michael awoke, and the children were up, ready for school. Nothing but smiles, Keagan was dressed in his best school clothes and the twins were eating quickly trying to get to school on time. Michael rushed up and put on his clothes.

We were both to check back into work today. I was to take Keagan into see Dr. Tate soon after school. I first took him to his class to see his teacher. She was so excited to see him back after I talked to her telling her that he was fine and for her to please send his missing work home and we'd try to help him catch up. She quickly introduced him to a couple more new students as if he was new. Keagan waved at his old friends. It seemed as if he never left them. They gathered around him hugging him telling him they were glad to see him. They all welcomed him back quickly walking him over to his seat. I could hear them questioning about what happened to him and what did he see when he was out of it.

He smiled, and just like the old Keagan, he began to tell them stories. It was a quick ride to work. Maddy greeted me at the front desk with my new schedule. She was so happy to see me she hugged me for a very long time. I was happy to be back to work. I went through my day laughing and talking to patients. I ate lunch with Michael and a few of his friends. I felt good all day. I picked Keagan up from school and then the twins. We headed to Dr. Tate's office from there. We waited in the waiting room for a while before the nurse came out to get Keagan. I left the twins in the waiting room to be with him and Dr. Tate.

He looked Keagan over and asked him question after question about his vision and whether or not he was having any headaches. He would shake his head no. The visit was very quick. Dr. Tate gave Keagan a clean bill of health "The bruises could be from him being a little anemic," he said looking at them holding Keagan's face. "They will go away in another week or so," he said smiling at Keagan as he jumped from the table.

"He's getting so tall," Dr. Tate said looking at his long legs. "He'll probably get to be at least six feet tall or taller," he said giving him a handshake. "You take care, Mrs. Philips," he said opening the door for us to all leave. We stopped at the grocery store on the way home for food for the house. I also could get all the things I needed for Keagan's birthday party. We shopped for everything we needed and went straight home. Kristine and I put all the groceries away and ordered Keagan a big beautiful cake.

It was to read Happy 13th Birthday Keagan; we were to pick it up on the Saturday morning of the party. The days went by quickly; the house was quiet for that week. The children were happy, and I was able to sleep without waking up at all. When Saturday came around, we woke early in the morning and began to prepare for Keagan's party we decorated the house. Kristine did most of the decorating. She decorated from the front to the back. Blue and gold balloons surrounded the pool chairs, and balloons and signs hung all over reading Happy Birthday Keagan.

By 2 in the afternoon that day the house was filled with Keagan's friends from school even his teacher showed up with her two children. The twins even invited their friends, everyone showed up from the hospital all bringing their children or their family members children. We laughed and the kids swam in the pool some of them even danced to the music. By dusk we were ready to sing happy birthday to Keagan. Michael took lots of pictures, and Kristine and her friends prepared the ice cream, laughing and joking around with the ice cream scoopers.

I watched   Keagan as he sat in front of his big cake; he was so excited and happy. It was if that those last few months never happened to him. I watched him smile big as we all sang happy birthday to him, and I thought, look at God's good grace. Thank you, Lord, I thought to myself as I watched him blow out all of his candles in one blow. Everyone clapped and screamed out "Yay! Keagan, Happy Birthday!" They said shouted. Michael handed him the knife to cut the cake. He cut the biggest piece of cake he could and everyone laughed as he tossed it on to his plate.

Thanks to Kristine and her friends everyone received a piece of cake and a scoop of ice cream. It was very quiet as everyone sat down to enjoy the ice cream and cake. When we finished, I gave away fun bags and thank you notes to everyone. Michael lit up the backyard, an d we all sat on the patio watching some of the children swim and play. It would be 10pm when everyone would begin to leave. Michael escorted most of them to the door. We thanked everyone for coming. Keagan was still putting away all of his gifts when they were leaving.

All of his friends were so happy he was back at school they hugged him and shook his hand as they left the house. After they were all gone, we began to clean the house as a family. We cleaned from the front to the back, Maddy and Dr. Green stayed and helped for a while before it became too much for them. Maddy helped me stack all of the dishes away in the dishwasher, and Dr. Green helped the boys clean the yard. It was well into midnight by the time we had it all cleaned up. The children went upstairs to wash and go to bed as Michael, and I continued putting everything back in its place. We both went up together and checked in with the children before going to shower together.

"It was a great day," Michael said pulling me toward him in the shower. "It was, a great day Michael, did you see how happy Keagan was?" I said as he kissed all over my neck. He shook his head yes as he kissed all over me. I wanted to wash, but Michael was eager to get to bed , it had been a while since we'd made love and Michael was ready. We got out of the shower quickly and onto the bathroom floor. Michael was so eager we didn't even make it to the bed. We made love all night until we were both tired.

When we were done I went back into the shower while Michael was still lying on the bathroom floor mat, he soon came in after me. I washed quickly and got out drying myself off. "Michael I'm thirsty, I'm going down to get cold water, do you want anything?" I asked as I dried myself. "Yes please, ice water in a glass," he said peeking out from the curtain. I went inside the bedroom and grabbed my robe from the closet and walked downstairs to get a drink. The house was quiet and dark. I didn't need the light, I knew my way through the dark room to the kitchen.

When I reached the refrigerator I opened the door quickly, and then closed it quickly, I had to get two glasses from the cabinet. I went over and reached into the cabinet I could see the light of the moon shining into the kitchen as I looked out back. On the grass sat the big dove with the orange-tinted wings, I didn't watch him. I just smiled and walked back over to the refrigerator with the glasses. I placed them down on the counter and opened the refrigerator with one hand and took out the pitcher of cold water.

I opened the freezer and reached for the ice, as soon as I did the hairs on my neck rose as if a cold wind blew over me and suddenly as I turned to see what was behind me. There was a cloud of darkness, and its hands reached out to grab me. I turned my back to it quickly and before I could pray the water pitcher dropped to the floor and my wings spread out as big as the room, at the tip of them shined his light. As I spin around to face the darkness, I was fearless in his grace.

Fin

About the Author

K.C McGee born March 7th 1972 to Mr. & Mrs. Ernest and Ruth Love in Santa Ana, CA. the 9th of ten children, graduated from high school in San Diego, CA. She then married young to her then high school sweetheart, and moved to Fort Drum NY following her husband to pursue his military career serving the US Army. After attending a program to became a bank teller for Key Bank of New York she worked as a Bank Teller on the military base, until they were moved to North Carolina where she began her career as a writer taking a creative writing classes and journalism classes for 3 years. Moving back to San Diego to care for her mother she became a stay at home mother caring for her mother and her five children. In 1992 her mother passed on, K.C continued to live in San Diego when her husband of eight years decided he no longer wanted to be a husband nor a father any longer. They divorced in 1993. When he left K.C began a life alone with her five children working for various family help centers in the county, while going to school part time, and eventually graduating with a Degree in Journalism from UCSD. K.C has always wanted to be a writer but never had the opportunity to fully focus on her career for she was alone taking care of her children. In 1996 she re-married a man who was serving in the US Navy and she began her life with him and her five children. They went on to have four more children living in a wonderful neighborhood in San Diego County, Raising their nine children and their dog Goldie. She is now on her journey to becoming a well-known writer building her legacy for her children. Today she is a published Author pursuing her dream.

www.ingramcontent.com/pod-product-compliance
Lightning Source LLC
Chambersburg PA
CBHW071329020726
47502CB00001B/16